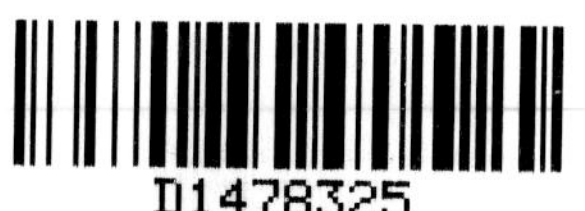

THE EDINBURGH EDITION OF THE WAVERLEY NOVELS

VOLUME SIXTEEN

SAINT RONAN'S WELL

EDINBURGH EDITION OF THE WAVERLEY NOVELS

to be complete in thirty volumes

Each volume will be published separately but original conjoint publication of certain works is indicated in the EEWN volume numbering [4a, b; 7a, b, etc.]. Where EEWN editors have been appointed, their names are listed

1 Waverley [1814]
2 Guy Mannering [1815] P.D. Garside, *Cardiff*
3 The Antiquary [1816] David Hewitt, *Aberdeen*
4a The Black Dwarf [1816] P.D. Garside
4b The Tale of Old Mortality [1816] Douglas Mack, *Stirling*
5 Rob Roy [1818] John and Winifred MacQueen, *Edinburgh*
6 The Heart of Mid-Lothian [1818] D. Hewitt and Alison Lumsden
7a The Bride of Lammermoor [1819] J.H. Alexander, *Aberdeen*
7b A Legend of the Wars of Montrose [1819] J.H. Alexander
8 Ivanhoe [1820] Graham Tulloch, *S. Australia*
9 The Monastery [1820] Penelope Fielding, *Trinity College, Dublin*
10 The Abbot [1820] Christopher Johnson, *Oxford*
11 Kenilworth [1821] J.H. Alexander
12 The Pirate [1822]
13 The Fortunes of Nigel [1822] Frank Jordan, *Miami, Ohio*
14 Peveril of the Peak [1822]
15 Quentin Durward [1823] G.A.M. Wood, *Stirling*
16 Saint Ronan's Well [1824] Mark Weinstein, *Nevada*
17 Redgauntlet [1824] G.A.M. Wood
18a The Betrothed [1825] J.B. Ellis, *Edinburgh*
18b The Talisman [1825] J.B. Ellis
19 Woodstock [1826]
20 Chronicles of the Canongate [1827] Claire Lamont, *Newcastle*
21 The Fair Maid of Perth [1828] A. Hook and D. Mackenzie, *Glasgow*
22 Anne of Geierstein [1829] J.H. Alexander
23a Count Robert of Paris [1831] Kurt Gamerschlag, *Bonn*
23b Castle Dangerous [1831]
24 *Stories from* The Keepsake [1828]
25a Introductions and Notes from the *Magnum Opus* edition of 1829–33
25b Introductions and Notes from the *Magnum Opus* edition of 1829–33

WALTER SCOTT

SAINT RONAN'S WELL

Edited by
Mark Weinstein

EDINBURGH
University
Press

COLUMBIA
University
Press

Edinburgh University Press
22 George Square, Edinburgh
Columbia University Press
562 West 113th Street, New York

Typeset in Linotronic Ehrhardt
by Speedspools, Edinburgh
and printed and bound in Great Britain
on acid-free paper at the University Press, Cambridge

ISBN 0 7486 0535 5 (Edinburgh edition)

British Library Cataloguing in Publication Data
Waverley Novels
Fiction
Scott, Sir Walter 1771–1832
New Edition
Hewitt, David, Editor-in-chief
Saint Ronan's Well
Mark Weinstein, editor

ISBN 0-231-10398-0 (Columbia edition)

Library of Congress Cataloging-in-Publication Data and LC Card Number available on request

FOREWORD

The Publication of *Waverley* in 1814 marked the emergence of the modern novel in the western world. It is difficult now to recapture the impact of this and the following novels of Scott on a readership accustomed to prose fiction either as picturesque romance, 'Gothic' quaintness, or presentation of contemporary manners. For Scott not only invented the historical novel, but gave it a dimension and a relevance that made it available for a great variety of new kinds of writing. Balzac in France, Manzoni in Italy, Gogol and Tolstoy in Russia, were among the many writers of fiction influenced by the man Stendhal called 'notre père, Walter Scott'.

What Scott did was to show history and society in motion: old ways of life being challenged by new; traditions being assailed by counter-statements; loyalties, habits, prejudices clashing with the needs of new social and economic developments. The attraction of tradition and its ability to arouse passionate defence, and simultaneously the challenge of progress and 'improvement', produce a pattern that Scott saw as the living fabric of history. And this history was rooted in *place*; events happened in localities still recognisable after the disappearance of the original actors and the establishment of new patterns of belief and behaviour.

Scott explored and presented all this by means of stories, entertainments, which were read and enjoyed as such. At the same time his passionate interest in history led him increasingly to see these stories as illustrations of historical truths, so that when he produced his final *Magnum Opus* edition of the novels he surrounded them with historical notes and illustrations, and in this almost suffocating guise they have been reprinted in edition after edition ever since. The time has now come to restore these novels to the form in which they were presented to their first readers, so that today's readers can once again capture their original power and freshness. At the same time, serious errors of transcription, omission, and interpretation, resulting from the haste of their transmission from manuscript to print can now be corrected.

David Daiches

EDINBURGH
University
Press

CONTENTS

ACKNOWLEDGEMENTS

The Scott Advisory Board and the editors of the Edinburgh Edition of the Waverley Novels wish to express their gratitude to The University Court of the University of Edinburgh *and its Press Committee for their vision in initiating and supporting the preparation of the first critical edition of Walter Scott's fiction. Those Universities which employ the editors have also contributed greatly in paying the editors' salaries, and awarding research leave and grants for travel and materials. Particular thanks are due to* The University of Aberdeen *and to the* University of Nevada, Las Vegas *for their support in the editing of* Saint Ronan's Well.

Although the edition is the work of scholars employed by universities, the project could not have prospered without the help of the sponsors cited below. Their generosity has met the direct costs of the initial research and of the preparation of the text of the first six novels to appear in this edition.

BANK OF SCOTLAND

The collapse of the great Edinburgh publisher Archibald Constable in January 1826 entailed the ruin of Sir Walter Scott who found himself responsible for his own private debts, for the debts of the printing business of James Ballantyne and Co. in which he was co-partner, and for the bank advances to Archibald Constable which had been guaranteed by the printing business. Scott's largest creditors were Sir William Forbes and Co., bankers, and the Bank of Scotland. On the advice of Sir William Forbes himself, the creditors did not sequester his property, but agreed to the creation of a trust to which he committed his future literary earnings, and which ultimately repaid the debts of over £120,000 for which he was legally liable.

In the same year the Government proposed to curtail the rights of the Scottish banks to issue their own notes; Scott wrote the 'Letters of Malachi Malagrowther' in their defence, arguing that the measure was neither in the interests of the banks nor of Scotland. The 'Letters' were so successful that the Government was forced to withdraw its proposal and to this day the Scottish Banks issue their own notes.

A portrait of Sir Walter appears on all current bank notes of the Bank of Scotland because Scott was a champion of Scottish banking, and because he was an illustrious and honourable customer not just of the Bank of Scotland itself, but also of three other banks now incorporated within it—the British Linen Bank which continues today as the merchant banking arm of the Bank of Scotland, Sir William Forbes and Co., and Ramsays, Bonars and Company.

Bank of Scotland's *support of the EEWN continues its long and fruitful involvement with the affairs of Walter Scott.*

P.F. CHARITABLE TRUST

The P.F. Charitable Trust is the main charitable trust of the Fleming family which founded and still has a controlling interest in the City firm of Robert Fleming Holdings Limited. *It was started in 1951 by Philip Fleming and has since been added to by his son, Robin, who is now Managing Trustee. The Board and the editors are most grateful to the Trust and Mr Robin Fleming for their generosity to the Edition.*

EDINBURGH UNIVERSITY DEVELOPMENT TRUST

The Edinburgh University General Council Trust, now incorporated within the Edinburgh University Development Trust, derived its funds from the contributions of graduates of the University. To the trustees, and to all whose gifts allowed the Trust to give a generous grant to the EEWN, the Board and the editors express their thanks.

The Board and editors also wish to thank Sir Gerald Elliot *for a gift from his charitable trust, and the British Academy and the Carnegie Trust for the Universities of Scotland for grants to facilitate specific aspects of EEWN research.*

LIBRARIES

Without the generous assistance of the two great repositories of Scott manuscripts, the National Library of Scotland *and the* Pierpont Morgan Library, *New York, it would not have been possible to have undertaken the editing of Scott's novels, and the Board and editors cannot overstate the extent to which they are indebted to their Trustees and staffs. In particular they wish to pay tribute to the late* Professor Denis Roberts, *Librarian of the National Library, who served on the Scott Advisory Board, who persuaded many of his colleagues in Britain and throughout the world to assist the Edition, and whose determination brought about the repatriation in 1986 of the Pforzheimer Library's Scott manuscripts and of the Interleaved Set of the Waverley Novels.*

SAINT RONAN'S WELL

The manuscript of Saint Ronan's Well *is part of the magnificent Scott collection of the Pierpont Morgan Library, an oasis of civility in midtown Manhattan. The editor is especially indebted to Ms Inge Dupont, Mr David Loggie, and Mr Robert Parks. The following libraries made available to the editor rare editions of* Saint Ronan's Well*: the British Library, the National Library of Scotland, Stanford University Library, Stirling University Library, University College Library, London, and University of Illinois Library, Champagne-Urbana.*

Thanks are also due to Dr J. H. Alexander, The Marjorie Barrick Foundation, Dr Ian Clark, Mr Elmer Curley, Professor David Daiches, Professor Tim Erwin, Professor Richard Harp, Dr David Hewitt, Dr Joan Pittock

Wesson (Director, The Thomas Reid Institute, University of Aberdeen), Mr Lyle Rivera and the University of Nevada, Las Vegas, Foundation, Dr Archie Turnbull, and Professor John Unrue. Special thanks are due to Dr Alison Lumsden, an extremely able researcher and reader of Scott's difficult manuscript.

To help editors solve specific problems, the Edinburgh Edition of the Waverley Novels has appointed the following as consultants: Professor David Nordloh, Indiana University (editorial practice); Dr Alan Bruford, University of Edinburgh, (popular beliefs and customs); Dr John Cairns, University of Edinburgh (Scots Law); Professor Thomas Craik, University of Durham (Shakespeare); Mr John Ellis, University of Edinburgh (medieval literature); Dr Caroline Jackson-Houlston, Oxford Polytechnic (popular song); Mr Roy Pinkerton, University of Edinburgh (classical literature); Mrs Mairi Robinson (language); Professor David Stevenson, University of St Andrews (history). Of these the editor of Saint Ronan's Well *is particularly grateful for the generous help of Dr Cairns, Professor Craik, Dr Jackson-Houlston, and Mrs Robinson.*

The general editor of Saint Ronan's Well *was David Hewitt.*

GENERAL INTRODUCTION

The Edinburgh Edition of the Waverley Novels is the first authoritative edition of Walter Scott's fiction. It is the first to return to what Scott actually wrote in his manuscripts and proofs, and the first to reconsider fundamentally the presentation of his novels in print. In the light of comprehensive research, the editors decided in principle that the text of the novels in the new edition should be based on the first editions, but that all those manuscript readings which had been lost through accident, error, or misunderstanding should be restored. As a result each novel in the Edinburgh Edition differs in thousands of ways from the versions we have been accustomed to read, and many hundreds of readings never before printed have been recovered from the manuscripts. The individual differences are often minor, but are cumulatively telling. The return to the original Scott produces fresher, less formal and less pedantic novels than we have known.

Scott was the most famous and prestigious novelist of his age, but he became insolvent in 1826 following the bankruptcy of his publishers, Hurst, Robinson and Co. in London and Archibald Constable and Co. in Edinburgh. In 1827 Robert Cadell, who had succeeded Constable as Scott's principal publisher, proposed the first collected edition of the complete Waverley Novels as one way of reducing the mountain of debt for which Scott was legally liable. Scott agreed to the suggestion and over the next few years revised the text of his novels and wrote introductions and notes. The edition was published in 48 monthly volumes from 1829 to 1833. The full story of the making of the Magnum Opus, as it was familiarly christened by Scott, is told in Jane Millgate's *Scott's Last Edition* (Edinburgh, 1987), but for present purposes what is significant is that the Magnum became the standard edition of Scott, and since his death in 1832 all editions of the Waverley Novels, with the exceptions of Claire Lamont's *Waverley* (Oxford, 1981), and Tony Inglis's *The Heart of Mid-Lothian* (London, 1994), have been based on it.

Because Scott prepared the Magnum Opus it has long been felt that it represented his final wishes and intentions. In a literal sense this must be so, but all readers who open the pages of any edition published since 1832 and are confronted with the daunting clutter of introductions, prefaces, notes, and appendices, containing a miscellaneous assemblage of historical illustration and personal anecdote, must feel that the creative power which took Britain, Europe and America by storm in the preceding decades is cabin'd, cribb'd, confin'd by its Magnum context. Just as the new matter of 1829–33 is not integral to the novels as they were originally conceived, neither are the revisions and additions to the text.

'Scholarly editors may disagree about many things, but they are in general agreement that their goal is to discover exactly what an author wrote and to determine what form of his work he wished the public to have.' Thus Thomas Tanselle in 1976 succinctly and memorably defined the business of textual editing. The editors of the Edinburgh Edition have made this goal their own, and have returned to the original manuscripts, to the surviving proofs, and to other textually relevant material to determine exactly what Scott wrote; they have also investigated each British edition and every relevant foreign edition published in Scott's lifetime. They have discovered that ever since they were written, the Waverley Novels have suffered from textual degeneration.

The first editions were derived from copies of Scott's manuscripts, but the pressure to publish quickly was such that they are not wholly reliable representations of what he wrote. Without exception, later editions were based on a preceding printed version, and so include most of the mistakes of their predecessors while adding their own, and in most cases Scott was not involved. There was an accumulation of error, and when Scott came to prepare the Magnum Opus he revised and corrected an earlier printed text, apparently unaware of the extent to which it was already corrupt. Thus generations of readers have read versions of Scott which have suffered significantly from the changes, both deliberate and accidental, of editors, compositors and proof-readers.

A return to authentic Scott is therefore essential. The manuscripts provide the only fully authoritative state of the texts of the novels, for they alone proceed wholly from the author. They are for the most part remarkably coherent; the shape of Scott's narratives seems to have been established before he committed his ideas to paper, although a close examination of what he wrote shows countless minor revisions made in the process of writing, and usually at least one layer of later revising. We are closest to Scott in the manuscripts, but they could not be the sole textual basis for the new edition. They give us his own words, free of non-authorial interventions, but they do not constitute the 'form of his work he wished the public to have'.

Scott expected his novels to be printed, usually in three volumes, and he structured his stories so that they fitted the three-volume division of the printed books. He expected minor errors to be corrected, words repeated in close proximity to each other to be removed, spelling to be normalised, and a printed-book style of punctuation, amplifying and replacing the marks he had provided in manuscript, to be inserted. There are no written instructions to the printers to this effect, but his acceptance of what was done implies approval, even although the imposition of the conventions of print had such a profound effect on the evolution of his text that the conversion of autograph text into print was less a question of transliteration than of translation.

This assumption of authorial approval is better founded for Scott than for any other writer. Walter Scott was in partnership with James Ballantyne in a firm of printers which Ballantyne managed and for which Scott generated much of the work. The contracts for new Scott novels were unusual, in that they always stipulated that the printing would be undertaken by James Ballantyne and Co., and that the publishers should have the exclusive right only to purchase and to manage the sales of an agreed number of copies. Thus production was controlled not by the publishers but by James Ballantyne and his partner, Walter Scott. The textually significant consequence of this partnership was a mutual trust to a degree uncommon between author and printer. Ballantyne was most anxious to serve Scott and to assist him in preparing the novels for public presentation, and Scott not only permitted his but actively sought it. Theirs was a unique business and literary partnership which had a crucial effect on the public form of the Waverley Novels.

Scott expected his novels to appear in the form and format in which they did appear, but in practice what was done was not wholly satisfactory because of the complicated way in which the texts were processed. Until 1827, when Scott acknowledged his authorship, the novels were published anonymously and so that Scott's well-known handwriting should not be seen in the printing works the original manuscripts were copied, and it was these copies, not Scott's original manuscripts, which were used in the printing house. Not a single leaf is known to survive but the copyists probably began the tidying and regularising. The compositors worked from the copies, and, when typesetting, did not just follow what was before them, but supplied punctuation, normalised spelling, and corrected minor errors. Proofs were first read in-house against the transcripts, and in addition to the normal checking for mistakes these proofs were used to improve the punctuation and the spelling.

When the initial corrections had been made, a new set of proofs went to James Ballantyne. He acted as editor, not just as proof-reader. He drew Scott's attention to gaps in the text and pointed out inconsistencies in detail; he asked Scott to standardise names; he substituted nouns for pronouns when they occurred in the first sentence of a paragraph, and inserted the names of speakers in dialogue; he changed incorrect punctuation, and added punctuation he thought desirable; he corrected grammatical errors and removed close verbal repetitions; he told Scott when he could not follow what was happening; and when he particularly enjoyed something he said so.

These annotated proofs were sent to the author, who sometimes accepted Ballantyne's suggestions and sometimes rejected them. He made many more changes; he cut out redundant words, and substituted the vivid for the pedestrian; he refined the punctuation; he sometimes reworked and revised passages extensively, and in so doing made the proofs a stage in the composition of the novels.

When Ballantyne received Scott's corrections and revisions, he transcribed all the changes on to a clean set of proofs so that the author's hand would not be seen by the compositors. Further revises were prepared. Some of these were seen and read by Scott but by and large he seems to have trusted Ballantyne to make sure that the earlier corrections and revisions had been correctly executed. When doing this Ballantyne did not just read for typesetting errors, but continued the process of punctuating and tidying the text. A final proof allowed the corrections to be inspected and the imposition of the type to be checked prior to printing.

One might imagine that after all this activity the first editions would be perfect, but this is far from being the case. There are usually in excess of 50,000 variants in the first edition of a three-volume novel when compared with the manuscript. The great majority are in accordance with Scott's general wishes as described above. But the intermediaries, as the copyist, compositors, proof-readers, and James Ballantyne are collectively known, made mistakes; they misread the manuscripts from time to time, and they did not always understand what Scott had written. This would not have mattered had there not also been procedural failures. The transcripts were not thoroughly checked against the original manuscripts. Scott himself does not seem to have read the proofs against the manuscripts and thus did not notice transcription errors which made sense in their context. And James Ballantyne continued his editing in post-authorial proofs; his changes may have been in the spirit of Scott's own critical proof-reading, but it is probable that his efforts were never inspected by the author.

The editors of the Edinburgh Edition of the Waverley Novels have studied every single variant in the first editions of all the novels they have worked on to date. There are a large number of small verbal differences, and the editors have come to the conclusion that the words originally written by Scott, though subsequently changed by the intermediaries, are nearly always justified by colloquial, dialect, or period usage. Similarly the punctuation supplied at times misinterprets the sense of the manuscript or the rhythm of speech, and the substitution of synonyms for repeated words was often effected too mechanically, changing meaning or spoiling rhetoric. It is not surprising that the intermediaries should make mistakes when translating the manuscripts into print. Even James Ballantyne's knowledge of language and history was limited compared to Scott's. He was a trusted and competent editor; he was honest about his likes and dislikes and was useful to Scott in giving voice to them. But his annotations and suggestions show that he did not appreciate the full variety of Scott's language, objected to any suggestion of the indelicate, and tidied the text by rule. Above all, his comments were made as Scott wrote, and without knowing the outcome of the story, and thus he was inevitably unaware of the architectonics of the complete work of art. His views were sometimes wrong, and Scott was sometimes wrong to give way to them.

The editors have normally chosen the first edition of a novel as base-text, for the first edition usually represents the culmination of the initial creative process, and, local failings excepted, usually seems closest to the form of his work he wished his public to have. After the careful collation of all pre-publication materials, and in the light of their investigation into the factors governing the writing and printing of the Waverley Novels, they have incorporated into the base-text readings which were lost in the production process through accident, error or misunderstanding. In certain cases they have also introduced into the base-texts revisions from printed texts which they believe to have emanated from Scott, or are consistent with the spirit of his own revision during the initial creative process. Only revisions which belong to the process and period of initial creation have been adopted. In addition, they have corrected various kinds of error, such as typographical and copy-editing mistakes including the misnumbering of chapters, inconsistencies in the naming of characters, egregious errors of fact that are not part of the fiction, and failures of sense which a simple emendation can restore. The result is an ideal text, which the first readers of the Waverley Novels would have read had the production process been less pressurised and more considered.

The 'new' Scott will be visible not only in the text but also in the context. The Magnum introductions and notes are not integral to the novels as they were originally conceived, and are therefore reserved for separate publication in the final volumes of the edition where they will be treated as a distinct, final phase of Scott's involvement in his fiction. Thus the novels appear as they were first presented. The Edinburgh Edition of the Waverley Novels offers a clean text; there are no footnotes or superscripts to detract from the pleasure of reading. It does not remove Scott's own introductions only to replace them with those of modern editors; the textual essays appear at the end, where they will be encountered only after reading Scott. The essays present a detailed history of the genesis and composition of the novel, a history of the evolution of the old text, and a description of the distinguishing features of the new. The textual apparatus does not include a full list of variants because for one of the major early works there would be at least 100,000 to record. Instead, the textual essays analyse and illustrate the evidence gleaned from the collation of the manuscripts and proofs (where these are extant) and of all relevant editions published in Scott's lifetime. All variants from the base-text are listed in the emendation list (but as variants from the Magnum are not, the scale of the change from old editions to the new is not immediately apparent).

And finally, there are explanatory notes and a glossary. Scott's reading was wide and voluminous, he was immensely knowledgeable in a range of disciplines, and he had a considerable understanding of the social organisation, customs and beliefs of contemporary and historical societies. Few readers are likely to appreciate the full extent of his learning without some assistance, and the notes at the end of this volume draw on a greater variety of expertise, and are more comprehensive, than any previously published. They are informative rather than expository; for instance, they identify all quotations, from the most obvious passages in the Bible and Shakespeare through to the truly recondite, but they leave the reader to consider their significance in each context. And the glossary for the first time attempts to cover comprehensively all Scott's period, dialectal, foreign, and obscure words.

The Edinburgh Edition of the Waverley Novels aims to provide an authoritative text of Scott's fiction, to give the reader the support required to appreciate the intellectual richness of his work, and to allow a new audience to share the excitement that the novels generated when they were first published. The editors are confident of fulfilling the first two aims. The reader must be judge of their success in the third.

DAVID HEWITT

SAINT RONAN'S WELL.

BY THE AUTHOR OF "WAVERLEY, QUENTIN DURWARD," &C.

"A jolly place," said he, "in times of old!
But something ails it now: the spot is curst."

WORDSWORTH.

IN THREE VOLUMES.

VOL. I.

EDINBURGH:

PRINTED FOR ARCHIBALD CONSTABLE AND CO. EDINBURGH:
AND HURST, ROBINSON, AND CO. LONDON.

1824.

SAINT RONAN'S WELL

VOLUME I

Chapter One

AN OLD-WORLD LANDLADY

But to make up my tale,
She breweth good ale,
And thereof maketh sale.
SKELTON

ALTHOUGH FEW, if any, of the countries of Europe, have increased so rapidly in wealth and cultivation as Scotland during the last half century, Sultan Mahmoud's owls might nevertheless have found in Caledonia, at any term within that flourishing period, their dowry of ruined villages. Accident or local advantages have, in many instances, transferred the inhabitants of ancient hamlets, from the situations which their predecessors chose, with more respect to security than convenience, to those in which their increasing industry and commerce could more easily expand itself; and hence places which stand distinguished in Scottish History, and which figure in David Macpherson's excellent historical map, can now only be discerned from the wild moor by the verdure which clothes their site, or, at best, by a few scattered ruins, resembling pinfolds, which mark the spot of their former existence.

The little village of Saint Ronan's, though it had not yet fallen into the state of entire oblivion we have described, was, about twenty years since, fast verging towards it. The situation had something in it so romantic, that it provoked the pencil of every passing tourist; and we will endeavour, therefore, to describe it in language which can scarce be less intelligible than some of their sketches, avoiding, however, for reasons which seem to us of weight, to give any more exact indication of the site, than that it is on the southern side of the Forth, and not above thirty miles distant from the English frontier.

A river of considerable magnitude pours its streams through a narrow vale, varying in breadth from two miles to a fourth of that distance, and which, being composed of rich alluvial soil, is, and has long been, enclosed, tolerably well inhabited, and cultivated with all the skill of Scottish agriculture. Either side of this valley is bounded by a chain of hills, which, on the right in particular, may be almost termed mountains. Little brooks arising in these ridges, and finding their way to the river, offer each its own little vale to the industry of the cultivator. Some of them bear fine large trees, which have as yet escaped the axe, and upon the banks of most there are scattered, from space to space, patches and fringes of natural copsewood, above and around which the bare banks of the stream arise, somewhat desolate in the colder months, but in summer glowing with dark purple heath, or with the golden lustre of the broom and gorse. This is a sort of scenery peculiar to those countries, which abound, like Scotland, in hills and in streams, and where the traveller is ever and anon discovering in some intricate and unexpected recess, a simple and sylvan beauty, which pleases him the more, that it seems to be peculiarly his own property as the first discoverer.

In one of these recesses, and so near its opening as to command the prospect of the river, the broader valley, and the opposite chain of hills, stood, and, unless neglect and desertion have completed their work, still stands, the ancient and decayed village of Saint Ronan's. The site was singularly picturesque, as the straggling street of the village ran up a very steep hill, on the side of which were clustered, as it were, upon little terraces, the cottages which composed the place, seeming, as in the Swiss towns on the Alps, to rise above each other towards the ruins of an old castle, which continued to occupy the crest of the eminence, and the strength of which had doubtless led the neighbourhood to assemble under its walls for protection. It must, indeed, have been a place of formidable defence, for, on the side opposite to the town, its walls rose straight up from the verge of a tremendous precipice, whose base was washed by Saint Ronan's burn, as the brook was entitled. On the southern side, where the declivity was less precipitous, the ground had been carefully levelled into successive terraces, which ascended to the summit of the hill, and were, or rather had been, connected by stair-cases of stone, rudely ornamented. In peaceful periods these terraces had been occupied by the gardens of the Castle, and in times of siege, they added to its security; for each commanded the other, so that they could be separately and successively defended, and all were exposed to the fire from the place itself—a massive square tower of the largest size, surrounded, as usual, by lower buildings, and a high embattled wall. On the northern side, a considerable mountain, of which the descent that lay between the eminence on which the Castle was situated seemed a detached portion, had been improved and deepened by three successive huge trenches. Another very deep trench was drawn in front of the main entrance from the east, where the principal gateway formed the termination of the street, which, as we have noticed, ascended from the village, and this last defence completed the fortifications of the tower.

In the ancient gardens of the Castle, and upon all sides of it excepting the western, which was precipitous, large old trees had found root, mantling the rock and the ancient and ruinous walls with their dusky verdure, and increasing the effect of the shattered pile which towered up from the centre.

Seated on the threshold of this ancient pile, where the "proud porter" had in former days "rear'd himself,"* a stranger had a complete and commanding view of the decayed village, the houses of which, to a fanciful imagination, might seem as if they had been suddenly arrested in hurrying down the precipitous hill, and fixed as if by magic in the whimsical arrangement which they now presented. It was like a sudden pause in one of Amphion's country-dances, when the huts which were to form the future Thebes were jigging it to his lute. But, to such an observer, the melancholy excited by the desolate appearance of the village soon overcame all mere light frolics of the imagination. Originally constructed on the humble plan used in the building of Scottish cottages about a century ago, the greater part of them had been long deserted, and their fallen roofs, blackened gables, and ruinous walls, shewed Desolation's triumph over Poverty. On some cottages the rafters, varnished with soot, were still standing, in whole or in part, like skeletons, and a few, wholly or partially covered with thatch, seemed still inhabited, though scarce habitable; for the smoke of the peat-fires, which prepared the humble meal of the indwellers, stole upwards, not only from the chimneys, its regular vent, but from various other crevices in the roofs. Nature, in the meanwhile, always changing, but renewing as she changes, was supplying, by the power of vegetation, the fallen and decaying marks of human labour. Small pollards, which had been formerly planted around the little gardens, had now waxed into huge and high forest trees; the fruit trees had extended their branches over the verges of the little yards, and the hedges had shot up into huge and irregular bushes; while quantities of dock, and nettles, and hemlock, hiding the ruined walls, were busily converting the whole scene of desolation into a picturesque forest-bank.

* See the old Ballad of King Estmere, in PERCY'S *Reliques*.

Two houses in Saint Ronan's were still in something like decent repair—places essential, the one to the spiritual weal of the inhabitants, the other to the accommodation of travellers. These were the clergyman's manse and the village inn. Of the former we need only say, that it formed no exception to the general rule by which the landed proprietors of Scotland seem to proceed in lodging their clergy, not only in the cheapest, but in the ugliest and most inconvenient house which the wit of masonry can contrive. It had the usual number of chimneys—two, namely—rising like asses ears at either end, which answered the purpose for which they were designed as ill as usual. It had all the ordinary leaks and inlets to the fury of the elements, which usually form the subject of the complaints of a Scottish incumbent to his brethren of the presbytery. And, to complete the picture, the clergyman being a bachelor, the pigs had unmolested admission to the garden and court-yard, broken windows were repaired with brown paper, and the disordered and squalid appearance of a low farm-house, occupied by a bankrupt tenant, dishonoured the dwelling of one, who, besides his clerical character, was a scholar and a gentleman, though a little of a humourist.

Beside the manse stood the kirk of Saint Ronan's, a little old mansion with a clay floor, and an assemblage of wretched pews, originally of carved oak, but heedfully clouted with white fir-deal. But the outside form of the church was elegant in the outline, having been built in Catholic times, when we cannot deny to the forms of ecclesiastical architecture that grace, which, as good Protestants, we refuse to their doctrine. The fabric hardly raised its grey and vaulted roof among the crumbling hills of mortality by which it was surrounded, and was indeed so small in size, and so much lowered in height by the graves on the outside, which ascended half way up the little Saxon windows, that it might itself have appeared only a funeral vault, or mausoleum of larger size. Its little square tower, with the ancient belfrey, alone distinguished it from such a monument. But when the grey-headed beadle turned the keys with his shaking hand, the antiquary was admitted into an ancient building, which, from the style of its architecture, and some monuments of the Mowbrays of Saint Ronan's, which the old man was accustomed to point out, was generally conjectured to be as early as the thirteenth century.

These Mowbrays of Saint Ronan's seem to have been at one time a very powerful family. They were allied to, and friends of the house of Douglas, at the time when the overgrown power of that heroic race made the Stuarts tremble on the Scottish throne. It followed that, when, as our old naive historian expresses it, "no one dared to strive with a Douglas, nor yet with a Douglas's man; for if he did, he was sure to come by the waur," the family of Saint Ronan's shared their prosperity, and became lords of almost the whole of the rich valley of which their mansion commanded the prospect. But upon the turning of the tide, in the reign of James II., they became despoiled of the greater part of these fair acquisitions, and succeeding events reduced their importance still farther. Nevertheless, they were, in the middle of the seventeenth century, still a family of considerable note; and Sir Reginald Mowbray, after the unhappy battle of Dunbar, distinguished himself by the obstinate defence of his Castle against the arms of Cromwell, who, incensed at the opposition which he had unexpectedly encountered in an obscure corner, caused the fortress to be dismantled and blown up with gunpowder.

After this catastrophe the old Castle was abandoned to ruin; but Sir Reginald, when, like Allan Ramsay's Sir William Worthy, he returned after the Revolution, built himself a house in the fashion of that later age, which he prudently suited in size to the diminished fortunes of his family. It was situated about the middle of the village, whose vicinity was not in these days judged any inconvenience, upon a spot of ground more level than was presented by the rest of the acclivity, where, as we said before, the houses were notched as it were into the side of the steep bank, with little more level ground about them than the spot occupied by their site. But the Laird's house had a court in front and a small garden behind, which again was connected with another garden, which, occupying three terraces, descended, in emulation of the orchards of the old Castle, almost to the banks of the stream.

The family continued to inhabit this new messuage until about fifty years before the commencement of our history, when it was much damaged by a casual fire; and the laird of the day, having just succeeded to a more pleasant and commodious dwelling at the distance of about three miles from the village, determined to abandon the habitation of his ancestors. As he cut down at the same time an ancient rookery, (perhaps to defray the expenses of the migration,) it became a common remark among the country folks, that the decay of Saint Ronan's began when Laird Laurence and the Crows flew off.

The deserted mansion, however, was not consigned to owls and birds of the desart; on the contrary, for many years it witnessed more fun and festivity than when it had been the sombre abode of a grave Scottish Baron of "auld lang syne." In short, it was converted into an inn, and marked by a huge sign, representing on the one side Saint Ronan catching hold of the devil's game-leg with his episcopal crook, as the story may be read in his veracious legend, and on the other the Mowbray arms. It was by far the best frequented public-house in that vicinity; and a thousand stories were told of the revels which had been held within its walls, and the gambols which had been achieved under the influence of its liquors. All this, however, had been long over.

> "A jolly place," said he, "in times of old!
> But something ails it now: the spot is curst."

The worthy couple (servants and favourites of the Mowbray family) who first kept the inn, had died reasonably wealthy, after long carrying on a flourishing trade, leaving behind them an only daughter. They had acquired by degrees not only the property of the inn itself, of which they were originally tenants, but of some remarkably good meadow-land by the side of the brook, which, when touched by a little pecuniary necessity, the Lairds of Saint Ronan's had disposed of piece-meal, as the readiest way to portion off a daughter, procure a commission for the younger son, and the like emergencies. So that Meg Dods, when she succeeded to her parents, was a considerable heiress, and, as such, had the honour of refusing three topping farmers, two bonnet-lairds, and a horse-couper, who successively made proposals to her.

Many bets were laid on the horse-couper's success, but the knowing ones were taken in. Determined to ride the fore-horse herself, Meg would admit no helpmate who might soon assert the rights of a master; and so, in single blessedness, and with all the despotism of Queen Bess herself, she ruled all matters with a high hand, not only over her men servants and maid servants, but over the stranger within her gates, who, if he ventured to oppose Meg's sovereign will and pleasure, or desired to have either fare or accommodation different from that which she chose to provide him, was instantly ejected with that answer which Erasmus tells us silenced all complaints in the German inns of his time, *Quære aliud hospitium*; or, as Meg expressed it, "Troop aff wi' ye to another public." As this amounted to a banishment equal to sixteen miles from Meg's residence, the unhappy party on whom it was passed had no other refuge save deprecating the wrath of his landlady, and implicit resignation to her will, and his own fate. It is but justice to Meg Dods to state, that though hers was a severe and almost despotic government, it could not be termed a tyranny, since it was exercised upon the whole for the good of the subject.

The vaults of the old Laird's cellar had not, even in his own day, been replenished with more excellent wines; the only difficulty was to prevail on Meg to look for the precise liquor you chose;—to which it may be added, that she often became restive when she thought a company had had "as much as did them good," and refused to furnish any more supplies. Then her kitchen was her pride and glory; she looked to the dressing of every dish herself, and there were some with which she suffered no one to interfere. Such were the cock-a-leeky, and the savoury minced collops, which rivalled in their way even the veal cutlets of our old friend Mrs Hall, at Ferrybridge. Meg's table-linen, bed-linen, and so forth, were always home-made, of the best quality, and in the best order; and a weary day was that to the chambermaid in which her lynx-eye discovered any neglect of the strict cleanliness which she constantly enforced. Indeed, considering Meg's country and calling, we were never able to account for her extreme and scrupulous cleanliness, unless by supposing that it afforded her the most apt and frequent pretext for scolding her maids; an exercise in which she displayed so much eloquence and energy, that we must needs suppose it to have been a favourite one.

We have only further to commemorate the moderation of Meg's reckonings, which, when they closed the banquet, often relieved the apprehensions, instead of saddening the heart, of the rising guest. A shilling for breakfast, three shillings for dinner, including a pint of old port, eighteen-pence for a snug supper—such were the charges of the inn of Saint Ronan's, under this landlady of the olden world, even after the nineteenth century had commenced; and they were ever tendered with the pious recollection, that her good father never charged half so much, but these weary times rendered it impossible for her to make the lawing less.

Notwithstanding all these excellent and rare properties, the inn at Saint Ronan's shared the decay of the village to which it belonged. This was owing to various circumstances. The high-road had been turned aside from the place, the steepness of the street being murder, (so the postillions declared,) to their post-horses. It was thought that Meg's stern refusal to treat them with liquor, or to connive at their exchanging for porter and whisky the corn which should feed their cattle, had no small influence on the opinion of these respectable gentlemen, and that a little cutting and levelling would have made the ascent easy enough; but let that pass. It was an injury which Meg did not easily forgive to the country gentlemen, most of whom she had recollected when children. "Their fathers," she said, "wad not have done the like of it to a lone woman." Then the decay of the village itself, which had formerly contained a set of feuars and bonnet-lairds, who, under the name of the Chirupping Club, contrived to drink twopenny, qualified with brandy or whisky, at least twice or thrice a-week, was some small loss.

The temper and manners of the landlady scared away all customers of that numerous class, who will not allow originality to be an excuse for the breach of decorum, and who, accustomed perhaps to little attendance at home, love to play the great man at an inn, and to have a certain number of bows, deferential speeches, and apologies, in answer to the G— d—n ye's which they bestow on the house, attendance, and entertainment. Woe to those who commenced this sort of barter in the Clachan of Saint Ronan's; well could Meg Dods pay them back, but it was in their own coin; and glad they were to escape from the house with eyes not quite scratched out, and ears not more deafened than if they had been within hearing of a pitched battle.

Nature had formed honest Meg for such encounters; and as her noble soul delighted in them, so her outward properties were in what Tony Lumpkin calls a concatenation accordingly. She had hair of a brindled colour, betwixt black and grey, which was apt to escape in elf-locks from under her mutch when she was thrown into violent agitation—long skinny hands, terminated by stout talons—grey eyes, thin lips, a robust person, a broad, though flat chest, capital wind, and a voice that could match a choir of fish-women. She was accustomed to say of herself in her more gentle moods, that her bark was worse than her bite; but what teeth could have matched a tongue, which, when in full career, might be heard from the Kirk to the Castle of Saint Ronan's?

These notable gifts, however, had no charms for the travellers of these light and giddy-paced times, and Meg's inn became less and less frequented. What carried the evil to the uttermost was, that a fanciful lady of rank in the neighbourhood chanced to recover of some imaginary complaint by the use of a mineral well about a mile and a half from the village; a fashionable doctor was found to write an analysis of the healing stream, with a list of sundry cures; a speculative builder took land in feu, and erected lodging-houses, shops, and even streets. At length a tontine subscription was obtained to erect an inn, which, for the more grace, was called a hotel; and so the desertion of Meg Dods became general.

She had still, however, her friends and well-wishers, many of whom thought, that as she was a lone woman, and known to be well to pass in the world, she would act wisely to retire from public life, and take down a sign which had no longer fascination for guests. But Meg's spirit scorned submission, direct or implied. "Her father's door," she said, "should be open to the road, till her father's bairn should be streekit and carried out at it with her feet foremost. It was not for the profit—there was little profit at it;—profit?—there was a dead loss; —but she wad not be dung by any of them—they maun hae a hottle, maun they?—and an honest public canna serve them—they may hoddle on that likes; but they shall see that Luckie Dods can hoddle on as lang as the best of them—Ay, though they had made a Tamteen of it, and linkit aw their breaths of lives, whilk are in their nostrils, on end of ilk other like a string of wild geese, and the langest liver bruick a', whilk was sinful presumption, she would match ilk ane of them as lang as her ain wind held out. And besides a' that," she concluded, "I see them a' down the black gate before I change my auld ways or charge them a penny mair than I have done this twenty years." Fortunate it was for Meg, since she had formed this doughty resolution, that although her inn had decayed in custom, her land had risen in value in a degree which more than compensated the balance on the wrong side of her book, and, joined to her usual providence and economy, enabled her to act up to her lofty purpose.

She prosecuted her trade too with every attention to its diminished income; shut up the windows of one half of her house, to baffle the tax-gatherer; retrenched her furniture; discharged her pair of post-horses, and pensioned off the old hump-backed postillion who drove them, retaining his services, however, as an occasional assistant to a still more aged hostler. To console herself for restrictions by which her pride was secretly wounded, she agreed with the celebrated Dick Tinto to re-paint her father's sign, which had become rather indecypherable; and Dick accordingly gilded the Bishop's crook, and augmented the horrors of the Devil's aspect, until it became a terror to all the younger fry of the school-house, and a sort of visible illustration of the terrors of the arch-enemy, with which the minister endeavoured to impress their infant minds.

Under this renewed symbol of her profession, Meg Dods, or Meg Dorts, as she was popularly termed, on account of her refractory humours, was still patronized by some steady customers. Such were the members of the Killnakelty Hunt, once famous on the turf and in the field, but now a set of venerable grey-headed sportsmen, who had sunk from fox-hounds to basket-beagles and coursing, and who made an easy canter on their quiet nags a gentle induction to a dinner at Meg's. "A set of honest decent men they were," Meg said; "had their sang and their joke—and what for no? Their bind was just a Scots pint over-head, and a tappit-hen to the bill, and no man ever saw them the waur o't. It was thae cockle-brained callants of the present day that would be mair owerta'en wi' a puir quart than douce folks were with a magnum."

Then there were a set of ancient brethren of the angle from Edinburgh who visited Saint Ronan's frequently in the spring and summer, a class of guests peculiarly acceptable to Meg, who permitted them more latitude in her premises than she was known to allow to any other body. "They were," she said, "pawky auld carles, that kenn'd whilk side their bread was buttered upon. Ye never heard of ony o' them ganging to the spring, as they behoved to ca' the stinking auld well yonder. Na, na—they were up in the morning—had their parritch, wi' maybe a thimblefull of brandy, and then awa up into the hills, eat their bit cauld meat on the heather, and came hame at e'en wi' the creel full of caller trouts, and had them to their dinner, and their quiet cogue of ale, and their drap punch, and were set singing their catches and glees, as they ca'd them, till ten o'clock, and then to bed, wi' God bless ye—and what for no?"

Thirdly, we may commemorate some ranting blades, who also came from the metropolis to visit Saint Ronan's, attracted by the humours of Meg, and still more by the excellence of her liquor, and the cheapness of her reckonings.—These were members of the Helter Skelter Club, of the Wildfire Club, and other associations formed for the express purpose of getting rid of care and sobriety. Such dashers occasioned many a racket in Meg's house, and many a *bourasque* in Meg's temper. Various were the arts of flattery and violence by which they endeavoured to get supplies of liquor, when Meg's conscience told her they had had too much already. Sometimes they failed, as when the croupier of the Helter Skelter got himself scalded with the mulled wine, in an unsuccessful attempt to coax this formidable virago by a salute; and the excellent president of the Wildfire received a broken head from the keys of the cellar, as he endeavoured to possess himself of these emblems of authority. But little did these dauntless officials care for the exuberant frolics of Meg's temper, which were to them only "pretty Fanny's way"—the *dulces Amaryllidis iræ*. And Meg, on her part, though she often called them "drunken ne'er-do-weels, and thorough-bred High Street blackguards," allowed no other person to speak ill of them in her hearing. "They were daft callants," she said, "and that was all—When the drink was in, the wit was out—ye could not pit an auld head upon young shouthers—a young cowt will canter, be it up-hill or down—And what for no?" was her uniform conclusion.

Nor must we omit, among Meg's steady customers, "faithful amongst the unfaithful found," the copper-nosed sheriff-clerk of the county, who, when summoned by official duty to that district, warmed by recollections of her double-brewed ale, and her generous Antigua, always advertised that his "Prieves," or "Comptis," or whatever other business was in hand, were to proceed on such a day and hour, "within the House of Margaret Dods, Vintner in Saint Ronan's."

We have only farther to notice Meg's mode of conducting herself towards chance travellers, who, knowing nothing of nearer or more fashionable accommodations, or perhaps consulting rather the state of their purse than their taste, stumbled upon her house of entertainment. Her reception of these was as precarious as the hospitality of a savage nation to sailors shipwrecked on their coast. If the guests seemed to have made her mansion their free choice—or if she liked their appearance (and her taste was very capricious)—above all, if they seemed pleased with what they got, and little disposed to criticize or give trouble, it was all very well. But if they had come to Saint Ronan's because the house at the Well was full—or if she disliked what the sailor calls the cut of their jibb—or if, above all, they were critical about their accommodations, none so likely as Meg to give them what in her country is called a *sloan*. In fact, she reckoned such persons a part of that ungenerous and ungrateful public, for whose sake she was keeping her house open at a dead loss, and who had left her, as it were, a victim to her public zeal.

Hence arose the different reports concerning the little inn of Saint Ronan's, which some favoured travellers praised as the neatest and most comfortable old-fashioned house in Scotland, where you had good attendance, and good cheer, at moderate rates; while others, less fortunate, could only talk of the darkness of the rooms, the homeliness of the old furniture, and the detestable bad humour of Meg Dods, the landlady.

Reader, if you come from the more sunny side of the Tweed—or even if, being a Scot, you have had the advantage to be born within the last twenty-five years, you may be induced to think this portrait of Queen Elizabeth, in Dame Quickly's piqued hat and green apron, somewhat overcharged in the features. But I appeal to my own contemporaries, who have known wheel-road, bridle-way, and foot-path, for thirty years, whether they do not, every one of them, remember Meg Dods—or somebody very like her. Indeed, so much is this the case, that about the period I mention, I should have been afraid to have rambled from the Scottish metropolis, in almost any direction, lest I had lighted upon some one of the sisterhood of Dame Quickly, who might suspect me of having showed her up to the public in the character of Meg Dods. At present, though it is possible some one or two of this peculiar class of wild-cats may still exist, their talons must be much impaired by age; and I think that they can do little more than sit, like the Giant Pope in the Pilgrim's Progress, at the door of their unfrequented caverns, and grin at the pilgrims over whom they used formerly to execute their despotism.

Chapter Two

THE GUEST

Quis novus hic hospes?
Dido apud Virgilium

Cha'am-maid! The Gemman in the front parlour!
BOOTS'S *free Translation of the Eneid*

IT WAS on a fine summer's day that a solitary traveller rode under the old-fashioned archway, and alighted in the court-yard of Meg Dods's inn, and delivered the bridle of his horse to the hump-backed postillion. "Bring my saddle-bags," he said, "into the house—or stay—I am abler, I think, to carry them than you." He then assisted the poor meagre groom to unbuckle the straps which secured the humble and now despised convenience, and meantime gave strict charges that his horse should be unbridled, and put into a clean and comfortable stall, the girths slacked, and a cloth cast over his loins; but that the saddle should not be removed until he himself came to see him dressed.

The companion of his travels seemed in the hostler's eye deserving of this care, being a strong active horse, fit either for the road or field, but rather high in bone from a long journey, though from the state of his skin it appeared the utmost care had been bestowed to keep him in condition. While the groom obeyed the stranger's directions, the latter, with his saddle-bags laid over his arm, entered the kitchen of the inn.

Here he found the landlady herself in none of her most blessed humours. The cook-maid was abroad on some errand, and Meg, in a close review of the kitchen apparatus, was making the unpleasing discovery, that trenchers had been broken or cracked, pots and saucepans not so accurately scoured as her precise notions of cleanliness required, which, joined to other detections of a more petty description, stirred her bile in no small degree; so that while she disarranged and arranged the *bink*, she maundered in an undertone, complaints and menaces against the absent delinquent.

The entrance of a guest did not induce her to suspend this agreeable amusement—she just glanced at him as he entered, then turned her back short on him, and continued her labour and her soliloquy of lamentation. Truth is, she thought she recognized in the person of the stranger, one of those useful envoys of the commercial community, called, by themselves and the waiters, *Travellers* par excellence—by others, Riders and Bagmen. Now against this class of customers Meg had peculiar prejudices; because, there being no shops in the old village of Saint Ronan's, the said commercial emissaries, for the convenience of their traffic, always took up their abode at the New Inn, or Hotel, in the rising and rival village called Saint Ronan's Well, unless when some straggler, by chance or dire necessity, was compelled to lodge himself at the Auld Town, as the place of Meg's residence began to be generally termed. She had, therefore, no sooner formed the hasty conclusion, that the individual in question belonged to this obnoxious class, than she resumed her former occupation, and continued to soliloquize and to apostrophize her absent hand-maidens, without ever appearing sensible of his presence.

"The hussy Beenie—the jaud Eppie—the deil's buckie of a callant! —Another plate gaen—they'll break me out of house and ha'!"

The traveller, who, with his saddle-bags rested on the back of a chair, had waited in silence for some note of welcome, now saw that ghost or no-ghost he must speak first, if he intended to have an answer.

"You are my old acquaintance, Mrs Margaret Dods?" said the stranger.

"What for no—and wha are ye that speers?" said Meg, in the same breath, and began to rub a brass candlestick with more vehemence than before—the dry tone in which she spoke indicating plainly, how little concern she took in the conversation.

"A traveller, good Mistress Dods, who comes to take up his lodging here for a day or two."

"I am thinking ye will be mista'en," said Meg; "there's nae room for bags or jaugs here—ye've mista'en your road, neighbour—ye maun e'en bundle yoursell a bit farther down hill."

"I see you have not got the letter I sent you, Mistress Dods?" said the guest.

"How should I, man?" answered the hostess; "they have ta'en awa' the post-office frae us—moved it down till the Spaw-well yonder, as they ca'd."

"Why, that is but a step off," observed the guest.

"Ye will get there the sooner," answered the hostess.

"Nay, but," said the guest, "if you had sent there for my letter, you would have learned——"

"I'm no wanting to learn ony thing at my years," said Meg. "If folk have ony thing to write to me about, they may gie the letter to John Hislop, the carrier, that has used the road these forty years. As for the letters at the post-mistress's, as they ca' her, down by yonder, they may bide in her shop-window, wi' the snaps and bawbee rows, till Beltane, or I loose them. I'll never file my fingers with them. Post-mistress, indeed!—Upsetting cutty! I mind her fou weel when she dreed penance for ante-nup——"

Laughing, but interrupting Meg in good time for the character of the post-mistress, the stranger assured her he had sent his fishing-rod and trunk by her confidential friend the carrier, and that he sincerely hoped she would not turn an old acquaintance out of her premises, especially as he believed he could not sleep in a bed within five miles of Saint Ronan's, if he knew that her Blue room was unengaged.

"Fishing-rod!—Auld acquaintance!—Blue room!" echoed Meg, in some surprise; and, facing round upon the stranger, and examining him with some interest and curiosity,—"Ye'll be nae bag-man, then, after a'?"

"No," said the traveller; "not since I have laid the saddle-bags out of my hands."

"Weel, I canna say but I am glad of that—I canna bide their yanking way of knapping English at every word.—I have kent decent lads amang them too—What for no?—But that was when they stopped up here whiles, like other douce folk; but since they gaed down, the hail flight of them, like a string of wild-geese, to the new-fashioned hottle yonder, I am tauld there are as mony hellicate tricks played in the travellers' room, as they behove to call it, as if it were fou of drunken young lairds."

"That is because they want you to keep good order among them, Mistress Margaret."

"Ay, lad?" replied Meg, "ye are a fine blaw-in-my-lug, to think to cuitle me aff sae cleverly!" And, facing about upon her guest, she honoured him with a more close and curious investigation than she had at first deigned to bestow on him.

All that she remarked was in her opinion rather favourable to the stranger. He was a well-made man, rather above than under the middle size, and apparently betwixt five-and-twenty and thirty years of age—for, although he might, at first glance, have passed for one who had attained the latter period, yet, on a nearer examination, it seemed as if the burning sun of a warmer climate than Scotland, and perhaps some fatigue, both of body and mind, had imprinted the marks of care and of manhood upon his countenance, without abiding the course of years. His eyes and teeth were excellent, and his other features, though they could be scarce termed handsome, expressed sense and acuteness; he bore, in his aspect, that ease and composure of manner, equally void of awkwardness and affectation, which is said emphatically to mark the gentleman; and, although neither the plainness of his dress, nor the total want of the usual attendants, allowed Meg to suppose him a wealthy man, she had little doubt that he was above the rank of her lodgers in general. Amidst these observations, and while she was in the course of making them, the good landlady was embarrassed with various obscure recollections of having seen the object of them formerly; but when, or on what occasion, she was quite unable to call to remembrance. She was particularly puzzled by the cold and sarcastic expression of a countenance, which she could not by any means reconcile with the recollections which it awakened. At length she said, with as much courtesy as she was capable of assuming,—"Either I have seen you before, sir, or some ane very like ye—Ye ken the Blue room, too, and you a stranger in these parts."

"Not so much a stranger as you may suppose, Meg," said the guest, assuming a more intimate tone, "when I call myself Frank Tyrrel."

"Tirl!" exclaimed Meg, with a tone of wonder—"It's impossible! You cannot be Francie Tirl, the wild callant that was fishing and bird's-nesting here seven or eight years syne—it canna be—Francie was but a callant!"

"But add seven or eight years to that boy's life, Meg," said the stranger gravely, "and you will find you have the man who is now before you."

"Even sae!" said Meg, with a glance at the reflection of her own countenance in the copper coffee-pot, which she had scoured so brightly, that it did the office of a mirror—"Just e'en sae—but folk maun grow auld or die.—But, Mr Tirl, for I maunna call you Francie now, I am thinking——"

"Call me what you please, good dame," said the stranger; "it has been so long since I heard any one call me by a name that sounded like former kindness, that such a one is more agreeable to me than a lord's title would be."

"Weel, then, Maister Frauncie—if it be no offence to you—I hope you are no Nabob?"

"Not I, I can safely assure you, my old friend;—but what an I were?"

"Naething—only maybe I might bid ye gang further, and be waur served.—Nabobs, indeed! the country's plagued wi' them—they have raised the price of eggs and poutry for twenty miles round—But what is my business?—they use almaist a' of them the Well down bye. They need it, ye ken, for the clearing of their copper complexions, that need scouring as much as my sauce-pans, that naebody can clean but mysell."

"Well, my good friend," said Tyrrel, "the upshot of all this is, that I am to stay and have dinner here."

"What for no?" replied Mrs Dods.

"And that I am to have the Blue room for a night or two—perhaps longer?"

"I dinna ken that," said the dame.—"The Blue room is the best—and they that get neist best, are no ill aff in this warld."

"Arrange it as you will," said the stranger, "I leave the whole matter to you, mistress.—Meantime, I will go see after my horse."

"The merciful man," said Meg, when her guest had left the kitchen, "is merciful to his beast.—He had aye something about him by ordinar, that callant—But eh, sirs! there is a sair change on his cheek-haffit since I saw him last!—He sall no want a good dinner for auld lang syne, that I'se engage for."

Meg set about the necessary preparations with all the natural energy of her disposition, which was so much exerted upon her culinary cares, that her two maids, on their return to the house, escaped the bitter reprimand which she had been previously conning over, in reward of their alleged slatternly negligence. Nay, so far did she carry her complaisance, that when Tyrrel crossed the kitchen to recover his saddle-bags, she formally rebuked Eppie for an idle taupie, for not carrying the gentleman's things to his room.

"I thank you, mistress," said Tyrrel; "but I have some drawings and colours in these saddle-bags, and I always like to carry them myself."

"Ay, and are you at the painting trade yet?" said Meg; "an unco slaister ye used to make with it lang syne."

"I cannot live without it," said Tyrrel; and taking the saddle-bags, was formally inducted by the maid into a snug apartment, where he soon had the satisfaction to behold a capital dish of minced collops, with vegetables, and a jug of excellent ale, placed on the table by the careful hand of Meg herself. He could do no less, in acknowledgment of the honour, than ask Meg for a bottle of the yellow seal, "if there was any of that excellent claret still left."

"Left?—ay is there, walth of it," said Meg; "I dinna gie it to every body—Ah! Mr Tirl, ye have not got ower your auld tricks!—I am sure, if ye are painting for your leeving, as you say, a little rum and water would come cheaper, and do ye as much good. But ye maun hae your ain way the day, nae doubt, if ye should never have it again."

Away trudged Meg, her keys clattering as she went, and after much rummaging, returned with such a bottle of claret as no fashionable tavern could have produced, had it been called for by a duke, or at a duke's price; and she seemed not a little gratified when her guest assured her he had not yet forgotten its excellent flavour. She retired after these acts of hospitality, and left the stranger to enjoy in quiet the excellent matters which she had placed before him.

But there was that in Tyrrel's spirits which defied the enlivening power of good cheer and of wine, which only maketh man's heart glad when that heart has no secret oppression to counteract its influence. Tyrrel found himself on a spot which he had loved in that delightful season, when youth and high spirits make all those flattering promises which are so ill kept to manhood. He drew his chair into the embrasure of the old-fashioned window, and throwing up the sash to enjoy the fresh air, suffered his thoughts to return to former days, while his eyes wandered over objects which they had not looked upon for several eventful years. He could behold beneath his eye, the lower part of the decayed village, as its ruins peeped from the umbrageous shelter with which they were shrouded. Still lower down, upon the little holm which formed its church-yard, was seen the Kirk of Saint Ronan's; and looking yet further, towards the junction of Saint Ronan's Burn with the river which traversed the larger dale or valley, he could see whitened, by the western sun, the rising houses, which were either newly finished, or in the act of being built, about the medicinal spring.

"Time changes all around us," such was the course of natural, though trite reflections, which flowed upon Tyrrel's mind; "wherefore should loves and friendships have a longer date than our dwellings and our monuments?" As he indulged these sombre recollections, his officious landlady disturbed their tenor by her entrance.

"I was thinking to offer you a dish of tea, Maister Francie, just for the sake of auld lang syne, and I'll gar the quean Beenie bring it here, and mask it mysell.—But ye arena done with your wine yet?"

"I am, indeed, Mrs Dods," answered Tyrrel; "and I beg you will remove the bottle."

"Remove the bottle, and the wine no half drank out!" said Meg, displeasure lowering on her brow; "I hope there is nae fault to be found wi' the wine, Maister Tirl?"

To this answer, which was put in a tone resembling defiance, Tyrrel submissively replied, by declaring, "the claret not only unexceptionable, but excellent."

"And what for dinna ye drink it then?" said Meg, sharply; "folk should never ask for mair liquor than they can mak a gude use of. Maybe ye think we have the fashion of the table-dot, as they ca' their new-fangled ordinary down by yonder, where a' the bits of vinegar cruets are put awa' into an awmry, as they tell me, and ilk ane wi' the bit dribbles of syndings in it, and a paper about the neck o't, to shew wha's aught it—there they stand like pothecaries' drugs—and no an honest Scots mutchkin will ane o' them haud, granting it were at the fowest."

"Perhaps," said Tyrrel, willing to indulge the spleen and prejudice of his old acquaintance, "perhaps the wine is not so good as to make full measure desirable."

"Ye may say that, lad—and yet them that sell it might afford a gude pennyworth, for they hae it for the making—maist feck of it ne'er saw France or Portugal. But as I was saying—this is no ane of their new-fangled places, where wine is put by for them that canna drink it—When the cork's drawn the bottle maun be drank out—and what for no?—unless it be corkit."

"I agree entirely, Meg," said her guest; "but my ride to-day has somewhat heated me—and I think a dish of the tea you promise me, will do me more good than to finish my bottle."

"Na, then, the best I can do for you is to put it by, to be sauce for the wild-ducks to-morrow; for I think ye said ye were to bide here for a day or twa."

"It is my very purpose, Meg, unquestionably," replied Tyrrel.

"Sae be it then," said Mrs Dods; "and then the liquor's no lost—it has been seldom sic claret as that has simmered in a sauce-pan, let me tell you that, neighbour;—and I mind the day, when head-ache or nae head-ache, ye wad hae been at the hinder-end of that bottle, and maybe anither, if ye could have gotten it wiled out of me. But then ye had your cousin to help you—Ah! he was a blithe bairn that Valentine Bulmer!—Ye were a canty callant too, Maister Francie, and muckle ado I had to keep ye baith in order when ye were on the ramble. But ye were a thought doucer than Valentine—But O! he was a bonnie bairn!—wi' een like diamonds, cheeks like roses, a head like a heather-tap—he was the first I ever saw wear a crap, as they ca' it, but a' body cheats the barber now—And he had a laugh that wad hae raised the dead!—What wi' flyting on him, and what wi' laughing at him, there was nae minding ony other body when that Valentine was in the house—but how is your cousin Valentine Bulmer, Maister Francie?"

Tyrrel looked down, and only answered with a sigh.

"Ay—and is it even sae?" said Meg; "and has the puir bairn been sae soon removed frae this fashious warld?—Ay—ay—we maun a' gang ae gate—crackit quart-stoups and geisen'd barrels—leaky quaighs are we a', and canna keep in the liquor of life—Ohon, sirs!—Was the puir lad Bulmer frae Bu'mer bay, where they land the Hollands, think ye, Maister Francie?—They whiles rin in a pickle tea there too—I hope that is good that I have made you, Maister Francie?"

"Excellent, my good dame," said Francis Tyrrel; but it was in a tone of voice which intimated that she had pressed upon a subject which awakened some unpleasant reflections.

"And whan did this puir lad die?" continued Meg, who was not without her share of Eve's qualities, and wished to know something concerning what seemed to affect her guest so particularly; but he disappointed her purpose, and at the same time awakened another train of sentiment in her mind, by turning again to the window, and looking upon the distant buildings at Saint Ronan's Well. As if he had observed for the first time these new objects, he said to Mistress Dods in an indifferent tone, "You have got some gay new neighbours yonder, mistress."

"Neighbours!" said Meg, her wrath beginning to arise, as it always did upon any allusion to this sore subject—"Ye may ca' them neighbours, if ye like—but the deil flee awa' wi' the neighbourhood for Meg Dods!"

"I suppose," said Tyrrel, as if he did not observe her displeasure, "that yonder is the Fox Hotel they told me of."

"The Fox!" said Meg; "I am sure it is the fox that has carried off a' my geese.—I might shut up house, Maister Francie, if it was the thing I lived by—me, that has seen a' our gentle-folks bairns, and gien them snaps and sugar-biscuit maist of them wi' my ain hand. They wad hae seen my father's roof-tree fa' down and smore me before they wad hae gien a boddle a piece to have propped it up—but they could a' link out their fifty pounds ower head to bigg a hottle at the well yonder and muckle they hae made o't—the bankrupt body, Sandie Lawson, has no paid them a bawbee of four terms' rent."

"Surely, mistress, I think that if the well became so famous for its cures, the least the gentlemen could have done was to make you the Priestess."

"Me priestess! I am nae Quaker, I wot, Maister Francie; and I never heard of ale-wife who turned preacher, except Luckie Buchan in the west. And if I were to preach, I think I have mair the spirit of a Scotswoman, than to preach in the very room they hae been dauncing in ilka night o' the week, Saturday itsel not excepted, and that till twal o'clock at night. Na, na, Maister Francie; I leave the like o' that to Mr Simon Chatterley, as they ca' the bit prelatical sprig of divinity from the town yonder, that plays at cards, and dances six days of the week, and on the seventh reads the Common Prayer-book in the ball-room, wi' Tam Simson, the drunken barber, for his clerk."

"I think I have heard of Mr Chatterley," said Tyrrel.

"Ye'll be thinking o' the sermon he has printed," said the angry dame, "where he compares their nasty puddle of a well yonder to the pool of Bethesda, like a foul-mouthed, fleeching, feather-headed fule as he is! He should hae ken'd that the place got a' its fame in the times of black papery; and though they pat it in Saint Ronan's name, I'll never believe for ane that the honest man had ony hand in't; for I have been tell'd by ane that suld ken, that he was nae Roman, but only a Cuddie, or Culdee, or such like.—But will ye not take anither dish of tea, Maister Fraunce? and a wee bit of the diet-loaf, raised wi' my ain fresh butter, Maister Fraunce? and no wi' greasy kitchen-fee, like the seed-cake down at the confectioner's yonder, that has as mony dead flees as carvy in it. Set him up for confectioner!—Wi' a penny of rye-meal, and anither of tryacle, and twa three carvy-seeds, I will make better confections than ever came out of his o'on."

"I have no doubt of that, Mrs Dods," said the guest; "and I only wish to know how these new comers were able to establish themselves against a house of such good reputation and old standing as yours?—It was the virtues of the mineral, I dare say; but how came the waters to receive a character all at once, mistress?"

"I dinna ken, sir—they used to be thought good for naething, but here and there a puir body's bairn, that had gotten the cruells, and could not afford a pennyworth of salts. But my Lady Penelope Penfeather had fa'an ill, it's like, as nae other body ever fell ill, and sae she was to be cured as nae other body was ever cured, which was naething mair than was reasonable—And my lady, ye ken, has wit at wull, and has a' the wise folk out from Edinburgh at her house at Windywa's yonder, which it is her leddyship's will and pleasure to call Air-castle—and they have a' their different turns, and some can clink verses, wi' their tale, as weel as Rob Burns or Allan Ramsay—and some rin up hill and down dale, knapping the chucky stanes to pieces wi' hammers, like sae mony road-makers run daft—they say it is to see how the warld was made!—And some that play on all manner of ten-stringed instruments—and a wheen sketching souls, that ye may see perched like craws on every craig in the country, e'en working at your ain trade, Maister Francie; forbye men that had been in foreign parts, or said they had been there, whilk was a' ane, ye ken; and maybe twa or three draggle-tailed misses, that wear her follies when she has dune wi' them, as her queans of maids wear her second-hand claithes. So, after her leddyship's happy recovery, as they ca'd it, down came the hail tribe of wild geese, and settled by the Well, to dine thereout on bare grund, like a wheen tinklers; and they had sangs, and tunes, and healths, nae doubt, in praise of the fountain, as they ca'd the well, and of Lady Penelope Penfeather; and, lastly, they behoved a' to take a solemn bumper of the spring, which, as I'm tauld, made unco havoc amang them or they wan hame; and this they called Picknick, and a plague to them! And sae the jig was begun after her leddyship's pipe, and mony a mad measure has been danced sin' syne; for down came masons and murgeon-makers, and preachers and player-folk, and episcopals and methodists, and fools and fiddlers, and papists and pye-bakers, and doctors and drugsters; bye the shop-folk, that sell trash and trumpery at three prices—and so up got the bonnie new Well, and down fell the honest auld toun of Saint Ronan's, where blithe decent folk had been heartsome eneugh for mony a day before ony o' them were born, or ony sic vapouring fancies kittled in their cracked brains."

"What said your landlord, the Laird of Saint Ronan's, to all this?" said Tyrrel.

"Is't *my* landlord ye are asking after, Maister Francie?—The Laird of Saint Ronan's is nae landlord of mine, and I think ye might hae minded that.—Na, na, thanks be to Praise! Meg Dods is baith landlord and landlady—ill eneugh to keep the doors open as it is, forbye facing Whitsunday and Martinmas—An auld leather pock there is, Maister Frauncie, in ane of worthy Maister Bindloose, the sheriff-clerk's pigeon-holes, in his dowcot of a closet in the burgh; and therein is baith charter and sasine, and special service to boot; and that will be chapter and verse for the property, speer whan ye list."

"I had quite forgotten," said Tyrrel, "that the inn was your own; though I remember you were a considerable landed proprietor."

"May be I am," replied Meg, "may be I am not; and if I be, what for no?—But as to what the laird, whose grandfather was my father's landlord, said to the new doings yonder—he just jumped at the ready penny, like a cock at a grossart, and feu'd the bonnie holm beside the Well, that they ca'd the Saint's of Wellholm, that was like the best land in his aught, to be carved, and bigged, and howked up, just at the pleasure of Jock Ashler the stane-mason, that ca's himsel an arkitect—there is nae living for new words in this new warld neither, and that is another vex to auld folks such as me.—It's a shame o' the young Laird, to let his auld patrimony gang the gate it is like to gang, and my heart is sair to see't, though it has but little cause to care what comes of him or his."

"Is it the same Mr Mowbray," said Mr Tyrrel, "who still holds the estate?—the old gentleman, you know, whom I had some dispute with——"

"About hunting moor-fowl upon the Springwell-head muirs," said Meg. "Ah lad! honest Mr Bindloose brought you neatly off there—Na, it was nae that honest man, but his son John Mowbray—the tother's slept down by in Saint Ronan's Kirk for this six or seven years."

"Did he leave," asked Tyrrel, with something of a faltering voice, "no other child than the present laird?"

"No other son," said Meg; "and there's e'en aneugh, unless he could have left a better ane."

"He died then," said Tyrrel, "excepting this son—without children?"

"By your leave, no!" said Meg; "there is the lassie Miss Clara, that keeps house for the laird, if it can be ca'd keeping house, for he is almost aye down at the Well yonder—so a sma' kitchen serves them at the Shaws."

"Miss Clara will have but a dull time of it there during her brother's absence?" said the stranger.

"Out no!—he has her aften jinketting about, and back and forward, wi' a' the fine flichtering fools that come yonder; and clapping palms wi' them, and linking at their dances and daffings. I wuss nae ill come o't, but it's a shame her father's daughter should keep company wi' a' that scauff and raff of students, and writers' 'prentices, and bagmen, and sic-like trash as are down at the Well yonder."

"You are severe, Meg," replied the guest. "No doubt Miss Clara's conduct deserves all sort of freedom."

"I am saying naething against her conduct," said the dame; "and there's nae ground to say ony thing that I ken of—But I wad hae like draw to like, Mr Frauncie.—I never quarrelled the ball that the gentry used to hae at my bit house a gude wheen years bygane—when they came, the auld folks in their coaches, wi' lang-tailed black horses, and a wheen gaillard gallants on their hunting horses, and mony a decent leddy behind her ain goodman, and mony a bonny smirking lassie on her pownie, and wha sae happy as they—And what for no? And then there was the farmers' ball, wi' the tight lads of yeomen with the brank new blues and buckskins—These were decent meetings—but then they were a' ae man's bairns that were at them, ilk ane ken'd ilk other—they danced farmers wi' farmers' daughters, at the tane, and gentles wi' gentle blood, at the t'other, unless maybe when some of the gentlemen of the Kilnakelty club would give me a round of the floor mysel, in the way of daffing and fun, and me no able to flyte on them for laughing—I am sure I never grudged these innocent pleasures, although it has cost me maybe a week's redding up, ere I got the better of the confusion."

"But, dame," said Tyrrel, "this ceremonial would be a little hard upon strangers like myself, for how were we to find partners in these family parties of yours?"

"Never you fash your thumb about that, Maister Francis," returned the landlady, with a knowing wink.—"Every Jack will find a Jill, gang the world as it may—And, at the warst o't, better hae some fashery in finding a partner for the night, than get yoked with ane that you may not be able to shake off the morn."

"And does that sometimes happen?" asked the stranger.

"Happen!—and is't amang the Well folk that you mean?" exclaimed the hostess. "Was it not the last season, as they ca't, no farther gane, that young Sir Bingo Binks, the English lad wi' the red coat, that keeps a mail-coach, and drives it himsell, gat cleekit with Miss Rachael Bonnyrig, the auld Lady Loupengirth's lang-legged daughter—and they danced sae lang thegither, that there was mair said than suld hae been said about it—and the lad would fain have louped back, but the auld leddy held him to his tackle, and the Commissary Court and somebody else made her Leddy Binks in spite of Sir Bingo's heart—and he has never daured take her to his friends in England, but they have just wintered and summered it at the Well ever since—and that is what the Well is good for!"

"And does Clara,—I mean does Miss Mowbray,—keep company with such women as these?" said Tyrrel, with a tone of interest which he checked as he proceeded with the question.

"What can she do, puir thing!" said the dame. "She maun keep the company that her brother keeps, for she is clearly dependent.—But, speaking of that, I ken what *I* have to do, and that is no little, before it darkens.—I have sat clavering with you ower lang, Maister Frauncie."

And away she marched with a resolved step, and soon the clear octaves of her voice were heard in shrill admonition to her handmaidens.

Tyrrel paused a moment in deep thought, then took his hat, paid a visit to the stable, where his horse saluted him with feathering ears, and that low amicable neigh, with which that animal acknowledges the approach of a loving and beloved friend. Having seen that the faithful creature was in every respect attended to, Tyrrel availed himself of the continued and lingering twilight, to visit the old Castle, which, upon former occasions, had been his favourite evening walk. He remained while the light permitted, admiring the prospect we attempted to describe in the first chapter, and comparing, as in his former reverie, the faded hues of the glimmering landscape to those of human life, when early youth and hope have ceased to gild them.

A brisk walk to the inn, and a light supper on a Welsh rabbit and the dame's home-brewed, were stimulants of livelier, at least more resigned thoughts—and the Blue bed-room, to the honours of which he had been promoted, received him a contented, if not a cheerful tenant.

Chapter Three

ADMINISTRATION

There must be government in all society—
Bees have their Queen, and stag herds have their leader;
Rome had her Consuls, Athens had her Archons,
And we, sir, have our Managing Committee.
The Album of Saint Ronan's

FRANCIS TYRREL was, in the course of the next day, formally settled in his own old quarters, where he announced his purpose of remaining for several days. The old-established carrier of the place brought his fishing-rod and travelling-trunk, with a letter to Meg, dated a week previously, desiring her to prepare to receive an old acquaintance. This annunciation, though something of the latest, Meg received with great complacency, observing, it was a civil attention in Maister Tirl; and that John Hislop, though he was not just sae fast, was far surer than ony post of them a', or express either. She also observed with satisfaction, that there was no gun-case along with her guest's baggage; "for that weary gunning had brought baith him and her into trouble—the lairds had cried out upon't, as if she made her house a howff for common fowlers and poachers; and yet how could she help twa daft hempie callants from taking a start and an owerloup? They had leave ower the neighbour's ground up to the march, and they werena just to ken meiths when the moorfowl got up."

In a day or two, her guest fell into such quiet and solitary habits, that Meg, herself the most restless and bustling of human creatures, began to be vexed, for want of the trouble which she expected to have had with him, experiencing, perhaps, the same sort of feeling, from his extreme and passive indifference on all points, that a good horseman has for the over-patient steed, which he can scarce feel under him. His walks were directed to the most solitary recesses among the neighbouring woods and hills—his fishing-rod was often left behind him, or carried merely as an apology for sauntering slowly by the banks of some little brooklet—and his success so indifferent, that Meg said the piper of Peebles would have killed a creelfull before Maister Fraunicie made out the half-dozen; so that he was obliged, for peace's sake, to vindicate his character, by killing a handsome salmon.

Tyrrel's painting, as Meg called it, went on equally slowly: He often, indeed, shewed her the sketches which he brought from his walks, and used to finish at home; but Meg held them very cheap.

What signified, she said, a wheen scrapes of paper, wi' black and white skarts upon them, that he ca'd bushes, and trees, and craigs!—Couldna he paint them wi' green, and blue, and yellow, like the other folk? "Ye will never mak your bread that way, Maister Frauncie. Ye suld munt up a muckle square of canvas, like Dick Tinto, and paint folks ainsells, that they like muckle better to see than ony craig in the hail water; and I wadna muckle objeck even to some of the wallers coming up and sitting to ye. They waste their time waur, I wis—and, I warrant, ye might mak a guinea a-head of them. Dick made twa, but he was an auld used hand, and folk maun creep before they gang."

In answer to these remonstrances, Tyrrel assured her, that the sketches with which he busied himself were held of such considerable value, that very often an artist in that line received much more high remuneration for these, than for portraits or coloured drawings. He added, that they were often taken for the purpose of illustrating popular poems, and hinted as if he himself was engaged in some labour of that nature.

Eagerly did Meg long to pour forth to Nelly Trotter, the fish-woman,—whose cart formed the only neutral channel of communication between the Auld Town and the Well, and who was in favour with Meg, because, as Nelly passed her door in her way to the Well, she always had the first choice of her fish,—the merits of her lodger as an artist. Luckie Dods had, in truth, been so much annoyed and bullied, as it were, with the report of clever persons, accomplished in all sorts of excellence, arriving day after day at the Hotel, that she was overjoyed in this fortunate opportunity to triumph over them in their own way; and it may be believed, that the excellencies of her lodger lost nothing by being trumpeted through her mouth.

"I maun hae the best o' the cart, Nelly—if you and me can gree—for it is for ane of the best of painters. Your fine fo'k down yonder would gie their lugs to look at what he has been doing—he gets gowd in goupins, for three downright skarts and three cross anes—And he is no an ungrateful lown, like Dick Tinto, that had nae suner my good five-and-twenty shillings in his pocket, than he gaed down to birl it awa' at their bonny hottle yonder, but a decent quiet lad, that kens when he is weel aff, and bides still at the auld howff—And what for no?—Tell them a' this, and hear what they will say till't."

"Indeed, mistress, I can tell ye that already, without stirring my shanks for the matter," answered Nelly Trotter; "they will e'en say that ye are ae auld fule, and me anither, that might hae some judgment in cock-bree or in scate-rumples, but maunna fash our beards about ony thing else."

"Wad they say sae, the frontless villains! and me been a house-keeper this thirty years!" exclaimed Meg; "I wadna hae them say't to my face. But I am no speaking without warrant—for what an I had spoken to the minister, lass, and shewn him ane of the loose skarts of paper that Maister Tirl leaves fleeing about his room?—and what an he had said he had kenn'd Lord Bidmore gie five guineas for the waur o't? and a' the warld kens he was lang tutor in the Bidmore family."

"Troth," answered her gossip, "I doubt if I was to tell a' this they would hardly believe me, mistress; for there are sae mony judges amang them, and they think sae muckle of themselves, and sae little of other folk, that unless ye were to send down the bit picture, I am no thinking they will believe a word that I can tell them."

"No believe what an honest woman says—let a be to say twa o' them?" exclaimed Meg; "O the unbelieving generation!—Weel, Nelly, since my back is up, ye sall tak down the picture, or sketching, or whatever it is; (though I thought sketchers were aye made of airn,) and shame wi' it the conceited crew that they are.—But see and bring't back wi' ye again, Nelly, for it's a thing of value; and trustna it out o' your hand, *that* I charge you, for I lippen no muckle to their honesty.—And, Nelly, ye may tell them he has an illustrated poem—*illustrated*—mind the word, Nelly—that is to be stuck as fou o' the like o' that, as ever turkey was larded wi' slabs o' bacon."

Thus furnished with her credentials, and acting the part of a herald betwixt two hostile countries, honest Nelly switched her little fish-cart downwards to Saint Ronan's Well.

In watering-places, as in other congregated assemblies of the human species, various kinds of government have been dictated by chance, caprice, or convenience; but, in almost all of them, some sort of direction has been adopted to prevent the consequences of anarchy. Sometimes the sole power has been vested in a Master of Ceremonies; but this, like other despotisms, has been of late unfashionable, and the powers of this great officer have been much limited even at Bath, where Nash once ruled with undisputed supremacy. Committees of management, chosen from amongst the most steady guests, have been in general resorted to, as a more liberal mode of sway, and to such was confided the administration of the infant republic of Saint Ronan's Well. This little senate, it must be observed, had the more difficult task in discharging their high duties, that, like those of other republics, their subjects were divided into two jarring and contending factions, who every day eat, drank, danced, and made merry together, hating each other all the while with all the animosity of political party, endeavouring, by every art, to secure the adherence of each guest who arrived, and ridiculing the absurdities and follies of each other, with all the bitterness and wit of which they were masters.

At the head of one of these parties, was no less a personage than Lady Penelope Penfeather, to whom the establishment owed its fame, nay, its existence; and whose influence could only have been balanced by that of the Lord of the Manor, Mr Mowbray of Saint Ronan's, or, as he was called usually by the company, The Squire, who was the leader of the faction.

The rank and fortune of the lady, her pretensions to beauty as well as talent, (though the former was something faded,) and the consequence which she arrogated to herself as a woman of fashion, drew round her painters, and poets, and philosophers, and men of science, and lecturers, and foreign adventurers, *et hoc genus omne.*

On the contrary, the Squire's influence as a man of family and property, in the immediate neighbourhood, who actually kept greyhounds, and at least talked of hunters and of racers, ascertained him the support of the whole class of bucks, half and whole bred, from the three next counties; and if more inducements were wanting, he could grant his favourites the privilege of shooting over his moors, which is enough to turn the head of a young Scotsman at any time. Mr Mowbray was of late especially supported in his pre-eminence, by a close alliance with Sir Bingo Binks, a sapient English Baronet, who, ashamed, as many thought, to return to his own country, had sat him down at the Well of Saint Ronan's, to enjoy the blessing which the Caledonian Hymen had so kindly forced on him, in the person of Miss Rachael Bonnyrig. As this gentleman actually drove a regular-built mail-coach, not in any respect differing from that of his Majesty, only that it was more frequently overturned, his influence with a certain set was irresistible, and the Squire of Saint Ronan's having the better sense of the two, contrived to reap the full benefit of the consequence attached to his friendship.

These two contending parties were so equally balanced, that the predominance of the influence of either was often determined by the course of the sun. Thus, in the morning and forenoon, when Lady Penelope led forth her herd to lawn and shady bower, whether to visit some ruined monument of ancient times, or eat their pic-nic luncheon, to spoil good paper with bad drawings, and good verses with repetition—In a word,

> To rave, recite, and madden round the land,

her ladyship's empire over the loungers seemed uncontrouled and absolute, and all things were engaged in the *tourbillon*, of which she formed the pivot and centre. Even the hunters, and shooters, and hard drinkers, were sometimes fain reluctantly to follow in her train, sulking, and quizzing, and flouting at her solemn festivals, besides encouraging the younger nymphs to giggle when they should have looked sentimental. But after dinner the scene was changed, and her ladyship's sweetest smiles, and softest invitations, were often insufficient to draw the neutral part of the company to the tea-room while the bottle continued to circulate; and on these occasions the Lady Penelope's suite was reduced to those whose constitution or finances rendered early retirement from the dining-parlour a matter of convenience, together with the more devoted and zealous of her own immediate dependents and adherents. Even the faith of the latter was apt to be debauched. Her ladyship's poet-laureate, in whose behalf she was teazing each new comer for subscriptions, got sufficiently independent to sing in her ladyship's presence, at supper, a song of rather equivocal meaning; and her chief painter, who was employed upon an illustrated copy of the Loves of the Plants, was, at another time, seduced into such a state of pot-valour, that, upon her ladyship's administering her usual dose of criticism upon his works, he not only bluntly disputed her judgment, but talked something of his right to be treated like a gentleman.

These feuds were taken up by the Managing Committee, who interceded for the penitent offenders upon the next morning, and obtained their re-establishment in Lady Penelope's good graces, upon moderate terms. Many other acts of moderating authority they performed, much to the assuaging of faction, and the quiet of the Wellers; and so essential was their government to the prosperity of the place, that, without them, Saint Ronan's spring would probably have been speedily deserted. We must, therefore, give a brief sketch of that potential Committee, which both factions, acting as if on a self-denying ordinance, had combined to invest with the reins of government.

Each of its members appeared to be selected, as Fortunio, in the fairy-tale, chose his followers, for their peculiar gifts.

First on the list stood the MAN OF MEDICINE, Dr Quentin Quackleben, who claimed right to regulate medical matters at the spring, upon the principle which, of old, assigned the property of a newly-discovered country to the first buccaneer who committed piracy on its shores. The acknowledgment of the doctor's merit, as having been first to proclaim and vindicate the merits of these healing fountains, had occasioned his being universally installed First Physician and Man of Science, which last qualification he could apply to all purposes, from the boiling of an egg to the giving a lecture. He was, indeed, qualified, like many of his profession, to spread both the bane and antidote before a dyspeptic patient, being as knowing a gastronome as Dr Redgill himself, or any other worthy physician who has written for the benefit of the *cuisine*, from Dr Moncrieff of Tippermalloch, to the late Dr Hunter of York, and Dr Kitchiner of London. But pluralities are always invidious, and therefore the Doctor prudently relinquished the office of caterer and head-carver to the Man of Taste, who occupied regularly, and *ex officio*, the head of the table, reserving to himself the occasional privilege of criticising, and a principal share in consuming, the good things which the common entertainment afforded. We have only to sum up this brief account of the learned Doctor, by informing the reader, that he was a tall, lean, beetle-browed man, with an ill-made black scratch-wig, that stared out on either side from his lantern jaws. He resided nine months out of the twelve at Saint Ronan's, and was supposed to make an indifferent good thing of it, especially as he played whist to admiration.

First in place, though perhaps second to the Doctor in real authority, was Mr Winterblossom; a civil sort of person, who was nicely precise in his address, wore his hair cued, and dressed with powder, had knee-buckles set with Bristol stones, and a seal-ring as large as Sir John Falstaff's. In his heyday he had a small estate, which he spent like a gentleman, by mixing with the gay world. He was, in short, one of those respectable links which connect the coxcombs of the present day with those of the last age, and could compare, in his own experience, the follies of both. In latter days, he had sense enough to extricate himself from his course of dissipation, though with impaired health and impoverished fortune.

Mr Winterblossom now lived upon a moderate annuity, and had discovered a way of reconciling his economy with much company and made dishes, by acting as perpetual president of the table-d'hote at the Well. Here he used to amuse the society by telling stories about Garrick, Foote, Bonnel Thornton, and Lord Kellie, and delivering his opinions on matters of taste and vertu. An excellent carver, he knew how to help each guest to what was precisely his due; and never failed to reserve a proper slice as the reward of his own labours. To conclude, he was possessed of some taste in the fine arts, at least in painting and music, although it was rather of the technical kind, than that which warms the heart and elevates the feelings. There was, indeed, about Mr Winterblossom, nothing that was either warm or elevated. He was shrewd, selfish, and sensual; the last of which qualities he screened from observation, under a specious varnish of exterior complaisance. Therefore, in his professed and apparent anxiety to do the honours of the table, to the most punctilious point of good breeding, he never permitted the attendants upon the public table to supply the wants of others until all his own private comforts had been fully arranged and provided for.

Mr Winterblossom was also distinguished for possessing a few curious engravings, and other specimens of art, with the exhibition of which he occasionally beguiled a wet morning at the public room. They were collected, "*viis et modis*," said the Man of Law, another distinguished member of the Committee, with a knowing cock of his eye to his next neighbour.

Of this person little need be said. He was a large-boned, loud-voiced, red-faced old man, named Micklewhame; a country writer, or attorney, who managed the matters of the Squire much to the profit of one or other,—if not of both. His nose stood forth in the middle of his broad vulgar face, like the style of an old sun-dial, twisted all of one side. He was as great a bully in his profession, as if it had been military instead of civil; conducted the whole technicalities concerning the cutting up the Saint's-Well haugh, so much lamented by Dame Dods, into building stances, and was on excellent terms with Doctor Quackleben, who always recommended him to make the wills of his patients.

After the Man of Law comes Captain Mungo MacTurk, a Highland lieutenant on half-pay, and that of ancient standing; one who preferred toddy of the strongest to wine, and in that fashion and cold drams finished about a bottle of whisky *per diem*, whenever he could come by it. He was called the Man of Peace, on the same principle which assigns to constables, Bow-street runners, and such like, who are perpetually and officially employed in scenes of riot, the title of peace-officers—that is, because by his valour he compelled others to act with discretion. He was the general referee in all those abortive quarrels, which, at a place of this kind, are so apt to occur at night, and to be quietly settled in the morning; and occasionally took up a quarrel himself, by way of taking down any guest who was unusually pugnacious. This occupation procured Captain MacTurk a good deal of respect at the Well; for he was precisely that sort of person, who is ready to fight with any one—whom no one could find an apology for declining to fight with,—in fighting with whom considerable danger was incurred, for he was ever and anon shewing that he could snuff a candle with a pistol ball,—and lastly, through fighting with whom no eclat or credit could redound to the antagonist. He always wore a blue coat and red collar, had a supercilious taciturnity of manner, ate sliced leeks with his cheese, and resembled in complexion a Dutch red-herring.

Still remains to be mentioned the Man of Religion—the gentle Mr Simon Chatterley, who had strayed to Saint Ronan's Well from the banks of Cam or Isis, and who piqued himself, first on his Greek, and secondly, on his politeness, especially to the ladies. During all the week days, as Dame Dods has already hinted, this reverend gentleman was the partner at the whist-table, or in the ball-room, to what maid or matron soever lacked a partner at either; and on the Sundays, he read prayers in the public room to the great edification of all who chose to attend. He was also a deviser of charades, and an unriddler of riddles; he played a little on the flute, and was Mr Winterblossom's principal assistant in contriving those ingenious and romantic paths, by which, as by the zig-zags which connect military parallels, you were enabled to ascend to the top of the hill behind the hotel, which commands so beautiful a prospect, at exactly that precise angle of ascent, which entitles a gentleman to offer his arm, and a lady to accept it with perfect propriety.

There was yet another member of this Select Committee, Mr Michael Meredith, who might be termed the Man of Mirth, or, if you please, the Jack Pudding to the company, whose business it was to crack the best joke, and sing the best song,—he could. Unluckily, however, this functionary was for the present obliged to absent himself from Saint Ronan's; for, not recollecting that he did not actually wear the privileged motley of his profession, he had passed some jest upon Captain MacTurk, which cut so much to the quick, that Mr Meredith was fain to go to goat-whey quarters, at some ten miles distance, and remain there in a sort of concealment, until the affair should be made up through the mediation of his brethren of the Committee.

Such were the honest gentlemen who managed the affairs of this rising settlement, with as much impartiality as could be expected. They were not indeed without their own secret predilections; for the lawyer and the soldier privately inclined to the party of the Squire, while the parson, Mr Meredith, and Mr Winterblossom, were more devoted to the interests of Lady Penelope; so that Doctor Quackleben alone, who probably recollected that the gentlemen were as liable to stomach complaints, as the ladies to disordered nerves, seemed the only person who preserved in word and deed the most rigid neutrality. Nevertheless, the interests of the establishment being very much at the heart of this honourable council, and each feeling his own profit, pleasure, or comfort, in some degree involved, they suffered not their private affections to interfere with their public duties, but acted each in his own sphere, for the public benefit of the whole community.

Chapter Four

THE INVITATION

Thus painters write their names at Co.
PRIOR

THE CLAMOUR which attends the removal of dinner from a public room had subsided; the clatter of plates, and knives and forks—the bustling tread of awkward boobies of country servants, kicking each other's shins, and wrangling, as they endeavour to rush out of the door three abreast—the clash of glasses and tumblers, borne to earth in the tumult—the shrieks of the landlady—the curses, not loud, but deep, of the landlord—had all passed away; and those of the company who had servants, had been accommodated by their respective Ganymedes with such remnants of their respective bottles of wine, spirits, &c., as the said Ganymedes had not previously drunken up, while the rest, broken in to such observance by Mr Winterblossom, waited patiently until the worthy president's own special and multifarious commissions had been executed by a tidy young woman and a lumpish lad, the regular attendants belonging to the house, but whom he permitted to wait on no one, till, as the hymn says,

All his wants were well supplied.

"And, Dinah—my bottle of pale sherry, Dinah—place it on this side—there is a good girl;—and, Toby—get my jug with the hot water—and let it be boiling—and don't spill it on Lady Penelope, if you can help it, Toby."

"No—for her ladyship has been in hot water to-day already," said the Squire; a sarcasm to which Lady Penelope only replied with a look of contempt.

"And, Dinah, bring the sugar—the soft East Indian sugar, Dinah—And a lemon, Dinah, one of those which came fresh to-day—go fetch it from the bar, Toby—and don't tumble down stairs, if you can help it.—And, Dinah—stay, Dinah—the nutmeg, Dinah, and the ginger, my good girl—And, Dinah—put the cushion up behind my back—and the footstool to my foot, for my toe is something the worse of my walk with your ladyship this morning to the top of Belvidere."

"Her ladyship may call it what she pleases in common parlance," said the writer; "but it must stand Munt-grunzie in the stamped paper, being so nominated in the ancient writs and evidents thereof."

"And, Dinah," continued the president, "lift up my handkerchief—

and—a bit of biscuit, Dinah—and—and I do not think I want any thing else—Look to the company, my good girl.—I have the honour to drink the company's very good health—Will your ladyship honour me by accepting a glass of negus?—I learned to make negus from old Dartineuf's son.—He always used East Indian sugar, and added a tamarind—it improves the flavour infinitely.—Dinah, see your father sends for some tamarinds—Dartineuf knew a good thing almost as well as his father—I met him at Bath in the year—let me see—Garrick was just taking leave, and that was in," &c. &c. &c.—"And what is this now, Dinah?" he said, as she put into his hand a roll of paper.

"Something that Nelly Trotter (Trotting Nelly, as the company called her,) brought from a sketching gentleman that lives at the woman's (thus bluntly did the upstart minx describe the reverend Mrs Margaret Dods,) at the Cleek'um of Aulton yonder"—A name, by the way, which the inn had acquired from the use which the saint upon the sign-post was making of his pastoral hook.

"Indeed, Dinah?" said Mr Winterblossom, gravely taking out his spectacles, and wiping them before he opened the roll of paper; "some boy's daubing, I suppose, whose pa and ma wish to get him into the Trustees' School, and so are beating about for a little interest.—But I am drained dry—I put three lads in last season; and if it had not been my particular interest with the secretary, who asks my opinion now and then, I could not have managed it. But giff gaff, says I.—Eh! What, in the devil's name, is this?—Here is both force and keeping—Who can this be, my lady?—Do but see the sky-line—why, this is really a little bit—an exquisite little bit—Who the devil can it be? and how can he have stumbled upon the dog-hole in the Old Town, and the snarling b—— I beg your ladyship ten thousand pardons—that kennels there?"

"I dare say, my lady," said a little miss of fourteen, her eyes growing rounder and rounder, and her cheeks redder and redder, as she found herself speaking, and so many folks listening—"O la! I dare say it is the same gentleman we met one day in the Low-wood walk, that looked like a gentleman, and yet was none of the company, and that you said was a handsome man."

"I did not say handsome, Maria," replied her ladyship; "ladies never say men are handsome—I only said he looked genteel and interesting."

"And that, my lady," said the young parson, bowing and smiling, "is, I will be judged by the company, the most flattering compliment of the two—We shall be jealous of this Unknown presently."

"Nay, but," continued the sweetly communicative Maria, with some real and some assumed simplicity, "your ladyship forgets—for you said presently after, you were sure he was no gentleman, for he did not run after you with your glove which you had dropped—and so I went back myself to find your ladyship's glove, and he never offered to help me, and I saw him closer than your ladyship did, and I am sure he is handsome, though he is not very civil."

"You speak a little too much and too loud, miss," said Lady Penelope, a natural blush reinforcing the *nuance* of rouge by which it was usually superseded.

"What say you to that, Squire Mowbray?" said the elegant Sir Bingo Binks.

"A fair challenge to the field, Sir Bingo," answered the Squire; "when a lady throws down the gauntlet, a gentleman may throw the handkerchief."

"I have always the benefit of *your* best construction, Mr Mowbray," said the lady with dignity. "I suppose Miss Maria has contrived this pretty story for your amusement. I can hardly answer to Mrs Digges, for bringing her into company where she receives encouragement to behave so."

"Nay, nay, my lady," said the president, "you must let the jest pass by; and since this is really such an admirable sketch, you must honour us with your opinion, whether the company can consistently with propriety make any advances to this man."

"In my opinion," said her ladyship, the angry spot still glowing on her brow; "there are enough of *men* among us already—I wish I could say gentlemen—As matters stand, I see little business *ladies* can have at Saint Ronan's."

This was an intimation which always brought the Squire back to good-breeding, which he could make use of when he pleased. He deprecated her ladyship's displeasure, until she told him, in returning good-humour, that she really would not trust him unless he brought his sister to be security for his future politeness.

"Clara, my lady," said Mowbray, "is a little wilful; and I believe your ladyship must take the task of unharbouring her into your own hands. What say you to a gipsy party up to my old shop?—it is a bachelor's house—you must not expect things in much order; but Clara would be honoured——"

The Lady Penelope eagerly accepted the proposal of something like a party, and, quite reconciled with Mowbray, began to inquire whether she might bring the strange artist with her; "that is," said her ladyship, looking to Dinah, "if he be a gentleman."

Here Dinah interposed her assurance, "that the gentleman at Meg Dorts's was quite and clean a gentleman, and an illustrated poet besides."

"An illustrated poet, Dinah!" said Lady Penelope; "you must mean an illustrious poet."

"I dares to say your ladyship is right," said Dinah, dropping her little curtesy.

A joyous flutter of impatient anxiety was instantly excited through all the blue-stocking faction of the company, nor were the news totally indifferent to the rest of the community. The former belonged to that class, who, like the young Ascanius, are ever beating about in quest of a tawny lion, though they are much more successful in now and then starting a great bore;* and the others, having left all their own ordinary affairs, and subjects of interest at home, were glad to make a matter of importance out of the most trivial occurrence. A mighty poet, said the former class—who could it possibly be?—All names were recited—all Britain scrutinized, from Highland hills to the Lakes of Cumberland—from Sydenham Common to Saint James's Place—even the Banks of the Bosphorus were explored for some name which might rank under this distinguished epithet.—And then, besides his illustrious poesy, to sketch so inimitably!—who *could* it be? And all the gapers, who had nothing of their own to suggest, answered with the antistrophe, "Who could it be?"

The Claret-club, which comprised the choicest and firmest adherents of Squire Mowbray and the Baronet—men who scorned that the reversion of one bottle of wine should furnish forth the feast of to-morrow, though caring nought about either of the fine arts in question, found an interest of their own, which centered in the same individual.

"I say, little Sir Bing," said the Squire, "this is the very fellow that we saw down at the Willow-slack on Saturday—he was tog'd gnostically enough, and cast twelve yards of line with one hand—the fly fell like a thistle-down on the water."

"Uich!" answered the party he addressed, in the accent of a dog choking in the collar.

"We saw him pull out the salmon yonder," said Mowbray; "you remember—clean fish—the tide-ticks on his gills—weighed, I dare say, a matter of eighteen pounds."

"Sixteen!" replied Sir Bingo, in the same tone of strangulation.

"None of your rigs, Bing!" said his companion,—"nearer eighteen than sixteen!"

"Nearer sixteen, by ——!"

"Will you go a dozen of blue on it to the company?" said the Squire.

* The one or the other was equally *in votis* to Ascanius,—

Optat aprum, aut fulvum descendere monte leonem.

Modern Trojans make a great distinction betwixt these two objects of chase.

"No, d—— me!" croaked the Baronet—"to our own set I will."

"Then, I say done!" quoth the Squire.

And "Done!" responded the Knight; and out came their red pocket-books.

"But who shall decide the bet?" said the Squire.—"The genius himself, I suppose; they talk of asking him here, but I suppose he will scarce mind quizzes like them."

"Write myself—John Mowbray," said the Baronet.

"You, Baronet!—you write! d—— me, that cock won't fight—you won't?"

"I will," growled Sir Bingo, more articulately than usual.

"Why, you can't!" said Mowbray. "You never wrote a line in your life, save those you were whipped for at school."

"I can write—I will write!" said Sir Bingo. "Two to one I will."

And there the affair rested, for the counsel of the company were in high consultation concerning the most proper manner of opening a communication with the mysterious stranger; and the voice of Mr Winterblossom, whose tones, originally fine, age had reduced to falsetto, was calling upon the whole party for "Order, order!" So that the bucks were obliged to lounge in silence, with both arms reclined on the table, and testifying, by coughs and yawns, their indifference to the matters in question, while the rest of the company debated upon them, as if they were matters of life and death.

"A visit from one of the gentlemen—Mr Winterblossom, if he would take the trouble,—in name of the company at large—would," Lady Penelope Penfeather presumed to think, "be a necessary preliminary to an invitation."

Mr Winterblossom was "quite of her ladyship's opinion, and would gladly have been the personal representative of the company at Saint Ronan's Well—but it was up hill—her ladyship knew his tyrant, the gout, was hovering upon the frontiers—there were other gentlemen, younger, and more worthy to fly at the ladies' command than an ancient Vulcan like him,—there was the valiant Mars and the eloquent Mercury."

Thus speaking, he bowed to Captain MacTurk and the Rev. Mr Simon Chatterley, and reclined in his chair, sipping his negus with the self-satisfied smile of one, who, by a pretty speech, has rid himself of a troublesome commission. At the same time, by an act probably of mental absence, he put in his pocket the drawing, which, after circulating around the table, had returned back to the chair of the President, being the point from which it had set out.

"By Cot, madam," said Captain MacTurk, "I should be proud to obey your Leddyship's commands—but, by Cot, I never call first on any man that never called upon me at all, unless it were to carry him a friend's message, or such like."

"Twig the old connoisseur," said the Squire to the Knight.—"He is condiddling the drawing."

"Go it, Johnnie Mowbray—pour it into him," whispered Sir Bingo.

"Thank ye for nothing, Sir Bingo," said the Squire, in the same tone. "Winterblossom is one of us—*was* one of us at least—and won't stand the ironing. He has his Wogdens still, that were right things in his day, and can hit the hay-stack with the best of us—But stay, they are hallooing on the parson."

They were indeed busied on all hands, to obtain Mr Chatterley's consent to wait on the Genius unknown; but though he smiled and simpered, and was absolutely incapable of saying No, he begged leave, in all humility, to decline their commission. "The truth was," he pleaded in his excuse, "that having one day walked to visit the old Castle of Saint Ronan's, and returning through the Auld Town, as it was popularly called, he had stopped at the door of the *Cleikum*, (pronounced *Anglice*, with the open diphthong,) in hopes to get a glass of syrup of capillaire, or a draught of something cooling; and had in fact expressed his wishes, and was knocking pretty loudly, when a sash-window was thrown suddenly up, and ere he was aware what was about to happen, he was soused with a deluge of water, (as he said,) while the voice of an old hag from within assured him, that if that did not cool him there was another biding him,—an intimation which induced him to retreat in all haste from the repetition of this shower-bath."

All laughed at the account of their chaplain's misfortune, the history of which seemed to be wrung from him reluctantly, by the necessity of assigning some weighty cause for declining to execute the ladies' commands. But the Squire and Baronet continued their mirth far longer than decorum allowed, flinging themselves back in their chairs, with their hands thrust into their side-pockets, and their mouths expanded with unrestrained enjoyment, until the sufferer, angry, disconcerted, and endeavouring to look scornful, incurred another general burst of laughter on all hands.

When Mr Winterblossom had succeeded in restoring some degree of order, he found the mishaps of the young divine proved as intimidating as ludicrous. Not one of the company chose to go Envoy Extraordinary to the dominions of Queen Meg, who might be suspected of paying little respect to the sanctity of an ambassador's person. And what was worse, when it was resolved that a civil card from Mr Winterblossom, in the name of the company, should be sent to the stranger, instead of a personal visit, Dinah informed them that she was sure no one about the house could be bribed to carry up a letter of the kind; for, when such an event had taken place two summers since, Meg, who construed it into an attempt to seduce from her tenement the invited guest, had so handled a plough-boy who carried the letter, that he fled the country-side altogether, and never thought himself safe till he was at a village ten miles off, where it was afterwards learned he enlisted with a recruiting party, chusing rather to face the French than to return within the sphere of Meg's displeasure.

Just while they were agitating this new difficulty, a prodigious clamour was heard without, which, to the first apprehensions of the company, seemed to be Meg, in all her terrors, come to anticipate their proposed invasion. Upon inquiry, however, it proved to be her gossip, Trotting Nelly, or Nelly Trotter, in the act of forcing her way up stairs, against the united strength of the whole household of the hotel, to reclaim Luckie Dods's picture, as she called it. This made the connoisseur's treasure tremble in his pocket, who, thrusting a half-crown into Toby's hand, exhorted him to give it her, and try his influence in keeping her back. Toby, who knew Nelly's nature, put the half-crown into his own pocket, and snatched up a gill-stoup of whisky from the sideboard. Thus armed, he boldly confronted the virago, and interposing a remora, which was able to check poor Nelly's course in her most determined moods, not only succeeded in averting the immediate storm which approached the company in general, and Mr Winterblossom in particular, but brought the guests the satisfactory information, that Trotting Nelly had agreed, after she had slept out her nap in the barn, to convey their commands to the Unknown of Cleikum of Aulton.

Mr Winterblossom, therefore, having authenticated his proceedings, by inserting in the Minutes of the Committee the authority which he had received, wrote his card in the best style of diplomacy, and sealed it with the seal of the Spaw, which represented something like a nymph, seated beside what was designed to represent an urn.

The rival factions, however, did not trust intirely to this official invitation. Lady Penelope was of opinion that they should find some way of letting the stranger—a man of talent unquestionably—understand that there were in the society to which he was invited, spirits of a more select sort, who felt worthy to intrude themselves on his solitude.

Accordingly, her ladyship imposed upon the elegant Mr Chatterley the task of expressing the desire of the company to see the unknown artist, in a neat occasional copy of verses. The poor gentleman's muse, however, proved unpropitious; for he was able to proceed no farther than two lines in half an hour, which, coupled with its variations, we insert from the blotted manuscript, as Dr Johnson has printed the alterations in Pope's version of the Iliad:

> 1. *Maids*. 2. *Dames*. *unity joining*.
> The [nymphs] of St Ronan's in [purpose combining]
> 1. *Swain*. 2. *Man*.
> To the [youth] who is great both in verse and designing,
> - - - - - - - - dining.

The eloquence of a prose billet was necessarily resorted to in the absence of the heavenly muse, and the said billet was secretly intrusted to the care of Trotting Nelly. The same trusty emissary, when refreshed by her nap among the pease-straw, and about to harness her cart for her return to the sea-coast, (in the course of which she was to repass the Aulton,) received another card, written, as he had threatened, by Sir Bingo Binks himself, who had given himself this trouble to secure the settlement of the bet; conjecturing that a man with a fashionable exterior, who could throw twelve yards of line at a cast with such precision, might consider the invitation of Winterblossom as that of an old twaddle, and care as little for the good graces of an affected blue-stocking and her coterie, whose conversation, in Sir Bingo's mind, relished of nothing but of weak tea and bread and butter. Thus the happy Mr Francis Tyrrel received, considerably to his surprise, no less than three invitations at once from the Well of Saint Ronan's.

Chapter Five

EPISTOLARY ELOQUENCE

> But how can I answer, since first I must read thee?
> PRIOR

DESIROUS of authenticating our more important facts, by as many original documents as possible, we have, after much research, enabled ourselves to present the reader with the following accurate transcripts of the notes intrusted to the care of Trotting Nelly. The first ran thus:

"Mr Winterblossom [of Silverhed] has the commands of Lady Penelope Penfeather, Sir Bingo and Lady Binks, Mr and Miss Mowbray [of Saint Ronan's,] and the rest of the company at the Hotel and Tontine Inn of Saint Ronan's Well, to express their hope that the gentleman lodged at the Cleikum Inn, Old Town of Saint Ronan's, will favour them with his company at the Ordinary, as early and as often as may suit his convenience. The COMPANY think it necessary to send this invitation, because, according to the RULES of the place, the Ordinary can only be attended by such gentlemen and ladies as lodge at Saint Ronan's Well; but they are happy to make a distinction in favour of a gentleman so distinguished for success in the fine arts as Mr —— ——, residing at Cleikum. If Mr —— —— should be inclined, upon becoming further acquainted with the COMPANY and RULES of the place, to remove his residence to the WELL, Mr Winterblossom, though he would not be understood to commit himself by a positive assurance to that effect, is inclined to hope that an arrangement might be made, notwithstanding the extreme crowd of the season, to accommodate Mr —— —— at the lodging-house, called Lilliput-hall. It will much conduce to facilitate this negotiation, if Mr —— —— would have the goodness to send an exact note of his stature, as Captain Rannletree seems disposed to resign the folding-bed at Lilliput-hall, on account of his finding it rather deficient in length. Mr Winterblossom begs farther to assure Mr —— —— of the esteem in which he holds his genius, and of his high personal consideration.

"For —— ——, Esquire,
Cleikum Inn,
Old-Town of Saint Ronan's.

"The Public Rooms,
Hotel and Tontine, Saint Ronan's Well, &c. &c. &c."

The above card was written (we love to be precise in matters concerning orthography,) in a neat, round, clerk-like hand, which, like Mr Winterblossom's character, in many particulars was most accurate and common-place, though betraying an affectation both of flourish and of precision.

The next billet was a contrast to the diplomatic gravity and accuracy of Mr Winterblossom's official communication, and ran thus, the young divine's academic jests and classical flowers of eloquence being mingled with some wild flowers from the teeming fancy of Lady Penelope.

"A choir of Dryads and Naiads, assembled at the healing spring of Saint Ronan's, have learned with surprise that a youth, gifted by Apollo, when the Deity was prodigal, with two of his most esteemed endowments, wanders at will among their domains, frequenting grove and river, without once dreaming of paying homage to its tutelary deities. He is, therefore, summoned to their presence, and prompt obedience will insure him forgiveness; but in case of contumacy, let him beware how he again essays either the lyre or the pallet.

"*Postscript.* The adorable Penelope, long enrolled among the Goddesses for her beauty and virtues, gives Nectar and Ambrosia, which mortals call tea and cake, at the Public Rooms, near the Sacred Spring, on Thursday evening, at eight o'clock, when the Muses never fail to attend. The stranger's presence is requested to participate in the delights of the evening.

"*Second Postscript.* A shepherd, ambitiously aiming at more accommodation than his narrow cot affords, leaves it in a day or two.

> Assuredly the thing is to be hired.
>
> *As You Like It.*

"*Postscript third.* Our Iris, whom mortals know as Trotting Nelly in her tartan cloak, will bring us the stranger's answer to our celestial summons."

This letter was written in a delicate Italian hand, garnished with fine hair-strokes and dashes, which were sometimes so dexterously thrown off as to represent lyres, pallets, vases, and other appropriate decorations, suited to the tenor of the contents.

The third epistle was a complete contrast to the other two. It was written in a coarse, irregular, school-boy half-text, which, however, seemed to have cost the writer as much pains as if it had been a specimen of the most exquisite calligraphy. And these were the contents:

"SUR—Jack Moobray has betted with me that the samon you killed Saturday last weyd ni to eiteen pounds,—I say nyer sixteen.—So you being a spurtsman, 'tis refer'd.—So hope you will come or send me't; do not doubt you will be on honour. The bet is a dozen of claret, to be drank at the hotel by our own sett, on Monday next; and we beg you will make one; and Moobray hopes you will come down.—Being, sir, your most humbel servant,—Bingo Binks, Baronet, and of Block-hall.

"*Postscript*—Have sent some loops of Indian gout, also some black hakkels of my groom's dressing; hope they will prove killing, as suiting rivre and season."

No answer was received to any of these invitations for more than three days; which, while it secretly rather added to than diminished the curiosity of the Wellers concerning the Unknown, occasioned much railing in public against him, as ill-mannered and rude.

Meantime, Francis Tyrrel, to his great surprise, began to find, like the philosopher, that he was never less alone than when alone. In the most silent and sequestered walks, to which the present state of his mind induced him to betake himself, he was sure to find some strollers from the Well, to whom he had become the object of so much solicitous interest. Quite innocent of the knowledge that he himself possessed the attraction which occasioned his meeting them so frequently, he began to doubt whether the Lady Penelope and her maidens—Mr Winterblossom and his grey pony—the parson and his short black coat and raven-grey pantaloons—were not either actually polygraphic copies of the same individuals, or possessed of a celerity of motion resembling omnipresence and ubiquity; for nowhere could he go without meeting them, and that oftener than once a day, in the course of his walks. Sometimes the presence of the sweet Lycoris was intimated by the sweet prattle in an adjacent shade; sometimes, when Tyrrel thought himself most solitary, the parson's flute was heard snoring forth Gramachree Molly; and if he betook himself to the river, he was pretty sure to find his sport watched by Sir Bingo or some of his friends.

The efforts which Tyrrel made to escape from this persecution, and the impatience of it which his manner indicated, procured him, among the Wellers, the name of the *Misanthrope;* and, once distinguished as an object of curiosity, he was the person most attended to, who could at the ordinary of the day give the most accurate account of where the Misanthrope had been, and how occupied in the course of the morning. And so far was Tyrrel's shyness from diminishing the desire of the Wellers for his society, that the latter feeling increased with the difficulty of gratification,—as the angler feels the most peculiar interest when throwing his fly for the most cunning and considerate trout in the pool.

In short, such was the interest which the excited imaginations of the company took in the Misanthrope, that, notwithstanding the unamiable qualities which the word expresses, there was only one of the society who did not desire to see the specimen at their rooms, for the purpose of examining him closely and at leisure; and the ladies were particularly desirous to inquire whether he was actually a Misanthrope? Whether he had been always a Misanthrope? What had induced him to become a Misanthrope? And whether there were no means of inducing him to cease to be a Misanthrope?

One individual only, as we have said, neither desired to see or hear more of the supposed Timon of Cleikum, and that was Mr Mowbray of Saint Ronan's. Through the medium of that venerable character John Pirner, professed weaver and practical black-fisher in the Aulton of Saint Ronan's, who usually attended Tyrrel, to shew him the casts of the river, carry his bag, and so forth, the Squire had ascertained that the judgment of Sir Bingo regarding the disputed weight of the fish was more correct than his own. This inferred an immediate loss of honour, besides the payment of a heavy bill. And the consequences might be yet more serious; nothing short of the emancipation of Sir

Bingo, who had hitherto been his convenient shadow and adherent, but who, if triumphant, confiding in his superiority of judgment upon so important a point, might either cut him altogether, or expect that, in future, the Squire, who had long seemed the planet of their set, should be content to roll around himself, Sir Bingo, in the capacity of a satellite.

The Squire, therefore, devoutly hoped, that Tyrrel's restive disposition might continue to prevent the decision of the bet, while, at the same time, he nourished a very reasonable degree of dislike to that stranger, who had been the direct occasion of the unpleasant predicament in which he found himself, by not catching a salmon weighing a pound heavier. He therefore openly censured the meanness of those who proposed taking further notice of Tyrrel, and referred to the unanswered letters, as a piece of impertinence which announced him to be no gentleman.

But though appearances were against him, and though he was in truth naturally inclined to solitude, and averse to the affectation and bustle of such a society, that part of Tyrrel's behaviour which indicated ill-breeding was easily accounted for, by his never having received the letters which required an answer. Trotting Nelly, whether unwilling to face her gossip, Meg Dods, without bringing back the drawing, or whether oblivious through the influence of the double dram with which she had been indulged at the Well, jumbled off with her cart to her beloved village of Scate-raw, from which she transmitted the letters by the first bare-legged gillie who travelled towards Aulton of Saint Ronan's; so that at last, but after a long delay, they reached the Cleikum Inn and the hands of Mr Tyrrel.

The arrival of these documents explained some part of the oddity of behaviour which had surprised him in his neighbours of the Well; and as he saw they had got somehow an idea of his being a lion extraordinary, and sensible that such is a character equally ridiculous, and difficult to support, he hastened to write to Mr Winterblossom a card in the style of ordinary mortals. In this he stated the delay occasioned by miscarriage of the letter, and his regret on that account—expressed his intention of dining with the company at the Well on the succeeding day, while he regretted that other circumstances, as well as the state of his health and spirits, would permit him this honour very infrequently during his residence in the country, and begged no trouble might be taken about his accommodation at the Well, as he was perfectly satisfied with his present residence. A separate note to Sir Bingo, said he was happy he could verify the weight of the fish, which he had noted in his diary; ("D—n the fellow, does he keep a dairy?" said the Baronet,) and though the result could only be particularly agreeable to one party, he should wish both winner and loser mirth with their wine;—he was sorry he was unable to promise himself the pleasure of participating in either. Inclosed was a signed note of the weight of the fish. Armed with this, Sir Bingo claimed his wine—triumphed in his judgment—swore louder and more articulately than ever he was known to utter any previous sounds, that this Tyrrel was a devilish honest fellow, and he trusted to be better acquainted with him; while the crest-fallen Squire, privately cursing the stranger by all his gods, had no mode of silencing his companion but by allowing his loss, and fixing a day for discussing the bet.

In the public rooms the *Company* examined even microscopically the response of the stranger to Mr Winterblossom, straining their ingenuity to discover in the most ordinary expressions, a deeper and esoteric meaning, expressive of something mysterious, and not meant to meet the eye. Mr Micklewhame, the writer, dwelt on the word *circumstances*, which he read with a peculiar emphasis.

"Ah, poor lad!" he concluded, "I doubt he sits cheaper at Meg Dorts's chimney-corner than he can do with the present company."

Doctor Quackleben, in the manner of a clergyman selecting a word from his text, as that which is to be particularly insisted upon, repeated in an under tone, the words, "*State of health?*—umph—state of health?—nothing acute—no one has been sent for, must be chronic —tending to gout, perhaps—or his shyness to society—light wild eye —irregular step—starting when met suddenly by a stranger, and turning abruptly and angrily away—Pray, Mr Winterblossom, let me have an order to look over the file of newspapers—it's very troublesome that restriction about consulting them."

"You know it is a necessary one, Doctor," said the president; "because so few of the good company read any thing else, that the old newspapers would have been worn to pieces long since."

"Well, well, let me have the order," said the Doctor; "I remember something of a gentleman run away from his friends—I must look at the description.—I believe I have a strait-jacket somewhere about the Dispensary."

While this suggestion appalled the male part of the company, who did not much relish the approaching dinner with a gentleman whose situation seemed so precarious, some of the younger Misses whispered to each other—"Ah, poor fellow!—and if it be as the Doctor supposes, my Lady, who knows what the cause of his illness may have been?—His *spirits* he complains of—ah, poor man!"

And thus, by the ingenious commentaries of the company at the Well, on as plain a note as ever covered the eighth part of a sheet of foolscap, the writer was deprived of his property, his reason, and his heart, "all or either, or one or other of them," as is briefly and distinctly expressed in the law phrase.

In short, so much was said pro and con, so many ideas started and theories maintained, concerning the disposition and character of the Misanthrope, that, when the company assembled at the usual time, before proceeding to dinner, they doubted, as it seemed, whether the expected addition to their society was to enter the room on his hands or his feet; and when "Mr Tyrrel" was announced by Toby, at the top of his voice, the gentleman who entered the room had so very little to distinguish him from others, that there was a momentary disappointment. The ladies, in particular, began to doubt whether the compound of talent, misanthropy, madness, and mental sensibility, which they had pictured to themselves, actually was the same with the genteel, and even fashionable-looking man whom they saw before them; who, though in a morning dress, which the distance of his residence, and the freedom of the place, made excusable, had, even in the minute points of his exterior, none of the negligence, or wildness, which might be supposed to attach to the vestments of a misanthropic recluse, whether sane or insane. As he paid his compliments round the circle, the scales seemed to fall from the eyes of those he spoke to; and they saw with surprise, that the exaggerations had existed entirely in their own preconceptions, and that whatever the fortunes, or rank in life, of Mr Tyrrel might be, his manners, without being showy, were gentlemanlike and pleasing.

He returned his thanks to Mr Winterblossom in a manner which made that gentleman recall his best breeding to answer the stranger's address in kind. He then escaped from the awkwardness of remaining the sole object of attention, by gliding gradually among the company, —not like an owl, which seeks to hide itself in a thicket, or an awkward and retired man, shrinking from the society into which he is compelled, but with the air of one who could maintain with ease his part in a higher circle. His address to Lady Penelope was adapted to the romantic tone of Mr Chatterley's epistle, to which it was necessary to allude. He was afraid, he said, he must complain to Juno of the neglect of Iris, for her irregularity in delivery of a certain ethereal command, which he had not dared to answer otherwise than by mute obedience —unless, indeed, as the import of the letter seemed to infer, the invitation was designed for some more gifted individual than him to whom chance had assigned it.

Lady Penelope by her lips, and many of the young ladies with their eyes, assured him there was no mistake in the matter; that he was really the gifted person whom the nymphs had summoned to their presence, and that they were well acquainted with his talents as a poet and a painter. Tyrrel disclaimed, with earnestness and gravity, the charge of poetry, and professed, that far from attempting the art itself, he "read with reluctance all but the productions of the very first-rate poets, and some of these—he was almost afraid to say—he should have liked better in humble prose."

"You have now only to disown your skill as an artist," said Lady Penelope, "and we must consider Mr Tyrrel as the falsest and most deceitful of his sex, who has a mind to deprive us of the opportunity of benefiting by the productions of his unparalleled endowments. I assure you I shall put my young friends on their guard. Such dissimulation cannot be without its object."

"And I," said Mr Winterblossom, "can produce a piece of real evidence against the culprit."

So saying, he unrolled the sketch which he had filched from Trotting Nelly, and which he had pared and pasted, (arts in which he was eminent,) so as to take out its creases, repair its breaches, and vamp it as well as my old friend Mrs Weir could repair the damages of time on a folio Shakespeare.

"The vara *corpus delicti*," said the writer, grinning and rubbing his hands.

"If you are so good as to call such scratches drawing," said Tyrrel, "I must stand so far confessed. I used to do them for my own amusement; but since my landlady, Mrs Dods, has of late discovered that I gain my livelihood by them, why should I disown it?"

This avowal, made without the least appearance either of shame or *retenue*, seemed to have a striking effect on the whole society. The president's trembling hand stole the sketch back to the portfolio, afraid doubtless it might be claimed in form, or else compensation expected by the artist. Lady Penelope was disconcerted, like a horse when it changes the leading foot in galloping. She had to recede from the respectful and easy footing on which he had contrived to place himself, to one which might express patronage on her own part, and dependence on Tyrrel's; and this could not be done in a moment.

The Man of Law murmured, "Circumstances—circumstances—I thought so!"

Sir Bingo whispered to his friend the Squire, "Run out—blown up—off the course—pity—d—d pretty fellow he has been!"

"A raff from the beginning!" whispered Mowbray.—"I never thought him anything else!"

"I'll hold ye a poney of that, my dear, and I'll ask him."

"Done, for a poney, provided you ask him in ten minutes," said the Squire; "but you dare not, Bingie—he has a d—d cross game look, with all that civil chaff of his."

"Done," said Sir Bingo, but in a less confident tone than before, and with a determination to proceed with some caution in the matter. —"I have got a rouleau above, and Winterblossom shall hold stakes."

"I have no rouleau," said the Squire; "but I'll fly a cheque on Micklewhame."

"See it be better than your last, for I won't be sky-larked again.—Jack, my boy, you are had."

"Not till the bet's won; and I shall see that walking dandy break your head, Bingie, before that," answered Mowbray. "Best speak to the Captain before hand—it is a hellish scrape you are running into—I'll let you off yet, Bingie, for a guinea forfeit.—See, I am just going to start the tattler."

"Start, and be d—d!" said Sir Bingo. "You are gotten, I assure you o' that, Jack." And with a bow and a shuffle, he went up and introduced himself to the stranger as Sir Bingo Binks.

"Had—honour—write—sir," were the only sounds which his throat, or rather his cravat, seemed to send forth.

"Confound the booby!" thought Mowbray; "he will get out of leading strings, if he goes on at this rate; and doubly confounded be this cursed tramper, who, the Lord knows why, has come hither from the Lord knows where, to drive the pigs through my game."

In the meantime, while his friend stood with his stop-watch in his hand, with a visage lengthened under the influence of these reflections, Sir Bingo, with an instinctive tact, which self-preservation seemed to dictate to a brain neither the most delicate nor subtle in the world, premised his inquiry by some general remark on fishing and field-sports. With all these, he found Tyrrel more than passably acquainted. Of fishing and shooting, particularly, he spoke with something like enthusiasm; so that Sir Bingo began to hold him in considerable respect, and to assure himself that he could not be now, or at least could not originally have been bred, the itinerant artist which he now gave himself out—and this, with the fast lapse of the time, induced him thus to address Tyrrel.—"I say, Mr Tyrrel—why, you have been one of us—I say——"

"If you mean a sportsman, Sir Bingo—I have been, and am a pretty keen one still," replied Tyrrel.

"Why, then, you did not always do them sort of things?"

"What sort of things do you mean, Sir Bingo?" said Tyrrel. "I have not the pleasure of understanding you."

"Why, I mean them sketches," said Sir Bingo. "I'll give you a handsome order for them, if you will tell me. I will, on my honour."

"Does it concern you particularly, Sir Bingo, to know anything of my affairs?"

"No—certainly—not immediately," answered Sir Bingo, with some hesitation, for he liked not the dry tone in which Tyrrel's answers were returned, half so well as a bumper of dry sherry; "only I said you were a d—d gnostic fellow, and I laid a bet you have not been always professional—that's all."

Mr Tyrrel replied, "A bet with Mr Mowbray, I suppose?"

"Yes—with Jack—you have hit—I hope I have done him?"

Tyrrel bent his brows, and looked first at Mr Mowbray, then at the Baronet, and, after a moment's thought, addressed the latter.—"Sir Bingo Binks, you are a gentleman of elegant inquiry and acute judgment.—You are perfectly right—I was *not* bred to the profession of an artist, nor did I practise it formerly, whatever I may do now; and so that question is answered."

"And Jack is diddled," said the Baronet, smiting his thigh in triumph, and turning towards the Squire and the stake-holder, with a smile of exultation.

"Stop a single moment, Sir Bingo," said Tyrrel; "take one word with you. I have a great respect for bets—it is part of an Englishman's charter to bet on what he thinks fit, and to prosecute his inquiries over hedge and ditch, as if he were steeple-hunting. But as I have satisfied you on the subject of two bets, that is sufficient compliance with the custom of the country; and therefore I request, Sir Bingo, you will not make me or my affairs the subject of any more wagers."

"I'll be d—d if I do," was the internal resolution of Sir Bingo. Aloud he muttered some apologies, and was heartily glad that the dinner-bell, sounding at the moment, afforded him an apology for shuffling off in a different direction.

Chapter Six

TABLE-TALK

And, sir, if these accounts be true,
The Dutch have mighty things in view;
The Austrians—I admire French beans,
Dear ma'am, above all other greens.
* * * * * * *
And all as lively and as brisk
As—Ma'am, d'ye choose a game at whisk?
Table-Talk

WHEN they were about to leave the room, Lady Penelope assumed Tyrrel's arm with a sweet smile of condescension, meant to make the honoured party understand in its full extent the favour conferred. But the unreasonable artist, far from intimating the least confusion at an attention so little to be expected, seemed to consider the distinction as one which was naturally paid to the greatest stranger present; and when he placed Lady Penelope at the head of the table, by Mr Winterblossom the president, and took a chair for himself betwixt her ladyship and Lady Binks, the provoking wretch appeared no more sensible of being exalted above his proper rank in society, than if he had been sitting by honest Mrs Blower from the Bow-head, who had come to the Well to carry off the dregs of the *Inflienzie*, which she scorned to term a surfeit.

Now this indifference puzzled Lady Penelope's game extremely, and irritated her desire to get at the bottom of Tyrrel's mystery, if there was one, and secure him to her own party. If you were ever at a watering-place, reader, you know that while the guests do not always pay the most polite attention to unmarked individuals, the appearance of a stray lion makes an interest as strong as it is reasonable, and the Amazonian chiefs of each coterie, like the hunters of Buenos-Ayres, prepare their cord and their loop, and manœuvre to the best advantage they can, each hoping to noose the unsuspicious monster, and lead him captive to her own menagerie. A few words concerning Lady Penelope Penfeather will explain why she practised this sport with even more than common zeal.

She was the daughter of an earl, possessed a showy person, and features which might be called handsome in youth, though now rather too much *prononcés* to render the term proper. The nose was become sharper; the cheeks had lost the roundness of youth; and as, during fifteen years that she had reigned a beauty and a ruling toast, the right man had not spoken, or, at least, had not spoken at the right time, her ladyship, now rendered sufficiently independent by the bequest of an old relation, spoke in praise of friendship, began to dislike the town in summer, and to "babble of green fields."

About the time Lady Penelope thus changed the tenor of her life, she was fortunate enough, with Dr Quackleben's assistance, to find out the virtues of Saint Ronan's spring; and, having contributed her share to establish the *Urbs in rure*, which had risen around it, she sat herself down as leader of the fashions in the little province which she had in a great measure both discovered and colonized. She was, therefore, justly desirous to compel homage and tribute from all who should approach the territory.

In other respects, Lady Penelope pretty much resembled the numerous class she belonged to. She was at bottom well-principled, but too thoughtless to let her principles control her humour, therefore not scrupulously nice in society. She was good-natured, but capricious and whimsical, and willing enough to be kind or generous, if it neither thwarted her humour, nor cost her much trouble; would have chaperoned a young friend anywhere, and moved the world for subscription tickets; but never troubled herself how much her giddy charge flirted, or with whom, so that, with a numerous class of Misses, her ladyship was the most delightful creature in the world. Then Lady Penelope had lived so much in society, knew so exactly when to speak, and how to escape from an embarrassing discussion by professing ignorance, while she looked intelligence, that she was not generally discovered to be a fool until she set up for being remarkably clever. This happened more frequently of late, when perhaps, as she could not but observe that the repairs of the toilette became more necessary, she might suppose that new lights, according to the poet, were streaming on her mind through the chinks that Time was making. Many of her friends, however, thought that Lady Penelope had better consulted her genius by remaining in mediocrity, as a fashionable and well-bred woman, than by parading her new-founded pretensions to taste and patronage; but such was not her own opinion, and, doubtless, her ladyship was the best judge.

On the other side of Tyrrel sat Lady Binks, lately the beautiful Miss Bonnyrig, who, during the last season, had made the company at the Well alternately admire, smile, and stare, by dancing the highest Highland fling, riding the wildest pony, laughing the loudest laugh at the broadest joke, and wearing the briefest petticoat of any nymph of Saint Ronan's. Few knew that this wild, hoydenish, half-mad humour, was only superinduced over her real character, for the purpose of—getting well married. She had fixed her eyes on Sir Bingo, and was aware of his maxim, that to catch him, "a girl must be bang up to everything;" and that he would choose a wife for the neck-or-nothing qualities which recommend a good hunter. She made out her catch-match, and she was miserable. Her wild good humour was entirely an assumed part of her character, which was passionate, ambitious, and thoughtful. Delicacy she had none—she knew Sir Bingo was a brute and a fool, even while she was hunting him down; but she had so far mistaken her own feelings, as not to have expected that when she became bone of his bone, she should feel so much shame and anger when she saw his folly expose him to be laughed at and plundered, and so disgusted when his brutality became intimately connected with herself. It is true, he was on the whole rather an innocent monster; and between bitting and bridling, coaxing and humouring, might have been made to pad on well enough. But the unhappy boggling which had taken place previous to the declaration of their private marriage, had so exasperated her spirits against her helpmate, that modes of conciliation were the last she was likely to adopt. Not only had the assistance of the Scottish Themis, so propitiously indulgent to the foibles of the fair, been resorted to on the occasion, but even Mars seemed ready to enter upon the tapis, if Hymen had not intervened. There was, *de par le monde*, a certain brother of the lady—an officer—and, as it happened, on leave of absence,—who alighted from a hack chaise at the Fox Hotel, at eleven o'clock at night, holding in his hand a slip of well-dried oak, accompanied by another gentleman, who, like himself, wore a military travelling-cap and a black stock. Out of the said chaise, as was reported by the trusty Toby, was handed a small reise-sac, an Andrea Ferrara, and a neat mahogany box, eighteen inches long, three deep, and some six broad. Next morning a solemn *palaver* (as the natives of Madagascar call their national convention,) was held at an unusual hour, at which Captain MacTurk and Mr Mowbray assisted; and the upshot was, that at breakfast the company were made happy by the information, that Sir Bingo had been for some weeks the happy bride-groom of their general favourite, which union, concealed for family reasons, he was now at liberty to acknowledge, and to fly with the wings of love to bring his sorrowing turtle from the shades to which she had retired, till the obstacles to their mutual happiness could be removed. Now, though all this sounded very smoothly, that gall-less turtle, Lady Binks, could never think of the tenor of the proceedings without the deepest feelings of resentment and contempt.

Besides all these unpleasant circumstances, Sir Bingo's family had refused to countenance her wish that he should bring her to his own seat; and hence a new shock to her pride, and new matter of contempt against poor Sir Bingo, for being ashamed and afraid to face down the opposition of his kinsfolks, for whose displeasure, though never attending to any good advice from them, he retained a childish awe.

The manners of the young lady were no less changed than was her temper; and, from being much too careless and free, were become reserved, sullen, and haughty. A consciousness that many scrupled to hold intercourse with her in society, rendered her disagreeably tenacious of her rank, and jealous of everything which appeared like neglect. She had constituted herself mistress of Sir Bingo's purse; and, unrestrained in the expenses of dress and equipage, chose, contrary to her maiden practice, to be rather rich and splendid than gay, and to command that attention by magnificence, which she no longer deigned to solicit by rendering herself either agreeable or entertaining. One secret source of her misery was the necessity of shewing deference to Lady Penelope Penfeather, whose understanding she despised, and whose pretensions to consequence, to patronage, and to literature, she had acuteness enough to see through, and to contemn; and this dislike was the more grievous, that she felt she depended a good deal on Lady Penelope's countenance for the situation she was able to maintain even among the not very select society of Saint Ronan's Well; and that, neglected by her, she must have dropped lower in the scale even there. Neither was Lady Penelope's kindness to Lady Binks extremely cordial. She partook in the ancient and ordinary dislike of single nymphs of a certain age, to those who make splendid alliances under their very eye—and she more than suspected the secret disaffection of the lady. But the name sounded well; and the style in which Lady Binks lived was a credit to the place. So they satisfied their mutual dislike with saying a few sharp things to each other occasionally, but all under the mask of civility.

Such was Lady Binks; and yet, being such, her dress, and her equipage, and carriages, were the envy of half the Misses at the Well, who, while she sat disfiguring with sullenness her very lovely face, (for it was as beautiful as her shape was exquisite,) only thought she was proud of having carried her point, and felt herself, with her large fortune and diamond bandeau, no fit company for the rest of the party. They submitted, therefore, with meekness to her domineering temper, though it was not the less tyrannical, that in her maiden state of hoyden-hood, she had been to some of them an object of slight and of censure; and Lady Binks had not forgotten the offences offered to Miss Bonnyrig. But the fair sisterhood submitted to her retaliations, as lieutenants endure the bullying of a rough and boisterous captain of the sea, with the secret determination to pay it home on their underlings, when they shall become captains themselves.

In this state of importance, yet of penance, Lady Binks occupied her place at the dinner-table, alternately disconcerted by some stupid speech of her lord and master, and by some slight sarcasm from Lady Penelope, to which she longed to reply, but dared not.

She looked from time to time at her neighbour Frank Tyrrel, but without addressing him, and accepted in silence the usual civilities which he proffered to her. She had remarked keenly his interview with Sir Bingo, and knowing by experience the manner in which her honoured lord was wont to retreat from a dispute in which he was unsuccessful, as well as his genius for getting into such perplexities, she had little doubt that he had sustained from the stranger some new indignity; whom, therefore, she regarded with a mixture of feeling, scarce knowing whether to be pleased with him for having given pain to him whom she hated, or angry with him for having affronted one in whose degradation her own was necessarily involved. There might be other thoughts—on the whole, she regarded him with much though with mute attention. He paid her but little in return, being almost entirely occupied in replying to the questions of the engrossing Lady Penelope Penfeather.

Receiving polite though rather evasive answers to her inquiries concerning his late avocations, her ladyship could only learn that Tyrrel had been travelling in several remote parts of Europe, and even of Asia. Baffled, but not repulsed, the lady continued her courtesy, by pointing out to him, as a stranger, several individuals of the company to whom she proposed introducing him, as persons from whose society he might derive either profit or amusement. In the midst of this sort of conversation, however, she suddenly stopped short.

"Will you forgive me, Mr Tyrrel," she said, "if I say I have been watching your thoughts for some moments, and that I have detected you? All the while that I have been talking of these good folks, and that you have been making such civil replies, that they might be with great propriety and utility inserted in the familiar dialogues, teaching foreigners how to express themselves in English upon ordinary occasions—your mind has been entirely fixed on that empty chair, which has remained there opposite betwixt our worthy president and Sir Bingo Binks."

"I own, madam," he answered, "I was a little surprised at seeing such a distinguished seat unoccupied, while the table is rather crowded."

"O, confess more, sir!—Confess that to a poet a seat unoccupied—the chair of Banquo—has more charms than if it were filled even as an alderman would fill it.—What if 'the Dark Ladye' should glide in and occupy it?—Would you have courage to stand the vision, Mr Tyrrel?—I assure you the thing is not impossible."

"*What* is not impossible, Lady Penelope?" said Tyrrel, somewhat surprised.

"Startled already?—Nay, then, I despair of your enduring the awful interview."

"What interview? who is expected?" said Tyrrel, unable with the utmost exertion to suppress some signs of curiosity, though he suspected the whole to be merely some mystification of her ladyship.

"How delighted I am," she said, "that I have found out where you are vulnerable!—Expected—did I say expected?—no, not expected.

> She glides, like Night, from land to land,
> She hath strange power of speech.

—But come, I have you at my mercy, and I will be generous and explain.—We call—that is, among ourselves you understand—Miss Clara Mowbray, the sister of that gentleman that sits next to Miss

Parker, the Dark Ladie, and that seat is left for her—for she was expected—no, not expected—I forget again!—but it was thought *possible* she might honour us to-day, when our feast was so full and piquant. —Her brother is our Lord of the Manor—and so they pay her that sort of civility to regard her as a visitor—and neither Lady Binks nor I think of objecting—She is a singular young person, Clara Mowbray—she amuses me very much—I am always rather glad to see her."

"She is not to come hither to-day," said Tyrrel; "am I so to understand your ladyship?"

"Why, it is past her time—even *her* time," said Lady Penelope—"dinner was kept back half an hour, and our poor invalids were famishing, as you may see by the deeds they have done since.—But Clara is an odd creature, and if she took it into her head to come hither at this moment, hither she would come.—She is very whimsical.—Many people think her handsome—but she looks so like something from another world, that she makes me always think of Mat Lewis's Spectre Lady."

And she repeated with much cadence,

> "There is a thing—there is a thing
> I fain would have from thee;
> I fain would have that gay gold ring,
> O warrior, give it me!

"And then you remember his answer:

> This ring Lord Brooke from his daughter took,
> And a solemn oath he swore,
> That that ladye my bride should be
> When this crusade was o'er.

"You do figures as well as landscapes, I suppose, Mr Tyrrel?—You shall make a sketch for me—a slight thing—for sketches, I think, shew the freedom of art better than finished pieces—I dote on the first coruscations of genius—flashing like lightning from the cloud!—You shall make a sketch for my own boudoir—my dear sulky den at Air Castle, and Clara Mowbray shall sit for the Ghost Ladye."

"That would be but a poor compliment to your ladyship's friend," replied Tyrrel.

"Friend? We do not get quite that length, though I like Clara very well.—Quite sentimental cast of face, I think I saw an antique in the Louvre very like her—(I was there in 1802)—quite an antique countenance—eyes something hollowed—care has dug caves for them, but they are caves of the most beautiful marble, arched with jet—a straight nose, and absolutely the Grecian mouth and chin—a profusion of long straight black hair, with the whitest skin you ever saw—as white as the whitest parchment—and not a shade of colour in her cheek—none whatever—If she would be naughty, and borrow a prudent touch of complexion, she might be called beautiful. Even as it is, many think her so, although surely, Mr Tyrrel, three colours are necessary to the female face. However, we used to call her the Melpomene of the Spring last season, as we called Lady Binks—who was not then Lady Binks—our Euphrosyne—Did we not, my dear?"

"Did we not what, madam?" said Lady Binks, in a tone something sharper than ought to have belonged to so beautiful a countenance.

"I am sorry I have started you out of your reverie, my love," answered Lady Penelope. "I was only assuring Mr Tyrrel that you were once Euphrosyne, though now so much under the banners of Il Penseroso."

"I do not know that I have been either one or the other," answered Lady Binks; "one thing I certainly am not—I am not capable of understanding your ladyship's wit and learning."

"Poor soul," whispered Lady Penelope to Tyrrel; "we know what we are, we know not what we may be.—And now, Mr Tyrrel, I have been your sibyl to guide you through this Elysium of ours, I think, in reward, I deserve a little confidence in return."

"If I had any to repose, which could be in the slightest degree interesting to your ladyship," answered Tyrrel.

"Oh! cruel man—he will not understand me!" exclaimed the lady —"In plain words then, a peep into your portfolio—just to see what objects you have rescued from natural decay, and rendered immortal by the pencil. You do not know—indeed, Mr Tyrrel, you do not know how I dote upon your 'serenely silent art,' second to Poetry—equal—superior perhaps—to Music."

"I really have little that could possibly be worth the attention of such a judge as your ladyship," answered Tyrrel; "such trifles as your ladyship has seen, I sometimes leave at the foot of the tree I have been sketching on them."

"As Orlando left his verses in the Forest of Ardennes?—Oh, the thoughtless prodigality!—Mr Winterblossom, do you hear this?—We must follow Mr Tyrrel in his walks, and glean what he leaves behind him."

Her ladyship was here disconcerted by some laughter on Sir Bingo's side of the table, which she chastised by an angry glance, and then proceeded emphatically.

"Mr Tyrrel—this must *not* be—this is not the way of the world, my good sir, to which even Genius must stoop its flight. We must consult the engraver—though perhaps you etch as well as you draw?"

"I should suppose so," said Mr Winterblossom, edging in a word with difficulty, "from the freedom of Mr Tyrrel's touch."

"I will not deny having spoiled a little copper now and then," said Tyrrel, "since I am charged with the crime by such good judges; but it has been only by way of experiment."

"Say no more," said the lady; "my darling wish is accomplished!—We have long desired to have the remarkable and most romantic spots of our little Arcadia here—spots consecrated to friendship, the fine arts, the loves and the graces, immortalized by the graver's art, faithful to its charge of fame—you shall labour on this task, Mr Tyrrel; we will all assist with notes and illustrations—we will all contribute—only some of us must be permitted to remain anonymous—fairy favours, you know, Mr Tyrrel, must be kept secret—And you shall be allowed the pillage of the Album—some sweet things there of Mr Chatterley's—and Mr Edgeit, a gentleman of your own profession, I am sure will lend his aid—Dr Quackleben will contribute some scientific notices.—And for subscription——"

"Financial—financial—your leddyship, I speak to order!" said the writer, interrupting Lady Penelope with a tone of impudent familiarity, which was meant doubtless for jocular ease.

"How am I out of order, Mr Micklewhame?" said her ladyship, drawing herself up.

"I speak to order!—No warrants for money can be extracted before intimation to the Committee of Management."

"Pray who mentioned money, Mr Micklewhame?" said her ladyship.—"That wretched old pettifogger," she added in a whisper to Tyrrel, "thinks of nothing else but his filthy pelf."

"Ye spake of subscription, my leddy, whilk is the same thing as money, differing only in respect of time—the subscription being a contract *de futuro*, and having a *tractus temporis in gremio*—And I have kenn'd mony honest folks in the company at the Well, complain of these subscriptions as a great abuse, as obliging them either to look unlike other folk, or to gie good lawful coin for ballants and picture-books, and things they caredna a pinch o' snuff for."

Several of the company, at the lower end of the table, assented both by nods and murmurs of approbation; and the orator was about to proceed, when Tyrrel with difficulty procured a hearing before the debate went farther, and assured the company that her ladyship's goodness had led her into an error; that he had no work in hand worthy of their patronage, and, with the deepest gratitude for Lady Penelope's goodness, had it not in his power to comply with her request. There was some tittering at her ladyship's expence, who, as the writer slyly observed, had been something *ultronious* in her patronage. Without attempting for the moment any rally, (as indeed the time which had passed since the removal of the dinner scarce permitted an opportunity,) Lady Penelope gave the signal for the ladies' retreat, and left the gentlemen to the circulation of the bottle.

Chapter Seven

THE TEA-TABLE

——While the cups
Which cheer, but not inebriate, wait on each.
COWPER

IT WAS common at the Well, for the fair guests occasionally to give tea to the company,—such at least as from their rank and leading in the little society, might be esteemed fit to constitute themselves patronesses of an evening; and the same lady generally carried the authority she had acquired into the ball-room, where two fiddles and a bass, at a guinea a night, with a *quantum sufficit* of tallow candles, (against the use of which Lady Penelope often mutinied,) enabled the company—to use the appropriate phrase—"to close the evening on the light fantastic toe."

On the present occasion, the lion of the hour, Mr Francis Tyrrel, had so little answered the high-wrought expectations of Lady Penelope, that she rather regretted having ever given herself any trouble about him, and particularly that of having manœuvred herself into the patronage of the tea-table for the evening, to the great expenditure of souchong and congo. Accordingly, her ladyship had no sooner summoned her own woman, and her *fille de chambre*, to make tea, with her page, footman, and postillion, to hand it about, (in which duty they were assisted by two richly-laced, and thickly powdered footmen of Lady Binks's, whose liveries put to shame the more modest garb of Lady Penelope's, and even dimmed the glory of the suppressed coronet upon the buttons,) than she began to vilipend and depreciate what had been so long the object of her curiosity.

"This Mr Tyrrel," she said, in a tone of authoritative decision, "seems after all a very ordinary sort of person—quite a commonplace man, who, she dared say, had considered his condition, in going to the old ale-house, much better than they had done for him, when they asked him to the Public Rooms. He had known his own place better than they did—there was nothing uncommon in his appearance or conversation—nothing at all *frappant*—she scarce believed he could even draw that sketch. Mr Winterblossom, indeed, made a great deal of it; but then all the world knew that every scrap of engraving or drawing, which Mr Winterblossom contrived to make his own, was, the instant it came into his collection, the finest thing that ever was seen—that was the way with collectors—their geese were all swans."

"And your ladyship's swan has proved but a goose, my dear Lady Pen," said Lady Binks.

"*My* swan, dearest Lady Binks! I really do not know how I have deserved the appropriation."

"Do not be angry, my dear Lady Penelope; I only mean, that for a fortnight and more you have spoke constantly *of* this Mr Tyrrel, and all dinner-time you spoke *to* him."

The fair company began to collect around, at hearing the word *dear* so often repeated in the same brief dialogue, which induced them to expect sport, and, like the vulgar on a similar occasion, to form a rink for the expected combatants.

"He sat betwixt us, Lady Binks," answered Lady Penelope, with dignity. "You had your usual head-ache, you know, and, for the credit of the company, I spoke for one."

"For *two*, if your ladyship pleases," replied Lady Binks. "I mean," she added, softening the expression, "for yourself and me."

"I am sorry," said Lady Penelope, "I should have spoke for one who can speak so smartly for herself, as my dear Lady Binks—I did not, by any means, desire to engross the conversation—-I repeat it, there is a mistake about this man."

"I think there is," said Lady Binks, in a tone which implied something more than mere assent to Lady Penelope's proposition.

"I doubt if he is an artist at all," said the Lady Penelope; "or if he is, he must be doing things for a Magazine, or Encyclopedia, or some such matter."

"*I* doubt, too, if he be a professional artist," said Lady Binks. "If so, he is of the very highest class, for I have seldom seen a better-bred man."

"There are very well-bred artists," said Lady Penelope. "It is the profession of a gentleman."

"Certainly," answered Lady Binks; "but the poorer class have often to struggle with poverty and dependance. In general society, they are like commercial people in presence of their customers; and that is a difficult part to sustain. And so you see them of all sorts—shy and reserved when they are conscious of merit—petulant and whimsical, by way of shewing their independence—intrusive, in order to appear easy—-and sometimes obsequious and fawning, when they chance to be of a mean spirit. But you seldom see them quite at their ease, and therefore I either hold this Mr Tyrrel to be an artist of the first class, raised completely above the necessity and degradations of patronage, or else no professional artist at all."

Lady Penelope looked at Lady Binks with much such a regard as Balaam may have cast upon his ass, when he discovered the animal's capacity for holding an argument with him. She muttered to herself—

"Mon âne parle, et même il parle bien."

But declining the altercation which Lady Binks seemed disposed to enter into, she replied with good humour, "Well, dearest Rachael, we will not pull caps about this man—nay, I think your good opinion of him gives him new value in my eyes. That is always the way with us girls, my good friend! We may confess it, when there are none of these conceited male wretches amongst us. We will know what he really is—he shall not wear fern-seed, and walk amongst us invisible thus—what say you, Maria?"

"Indeed, I say, dear Lady Penelope," answered Miss Digges, whose ready chatter we have already introduced to the reader, "he is a very handsome man, though his nose is too big, and his mouth too wide—but his teeth are like pearl—and he has such eyes!—especially when your ladyship spoke to him. I don't think you looked at his eyes—they are quite deep and dark, and full of glow, like what you read to us in the letter from that lady, about Robert Burns."

"Upon my word, miss, you come on finely," said Lady Penelope.—"One had need take care what they read or talk about before you, I see.—Come, Jones, have mercy upon us—put an end to that symphony of tinkling cups and saucers, and let the first act of the tea-table begin, if you please."

"Does her leddyship mean the grace?" said honest Mrs Blower, for the first time admitted into this worshipful society, and busily employed in arranging an Indian handkerchief, that might have made a main-sail for one of her husband's smuggling luggers, which she spread carefully on her knees, to prevent damage to a flowered silk gown from the repast of tea and cake, to which she proposed to do due honour,—"Does her leddyship mean the grace? I see the minister is just coming in.—Her leddyship waits till ye say a blessing, an ye please, sir."

This was addressed to Mr Simon Chatterley, who had just entered the room with a graceful sliding step. He bent on the honest woman a stare of astonishment through his quizzing-glass, and slid on to the tea-table.

Mr Winterblossom, who toddled after the chaplain, his toe having given him an alert hint to quit the dining-table, though he saw every feature in the poor woman's face swoln with desire to procure information concerning the ways and customs of the place, passed on the other side of the way, regardless of her agony of curiosity.

A moment after, she was relieved by the entrance of Dr Quackleben, whose maxim being, that one patient was as well worth attention as another, and who knew by experience, that the honoraria of a godly wife of the Bowhead were as apt to be forth-coming, (if not more so,) as my Lady Penelope's, he e'en sat himself quietly down by Mrs Blower, and proceeded with the utmost kindness to inquire after her health, and to hope she had not forgotten taking a table-spoonful of spirits burned to a *residuum*, in order to qualify the crudities.

"Indeed, Doctor," said the honest woman, "I loot the brandy burn as lang as I dought look at the guid creature wasting its sell that gate—and then, when I was fain to put it out for very thrift, I did take a thimble-full of it, (although it is not the thing I am used to, Dr Keckleben;) and I winna say but that it did me good."

"Unquestionably, madam," said the Doctor. "I am no friend to the use of alcohol in general, but there are particular cases—there are particular cases, Mrs Blower—My venerated instructor, one of the greatest men in our profession that ever lived, took a wine-glass of old rum, mixed with sugar, every day after his dinner."

"Ay, dear heart, he would be a comfortable doctor that," said Mrs Blower. "He wad maybe ken something of my case. Is he living, think ye, sir?"

"Dead for many years, madam," said Dr Quackleben; "and there are but few of his pupils that can fill his place, I assure ye. If I could be thought an exception, it is only because I was a favourite. Ah! blessings on the old red cloak of him!—It covered more of the healing science than the gowns of a whole modern university."

"There is ane, sir," said Mrs Blower, "that has been muckle recommended about Edinburgh—Macgregor, I think they ca' him—fo'k come far and near to see him."

"I know who you mean, ma'am—a clever man—no denying it—a clever man—but there are certain cases—yours, for example—and I think many that come to drink this water—which I cannot say I think he perfectly understands—hasty—very hasty and rapid. Now I—I give the disease its own way at first—then watch it, Mrs Blower—watch the turn of the tide."

"Ay, troth, that's true," responded the widow; "John Blower was aye watching turn of tide, puir man."

"Then he is a starving Doctor, Mrs Blower—reduces diseases as soldiers do towns—by famine, not considering that the friendly inhabitants suffer as much as the hostile garrison—a-hem!"

Here he gave an important and emphatic cough, and then proceeded.

"I am no friend either to excess or to violent stimulus, Mrs Blower—but nature must be supported—a generous diet—cordials judiciously thrown in—not without the advice of a medical man—that is my opinion, Mrs Blower, to speak as a friend—others may starve their patients if they have a mind."

"It wadna do for me, the starving, Dr Keekerben," said the alarmed relict,—"it wadna do for me at a'—Just a' I can do to wear through the day with the sma' supports that nature requires—not a soul to look after me, Doctor, since John Blower was taen awa.—Thank ye kindly, sir, (to the servant who handed the tea,)—thank ye, my bonny man, (to the page who served the cake)—Now, dinna ye think, Doctor, (in a low and confidential voice,) that her leddyship's tea is rather of the weakliest—water bewitched, I think—and Mrs Jones, as they ca' her, has cut the seed-cake very thin."

"It is the fashion, Mrs Blower," answered Dr Quackleben; "and her ladyship's tea is excellent. But your taste is a little chilled, which is not uncommon at the first use of the waters, so that you are not sensible of the flavour—we must support the system—reinforce the digestive powers—give me leave—you are a stranger, Mrs Blower, and we must take care of you—I have an elixir which will put that matter to rights in a moment."

So saying, Dr Quackleben pulled from his pocket a small portable case of medicines—"Catch me without my tools—" he said, "here I have the real useful pharmacopeia—the rest is all humbug and hard names—this little case, with a fortnight or month, spring and fall, at Saint Ronan's Well, and no one will die till his day come."

Thus boasting, the Doctor drew from his case a large vial or small flask, full of a high-coloured liquid, of which he mixed three teaspoonfulls in Mrs Blower's cup, who, immediately afterwards, allowed that the flavour was improved beyond all belief, and that it was "vera comfortable and restorative indeed."

"Will it not do good to my complaints, Doctor?" said Mr Winterblossom, who had strolled towards them, and held out his cup to the physician.

"I by no means recommend it, Mr Winterblossom," said Dr Quackleben, shutting up his case with great coolness; "your case is œdomatous, and you treat it your own way—you are as good a physician as I am, and I never interfere with another practitioner's patient."

"Well, Doctor," said Winterblossom, "I must wait till Sir Bingo comes in: he has a hunting-flask usually about him, which contains as good medicine as yours to the full."

"You will wait for Sir Bingo some time," said the Doctor, "he is a gentleman of sedentary habits—he has ordered another magnum."

"Sir Bungo is an unco name for a man o' quality, dinna ye think sae, Dr Cacklehen?" said Mrs Blower. "John Blower, when he was a wee bit 'in the wind's eye', as he ca'd it, puir fallow—used to sing a sang about a dog they ca'd Bungo, that suld hae belanged to a farmer."

"Our Bingo is but a puppy yet, madam—or if a dog, he is a sad dog," said Mr Winterblossom, applauding his own wit, by one of his own inimitable smiles.

"Or a mad dog, rather," said Mr Chatterley, "for he drinks no water;" and he also smiled gracefully at the thoughts of having trumped, as it were, the president's pun.

"Twa pleasant men, Doctor," said the widow, "and so is Sir Bungy too for that matter; but O! is na it a pity he should bide sae lang by the bottle? It was puir John Blower's fau't too, that weary tippling; when he wan to the lee-side of a bowl of punch, there was nae raising him.—But they are taking awa' the things, and, Doctor, is it not an awfu' thing that the creature-comforts should hae been used without grace or thanksgiving?—that Mr Chitterling, if he really be a minister, has muckle to answer for, that he neglects his Master's service."

"Why, madam," said the Doctor, "Mr Chatterley is scarce arrived at the rank of a minister plenipotentiary."

"A minister potentiary—ah, Doctor, I doubt that is some jeest of yours," said the widow; "that's sae like puir John Blower. When I wad hae had him gie up the Lovely Peggy, ship and cargo, (the vesshel was named after me, Doctor Kittleben,) to be remembered in the prayers o' the congregation, he wad sae to me, 'they may pray that stand the risk, Peggy Bryce, for I've made insurance.' He was a merry man, Doctor; but he had the root of the matter in him, for a' his light way of speaking, as deep as ony skipper that ever loosed anchor from Leith Roads. I hae been a forshaken creature since his death—O the weary days and nights that I have had!—and the weight on the spirits—the spirits—the spirits, Doctor!—though I canna sae I hae been easier since I hae been at the Wall than even now—if I kenned what I was awing ye for elickstir, Doctor, for it's doun me muckle heart's good, forbye the opening of my mind to you?"

"Fie, fie, ma'am," said the Doctor, as the widow pulled out a seal-skin pouch, such as sailors carry tobacco in, but apparently well stuffed with bank-notes,—"Fie, fie, madam—I am no apothecary—I have my diploma from Leyden—a regular physician, madam,—the elixir is heartily at your service; and should you want any advice, no man will be prouder to assist you than your humble servant."

"I am sure I am muckle obliged to your kindness, Dr Kickalpin," said the widow, folding up her pouch, "this was puir John Blower's *spleuchan*, as they ca' it—I e'en wear it for his sake. He was a kind man, and left me comfortable in warld's gudes; but comforts hae their cumbers,—to be a lone woman is a sair weird, Dr Kittlepin."

Dr Quackleben drew his chair a little nearer that of the widow, and entered into a closer communication with her, in a tone doubtless of more delicate consolation than was fit for the ears of the company at large.

One of the chief delights of a watering-place is, that every one's affairs seem to be put under the special surveillance of the whole company, so that, in all probability, the various flirtations, *liaisons*, and so forth, which naturally take place in the society, are not only the subject of amusement to the parties engaged, but also to the lookers on; that is to say, generally speaking, to the whole community, of which for the time the said parties are members. Lady Penelope, the presiding goddess of the region, watchful over all her circle, was not long of observing that the Doctor seemed to be suddenly engaged in close communication with the widow, and even ventured to take hold of her fair plump hand, with a manner which partook at once of the gallant, and of the medical adviser.

"For the love of Heaven," said her ladyship, "who can that comely dame be, on whom our excellent and learned Doctor looks with such uncommon regards?"

"Fat, fair, and forty," said Mr Winterblossom; "that is all I know of her—a mercantile person."

"A carrack, Sir President," said the chaplain, "richly laden with colonial produce, by name the Lovely Peggy Bryce—no master—the late John Blower of North Leith having pushed off his boat for the Stygian Creek, and left the vessel without a hand on board."

"The Doctor," said Lady Penelope, turning her glass towards them, "seems willing to play the part of pilot."

"I dare say he will be willing to change her name and register," said Mr Chatterley.

"He can do no less in common requital," said Winterblossom. "She has changed his name six times in the five minutes which I stood within hearing of them."

"What do you think of the matter, my dear Lady Binks?" said Lady Penelope.

"Madam?" said Lady Binks, starting from a reverie, and answering as one who either had not heard, or did not understand the question.

"I mean, what think you of what is going on yonder?"

Lady Binks turned her glass in the direction of Lady Penelope's glance, fixed the widow and the Doctor with one bold fashionable stare, and then dropping her hand slowly, said with indifference, "I really see nothing there worth thinking about."

"I dare say it is a fine thing to be married," said Lady Penelope; "one's thoughts, I suppose, are so much engrossed with one's own perfect happiness, that they have neither time nor inclination to laugh like other folks. Miss Rachael Bonnyrig would have laughed till her eyes run over, had she seen what Lady Binks cares so little about—I dare say it must be an all-sufficient happiness to be married."

"He would be a happy man that could convince your ladyship of that in good earnest," said Mr Winterblossom.

"Oh, who knows—the whim may strike me," replied the lady; "but no—no—no;—and that is three times."

"Say it sixteen times more," said the gallant president, "and let nineteen nay-says be a grant."

"If I should say a thousand Noes, there exists not the alchemy in living man that can extract one Yes out of the whole mass," said her ladyship. "Blessed be the memory of good Queen Bess!—She set us all an example to keep power when we have it.—What noise is that?"

"Only the usual after-dinner quarrel," said the divine. "I hear the captain's voice, else most silent, commanding them to keep peace, in the devil's name and that of the ladies."

"Upon my word, dearest Lady Binks, this is too bad of that lord and master of yours, and of Mowbray, who might have more sense, and of the rest of that claret-drinking set, to be quarrelling and alarming our nerves every evening with presenting their pistols perpetually at each other, like sportsmen confined to the house upon a rainy 12th of August. I am tired of the Peace-maker—he but skins the business up to have it break out elsewhere.—What think you, love, if we were to give out in orders, that the next quarrel which may arise, shall be *bona fide* fought to an end?—We will all go out and see it, and wear the colours on each side; and if there should come a funeral, we will attend it in a body.—Weeds are so becoming!—Are they not, my dear Lady Binks? Look at Widow Blower in her deep blacks—don't you envy her, my love?"

Lady Binks seemed about to make a sharp and hasty answer, but checked herself, perhaps under the recollection that she could not prudently come to an open breach with Lady Penelope.—At the same moment the door opened, and a lady dressed in a riding-habit, and wearing a black veil over her hat, appeared at the entry of the apartment.

"Angels and ministers of grace!" exclaimed Lady Penelope, with her very best tragic start—"my dearest Clara, why so late? and why thus? Will you step to my dressing-room—Jones will get you one of my gowns—we are just of a size, you know—do, pray—let me be vain of something of my own for once by seeing you wear it."

This was spoken in the fondest tone of female friendship, and at the same time the fair hostess bestowed on Miss Mowbray one of those tender caresses, which ladies, God bless them, sometimes bestow on each other with unnecessary prodigality, to the great discontent and envy of the male spectators.

"You are fluttered, my dearest Clara—you are feverish—I am sure you are," continued the sweetly anxious Lady Penelope; "let me persuade you to lie down."

"Indeed you are mistaken, Lady Penelope," said Miss Mowbray, who seemed to receive much as a matter of course her ladyship's profusion of affectionate politeness;—"I am heated, and my pony trotted hard, that is the whole mystery.—Let me have a cup of tea, Mrs Jones, and the matter is ended."

"Fresh tea, Jones, directly," said Lady Penelope, and led her passive friend to her own corner, as she was pleased to call the recess, in which she held her little court—ladies and gentlemen courtsying and bowing as she passed; to which civilities the new guest made no more return, than the most ordinary politeness rendered unavoidable.

Lady Binks did not rise to receive her, but she sate upright in her chair, and bent her head very stiffly; a courtsy which Miss Mowbray returned in the same stately manner, without farther greeting on either side.

"Now, wha can that be, Doctor?" said the Widow Blower—"mind ye have promised to tell me all about the grand folk—wha can that be that Lady Penelope halds such a racket wi'?—and what for does she come wi' a habit and a beaver-hat, when we are a' (a glance at her own gown) in our silks and satins?"

"To tell you who she is, my dear Mrs Blower, is very easy," said the officious Doctor. "She is Miss Clara Mowbray, sister to the Lord of the Manor—the gentleman who wears the green coat, with an arrow on the cape. To tell why she wears that habit, or does anything else, would be rather beyond doctor's skill. Truth is, I have always thought she was a little—a very little—touched—call it nerves—hypochondria—or what you will."

"Lord help us, puir thing!" said the compassionate widow.—"And troth it looks like it. But it is a shame to let her go loose, Doctor—she might hurt hersell, or somebody. See, she has ta'en the knife!—O, it's only to cut a shave of the diet-loaf. She winna let the powder-monkey of a boy help her. There is judgment in that though, Doctor, for she can cut thick or thin as she likes.—Dear me! she has not taken mair than a crumb, that ane would pit between the wires of a canary-bird's cage, after all.—I wish she would lift up that lang veil, or put aff that riding-skirt, Doctor. She should really be shewed the regulations, Doctor Kickelshin."

"She cares about no rules we can make, Mrs Blower," said the Doctor; "and her brother's will and pleasure, and Lady Penelope's whim of indulging her, carry her through in everything. They should take advice on her case."

"Ay, truly, it's time to take advice, when young creatures like her caper in amang dressed leddies, just as if they were come from scampering on Leith sands.—Such a wark as my leddy makes wi' her, Doctor! Ye would think they were baith fools of a feather."

"They might have flown on one wing, for what I know," said Dr Quackleben; "but there was early and sound advice taken in Lady Penelope's case. My friend, the late Earl of Featherhead, was a man of judgment—did little in his family but by rule of medicine—so that, what with the waters, and what with my own care, Lady Penelope is only freakish—fanciful—that's all—and her quality bears it out—the peccant principle might have broken out under other treatment."

"Ay—she has been weel-friended," said the widow; "but this bairn Mowbray, puir thing! how came she to be sae left to hersell?"

"Her mother was dead—her father thought of nothing but his sports," said the Doctor. "Her brother was educated in England, and cared for nobody but himself, if he had been here—what education she got was at her own hand—what reading she read was in a library full of old romances—what friends or company she had was what chance sent her—then no family-physician, not even a good surgeon within ten miles! And so you cannot wonder if the poor thing became unsettled."

"Puir thing!—no doctor!—nor even a surgeon!—But, Doctor," said the widow, "maybe the puir thing had the enjoyment of her health ye ken, and then——"

"Ah? ha, ha!—why *then*, madam, she needed a physician far more than if she had been delicate. A skilful physician, Mrs Blower, knows how to bring down that robust health, which is a very alarming state of the frame when it is considered *secundum artem*. Most sudden deaths happen when people are in a robust state of health. Ah! that state of perfect health is what the doctor dreads most on behalf of his patient."

"Ay, ay, Doctor?—I am quite sensible, nae doubt," said the widow, "of the great advantage of having a skeelfu' person about ane."

Here the Doctor's voice, in his earnestness to convince Mrs Blower of the danger of supposing herself capable of living and breathing without a medical man's permission, sunk into a soft pleading tone, of which our reporter could not catch the sound. He was, as great orators will sometimes be, "inaudible in the gallery."

Meantime, Lady Penelope overwhelmed Clara Mowbray with her caresses. In what degree her ladyship, at her heart, loved this young person, might be difficult to ascertain,—probably in the degree in which a child loves a new toy. But Clara was a toy not always to be come by—as whimsical in her way as her ladyship in her own, only that poor Clara's singularities were real, and her ladyship's chiefly affected. Without adopting the harshness of the Doctor's conclusions concerning the former, she was certainly unequal in her spirits; and her occasional fits of levity were chequered by very long intervals of sadness. Her levity also appeared, in the world's eye, greater than it really was, for she had never been under the restraint of society which was really good, and entertained an undue contempt for that which she sometimes mingled with; having unhappily none to teach her the important truth, that some forms and restraints are to be observed, less in respect to others than to ourselves. Her dress, her manners, and her ideas, were therefore very much her own; and though they became her wonderfully, yet, like Ophelia's garlands, and wild snatches of melody, they were calculated to excite compassion and melancholy, even while they amused the observer.

"And why came you not to dinner?—We expected you—your throne was prepared."

"I had scarce come to tea," said Miss Mowbray, "of my own free will. But my brother says your ladyship proposes to come to Shaws-Castle, and he insisted it was quite right and necessary, to confirm you in so flattering a purpose, that I should come and say, Pray do, Lady Penelope; and so now here am I to say, Pray, do come."

"Is an invitation so flattering limited to me alone, my dear Clara?—Lady Binks will be jealous."

"Bring Lady Binks, if she has the condescension to honour us—[a bow was very stiffly exchanged between the ladies]—bring Mr Springblossom—Winterblossom—and all the lions and lionesses—we have room for the whole collection. My brother, I suppose, will bring his own particular regiment of bears, which, with the usual assortment of monkeys seen in all caravans, will complete the menagerie. How you are to be entertained at Shaws-Castle, is, I thank Heaven, not my business, but John's."

"We shall want no formal entertainment, my love," said Lady Penelope; "a *déjeuner à la fourchette*—we know, Clara, you would die of doing the honours of a formal dinner."

"Not a bit; I should live long enough to make my will, and bequeath all large parties to Old Nick, who invented them."

"Miss Mowbray," said Lady Binks, who had been thwarted by this free-spoken young lady, both in her former character of a coquette and romp, and in that of a prude, which she at present wore—"Miss Mowbray declares for

> Champagne and a chicken at last."

"The chicken, without the champagne, if you please," said Miss Mowbray; "I have known ladies pay dear to have champagne on the board.—By the by, Lady Penelope, you have not your collection in the same order and discipline as Pidcock and Polito.—There was much growling and snarling in the lower den when I passed it."

"It was feeding-time, my love," said Lady Penelope; "and the lower animals of every class become pugnacious at that hour—you see all our safer and well-conditioned animals are loose, and in good order."

"Oh, yes—in the keeper's presence, you know—Well, I must venture to cross the hall again among all that growling and grumbling—I would I had the prince Ahmed's quarters of mutton to toss among them if they should break out—He, I mean, who fetched water from the Fountain of Lions. However, on second thoughts, I will take the back way, and avoid them.—What says honest Bottom?—

> For if they should as lions come in strife
> Into such place, 'twere pity of their life."

"Shall I go with you, my dear?" said Lady Penelope.

"No—I have too great a soul for that—I think some of them are only lions as far as the hide is concerned."

"But why would you go so soon, Clara?"

"Because my errand is finished—have I not invited you and yours? and would not Lord Chesterfield himself allow I have done the polite thing?"

"But you have spoke to none of the company—how can you be so odd, my love?" said her ladyship.

"Why, I spoke to them all when I spoke to you and Lady Binks—but I am a good girl, and will do as I am bid."

So saying, she looked round the company, and addressed each of them with an affectation of interest and politeness.

"Mr Winterblossom, I hope the gout is better—Mr Robert Rymar—(I have escaped calling him Thomas for once)—I hope the public give encouragement to the muses—Mr Keelavine, I trust your pencil is busy—Mr Chatterley, I have no doubt your flock improves—Dr Quackleben, I trust your patients recover.—These are all the especials of the worthy company I know—for the rest, health to the sick, and pleasure to the healthy."

"You are not going in reality, my love?" said Lady Penelope; "these hasty rides agitate your nerves—they do, indeed—you should be cautious—Shall I speak to Quackleben?"

"To neither quack nor quackle, on my account, my dear lady.—It is not as you would seem to say, by your winking at Lady Binks—it is not, indeed—I shall be no Lady Clementina, to be the wonder and pity of the spring of Saint Ronan's—No Ophelia neither—though I will say with her, Good night, ladies—Good night, sweet ladies!—and now—not my coach, my coach—but my horse, my horse!"

So saying, she tripped out of the room by a side passage, leaving the ladies looking at each other significantly, and shaking their heads with looks of much import.

"Something has ruffled the poor unhappy girl," said Lady Penelope; "I never saw her so very odd before."

"Were I to speak my mind," said Lady Binks, "I think, as Mrs Highmore says in the farce, her madness is but a poor excuse for her impertinence."

"Oh fie! my sweet Lady Binks," said Lady Penelope, "spare my poor favourite! You, surely, of all others, should forgive the excesses of an amiable eccentricity of temper.—Forgive me, my love, but I must defend an absent friend—My Lady Binks, I am very sure, is too generous and candid to

> Hate for arts which caused herself to rise."

"Not being conscious of any high elevation, my lady," answered Lady Binks, "I do not know any arts I have been under the necessity of practising to attain it. I suppose a Scots lady of ancient family may become the wife of an English baronet, and no very extraordinary great cause to wonder at it."

"No, surely—but people in this world will, you know, wonder at nothing," answered Lady Penelope.

"If you envy me my poor quiz Sir Bingo, I'll get you a better, Lady Pen."

"I don't doubt your talents, my dear, but when I want one, I will get one for myself.—But here comes the whole party of quizzes.—Joliffe, offer the gentlemen tea—then get the floor ready for the dancers, and set the card-tables in the next room."

Chapter Eight

AFTER DINNER

They draw the cork, they broach the barrel,
And first they kiss, and then they quarrel.
PRIOR

IF THE READER has attended much to the manners of the canine race, he may have remarked the very different manner in which the individuals of the different genders carry on their quarrels among each other. The females are testy, petulant, and very apt to indulge their impatient dislike of each other's presence, or the spirit of rivalry which it produces, in a sudden bark and snap, which last is generally made as much at advantage as possible. But these ebullitions of peevishness lead to no very serious or prosecuted conflict; the affair begins and ends in a moment. Not so the ire of the male dogs, which, once produced, and excited by growls of mutual offence and defiance, leads generally to a fierce and obstinate contest; in which if the parties be dogs of game, and well matched, they grapple, throttle, tear, roll each other in the kennel, and can only be separated by choking them with their own collars, till they lose wind and hold at the same time, or by surprising them out of their wrath by sousing them with cold water.

The simile, though a currish one, will hold good in its application to the human race. While the ladies in the tea-room of the Fox Hotel were engaged in the light snappish velitation or skirmish, which we have described, the gentlemen who remained in the parlour were more than once like to have quarrelled more seriously.

We have mentioned the weighty reasons which induced Mr Mowbray to look upon the stranger whom a general invitation had brought into their society, with unfavourable prepossessions; and these were far from being abated by the demeanour of Tyrrel, which, though perfectly well-bred, indicated a sense of equality, which the young Laird of Saint Ronan's considered as extremely presumptuous.

As for Sir Bingo, he already began to nourish the genuine hatred always entertained by a mean spirit against an antagonist, before whom it is conscious of having made a dishonourable retreat. He forgot not the manner, look, and tone, with which Tyrrel had checked his unauthorized intrusion; and though he had sunk beneath it at the moment, the recollection rankled in his heart as an affront to be avenged. As he drank his wine, courage, the want of which was, in his more sober moments, a check upon his bad temper, began to inflame his malignity, and he ventured upon several occasions to shew his spleen, by contradicting Tyrrel more flatly than good manners permitted upon so short an acquaintance, and without any provocation. Tyrrel saw his ill humour and despised it, as that of an overgrown school-boy, whom it was not worth his while to answer according to his folly.

One of the apparent causes of the Baronet's rudeness was indeed childish enough. The company were talking of shooting, the most animating topic of conversation among Scottish country gentlemen of the younger class, and Tyrrel had mentioned something of a favourite setter, an uncommonly handsome dog, from which he had been for some time separated, but which he expected would rejoin him in the course of next week.

"A setter!" retorted Sir Bingo, with a sneer; "a pointer I suppose you mean."

"No, sir," said Tyrrel; "I am perfectly aware of the difference betwixt a setter and a pointer, and I know the old-fashioned setter is become unfashionable among modern sportsmen. But I love my dog as a companion, as well as for his merits in the field; and a setter is more sagacious, more attached, and fitter for his place on the hearth-rug, than a pointer—not," he added, "from any deficiency of intellects on the pointer's part, but he is generally so abused while in the management of brutal breakers and grooms, that he loses all excepting his professional accomplishments, of finding and standing steady to game."

"And who the d—l desires he should have more?" said Sir Bingo.

"Many people, Sir Bingo," replied Tyrrel, "have been of opinion, that both dogs and men may follow sport indifferently well, though they do happen, at the same time, to be fit for mixing in friendly intercourse in society."

"That is for licking trenchers, and scratching copper, I suppose," said the Baronet *sotto voce;* and added, in a louder and more distinct tone,—"He never before heard that a setter was fit to follow any man's heels but a poacher's."

"You know it now then, Sir Bingo," answered Tyrrel; "and I hope you will not fall into so great a mistake again."

The Peace-maker here seemed to think his interference necessary, and, surmounting his taciturnity, made the following pithy speech:—"By Cot! and do you see, as you are looking for my opinion, I think there is no dispute in the matter—because, by Cot! it occurs to me, d'ye see, that you are both right, by Cot! It may do fery well for my excellent friend Sir Bingo, who hath stables, and kennels, and what not, to maintain the six filthy prutes that are yelping and yowling all the tay, and all the neight too, under my window, by Cot!—And if they are yelping and yowling there, may I never die but I wish they were yelping and yowling somewhere else. But then there is many a man who may be as cood a gentleman at the bottom as my worthy friend Sir Bingo, though it may be that he is poor—and if he is poor—and as if it might be my own case, or that of this honest gentleman, Mr Tirl, is that a reason or a law, that he is not to keep a prute of a tog, to help him to take his sports and his pleasures? and if he has not a stable or a kennel to put the crature into, must he not keep it in his pit of ped-room, or upon his parlour, seeing that Luckie Dods would make the kitchen too hot for the paist—and so, if Mr Tirl finds a setter more fitter for his purpose than a pointer, by Cot, I know no law against it, else may I never die the black death."

If this oration appear rather long for the occasion, the reader must recollect that Captain MacTurk had in all probability the trouble of translating it from the periphrastic language of Ossian, in which it was originally conceived in his own mind.

The Man of Law replied to the Man of Peace, "Ye are mistaken for ance in your life, Captain, for there is a law against setters; and I will undertake to prove them to be the 'lying dogs' which are mentioned in the auld Scots statute, and which all and sundry are discharged to keep, under a penalty of——"

Here the Captain broke in with a very solemn mien and dignified manner—"By Cot, Master Micklewhame, and I shall be asking what you mean by talking to me of peing mistaken, and about lying togs, sir —pecause I would have you to know, and to pelieve, and to very well consider, that I never was mistaken in my life, sir, unless it was when I took you for a gentleman."

"No offence, Captain," said Mr Micklewhame; "dinna break the wand of peace, man, you that should be the first to keep it.—He is as cankered," continued the Man of Law, apart to his patron, "as an auld Hieland terrier, that snaps at whatever comes near it—but I tell you ae thing, Saint Ronan's, and that is on soul and conscience, that I believe this is the very lad Tirl, that I raised a summons against before the justices—him and another hempie—in your father's time, for shooting on the Springwellhead muirs."

"The devil you did, Mick!" replied the Lord of the Manor, also aside;—"Well, I am obliged to you for giving me some reason for the ill thoughts I had of him—I knew he was some trumpery scamp.—I'll blow him, by——"

"Whisht—stop—hush—haud your tongue, Saint Ronan's—keep a calm sough—ye see, I intented the process, by your worthy father's desire, before the Quarter Sessions—but I ken na—The auld sheriff clerk stood the lad's friend—and some of the justices thought it was but a mistake of the marches, and sae we couldna get a judgment—and your father was very ill of the gout, and I was feared to vex him, and fain to let the process sleep, for fear they had been assoilzied.—Sae ye had better gang cautious to wark, Saint Ronan's, for though they were summoned, they were na convict."

"Could you not take up the action again?" said Mr Mowbray.

"Whew! it's been prescribed sax or seven years syne. It is a great shame, Saint Ronan's, that the game laws, whilk are the very best protection that is left to country gentlemen against the encroachment of their inferiors, rin sae short a course of prescription—a poacher may just jink ye back and forward like a flea in a blanket, (wi' pardon) —hap ye out of ae county and into anither at their pleasure, like pyots —and unless ye get your thumb-nail on them in the very nick o' time, ye may dine on a dish of prescription, and sup upon an absolvitor."

"It is a shame, indeed," said Mowbray, turning from his confidant and agent, and addressing himself to the company in general, yet not without a peculiar look directed to Tyrrel.

"What is a shame, sir?" said Tyrrel, conceiving that the observation was particularly addressed to him.

"That we should have so many poachers upon our muirs, sir," answered Saint Ronan's. "I sometimes regret having countenanced the Well here, when I think how many guns it has brought on my property every season."

"Hout, fie! hout away, Saint Ronan's!" said his Man of Law; "no countenance the Waal? What would the country-side be without it, I would be glad to ken? It's the greatest improvement that has been made in this country since the year forty-five. Na, na, it's no the Waal that's to blame for the poaching and delinquencies on the game.—We maun to the Aul' Town for the howf of that kind of cattle. Our rules at the Waal are clear, and express again trespassers."

"I can't think," said the Squire, "what made my father sell the property of the old change-house yonder, to the hag that keeps it open out of spite, I think, and to harbour poachers and vagabonds—I can't conceive what made him do so foolish a thing!"

"Probably because your father wanted money, sir," said Tyrrel drily; "and my worthy landlady, Mrs Dods, had got some.—You know, I presume, sir, that I lodge there."

"Oh, sir," replied Mowbray, in a tone betwixt scorn and civility, "you cannot suppose the present company is alluded to; I only presumed to mention a fact, that we have been annoyed with unqualified people shooting on our grounds, without either liberty or licence.—

And I hope to have her sign taken down for it—that is all—There was the same plague in my father's days I think, Mick?"

But Mr Micklewhame, who did not like Tyrrel's looks so well as to induce him to become approver on the occasion, replied with an inarticulate grunt, addressed to the company, and a private admonition to his patron's own ear, "to let sleeping dogs lie."

"I can scarce forbear the fellow," said Saint Ronan's; "and yet I cannot well tell where my dislike to him lies—but it would be d——d folly to turn out with him for nothing; and so, honest Mick, I will be as quiet as I can."

"And that you may be so," said Micklewhame, "I think you had best take no more wine."

"I think so too," said the Squire; "for each glass I drink in his company gives me the heart-burn—yet the man is not different from other raffs either—but there is something about him intolerable to me."

So saying, he pushed back his chair from the table, and—*regis ad exemplar*—after the pattern of the Laird, all the company arose.

Sir Bingo got up with reluctance, which he testified by two or three deep growls, as he followed the rest of the company into the outer apartment, which served as an entrance-hall, and divided the dining-parlour from the tea-room, as it was called. Here, while the party were assuming their hats, for the purpose of joining the ladies' society, (which old-fashioned folks used only to take up for that of going into the open air,) Tyrrel asked a smart footman, who stood betwixt him and that part of his property, to hand him the hat which lay on the table beyond.

"Call your own servant, sir," answered the fellow, with the true insolence of a pampered menial.

"Your master," answered Tyrrel, "ought to have taught you good manners, my friend, before bringing you here."

"Sir Bingo Binks is my master," said the fellow, in the same insolent tone as formerly.

"Now for it, Bingie," said Mowbray, who was aware that the Baronet's pot-courage had arrived at fighting-pitch.

"Yes!" said Sir Bingo aloud, and more articulately than usual—"The fellow is my servant—what has any one to say to it?"

"I at least have my mouth stopped," answered Tyrrel, with perfect composure. "I should have been surprised to have found Sir Bingo's servant better bred than himself."

"What d'ye mean by that, sir?" said Sir Bingo, coming up in an offensive attitude, for he was no mean pupil of the Fives-Court—"What d'ye mean by that? D—n you, sir! I'll serve you out before you can say dumpling."

"And I, Sir Bingo, unless you presently lay aside that look and manner, will knock you down before you can cry help."

The visitor held in his hand a slip of oak, with which he gave a flourish, that, however slight, intimated some acquaintance with the noble art of single-stick. From this demonstration Sir Bingo thought it prudent somewhat to recoil, though backed by a party of friends, who, in their zeal for his honour, would rather have seen his bones broken in conflict bold, than his honour injured by a discreditable retreat; and Tyrrel seemed to have some inclination to indulge them. But, at the very instant when his hand was raised with a motion of no doubtful import, a whispering voice, close to his ear, pronounced the emphatic words—"Are you a man?"

Not the thrilling tone with which our inimitable Siddons used to electrify the scene, when she uttered the same whisper, ever had a more powerful effect upon an auditor, than had these unexpected sounds on him, to whom they were now addressed. Tyrrel forgot every thing—his quarrel—the circumstances in which he was placed—the company. The crowd was to him at once annihilated, and life seemed to have no other object than to follow the person who had spoken. But suddenly as he turned, the disappearance of the monitor was at least equally so, for, amid the group of common-place countenances with which he was surrounded, there was none which assorted to the tone and words, which possessed such a power over him. "Make way," he said, to those who surrounded him; and it was in the tone of one who was prepared, if necessary, to make way for himself.

Mr Mowbray, of Saint Ronan's, stepped forward. "Come, sir," said he, "this will not do—you have come here, a stranger amongst us, to assume airs and dignities, which, by G—d, would become a duke or a prince! We must know who or what you are, before we permit you to carry your high tone any farther."

This address seemed at once to arrest Tyrrel's anger, and his impatience to leave the company. He turned to Mowbray, collected his thoughts for an instant, and then answered him thus:—"Mr Mowbray, I seek no quarrel with any one here—with you, in particular, I am most unwilling to have any disagreement. I came here by invitation, not certainly expecting much pleasure, but, at the same time, supposing myself secure from incivility. In the last point, I find myself mistaken, and therefore wish the company good night. I must also make my adieu to the ladies."

So saying, he walked several steps, yet, as it seemed, rather irresolutely, towards the door of the card-room—and then, to the increased surprise of the company, stopped suddenly, and muttering something about the "unfitness of the time," turned on his heel, and bowing haughtily, as there was way made for him, walked in the opposite direction towards the door which led to the outer hall.

"D—n me, Sir Bingo, will you let him off?" said Mowbray, who seemed to delight in pushing his friend into new scrapes—"To him, man—to him—he shews the white feather."

Sir Bingo, thus encouraged, planted himself with a look of defiance, exactly between Tyrrel and the door; upon which the retreating guest, bestowing on him most emphatically the epithet Fool, seized him by the collar, and flung him out of his way with some violence.

"I am to be found at the Old Town of Saint Ronan's by whomsoever has any concern with me."—Without waiting the issue of this aggression farther than to utter these words, Tyrrel left the hotel. He stopped in the court-yard, however, with the air of one uncertain whither he intended to go, and who was desirous to ask some question, which seemed to die upon his tongue. At length his eye fell upon a groom, who stood not far from the door of the inn, holding in his hand a handsome pony, with a side-saddle.

"Whose——" said Tyrrel—but the rest of the question he seemed unable to utter.

The man, however, replied, as if he had heard the whole interrogation.—"Miss Mowbray's, sir, of Saint Ronan's—she leaves directly—and so I am walking the pony—a clever thing, sir, for a lady."

"She returns to Shaws-Castle by the Bucklane road?"

"I suppose so, sir," said the groom. "It is the nighest, and Miss Clara cares little for rough road. Zounds! She can spank it over wet and dry."

Tyrrel turned away from the man, and hastily left the hotel—not, however, by the road which led to the Aulton, but by a foot-path among the natural copse-woods, which, following the course of the brook, intersected the usual horse-road to Shaws-Castle, the seat of Mr Mowbray, at a romantic spot called the Buckstane.

In a small peninsula, formed by a winding of the brook, was situated, on a rising hillock, a large rough-hewn pillar of stone, said by tradition to commemorate the fall of a stag of unusual speed, size, and strength, whose flight, after having lasted through a whole summer's day, had there terminated in death, to the honour and glory of some ancient Baron of Saint Ronan's, and of his staunch hounds. During the periodical cuttings of the copse, which the necessities of the family of Saint Ronan's brought round more frequently than Pontey would have recommended, some oaks had been spared in the neighbourhood of this massive obelisk, old enough perhaps to have heard the whoop and halloo, which followed the fall of the stag, and to have witnessed the raising of the rude monument, by which that great event was commemorated. These trees, with their broad spreading boughs, made a twilight even of noon-day; and, now that the sun was approaching its setting point, their shade already anticipated night. This was especially the case where three or four of them stretched their arms over a deep gully, through which winded the horse-path to Shaws-Castle, at a point about a pistol-shot distant from the Buckstane. As the principal access to Mr Mowbray's mansion was by a carriage-way, which passed in a different direction, the present path was left almost in a state of nature, full of large stones, and broken by gullies, delightful, from the varied character of its banks, to the picturesque traveller, and most inconvenient, nay dangerous, to him who had a stumbling horse.

The foot-path to the Buckstane, which here joined the bridle-road, had been constructed, at the expence of a subscription, under the direction of Mr Winterblossom, who had taste enough to see the beauties of this secluded spot, which was exactly such as in earlier times might have harboured the ambush of some marauding chief. This recollection had not escaped Tyrrel, to whom the whole scenery was familiar, and who now hastened to the spot, as one which peculiarly suited his present purpose. He sat down behind one of the large projecting trees, and, screened by its enormous branches from observation, was enabled to watch the road from the Hotel for a considerable part of its extent, whilst he was himself invisible to any who might travel upon it.

Meanwhile his sudden departure excited a considerable sensation among the party whom he had just left, and who were induced to form conclusions not very favourable to his character. Sir Bingo, in particular, blustered loudly and more loudly, in proportion to the increasing distance betwixt himself and his antagonist, declaring his resolution to be revenged on the scoundrel for his insolence—to drive him from the neighbourhood,—and I know not what other menaces of formidable import. The devil, in the old stories of *diablerie*, was always sure to start up at the elbow of any one who nursed diabolical purposes, and only wanted a little backing from the foul fiend to carry his imaginations into action. The noble Captain MacTurk had so far this property of his infernal majesty, that the least hint of an approaching quarrel drew him always to the vicinity of the party concerned. He was now at Sir Bingo's side, and was taking his own view of the matter, in his character of peace-maker.

"By Cot! and it's very exceedingly true, my goot friend, Sir Binco—and as you say, it concerns your honour, and the honour of the place, and credit and character of the whole company, by Cot! that this matter be properly looked after; for, as I think, he laid hands on your body, my excellent goot friend."

"Hands, Captain MacTurk!" exclaimed Sir Bingo, in some confusion; "no, blast him—not so bad as that neither—if he had, I should have handed *him* over the window—but, by——, the fellow had the impudence to offer to collar me—I had just stepped back to square at him, when, curse me, the blackguard ran away."

"Right, vara right, Sir Bingo," said the Man at Law, "a vara perfect blackguard, a poaching sorning sort of fallow, that I will have scoured out of the country before he be three days aulder. Fash you your beard nae further about the matter, Sir Bingo."

"By Cot, but I can tell you, Mr Meiklewhame," said the Man of Peace, with great solemnity of visage, "that you are scalding your lips in other folks' kale, and that it is necessary for the credit, and honour, and respect of this company, at the Well of Saint Ronan's, that Sir Bingo goes by more competent advice than yours upon the present occasion, Mr Meiklewhame; for though your counsel may do very well in a small-debt court, here, do you see, Mr Meiklewhame, is a question of honour, which is not a thing in your line, as I take it."

"No, by George! is it not," answered Micklewhame; "e'en take it all to yoursell, Captain, and muckle ye are likely to make on't."

"Then," said the Captain, "Sir Binco, I will peg the favour of your company to the smoking room, where we may have a segar and a glass of gin-twist; and we will consider how the honour of the company must be supported and upholden upon the present conjuncture."

The Baronet complied with this invitation, as much, perhaps, in consequence of the medium through which the Captain intended to convey his warlike counsels, as for the pleasure with which he anticipated the result of these counsels themselves. He followed the military step of his leader, whose stride was more stiff, and his form more perpendicular, when exalted by the consciousness of an approaching quarrel, to the smoking-room, where, sighing as he lighted his segar, Sir Bingo prepared to listen to the words of wisdom and valour, as they should flow in mingled stream from the lips of Captain MacTurk.

Meanwhile the rest of the company joined the ladies. "Here has been Clara," said Lady Penelope to Mr Mowbray; "here has been Miss Mowbray amongst us, like the ray of a sun which does but dazzle and die."

"Ah, poor Clara," said Mowbray; "I thought I saw her thread her way through the crowd a little while since, but I was not sure."

"Well," said Lady Penelope, "she has asked us all up to Shaws-Castle on Thursday, to a *déjeuner à la fourchette*—I trust you confirm your sister's invitation, Mr Mowbray?"

"Certainly, Lady Penelope," replied Mowbray; "and I am truly glad Clara has had the grace to think of it—How we shall acquit ourselves is a different question, for neither she nor I are much accustomed to play host or hostess."

"Oh! it will be delightful, I am sure," said Lady Penelope; "Clara has a grace in every thing she does; and you, Mr Mowbray, can be a perfectly well-bred gentleman—when you please."

"That qualification is severe—well—good manners be my speed —I will certainly please to do my best, when I see your ladyship at Shaws-Castle, which has seen no company this many a day.—Clara and I have lived a wild life of it, each in their own way."

"Indeed, Mr Mowbray," said Lady Binks, "if I might presume to speak—I think you do suffer your sister to ride about a little too much without an attendant. I know Miss Mowbray rides as woman never rode before, but still an accident may happen."

"An accident?" replied Mowbray—"Ah, Lady Binks, accidents happen as frequently when ladies *have* attendants as when they want them."

Lady Binks, who, in her maiden state, had cantered a good deal about these woods under Sir Bingo's escort, coloured, looked spiteful, and was silent.

"Besides," said John Mowbray, more lightly, "where is the risk after all? There are no wolves in our woods to eat up our pretty Red-Riding Hoods; and no lions either—except those of Lady Penelope's train."

"Who draw the car of Cybele," said Mr Chatterley.

Lady Penelope luckily did not understand the allusion, which was indeed better intended than imagined.

"Apropos!" she said; "what have you done with the great lion of the day? I see Mr Tyrrel nowhere—Is he finishing an additional bottle with Sir Bingo?"

"Mr Tyrrel, madam," said Mowbray, "has acted successively the lion rampant, and the lion passant; he has been quarrelsome, and he has run away—fled from the ire of your doughty knight, Lady Binks."

"I am sure I hope not," said Lady Binks; "my Chevalier's unsuccessful campaigns have been unable to overcome his taste for quarrels —a victory would make a fighting-man of him for life."

"That might bring its own consolations," said Winterblossom, apart to Mowbray; "quarrellers do not usually live long."

"No, no," replied Mowbray, "the lady's despair which broke out just now, even in her own despite, is quite natural—absolutely legitimate. Sir Bingo will give her no chance that way."

Mowbray then made his bow to Lady Penelope, and in answer to her request that he would join the ball or card-table, observed, that he had no time to lose; that the heads of the old domestics at Shaws-Castle would be by this time absolutely turned, by the apprehensions of what Thursday was to bring forth; and that as Clara would certainly give no directions for the necessary arrangements, it was necessary that he should take that trouble himself.

"If you ride smartly," said Lady Penelope, "you may save even a temporary alarm, by overtaking Clara, dear creature, ere she gets home—She sometimes suffers her pony to go at will along the lane, as slow as Betty Foy's."

"Ah, but then," said little Miss Digges, "Miss Mowbray sometimes gallops as if the lark was a snail to her pony—and it quite frights one to see her."

The Doctor touched Mrs Blower, who had approached so as to be on the verge of the genteel circle, though she did not venture within it, —they exchanged sagacious looks, and a most pitiful shake of the head. Mowbray's eye happened at that moment to glance on them; and doubtless, notwithstanding their hasting to compose their countenances to a different expression, he comprehended what was passing through their minds;—and perhaps it awoke a corresponding note in his own. He took his hat, and with a cast of thought upon his countenance which it seldom wore, left the apartment. A moment afterwards his horse's feet were heard spurning the pavement, as he started off at a sharp pace.

"There is something singular about these Mowbrays to-night," said Lady Penelope.—"Clara, poor dear angel, is always particular; but I should have thought Mowbray had too much worldly wisdom to be fanciful.—What are you consulting your *Souvenir* for with such attention, my dear Lady Binks?"

"Only for the age of the moon," said her ladyship, putting the little tortoise-shell bound calendar into her reticule; and having done so, she proceeded to assist Lady Penelope in the arrangements for the evening.

Chapter Nine

THE MEETING

> We meet as shadows in the land of dreams,
> Which speak not but in signs —
>
> ANONYMOUS

BEHIND one of the old oaks which we have described in the preceding chapter, shrouding himself from observation like a hunter watching for his game, or an Indian for his enemy, but with different, very different purpose, Tyrrel lay on his breast near the Buckstane, his eye on the horse-road which winded down the valley, and his ear alertly awake to every sound which mingled with the passing breeze, or the ripple of the brook.

"To have met her in yonder congregated assembly of brutes and fools"—such was a part of his internal reflections,—"had been little less than an act of madness—madness almost equal in its degree to that cowardice which has hitherto prevented my approaching her, when our eventful meeting might have taken place unobserved.—But now—now—my resolution is as fixed as the place is itself favourable. I will not wait till some chance again shall throw us together, with an hundred malignant eyes to watch, and wonder, and stare, and try in vain to account for the expression of feelings which I might find it impossible to suppress.—Hark—hark!—I hear the tread of a horse—No—it was the changeful sound of the water rushing over the pebbles. Surely she cannot have taken the other road to Shaws-Castle!—-No —the sounds become distinct—her figure is visible on the path, coming swiftly forwards.—Have I the courage to shew myself?—I have—the hour is come, and what must be shall be."

Yet this resolution was scarce formed ere it began to fluctuate, when he reflected upon the fittest manner of carrying it into execution. To shew himself at a distance, might give the lady an opportunity of turning back and avoiding the interview which he had determined upon—to hide himself till the moment when her horse, in rapid motion, should pass his lurking-place, might be attended with danger to the rider—and while he hesitated which course to pursue, there was some chance of his missing the opportunity of presenting himself to Miss Mowbray at all. He himself was sensible of this, formed a hasty and desperate resolution not to suffer the present moment to escape, and, just as the ascent induced the pony to slacken its pace, Tyrrel stood in the middle of the defile, about six yards distant from the young lady.

She pulled up the reins, and stopped as if arrested by a thunderbolt. —"Clara!"—"Tyrrel!" These were the only words which were exchanged between them, until Tyrrel, moving his feet as slowly as if they had been of lead, began gradually to diminish the distance which lay between them. It was then that, observing his closer approach, Miss Mowbray called out with great eagerness,—"No nearer—no nearer!—So long have I stood your presence—but if you approach me more closely, I shall be mad indeed."

"What do you fear?" said Tyrrel, in a hollow voice—"What can you fear?" and he continued to draw nearer, until they were within a pace of each other.

Clara, meanwhile, dropping her bridle, clasped her hands together, and held them up towards Heaven, muttering, in a voice scarce audible, "Great God!—if this apparition be formed by my heated fancy, let it pass away; if it be real—enable me to endure its presence! —Tell me, I conjure you—are you Francis Tyrrel in blood and body, or is this but one of those wandering visions, that have crossed my path and glared on me, but without daring to abide my steadfast glance?"

"I am Francis Tyrrel," answered he, "in blood and body, as much as she to whom I speak is Clara Mowbray."

"Then God have mercy on us both!" said Clara, in a tone of deep feeling.

"Amen!" said Tyrrel. "But what avails this excess of agitation?—You saw me but now, Miss Mowbray—your voice still rings in my ears—You saw me but now—you spoke to me—and that when I was among strangers—Why not preserve your composure, when we are where no human eye can see—no human ear can hear?"

"Is it so?" said Clara; "and was it indeed yourself whom I saw even now?—I thought so, and something I said at the time—but my brain has been but ill-settled since we last met—But I am well now—quite well—I have invited all the people yonder to come up to Shaws-Castle—my brother desired me to do it—I hope I shall have the pleasure of seeing Mr Tyrrel there—though I think there is some old grudge between my brother and you."

"Alas! Clara, you mistake. Your brother I have scarce seen," replied Tyrrel, much distressed, and apparently uncertain in what tone to address her, which might soothe, and not irritate her mental malady, of which he could now entertain no doubt.

"True—true," she said, after a moment's reflection, "my brother was then at college. It was my father, my poor father, whom you had some quarrel with.—But you will come to Shaws-Castle on Thursday, at two o'clock?—John will be glad to see you—he can be kind when he pleases—And then we will talk of old times—I must get on to have things ready—Good evening."

She would have passed him, but he took gently hold of the rein of her bridle.—"I will walk with you, Clara," he said; "the road is rough and dangerous—you ought not to ride fast.—I will walk along with you, and we will talk of former times now, more conveniently than in company."

"True—true—very true, Mr Tyrrel—it shall be as you say. My brother obliges me to go into company sometimes at that hateful place down yonder; and I do so because he likes it, and because the folks let me have my own way, and come and go as I list. Do you know, Tyrrel, that very often when I am there, and John has his eye on me, I can carry it on as gaily as if you and I had never met?"

"I would to God we never had," said Tyrrel, in a trembling voice, "since this is to be the end of all!"

"And wherefore should not sorrow be the end of sin and of folly? And when did happiness come of disobedience?—And when did sound sleep visit a bloody pillow? That is what I say to myself, Tyrrel, and that is what you must learn to say too, and then you will bear your burthen as cheerfully as I endure mine—if we have no more than our deserts, why should we complain?—You are shedding tears, I think—is not that childish?—they say it is a relief—if so, weep on, and I will look another way."

Tyrrel walked on by the pony's side, in vain endeavouring to compose himself so as to reply.

"Poor Tyrrel," said Clara, after she had remained silent for some time—"Poor Frank Tyrrel!—Perhaps you will say in your turn, Poor Clara—but I am not so poor in spirit as you—the blast may bend, but it shall never break me."

There was another long pause, for Tyrrel was unable to determine with himself in what strain he could address the unfortunate young lady, without awakening recollections equally painful to her feelings, and dangerous, when her precarious state of health was considered. At length she herself proceeded:—

"What needs all this, Tyrrel?—and indeed, why came you here?—Why did I find you but now brawling and quarrelling among the loudest of the brawlers and quarrellers of yonder idle and dissipated debauchees?—You were used to have more temper—more sense. Another person—ay, another that you and I once knew—he might have committed such a folly, and he would have acted perhaps in character—But you, who pretend to wisdom—for shame, for shame! —And indeed, when we talk of that, what wisdom was there in coming hither at all?—or what good purpose can your remaining here serve? —Surely you need not come, either to renew your own unhappiness or to augment mine."

"To augment yours—God forbid!" answered Tyrrel. "No—I came hither only because, after so many years of wandering, I longed to revisit the spot where all my hopes lay buried."

"Ay—buried is the word," she replied, "crushed down and buried when they budded fairest. I often think of it, Tyrrel; and there are times when, Heaven help me! I can think of little else.—Look at me—you remember what I was—see what grief and solitude have made me."

She flung back the veil which surrounded her riding-hat, and which had hitherto hid her face. It was the same countenance which he had formerly known in all the bloom of early beauty; but though the beauty remained, the bloom was fled forever—Not the agitation of exercise—not that which arose from the pain and confusion of this unexpected interview, had called to poor Clara's cheek even the momentary semblance of colour. Her complexion was marble-white, like that of the finest piece of statuary.

"Is it possible?" said Tyrrel; "can grief have made such ravages?"

"Grief," replied Clara, "is the sickness of the mind, and its sister is the sickness of the body—they are twin-sisters, Tyrrel, and are seldom long separate. Sometimes the body's disease comes first, and dims our eyes and palsies our hands, before the fire of our mind and of our intellect is quenched.—But mark me—soon after comes her cruel sister with her urn, and sprinkles cold dew on our hopes and our loves, our memory, our recollections, and our feelings, and shews us that they cannot survive the decay of our bodily powers."

"Alas!" said Tyrrel, "is it come to this?"

"To this," she replied, speaking from the rapid and irregular train of her own ideas, rather than comprehending the purport of his sorrowful exclamation,—"to this it must ever come, while immortal souls are wedded to the perishable substance of which our bodies are composed. There is another state, Tyrrel, in which it will be otherwise—God grant our time of enjoying it were come!"

She fell into a melancholy pause which Tyrrel was afraid to disturb. The quickness with which she spoke, marked but too plainly the irregular succession of thought, and he was obliged to restrain the agony of his own feelings, rendered more acute by a thousand painful recollections, lest, by giving way to his expressions of grief, he should throw her into a still more disturbed state of mind.

"I did not think," she proceeded, "that after so horrible a separation, and so many years, I could have met you thus calmly and reasonably. But although what we were formerly to each other can never be forgotten, it is now all over, and we are now only friends—Is it not so?"

Tyrrel was unable to reply.

"But I must not remain here," she said, "till the evening grows darker on me.—We shall meet again, Tyrrel—meet as friends—nothing more—You will come up to Shaws-Castle and see me?—no need of secrecy now—my poor father is in his grave, and his prejudices sleep with him—my brother John is kind, though he is stern and severe sometimes—Indeed, Tyrrel, I believe he loves me, though he has taught me to tremble at his frown when I am in spirits, and talk too much—But he loves me, at least I think so, for I am sure I love him; and I try to go down amongst them yonder, and to endure their folly, and, all things considered, I do carry on the farce of life wonderfully well—We are but actors, you know, and the world but a stage."

"And ours has been a sad and a tragic scene," said Tyrrel, unable in the bitterness of his heart any longer to refrain from speech.

"It has indeed—but, Tyrrel, when was it otherwise with engagements formed in youth and in folly? You and I would, you know, become men and women, while we were yet scarcely more than children—We have run, while yet in our nonage, through the passions and adventures of youth, and therefore we are now old before our day, and the winter of our life has come on ere its summer was well begun.—O Tyrrel! often and often have I thought of this—thought of it often?—Alas! when will the time come that I shall be able to think of anything else!"

She sobbed bitterly, and her tears began to flow with a freedom which they had not probably enjoyed for a length of time. Tyrrel walked on by the side of her horse, which now prosecuted its road homewards, unable to devise a proper mode of addressing the unfortunate young lady, and fearing alike to awaken her passions and his own. Whatever he might have proposed to say, was disconcerted by the plain indications that her mind was clouded, more or less slightly, with a shade of insanity, which deranged, though it could not destroy, her powers of judgment.

At length he asked her, with as much calmness as he could assume —if she were contented—if aught could be done to render her situation more easy—if there was aught of which she could complain which he might be able to remedy? She answered gently, that she was calm and resigned, when her brother would permit her to stay at home; but that when she was brought into society, she experienced such a change as that which the water of the brook that slumbered in a crystalline pool of the rock might be supposed to feel, when gliding from its quiet bed, it becomes involved in the hurry of the cataract.

"But my brother Mowbray," she said, "thinks he is right,—and perhaps he is so. There are things on which we may ponder too long; —and were he mistaken, why should I not constrain myself in order to please him?—there are so few left to whom I can now give either pleasure or pain—I am a gay girl, too, in conversation, Tyrrel—still as gay for a moment, as when you used to chide me for my folly. So, now I have told you all,—I have one question to ask on my part—one question—if I had but breath to ask it—Is *he* still alive?"

"He lives," answered Tyrrel, but in a tone so low, that nought but the eager attention which Miss Mowbray paid could possibly have caught such feeble sounds.

"Lives!" she exclaimed,—"lives!—he lives, and the blood on your hand is not then indelibly imprinted—O Tyrrel, did you but know the joy which this assurance gives to me!"

"Joy!" replied Tyrrel—"joy that the wretch lives who has poisoned our happiness for ever—lives, perhaps, to claim you for his own?"

"Never, never shall he—dare he do so," replied Clara, wildly, "while water can drown, cords strangle, steel pierce—while there is a precipice on the hill, a pool in the river—never—never!"

"Be not thus agitated, my dearest Clara," said Tyrrel; "I spoke I know not what—he lives indeed—but far distant, and, I trust, never again to re-visit Scotland."

He would have said more, but that, agitated with fear or passion, she struck her horse impatiently with her riding-whip. The spirited pony, thus stimulated and at the same time restrained, became intractable, and reared so much, that Tyrrel, fearful of the consequences, and trusting to Clara's skill as a horsewoman, thought he best consulted her safety in letting go the reins. The animal instantly sprung forwards on the broken and hilly path at a very rapid pace, and was soon lost to Tyrrel's anxious eyes.

As he stood pondering whether he ought not to follow Miss Mowbray towards Shaws-Castle, in order to be satisfied that no accident had befallen her on the road, he heard the tread of a horse's feet advancing hastily in the same direction, leading from the Hotel. Unwilling to be observed at this moment, he stepped aside under shelter of the underwood, and presently afterwards saw Mr Mowbray of Saint Ronan's, followed by a groom, ride hastily past his lurking-place, and pursue the same road which had been just taken by his sister. Their presence seemed to assure Miss Mowbray's safety, and so removed Tyrrel's chief reason for following her. Involved in deep and melancholy reflection upon what had passed, nearly satisfied that his longer residence in Clara's vicinity could only add to her unhappiness and his own, yet unable to tear himself from that neighbourhood, or to relinquish feelings which had become entwined with his heart-strings, he returned to his lodgings in the Aulton, in a state of mind very little to be envied.

Tyrrel, on entering his apartment, found that it was not lighted, nor were the Abigails of Mrs Dods quite so alert as a waiter at Long's might have been, to supply him with candles. Unapt at any time to exact much personal attendance, and desirous to shun at that moment the necessity of speaking to any person whatsoever, even on the most trifling subject, he walked down into the kitchen to supply himself with what he wanted. He did not at first observe that Mrs Dods herself was present in this the very centre of her empire, far less that a lofty air of indignation was seated on that worthy matron's brow. At first it only vented itself in broken soliloquy and interjections; as, for example,

"Vera bonnie wark this!—vera bonnie wark, indeed!—a decent house to be disturbed at these hours—Keep a public—as weel keep a bedlam!"

Finding these murmurs attracted no attention, the dame placed herself betwixt her guest and the door, to which he was now retiring with his lighted candle, and demanded of him what was the meaning of such behaviour.

"Of what behaviour, madam?" said her guest, repeating her question in a tone of sternness and impatience so unusual with him, that perhaps she was sorry at the moment that she had provoked him out of his usual patient indifference; nay, she might even feel intimidated at the altercation she had provoked, for the resentment of a quiet and patient person has always in it something formidable to the professed and habitual grumbler. But her pride was too great to think of a retreat, after having sounded the signal for contest, and so she continued, though in a tone somewhat lowered.

"Maister Tirl, I wad but just ask you, that are a man of sense, whether I hae ony right to take your behaviour weel? Here have you been these ten days and mair, eating the best and drinking the best, and taking up the best room in my house; and now to think of your gaun down and taking up with yon idle hare-brained cattle at the Waal—I maun e'en be plain wi' ye—I like nane of the fair-fashioned folk that can say My Jo, and think it no; and therefore——"

"Mrs Dods," said Tyrrel, interrupting her, "I have no time at present for trifles—I am obliged to you for your attention while I have been in your house; but the disposal of my time, here or elsewhere, must be according to my own ideas of pleasure or business—If you are tired of me as a guest, send in your bill to-morrow."

"My bill?" said Mrs Dods; "my bill to-morrow? And what for no wait till Saturday, when it may be cleared atween us, plack and bawbee, as it was on Saturday last?"

"Well—we will talk of it to-morrow, Mrs Dods—Good night." And he withdrew accordingly.

Luckie Dods stood ruminating for a moment. "The deil's in him," she said, "for he winna bide being thrawn. And I think the deil's in me too for thrawing him, sic a canny lad, and sae gude a customer.—Odd, I am judging he has something on his mind—want of siller it canna be—I am sure if I thought that, I wadna care about my small thing.—But want o' siller it canna be—he pays ower the shillings as if they were sclate stanes, and that's no the way that folks part wi' their siller when there is but little o't—I ken weel eneugh how a customer looks that's near the grund of the purse.—Weel! I hope he winna mind onything of this nonsense splore the morn, and I'll try to guide my tongue something better—Hegh, sirs! but, as the minister says, it's an unruly member—troth, I am whiles ashamed o't mysel."

Chapter Ten

RESOURCES

Come, let me have thy counsel, for I need it;
Thou art of those, who better help their friends
With sage advice, than usurers with gold,
Or brawlers with their swords—I'll trust to thee,
For I ask only from thee words, not deeds.
The Devil hath met his Match

THE DAY of which we last gave the events chanced to be Monday, and two days therefore intervened betwixt it and that for which the entertainment was fixed, which was to assemble the flower of the company now at Saint Ronan's Well in the halls of the Lord of the Manor. The interval was but brief for the preparations necessary on an occasion so unusual; since the house, though delightfully situated, was in very indifferent repair, and for years had never received any visitors, except when by chance some blithe bachelor or fox-hunter shared the hospitality of Mr Mowbray; an event which became daily more and more uncommon; for, as he himself almost lived at the Well, he contrived his companions should be entertained where it could be done without expense to himself. Besides, the health of his sister afforded an irresistible apology to any of those old-fashioned Scottish gentlemen, who might be too apt, (in the rudeness of more primitive days,) to consider a friend's house as their own. Mr Mowbray was now, however, to the great delight of all his companions, nailed down, by invitation given and accepted, and they looked forward to the accomplishment of his promise, with the eagerness that the promise of some entertaining novelty never fails to produce amongst idlers.

A good deal of trouble accordingly devolved on Mr Mowbray, and his trusty agent Mr Micklewhame, before something like decent preparation could be made for the ensuing entertainment; and they were left to their unassisted endeavours by Clara, who, during both the Tuesday and Wednesday, obstinately kept herself secluded; nor could her brother, either by threats or flattery, extort from her any light concerning her purpose on the approaching and important Thursday. To do John Mowbray justice, he loved his sister as much as he was capable of loving anything but himself; and when, after several arguments, he had the mortification to find that she was not to be prevailed on to afford her assistance, he, without complaint, quietly set himself to do the best he could by his own unassisted judgment to put things in some order to receive his guests.

This was not so easy a task as might be supposed; for Mowbray was ambitious of that character of ton and elegance, which masculine faculties alone are seldom capable of attaining on such momentous occasions. The solid materials of a collation were indeed to be obtained for money from the next market town, and were purchased accordingly; but he felt it was likely to present the vulgar plenty of a farmer's feast, instead of the elegant entertainment, which might be announced in a corner of the county paper, as given by John Mowbray, Esq. of Saint Ronan's, to the gay and fashionable company assembled at that celebrated spring. There was like to be all sorts of error and irregularity in dishing, and in sending up; for Shaws-Castle boasted neither an accomplished house-keeper, nor a kitchen-maid with a hundred pair of hands to execute her mandates. Everything domestic was on the minutest system of economy consistent with ordinary decency, excepting in the stables, which were excellent and well kept. But can a groom of the stable perform the labours of a groom of the chambers? or can the game-keeper arrange in tempting order the carcases of the birds he has shot, strew them with flowers, and garnish them with piquant sauces? It would be as reasonable to expect a gallant soldier to act as undertaker, and conduct the funeral of the enemy he has slain.

In a word, Mowbray talked, and consulted, and advised, and squabbled, with the deaf cook, and a little old man whom he called the butler, until he at length perceived so little chance of bringing order out of confusion, or making the least advantageous impression on such obdurate understandings as he had to deal with, that he fairly committed the whole matter of the collation, with two or three hearty curses, to the charge of the officials principally concerned, and proceeded to take the state of the furniture and apartments under his consideration.

Here he found himself almost equally helpless; for what male wit is adequate to the thousand little coquetries practised in such arrangements? how can mere masculine eyes judge of the degree of *demi-jour* which is to be admitted into a decorated apartment, or discriminate where the broad light should be suffered to fall on a tolerable picture, where it should be excluded, lest the stiff daub of a periwigged grandsire should become too ridiculously prominent? And if men are unfit for weaving such a fairy web of light and darkness as may best suit furniture, ornaments, and complexions, how shall they be adequate to the yet more mysterious office of arranging, while they disarrange, the various movables in the apartment? so that while all has the air of negligence and chance, the seats are placed as if they had been transported by a wish to the spot most suitable for accommodation; stiffness and confusion are at once avoided, the company are neither limited to a formal circle of chairs, nor exposed to break their noses over wandering stools; but the arrangements seem to correspond to what ought to be the tone of the conversation, easy, without being confused, and regulated, without being constrained or stiffened.

Then how can a clumsy male wit attempt the arrangement of all the *chiffonerie* by which old snuff-boxes, heads of canes, pomander boxes, lamer beads, and all the trash usually found in the pigeon-holes of the bureaus of old-fashioned ladies, may be now brought into play, by throwing them, carelessly grouped with other unconsidered trifles, such as are to be seen in the windows of a pawnbroker's shop, upon a marble *encoignure*, or a mosaic work table, thereby turning to advantage the trash and trinketry, which all the old maids or magpies, who have inhabited the mansion for a century, have contrived to accumulate. With what admiration of the ingenuity of the fair artist have I sometimes pried into these miscellaneous groupes of *pseudo-bijouterie*, and seen the great grandsire's thumb-ring couchant with the coral and bells of the first-born—and the boatswain's whistle of some old naval uncle, or his silver tobacco-box, redolent of Oronoko, happily grouped with the mother's ivory comb-case, still odorous of musk, and with some virgin aunt's tortoise-shell spectacle-case, and the eagle's talon of ebony, with which, in the days of long and stiff stays, our grandmothers were wont to alleviate any little irritation in their back or shoulders. Then there was the silver strainer, on which, in more economical times than ours, the lady of the house placed the tea-leaves, after the very last drop had been exhausted, that they might afterwards be hospitably divided among the company, to be eaten with sugar, and with bread and butter. Blessings upon a fashion which has rescued from the claws of abigails, and the melting-pot of the silversmith, those neglected *cimelia*, for the benefit of antiquaries and the decoration of side-tables! But who shall presume to place them there, unless under the direction of female taste? and of that Mr Mowbray, though possessed of a large stock of such treasures, was for the present entirely deprived.

This digression upon his difficulties is already too long, or I might mention the laird's inexperience in the art of making the worse appear the better garnishment, of hiding a darned carpet with a floor-cloth, and flinging a shawl over a faded and thread-bare sofa. But I have said enough, and more than enough, to explain his dilemma to any unassisted bachelor, who, without mother, sister, or cousin, without skilful housekeeper, or experienced clerk of the kitchen, or valet of parts and figure, adventures to give an entertainment, and aspires to make it elegant and *comme il faut*.

The sense of his insufficiency was the more vexatious to Mowbray, as he was aware he would find sharp critics in the ladies, and particularly in his regular rival, Lady Penelope Penfeather. He was, therefore, incessant in his exertions; and for two whole days ordered and disordered, demanded, commanded, countermanded, and reprimanded, without pause or cessation. The companion, for he could not be termed an assistant of his labours, was his trusty agent, who trotted from room to room after him, affording him exactly the same degree of sympathy which a dog doth to his master when distressed in mind, by looking in his face from time to time with a piteous gaze, to assure him that he partakes of his trouble, though he neither comprehends the cause or the extent of it.

At length, when Mowbray had got some matters arranged to his mind, and abandoned a great many which he would willingly have put in better order to the guidance of chance, he sat down to dinner upon the Wednesday preceding the appointed day, with his worthy aid-de-camp, Mr Micklewhame; and, after bestowing a few muttered curses upon the whole concern, and the fantastic old maid who had brought him into the scrape, declared that all things might now go to the devil their own way, for so sure as his name was John Mowbray, he would trouble himself no more about them.

Keeping this doughty resolution, he sat down to dinner with his counsel learned in the law; and speedily they dispatched the dish of chops which was set before them, and the better part of the bottle of old port, which served for its menstruum.

"We are well enough now," said Mowbray, "though we have had none of their d—d kickshaws."

"A wame-fou' is a wame-fou'," said the writer, swabbing his greasy chops, "whether it be of the barley-meal or the bran."

"A cart-horse thinks so," said Mowbray; "but we must do as others do, and gentlemen and ladies are of a different opinion."

"The waur for themselves and the country baith, Saint Ronan's—it's the jinketting and the jirbling with tea and with trumpery that brings our nobles to ninepence, and mony a het ha'-house to a hired lodging in the Abbey."

The young gentleman paused for a few minutes—filled a bumper, and pushed the bottle to the Senior—then said abruptly, "Do you believe in luck, Mick?"

"In luck," answered the attorney, "what do you mean by the question?"

"Why, because I believe in luck myself—in a good or bad run of luck at cards."

"You wad have mair luck the day if you had never touched them," replied his confidant.

"That is not the question now," said Mowbray; "but what I wonder at is the wretched chance that has attended us miserable Lairds of Saint Ronan's for more than a hundred years, that we have always been getting worse in the world, and never better. Never has there been such a back-sliding generation, as the parson would say. Half the country once belonged to my ancestors, and now the last furrows of it seem to be flying."

"Fleeing!" said the writer, "they are barking and fleeing baith.—This Shaws-Castle here, I'se warrant it flee up the chimney after the rest, were it not weel fastened down with your grandfather's tailzie."

"Damn the tailzie!" said Mowbray; "if they had meant to keep up their estate, they should have entailed it when it was worth keeping;—to tie a man down to such an insignificant thing as Saint Ronan's, is like tethering a horse on six roods of a Highland moor."

"Ye have broke weel in on the mailing by your feus down at the Well," said Micklewhame, "and raxed ower the tether maybe a wee bit farther than ye had any right to do."

"It was by your advice, was it not?" said the laird.

"I'se ne'er deny it, Saint Ronan's," said the writer; "but I am such a good-natured guse, that I just set about pleasing you as an auld wife pleases a bairn."

"Ay," said the man of pleasure, "when she reaches it a knife to cut its own fingers with.—These acres would have been safe enough, if it had not been for your damned advice."

"And yet you were grumbling e'en now," said the man of business, "that you have not the power to gar the whole estate flee like a wild duck across a bog. Troth, you need care little about it; for if you have incurred an irritancy—and sae thinks Mr Wisebehind, the advocate, upon an A. B. memorial, that I laid before him—your sister, or your sister's goodman, if she should take the fancy to marry, might bring a declarator, and evict Saint Ronan's frae ye in the course of twa or three sessions."

"My sister will never marry," said John Mowbray.

"That's easily said," replied the writer; "but as broken a ship's come to land. If ony body kend o' the chance she has of the estate, there's mony a weel-doing man would think little of the bee in her bonnet."

"Harkye, Mr Micklewhame," said the laird, "I will be obliged to you if you will speak of Miss Mowbray with the respect due to her father's daughter, and my sister."

"Nae offence, Saint Ronan's, nae offence," answered the man of law; "but ilka man maun speak sae as to be understood, that is, when he speaks about business. Ye ken yoursel, that Miss Clara is na just like other folks; and were I you—it's my duty to speak plain—I wad e'en gie in a bit scroll of a petition to the Lords, to be appointed Curator Bonis, in respect of her incapacity to manage her own affairs."

"Micklewhame," said Mowbray, "you are a——" and there he stopped short.

"What am I, Mr Mowbray?" said Micklewhame, somewhat sternly —"What am I? I wad be glad to ken what I am."

"A very good lawyer, I dare say," replied Saint Ronan's, who was too much in the power of this agent to give way to his first impulse. "But I must tell you, that rather than take such a measure against poor Clara, as you recommend, I would give her up the estate, and become an ostler or a postilion for the rest of my life."

"Ah, Saint Ronan's," said the man of law, "if you had wished to keep up the auld house, you should have taken another trade, than to become an ostler or a postilion. What ailed you, man, to have been a lawyer as weel as other folks? My auld master had a wee bit Latin about *rerum dominos gentemque togatam*, whilk signified, he said, that all lairds should be lawyers."

"All lawyers are likely to become lairds, I think," replied Mowbray; "they purchase our acres by the thousand, and pay us, according to the old story, with a multiplepoinding, as your learned friends call it, Mr Micklewhame."

"Weel—and mightna you have purchased as weel as other folk?"

"Not I," replied the laird. "I have no turn for that service. I should only have wasted bombazine on my shoulders, and flour upon my three-tailed wig—should but have lounged away my mornings in the Outer-House, and my evenings at the playhouse, and acquired no more law than what would have made me a wise Justice at a Small-debt Court."

"If you gained little, you would have lost as little," said Micklewhame; "and albeit you were nae great gun at the bar, ye might aye have gotten a Sheriffdom, or a Commissaryship, amang the lave, to keep the banes green; and sae ye might have saved your estate from deteriorating, if ye didna mend it mickle."

"Yes, but I could not have had the chance of doubling it, as I might have done," answered Mowbray, "had that inconstant jade, Fortune, but stood a moment faithful to me. I tell you, Mick, that I have been, within this twelvemonth, worth a hundred thousand—worth fifty thousand—worth nothing, but the remnant of this wretched estate, which is too little to do one good while it is mine, though, were it sold, I could start again, and mend my hand a little."

"Ay, ay, just fling the helve after the hatchet—that's a' you think of. What signifies winning a hundred thousand pounds, if you were to lose them a' again?"

"What signifies it?" replied Mowbray. "Why, it signifies as much to a man of spirit, as having won a battle signifies to a general—no matter that he is beaten afterwards in his turn, he knows there is luck for him as well as others, and so he has spirit to try it again. Here is the young Earl of Etherington will be amongst us in a day or two—they say he is up to everything—if I had but five hundred to begin with, I should be soon up to him."

"Mr Mowbray," said Micklewhame, "I am sorry for ye. I have been your house's man-of-business—I may say, in some measure, your servant—and now I am to see an end of it all, and just by the lad that I thought maist likely to set it up again better than ever; for, to do ye justice, you have aye had an ee to your ain interest, sae far as your lights gaed. It brings tears into my auld een."

"Never weep for the matter, Mick," answered Mowbray; "some of it will stick, my old boy, in your pockets, if not in mine—your service will not be altogether gratuitous, my old friend—the labourer is worthy of his hire."

"Weel I wot is he," said the writer; "but double fees would hardly carry folk through some warks. But if ye will have siller, ye maun have siller—but, I warrant, it goes just where the rest gaed."

"No, by twenty devils!" exclaimed Mowbray, "to fail this time is impossible—Jack Wolverine was too strong for Etherington at anything he could name; and I can beat Wolverine from the Land's-End to Johnnie Groat's—but there must be something to go upon—the blunt must be had, Mick."

"Very likely—nae doubt—that is always provided it *can* be had," answered the legal adviser.

"That's your business, my old cock," said Mowbray. "This youngster will be here perhaps to-morrow, with money in both pockets—he takes up his rents as he comes down, Mick—think of that, my old friend."

"Weel for them that has rents to take up," said Micklewhame; "ours are lying rather ower low to be lifted at present.—But are ye sure this Earl is a man to mell with?—are ye sure ye can win of him, and that if you do, he can pay his losings, Mr Mowbray?—because I have kend mony ane come for wool, and gang hame shorn; and though ye are a clever young gentleman, and I am bound to suppose ye ken as much about life as most folk, and all that; yet some gate or other ye have aye come off at the losing hand, as ye have ower mickle reason to ken this day—howbeit——"

"Oh, the devil take your gossip, my dear Mick! If you can give no help, spare drowning me with your pother.—Why, man, I was a fresh hand—had my apprentice-fees to pay—and these are no trifles, Mack.—But what of that?—I am free of the company now, and can trade on my own bottom."

"Aweel, aweel, I wish it may be sae," said Micklewhame.

"It will be so, and it shall be so, my trusty friend," replied Mowbray, cheerily, "so you will but help me to the stock to trade with."

"The stock?—what d'ye ca' the stock? I ken nae stock that ye have left."

"But *you* have plenty, my old boy—Come, sell out a few of your three per cents; I will pay difference—interest—exchange—everything."

"Ay, ay—everything or naething," answered Micklewhame; "but as ye are sae very pressing, I hae been thinking—Whan is the siller wanted?"

"This instant—this day—to-morrow at farthest!" exclaimed the proposed borrower.

"Wh—ew!" whistled the lawyer, with a long prolongation of the note; "the thing is impossible."

"It must be, Mack, for all that," answered Mr Mowbray, who knew by experience that *impossible*, when uttered by his accommodating friend in this tone, only, when interpreted, meant extremely difficult.

"Then it must be by Miss Clara selling her stock, now that ye speak of stock," said Micklewhame; "I wonder ye didna think of this before."

"I wish you had been dumb rather than that you had mentioned it now," said Mowbray, starting, as if stung by an adder—"What, Clara's pittance!—the trifle my aunt left her for her own fanciful expenses—her own little private store, that she puts to so many good purposes—Poor Clara, that has so little!—And why not rather your own, Master Micklewhame, who call yourself the friend and servant of our family?"

"Ay, Saint Ronan's," answered Micklewhame, "that is a' very true —but service is nae inheritance; and as for friendship, it begins at hame, as wise folks have said lang before our time. And for that matter, I think they that are maist sib should take maist risk. You are nearer and dearer to your sister, Saint Ronan's, than you are to poor

Saunders Micklewhame, that hasna sae mickle gentle blood as would supper up a hungry flea."

"I will not do this," said Saint Ronan's, walking up and down with much agitation; for, selfish as he was, he loved his sister, and loved her the more on account of those peculiarities which rendered his protection indispensable to her comfortable existence—"I will not," he said, "pillage her, come on't what will. I will rather go a volunteer to the continent, and die like a gentleman."

He continued to pace the room in a moody silence, which began to disturb his companion, who had not been hitherto accustomed to see his patron take matters so deeply. At length he made an attempt to attract the attention of the silent and sullen ponderer.

"Mr Mowbray"—no answer—"I was saying, Saint Ronan's"—still no reply. "I have been thinking about this matter—and——"

"And *what*, sir?" said Saint Ronan's, stopping short, and speaking in a stern tone of voice.

"And to speak truth, I see little feasibility in the matter ony way; for if ye had the siller in your pocket to-day, it wad be a' in the Earl of Etherington's the morn."

"Pshaw! you are a fool."

"That is not unlikely," answered Micklewhame; "but so is Sir Bingo Binks, and yet he's had the better of you, Saint Ronan's, this twa or three times."

"It is false!—he has not," answered Saint Ronan's, fiercely.

"Weel I wot," resumed Micklewhame, "he took you in about the salmon fish, and some other wager ye lost to him this very day."

"I tell you once more, Micklewhame, you are a fool, and no more up to my trim than you are to the longitude.—Bingo is got shy—I must give him a little line, that is all—then I shall strike him to purpose—I am as sure of him as I am of the other—I know the fly they will both rise to—this cursed want of five hundred will do me out of ten thousand."

"If you are so certain of being the bangster—so very certain, I mean, of sweeping stakes, what harm will Miss Clara come to by your having the use of her siller? you can make it up to her for the risk ten times told."

"And so I can, by heaven!" said Saint Ronan's. "Mick, you are right, and I am a scrupulous, chicken-hearted fool. Clara shall have a thousand for her poor five hundred—she shall, by ——. And I will carry her to Edinburgh for a season, or perhaps to London, and we will have the best advice for her case, and the best company to divert her. And if they think her a little odd—why, d—n me, I am her brother, and will bear her through it. Yes—yes—you're right; there can be no hurt in borrowing five hundred of her for a few days, when such profit may be made on't, both for her and me.—Here, fill the glasses, my old boy, and drink success to it, for you are right."

"Here is success to it, with all my heart," answered Micklewhame, heartily glad to see his patron's sanguine temper arrive at this desirable conclusion, and yet desirous to hedge on his own credit; "but it is *you* are right, and not *me*, for I advise nothing excepting on your assurances, that you can make your ain of this English earl, and of this Sir Bingo—and if ye can but do that, I am sure it would be unwise and unkind in ony ane of your friends to stand in your light."

"True, Mick, true," answered Mowbray.—"And yet dice and cards are but bones and pasteboard, and the best horse ever started may slip a shoulder before he get to the winning-post—and so I wish Clara's venture had not been in such a bottom.—But, hang it, care killed a cat —I can hedge as well as any one, if the odds turn up against me. So let us have the cash, Mick."

"Aha! but there go two words to that bargain—the stock stands in my name, and Tam Turnpenny the banker's, as trustees for Miss Clara—Now, get you her letter to us, desiring us to sell out and to pay you the proceeds, and Tam Turnpenny will let you have five hundred pounds *instanter*, on the faith of the transaction; for I fancy you would desire a' the stock to be sold out, and it will produce more than six hundred, or seven hundred pounds either—and I reckon you will be for selling out the whole—it's needless making twa bites of a cherry."

"True," answered Mowbray; "since we must be rogues, or something like it, let us make it worth our while at least; so give me a form of the letter, and Clara shall copy it—that is, if she consents; for you know she can keep her own opinion as well as any other woman in the world."

"And that," said Micklewhame, "is as the wind will keep its way, preach to it as ye like. But if I might advise about Miss Clara—I wad say naething mair than that I was stressed for the penny money; for I mistake her mickle if she would like to see you ganging to pitch and toss wi' this lord and tither baronet for her aunt's three per cents—I ken she has some queer notions—she gies away the feck of the dividends on that very stock in downright charity."

"And I am in jeopardy to rob the poor as well as my sister," said Mowbray, filling once more his own glass and his friend's. "Come, Mack, no skylights—here is Clara's health—she is an angel—and I am—what I will not call myself, and suffer no other man to call me.— But I shall win this time—I am sure I shall, since Clara's fortune depends upon it."

"Now, I think, on the other hand," said Micklewhame, "that if anything should chance wrang, and Heaven kens that the best laid schemes will gang ajee, it will be a great comfort to think that the ultimate losers will only be the poor folk, that have the parish between them and absolute starvation—if your sister spent her ain siller, it would be a very different story."

"Hush, Mack—for God's sake, hush, mine honest friend," said Mowbray; "it is quite true; thou art a rare counsellor in time of need, and hast as happy a manner of reconciling a man's conscience with his necessities, as might set up a score of casuists; but beware, my most zealous counsellor and confessor, how you drive the nail too far—I promise you some of the chaffing you are at just now rather abates my pluck.—Well—give me your scroll—I will to Clara with it—though I would rather meet the best shot in Britain, with ten paces of green sod betwixt us." So saying, he left the apartment.

Chapter Eleven

FRATERNAL LOVE

Nearest of blood should still be next in love;
And when I see these happy children playing,
While William gathers flowers for Ellen's ringlets,
And Ellen dresses flies for William's angle,
I scarce can think, that in advancing life,
Coldness, unkindness, interest, or suspicion,
Can e'er divide that unity so sacred,
Which Nature bound at birth.

ANONYMOUS

WHEN MOWBRAY had left his dangerous adviser, in order to steer the course which his agent had indicated, without offering to recommend it, he went to the little parlour which his sister was wont to term her own, and in which she spent great part of her time. It was fitted up with a sort of fanciful neatness; and in its perfect arrangement and good order, formed a strong contrast to the other apartments of the old and neglected mansion-house. A number of little articles lay on the work-table, indicating the elegant, and, at the same time, the unsettled turn of the inhabitant's mind. There were unfinished drawings, blotted music, needle-work of various kinds, and many other little female tasks, all undertaken with zeal, and so far prosecuted with art and elegance, but all flung aside before any of them was completed.

Clara herself sat upon a little low couch by the window, reading, or at least turning over the leaves of a book, in which she seemed to read.

But instantly starting up when she saw her brother, she ran towards him with the most cordial cheerfulness.

"Welcome, welcome, my dear John; this is very kind of you to come to visit your recluse sister. I have been trying to nail my eyes and my understanding to a stupid book here, because they say too much thought is not quite good for me. But, either the man's dulness, or my want of the power of attending, makes my eyes pass over the page, just as one seems to read in a dream, without being able to comprehend one word of the matter. You shall talk to me, and that will do better. What can I give you to shew that you are welcome? I am afraid tea is all I have to offer, and that you set too little store by."

"I shall be glad of a cup at present," said Mowbray, "for I wish to speak with you."

"Then Jessy shall make it ready instantly," said Miss Mowbray, ringing, and giving orders to her waiting-maid—"but you must not be ungrateful, John, and plague me with any of the ceremonial for your fete—'sufficient for the day is the evil thereof.' I will attend and play my part as prettily as you can desire; but to think of it beforehand, would make both my head and heart ache; and so I beg you will spare me on the subject."

"Why, you wild kitten," said Mowbray, "you turn every day more shy of human communication—we shall have you take the woods, one day, and become as savage as the Princess Caraboo. But I will plague you about nothing if I can help it. If matters go not smooth on the great day, they must e'en blame the dull male head that had no fair lady to help him in his need. But, Clara, I had something more material to say to you—something indeed of the last importance."

"What is it?" said Clara, in a tone of voice approaching to a scream —"In the name of God, what is it? You know not how you terrify me."

"Nay, you start at a shadow, Clara," answered her brother. "It is no such uncommon matter neither—good faith, it is the most common distress in the world, so far as I know the world—I am sorely pinched for money."

"Is that all?" replied Clara, in a tone which seemed to her brother as much to under-rate the difficulty, when it was explained, as her fears had exaggerated it before she heard its nature.

"Is that all? Indeed it is all, and comprehends a great deal of vexation. I shall be hard run unless I can get a certain sum of money—and I must e'en ask you if you can help me?"

"Help you? Yes, with all my heart—but you know my purse is a light one—more than half of my last dividend is in it, however, and I am sure, John, I will be happy if it can serve you—especially as it will at least shew that your wants are but small ones."

"Alas, Clara, if you would help me, you must draw the neck of the goose which lays the golden egg—you must lend me the whole stock."

"And why not, John, if it will do you a kindness? Are you not my natural guardian? Are you not a kind one? And is not my little fortune entirely at your disposal? You will, I am sure, do all for the best."

"I fear I may not," said Mowbray, starting from her, and more distressed by her sudden and unsuspicious compliance, than he would have been by difficulties, or a remonstrance. In the latter case, he would have stifled the pangs of conscience amid the manœuvres which he must have resorted to for obtaining her acquiescence. As matters stood, there was all the difference that there is between slaughtering a tame and unresisting animal, and pursuing wild game, until the animation of the sportsman's exertions overcomes the internal sense of his own cruelty. The same idea occurred to Mowbray himself.

"By G——," he said, "this is like shooting the bird sitting.—Clara," he added, "I fear this money will scarce be employed as you would wish."

"Employ it as you please yourself, my dearest brother, and I will believe it is all for the best."

"Nay, I am doing for the best," he replied; "at least, I am doing what must be done, for I see no other way through it—so all you have to do is to copy this paper, and bid adieu to bank dividends—for a little while at least. I trust soon to double this little matter for you, if Fortune will but stand my friend."

"Do not trust to Fortune, John," said Clara, smiling, though with an expression of deep melancholy. "Alas! she has never been a friend to our family—not at least for many a day."

"She favours the bold, say my old grammatical exercises," answered her brother, "and I must trust her, were she as changeable as a weathercock.—And yet—if she should jilt me!—What will you do —what will you say, Clara, if I am unable, contrary to my hope, trust, and expectation, to repay you this money within a short time?"

"Do?" answered Clara; "I must do without it, you know; and for saying, I will not say a word."

"True," replied Mowbray, "but your little expenses—your charities —your halt and blind—your round of paupers?"

"Well, I can manage all that too. Look you here, John, how many half-worked trifles there are. The needle or the pencil is the resource of all distressed heroines, you know; and I promise you, though I have been a little idle and unsettled of late, yet, when I do set about it, no Emmeline or Ethelinde of them all ever sent such loads of trumpery to market as I shall, or made such wealth as I will do. I dare say Lady

Penelope, and all the gentry at the Well, will purchase, and will raffle, and do all sort of things to encourage the pensive performer. I will send them such lots of landscapes with sap-green trees, and such mazareen-blue rivers, and portraits that will terrify the originals themselves—and handkerchiefs and turbans, with needlework scallopped exactly like the walks on the Belvidere—Why, I shall become a little fortune in the first season."

"No, Clara," said John, gravely, for a virtuous resolution had gained the upperhand in his bosom, while his sister ran on in this manner,—"We will do something better than all this. If this kind help of yours does not fetch me through, I am determined I will cut the whole concern. It is but standing a laugh or two, and hearing a gay fellow say, Damme, Jack, are ye turned clod-hopper at last?—that is the worst. Dogs, horses, and all, shall go to the hammer; we will keep nothing but your pony, and I will trust to a pair of excellent legs. There is enough left in the old acres to keep us in the way you like best, and that I will learn to like. I will work in the garden, and work in the forest, mark my own trees, and cut them myself, keep my own accounts, and send Saunders Micklewhame to the devil."

"That last is the best resolution of all, John," said Clara; "and if such a day should come round, I would be the happiest of living creatures—I would not have a grief left in the world—if I had, you should never see or hear of it—it should lie here," she said, pressing her hand on her bosom, "buried as deep as a funereal urn in a cold sepulchre. Oh! could we not begin such a life to-morrow? If it is absolutely necessary that this trifle of money should be got rid of first, throw it into the river, and think you have lost it amongst gamblers and horse-jockeys."

Clara's eyes, which she fondly fixed on her brother's face, glowed through the tears which her enthusiasm called into them, while she thus addressed him. Mowbray, on his part, kept his looks fixed on the ground, with a flush on his cheek, that expressed at once false pride and real shame.

At length he looked up:—"My dear girl," he said, "how foolishly you talk, and how foolishly I, that have twenty things to do, stand here listening to you! All will go smooth on *my* plan—if it should not, we have yours in reserve, and I swear to you I will adopt it. The trifle which this letter of yours enables me to command, may have luck in it, and we must not throw up the cards while we have a chance of the game.—Were I to cut from this moment, these few hundreds would make us little better or little worse—so you see we have two strings to our bow. Luck is sometimes against me, that is true—but upon true principle, and playing on the square, I can manage the best of them, or my name is not Mowbray. Adieu, my dearest Clara." So saying, he kissed her cheek with a more than usual degree of affection.

Ere he could raise himself from his stooping posture, she threw her arm kindly over his neck, and said with a tone of the deepest interest, "My dearest brother, your slightest wish has been, and ever shall be, a law to me—Oh! if you would but grant me one request in return!"

"What is it, you silly girl?" said Mowbray, gently disengaging himself from her hold.—"What is it you can have to ask that needs such a solemn preface?—Remember, I hate prefaces; and when I happen to open a book, always skip them."

"Without preface, then, my dearest brother, will you, for my sake, avoid those quarrels in which the people yonder are eternally engaged? I never go down there but I hear of some new brawl; and I never lay my head down to sleep, but I dream that you are the victim of it. Even last night——"

"Nay, Clara, if you begin to tell your dreams, we shall never have done. Sleeping, to be sure, is the most serious employment of your life—for as to eating, you hardly match a sparrow; but I entreat you to sleep without dreaming, or to keep your visions to yourself.—Why do you keep such fast hold of me?—What on earth can you be afraid of?—Surely you do not think the block-head Binks, or any other of the good folks below yonder, dared to turn on me? Egad, I wish they would pluck up a little mettle, that I might have an excuse for drilling them. Gad, I would soon teach them to follow at heel."

"No, John," replied his sister; "it is not of such men as these that I have any fear—and yet, cowards are sometimes driven to desperation, and become more dangerous than better men—yet it is not such as these that I fear. But there are men in the world whose qualities are beyond their seeming—whose spirit and courage lie hidden, like metals in the mine, under an unmarked or a plain exterior.—You may meet with such—you are rash and headlong, and apt to exercise your wit without always weighing consequences, and thus——"

"On my word, Clara," answered Mowbray, "you are in a most sermonizing humour this morning!—the parson himself could not have been more logical or profound. You have only to divide your discourse into heads, and garnish it with conclusions for use, and conclusions for doctrine, and it might be preached before a whole presbytery, with every chance of instruction and edification. But I am a man of the world, my little Clara; and though I wish to go in death's way as little as possible, I must not fear the Raw-head and Bloody Bones neither.—And who the devil is to put the question to me?—I must know that, Clara, for you have some especial person in your eye when you bid me take care of quarrelling."

Clara could not become paler than was her usual complexion; but her voice faultered as she eagerly assured her brother, that she had no particular person in her thoughts.

"Clara," said her brother, "do you remember, when there was a report of a bogle in the upper orchard, when we were both children?—Do you remember how you were perpetually telling me to take care of the bogle, and keep away from its haunts?—And do you remember my going on purpose to detect the bogle, finding the cow-boy, with a sheet about him, busied in pulling pears, and treating him to a handsome drubbing?—I am the same Jack Mowbray still, as ready to face danger, and unmask imposition; and your fears, Clara, will only make me watch more closely, till I find out the real object of them. If you warn me of quarrelling with some one, it must be because you know some one who is not unlikely to quarrel with me. You are a flighty and a fanciful girl, but you have sense enough not to trouble either yourself or me on a point of honour, save when there is some real reason for it."

Clara once more protested, and it was with the deepest anxiety to be believed, that what she had said arose only from the general consequences which she apprehended from the line of conduct her brother had adopted, and which, in her apprehension, was so like to engage him in the broils which divided the good company at the Spaw. Mowbray listened to her apology with an air of doubt, or rather incredulity; and at length replied, "Well, Clara, whether I am right or wrong in my guess, it would be cruel to torment you any more, remembering what you have just done for me. But do justice to your brother, John, and believe, that when you have anything to ask of him, an explicit declaration of your wishes will answer your purpose much better than any ingenious oblique attempts to influence me. Give up all thoughts of such, my dear Clara—you are but a poor manœuvrer, but were you the very Machiavel of your sex, you should not turn the flank of John Mowbray."

He left the room as he spoke, and did not return, though his sister twice called upon him.—It is true that she uttered the word brother so faintly, that perhaps the sound did not reach his ears.—"He is gone," she said, "and I have had no power to speak out! I am like the unhappy creatures, who, it is said, lie under a potent charm, that prevents them alike from shedding tears and from confessing their crimes—Yes, there is a spell on this unhappy heart, and either that must be dissolved, or this must break."

Chapter Twelve

THE CHALLENGE

> A slight note I have about me, for the delivery of which you must excuse me. It is an office that friendship calls upon me to do, and no way offensive to you, as I desire nothing but right on both sides.
>
> *King and No King*

THE INTELLIGENT READER may recollect, that Tyrrel departed from the Fox Hotel on terms not altogether so friendly towards the company as those under which he entered it. Indeed it occurred to him, that he might probably have heard something farther on the subject, though, amidst matters of deeper and more anxious consideration, the idea only passed hastily through his mind; and two days having gone over without any message from Sir Bingo Binks, the whole affair glided entirely out of his memory.

The truth was, that although never old woman took more trouble to collect and blow up with her bellows the embers of her decayed fire, than Captain MacTurk kindly undertook, for the purpose of puffing into a flame the dying sparkles of the Baronet's courage; yet two days were spent in fruitless conferences before he could attain the desired point. He found Sir Bingo on these different occasions in all sort of different moods of mind, and disposed to view the thing in all shades of light, except what the Captain thought was the true one.—He was in a drunken humour—in a sullen humour—in a thoughtless and vilipending humour—in every humour but a fighting one. And when Captain MacTurk talked of the reputation of the company at the Well, Sir Bingo pretended to take offence, said the company might go to the devil, and hinted that he did them sufficient honour by gracing them with his countenance, but did not mean to constitute them any judges of his affairs. The fellow was a raff, and he would have nothing to do with him.

Captain MacTurk would willingly have taken measures against the Baronet, as in a state of contumacy, but was opposed by Winterblossom and other members of the committee, who considered Sir Bingo as too important and illustrious a member of their society to be rashly expelled from a place not honoured by the residence of many persons of rank; and finally insisted that nothing should be done in the matter without the advice of Mowbray, whose preparations for his solemn festival upon the following Thursday, had so much occupied him that he had not lately appeared at the Well.

In the meanwhile, the gallant Captain seemed to experience as much distress of mind, as if some stain had lain on his own most unblemished of reputations. He went up and down upon the points of his toes, rising up on his instep with a jerk which at once expressed vexation and defiance—He carried his nose turned up in the air, like that of a pig when he snuffs the approaching storm—He spoke in monosyllables when he spoke at all; and what perhaps illustrated in the strongest manner the depth of his feelings, he refused, in face of the whole company, to pledge Sir Bingo in a glass of the Baronet's peculiar cogniac.

At length, the whole Well was alarmed by the report brought by a smart outrider, that the young Earl of Etherington, supposed to be rising on the horizon of fashion as a star of the first magnitude, intended to pass an hour, or a day, or a week, as it might happen, (for his lordship could not be supposed to know his own mind,) at Saint Ronan's Well.

This suddenly put all in motion. Almanacks were opened to ascertain his lordship's age, inquiries were made concerning the extent of his fortune, his habits were quoted, his tastes were guessed at; and all that the ingenuity of the Managing Committee could devise was resorted to, in order to recommend their Spaw to this favourite of fortune. An express was dispatched to Shaws-Castle with the agreeable intelligence, which fired the train of hope that led to Mowbray's appropriation of his sister's capital. He did not, however, think proper to obey the summons to the Spring; for, not being aware in what light the Earl might regard the worthies there assembled, he did not desire to be found by his lordship in any strict connection with them.

Sir Bingo Binks was in a different situation. The bravery with which he had endured the censure of the place began to give way, when he considered that a person of such distinction as that which public opinion attached to Lord Etherington, should find him bodily indeed at Saint Ronan's, but, so far as society was concerned, on the road towards the ancient city of Coventry; and his banishment thither, incurred by that most unpardonable offence in modern morality, a solecism in the code of honour. Though sluggish and inert when called to action, the Baronet was by no means an absolute coward; or, if so, he was of that class which fights when reduced to extremity. He manfully sent for Captain MacTurk, who waited upon him with a grave solemnity of aspect, which instantly was exchanged for a radiant joy, when Sir Bingo, in few words, empowered him to carry a message to that damned strolling artist, by whom he had been insulted three days since.

"By Cot," said the Captain, "my exceedingly good and excellent friend, and I am happy to do such a favour for you! And it's well you have thought of it yourself; because, if it had not been for some of our very goot and excellent friends, that would be putting their spoon into other folks' dish, I should have been asking you a civil question myself, how you came to dine with us, with all that mud and mire which Mr Tyrrel's grasp has left upon the collar of your coat—you understand me.—But it is much better as it is, and I will go to the man with all the speed of light; and though, to be sure, it should have been sooner thought of, yet let me alone to make an excuse for that, just in my own civil way—better late thrive than never do well, you know, Sir Binco; and if you have made him wait a little while for his morning, you must give him the better measure, my darling."

So saying, he awaited no reply, lest peradventure the commission with which he was so hastily and unexpectedly charged, should have been clogged with some conditions of compromise. No such proposal, however, was made on the part of the doughty Sir Bingo, who eyed his friend as he hastily snatched up his rattan to depart, with a dogged look of obstinacy, expressive, to use his own phrase, of a determined resolution to come up to the scratch; and when he heard the Captain's parting footsteps, and the door slam behind him, he valiantly whistled a few bars of Jenny Sutton, in token he cared not a farthing how the matter was to end.

With a swifter pace than his half-pay leisure usually encouraged, or than his habitual dignity permitted, Captain MacTurk cleared the ground betwixt the Spring and its gay vicinity, and the ruins of the Aulton, where reigned our friend Meg Dods, the sole assertor of its ancient dignities. To the door of the Cleikum Inn the Captain addressed himself, as one too much accustomed to war to fear a rough reception; although at the very first aspect of Meg, who presented herself in the gateway, his military experience taught him that his entrance into the place would, in all probability, be disputed.

"Is Master Tyrrel at home?" was the question; and the answer was conveyed, by the counter-interrogation, "Wha may ye be that speers?"

As the most polite reply to this question, and an indulgence, at the same time, of his own taciturn disposition, the Captain presented to Luckie Dods the fifth part of an ordinary playing card, much grimed with snuff, which bore on its blank side his name and quality. But Luckie Dods rejected the information thus tendered, with contemptuous scorn.

"Nane of your deil's play-books for me," said she; "it's an ill world since sic prick-my-dainty doings came in fashion—It's an ill tongue that canna tell its ain name, and I'll hae nane of your scarts upon pasteboard."

"I am Captain MacTurk, of the —— regiment," said the Captain, disdaining further answer.

"MacTurk?" repeated Meg, with an emphasis, which induced the owner of the name to reply, "Yes, honest woman—MacTurk—Hector MacTurk—Have you ony objections to my name, good wife?"

"Nae objections have I," answered Meg; "it's e'en an excellent name for a heathen.—But, Captain MacTurk, since sae it be that ye are a captain, ye may e'en face about and march your ways hame again, to the tune of Dumbarton drums; for ye are ganging to have nae speech of Mr Tyrrel, or ony lodger of mine."

"And wherefore not?" demanded the veteran; "and is this of your own foolish head, honest woman, or has your lodger left such orders?"

"Maybe he has and maybe no," answered Meg, sturdily; "and I ken nae mair right that ye suld ca' me honest woman, than I have to ca' you honest man, whilk is as far frae my thoughts as it wad be from heaven's truth."

"The woman is delireet!" said Captain MacTurk; "but coom, coom—a gentlemans is not to be misused in this way when he comes on a gentleman's business; so make you a bit room on the doorstane, that I may pass by you, or I will make room for myself, by Cot, to your small pleasure."

And so saying, he assumed the air of a man who was about to make good his passage. But Meg, without deigning farther reply, flourished around her head the hearth-broom, which she had been employing to its more legitimate purpose, when disturbed in her housewifery by Captain MacTurk.

"I ken your errand weel aneugh, Captain,—and I ken yersell. Ye are ane of the folk that gang about yonder setting folks by the lugs, as callants set their collies to fight. But ye sall come to nae lodger o' mine, let a be Mr Tirl, with ony such ungodly errand; for I am ane that will keep God's peace and the King's within my dwelling."

So saying, and in explicit token of her peaceable intentions, she again flourished her broom.

The veteran instinctively threw himself under Saint George's guard, and drew two paces back, exclaiming, "That the woman was either mad, or as drunk as whisky could make her;" an alternative which afforded Meg so little satisfaction, that she fairly rushed on her retiring adversary, and began to use her weapon to fell purpose.

"Me drunk, ye scandalous blackguard! (a blow with the broom interposed as parenthesis,) me that am fasting from all but sin and bohea!" (another whack.)

The Captain, swearing, exclaiming, and parrying, caught the blows as they fell, shewing much dexterity in single-stick. The people began to gather; and how long his gallantry might have maintained itself against the spirit of self-defence and revenge, is rather uncertain, when the arrival of Tyrrel, returned from a short walk, put a period to the contest.

Meg, who had a great respect for her guest, began to feel ashamed of her own violence, and slunk into the house; observing, however, that she trowed she had made her hearth-broom and the auld heathen's pow right weel acquainted. The tranquillity which ensued upon her departure, gave Tyrrel an opportunity to ask the Captain, whom he at length recognized, the meaning of this singular affray, and whether the visit was intended for him; to which the veteran replied very discomposedly, that "he sald have known that long enough ago, if he had had decent people to open his door, and answer a civil question, instead of a flyting madwoman, who was worse than an eagle," he said, "or a mastiff bitch, or a she-bear, or any other beast in the creation."

Half suspecting his errand, and desirous to avoid unnecessary notoriety, Tyrrel, as he shewed the Captain to the parlour he called his own, entreated him to excuse the rudeness of his landlady, and to pass from the topic to that which had procured him the honour of this visit.

"And you are right, my good Master Tyrrel," said the Captain, pulling down the sleeves of his coat, adjusting his handkerchief and breast-ruffle, and endeavouring to recover the composure of manner becoming his mission, but still adverting indignantly to the usage he had received—"By ——, if she had but been a man, if it were the King himself—However, Mr Tyrrel, I am come on a civil errand—and very civilly I have been treated—the auld bitch should be set in the stocks, and be tamned.—My friend, Sir Bingo—By ——, I shall never forget that woman's insolence—if there be a constable or a cat-a-nine-tails within ten miles——"

"I perceive, Captain," said Tyrrel, "that you are too much disturbed at this moment to enter upon the business which has procured me the honour of a visit—if you will step into my bed-room, and make use of some cold water and a towel, it will give you the time to compose yourself a little."

"I shall do no such thing, Mr Tyrrel," answered the Captain, snappishly; "I do not want to be composed at all, and I do not want to stay in this house a minute longer than to do my errand to you on my friend's behalf—And as for this tamned woman Dods——"

"You will in that case forgive my interrupting you, Captain MacTurk, as I presume your errand to me can have no reference to this strange quarrel with my landlady, with which I have nothing to——"

"And if I thought that it had, sir," said the Captain, interrupting Tyrrel in his turn, "you should have given me satisfaction before you were a quarter of an hour older—Oh, I would give five pounds to the pretty fellow that would say, Captain MacTurk, the woman did right!"

"I certainly will not be that person you wish for, Captain," replied Tyrrel, "because I really do not know who was in the right or wrong; but I am certainly sorry that you should have met with ill usage, when your purpose was to visit me."

"Well, sir, if you are concerned, so am I, and there is an end of it.—And touching my errand to you—you cannot have forgotten that you treated my friend, Sir Bingo Binks, with singular incivility."

"I recollect nothing of the kind, Captain," replied Tyrrel. "I remember that the gentleman, so called, took some uncivil liberties in laying foolish bets concerning me, and that I treated him, in respect to the rest of the company, and the ladies in particular, with a great degree of moderation and forbearance."

"And you must have very fine ideas of forbearance, when you took my good friend by the collar of the coat, and lifted him out of your way as if he had been a puppy dog! My good Mr Tyrrel, I can assure you he does not think that you have forborne him at all, and he has no purpose to forbear you; and I must either carry back a sufficient apology, or you must meet in a quiet way, with a good friend on each side.—And this was the errand I came on, when this tamned woman, with the hearth-broom, who is an enemy to all quiet and peaceable proceedings——"

"We will forget Mrs Dods for the present, if you please, Captain MacTurk," said Tyrrel—"and to speak to the present subject, you will permit me to say, that I think this summons comes a little of the latest. You know best as a military man, but I have always understood that such differences are usually settled immediately after they occur—not that I intend to baulk Sir Bingo's inclinations upon the score of delay, or any other account."

"I dare say you will not—I dare say you will not, Mr Tyrrel," answered the Captain—"I am free to think that you know better what belongs to a gentleman.—And as to time—look you, my good sir, there are different sorts of people in this world, as there are different sorts of fire-arms. There is your hair-triggered rifles, that go off just at the right moment, and in the twinkling of an eye, and that, Mr Tyrrel, is your true man of honour;—and there is a sort of person that takes a thing up too soon, and sometimes backs out of it, like your rubbishy Birmingham pieces, that will at one time go off at half-cock, and at another time burn priming without going off at all;—then again there are pieces that hang fire—or I should rather say, that are like the match-locks which the black fellows use in the East Indies—there must be some blowing of the match, and so forth, which occasions delay, but the piece carries true enough after all."

"And your friend Sir Bingo's valour is of this last kind, Captain—I presume, that is the inference? I should have thought it more like a boy's cannon, which is fired by means of a train, and is but a pop-gun after all."

"I cannot allow of such comparisons, sir," said the Captain; "you will understand that I come here as Sir Bingo's friend, and a reflection on him will be an affront to me."

"I disclaim all intended offence to you, Captain—I have no wish to extend the number of my adversaries, or to add to them the name of a gallant officer like yourself," replied Tyrrel.

"You are too obliging, sir," said the Captain, drawing himself up with dignity. "By ——, and that was said very handsomely!—Well, sir, and shall I not have the pleasure of carrying back any explanation from you to Sir Bingo?—I assure you it would give me pleasure to make this matter handsomely up."

"To Sir Bingo, Captain MacTurk, I have no apology to offer—I think I treated him more gently than his impertinence deserved."

"Och, och!" sighed the Captain, with a strong Highland intonation; "then, there is no more to be said, but just to settle time and place; for pistols, I suppose, must be the weapons."

"All these matters are quite the same to me," said Tyrrel; "only in respect of time, I should wish it to be as speedy as possible—What say you to *one* afternoon this very day?—You may name the place."

"At one afternoon," replied the Captain deliberately, "Sir Bingo will attend you—the place may be the Buckstane; for as the whole company go to the water-side to-day to eat a kettle of fish, there will be no risk of interruption.—And who shall I speak to, my good friend, on your side of the quarrel?"

"Really, Captain," replied Tyrrel, "that is a puzzling question—I have no friend here—I suppose you could hardly act for both?"

"It would be totally, absolutely, and altogether out of the question, my good friend," replied MacTurk. "But if you will trust to me, I will bring up a friend on your part from the Well, who, though you never saw him before, will settle matters for you as well as if you had been intimates for twenty years—and I will bring up th'ould Doctor, if I can get him from the petticoat-string of that fat widow Blower, that he has strung himself upon."

"I have no doubt you will do everything with perfect accuracy,

Captain. At one o'clock, then, we meet at the Buckstane—Stay, permit me to see you to the door."

"By ——, and it is not altogether so unnecessary," said the Captain; "for the tamned woman with the besom might have some advantage in that long dark passage, knowing the ground better than I do—tamn her, I will have amends on her, if there be whipping-post, or ducking-stool, or a pair of stocks in the parish!" And so saying, the Captain trudged off, his spirits ever and anon agitated by recollection of the causeless aggression of Meg Dods, and again composed to a state of happy serenity by the recollection of the agreeable arrangement which he had made between Mr Tyrrel, and his friend Sir Bingo Binks.

We have heard of men of undoubted benevolence of character and disposition, whose principal delight was to see a miserable criminal, degraded alike by his previous crimes, and the sentence which he had incurred, conclude a vicious and wretched life, by an ignominious and painful death. It was some such inconsistency of character which induced honest Captain MacTurk, who had really been a meritorious officer, and was an honourable and well-intentioned man, to place his chief delight in setting his friends by the ears, and then acting as umpire in the dangerous rencontres, which, according to his code of honour, were absolutely necessary to restore peace and cordiality. We leave the explanation of such anomalies to the labours of craniologists, for they seem to defy all the researches of the Ethic philosopher.

Chapter Thirteen

DISAPPOINTMENT

Evans. I pray you now, good Master Slender's serving man, and friend Simple, by your name, which way have you looked for Master Caius?

Slender. Marry, sir, the City-ward, the Park-ward, every way; Old Windsor way, and every way.

Merry Wives of Windsor

SIR BINGO BINKS received the Captain's communication with the same dogged sullenness he had displayed at sending the challenge; a most ungracious *humph*, ascending, as it were, from the very bottom of his stomach, through the folds of a Belcher handkerchief, intimating his acquiescence in a tone nearly as gracious as that with which the drowsy traveller acknowledges the intimation of the slip-shod ostler, that it is on the stroke of five, and the horn will sound in a minute.

Captain MacTurk by no means considered this ejaculation as expressing a proper estimate of his own trouble and services. "Humph," he replied, "and what does that mean, Sir Binco? Have not I here had the trouble to put you just into the neat road; and would you have been able to make a handsome affair out of it all, after you had let it hang so long in the wind, if I had not taken on myself to make it agreeable to the gentleman, and cooked as neat a mess out of it as I have seen a Frenchman do out of a stale sprat?"

Sir Bingo saw it was necessary to mutter some intimation of acquiescence and acknowledgment, which, however inarticulate, was sufficient to satisfy the veteran, to whom the adjustment of a personal affair of this kind was a labour of love, and who now, kindly mindful of his promise to Tyrrel, hurried away as if he had been about the most charitable action upon earth, to secure the attendance of some one as a witness on the stranger's part.

Mr Winterblossom was the person whom MacTurk had in his own mind pitched upon as the fittest person to perform this act of benevolence; and he lost no time in communicating his wish to that worthy gentleman. But Mr Winterblossom, though a man of the world, and well enough acquainted with such matters, was by no means so passionately addicted to them as was the man of peace, Captain Hector MacTurk. As a *bon vivant*, he hated trouble of any kind, and the shrewd selfishness of his disposition enabled him to foresee that a good deal might accrue to all concerned in the course of this business. He, therefore, coolly replied, that he knew nothing of Mr Tyrrel—not even whether he was a gentleman or not; and besides, he had received no regular application in his behalf—he did not, therefore, feel himself at all inclined to go to the field as his second. His refusal drove the poor Captain to despair. He conjured his friend to be more public-spirited, and entreated him to consider the reputation of the Well, which was to them as a common country, and the honour of the company to which they both belonged, and of which Mr Winterblossom was in a manner the proper representative, as being, with consent of all, the perpetual president. He reminded him how many quarrels had been nightly undertaken and departed from on the ensuing morning, without any suitable consequences—said, that people began to talk of the place oddly; and that, for his own part, he found his honour so nearly touched, that he had begun to think he himself would be obliged to bring somebody or other to account for the general credit of the Well; and now, just when the most beautiful occasion had arisen to put everything on a handsome footing, it was hard—it was cruel—it was most unjustifiable—in Mr Winterblossom to decline so simple a matter as was requested of him.

Dry and taciturn as the Captain was on all ordinary occasions, he proved on the present eloquent and almost pathetic; for the tears came into his eyes when he recounted the various quarrels which had become addled, notwithstanding his best endeavours to hatch them into an honourable meeting; and here was one at length just chipping the shell like to be smothered for want of the most ordinary concession on the part of Mr Winterblossom. In short, that gentleman could not hold out any longer. "It was," he said, "a very foolish business, he thought; but to oblige Sir Bingo and Captain MacTurk, he had no objection to walk with them about noon as far as the Buckstane, although he must observe the day was hazy, and he had felt a prophetic twinge or two, which looked like a visit of his old acquaintance podagra."

"Never mind that, my excellent friend," said the Captain, "a sup out of Sir Bingo's flask is like enough to put that to rights; and by my soul it is not the thing he is like to leave behind him on this sort of errand, unless I be far mistaken in my man."

"But," said Winterblossom, "although I comply with your wishes thus far, Captain MacTurk, I by no means undertake for certain to back this same Master Tyrrel, of whom I know nothing at all, but only agree to go to the place in hopes of preventing mischief."

"Never fash your beard about that, Mr Winterblossom," replied the Captain; "for a little mischief, as you call it, is become a thing absolutely necessary to the credit of the place; and I am sure, whatsoever be the consequences, they cannot in the present instance be very fatal to anybody; for here is a young fellow that, if he should have a misfortune, nobody will miss, for nobody knows him; and then here is Sir Bingo, whom everybody knows so well, that they will miss him all the less."

"And there will be Lady Bingo, a wealthy widow," said Winterblossom, throwing his hat upon his head with the grace of former days, and sighing to see, as he looked in the mirror, how much time, that had whitened his hair, rounded his stomach, wrinkled his brow, and bent down his shoulders, had disqualified him, as he expressed it, "from entering for such a plate."

Secure of Winterblossom, the Captain's next anxiety was to obtain the presence of Dr Quackleben, who, although he wrote himself M.D., did not by any means decline practice as a surgeon when any job offered for which he was like to be well paid, as was warranted in the present instance, the wealthy Baronet being a party principally concerned. The Doctor, therefore, like the eagle scenting the carnage, seized at the first word with alacrity the huge volume of morocco leather which formed his case of portable instruments, and uncoiled before the Captain with ostentatious display, its formidable and glittering contents, upon which he began to lecture as upon a copious and interesting text, until the man of war thought it necessary to give him a word of caution.

"Och," says he, "I do pray you, Doctor, to carry that packet of yours under the breast of your coat, or in your pocket, or somewhere out of sight, and by no means to produce or open it before the parties. For although scalpels, and tourniquets, and pincers, and the like, are very ingenious implements, and pretty to behold, and are also useful when time and occasion call for them, yet I have known the sight of them take away a man's fighting stomach, and so lose their owner a job, Dr Quackleben."

"By my faith, Captain MacTurk," said the Doctor, "you speak as if you were graduated!—I have known these treacherous articles play their master many a cursed trick. The very sight of my forceps, without the least effort on my part, once cured an inveterate tooth-ache of three days' duration, prevented the extraction of a carious molindinar, which it was the very end of their formation to achieve, and sent me home minus a guinea.—But hand me that great-coat, Captain, and we will place the instruments in ambuscade, until they are called into action in due time. I should think something will happen—Sir Bingo is a sure shot at a moor-cock."

"Cannot say," replied MacTurk; "I have known the pistol shake many a hand that held the fowling-piece fast enough. Yonder Tyrrel looks like a tevilish cool customer—I watched him the whole time I was delivering my errand, and I can promise you he is mettle to the back-bone."

"Well—I will have my bandages ready *secundum artem*," replied the man of medicine. "We must guard against hæmorrhage—Sir Bingo is a plethoric subject.—One o'clock, you say—at the Buckstane—I will be punctual."

"Will you not walk with us?" said Captain MacTurk, who seemed willing to keep his whole convoy together on this occasion, lest, peradventure, any of them had fled from under his patronage.

"No," replied the Doctor, "I must first make an apology to worthy Mrs Blower, for I had promised her my arm down to the river-side, where they are all to eat a kettle of fish."

"By Cot, and I hope we shall make them a prettier kettle of fish than was ever seen at Saint Ronan's," said the Captain, rubbing his hands.

"Don't say *we*, Captain," replied the cautious Doctor; "I for one have nothing to do with the meeting—wash my hands of it—no, no, I cannot afford to be clapt up as accessory.—You ask me to meet you at the Buckstane—no purpose assigned—I am willing to oblige my worthy friend, Captain MacTurk—walk that way, thinking of nothing particular—hear the report of pistols—hasten to the spot—fortunately just in time to prevent the most fatal consequences—chance most opportunely to have my case of instruments with me—indeed, generally walk with them about me—*nunquam non paratus*—then give my professional definition of the wound and state of the patient. That is the way to give evidence, Captain, before sheriffs, coroners, and such sort of folks—never commit oneself—it is a rule of our profession."

"Well, well, Doctor," answered the Captain, "you know your own ways best; and so you are but there to give a chance of help in case of accident, all the laws of honour will be fully complied with. But it would be a foul reflection upon me, as a man of honour, if I did not take care that there should be somebody to come in thirdsman between Death and my principal."

At the awful hour of one afternoon, there arrived upon the appointed spot Captain MacTurk, leading to the field the valorous Sir Bingo, not exactly straining like a greyhound in the slips, but rather looking moody like a butcher's bull-dog, which knows he must fight since his master bids him. Yet the Baronet shewed no outward flinching or abatement of courage, excepting, that the tune of Jenny Sutton, which he had whistled without intermission since he left the Hotel, had, during the last half mile of their walk, sunk into silence; although, to look at the muscles of the mouth, projection of the lip, and vacancy of the eye, it seemed as if the notes were still passing through his mind, and that he whistled Jenny Sutton in his imagination. Mr Winterblossom came two minutes after this happy pair, and the Doctor was equally punctual.

"Upon my soul," said the former, "this is a mighty silly affair, Sir Bingo, and might, I think, be easily taken up at less risk to all parties, than a meeting of this kind. You should recollect, Sir Bingo, that you have much depending upon your life—you are a married man, Sir Bingo."

Sir Bingo turned the quid in his mouth, and squirted out the juice in a most coachman-like manner.

"Mr Winterblossom," said the Captain, "Sir Bingo has in this matter put himself in my hands, and unless you think yourself more able to direct his course than I am, I must frankly tell you, that I will be disobliged by your interference. You may speak to your own friend as much as you please; and if you find yourself authorized to make any proposal, I will be desirous to lend an ear to it on the part of my worthy principal, Sir Bingo. But I will be plain with you, that I do not greatly approve of settlements upon the field, though I hope I am a quiet and peaceable man; yet here is our honour to be looked after in the first place; and moreover, I must insist that every proposal for accommodation shall originate with your party or yourself."

"*My* party?" answered Winterblossom; "why really, though I came hither at your request, Captain MacTurk, yet I must see more of the matter, ere I can fairly pronounce myself second to a man I never saw but once."

"And, perhaps, may never see again," said the Doctor, looking at his watch; "for it is ten minutes past the hour, and here is no Mr Tyrrel."

"Hey! what's that you say, Doctor?" said the Baronet, wakened from his apathy.

"He speaks tamned nonsense," said the Captain, looking at a huge, old-fashioned, turnip-shaped watch, with a blackened silver dial-plate. "It is not above three minutes after one by the true time, and I will uphold Mr Tyrrel to be a man of his word—never saw a man take a thing more coolly."

"Not more coolly than he takes his walk this way," said the Doctor; "for the hour is as I tell you—remember, I am professional—have pulses to count by the second and half-second—my time-piece must go as true as the sun."

"And I have mounted guard a thousand times by my watch," said the Captain; "and I defy the devil to say that Hector MacTurk did not always discharge his duty to the twentieth part of the fraction of a second—it was my great grandmother Lady Killbracklin's, and I will maintain its reputation against any time-piece that ever went upon wheels."

"Well, then, look at your own watch, Captain," said Winterblossom, "for time stands still with no man, and while we speak the hour advances. On my word, I think this Mr Tyrrel intends to humbug us."

"Hey! what's that you say?" said Sir Bingo, once more starting from his sullen reverie.

"I shall not look at my watch upon no such matter," said the Captain; "nor will I any way be disposed to doubt your friend's honour, Mr Winterblossom."

"*My* friend?" said Mr Winterblossom; "I must tell you once more, Captain, that this Mr Tyrrel is no friend of mine—none in the world. He is your friend, Captain MacTurk; and I own, if he keeps us waiting much longer on this occasion, I will be apt to consider his friendship as of very little value."

"And how dare you then say that the man is my friend?" said the Captain, knitting his brows in a most formidable manner.

"Pooh! pooh! Captain," answered Winterblossom, coolly, if not contemptuously—"keep all that for silly boys; I have lived in the world too long either to provoke quarrels, or to care about them. So reserve your fire; it is all thrown away on such an old cock as I am. But I really wish we knew whether this fellow means to come—twenty minutes past the hour—I think it is odds that you are bilked, Sir Bingo."

"Bilked! hey!" cried Sir Bingo; "by Gad, I always thought so—I wagered with Mowbray he was a raff—I am had, by Gad. I'll wait no longer than the half hour, by Gad, were he a field-marshal."

"You will be directed in that matter by your friend, if you please, Sir Bingo," said the Captain.

"D—n me if I will," returned the Baronet—"Friend? a pretty friend, to bring me out here on such a fool's errand! I knew the fellow was a raff—but I never thought you, with all your chaff about honour, such a d—d spoon as to bring a message from a fellow who has fled the pit!"

"If you regret so much having come here to no purpose," said the Captain, in a very lofty tone, "and if you think I have used you like a spoon, as you say, I will have no objection in life to take Mr Tyrrel's place, and serve your occasion, my boy!"

"By ——! and if you like it, you may fire away, and welcome," said Sir Bingo; "and I'll spin a crown for first shot, for I do not understand being brought here for nothing, d—n me!"

"And there was never man alive so ready as I am to give you something to stay your stomach," said the irritable Highlander.

"Oh fie, gentlemen! fie, fie, fie!" exclaimed the pacific Mr Winterblossom; "For shame, Captain—out upon you, Sir Bingo, are you mad?—what, principal and second!—the like was never heard of."

The parties were in some degree recalled to their more cool recollections by this expostulation, yet continued a short quarter-deck walk to and fro, upon parallel lines, looking at each other sullenly as they passed, and bristling like two dogs who have a mind to quarrel, yet hesitate to commence hostilities. During this promenade, also, the perpendicular and erect carriage of the veteran, rising on his toes at every step, formed a whimsical contrast with the heavy loutish shuffle of the bulky Baronet, who had, by dint of practice, very nearly attained that most enviable of all carriages, the gait of a shambling Yorkshire ostler. His coarse spirit was now thoroughly kindled, and like iron, or any other baser metal, which is slow in receiving heat, it retained long the smouldering and angry spirit of resentment which had originally brought him to the place, and now rendered him willing to wreak his uncomfortable feelings upon the nearest object which occurred, since the first purpose of his coming thither was frustrated. In his own phrase, his pluck was up, and feeling himself in a fighting humour, he thought it a pity, like Bob Acres, that so much good courage should be thrown away. As, however, that courage after all consisted chiefly in ill humour; and as in the demeanour of the Captain, he read nothing deferential or deprecatory of his wrath, he began to listen with more attention to the arguments of Mr Winterblossom, who entreated them not to sully, by private quarrel, the honour they had that day so happily acquired without either blood or risk.

"It was now," he said, "three quarters of an hour past the time appointed for this person, who calls himself Tyrrel, to meet Sir Bingo Binks. Now, instead of standing squabbling here, which serves no purpose, I propose we should reduce to writing the circumstances which attend this affair, for the satisfaction of the company at the Well, and that the memorandum shall be regularly attested by our subscriptions; after which, I shall farther humbly propose that it be subjected to the revision of the Committee of Management."

"I object to any revision of a statement to which my name shall be appended," said the Captain.

"Right—very true, Captain," said the complaisant Mr Winterblossom; "undoubtedly you know best, and your signature is completely sufficient to authenticate this transaction—however, as it is the most important which has occurred since the Spring was established, I propose we shall all sign the *procès verbal*, as I may term it."

"Leave me out, if you please," said the Doctor, not much satisfied that both the original quarrel and the bye-battle had passed over without any occasion for the offices of a Machaon; "leave me out, if you please; for it does not become me to be ostensibly concerned in any proceedings, which have had for their object a breach of the peace. And for the importance of waiting here for an hour, on a fine afternoon, it is my opinion there was a more important service done to the Well of Saint Ronan's, when I, Quentin Quackleben, M.D. cured Lady Penelope Penfeather of her seventh attack upon the nerves, attended with febrile symptoms."

"No disparagement to your skill at all, Doctor," said Mr Winterblossom; "but I conceive the lesson which this fellow has received will be a great means to prevent improper persons from appearing at the Spring hereafter; and, for my part, I shall move that no one be invited to dine at the table in future, till his name is regularly entered as a member of the company, in the lists at the public room. And I hope both Sir Bingo and the Captain will receive the thanks of the company, for their spirited conduct in expelling the intruder.—Sir Bingo, will you allow me to apply to your flask—a little twinge I feel, owing to the dampness of the grass."

Sir Bingo, soothed by the consequence he had acquired, readily imparted to the invalid a thimbleful of his cordial, which, we believe, had been prepared by some canny chemist in the wilds of Glenlivat. He then filled a bumper, and extended it towards the veteran, as an unequivocal symptom of reconciliation. The real turbinacious flavour no sooner reached the nose of the Captain, than the beverage was turned down his throat with symptoms of most unequivocal applause.

"I shall have some hope of the young fellows of this day," he said, "now that they begin to give up their Dutch and French distilled waters, and stick to genuine Highland ware. By ——, it is the only liquor fit for a gentleman to drink in a morning, if he can have the good fortune to come by it."

"Or after dinner either, Captain," said the Doctor, to whom the glass had passed in rotation; "it is worth all the wines in France for flavour, and more cordial to the system besides."

"And now," said the Captain, "that we may not go off the ground with anything on our stomachs worse than the whisky, I can afford to say (as Captain Hector MacTurk's character is tolerably well established,) that I am sorry for the little difference that has occurred betwixt me and my worthy friend, Sir Bingo."

"And since you are so civil, Captain," said Sir Bingo; "why, I am sorry too—only it would put the devil out of temper to lose so fine a fishing day—wind south—fine air on the pool—water settled from the flood—just in trim—and I dare say three pairs of hooks have passed over my cast before this time."

He closed this elaborate lamentation with a libation of the same cordial which he had imparted to his companions; and they returned in a body to the Hotel, where the transactions of the morning were soon afterwards announced to the company, by the following program:—

STATEMENT

"Sir Bingo Binks, baronet, having found himself aggrieved by the uncivil behaviour of an individual calling himself Francis Tirrel, now or lately a resident at the Cleikum Inn, Aulton of Saint Ronan's; and having empowered Captain Hector MacTurk to wait upon the said Mr Tirrel to demand an apology, under the alternative of personal satisfaction, according to the laws of honour and the practice of gentlemen, the said Tirrel voluntarily engaged to meet the said Sir Bingo Binks, baronet, at the Buckstane, near Saint Ronan's Burn, upon this present day, being Wednesday —— August. In consequence of which appointment, we, the undersigned, did attend at the place named, from one o'clock till two, without seeing or hearing anything whatsoever of the said Francis Tirrel, or any one in his behalf. Which fact we make thus publicly known, that all men, and particularly the distinguished company assembled at the Fox Hotel, may be duly apprized of the behaviour of the said Francis Tirrel, in case of his again presuming to intrude himself into the society of persons of honour.

"The Fox Inn and Hotel, Saint Ronan's Well—August, 18—.

(Signed)

"BINGO BINKS.
"HECTOR MACTURK.
"PHILIP WINTERBLOSSOM."

A little lower followed this separate attestation:—

"I, Quentin Quackleben, M.D., F.R.S., D.E., B.L., X.Z., &c. &c., being called upon to attest what I know in the said matter, do hereby verify, that, being by accident at the Buckstane, near Saint Ronan's Burn, on this present day, at the hour of one afternoon, and chancing to remain there for the space of nearly an hour, conversing with Sir Bingo Binks, Captain MacTurk, and Mr Winterblossom, we did not, during that time, see or hear anything of or from the person calling himself Francis Tyrrel, whose presence at that place seemed to be expected by the gentlemen I have just named." This affiche was dated like the former, and certified under the august hand of Quentin Quackleben, M.D., &c. &c. &c.

Again, and prefaced by the averment that an improper person had been lately introduced into the company at Saint Ronan's Well, there came forth a legislative enactment, on the part of the Committee, declaring "that no one shall in future be invited to the dinners, or balls, or other entertainments of the Well, until their names shall be regularly entered in the books kept for the purpose at the rooms." Lastly, there was a vote of thanks to Sir Bingo Binks and Captain MacTurk for their spirited conduct, and the pains which they had taken to exclude an improper person from the company at Saint Ronan's Well.

These annunciations speedily became the magnet of the day. All idlers crowded to peruse them; and it would be endless to notice the "God bless me's"—the "Lord have a care of us"—the "Saw you ever the like's" of gossips, any more than the "Dear me's" and "Oh, laa's" of the titupping misses, and the oaths of the pantalooned or buskin'd beaux. The character of Sir Bingo rose like the stocks at the news of a dispatch from the Duke of Wellington, and, what was extraordinary, attained some consequence even in the estimation of his lady. All shook their head at the recollection of the unlucky Tyrrel, and found out much in his manner and address which convinced them that he was but an adventurer and swindler. A few, however, less partial to the Committee of Management, (for wherever there is an administration, there will soon arise an opposition,) whispered among themselves, that, to give the fellow his due, the man, be what he would, had only come among them, like the devil, when he was called for—And honest Dame Blower blessed herself when she heard of such blood-thirsty doings as had been intended, and "thanked God that honest Doctor Kickherben had come to nae harm amang a' their nonsense."

END OF VOLUME FIRST

SAINT RONAN'S WELL

VOLUME II

Chapter One

THE CONSULTATION

Clown. I hope here be proofs.—
Measure for Measure

THE BOROUGH of —— lies, as all the world knows, about fourteen miles distant from Saint Ronan's, being the county town of that shire, which, as described in the Tourist's Guide, numbers among its objects of interest, that gay and popular watering-place, whose fame, no doubt, will be greatly enhanced by the present annals of its earlier history. As it is at present unnecessary to be more particular concerning the scene of our story, we will fill up the blank left in the first name with the fictitious appellation of Marchthorn, having often found ourselves embarrassed in the course of a story, by the occurrence of an ugly hiatus, which we cannot always at first sight fill up, with the proper reference to the rest of the narrative.

Marchthorn, then, was an old-fashioned Scottish town, the street of which, on market-day, shewed a good number of stout great-coated yeomen, bartering or dealing for the various commodities of their farms; and on other days of the week, only a few forlorn burghers, crawling about like half-awakened flies, and watching the town steeple till the happy sound of twelve strokes from Time's oracle should tell them it was time to take their meridian. The narrow windows of the shops intimated very imperfectly the miscellaneous contents of the interior, where every merchant, as the shopkeepers of Marchthorn were termed, *more Scottico*, sold everything that could be thought of. As for manufactures, there were none, excepting that of the careful Town-Council, who were nightly busied in preparing the warp and woof, which, at the end of every six or seven years, the town of Marchthorn contributed, for the purpose of weaving the fourth part of a member of Parliament.

In such a town it usually happens that the Sheriff-clerk, especially supposing him agent for several lairds of the higher order, is possessed of one of the best-looking houses; and such was that of Mr Bindloose. None of the smartness of the brick-built and brass-hammered mansion of a southern attorney appeared indeed in this mansion, which was a tall, thin, grim-looking building, in the centre of the town, with narrow windows and projecting gables, notched into that sort of descent, called crow-steps, and having the lower casements defended by stancheons of iron; for Mr Bindloose, as frequently happens, kept a branch of one of the national banks, which had been lately established in the town of Marchthorn.

Towards the door of this tenement, there advanced slowly up the ancient, but empty streets of this famous borough, a vehicle, which, had it appeared in Piccadilly, would have furnished unremitted laughter for a week, and conversation for a twelvemonth. It was a two-wheeled vehicle, which claimed none of the modern appellations of tilbury, tandem, dennet, or the like; but aspired only to the humble name of that almost forgotten accommodation, a whisky; or, according to some authorities, a tim-whisky. Green was, or had been, its original colour, and it was placed sturdily and safely low upon its little old-fashioned wheels, which bore much less than the usual proportion to the size of the carriage which they sustained. It had a calash head, which had been pulled up, in consideration to the dampness of the morning air, or to the retiring delicacy of the fair form which, shrouded by leathern curtains, tenanted this venerable specimen of antediluvian coach-building.

But, as this fair and modest dame no way aspired to the skill of a charioteer, the management of a horse, which seemed as old as the carriage he drew, was in the exclusive charge of an old fellow in a postilion's jacket, whose grey hairs escaped on each side of an old-fashioned velvet jockey-cap, and whose left shoulder was so considerably elevated above his head, that it seemed as if, with little effort, his neck might have been tucked under his arm, like that of a roasted grouse-cock. This gallant equerry was mounted on a steed as old as that which toiled betwixt the shafts of the carriage, and which he guided by a leading rein. Goading one animal with his single spur, and stimulating the other with his whip, he effected a reasonable trot upon the causeway, which only terminated when the whisky stopped at Mr Bindloose's door—an event of importance enough to excite the curiosity of the inhabitants of that and the neighbouring houses. Wheels were laid aside, needles left sticking in the half-finished seams, and many a nose, spectacled and unspectacled, was popped out of the adjoining windows, which had the good fortune to command a view of Mr Bindloose's front-door. The faces of two or three giggling clerks were visible at the barred casements of which we have spoken, much amused by the descent of an old lady from this respectable carriage, whose dress and appearance might possibly have been fashionable at the time when her equipage was new. A satin cardinal, lined with grey squirrels' skin, and a black silk bonnet, trimmed with crape, were garments which did not now excite the respect, which in their fresher days they had doubtless commanded. But there was that in the features of the wearer, which would have commanded Mr Bindloose's best regard, though it had appeared in far worse attire; for he beheld the face of an ancient customer, who had always paid her law expenses with the ready penny, and whose accompt with the bank was balanced by a very respectable sum at her credit. It was, indeed, no other than our respected friend, Mrs Dods of the Cleikum Inn, Saint Ronan's, Aulton.

Now her arrival intimated matter of deep import. Meg was a person of all others most averse to leave her home, where, in her own opinion at least, nothing went on well without her immediate superintendance. Limited, therefore, as was her sphere, she remained fixed in the centre thereof; and few as were her satellites, they were under the necessity of performing their revolutions around her, while she herself continued stationary. Saturn, therefore, would be scarce more surprised at a call from the Sun, than Mr Bindloose at this unexpected visit of his old client. In one breath he rebuked the inquisitive impertinence of his clerks, in another stimulated his housekeeper, old Hannah—for Mr Bindloose was a bluff bachelor—to get tea ready in the green parlour; and while yet speaking, was at the side of the whisky, unclasping the curtains, rolling down the apron, and assisting his old friend to dismount.

"The japanned tea-cadie, Hannah—the best bohea—bid Tib kindle a spark of fire—the morning's damp—draw in the giggling faces of ye, ye damned idle scoundrels, or laugh at your ain toom pouches—it will be lang or your weel-doing fill them." This was spoken, as the honest lawyer himself might have said, *in transitu*, the rest by the side of the carriage. "My stars, Mrs Dods, and is this really your ain sell, *in propria persona?*—Wha lookit for you at such a time of day?—Anthony, hows a' wi' ye, Anthony?—so ye hae taen the road again, Anthony—help us down wi' the apron, Anthony—that will do. —Lean on me, Mrs Dods—help your mistress, Anthony—put the horses in my stable—the lads will give you the key.—Come away, Mrs

Dods—I am blithe to see you straight your legs on the causeway of our auld borough ance again—come in by, and we'll see to get you some breakfast, for ye hae been asteer early this morning."

"I am a sair trouble to you, Mr Bindloose," said the old lady, accepting the offer of his arm, and accompanying him into the house; "I am e'en a sair trouble to you, but I could not rest till I had your advice on something of moment."

"Happy will I be to serve you, my gude auld acquaintance," said the Clerk; "but sit you down—sit you down—sit ye down, Mrs Dods—meat and mess never hindered wark. Ye are something overcome wi' your travel—the spirit canna aye bear through the flesh, Mrs Dods; ye should remember that your life is a precious ain, and ye should take care of your health, Mrs Dods."

"My life precious?" exclaimed Meg Dods; "nane o' your willy-whaing, Mr Bindloose—Deil ane wad miss the auld girning ale-wife, Mr Bindloose, unless it were here and there a puir body, and maybe the auld house-tyke, that wadna be sae weel guided, puir fallow."

"Fie, fie! Mrs Dods," said the Clerk, in a tone of friendly rebuke; "it vexes an auld friend to hear ye speak of yourself in that respectless sort of a way; and, as for quitting us, I bless God I have not seen you look better this half score of years. But maybe you will be thinking of setting your house in order, which is the act of a carefu' and of a Christian woman—O! it's an awful thing to die intestate, if we had grace to consider it."

"Aweel, I daur say I'll consider that some day soon, Mr Bindloose; but that's no my present errand."

"Be it what it like, Mrs Dods, ye are right heartily welcome here, and we have a' the day to speak of the business in hand—*festina lente*, that is the true law language—hoolly and fairly as one may say—ill treating of business with an empty stomach—and here comes your tea, and I hope Hannah has made it to your taste."

Meg sipped her tea—confessed Hannah's skill in the mysteries of the Chinese herb—sipped again, then tried to eat a bit of bread and butter, with very indifferent success; and notwithstanding the lawyer's compliment to her good looks, seemed, in reality, on the point of becoming ill.

"In the deil's name, what is the matter?" said the lawyer, too well read in a profession where sharp observation is peculiarly necessary, to suffer these symptoms of agitation to escape him. "Ay, dame, ye are taking this business of yours deeper to heart than ever I kend you take onything. Ony o' your banded debtors failed, or like to fail? What then, cheer ye up—you can afford a little loss, and it canna be ony great matter, or I would have heard of it."

"In troth, but it *is* a loss, Mr Bindloose; and what say ye to the loss of a friend?"

This was a possibility which had never entered the lawyer's long list of calamities, and he was at some loss to conceive what the old lady could possibly mean by so sentimental an effusion. But just as he began to come out with his "Ay, ay, we are all mortal, *Vita incerta, mors certissima!*" and two or three more pithy reflections, which he was in the habit of uttering after funerals, when the will of the deceased was about to be opened, Mrs Dods was pleased to stand the expounder of her own oracle.

"I see how it is, Mr Bindloose," she said; "I maun tell my ain ailment, for you are no likely to guess it; and so, if ye will shut the door, and see that nane of your giggling callants are listening in the passage, I will e'en tell you how things stand with me."

Mr Bindloose hastily arose to obey her commands, gave a cautionary glance into the Bank-office, and saw that his idle apprentices were fast at their desks—turned the key upon them, as if it were in a fit of absence, and then returned, not a little curious to know what could be the matter with his old friend; and leaving off all further attempts to put cases, he quietly drew his chair near hers, and awaited her own time to make her communication.

"Mr Bindloose," said she, "I am no sure that you may mind, about six or seven years ago, that there were twa daft English callants, lodgers of mine, that had some trouble from auld Saint Ronan's about shooting on the Springwell-head muirs."

"I mind it as weel as yesterday, Mistress," said the Clerk; "by the same token you gave me a note for my trouble, (which wasna worth speaking about,) and bade me no bring in a bill against the puir bairns —ye had aye a kind heart, Mrs Dods."

"Maybe, and maybe no, Mr Bindloose—that is just as I find folk.— But concerning these lads, they baith left the country, and, as I think, in some ill blude wi' ane another, and now the auldest and the doucest of the twa came back again about a fortnight sin syne, and has been my guest ever since."

"Aweel, and I trust he is not at his auld tricks again, goodwife," answered the Clerk. "I havena sae mickle to say either wi' the new Sherriff or the Bench of Justices as I used to hae, Mistress Dods—and the pro-fiscal is very severe on poaching, being borne out by the new Association—few of our auld friends of the Killnakelty are able to come to the sessions now, Mrs Dods."

"The waur for the country, Mr Bindloose—they were decent, considerate men, that didna plague a puir herd callant mickle about a moorfowl or a mawkin, unless he turned common fowler—Sir Robert

Ringhorse used to say, the herd lads shot as mony gledes and pyots as they did game.—But new lords new laws—naething but fine and imprisonment, and the game no a feather the plentier.—If I wad hae a brace or twa of birds in the house, as everybody looks for them after the twelfth—I ken what they are like to cost me—and what for no?—risk maun be paid for.—There is John Pirner himsell has keepit the muir-side thirty years in spite of a' the lairds in the country, that shoots, he tells me, now-a-days, as if he felt a rape about his neck."

"It wasna about ony game business, then, that you wanted advice?" said Bindloose, who, though somewhat of a digresser himself, made little allowance for the excursions of others from the subject in hand.

"Indeed is it no, Mr Bindloose," said Meg; "but it is e'en about this unhappy callant that I spoke to ye about.—Ye maun ken I have cleikit a particular fancy to this lad, Francie Tirl—a fancy that whiles surprises my very sell, Mr Bindloose, only that there is nae sin in it."

"None—none in the world, Mrs Dods," said the lawyer, thinking at the same time within his own mind, "Oho! the mist begins to clear up—the young poacher has hit the mark, I see—winged the old barren grey-hen!—ay, ay—a marriage-contract, no doubt—but I maun gie her line.—Ye are a wise woman, Mrs Dods," he continued aloud, "and can doubtless consider the chances and the changes of human affairs."

"But I could never have considered what has befallen this puir lad, Mr Bindloose, through the malice of wicked men.—He lived then at the Cleikum, as I tell you, for mair than a fortnight, as quiet as a lamb on a lea-rig—a decenter lad never came within my doors—ate and drank aneugh for the gude of the house, and nae mair than was for his ain gude, whether of body or soul—cleared his bills ilka Saturday at e'en, as regular as Saturday came round."

"An admirable customer, no doubt, Mrs Dods," said the lawyer.

"Never was the like of him for that matter," answered the honest dame. "But to see the malice of men!—Some of thae land-loupers and gill-flirts down at the filthy puddle yonder, that they ca' the Waal, had heard of this puir lad, and the bits of pictures that he made fashion of drawing, and they maun cuitle him awa doun to the hottle, where mony a bonnie story they had clecked, Mr Bindloose, baith of Mr Tirl and of mysell."

"A Commissary Court business," said the writer, going off again upon a false scent. "I shall trim their jackets for them, Mrs Dods, if you can but bring tight evidence of the facts—I will soon bring them to fine and palinode—I will make them repent meddling with your good name."

"My gude name! What the sorrow is the matter wi' my name, Mr

Bindloose? I think ye hae been at the wee cappie this morning, for as early as it is—My gude name!—if onybody touched my gude name, I would neither fash counsel nor commissary—I wad be down amang them like a jer-faulcon amang a wheen wild geese, and the best amang them that dared to say onything of Meg Dods bye what was honest and civil, I wad sune see if her cockernonnie was made of her ain hair or other folks'. *My* gude name, indeed!"

"Weel, weel, Mistress Dods, I was mista'en, that's a'," said the writer, "I was mista'en; and I dare to say you would hauld your ain wi' your neighbours as weel as ony woman in the land—But let us hear now what the grief is in one word."

"In one word, then, Clerk Bindloose, it is little short of—murther," said Meg in a low tone, as if the very utterance of the word startled her.

"Murther—murther, Mrs Dods—it cannot be—there is not a word of it in the Sheriff-office—there could not be murther in the country, and we not hear of it—for God's sake, take heed what you say, woman, and dinna get yourself into trouble."

"Mr Bindloose, I can but speak according to my lights," said Mrs Dods; "you are in a sense a judge in Israel, at least you are one of the scribes having authority—and I tell you, with a wae and bitter heart, that this puir callant of mine that was lodging in my house has been murthered or kidnapped awa' amang thae banditti folk down at the New Waal; and I'll have the law put in force against them, if it should cost me a hundred pounds."

The Clerk stood much astonished at the nature of Meg's accusation, and the pertinacity with which she seemed disposed to insist upon it.

"I have this comfort," she continued, "that whatever has happened, it has been by no fault of mine, Mr Bindloose; for weel I wot, before that blood-thirsty auld half-pay Philistine, MacTurk, got to speech of him, I clawed his cantle to some purpose with my hearth-besom.—But the poor simple bairn himsel, that had nae mair knowledge of the wickedness of human nature than a calf has of a flesher's gully, he threappit to see the auld hardened blood-shedder, and trysted wi' him to meet wi' some of the gang at an hour certain that vera day, and awa he gaed to keep tryste, but since that hour naebody ever has set een on him.—-And the man-sworn villains now want to put a disgrace on him, and say that he fled the country rather than face them!—a likely story—fled the country for them!—and leave his bill unsettled—he that was sae regular—and his portmantle and his fishing-rod, and the pencils and pictures he held sic a wark about!—It's my faithful belief, Mr Bindloose—and ye may trust me or no as ye like—that he had some foul play between the Cleikum and the Buckstane. I have thought it, and I have dreamed it, and I will be at the bottom of it, or my name is not Meg Dods, and that I wad have them a' to reckon on.—Ay, ay, that is right, Mr Bindloose, tak out your pen and ink-horn, and let us set about it to purpose."

With considerable difficulty, and at the expense of much cross-examination, Mr Bindloose extracted from his client a detailed account of the proceedings of the company at the Well towards Tyrrel, so far as they were known to, or suspected by, Meg, making notes, as the examination proceeded, of what appeared to be matter of consequence. After a moment's consideration, he asked the dame the very natural question, how she came to be acquainted with the material fact, that a hostile appointment was made between Captain MacTurk and her lodger, when, according to her own account, it was made *intra parietes*, and *remotis testibus?*

"Ay, but we victuallers ken weel aneugh what goes on in our own houses," said Meg—"and what for no?—If ye *maun* ken a' about it, I e'en listened through the key-hole of the door."

"And do you say you heard them settle an appointment for a duel?" said the Clerk; "and did you no take ony measures to hinder mischief, Mrs Dods, having such a respect for this lad as you say you have, Mrs Dods?—I really wadna have looked for the like of this at your hand."

"In truth, Mr Bindloose," said Meg, putting her apron to her eyes, "and that's what vexes me mair than a' the rest, and ye needna say mickle to ane whose heart is e'en the sairer that she has been a thought to blame. But there has been mony a challenge, as they ca' it, passed in my house when thae daft lads of the Wild-fire Club and the Helter-skelter were upon their rambles; and they had aye sense aneugh to make it up without fighting, sae that I really did not apprehend ony-thing like mischief.—And ye maun think, moreover, Mr Bindloose, that it would have been an unco thing if a guest, in a decent and creditable public like mine, was to have cried coward before ony of thae land-louping black-guards that live down at the hottle yonder."

"That is to say, Mrs Dods, you were desirous your guest should fight for the honour of your house," said Bindloose.

"What for no, Mr Bindloose?—Isna that kind of fray aye about honour? and what for should the honour of a substantial, four-nooked, sclated house of three stories, no be foughten for as weel as the credit of ony of these feckless callants that make such a fray about their reputation?—I promise you my house, the Cleikum, stood in the Auld Town of Saint Ronan's before they were born, and it will stand there after they are hanged, as I trust some of them are like to be."

"Well, but perhaps your lodger had less zeal for the honour of the house, and has quietly taken himself out of harm's way," said Mr

Bindloose; "for if I understand your story, this meeting never took place."

"Have less zeal! Mr Bindloose, ye little ken him—I wish ye had seen him when he was angry!—I dared hardly face him mysell, and there are na mony folk that I am feared for—Meeting! there was nae meeting, I trow—they never dared to face him fairly—but I am sure waur came of it than ever would have come of a meeting; for Anthony heard twa shots gang aff as he was watering the auld naig down at the burn, and that is not far frae the foot-path that leads to the Buckstane. I was angry at him for na making in to see what the matter was, but he thought it was auld Pirner out wi' the double barrel, and he wasna keen of making himsel a witness, in case he suld have been caa'd on in the poaching court."

"Well," said the Sheriff-clerk, "and I dare say he did hear a poacher fire a couple of shots—nothing more likely. Believe me, Mrs Dods, your guest had no fancy for the party Captain MacTurk invited him to—and being a quiet sort of man, he has just walked away to his own home, if he has one—I am really sorry you have given yourself the trouble of this long journey about so simple a matter."

Mrs Dods remained with her eyes fixed on the ground in a very sullen and discontented posture, and when she spoke it was in a tone of corresponding displeasure.

"Aweel—aweel—live and learn, they say—I thought I had a friend in you, Mr Bindloose—I am sure I aye took your party when folk mis-caa'd ye, and said ye were this, that, and the other thing, and little better than an auld sneck-drawing loon, Mr Bindloose.—And ye have aye keepit my penny of money, though, nae doubt, Tam Turnpenny lives nearer me, and they say he allows half a per cent mair than ye do if the siller lies, and mine is but seldom steered."

"But ye have not the Bank's security, madam," said Mr Bindloose, reddening. "I say harm of nae man's credit—ill would it beseem me—but there is a difference between Tam Turnpenny and the Bank, I trow."

"Weel, weel, Bank here Bank there, I thought I had a friend in you, Mr Bindloose; and here am I, come from my ain house all the way to yours for sma' comfort, I think."

"My stars, madam," said the perplexed scribe, "what would you have me to do in such a blind story as yours, Mrs Dods?—Be a thought reasonable—consider that there isna *Corpus delicti*."

"*Corpus delicti?* and what's that?" said Meg; "something to be paid for, nae doubt, for your hard words a' end in that.—And what for suld I no have a Corpus delicti, or a Habeas Corpus, or ony other Corpus that I like, sae lang as I am willing to lick and lay down the ready sill—?"

"Lord help and pardon us, Mrs Dods, ye mistake the matter a'thegether! When I say there is no Corpus delicti, I mean to say there is no proof that a crime has been committed."

"And does the man say that murder is not a crime, than?" answered Meg, who had taken her own view of the subject too strongly to be subverted by any other—"Weel I wot it's a crime, baith by the law of God and man, and mony a pretty man has been strapped for it."

"I ken all that very weel," answered the writer; "but, my stars, Mrs Dods, there is nae evidence of murder in this case—nae proof that a man has been slain—nae production of his dead body—and that is what we call the Corpus delicti."

"Weel, than, the de'il lick it out of ye," said Meg, rising in wrath, "for I will awa hame again; and as for the puir lad's body, I'll hae it fand, if it costs me turning the earth for three miles round wi' pick and shool—if it were but to give the puir bairn Christian burial, and to bring punishment on MacTurk and the murthering crew at the Waal, and to shame an auld doited fule like yoursell, John Bindloose."

She rose in wrath to call her vehicle; but it was neither the interest nor the intention of the writer that his customer and he should part on such indifferent terms. He implored her patience, and reminded her that the horses, poor things, had but just come off their stage—an argument which sounded irresistible in the ears of the old she-publican, in whose early education due care of the post-cattle mingled with the most sacred duties. She therefore resumed her seat again in a sullen mood, and Mr Bindloose was cudgelling his brains for some argument which might bring the old lady to reason, when his attention was drawn by a noise in the passage.

Chapter Two

A PRAISER OF PAST TIMES

——Now your traveller,
He and his tooth-pick at my worship's mess.
King John

THE NOISE stated at the conclusion of last chapter to have disturbed Mr Bindloose, was the rapping of one, as in haste and impatience, at the Bank-office door, which office was held in an apartment of the Banker's house, opening on the left hand of his passage, as the parlour in which he had received Mrs Dods opened upon the right.

In general, this office was patent to all having business there; but at present, whatever might be the hurry of the party who knocked, the clerks within the office could not admit him, being themselves made prisoners by the prudent jealousy of Mr Bindloose, to prevent their listening to his consultation with Mrs Dods. They therefore answered the angry and impatient knocking of the stranger only with stifled giggling from within, finding it no doubt an excellent joke, that their master's precaution was thus interfering with their own discharge of duty.

With one or two hearty curses upon them, as the regular plagues of his life, Mr Bindloose darted into the passage, and admitted the stranger into his official apartment. The doors both of the parlour and office remaining open, the ears of Luckie Dods, experienced, as the reader knows, in collecting intelligence, could partly overhear what passed. The conversation seemed to regard a cash transaction of some importance, as Meg became aware when the stranger raised a voice which was naturally sharp and high, as he did when uttering the following words, towards the close of a conversation which had lasted about five minutes—"Premium?—not a pice, sir—not a cowrie—not a farthing—premium for a Bank of England bill?—d'ye take me for a fool, sir?—do not I know that you call forty days par when you give remittances to London?"

Mr Bindloose was here heard to mutter something indistinctly about "the custom of the trade."

"Custom?" retorted the stranger, "no such thing—damn'd bad custom, if it is one—don't tell me of customs—'Sbodikins, man, I know the rate of exchange all over the world, and have drawn bills from Timbuctoo—My friends in the Strand filed it along with Bruce's from Gondar—talk to me of premium on a Bank of England post-bill!—What d'ye look at the bill for?—D'ye think it doubtful?—I can change it."

"By no means necessary," answered Bindloose, "the bill is quite right, but it is usual to indorse, sir."

"Certainly—reach me a pen—d'ye think I can write with my rattan?—What sort of ink is this?—yellow as curry sauce—never mind—there is my name—Peregrine Touchwood—I got it from the Willoughbies, my Christian name—Have I my full change here?"

"Your full change, sir," answered Bindloose.

"Why, you should give *me* a premium, friend, instead of my giving you one."

"It is out of our way, I assure you, sir," said the Banker, "quite out of our way—but if you would step into the parlour and take a cup of tea——"

"Why, ay," said the stranger, his voice sounding more distinctly as (talking all the while, and ushered along by Mr Bindloose) he left the office and moved towards the parlour, "a cup of tea were no such bad thing, if one could come by it genuine—but as for your premium——" So saying, he entered the parlour and made his bow to Mrs Dods, who, seeing what she called a decent, purpose-like body, and aware that his pocket was replenished with English and Scotch paper currency, returned the compliment with her best courtsey.

Mr Touchwood, when surveyed more at leisure, was a short, stout, active man, who, though sixty years of age and upwards, retained in his sinews and frame the elasticity of an earlier period. His countenance expressed self-confidence, and something like a contempt for those who had neither seen nor endured so much as he had himself. His short black hair was mingled with grey, but not entirely whitened by it. His eyes were jet-black, deep-set, small, and sparkling, and contributed, with a short up-turned nose, to express an irritable and choleric habit. His complexion was burned to a brick-colour by the vicissitudes of climate, to which it had been subjected; and his face, which, at the distance of a yard or two, seemed hale and smooth, appeared, when closely examined, to be seamed by a million of wrinkles, crossing each other in every direction possible, but as fine as if drawn by the point of a very small needle. His dress was a blue coat and buff waistcoat, half boots remarkably well blacked, and a silk handkerchief tied with military precision. The only antiquated part of his dress was a cocked hat of equilateral dimensions, in the button-hole of which he wore a very small cockade. Mrs Dods, accustomed to judge of persons by their first appearance, said, that in the three steps which he made from the door to the tea-table, she recognized, without the possibility of mistake, the gait of a person who was well to pass in the world; "and that," she added with a wink, "is what we victuallers are seldom deceived in. If a gold-laced waistcoat has an empty pouch, the plain swan's-down will be the braver of the twa."

"A drizzling morning, good madam," said Mr Touchwood, as if with a view of sounding what sort of company he had got into.

"A fine saft morning for the crap, sir," answered Mrs Dods, with equal solemnity.

"Right, my good madam; *soft* is the very word, though it has been some time since I heard it. I have cast a double hank about the round world since I last heard of a soft morning."

"You will be from these parts, then?" said the writer, ingeniously putting a case, which, he hoped, would induce the stranger to explain himself. "And yet, sir," he added, after a pause, "I was thinking that Touchwood is not a Scottish name, at least that I ken of."

"Scottish name?—no," replied the traveller; "but a man may have been in these parts before, without being a native—or, being a native, he may have had some reason to change his name—there are many reasons why men change their names."

"Certainly, and some of them very good ones," said the lawyer; "as in the common case of an heir of entail, where deed of provision and tailzie is maist ordinarily implemented by taking up name and arms."

"Ay, or in the case of a man having made the country too hot for him under his own proper appellative," said Mr Touchwood.

"That is a supposition, sir," replied the lawyer, "which it would ill become me to put.—But at any rate, if you knew this country formerly, ye cannot but be marvellously pleased with the change we have been making since the American war—hill-sides bearing clover instead of heather—rents doubled, trebled, quadrupled—the auld reekie dungeons powed down, and gentlemen living in as good houses as you will see anywhere in England."

"Much good may it do them, for a pack of fools!" replied Mr Touchwood, hastily.

"You do not seem much pleased with our improvements, sir," said the banker, astonished to hear a dissentient voice where he conceived all men were unanimous.

"Pleased?" answered the stranger—"Yes, as much pleased as I am with the devil, who, I believe, set many of them agoing. Ye have got an idea that everything must be changed—Unstable as water, ye shall not excel—I tell ye, there have been more changes in this poor nook of yours within the last forty years, than in the great empires of the East for the space of four thousand, for what I know."

"And why not," replied Bindloose, "if they be changes for the better?"

"But they are *not* for the better," replied Mr Touchwood, eagerly. "I left your peasantry as poor as rats indeed, but honest and industrious, enduring their lot in this world with firmness, and looking forward to the next with hope—Now they are mere eye-servants—looking at their watches, forsooth, every ten minutes, least they should work for their master half an instant after loosing-time—And then, instead of studying the Bible on the weekdays, to kittle the clergyman with doubted points of controversy on the Sabbath, they glean all their theology from Tom Paine and Voltaire."

"Weel I wot the gentleman speaks truth," said Mrs Dods. "I fand a bundle of their bawbee blasphemies in my ain kitchen—But I trow I made a clean house of the packman loon that brought them!—No content wi' turning the tawpies' heads wi' ballats, and driving them daft wi' ribbands, to cheat them out of their precious souls, and gie them the deevil's ware, that I suld say sae, in exchange for the siller that suld support their puir father that's aff wark and bed-ridden."

"Father! madam," said the stranger; "they think no more of their father than Regan or Goneril."

"In gude troth, ye have skeel of our sect, sir," replied the dame; "they are *gomerils*, every one of them—I tell them sae every hour of the day, but catch them profiting by the doctrine."

"And then the brutes are turned mercenary, madam," said Mr Touchwood. "I remember when a Scotsman would have scorned to touch a shilling that he had not earned, and yet was as ready to help a stranger as an Arab of the desert. And now I did but drop my cane the other day as I was riding—a fellow who was working at the hedge, made three steps to lift it—I thanked him, and my friend threw his hat on his head, and 'damned my thanks, if that were all'—Saint Giles could not have excelled him."

"Weel, weel," said the Banker, "that may be a' as you say, sir, and nae doubt wealth makes wit waver; but the country's wealthy, that cannot be denied, and wealth, sir, ye ken——"

"I know wealth makes itself wings," answered the cynical stranger; "but I am not quite sure we have it even now. You make a great show, indeed, with building and cultivation; but stock is not capital, any more than the fat of a corpulent man is health or strength."

"Surely, Mr Touchwood, a set of landlords, living like lords in good earnest, and tenants with better housekeeping than the lairds used to have, and facing Whitsunday and Martinmas as I would face my breakfast—if these are not signs of wealth, I do not know where to seek for them."

"They are signs of folly, sir," replied Touchwood; "folly that is poor, and renders itself poorer by desiring to be thought rich; and how they come by the means they are so ostentatious of, you, who are a banker, perhaps can tell me better than I can guess."

"There is maybe a bill discounted now and then, Mr Touchwood; but men must have accommodation, or the world would stand still—accommodation is the grease that makes the wheels go."

"Ay, makes them go down hill to the devil," answered Touchwood. "I left you bothered about one Air bank, but the whole country is an Air bank now, I think—and who is to pay the piper?—But it is all one—I will see little more of it—it is a perfect Babel, and would turn the head of a man who has spent his life with people who love sitting better than running, silence better than speaking, who never eat but when they are hungry, never drink but when thirsty, never laugh without a jest, and never speak but when they have something to say. But here, it is all run, ride, and drive—froth, foam, and flippancy—no steadiness—no character."

"I'll lay the burthen of my life," said Dame Dods, looking towards her friend Bindloose, "that the gentleman has been at the new Spaw-waal yonder."

"Spaw do you call it, madam?—If you mean the new establishment yonder at Saint Ronan's, it is the very fountain-head of folly and coxcombry—a Babel for noise, and a Vanity-fair for nonsense."

"Sir, sir!" exclaimed Dame Dods, delighted with the unqualified sentence passed upon her fashionable rivals, and eager to testify her respect for the judicious stranger who had pronounced it,—"will you let me have the pleasure of pouring you out a dish of tea?" And so saying, she took bustling possession of the administration which had hitherto remained in the hands of Mr Bindloose himself. "I hope it is to your taste, sir," she continued, when the traveller had accepted her courtesy with the grateful acknowledgment which men addicted to speak a great deal, usually shew to a willing auditor.

"It is as good as we have any right to expect, ma'am," answered Mr Touchwood; "not quite like what I have drunk at Canton with old Fong Qua—but the Celestial Empire does not send its best tea to Leadenhall-Street, nor does Leadenhall-Street send its best to Marchthorn."

"That may be very true, sir," replied the dame; "but I will venture to say that Mr Bindloose's tea is mickle better than you had at the Spaw-waal yonder."

"Tea, madam!—I saw none—Ash leaves and black-thorn leaves were brought in in painted canisters, and handed about by powder-monkeys in livery, and consumed by those who liked it, amid the chattering of parrots, and the squalling of kittens. I longed for the days of the Spectator, when I might have laid my penny on the bar, and retired without ceremony—But no—this blessed decoction was circulated under the auspices of some half-crazed blue-stocking or other, and we were saddled with all the formality of an entertainment, for this miserable allowance of a cockle-shell full of cat-lap per head."

"Weel, sir, all I can say is, that if it had been my luck to have served ye at the Cleikum Inn, which our folks have kept for these twa generations, I canna pretend to say ye should have had such tea as ye have been used to in foreign parts where it grows, but the best I had I wad have gi'en it to a gentleman of your appearance, and never charged mair than sixpence in all my time, and my father's before me."

"I wish I had known the old Inn was still standing, madam," said the traveller; "I should certainly have been your guest, and sent down for the water every morning—the doctors insist I must use Cheltenham, or some substitute, for the bile—though, d—n them, I believe it's only to hide their own ignorance. And I thought this Spaw would have been the least evil of the two; but I have been fairly overreached—one might as well live in the inside of a bell. I think young Saint Ronan's must be mad, to have established such a Vanity-fair upon his father's old property."

"Do ye ken this Saint Ronan's that now is?" inquired the dame.

"By report only," said Mr Touchwood; "but I have heard of the family, and I think I have read of them, too, in Scottish history. I am sorry to understand they are lower in the world than they have been—this young man does not seem to take the best way to mend matters, spending his time among gamblers and black-legs."

"I should be sorry if it were so, sir," said honest Meg Dods, whose hereditary respect for the family always kept her from joining in any scandal affecting the character of the young Laird—"My forbears, sir, have had kindness frae his; and although maybe he may have forgotten all about it, it wad ill become me to say onything of him that should not be said of his father's son."

Mr Bindloose had not the same motive for forbearance: he declaimed against Mowbray as a thoughtless dissipator of his own fortune, and that of others. "I have some reason to speak," he said, "having two of his notes for L.100 each, which I discounted out of mere kindness and respect for his ancient family, and which he thinks nae mair of retiring, than he does of paying the national debt—And here has he been raking every shop in Marchthorn, to fit out an entertainment for all the fine folk in the Well yonder; and tradesfolks are obliged to take his acceptances for their furnishings. But they may cash his bills that will; I ken ane that will never advance a bawbee on ony paper that has John Mowbray either on the back or front of it. He had mair need to be paying the debts which he has made already, than making new anes, that he may feed fules and flatterers."

"I believe he is like to lose his preparations too," said Mr Touchwood; "for the entertainment has been put off, as I heard, in consequence of Miss Mowbray's illness."

"Ay, ay, puir thing!" said Dame Margaret Dods; "her health has been unsettled for this mony a day."

"Something wrong here they tell me," said the traveller, pointing to his own forehead significantly.

"God only kens," replied Mrs Dods; "but I rather suspect the heart than the head—the puir thing is hurried here and there, and down to the Waal, and up again, and nae society or quiet at hame; and a' thing ganging this unthrifty gait—nae wonder she is no that weel settled."

"Well," replied Touchwood, "she is worse they say than she has been, and that has occasioned the party at Shaws-Castle having been put off. Besides, now this fine young lord has come down to the Well, undoubtedly they will wait her recovery."

"A lord!" ejaculated Dame Dods; "a lord come down to the Waal —they will be neither to haud nor to bind now—ance wood and aye waur—a lord!—set them up and shute them forward—a lord!—the Lord have a care o' us!—a lord at the hottle!—Mr Touchwood, it's my mind he will only prove to be a Lord of Session."

"Nay, not so, my good lady—he is an English lord, and, as they say, a Lord of Parliament—but some folks pretend to say there is a flaw in the title."

"I'll warrant is there—a dozen of them!" said Meg, with alacrity, for she could by no means endure to think on the accumulation of dignity like to accrue to the rival establishment, from its becoming the residence of an actual nobleman. "I'll warrant he'll prove a land-louping lord on their hand, and they will be e'en cheap o' the loss—And he has come down out of order it's like, and nae doubt he'll no be lang there before he will recover his health, for the credit of the Spaw."

"Faith, madam, his present disorder is one which the Spaw will hardly cure—he is shot in the shoulder with a pistol-bullet—a robbery attempted, it seems—that is one of your new accomplishments—no such thing happened in Scotland in my time—men would have sooner expected to meet with the phœnix than with a highwayman."

"And where did this happen, if you please, sir?" asked the man of bills.

"Somewhere near the old village," replied the stranger; "and, if I am rightly informed, upon Wednesday last."

"This explains your twa shots, I am thinking, Mrs Dods," said Mr Bindloose; "your groom heard them on the Wednesday—it must have been this attack on the stranger nobleman."

"Maybe it was, and maybe it was not," said Mrs Dods; "but I'll see gude reason before I give up my ain judgment in that case. I wad like to ken if this gentleman," she added, returning to the subject from which Mr Touchwood's interesting conversation had for a few minutes diverted her thoughts, "has heard aught of Mr Tyrrel?"

"If you mean the person to whom this paper relates," said the stranger, taking a printed hand-bill from his pocket, "I heard of little else—the whole place rang of him, till I was almost as sick of Tyrrel as William Rufus was. Some idiotical quarrel which he had engaged in, and which he had not fought out, as their wisdom thought he should have done, was the principal cause of censure. That is another folly now, which has gained ground among you. Formerly, two old proud lairds, or cadets of good family, perhaps quarrelled, and had a rencontre, or fought a duel after the fashion of their old Gothic ancestors; but men who had no grandfathers never dreamt of such folly—And here the folks denounce a trumpery dauber of canvass, for such I understand to be this hero's occupation, as if he were a field-officer, who made valour his profession; and who, if you deprived him of his honour, was like to be deprived of his bread at the same time.—Ha, ha, ha! it reminds one of Don Quixote, who took his neighbour, Samson Carrasco, for a knight-errant."

The perusal of this paper, which contained the notes formerly laid before the reader, containing the statement of Sir Bingo, and the censure which the company at the Well had thought fit to pass upon his affair with Mr Tyrrel, induced Mr Bindloose to say to Mrs Dods, with as little exultation on the superiority of his own judgment, as human nature would permit,—

"Ye see now that I was right, Mistress Dods, and that there was nae earthly use in your fashing yoursell wi' this lang journey—The lad has just taen the bent, rather than face Sir Bingo; and troth, I think him the wiser of the twa for sae doing—there ye hae print for it."

"Ye may be mistaen for a' that your ainsell; for as wise as ye are, Mr Bindloose, I shall hae that matter mair strictly inquired into."

This led to a renewal of the altercation concerning the probable fate of Tyrrel, in the course of which the stranger was induced to take some interest in the subject.

At length, Mrs Dods receiving no countenance from the experienced lawyer, for the hypothesis she had formed, rose, in something like displeasure, to order her whisky to be prepared. But hostess as she was herself, when in her own dominions, she reckoned without her host in the present instance; for the hump-backed postilion, as absolute in his department as Mrs Dods herself, declared that the cattle would not be fit for the road these two hours yet. The good lady was therefore obliged to await his pleasure, bitterly lamenting all the while the loss which a house of public entertainment was sure to sustain by the absence of the landlord or landlady, and anticipating a long list of broken dishes, miscalculated reckonings, unarranged chambers, and other disasters, which she was to expect at her return. Mr Bindloose, however, zealous to recover the regard of his good friend and client, which he had in some degree forfeited by contradicting her on a favourite subject, did not choose to offer the unpleasing, though obvious topic of consolation, that an unfrequented inn is little exposed to the accidents she apprehended. On the contrary, he condoled with her very cordially, and went so far as to hint, that if Mr Touchwood had come to Marchthorn with post-horses, as he supposed from his dress, she could have the advantage of them to return with more dispatch to Saint Ronan's.

"I am not sure," said Mr Touchwood, suddenly, "but I may return there myself. In that case I will be glad to set this good lady down, and to stay a few days at her house, if she will receive me.—I respect a woman like you, ma'am, who pursue the occupation of your father—I have been in countries, ma'am, where people have followed the same trade, from father to son, for thousands of years—And I like the fashion—it shews a steadiness and sobriety of character."

Mrs Dods made a joyous countenance at this proposal, protesting that all should be done in her power to make things agreeable; and while her good friend, Mr Bindloose, expatiated upon the comfort her new guest would experience at the Cleikum, she silently contemplated with delight the prospect of a speedy and dazzling triumph, by carrying off a creditable customer from her showy and successful rival at the Well.

"I shall be easily accommodated, ma'am," said the stranger; "I have travelled too much and too far to be troublesome. A Spanish venta, a Persian khan, or a Turkish caravanserail, is all the same to me—only, as I have no servant—indeed, never can be plagued with one of these idle loiterers,—I must beg you will send to the Well for a bottle of the water on such mornings as I cannot walk there myself—I find it is really of some service to me."

Mrs Dods readily promised compliance with this reasonable request; graciously conceding, that there "could be nae ill in the water itsell, but maybe some gude—it was only the New Inn, and the daft havrels that they ca'd the Company, that she misliked. Folk had a jest that Saint Ronan dookit the Deevil in the waal, which gar'd it taste aye since of brimstone—but she dared say that was a' papist nonsense, for she was tell't by him that kenn'd weel, and that was the minister himsell, that Saint Ronan was nane of your idolatrous Roman saunts, but a Chaldee, (meaning probably a Culdee,) whilk was doubtless a very different story."

Matters being thus arranged to the satisfaction of both parties, the post-chaise was ordered, and speedily appeared at the door of Mr Bindloose's mansion. It was not without a private feeling of reluctance, that honest Meg mounted the step of a vehicle, on the door of which was painted, "FOX INN AND HOTEL, SAINT RONAN'S WELL;" but it was too late to start such scruples.

"I never thought to have entered ane o' their hurley-hackets," she said, as she seated herself; "and sic a like thing as it is—scarce room for twa folks!—Weel I wot, Mr Touchwood, when I was in the hiring line, our twa chaises wad hae carried, ilk ane o' them, four grown folk and as mony bairns. I trust that doiled creature, Anthony, will come awa' back with my whisky and the cattle as soon as they have had their feed.—Are ye sure ye hae room eneugh, sir?—I wad fain hotch mysell farther yont."

"O, ma'am, I am accustomed to all sorts of conveyances—a dooly, a litter, a cart, a palanquin, or a post-chaise, are all alike to me—I think I could be an inside with Queen Mab in a nut-shell, rather than not get forward.—Begging you many pardons, if you have no particular objections, I will light my sheroot," &c. &c. &c.

Chapter Three

THE CLERGYMAN

> A man he was to all the country dear,
> And passing rich with forty pounds a-year.
> DRYDEN, *from Chaucer*

MRS DODS'S conviction, that her friend Tyrrel had been murdered by the sanguinary Captain MacTurk, remained firm and unshaken; but some researches for the supposed body having been fruitless, as well as expensive, she began to give up the matter in despair. "She had done her duty"—"she left the matter to them that had a charge anent such things"—and "Providence would bring the mystery to light in his own fitting time." Such were the moralities with which the good dame consoled herself; and, with less obstinacy than Mr Bindloose had expected, she retained her opinion without changing her banker and man of business.

Perhaps Meg's acquiescent inactivity in a matter which she had threatened to probe so deeply, was partly owing to the place of poor Tyrrel being supplied in her blue chamber, and in her daily thoughts and cares, by her new guest, Mr Touchwood; in possessing whom, a deserter as he was from the Well, she obtained, according to her view of the matter, a decided triumph over her rivals. It sometimes required, however, the full force of this reflection, to induce Meg, old and crabbed as she was, to submit to the various caprices and exactions of attention which were displayed by her new lodger. Never any man talked so much as Mr Touchwood, of his habitual indifference to food, and accommodation in travelling; and probably there never was any traveller who gave more trouble in a house of entertainment. He had his own whims about cookery; and when these were contradicted, especially if he felt at the same time a twinge of incipient gout, one would have thought he had taken his lessons in the pastry-shop of

Bedreddin Hassan, and was ready to renew the scene of the unhappy cream-tart, which was compounded without pepper. Every now and then he started some new doctrine in culinary matters, which Mrs Dods deemed a heresy; and then the very house rang with their disputes. Again, his bed must necessarily be made at a certain angle from the pillow to the foot-posts; and the slightest deviation from this disturbed, he said, his nocturnal rest, and did certainly ruffle his temper. He was equally whimsical about the brushing of his clothes, the arrangement of the furniture in his apartment, and a thousand minutiæ, which, in conversation, he seemed totally to contemn.

It may seem singular, but such is the inconsistency of human nature, that a guest of this fanciful and capricious disposition, gave much more satisfaction to Mrs Dods than her quiet and indifferent friend, Mr Tyrrel. If her present lodger could blame, he could also applaud; and no artist, conscious of such skill as Mrs Dods possessed, is indifferent to the praises of such a connoisseur as Mr Touchwood. The pride of art comforted her for the additional labour; nor was it a matter unworthy of this most honest publican's consideration, that the guests who give most trouble, are usually those who incur the largest bills, and pay them with the best grace. On this point Touchwood was a jewel of a customer. He never denied himself the gratification of the slightest whim, whatever expense he might incur himself, or whatever trouble he might give to those about him; and all was done under protestation, that the matter in question was the most indifferent thing to him in the world. "What the devil did he care for Burgess's sauces, he that had eat his kouscousou, spiced with nothing but the sand of the desert? only it was a shame for Mrs Dods to want what every decent house, above the rank of an alehouse, ought to be largely provided with."

In short, he fussed, fretted, commanded, and was obeyed; kept the house in hot water, and yet was so truly good-natured when essential matters were in discussion, that it was impossible to bear him the least ill-will; so that Mrs Dods, though in a moment of spleen she sometimes wished him at the top of Tintock, always ended by singing forth his praises. She could not, indeed, help suspecting that he was a Nabob, as well from his conversation about foreign parts, as from his freaks of indulgence to himself, and generosity to others,—attributes she understood to be proper to most "Men of Ind." But although the reader has heard her testify a general dislike to this species of Fortune's favourites, Mrs Dods had sense enough to know, that a Nabob living in the neighbourhood, who raises the price of eggs and poultry upon the good housewives around, was very different from a Nabob residing within her own gates, drawing all his supplies from her own larder, and paying, without hesitation or question, whatever bills her conscience permitted her to send in. In short, to come back to the point at which we perhaps might have stopped sometime since, landlady and guest were very much pleased with each other.

But Ennui finds entrances into every scene, when the gloss of novelty is over; and the fiend began to seize upon Mr Touchwood just when he had got all matters to his mind in the Cleikum Inn—had instructed Dame Dods in the mysteries of currie and mullegatawny—drilled the chambermaid into the habit of making his bed at the angle recommended by Sir John Sinclair—and made some progress in instructing the hump-backed postilion in the Arabian mode of grooming. Pamphlets and newspapers, sent from London and from Edinburgh by loads, proved inadequate to rout this invader on Mr Touchwood's comfort; and, at last, he bethought himself of company. The natural resource would have been the Well—but the traveller had a holy shivering of awe, which crossed him at the very recollection of Lady Penelope, who had worked him rather hard during his former brief residence; and although Lady Binks's beauty might have charmed an Asiatic, by the plump graces of its contour, our Senior was past the thoughts of a Sultana and a haram. At length a bright idea crossed his mind, and he suddenly demanded of Mrs Dods, who was pouring out his tea for breakfast, into a large cup of a very particular species of china, of which he had presented her with a service on condition of her rendering him this personal service,—

"Pray, Mrs Dods, what sort of a man is your minister?"

"He's just a man like other men, Mr Touchwood," replied Meg Dods; "what sort of man should he be?"

"A man like other men—ay—that is to say, he has the usual complement of legs and arms, eyes and ears—But is he a sensible man?"

"No muckle o' that, sir," answered Dame Dods; "for if he was drinking this very tea that ye gat doun from London wi' the mail, he wad mistake it for common bohea."

"Then he has not all his organs—wants a nose, or the use of one at least," said Mr Touchwood; "the tea is right gunpowder—a perfect nosegay."

"Aweel, that may be," said the landlady; "but I have gi'en the minister a dram frae my ain best bottle of real Coniac brandy, and may I never stir frae the bit, if he didna commend my whisky when he set down the glass! There is no ane o' them in the Presbytery but himsell—ay, or in the Synod either—but wad hae kenn'd whisky frae brandy."

"But what *sort* of man is he?—Has he learning?" demanded Touchwood.

"Learning?—aneugh o' that," answered Meg, "just dung donnart wi' learning—lets a' things about the Manse gang whilk gate they will, sae they dinna plague him upon the score. An awfu' thing it is to see sic an ill-redd-up house!—If I had the twa tawpies that sorn upon the honest man ae week under my drilling, I think I wad shew them how to sort a lodging."

"Does he preach well?" asked the guest.

"Oh, weel aneugh, weel aneugh—sometimes he will fling in a lang word or a bit of learning that our farmers and bannet lairds canna sae weel follow—but what of that, as I am aye telling them?—they that pay stipend get aye the mair for their siller."

"Does he attend to his parish?—Is he kind to the poor?"

"Ower mickle o' that, Mr Touchwood—I am sure he makes the Word gude, and turns not away from those that ask o' him—his very pocket is picked by a wheen ne'er-do-weel blackguards, that gae sorning through the country."

"Sorning through the country, Mrs Dods?—what would you think if you had seen the fakirs, the dervises, the bonzes, the Imams, the monks, and the mendicants, that I have seen?—But go on, never mind—does this minister of yours come much into company?"

"Company?—gae wa'," replied Meg, "he keeps nae company at a', neither in his ain house or ony gate else. He comes doon in the morning in a lang ragged night-gown, like a potato bogle, and down he sits amang his books; and if they dinna bring him something to eat, the puir demented body has never the heart to cry for aught, and he has been kenn'd to sit for ten hours thegither, black fasting, whilk is a' mere papestrie, though he does it just out o' forget."

"Why, landlady, in that case, your parson is anything but the ordinary kind of man you described him—Forget his dinner!—the man must be mad—he shall dine with me to-day—he shall have such a dinner as I'll be bound he won't forget in a hurry."

"Ye'll maybe find that easier said than dune," said Mrs Dods; "the honest man hasna, in a sense, the true taste of his mouth—forbye, he never dines out of his ain house—that is, when he dines at a'—A drink of milk and a bit of bread serves his turn, or maybe a cauld potato.—It's a heathenish fashion of him, for as good a man as he is, for surely there is nae Christian man but loves his own bowels."

"Why, that may be; but I have known many who took so much care of their own bowels, my good dame, as to have none for any one else.—But come—bustle to the work—get us as good a dinner for two as you can set out—have it ready at three to an instant—get the old hock I had sent out from Cockburn's—a bottle of the particular Sherry—and another of your own old claret—fourth binn, you know, Meg.—And stay, he is a priest, and must have port—have all ready, but don't bring the wine into the sun, as that silly fool Beck did the other day.—I can't go down to the larder myself, but let us have no blunders."

"Nae fear, nae fear," said Meg, with a toss of the head, "I need naebody to look into my larder but mysell, I trow—but it's an unco order of wine for twa folk, and ane o' them a minister."

"Why, you foolish person, is there not the woman up the village that has just brought another fool into the world, and will she not need sack and caudle, if we leave some of our wine?"

"A gude ale-posset wad set her better," said Meg; "however, if it's your will, it shall be my pleasure.—But the like of sic a gentleman as yoursell never entered my doors."

The traveller was gone before she had completed the sentence; and, leaving Meg to bustle and maunder at her leisure, away he marched, with the haste that characterized all his motions when he had any new project in his head, to form an acquaintance with the minister of Saint Ronan's, whom, while he walks down the street to the Manse, we will endeavour to introduce to the reader.

The Rev. Josiah Cargill was the son of a small farmer in the south of Scotland; and a weak constitution, joined to the disposition for study which frequently accompanies infirm health, induced his parents, though at the expense of some sacrifices, to educate him for the ministry. They were the rather led to submit to the privations which were necessary to support this expense, because they conceived, from their family traditions, that he had in his veins some portion of the blood of that celebrated Boanerges of the Covenant, Donald Cargill, who was slain by the persecutors at the town of Queensferry, in the melancholy days of Charles II., merely because, in the plenitude of his sacerdotal power, he had cast out of the church, and delivered over to Satan by a formal excommunication, the King and Royal Family, with all the ministers and courtiers thereunto belonging. But if Josiah really derived himself from this uncompromising champion, the heat of the family spirit which he might have inherited was qualified by the sweetness of his own disposition, and the quiet temper of the times in which he had the good fortune to live. He was characterized by all who knew him as a mild, gentle, and studious lover of learning, who, in the quiet prosecution of his own sole object, the acquisition of knowledge, and especially that connected with his profession, had the utmost indulgence for all whose pursuits were different from his own. His sole relaxations were those of a gentle, mild, and pensive temper, and were limited to a ramble, almost always solitary, among the woods and hills, in praise of which he was sometimes guilty of a sonnet, but rather because he could not help the attempt, than as proposing to himself the fame or the rewards which attend the successful poet. Indeed, far from seeking to insinuate his fugitive pieces into magazines or newspapers, he blushed at his poetical attempts while alone, and, in fact, was rarely so indulgent to his vein as even to commit them to paper.

From the same maid-like modesty of disposition, our student suppressed a strong natural turn towards drawing, although he was repeatedly complimented upon the few sketches which he made, by some whose judgment was generally admitted. It was, however, this neglected talent, which, like the swift feet of the stag in the fable, was fated to render him a service which he might in vain have expected from his worth and learning.

My Lord Bidmore, a distinguished connoisseur, chanced to be in search of a private tutor for his son and heir, the Honourable Augustus Bidmore, and for this purpose had consulted the Professor of Theology, who passed before him in review several favourite students, any of whom he conceived well suited for the situation; but still his answer to the important and unlooked-for question, "Did the candidate understand drawing?" was answered in the negative. The Professor, indeed, added his opinion, that such an accomplishment was neither to be desired nor expected in a student of theology; but, pressed hard with this condition as a *sine qua non*, he at length did remember a dreaming lad about the Hall, who seldom could be got to speak above his breath, even when delivering his essays, but was said to have a strong turn for drawing. This was enough for my Lord Bidmore, who contrived to obtain a sight of some of young Cargill's sketches, and was satisfied that, under such a tutor, his son could not fail to maintain that character for hereditary taste which his father and grandfather had acquired at the expense of a considerable estate, the representative value of which was now the painted canvass in the great gallery at Bidmore-House.

Upon following up the inquiry concerning the young man's character, he was found to possess all the other necessary qualifications of learning and morals, in a greater degree than perhaps Lord Bidmore might have required; and, to the astonishment of his fellow-students, but more especially to his own, Josiah Cargill was promoted to the desired and desirable situation of private tutor to the Honourable Mr Bidmore.

Mr Cargill did his duty ably and conscientiously, by a spoiled though good-humoured lad, of weak health and very ordinary parts. He could not, indeed, inspire into him any portion of the deep and noble enthusiasm which characterizes the youth of genius; but his pupil made such progress in each branch of his studies as his capacity enabled him to attain. He understood the learned languages, and could be very learned on the subject of various readings—he pursued science, and could class shells, pack mosses, and arrange minerals—he drew without taste, but with much accuracy; and although he attained no commanding height in any pursuit, he knew enough of many studies, literary and scientific, to fill up his time, and divert from temptation a head which was none of the strongest in point of resistance.

Miss Augusta Bidmore, his lordship's only other child, received also the instructions of Cargill in such branches of science as her father chose she should acquire, and her tutor was capable to teach. But her progress was as different from that of her brother, as the fire of heaven differs from that grosser element which the peasant piles upon his smouldering hearth. Her acquirements in Italian and Spanish literature, in history, in drawing, and in all elegant learning, were such as to enchant her teacher, while at the same time it kept him on the stretch, lest, in her successful career, the scholar should outstrip the master.

Alas! such intercourse, fraught as it is with dangers arising out of the best and kindest, as well as the most natural feelings on either side, proved in the present, as in many other instances, fatal to the peace of the preceptor. Every feeling heart will excuse a weakness which we will presently find carried with it its own severe punishment. Cadenus, indeed, believe him who will, has assured us, that, in such a perilous intercourse, he himself preserved the limits which were unhappily transgressed by the unfortunate Vanessa, his more impassioned pupil.—

The innocent delight he took
To see the virgin mind her book,
Was but the master's secret joy,
In school to hear the finest boy.

But Josiah Cargill was less fortunate, or less cautious. He suffered his fair pupil to become inexpressibly dear to him, before he discovered the precipice towards which he was moving under the direction of a blind and misplaced passion. He was indeed utterly incapable of availing himself of the opportunities afforded by his situation, to involve his pupil in the toils of a mutual passion. Honour and gratitude alike forbade such a line of conduct, even had it been consistent with the natural bashfulness, simplicity, and innocence of his disposition. To sigh and suffer in secret, to form resolutions of separating himself from a situation so fraught with danger, and to postpone from day to day the accomplishment of a resolution so prudent, was all to which the tutor found himself equal; and it is not improbable, that the veneration with which he regarded his patron's daughter, with the utter hopelessness of the passion which he nourished, tended to render his love yet more pure and disinterested.

At length, the line of conduct which reason had long since recommended, could no longer be the subject of procrastination. Mr Bidmore was destined to foreign travel for a twelvemonth, and Mr Cargill received from his patron the alternative of accompanying his pupil, or retiring upon a suitable provision, the reward of his past instructions. It can hardly be doubted which he preferred; for while he was with young Bidmore, he did not seem entirely separated from his sister. He was sure to hear of Augusta frequently, and to see some part, at least, of the letters which she was to write to her brother: he might also hope to be remembered in these letters as her "good friend and tutor;" and to these consolations his quiet, contemplative, and yet enthusiastic disposition, clung as to a secret source of pleasure, the only one which life seemed to open to him.

But fate had a blow in store for him, which he had not anticipated. The chance of Augusta changing her maiden condition for that of a wife, probable as her rank, beauty, and fortune rendered such an event, had never once occurred to him; and although he had imposed upon himself the unwavering belief that she never could be his, he was inexpressibly affected by the intelligence that she had become the property of another.

The honourable Mr Bidmore's letters to his father soon after announced that poor Mr Cargill had been seized with a nervous fever, and again, that his reconvalescence was attended with so much debility, it seemed both of mind and body, as entirely to destroy his utility as a travelling companion. Shortly after this the travellers separated, and Cargill returned to his native country alone, indulging upon the road in a melancholy abstraction of mind, which he had suffered to grow upon him since the mental shock which he had sustained, and which in time became the most characteristical feature of his demeanour. His meditations were not even disturbed by any anxiety about his future subsistence, although the cessation of his employment seemed to render that precarious. For this, however, Lord Bidmore had made provision; for, though a coxcomb where the fine arts were concerned, he was in other particulars a just and honourable man, who felt a sincere pride in having drawn the talents of Cargill from obscurity, and entertained due gratitude for the manner in which he had achieved the important task entrusted to him in his family.

His lordship had privately purchased from the Mowbray family the patronage or advowson of the living of Saint Ronan's, then held by a very old incumbent, who died shortly afterwards; so that upon arriving in England he found himself named to the vacant living. So indifferent, however, did Cargill feel himself towards this preferment, that he might not possibly have taken the trouble to go through the necessary steps previous to his ordination, had it not been on account of his mother, now a widow, and unprovided for, unless by the support which he afforded her. He visited her in her small retreat in the suburbs of Marchthorn, heard her pour out her gratitude to Heaven, that she should have been granted life enough to witness her son's promotion to a charge, which, in her eyes, was more honourable and desirable than an Episcopal see—heard her chalk out the life which they were to lead together in the humble independence which had thus fallen on him—he heard all this, and had no power to crush her hopes and her triumph by the indulgence of his own romantic feelings. He passed almost mechanically through the usual forms, and was inducted into the living of Saint Ronan's.

Although fanciful and romantic, it was not in Josiah Cargill's nature to yield to unavailing melancholy; yet he sought relief not in society, but in solitary study. His seclusion was the more complete, that his mother, whose education had been as much confined as her fortunes, felt awkward under her new dignities, and willingly acquiesced in her son's secession from society, and spent her whole time in superintending the little household, and in her way providing for all emergencies, the occurrence of which might call Josiah out of his favourite book-room. As old age rendered her inactive, she began to regret the incapacity of her son to superintend his own household, and talked something of matrimony, and the mysteries of the muckle wheel. To these admonitions Mr Cargill returned only slight and evasive answers; and when the old lady slept in the village churchyard, at a reverend old age, there was no one to perform the office of superintendent in the minister's family. Neither did Josiah Cargill seek for any, but patiently submitted to all the evils with which a bachelor estate is attended, and which were at least equal to those which beset the renowned Mago-Pico during his state of celibacy. His butter was ill churned, and declared by all but himself and the quean who made it, altogether uneatable; his milk was burned in the pan, his fruit and vegetables were stolen, and his black stockings mended with blue and white thread.

For all these things the minister cared not, his mind ever bent upon far different matters. Do not let my fair readers do Josiah more than justice, or suppose that, like Beltenebros in the desert, he remained for years the victim of an unfortunate and misplaced passion. No—to the shame of the male sex be it spoken, that no degree of hopeless love, however desperate and sincere, can ever continue for years to embitter life. There must be hope—there must be uncertainty—there must be reciprocity, to enable the tyrant of the soul to secure a dominion of very long duration over a manly and well constituted mind, which is itself desirous to *will* its freedom. The memory of Augusta had long faded from Josiah's thoughts, or was remembered only as a pleasing, but melancholy and unsubstantial dream, while he was straining forward in pursuit of a yet nobler and coyer mistress, in a word, of Knowledge herself.

Every hour that he could spare from his parochial duties, which he discharged with zeal honourable to his heart and head, was devoted to his studies, and spent among his books. But this chase of wisdom, though in itself interesting and dignified, was indulged to an excess which diminished the respectability, nay, the utility, of the deceived student; and he forgot, amid the luxury of deep and dark investigations, that society has its claims, and that the knowledge which is unimparted, is necessarily a barren talent, and is lost to society, like the miser's concealed hoard, by the death of the proprietor. His studies also were under the additional disadvantage, that, being pursued for the gratification of a desultory longing after knowledge, and directed to no determined object, they turned on points rather curious than useful, and while they served for the amusement of the student himself, promised little utility to mankind at large.

Bewildered amid abstruse researches, metaphysical and historical, Mr Cargill, living only for himself and his books, acquired many ludicrous habits, which expose the secluded student to the ridicule of the world, and which tinged, though they did not altogether obscure, the natural civility of an amiable disposition, as well as the acquired habits of politeness which he had learned in the good society that frequented Lord Bidmore's mansion. He not only indulged in neglect of dress and appearance, and all those ungainly tricks which men are apt to acquire by living very much alone, but besides, and especially, he became probably the most abstracted and absent man of a profession peculiarly liable to cherish such habits. No man fell so regularly into the painful dilemma of mistaking, or, in Scottish phrase, *misken-ning* the person he spoke to, or more frequently inquired at an old maid after her husband, at a childless wife after her young people, at the distressed widower after the wife at whose funeral he himself had assisted but a fortnight before; and none was ever more familiar with strangers whom he had never seen, or seemed more estranged from those who had a title to think themselves well known to him. The worthy man perpetually confounded sex, age, and calling; and when a blind beggar extended his hand for charity, he has been known to return the civility by taking off his hat, making a low bow, and hoping his worship was well.

Among his brethren, Mr Cargill alternately commanded respect by the depth of his erudition, and gave occasion to laughter from his odd peculiarities. On the latter occasions he used abruptly to withdraw from the ridicule he had provoked; for, notwithstanding the general mildness of his character, his solitary habits had engendered a testy impatience of contradiction, and a keener sense of pain, arising from the satire of others, than was natural to his unassuming character. As for his parishioners, they enjoyed, as may reasonably be supposed, many a hearty laugh at their pastor's expense, and were sometimes, as Mrs Dods hinted, more astonished than edified by his learning; for in pursuing a point of biblical criticism, he did not altogether remember that he was addressing a popular and unlearned assembly, not delivering a *concio ad clerum*—a mistake, not arising from any conceit of his learning, or wish to display it, but from the same absence of mind which induced an excellent divine, when preaching before a party of criminals condemned to death, to break off by promising the wretches, who were to suffer next morning, "the rest of the discourse at the first proper opportunity." But all the neighbourhood acknowledged Mr Cargill's serious and devout discharge of his ministerial duties; and the poorer parishioners forgave his innocent peculiarities, in consideration of his unbounded charity; while the heritors, if they ridiculed the abstractions of Mr Cargill on some subjects, had the grace to recollect that they had prevented him from suing an augmentation of stipend, according to the fashion of the clergy around him, or from demanding at their hands a new manse, or the repair of the old one. He once, indeed, wished that they would amend the roof of his book-room, which "rained in" in a very pluvious manner; but receiving no direct answer from our friend Micklewhame, who neither relished the proposal nor saw means of eluding it, the minister quietly made the necessary repairs at his own expense, and gave the heritors no farther trouble on the subject.

Such was the worthy divine whom our *bon vivant* at the Cleikum Inn hoped to conciliate by a good dinner and Cockburn's particular; an excellent menstruum in most cases, but not likely to be very efficacious on the present occasion.

Chapter Four

THE ACQUAINTANCE

'Twixt us thus the difference trims:—
Using head instead of limbs,
  You have read what I have seen;
Using limbs instead of head,
I have seen what you have read—
  Which way does the balance lean?
BUTLER

OUR TRAVELLER, rapid in all his resolutions and motions, strode stoutly down the street, and arrived at the Manse, which was, as we have already described it, all but absolutely ruinous. The total desolation and want of order about the door, would have argued the place uninhabited, had it not been for two or three miserable tubs with suds, or such like sluttish contents, which were left there, that those who broke their shins amongst them might receive a sensible proof, that "here the hand of woman had been." The door being half off its hinges, the entrance was for the time protected by a broken harrow, which must necessarily be removed before entry could be obtained. The little garden, which might have given an air of comfort to the old house had it been kept in any order, was abandoned to a desolation, of which that of the sluggard was only a type; and the minister's man, an attendant always proverbial for doing half work, and who seemed in the present instance to do none, was seen among docks and nettles, solacing himself with the few gooseberries which remained on some moss-grown bushes. To him Mr Touchwood called loudly, inquiring after his master; but the clown, conscious of being taken in flagrant delict, as the law says, fled from him like a guilty thing, instead of obeying his summons, and was soon heard *hupping* and *jeeing* to the cart, which he had left on the other side of the broken wall.

Disappointed in his application to the man-servant, Mr Touchwood knocked with his cane, at first gently, then harder, hollowed, bellowed, and shouted, in hope of calling the attention of some one within doors, but received not a word in reply. At length, thinking that no trespass could be committed upon so forlorn and deserted an establishment, he removed the obstacles to entrance with such a noise as he thought must necessarily have alarmed some one, if there was any live person about the house at all. All was still silent; and, entering a passage where the damp walls and broken flags corresponded to the appearance of things without doors, he opened a door to the left, which, wonderful to say, still had a latch remaining, and found himself in the parlour, and in the presence of the person whom he came to visit.

Amid a heap of books and other literary lumber, which had accumulated around him, sat, in his well-worn leathern elbow-chair, the learned minister of Saint Ronan's; a thin, spare man, beyond the middle age, of an adust complexion, but with eyes which, though now obscured and vacant, had been once bright, soft, and expressive, and his features seemed interesting, the rather that, notwithstanding the carelessness of his dress, he was in the habit of performing his ablutions with eastern precision; for he had forgot neatness, but not cleanliness. His hair might have appeared much more disorderly, had it not been thinned by time, and disposed chiefly around the sides of his countenance and the back part of his head; black stockings, ungartered, marked his professional dress, and his feet were thrust into the old slip-shod shoes, which served him instead of slippers. The rest of his garments, so far as visible, consisted in a plaid night-gown wrapt in long folds round his stooping and emaciated length of body, and reaching down to the slippers aforesaid. He was so intently engaged in studying the book before him, a folio of no ordinary bulk, that he totally disregarded the noise which Mr Touchwood made in entering the room, as well as the coughs and hems with which he thought proper to announce his presence.

No notice being taken of these inarticulate signals, Mr Touchwood, however great an enemy he was to ceremony, saw the necessity of introducing his business, as an apology for his intrusion.

"Hem! sir—Ha, hem!—you see before you a person in some distress for want of society, who has taken the liberty to call on you as a good pastor, who may be, in Christian charity, willing to afford him a little of your company, since he is tired of his own."

Of this speech Mr Cargill only understood the words "distress" and "charity," sounds with which he was well acquainted, and which never failed to produce some effect on him. He looked at his visitor with lack-lustre eye, and, without correcting the first opinion which he had formed, although the stranger's plump and sturdy frame, as well as his nicely-brushed coat, glancing cane, and, above all, his upright and self-satisfied manner, resembled in no respect the dress, form, or bearing of a mendicant, he quietly thrust a shilling into his hand, and relapsed into the studious contemplation which the entrance of Mr Touchwood had interrupted.

"Upon my word, my good sir," said his visitor, surprised at a degree of absence of mind which he could hardly have conceived possible, "you have entirely mistaken my object."

"I am sorry my mite is insufficient, my friend," said the clergyman, without again raising his eyes, "it is all I have at present to bestow."

"If you will have the kindness to look up for a moment, my good sir," said the traveller, "you may possibly perceive that you labour under a considerable mistake."

Mr Cargill raised his head, recalled his attention, and, seeing that he had a well-dressed, respectable looking person before him, he exclaimed in much confusion, "Ha!—yes—on my word, I was so immersed in my book—I believe—I think I have the pleasure to see my worthy friend, Mr Lavender?"

"No such thing, Mr Cargill," replied Mr Touchwood. "I will save you the trouble of trying to recollect me—you never saw me before.—But do not let me disturb your studies—I am in no hurry, and my business can wait your leisure."

"I am much obliged," said Mr Cargill; "have the goodness to take a chair, if you can find one—I have a train of thought to recover—a slight calculation to finish—and then I am at your command."

The visitor found among the broken furniture, not without difficulty, a seat strong enough to support his weight, and sat down, resting upon his cane, and looking attentively at his host, who very soon became totally insensible of his presence. A long pause of total silence ensued, only disturbed by the rustling leaves of the folio from which Mr Cargill seemed to be making extracts, and now and then by a little exclamation of surprise and impatience, when he dipped his pen, as happened once or twice, into his snuff-box, instead of the ink-standish which stood beside it. At length, just as Mr Touchwood began to think the scene as tedious as it was singular, the abstracted student raised his head, and spoke as if in soliloquy, "From Acon, Accor, or Saint John D'Acre, to Jerusalem, how far?"

"Twenty-three miles north north-west," answered his visitor, without hesitation.

Mr Cargill expressed no more surprise than if he had found the distance on the map, and, indeed, was not probably aware of the medium through which his question had been solved; and it was the tenor of the answer alone which he attended to in his reply.—"Twenty-three miles—Ingulphus," laying his hand on the volume, "and Jeffrey Winesauf do not agree in this."

"They may both be d—d, then, for blockheads," answered the traveller.

"You might have contradicted their authority without using such an expression," said the divine gravely.

"I cry you mercy, Doctor," said Mr Touchwood; "but would you compare these parchment fellows with me, that have made my legs my compasses over great part of the inhabited world?"

"You have been in Palestine, then?" said Mr Cargill, drawing himself upright in his chair, and speaking with eagerness and with interest.

"You may swear that, Doctor, and at Acre too. Why, I was there the month after Boney had found it too hard a nut to crack.—I dined with Sir Sydney's chum, old Djezzar Pacha, and an excellent dinner we had, but for a dessert of noses and ears brought on after the last remove, which spoiled my digestion. Old Djezzar thought it so good a joke, that you hardly saw a man in Acre whose face was not as flat as the palm of my hand—Gad, I respect my olfactory organ, and set off the next morning as fast as the most cursed hard-trotting dromedary which ever fell to poor pilgrim's lot could contrive to tramp."

"If you have really been in the Holy Land, sir," said Mr Cargill, whom the reckless gaiety of Mr Touchwood's manner rendered somewhat suspicious of a trick, "you will be able materially to enlighten me on the subject of the Crusades."

"They happened before my time, Doctor," replied the traveller.

"You are to understand that my curiosity refers to the geography of the countries where these events took place," answered Mr Cargill.

"O! as to that matter, you are lighted on your feet," said Mr Touchwood; "for the time present I can fit. Turk, Arab, Copt, and Druse, I know every one of them, and can make you as well acquainted with them as myself. Without stirring a step beyond your threshold, you shall know Syria as well as I do.—But one good turn deserves another—in that case, you must have the goodness to dine with me."

"I go seldom abroad, sir," said the minister, with a good deal of hesitation, for his habits of solitude and seclusion could not be entirely overcome, even by the expectation raised by the traveller's discourse; "yet I cannot deny myself the pleasure of waiting on a gentleman possessed of so much experience."

"Well then," said Mr Touchwood, "three be the hour—I never dine later, and always to a minute—and the place, the Cleikum Inn, up the way; where Mrs Dods is at this moment busy in making ready such a dinner as your learning has seldom seen, Doctor, for I brought the receipts from the four different quarters of the globe."

Upon this treaty they parted; and Mr Cargill, after musing for a short while upon the singular chance which had sent a living man to answer those doubts for which he was in vain consulting ancient authorities, at length resumed, by degrees, the train of reflection and investigation which Mr Touchwood's visit had interrupted, and in a short time lost all recollection of his episodical visitor, and of the engagement which he had formed.

Not so Mr Touchwood, who, when not occupied with business of real importance, had the art, as the reader may have observed, to make a prodigious fuss about nothing at all. Upon the present occasion, he bustled in and out of the kitchen, till Mrs Dods lost patience, and threatened to pin the dishclout to his tail; a menace which he pardoned, in consideration, that in all the countries which he had visited, which are sufficiently civilized to boast of cooks, these artists, toiling in their fiery element, have a privilege to be testy and impatient. He therefore retreated from the torrid region of Mrs Dods's microcosm, and employed his time in the usual devices of loiterers, partly by walking for an appetite, partly by observing the progress of his watch towards three o'clock, when he had happily succeeded in getting one. His table, in the blue parlour, was displayed with two covers, after the fairest fashion of the Cleikum Inn; yet the landlady, with a look "civil but sly," contrived to insinuate a doubt whether the clergyman would come, "when a' was dune."

Mr Touchwood scorned to listen to such an insinuation until the fated hour arrived, and brought with it no Mr Cargill. The impatient entertainer allowed five minutes for difference of clocks, and variation of time, and other five for the procrastination of one who went little into society. But no sooner were the last five minutes expended, than he darted off for the Manse, not, indeed, much like a greyhound or a deer, but with the momentum of a corpulent and well-appetized elderly gentleman, who is in haste to secure his dinner. He bounced without ceremony into the parlour, where he found the worthy divine, clothed in the same plaid night-gown, and seated in the very elbow-chair in which he had left him five hours before. His sudden entrance recalled to Mr Cargill, not an accurate, but something of a general recollection, of what had passed in the morning, and he hastened to apologize with "Ha!—indeed—already?—upon my word, Mr A—a—, I mean my dear friend—I am afraid I have used you ill —I forgot to order any dinner—but we will do our best.—Eppie—Eppie!"

Not at the first, second, nor third call, but *ex intervallo*, as the lawyers express it, Eppie, a bare-legged, shock-headed, thick-ankled, red-armed wench, entered, and announced her presence by an emphatic "What's your wull?"

"Have you got anything in the house for dinner, Eppie?"

"Naething but bread and milk, plenty o't—what should I have?"

"You see, sir," said Mr Cargill, "you are like to have a Pythagorean entertainment; but you are a traveller, and have doubtless been in your time thankful for bread and milk."

"But never when there was anything better to be had," said Mr

Touchwood. "Come, Doctor, I beg your pardon, but your wits are fairly gone a wool-gathering: it was *I* invited *you* to dinner, up at the Inn yonder, not you me."

"On my word, and so it was," said Mr Cargill; "I knew I was quite right—I knew there was a dinner engagement betwixt us, I was sure of that, and that is the main point.—Come, sir, I wait upon you."

"Will you not first change your dress?" said the visitor, seeing with astonishment that the divine proposed to attend him in his plaid night-gown; "why, we shall have all the boys in the village after us—why, you will look an owl in sunshine, and they will flock round you like so many hedge-sparrows."

"I will get my clothes instantly," said the worthy clergyman; "I will get ready directly—I am really ashamed to keep you waiting, my dear Mr—eh—eh—your name has this instant escaped me."

"It is Touchwood, sir, at your service; I do not believe you ever heard it before," answered the traveller.

"True—right—no more I have—well, my good Mr Touchstone, will you sit down an instant until we see what we can do?—strange slaves we make ourselves to these bodies of ours, Mr Touchstone—the clothing and the sustaining of them costs us much thought and leisure, which might be better employed in catering for the wants of our immortal spirits."

Mr Touchwood thought in his heart that never had Bramin or Gymnosophist less reason to reproach himself with excess in the indulgence of the table, or of the toilette, than the sage before him; but he assented to the doctrine, as he would have done to any minor heresy, rather than protract matters by farther discussing the point at present. In a short time the minister was dressed in his Sunday's suit, without any farther mistake than turning one of his black stockings inside out; and Mr Touchwood, happy as was Boswell when he carried off Dr Johnson in triumph to dine with Strahan and John Wilkes, had the pleasure of escorting him to the Cleikum Inn.

In the course of the afternoon they became more familiar, and the familiarity led to their forming a considerable estimate of each other's powers and acquirements. It is true, the traveller thought the student too pedantic, too much attached to systems, which, formed in solitude, he was unwilling to renounce, even when contradicted by the voice and testimony of experience; and, moreover, considered his utter inattention to the quality of what he eat and drank, as unworthy of a rational, that is, of a cooking creature, or of a being, who, as defined by Johnson, holds his dinner the most important business of the day. Cargill did not act up to this definition, and was, therefore, in the eyes of his new acquaintance, so far ignorant and uncivilized.

What then? He was still a sensible, intelligent man, however abstemious and bookish.

On the other hand, the divine could not help regarding his new friend as something of an epicure or belly-god, nor could he observe in him either the perfect education, or the polished bearing, which mark the gentleman of rank, and of which, while he mingled with the world, he had become a competent judge. Neither did it escape him, that in the catalogue of Mr Touchwood's defects, occurred that of many travellers, a slight disposition to exaggerate his own personal adventures, and to prose concerning his own exploits. But then his acquaintance with Eastern manners, existing now in the same state in which they existed during the time of the Crusades, formed a living commentary on the works of William of Tyre, Raymund of Saint Giles, the Moslem annal of Abulfaragi, and other historians of the dark period, with which his studies were at present occupied.

A friendship, a companionship at least, was therefore struck up hastily betwixt these two originals; and to the astonishment of the whole parish of Saint Ronan's, the minister thereof was seen once more leagued and united with an individual of his species, generally called among them the Cleikum Nabob. Their intercourse sometimes consisted in long walks, which they took in company, traversing, however, as limited a space of ground, as if it had been actually roped in for their pedestrian exercise. Their parade was, according to circumstances, a low haugh at the nether end of the ruinous hamlet, or the esplanade in the front of the old castle; and, in either case, the direct longitude of their promenade never exceeded a hundred yards. Sometimes, too, though rarely, the divine took share of Mr Touchwood's meal, though less splendidly set forth than when he was first invited to partake of it; for, like the ostentatious owner of the gold cup in Parnell's Hermit,

> ——Still he welcomed, but with less of cost.

On these occasions, the conversation was not of the regular and compacted nature, which passes betwixt men, as they are ordinarily termed, of this world. On the contrary, the one party was often thinking of Saladin and Cœur de Lion, when the other was haranguing on Hyder Ali and Sir Eyre Coote. Still, however, the one spoke, and the other seemed to listen; and, perhaps, the lighter intercourse of society, where amusement is the sole object, can scarcely rest on a safer basis.

It was upon one of the evenings when the learned divine had taken his place at Mr Touchwood's social board, or rather at Mrs Dods's,—for a cup of excellent tea, the only luxury which Mr Cargill continued to partake of with some complacence, was the regale before them,— when a card was delivered to the Nabob.

"Mr and Miss Mowbray see company at Shaws-Castle on the twentieth current, at two o'clock—a déjeuner—dresses in character admitted—a dramatic picture."—"See company? the more fools they," he continued, by way of comment. "See company?—choice phrases are ever commendable—and this piece of pasteboard is to intimate that one may go and meet all the fools of the parish, if they have a mind—in my time they asked the honour, or the pleasure, of a stranger's company. I suppose, by and by, we shall have in this country the ceremonial of a Bedouin's tent, where every ragged Hadgi, with his green turban, comes in slap without leave asked, and has his black paw among the rice, with no other apology than Salam Alicum.— 'Dresses in character—Dramatic picture'—what new Tomfoolery can that be?—but it does not signify.—Doctor! I say, Doctor!—but he is in the seventh heaven—I say, Mother Dods, you who know all the news—Is this the feast that was put off until Miss Mowbray should be better?"

"Troth is it, Mr Touchwood—they are no in the way of giving twa entertainments in one season—no very wise to gie ane maybe—but they ken best."

"I say, Doctor, Doctor!—D—n him, he is charging the Moslemah with stout King Richard—I say, Doctor, do you know anything of these Mowbrays?"

"Nothing extremely particular," answered Mr Cargill, after a pause; "it is an ordinary tale of greatness, which blazes in one century, and is extinguished in the next. I think Camden says, that Thomas Mowbray, who was Grand-Marshall of England, succeeded to that high office, as well as to the Dukedom of Norfolk, as grandson of Roger Bigot, in 1301."

"Pshaw, man, you are back into the 14th century—I mean these Mowbrays of Saint Ronan's—now, don't fall asleep again till you have answered my question—and don't look so like a startled hare—I am speaking no treason."

The clergyman floundered a moment, as is usual with an absent man who is recovering the train of his ideas, or a somnambulist, when he is suddenly awakened, and then answered, still with hesitation.

"Mowbray of Saint Ronan's?—ha—eh—I know—that is—I did know the family."

"Here they are going to give a masquerade, a *bal paré*, private theatricals, I think, and what not," handing him the card.

"I saw something about this a fortnight ago," said Mr Cargill; "indeed, I either had a ticket myself, or I saw such a one as that."

"Are you sure you did not attend the party, Doctor?" said the Nabob.

"Who attend? I? you are jesting, Mr Touchwood."

"But are you quite positive?" demanded Mr Touchwood, who had observed, to his infinite amusement, that the learned and abstracted scholar was so conscious of his own peculiarities, as never to be very sure on any such subject.

"Positive!" he repeated with embarrassment; "my memory is so wretched that I never like to be positive—but had I done anything so far out of my usual way, I must have remembered it, one would think —and—I *am* positive I was not there."

"Neither could you, Doctor," said the Nabob, laughing at the process by which his friend reasoned himself into confidence; "for it did not take place—it was adjourned, and this is the second invitation—there will be one for you, as you had a card to the former.—Come, Doctor, you must go—you and I will go together—I as an Imaum—I can say my Bismillah with any Hadgi of them all—You as a cardinal, or what you like best."

"Who, I?—it is unbecoming my station, Mr Touchwood," said the clergyman—"a folly altogether inconsistent with my habits."

"All the better—you shall change your habits."

"You had better gang up and see them, Mr Cargill," said Mrs Dods; "for it's maybe the last sight ye may see of Miss Mowbray—they say she is to be married and off to England ane of thae odd-come-shortlies, wi' some of the gowks about the Waal down bye."

"Married!" said the clergyman; "it is impossible!"

"But whare's the impossibility, Mr Cargill, when ye see folk marry every day, and buckle them yoursell into the bargain?—Maybe ye think the puir lassie has a bee in her bannet; but ye ken yoursell if naebody but wise folk were to marry, the warld wad be ill peopled. I think it's the wise folk that keep single, like yoursell and me, Mr Cargill.—God guide us!—are ye no weel?—will ye taste a drap o' something?"

"Sniff at my ottar of roses," said Mr Touchwood; "the scent would revive the dead—why, what in the devil's name is the meaning of this? —you were quite well just now."

"A sudden qualm," said Mr Cargill, recovering himself.

"Oh! Mr Cargill," said Dame Dods, "this comes of your lang fasts."

"Right, dame," subjoined Mr Touchwood; "and of breaking them with sour milk and pease bannock—the least morsel of Christian food is rejected by the stomach, just as a small gentleman refuses the visit of a creditable neighbour, least he see the nakedness of the land—ha! ha!"

"And there is really a talk of Miss Mowbray of Saint Ronan's being married?" said the clergyman.

"Troth is there," said the dame; "it's Trotting Nelly's news; and though she likes a drappie, I dinna think she would invent a lee or carry ane—at least to me, that am a gude customer."

"This must be looked to," said Mr Cargill, as if speaking to himself.

"In troth, and so it should," said Dame Dods; "it's a sin and a shame if they should employ the tinkling cymbal they ca' Chatterley, and sic a presbyterian trumpet as yoursell in the land, Mr Cargill; and if ye will take a fule's advice, ye winna let the multure be taen by your ain mill, Mr Cargill."

"True, true, good Mother Dods," said the Nabob; "gloves and hatbands are things to be looked after, and Mr Cargill had better go down to this cursed festivity with me, in order to see after his own interest."

"I must speak with the young lady," said the clergyman, still in a brown study.

"Right, right, my boy of blackletter," said the Nabob; "with me you shall go, and we'll bring them to submission to mother-church, I warrant you—Why, the idea of being cheated in such a way, would scare a Santon out of his trance.—What dress will you wear?"

"My own, to be sure," said the divine, starting from his reverie.

"True, thou art right again—they may want to knit the knot on the spot, and who would be married by a parson in masquerade?—We go to the entertainment though—it is a done thing."

The clergyman assented, provided he should receive an invitation; and as that was found at the Manse, he had no excuse for retreating, even if he had seemed to desire one.

Chapter Five

FORTUNE'S FROLICS

Count Basset. We gentlemen, whose carriages run on the four aces, are apt to have a wheel out of order.

The Provoked Husband

OUR HISTORY must now look a little backwards; and although it is rather foreign to our natural style of composition, it must speak more in narrative, and less in dialogue, rather telling what happened, than its effects upon the actors. Our promise, however, is only conditional, for we foresee temptations which may render it difficult for us exactly to keep it.

The arrival of the young Earl of Etherington at the salutiferous fountain of Saint Ronan's had produced the strongest sensation; especially, as it was joined with the singular accident of the attempt upon his lordship's person, as he took a short cut through the woods upon foot, at a distance from his equipage and servants. The gallantry with which he beat off the highwayman, was only equal to his generosity; for he declined making any researches after the poor devil, although he had received a severe wound in the scuffle.

Of the "three black Graces," as they have been termed by one of the most pleasant companions of our time, Law and Physic hastened to do homage to Lord Etherington, represented by Mr Micklewhame and Dr Quackleben, while Divinity, as favourable, though more coy, in the person of the Reverend Mr Simon Chatterley, stood on tiptoe to offer any service in her power.

For the honourable reason already assigned, his lordship, after thanking Mr Micklewhame, and hinting, that he might have different occasion for his services, declined his offer to search out the delinquent by whom he had been wounded; while to the care of the Doctor he subjected the cure of a smart flesh-wound in the arm, together with a slight scratch on the temple; and so very genteel was his behaviour on the occasion, that the Doctor, in his anxiety for his safety, enjoined him a month's course of the waters, if he would enjoy the comfort of a complete and perfect recovery. Nothing so frequent, he could assure his lordship, as the opening of cicatrized wounds; and the waters of Saint Ronan's spring being, according to Dr Quackleben, a remedy for all the troubles which flesh is heir to, could not fail to equal those of Barèges, in facilitating the discharge of all splinters or extraneous matter, which a bullet may chance to incorporate with the human frame, to its great annoyance. For he was wont to say, that although he could not declare the waters which he patronized to be an absolute *panpharmacon*, yet he would with word and pen maintain, that they possessed the principal virtues of the most celebrated medicinal springs in the known world. In short, the love of Alpheus for Arethusa was a mere jest, compared to that which the Doctor entertained for his favourite fountain.

The new and noble guest, whose arrival so much illustrated these scenes of convalescence and of gaiety, was not at first seen so much at the ordinary, and other places of public resort, as had been the hope of the worthy company assembled. His health and his wound proved an excuse for making his visits to the society few and far between.

But when he did appear, his manners and person were infinitely captivating; and even the carnation-coloured silk-handkerchief, which suspended his wounded arm, together with the paleness and languor which loss of blood had left on his handsome and open countenance, gave a grace to the whole person, which many of the ladies declared irresistible. All contended for his notice, attracted at once by his affability, and piqued by the calm and easy nonchalance with which it seemed to be blended. The scheming and selfish Mowbray, the coarse-minded and brutal Sir Bingo, accustomed to consider themselves, and to be considered, as the first men of the party, sunk into comparative insignificance. But chiefly Lady Penelope threw out the captivations of her wit and her literature; while Lady Binks, trusting to her natural charms, endeavoured equally to attract his notice. The other nymphs of the Spaw held a little back, upon the principle of that politeness, which, at continental hunting parties, affords the first shot at a fine piece of game, to the person of the highest rank present; but the thought throbbed in many a fair bosom, that their ladyships might miss their aim, in spite of the advantages thus allowed them, and that there might then be room for less exalted, but perhaps not less skilful, markswomen, to try their skill.

But while the Earl thus withdrew from public society, it was necessary, at least natural, that he should choose some one with whom to share the solitude of his own apartment; and Mowbray, superior in rank to the half-pay whisky-drinking Captain MacTurk; in dash to Winterblossom, who was broken down, and turned twaddle; and in tact and sense to Sir Bingo Binks, easily manœuvred himself into his lordship's more intimate society; and internally thanking the honest footpad, whose bullet had been the indirect means of secluding his intended victim from all society but his own, he gradually began to feel the way, and prove the strength of his antagonist, at the various games of skill and hazard which he introduced, apparently with the sole purpose of relieving the tædium of a sick-chamber.

Micklewhame, who felt, or affected, the greatest possible interest in his patron's success, and who watched every opportunity to inquire how his schemes advanced, received at first such favourable accounts as made him grin from ear to ear, rub his hands, and chuckle forth such bursts of glee as only the success of triumphant roguery could have extorted from him. Mowbray looked grave, however, and checked his mirth.

"There was something in it after all," he said, "that he could not perfectly understand.—Etherington, an used hand—d—d sharp—up to everything, and yet he lost his money like a baby."

"And what the matter how he loses it, so you win it like a man?" said his legal friend and adviser.

"Why, hang it, I cannot tell," replied Mowbray—"were it not that I think he has scarce the impudence to propose such a thing to succeed, curse me but I should think he was coming the old soldier over me, and keeping up his game.—But no—he can scarce have the impudence to think of that.—I find, however, he has done Wolverine—cleaned out poor Tom—though Tom wrote to me the precise contrary, yet the truth has since come out—Well, I shall avenge him, for I see his lordship is to be had as well as other folks."

"Weel, Mr Mowbray," said the lawyer, in a tone of affected sympathy, "ye ken your own ways best—but the heavens will bless a moderate mind. I would not like to see ye ruin this poor lad *funditus*, that is to say, out and out.—To lose some of the ready will do him no great harm, and maybe give him a lesson he may be the better of as long as he lives—but I wad not, as an honest man, wish you to go deeper—you should spare the lad, Mr Mowbray."

"Who spared *me*, Micklewhame?" said Mowbray, with a look and tone of deep emphasis—"No, no—he must go through the mill—money and money's worth.—His seat is called Oakendale—think of that, Mick—Oakendale! Oh, name of thrice happy augury!—Speak not of mercy, Mick—the squirrels of Oakendale must be dismounted, and learn to go a-foot.—What mercy can this wandering lord of Troy expect among the Greeks?—the Greeks!—I am a very Suliote—the bravest of Greeks.

> I think not of pity, I think not of fear,
> He neither must know who would serve the Vizier.

And necessity, Mick," he concluded, with a tone something altered, "necessity is as unrelenting a leader as any Vizier or Pacha, whom Scanderbeg ever fought with, or Byron has sung."

Micklewhame echoed his patron's ejaculation with a sound betwixt a whine, a chuckle, and a groan; the first being designed to express his pretended pity for the destined victim; the second, his sympathy with his patron's prospects of success; and the third being a sound admonitory of the dangerous courses through which his object was to be pursued.

Suliote as he boasted himself, Mowbray had, soon after this conversation, some reason to admit, that,

> When Greek meets Greek, then comes the tug of war.

The light skirmishing betwixt the parties was ended, and the serious battle commenced with some caution on either side; each perhaps desirous of being master of his opponent's system of tactics, before exposing his own. Piquet, the most beautiful game at which a man can make sacrifice of his fortune, was one at which Mowbray had, for his misfortune perhaps, been accounted, from an early age, a great proficient, and in which the Earl of Etherington, with less experience, proved no novice. They now played for such stakes as Mowbray's state of fortune rendered considerable to him, though his antagonist appeared not to regard the amount. And they played with various success; for, though Mowbray at times returned with a smile of confidence the inquiring looks of his friend Micklewhame, there were other occasions on which he seemed to evade them, as if his own had a sad confession to make in reply.

These alternations, though frequent, did not occupy, after all, many days; for Mowbray, a friend of all hours, spent much of his time in Lord Etherington's apartment, and these few days were days of battle. In the meantime, as his lordship was now sufficiently recovered to join the party at Shaws-Castle, and Miss Mowbray's health being announced as restored, that proposal was renewed, with the addition of a dramatic entertainment, the nature of which we shall afterwards have occasion to explain. Cards were anew issued to all those who had been formerly included in the invitation, and of course to Mr Touchwood, as formerly a resident at the Well, and now in the neighbourhood; it being previously agreed among the ladies, that a Nabob, though sometimes a dingy or damaged commodity, was not to be rashly or unnecessarily neglected. As to the parson, he had been asked, of course, as an old acquaintance of the Mowbray family, not to be left out when the friends of the family were invited on a great scale; but his habits were well known, and it was no more expected that he would leave his manse on such an occasion, than that the kirk should loosen itself from its foundations.

It was after these arrangements had been made, that the Laird of Saint Ronan's suddenly entered Micklewhame's private apartment with looks of exultation. The worthy scribe turned his spectacled nose towards his patron, and holding in one hand the bunch of papers which he had been just perusing, and in the other the tape with which he was about to tie them up again, suspended that operation to await with open eyes and ears the communication of Mowbray.

"I have done him!" he said, exultingly, yet in a tone of voice lowered almost to a whisper; "capotted his lordship for this bout—doubled my capital, Mick, and something more.—Hush, don't interrupt me—we must think of Clara now—she must share the sunshine, should it prove but a blink before a storm.—You know, Mick, these two d—d women have settled that they will have something like a *bal paré* on this occasion, a sort of theatrical exhibition, and that those who like it shall be dressed in character.—I know their meaning—they think Clara has no dress fit for such tom-foolery, and so they hope to eclipse her; Lady Pen, with her old-fashioned, ill-set diamonds, and my Lady Binks, with the new-fashioned finery which she swopt her character for. But Clara shan't be borne down so, by ——. I got that affected slut, Lady Pen's maid, to tell me what her mistress had set her mind on, and she is to wear a Grecian habit, forsooth, like one of Will Allan's eastern subjects.—But here's the rub—there is only one shawl for sale in Edinburgh that is worth shewing off in, and that is at the Gallery of Fashion.—Now, Mick, that shawl must be had for Clara, with the other trangums of muslin and lace, and so forth, which you will find marked in the paper there.—Send instantly and secure it, for, as Lady Penelope writes by to-morrow's post, your order can go by to-night's mail—There is a note for L.100."

From a mechanical habit of never refusing anything, Micklewhame readily took the note, but, having looked at it through his spectacles, he continued to hold it in his hand as he remonstrated with his patron. —"This is a' very kindly meant, Saint Ronan's—very kindly meant; and I wad be the last to say that Miss Clara does na merit respect and kindness at your hand; but I doubt mickle if she would care a bodle for thae braw things. Ye ken yoursell, she seldom alters her fashions.—Odd, she thinks her riding-habit dress aneugh for ony company; and if you were ganging by good looks, so it is—if she had a thought mair colour, poor dear."

"Well, well," said Mowbray, impatiently, "let me alone to reconcile a woman and a fine dress."

"To be sure, ye ken best," said the writer; "but, after a', now, wad it no be better to lay by this hundred pound in Tam Turnpenny's, in case the young lady should want it afterhand, just for a sair foot?"

"You are a fool, Mick; what signifies healing a sore foot, when there will be a broken heart in the case?—No, no—get the things as I desire you—we will blaze them down for one day at least, perhaps it will be the beginning of a proper dash."

"Weel, weel, I wish it may be so," answered Micklewhame; "but this young Earl—hae ye found the weak point?—Can ye get a decerniture against him, with expenses?—that is the question."

"I wish I could answer it," said Mowbray, thoughtfully.—"Confound the fellow—he is a cut above me in rank and in society too—belongs to the great clubs, and is in with the Superlatives and Inaccessibles, and all that sort of folk.—My training has been a peg lower—but, hang it, there are better dogs bred in the kennel than in the parlour. I am up to him, I think—at least I will soon know, Mick, whether I am or no, and that is always one comfort. Never mind—do you execute my commission, and take care you name no names—I must save my little Abigail's reputation."

They parted, Micklewhame to execute his patron's commission—his patron to bring to the test those hopes, the uncertainty of which he could not disguise from his own sagacity.

Trusting to the continuance of his run of luck, Mowbray resolved to bring affairs to a crisis that same evening. Everything seemed in the outset to favour his purpose. They had dined together in Lord Etherington's apartments—his state of health interfered with the circulation of the bottle, and a drizzly autumnal evening rendered walking disagreeable, even had they gone no farther than the private stable where Lord Etherington's horses were kept, under the care of a groom of superior skill. Cards were naturally, almost necessarily, resorted to, as the only alternative for helping away the evening, and piquet was, as formerly, chosen for the game.

Lord Etherington seemed at first indolently careless and indifferent about his play, suffering advantages to escape him, of which, in a more attentive state of mind, he could not have failed to avail himself. Mowbray upbraided him with his carelessness, and proposed a deeper stake, in order to interest him in the game. The young nobleman complied; and in the course of a few hands, the gamesters became both deeply engaged in watching and profiting by the changes of fortune. These were so many, so varied, and so unexpected, that the very souls of the players seemed at length centered in the event of the struggle; and, by dint of doubling stakes, the accumulated sum of a thousand pounds and upwards, upon each side, came to be staked in the issue of the game.—So large a risk included all those funds which Mowbray commanded by his sister's kindness, and nearly all his previous winnings, so to him the alternative was victory or ruin. He could not hide his agitation, however desirous to do so. He drank wine to supply himself with courage—he drank water to cool his agitation; and at length bent himself to play with as much care and attention as he felt himself enabled to command.

In the first part of the game their luck appeared tolerably equal, and the play of both befitting gamesters who had dared to place such a sum on the cast. But, as it drew towards a conclusion, fortune altogether deserted him who stood most in need of her favour, and Mowbray, with silent despair, saw his fate depend on a single trick, and that with every odds against him, for Lord Etherington was elder hand. But how can Fortune's favours secure any one who is not true to himself? —By an infraction of the laws of the game, which could only have been expected from the veriest bungler that ever touched a card, Lord Etherington called a point without shewing it, and by the ordinary rule, Mowbray was entitled to count his own—and in the course of that and the next hand, gained the game and swept the stakes. Lord Etherington shewed chagrin and displeasure, and seemed to think that the rigour of the game had been more insisted upon than in courtesy ought to have been, when men were playing for so small a stake. Mowbray did not understand this logic. A thousand pounds, he said, were in his eyes no nut-shells; the rules of piquet were insisted on by all but boys and women; and for his part, he had rather not play at all than not play the game.

"So it would seem, my dear Mowbray," said the Earl; "for on my soul, I never saw so disconsolate a visage as thine during that unlucky game—it withdrew all my attention from my hand; and I may safely say, your rueful countenance has stood me in a thousand pounds. If I could transfer thy long visage to canvass, I should have both my revenge and my money; for a correct resemblance would be worth not a penny less than the original has cost me."

"You are welcome to your jest, my lord," said Mowbray, "it has been well paid for; and I will serve you in ten thousand at the same rate.—What say you?" he said, taking up and shuffling the cards, "will you do yourself more justice in another game?—Revenge, they say, is sweet."

"I have no appetite for it this evening," said the Earl, gravely; "if I had, Mowbray, you might come by the worse. I do not *always* call a point without shewing it."

"Your lordship is out of humour with yourself for a blunder that might happen to any man—it was as much my good luck as a good hand would have been, and so Fortune be praised."

"But what if with this Fortune had nought to do?" replied Lord Etherington.—"What if, sitting down with an honest fellow and a friend like yourself, Mowbray, a man should rather choose to lose his own money, which he could afford, than to win what it might distress his friend to part with?"

"Supposing a case so far out of supposition, my lord—for, with submission, the allegation is easily made, and is totally incapable of proof—I should say, no one had a right to think for me in such a particular, or to suppose that I played for a higher stake than was convenient."

"And thus the poor devil," replied Lord Etherington, "would lose his money, and run the risk of a quarrel into the boot!—We will try it another way—Suppose this good-humoured and simple-minded gamester had a favour of the deepest import to ask of his friend, and judged it better to prefer his request to a winner than to a loser."

"If this applies to me, my lord," replied Mowbray, "it is necessary I should learn how I can oblige your lordship."

"That is a word soon spoken, but so difficult to be recalled, that I am almost tempted to pause—but yet it must be said.—Mowbray, you have a sister."

Mowbray started.—"I have indeed a sister, my lord; but I can conceive no case in which her name can enter with propriety into our present discussion."

"Again in the menacing mood!" said Lord Etherington, in his former tone; "now, here is a pretty fellow—he would first cut my throat for having won a thousand pounds from me, and then for offering to make his sister a countess."

"A countess, my lord?" said Mowbray. "You are but jesting—You have never even seen Clara Mowbray."

"Perhaps not—but what then?—I may have seen her picture, as Puff says in The Critic, or fallen in love with her from rumour—or, to save farther suppositions, as I see they render you impatient, I may be satisfied with knowing that she is a beautiful and accomplished young lady, with a large fortune."

"What fortune do you mean, my lord?" said Mowbray, recollecting with alarm some claims, which, according to Micklewhame's view of the subject, his sister might form upon his property.—"What estate?—there is nought belongs to our family, save these lands of Saint Ronan's, or what is left of them; and of these I am, my lord, undoubted heir of entail in possession."

"Be it so," said the Earl, "for I have no claim on your mountain realms here, which are, doubtless,

—— renown'd of old
For knights, and squires, and barons bold;

my views respect a much richer, though less romantic domain—a large manor, hight Nettlewood-House, old, but standing in the midst of such glorious oaks—three thousand acres of land, arable, pasture, and woodland, exclusive of the two closes, occupied by Widow Hodge and Goodman Trampclod—manorial rights—mines and minerals—and the devil knows how many good things beside, all lying in the vale of Bever."

"And what has my sister to do with all this?" asked Mowbray, in great surprise.

"Nothing; but that it belongs to her when she becomes Countess of Etherington."

"It is, then, your lordship's property already?"

"No, by Jove! nor can it, unless your sister honours me with her approbation of my suit," replied the Earl.

"This is a sorer puzzle than one of Lady Penelope's charades, my lord," said Mr Mowbray; "I must call in the assistance of the Reverend Mr Chatterley."

"You shall not need," said Lord Etherington; "I will give you the key, but listen to me with patience.—You know that we nobles of

England, less jealous of our sixteen quarters than those on the continent, do not take scorn to line our decayed ermines with a little cloth of gold from the city; and my grandfather was lucky enough to get a wealthy wife, with a halting pedigree,—rather a singular circumstance, considering that her father was a countryman of yours. She had a brother, however, still more wealthy than herself, and who increased his fortune by continuing to carry on the trade which had first enriched his family. At length he summed up his books, washed his hands of commerce, and retired to Nettlewood, to become a gentleman; and here my much respected grand-uncle was seized with the rage of making himself a man of consequence. He tried what marrying a woman of family would do; but he soon found that whatever advantage his family might derive from his doing so, his own condition was but little illustrated. He next resolved to become a man of family himself. His father had left Scotland when very young, and bore, I blush to say, the vulgar name of Scrogie. This hapless dissyllable my uncle carried in person to the herald office in Scotland; but neither Lyon, nor Marchmont, nor Islay, nor Snadoun, neither herald nor pursuivant, would patronize Scrogie.—Scrogie!—there could nothing be made out of it—so that my worthy relative had recourse to the surer side of the house, and began to found his dignity on his mother's name of Mowbray. In this he was much more successful, and I believe some sly fellow stole for him a slip from your own family tree, Mr Mowbray of Saint Ronan's, which, I dare say, you have never missed. At any rate, for his *argent* and *or*, he got a handsome piece of parchment, blazoned with a white lion for Mowbray, to be borne quarterly, with three stunted or scrog-bushes for Scrogie, and became thenceforth Mr Scrogie Mowbray, or rather, as he subscribed himself, Reginald (his former Christian name was Ronald,) S. Mowbray. He had a son who most undutifully laughed at all this, refused the honours of the high name of Mowbray, and insisted on retaining his father's original appellative of Scrogie, to the great annoyance of his said father's ears, and damage of his temper."

"Why, faith, betwixt the two," said Mowbray, "I own I should have preferred my own name, and I think the old gentleman's taste rather better than the young one's."

"True, but both were wilful, absurd originals, with a happy obstinacy of temper, whether derived from Mowbray or Scrogie I know not, but which led them so often into opposition, that the offended father, Reginald S. Mowbray, turned his recusant son Scrogie fairly out of doors; and the fellow would have paid for his plebeian spirit with a vengeance, had he not found refuge with a surviving partner of the original Scrogie of all, who still carried on the lucrative branch of traffic by which the family had been first enriched. I mention these particulars to account, in so far as I can, for the singular predicament in which I now find myself placed."

"Proceed, my lord," said Mr Mowbray; "there is no denying the singularity of your story, and I presume you are quite serious in giving me such an extraordinary detail."

"Entirely so, upon my honour—and a most serious matter it is, as you will presently find. When my worthy uncle, Mr S. Mowbray, (for I will not call him Scrogie even in the grave,) paid his debt to nature, everybody concluded he would be found to have disinherited his son, the unfilial Scrogie, and so far everybody was right—But it was also generally believed that he would settle the estate on my father, Lord Etherington, the son of his sister, and therein every one was wrong. For my excellent grand-uncle had pondered with himself, that the favoured name of Mowbray would take no advantage, and attain no additional elevation, if his estate of Nettlewood, (otherwise called Mowbray-Park,) should descend to our family without any condition; and with the assistance of a sharp attorney, he settled it on me, then a school-boy, *on condition* that I should, before attaining the age of twenty-five complete, take unto myself in holy wedlock a young lady of good fame, of the name of Mowbray, and, by preference, of the house of Saint Ronan's, should a damsel of that house exist.—Now my riddle is read."

"And a very extraordinary one it is," replied Mowbray, thoughtfully.

"Confess the truth," said Lord Etherington, laying his hand on his shoulder; "you think the story will bear a grain of a scruple of doubt, if not a whole scruple itself?"

"At least, my lord," answered Mowbray, "your lordship will allow, that, being Miss Mowbray's only near relation, and sole guardian, I may, without offence, pause upon a suit for her hand, made under such odd circumstances."

"If you have the least doubt either respecting my rank or fortune, I can give, of course, the most satisfactory references," said the Earl of Etherington.

"That I can easily believe, my lord," said Mowbray; "nor do I in the least fear deception, where detection would be so easy. Your lordship's proceedings towards me, too, (with a conscious glance at the bills he still held in his hand,) have, I admit, been such as to intimate some such deep cause of interest as you have been pleased to state. But it seems strange that your lordship should have permitted years to glide away, without so much as inquiring after the young lady, who, I believe, is the only person qualified, as your grand-uncle's will requires, with whom you can form an alliance. It appears to me, that long before now, this matter ought to have been investigated; and that, even now, it would have been more natural and more decorous to have at least seen my sister before proposing for her hand."

"On the first point, my dear Mowbray," said Lord Etherington, "I am free to own to you, that, without meaning your sister the least affront, I would have got rid of this clause if I could; for every man would fain choose a wife for himself, and I feel no hurry to marry at all. But the rogue-lawyers, after taking fees, and keeping me in hand for years, have at length roundly told me the clause must be complied with, or Nettlewood must have another master. So I thought it best to come down here in person, in order to address the fair lady; but as accident has hitherto prevented my seeing her, and as I found in her brother a man who understands the world, I hope you will not think the worse of me, that I have endeavoured in the outset to make you my friend. Truth is, I shall be twenty-five in the course of a month; and without your favour, and the opportunities which only you can afford me, that seems a short time to woo and win a lady of Miss Mowbray's merit."

"And what is the alternative if you do not form this proposed alliance, my lord?" said Mowbray.

"The bequest of my grand-uncle lapses," said the Earl, "and fair Nettlewood, with its old house, and older oaks, manorial rights, and all, devolves on a certain cousin-german of mine, whom Heaven of his mercy confound!"

"You have left yourself little time to prevent such an event, my lord," said Mowbray; "but things being as I now see them, you shall have what interest I can give you in the affair.—We must stand, however, on more equal terms, my lord—I will condescend so far as to allow it would have been inconvenient for me at this moment to have *lost* that game, but I cannot in the circumstances think of acting as if I had fairly won it. We must draw stakes, my lord."

"Not a word of that, if you really mean me kindly, my dear Mowbray. The blunder was a real one, for I was thinking, as you may suppose, on other things than the shewing my point—All was fairly lost and won.—I hope I shall have opportunities of offering real services, which may perhaps give me some right to your partial regard—at present we are on an equal footing on all sides—perfectly so."

"If your lordship thinks so," said Mowbray,—and then passing rapidly to what he felt he could say with more confidence,—"Indeed, at any rate, no personal obligation to myself could prevent my doing my full duty as guardian to my sister."

"Unquestionably, I desire nothing else," replied the Earl of Etherington.

"I must therefore understand that your lordship is quite serious in your proposal; and that it is not to be withdrawn, even if upon acquaintance with Miss Mowbray, you should not perhaps think her so deserving of your lordship's attentions, as report may have spoken her."

"Mr Mowbray," replied the Earl, "the treaty between you and me shall be as definitive as if I were a sovereign prince, demanding in marriage the sister of a neighbouring sovereign, whom, according to royal etiquette, he neither has seen nor could see. I have been quite frank with you, and have stated to you that my present motives for entering upon negotiation are not personal, but territorial; when I know Miss Mowbray, I have no doubt they will be otherwise. I have heard she is beautiful."

"Something of the palest, my lord," answered Mowbray.

"A fine complexion is the first attraction which is lost in the world of fashion, and that which it is easiest to replace."

"Dispositions, my lord, may differ," said Mowbray, "without faults on either side. I presume your lordship has inquired into my sister's. She is amiable, accomplished, sensible, and high-spirited; but yet——"

"I understand you, Mr Mowbray, and will spare you the pain of speaking out. I have heard Miss Mowbray is in some respects—particular; to use a broader word—a little whimsical.—No matter. She will have the less to learn when she becomes a countess, and a woman of fashion."

"Are you serious, my lord?" said Mowbray.

"I am—and I will speak my mind still more plainly. I have good temper, and excellent spirits, and can endure a good deal of singularity in those I live with. I have no doubt your sister and I will live happily together—But in case it should prove otherwise, arrangements may be made previously, which will enable us to live happily apart.—My own estate is large, and Nettlewood will bear dividing."

"Nay, then," said Mowbray, "I have little more to say—nothing indeed remains for inquiry, so far as your lordship is concerned.—But my sister must have free liberty of choice—so far as I am concerned, your lordship's suit has my interest."

"And I trust we may consider it as a done thing?"

"With Clara's approbation—certainly," answered Mowbray.

"I trust there is no chance of personal repugnance on the young lady's part?"

"I anticipate nothing of the kind, my lord, as I presume there is no reason for any; but young ladies will be capricious, and if Clara, after I have done and said all that a brother ought to do, should remain repugnant, there is a point in the exertion of my influence which it would be cruelty to pass."

The Earl of Etherington walked a turn through the apartment, then paused, and said, in a grave and doubtful tone, "In the meanwhile, I am bound, and the young lady is free, Mowbray? Is this quite fair?"

"It is what happens in every case, my lord, where a gentleman proposes for a lady," answered Mowbray; "he must remain, of course, bound by his offer, until, within a reasonable time, it is accepted or rejected. It is not my fault that your lordship has declared your wishes to me, before ascertaining Clara's inclination. But as yet the matter is between ourselves—I make you welcome to draw back if you think proper. Clara Mowbray needs not push for a catch-match."

"Nor do I desire," said the young nobleman, "any time to reconsider the resolution which I have confided to you. I am not in the least fearful that I shall change my mind on seeing your sister, and I am ready to stand by the proposal which I have made to you.—If, however, you feel so extremely delicately on my account," he continued, "I can see and even converse with Miss Mowbray at this fete of yours, without the necessity of being at all presented to her—The character which I have assumed in a manner obliges me to wear a mask."

"Certainly," said the Laird of Saint Ronan's, "and I am glad, for both our sakes, your lordship thinks of taking a little law upon this occasion."

"I shall profit nothing by it," said the Earl; "my doom is fixed before I start—but if this mode of managing the matter will save your conscience, I have no objection to it—it cannot consume much time, which is what I have to look to."

They then shook hands and parted, without any farther discourse which could interest the reader.

Mowbray was glad to find himself alone, in order to think over what had happened, and to ascertain the state of his own mind, which at present was puzzling even to himself. He could not but feel that much greater advantages of every kind might accrue to himself and his family from the alliance of the wealthy young Earl, than could have been derived from any share of his spoils which he had proposed to gain by superior address in play, or greater skill on the turf. But his pride was hurt when he recollected, that he had placed himself entirely in Lord Etherington's power; and the escape from absolute ruin which he had made, solely by the sufferance of his opponent, had nothing in it consolatory to his wounded feelings. He was lowered in his own eyes, when he recollected how completely the proposed victim of his ingenuity had seen through his schemes, and only abstained from baffling them entirely, because to do so suited best with his own. There was a shade of suspicion, too, which he could not entirely eradicate from his mind.—What occasion had this young nobleman to preface, by the voluntary loss of a brace of thousands, a proposal which must have been acceptable in itself, without any such sacrifice? And why should he, after all, have been so eager to secure his accession to the proposed alliance, before he had even seen the lady who was the object of it? However hurried for time, he might have waited the event at least of the entertainment at Shaws-Castle, at which Clara was necessarily obliged to make her appearance?—Yet such conduct, however unusual, was equally inconsistent with any sinister intentions; since the sacrifice of a large sum of money, and the declaration of his views upon a portionless young lady of family, could scarcely be the preface to any unfair practice. So that, upon the whole, Mowbray settled, that what was uncommon in the Earl's conduct arose from the hasty and eager disposition of a rich young Englishman, to whom money is of little consequence, and who is too headlong in pursuit of the favourite plan of the moment, to proceed in the most rational or most ordinary manner. If, however, there should prove anything farther in the matter than he could at present discover, Mowbray promised himself that the utmost circumspection on his part could not fail to discover it, and that in full time to prevent any ill consequences to his sister or himself.

Immersed in such cogitations, he avoided the inquisitive presence of Mr Micklewhame, who, as usual, had been watching for him to learn how matters were going on; and although it was now late, he mounted his horse, and rode hastily to Shaws-Castle. On the way, he deliberated with himself whether to mention to his sister the application which had been made to him, in order to prepare her to receive the young Earl as a suitor, favoured with her brother's approbation. "But no, no, no;" such was the result of his contemplation. "She might take it into her head that his thoughts were bent less upon having her for a countess, than on obtaining possession of his granduncle's estate.—We must keep quiet until her personal appearance and accomplishments may appear at least to have some influence upon his choice.—We must say nothing till this blessed entertainment has been given and received."

Chapter Six

A LETTER

Has he so long held out with me untired,
And stops he now for breath?—Well—Be it so.
Richard III

MOWBRAY had no sooner left the Earl's apartment, than the latter commenced an epistle to a friend and associate, which we lay before the readers, as best calculated to illustrate the views and motives of the writer. It was addressed to Captain Jekyl, of the —— regiment of Guards, at the Green Dragon, Harrogate, and was of the following tenor.—

"DEAR HARRY,

"I have expected you here these ten days past, anxiously as ever man was looked for; and have now to charge your absence as high treason to your sworn allegiance. Surely you do not presume, like one of Napoleon's new-made monarchs, to grumble for independence, as if your greatness were of your own making, or as if I had picked you out of the whole Saint James's coffee-house to hold my back-hand for your sake, forsooth, not for my own? Wherefore, lay aside all your own proper business, be it the pursuit of dowagers, or the plucking of pigeons, and instantly repair to this place, where I may speedily want your assistance.—*May* want it, said I? Why, most negligent of friends and allies, I *have* wanted it already, and that when it might have done me yeoman's service. Know that I have had an affair since I came hither—have got hurt myself, and have nearly shot my friend; and if I had, I might have been hanged for it, for want of Harry Jekyl to bear witness in my favour. I was so far on my road to this place, when, not choosing, for certain reasons, to pass through the old village, I struck by a foot-path into the woods which separate it from the new Spaw, leaving my carriage and people to go the carriage-way. I had not walked half a mile when I heard the footsteps of some one behind, and, looking round, what should I behold but the face in the world which I most cordially hate and abhor—I mean that which stands on the shoulders of my right trusty and well-beloved cousin and counsellor, Saint Francis. He seemed as much confounded as I was at our unexpected meeting; and it was a minute ere he found breath to demand what I did in Scotland, contrary to my promise, as he was pleased to express it.—I retaliated, and charged him with being here, in contradiction to his.—He justified, and said he had only come down upon the express information that I was upon my road to Saint Ronan's.—Now, Harry, how the devil should he have known this, hadst thou been quite faithful? for I am sure, to no ear but thine own did I breathe a whisper of my purpose—Next, with the insolent assumption of superiority, which he founds on what he calls the rectitude of his purpose, he proposed we should both withdraw from a neighbourhood into which we could bring nothing but wretchedness.—I have told you how difficult it is to cope with the calm and resolute manner that the devil gifts him with on such occasions; but I was determined he should not carry the day this time. I saw no chance for it, however, but to put myself into a towering passion, which, thank Heaven, I can always do on short notice.—I charged him with having imposed formerly on my youth, and made himself judge of my rights; and I accompanied my defiance with the strongest terms of irony and contempt, as well as with demand of instant satisfaction. I had my travelling pistols with me, (*et pour cause*,) and, to my surprise, my gentleman was equally provided.—For fair play's sake, I made him take one of my pistols —right Kuchenritters—a brace of balls in each, but that circumstance I forgot.—He would fain have argued the matter a little longer; but I thought at the time, and think still, that the best arguments which he and I can exchange, must come from the point of the sword, or the muzzle of the pistol.—We fired nearly together, and I think both dropped—I am sure I did, but recovered in a minute, with a damaged arm and a scratch on the temple—it was the last which stunned me —so much for double-loaded pistols.—My friend was invisible, and I had nothing for it but to walk to the Spaw, bleeding all the way like a calf, and tell a raw-head and bloody-bone story about a footpad, which, but for my earldom, and my gory locks, no one would have believed.

"Shortly after, when I had been installed in a sick room, I had the mortification to learn, that my own impatience had brought all this mischief upon me, at a moment when I had every chance of getting rid of my friend without trouble, had I but let him go on his own errand; for it seems he had an appointment that morning with a booby Baronet, who is said to be a bullet-slitter, and would perhaps have rid me of Saint Francis without any trouble or risk on my part. Meantime, his non-appearance at this rendezvous has placed Master Francis Tyrrel, as he chooses to call himself, in the worst odour possible with the gentry at the Spring, who have denounced him as a coward and no gentleman.—What to think of the business myself, I know not; and I much want your assistance to see what can have become of this fellow, who, like a spectre of ill omen, has so often thwarted and baffled my best plans. My own confinement renders me inactive, though my wound is fast healing. Dead he cannot be; for, had he been mortally wounded, we should have heard of him somewhere or other—he could not have vanished from the earth like a bubble of the elements. Sound he cannot be; for, besides that I am sure I saw him stagger and drop, firing his pistol as he fell, I know him well enough to swear, that, had he not been severely wounded, he would have first pestered me with his accursed presence and assistance, and then walked forward with his usual composure to settle matters with Sir Bingo Binks. No—no—Saint Francis is none of those who leave such jobs half finished—it is but doing him justice to say, he has the devil's courage to back his own deliberate impertinence. But then, if wounded severely, he must be still in this neighbourhood, and probably in concealment—this is what I must discover, and I want your assistance in my inquiries among the natives.—Haste hither, Harry, as ever you look for good at my hand.

"A good player, Harry, always studies to make the best of bad cards—and so I have endeavoured to turn my wound to some account; and it has given me the opportunity to secure Monsieur le Frere in my interests. You say very truly, that it is of consequence to me to know the character of this new actor on the disordered scene of my adventures.—Know, then, he is that most incongruous of all monsters—a Scotch buck—how far from being buck of the season you may easily judge. Every point of national character is opposed to the pretensions of this luckless race, when they attempt to take on them a personage which is assumed with so much facility by their brethren of the Isle of Saints. They are a shrewd people, indeed, but so destitute of ease, grace, and pliability of manners, and insinuation of address, that they eternally seem to suffer actual misery in their attempts to look gay and careless. Then their pride heads them back at one turn, their poverty at another, their pedantry at a third, their *mauvaise honte* at a fourth; and with so many obstacles to make them bolt off the course, it is positively impossible they should win the plate. No, Harry, it is the grave folks that have to fear a Caledonian invasion—they will make no conquests in the world of fashion. Excellent bankers they may be, for they are eternally calculating how to add interest to principal;—good soldiers; for they are, if not such heroes as they would be thought, as brave, I suppose, as their neighbours, and much more amenable to discipline;—lawyers they are born; indeed every country gentleman is bred one, and their patient and crafty disposition enables them, in other lines, to submit to hardships which others could not bear, and avail themselves of advantages which others would let pass under their noses unavailingly. But assuredly Heaven did not form the Caledonian for the gay world; and his efforts at ease, grace, and gaiety, resemble only the clumsy gambols of the ass in the fable. Yet he has his sphere too, (in his own country only,) where the character which he assumes is allowed to pass current. This Mowbray, now—this brother-in-law of mine, might do pretty well at a Northern Meeting, or the Leith races, where he could mingle with brother thanes and give five minutes to the sport of the day, and the next half hour to county politics, or to farming; but it is scarce necessary to tell you, Harry, that this will not pass on the better side of the Tweed.

"Yet, for all I have told you, this trout was not easily tickled; nor should I have made much of him, had he not, in the plenitude of his northern conceit, entertained that notion of my being a good subject of plunder, which you had contrived (blessing on your contriving brain) to insinuate into him by means of Wolverine. He commenced this hopeful experiment, and, as you must have anticipated, caught a Tartar with a vengeance. Of course, I used my victory only so far as to secure his interest in accomplishing my principal object; and yet, I could see my gentleman's pride was so much injured in the course of the negotiation, that not all the advantages which the match offered to his damned family, were able to subdue the chagrin arising from his defeat. He did gulp it down though, and we are friends and allies, for the present at least—not so cordially so, however, as to lead me to trust him with the whole of the strangely complicated tale. The circumstance of the will it was necessary to communicate, as affording a sufficiently strong reason for urging my suit; and the disclosure enabled me for the present to dispense with farther confidence.

"You will observe, that I stand by no means secure; and besides the chance of my cousin's re-appearance—a certain event, unless he is worse than I dare hope for—I have perhaps to expect the fantastic repugnance of Clara herself, or some sulky freak on her brother's part. —In a word—and let it be such a one as conjurors raise the devil with —Harry Jekyl, I *want* you.

"As well knowing the nature of my friend, I can assure him that his own interest, as well as mine, may be advanced by your coming hither on duty. Here is a blockhead, whom I already mentioned, Sir Bingo Binks, with whom something may be done worth *your* while, though scarce worth *mine*. The Baronet is a perfect buzzard, and when I came here he was under Mowbray's training. But the awkward Scotchman had plucked half-a-dozen pen-feathers from his wing with so little precaution, that the Baronet had become frightened and shy, and is now in the act of rebelling against Mowbray, whom he both hates and fears—the least backing from a knaving hand like you, and the bird becomes your own, feathers and all.—Moreover,

> —— by my life,
> This Bingo hath a mighty pretty wife.

A lovely woman, Harry—rather plump, and above the middle size—quite your taste—A Juno in beauty, looking with such scorn on her husband, whom she despises and hates, and looking, as if she *could* look so differently on any one whom she might like better, that, on my faith, 'twere sin not to give her occasion. If you please to venture your luck, either with the knight or the lady, you shall have fair play, and no interference—that is, provided you appear upon this summons; for, otherwise, I may be so placed, that the affairs of the knight and the lady may fall under my own immediate cognizance. And so, Harry, if you wish to profit by these hints, you had best make haste, as well for your own concerns, as to assist me in mine.—Yours, Harry, as you behave yourself,

"ETHERINGTON."

Having finished this eloquent and instructive epistle, the young Earl demanded the attendance of his own valet Solmes, whom he charged to put it into the post-office without delay, and with his own hand.

Chapter Seven

THEATRICALS

> ——The play's the thing.
> *Hamlet*

THE IMPORTANT DAY had now arrived, the arrangement for which had for some time occupied all the conversation and thoughts of the good company at the Well of Saint Ronan's. To give it, at the same time, a degree of novelty and consequence, Lady Penelope Penfeather had long since suggested to Mr Mowbray, that the more gifted and accomplished part of the guests might contribute to furnish out entertainment for the rest, by acting a few scenes of some popular drama; an accomplishment in which her self-conceit assured her that she was peculiarly qualified to excel. Mr Mowbray, who seemed on this occasion to have thrown the reins entirely into her ladyship's hands, made no objection to the plan which she proposed, excepting that the old-fashioned hedges and walks of the garden at Shaws-Castle must necessarily serve for stage and scenery, as there was no time to fit up the old hall for the exhibition of the proposed theatricals.

But upon inquiry among the company, this plan was wrecked upon the ordinary shelve, the difficulty namely of finding performers who would consent to assume the lower characters of the drama. For the first parts there were candidates more than enough; but most of these were greatly too high-spirited to play the fool, excepting they were permitted to top the part. Then amongst the few unambitious underlings, who could be coaxed or cajoled to undertake subordinate characters, there were so many bad memories, and short memories, and treacherous memories, that at length the plan was resigned in despair.

A substitute, proposed by Lady Penelope, was next considered. It was proposed to act what the Italians call a Comedy of Character; that is, not an exact drama, in which the actors deliver what is set down for them by the author; but one in which, the plot having been previously fixed upon, and a few striking scenes adjusted, the actors are expected to supply the dialogue extempore, or, as Petruchio says, from their mother wit. This is an amusement which affords much entertainment in Italy, particularly in the state of Venice, where the characters of their drama have been long since all previously fixed, and are handed down by tradition; and this species of drama, though rather belonging to the masque than the theatre, is distinguished by the name of Commedia dell' arte.* But the shame-faced character of Britons is still more alien to a species of display, where there is a constant and extemporaneous demand for wit, or the sort of ready small talk which supplies its place, than to the regular exhibitions of the drama, where the author, standing responsible for language and sentiment, leaves to the presenters of the scene only the trouble of finding enunciation and action.

But the ardent and active spirit of Lady Penelope, still athirst after novelty, though baffled in her two first projects, brought forward a third, in which she was more successful. This was the proposal to combine a certain number, at least, of the guests, properly dressed for the occasion, as representing some well-known historical or dramatic characters, in a group, having reference to history, or to a scene of the drama. In this representation, which may be called playing a picture, action, even pantomimical action, was not expected; and all that was required of the performers, was to throw themselves into such a group as might express a marked and striking point of an easily remembered scene, but when the actors are at a pause, and without either speech or motion. In this species of representation there was no tax, either on the invention or memory of those who might undertake parts; and

* See Mr William Stewart Rose's very interesting Letters from the North of Italy, Vol. I. Letter XXX., where this curious subject is treated with the information and precision which distinguish that accomplished author.

what recommended it still farther to the good company, there was no marked difference betwixt the hero and heroine of the group, and the less distinguished characters by whom they were attended on the stage; and every one who had confidence in a handsome shape and a becoming dress, might hope, though standing in not quite so broad and favourable a light as the principal personages, to draw, nevertheless, a considerable portion of attention and applause. This motion, therefore, that the company, or such of them as might choose to appear properly dressed for the occasion, should form themselves into one or more groups, which might be renewed and varied as often as they pleased, was hailed and accepted as a bright idea, which assigned to every one a share of the importance attached to its probable success.

Mowbray, on his side, promised to contrive some arrangement which should separate the actors in this mute drama from the spectators, and enable the former to vary the amusement, by withdrawing themselves from the scene, and again appearing upon it under a different and new combination. This plan of exhibition, where fine clothes and affected attitudes supplied all draughts upon fancy or talent, was highly agreeable to most of the ladies present; and even Lady Binks, whose discontent seemed proof against every effort that could be proposed to soothe it, acquiesced in the project, with perfect indifference indeed, but with something less of sullenness than usual.

It now only remained to rummage the circulating library, for some piece of sufficient celebrity to command attention, and which should be at the same time suited to the execution of their project. Bell's British Theatre, Miller's Modern and Ancient Drama, and about twenty odd volumes, in which stray tragedies and comedies were associated, like the passengers in a mail-coach, without the least attempt at selection or arrangement, were all examined in the course of their researches. But Lady Penelope declared loftily and decidedly for Shakespeare, as the author whose immortal works were fresh in every one's recollection. Shakespeare was therefore chosen, and from his works the Midsummer Night's Dream was selected, as the play which afforded the greatest variety of characters, and most scope of course for the intended representation. An active competition presently occurred among the greater part of the company, for such copies of the Midsummer Night's Dream, or the volume of Shakespeare containing it, as could be got in the neighbourhood; for, notwithstanding Lady Penelope's declaration, that every one who could read had Shakespeare's plays by heart, it appeared that such of his dramas as have not kept possession of the stage, were very little known at Saint Ronan's, save among those people who are emphatically called readers.

The adjustment of the parts was the first subject of consideration, so soon as those who intended to assume characters had refreshed their recollection on the subject of the piece. Theseus was unanimously assigned to Mowbray, the giver of the entertainment, and therefore justly entitled to represent the Duke of Athens. The costume of an Amazonian, crest and plume, a tucked-up vest, and a tight buskin of sky-blue silk, buckled with diamonds, reconciled Lady Binks to the part of Hippolyta. The superior stature of Miss Mowbray to Lady Penelope, made it necessary that the former should perform the part of Helena, and her ladyship rest contented with the shrewish character of Hermia. It was resolved to compliment the young Earl of Etherington with the part of Lysander, which, however, his lordship declined, and, preferring comedy to tragedy, refused to appear in any other character than that of the magnanimous Bottom; and he gave them such a humorous specimen of his quality in that part, that all were delighted at once with his condescension in assuming, and his skill in performing, the presenter of Pyramus.

The part of Egeus was voted to Captain MacTurk, whose obstinacy in refusing to appear in any other than the full Highland garb, had nearly disconcerted the whole affair. At length this obstacle was got over, on the authority of Childe Harold, who remarks the similarity betwixt the Highland and Grecian costume; and the company, dispensing with the difference of colour, voted the Captain's variegated kilt of the MacTurk tartan to be the kirtle of a Grecian mountaineer, Egeus to be a Mainot, and the Captain to be Egeus. Chatterley and the painter, walking gentlemen by profession, agreed to walk through the parts of Demetrius and Lysander, the two Athenian lovers; and Mr Winterblossom, after many excuses, was bribed by Lady Penelope with an antique, or supposed antique cameo, to play the part of Philostratus, master of the revels, providing his gout would permit him to remain so long upon the turf, which was to be their stage.

Muslin trowsers, adorned with spangles, a voluminous turban of silver gauze, and wings of the same, together with an embroidered slipper, with a pretty ankle peeping out above it, converted at once Miss Digges into Oberon, the King of Shadows, whose sovereign gravity, however, was somewhat indifferently represented by the silly gaiety of Miss in her Teens, and the uncontrolled delight which she felt in her fine clothes. A younger sister represented Titania; and two or three subordinate elves were selected, among families attending the salutiferous fountain, who were easily persuaded to let their children figure in fine clothes at so juvenile an age, though they shook their head at Miss Digges and her pantaloons, and no less at the liberal display of Lady Binks's right leg, with which the Amazonian garb gratified the public of Saint Ronan's.

Dr Quackleben was applied to to play Wall, by the assistance of such a wooden horse, or screen, as clothes are usually dried upon; the old Attorney stood for Lion; and the other characters of Bottom's drama were easily found among the unnamed frequenters of the Spring. Dressed rehearsals, and so forth, went merrily on—all voted there was a play fitted.

But even the Doctor's eloquence could not press Mrs Blower into the scheme, although she was particularly wanted to present Thisbe.

"Truth is," she replied, "I dinna greatly like stage-plays. John Blower, honest man, as sailors are aye for some spree or another, wad take me ance to see ane Mrs Siddons—I thought we should hae been crushed to death before we gat in—a' my things riven aff my back, forbye the four lily-white shillings that it cost us—and than in came three frightsome carlines wi' besoms, and they wad bewitch a sailor's wife—I was lang eneugh there—and out I wad be, and out John Blower gat me, but wi' nae sma' fight and fend.—My Lady Penelope Penfitter, and the great folk, may just take it as they like; but in my mind, Dr Cacklehen, it's a mere blasphemy for folk to gar themselves look otherwise than their Maker made them."

"You mistake the matter entirely, my dear Mrs Blower," said the Doctor; "there is nothing serious intended—a mere *placebo*—just a divertisement to cheer the spirits, and assist the effect of the waters—cheerfulness is a great promoter of health."

"Dinna tell me o' health, Dr Kittlepin!—Can it be for the puir body McDurk's health to gang about like a tobacconist's sign in a frosty morning, with his poor wizened houghs as blue as a blawart?—weel I wot he is a humbling spectacle. Or can it gie onybody health or pleasure either to see your ainsell, Doctor, ganging about wi' a claise screen tied to your back, covered wi' paper, and painted like a stane and lime wa'?—I'll gang to see nane of their vanities, Dr Kittlehen; and if there is nae other decent body to take care o' me, as I dinna like to sit a haill afternoon by mysell, I'll e'en gae doun to Mr Sowerbrowst the maltster's—he is a pleasant, sensible man, and a sponsible man in the world."

"Confound Sowerbrowst," thought the Doctor; "if I had thought he was to come across me in my line of practice, he should not have got the better of his dispepsy so easily.—My dear Mrs Blower," he continued, but aloud, "it is a foolish affair enough, I must confess; but every person of style and fashion at the Well has settled to attend this exhibition; there has been nothing else talked of for this month through the whole country, and it will be a year before it is forgotten. And I would have you consider how ill it will look, my dear Mrs

Blower, to stay away—nobody will believe you had a card—no, not though you were to hang it round your neck like a label round a vial of tincture, Mrs Blower."

"If ye thought *that*, Doctor Kickherben," said the widow, alarmed at the idea of losing cast, "I wad e'en gang to the show, like other folk; sinful and shameful if it be, let them that make the sin bear the shame. But then I will put on nane of their Popish disguises—me that has lived in North Leith, baith wife and lass, for I shanna say how mony years, and has a character to keep up baith with saint and sinner.—And then, whase to take care of me, since you are gaun to make a lime-and-stane wa' of yoursell, Doctor Kickinben?"

"My dear Mrs Blower, if such is your determination, I will not make a wall of myself. Her ladyship must consider my profession—she must understand it is my function to look after my patients, in preference to all the stage-plays in this world—and to attend on a case like yours, Mrs Blower, it is my duty to sacrifice, were it called for, the whole drama, from Shakespeare to O'Keefe."

On hearing this magnanimous resolution, the widow's heart was greatly cheered; for, in fact, she might probably have considered the Doctor's perseverance in the plan, of which she had expressed such high disapprobation, as little less than a symptom of absolute defection from his allegiance. By an accommodation, therefore, which suited both parties, it was settled that the Doctor should attend his loving widow to Shaws-Castle without mask or mantle; and that the painted screen should be transferred from Quackleben's back to the broad shoulders of a briefless barrister, well qualified for the part of Wall, since the composition of his skull might have rivalled in solidity the mortar and stone of the most approved builder.

We must not pause to dilate upon the various labours of body and spirit which preceded the intervening space, betwixt the settlement of this gay scheme, and the time appointed to carry it into execution. We will not attempt to describe how the wealthy, by letter and by commissioners, urged their researches through the stores of the Gallery of Fashion for specimens of oriental finery—how they that were scant of diamonds supplied their place with paste and Bristol stone—how the country dealers were driven out of patience by the demand for goods of which they had never before heard the name—and, lastly, how the busy fingers of the more economical damsels twisted handkerchiefs into turbans, and converted petticoats into pantaloons, shaped and sewed, cut and clipped, and spoiled many a decent gown and petticoat, to produce something like a Grecian habit.—Who can describe the wonders wrought by active needles and scissars, aided by thimbles and thread, upon silver gauze, and sprigged muslin? or who can shew how, if the fair nymphs of the Spring did not entirely succeed in attaining the desired resemblance to heathen Greeks, they at least contrived to get rid of all similitude to sober Christians.

Neither is it necessary to dwell upon the various schemes of conveyance which were resorted to, in order to transfer the beau monde of the Spaw to the scene of revelry at Shaws-Castle. These were various as the fortunes and pretensions of the owners; from the lordly curricle, with its outriders, to the humble taxed cart, nay, untaxed cart, which conveyed the personages of less rank. For the latter, indeed, the two post-chaises at the Inn seemed converted into hourly stages, so often did they come and go between the Hotel and the Castle—a glad day for the postilions, and a day of martyrdom for the poor post-horses; so seldom is it that every department of any society, however constituted, can be injured or benefited by the same occurrence.

Such, indeed, was the penury of vehicular conveyance, that applications were made in manner most humble, even to Meg Dods herself, entreating she would permit her old whisky to *ply* (for such might have been the phrase) at Saint Ronan's Well, for that day only, and that upon good cause shewn. But not for sordid lucre would the undaunted spirit of Meg compound her feud with her neighbours of the detested Well. "Her carriage," she briefly replied, "was engaged for her ain guest and the minister, and deil anither body's fit should gang intill't. Let every herring hing by its ain head." And, accordingly, at the duly appointed hour, creaked forth the leathern convenience, in which, carefully screened by the curtains from the gaze of the fry of the village, sat Nabob Touchwood, in the costume of an Indian merchant, or Shroff, as they are termed. The clergyman would not, perhaps, have been so punctual, had not a set of notes and messages from his friend at the Cleikum Inn, following each other as thick as the papers which decorate the tail of a school-boy's kite, kept him so continually on the alert from daybreak till noon, that Mr Touchwood found him completely dressed; and the whisky was only delayed for about ten minutes before the door of the manse, a space employed by Mr Cargill in searching for the spectacles, which were actually discovered upon his own nose.

At length, seated by the side of his new friend, Mr Cargill arrived safe at Shaws-Castle, the gate of which mansion was surrounded by a screaming group of children, so extravagantly delighted at seeing the strange figures to whom each successive carriage gave birth, that even the stern brow and well-known voice of Johnnie Tirlsneck, the beadle, though stationed in the court on express purpose, was not equal to the task of controlling them. These noisy intruders, however, who, it was believed, were somewhat favoured by Clara Mowbray, were excluded from the court which opened before the house, by a couple of grooms or helpers armed with their whips, and could only salute, with their shrill and wondering hailing, the various personages, as they passed down a short avenue leading from the exterior gate.

The Cleikum Nabob and the Minister were greeted with shouts not the least clamorous; which the former merited by the ease with which he wore the white turban, and the latter, by the infrequency of his appearance in public, and both, by the singular association of a decent clergyman of the church of Scotland, in a dress more old-fashioned than could now be produced in the General Assembly, walking arm in arm, and seemingly in the most familiar terms, with a Parsee merchant. They stopped a moment at the gate of the court-yard to admire the front of the old mansion, which had been disturbed with so unusual a scene of gaiety.

Shaws-Castle, though so named, presented no appearance of defence; and the present edifice had never been designed for more than the accommodation of a peaceful family, having a low, heavy front, loaded with some of that meretricious ornament, which, uniting, or rather confounding, the Gothic and Grecian architecture, was much used during the reigns of James VI. of Scotland, and his unfortunate son. The court formed a small square, two sides of which were occupied by such buildings as were required for the family, and the third by the stables, the only part of the edifice which had received any repairs, the present Mr Mowbray having put them into excellent order. The fourth side of the square was shut up by a screen wall, through which a door opened to the short avenue; the whole being a kind of structure which may be still found on those old Scottish properties, where a rage to render their place *Parkish*, as was at one time the prevailing phrase, has not induced the owners to pull down the venerable and sheltering appendages with which their wiser fathers had screened their mansion, and to lay the whole open to the keen north-east; much after the fashion of a spinster of fifty, who chills herself to gratify the public, by an exposure of her thin red elbows, and shrivelled neck and bosom.

A double door, thrown hospitably open on the present occasion, admitted the company into a dark and low hall, where Mowbray himself, wearing the under dress of Theseus, but not having yet assumed his ducal cap and robes, stood to receive his guests with due courtesy, and to indicate to each the road allotted to him. For those who were to take share in the representation of the morning, were conducted to an old saloon, destined for a green-room, and which communicated with a series of apartments on the right, hastily fitted with accommodations for arranging and completing their toilette;

while those who took no part in the intended drama, were ushered to the left, into a large, unfurnished, and long disused dining parlour, where a sashed door opened into the gardens, crossed with yew and holly hedges, still trimmed and clipped by the old grey-headed gardener, upon those principles which a Dutchman thought worthy of commemorating in a didactic poem upon the *Ars Topiaria.*

A little wilderness, surrounding a beautiful piece of the smoothest turf, and itself bounded by such high hedges as we have described, had been selected as the stage most proper for the exhibition of the intended dramatic picture. It afforded many facilities; for a rising bank exactly in front was accommodated with seats for the spectators, who had a complete view of the sylvan theatre, the bushes and shrubs having been cleared away in front, and the place supplied with a temporary screen, which, being withdrawn by the domestics appointed for that purpose, was to serve for the rising of the curtain. A covered trellice, which passed through another part of the garden, and terminated with a private door opening from the right wing of the building, seemed as if it had been planted on purpose for the proposed exhibition, as it served to give the personages of the drama a convenient and secret access from their green-room to the place of representation. Indeed, the dramatis personæ, at least those who adopted the management of the matter, were induced, by so much convenience, to extend, in some measure, their original plan; and, instead of one group, as had been at first proposed, they now found themselves able to exhibit to the good company a succession of three or four, selected and arranged from different parts of the drama; thus giving some duration, as well as some variety, to the entertainment, besides the advantage of separating and contrasting the tragic and the comic scenes.

After wandering about amongst the gardens, which contained little to interest any one, and endeavouring to recognize some characters, who, accommodating themselves to the humour of the day, had ventured to appear in the various disguises of ballad-singers, pedlars, shepherds, Highlanders, and so forth, the company began to draw together towards the spot where the seats prepared for them, and the screen drawn in front of the bosky stage, induced them to assemble, and excited expectation, especially as a scroll in front of the esplanade set forth, in the words of the play, "This green plot shall be our stage, this hawthorn brake our tyring house, and we will do it in action." A delay of about ten minutes began to excite some suppressed murmurs of impatience among the audience, when the touch of Gow's fiddle suddenly burst from a neighbouring hedge, behind which he had established his little orchestra. All were of course silent,

As through his dear strathspeys he bore with Highland rage.

And when he changed his strain to an adagio, and suffered his music to die away in the plaintive notes of Roslin Castle, the echoes of the old walls were, after long slumber, awakened by that enthusiastic burst of applause, with which the Scotch usually receive and reward their country's gifted minstrel.

"He is his father's own son," said Touchwood to the clergyman, for both had gotten seats near about the centre of the place of audience. "It is many a long year since I listened to old Niel at Inver, and, to say truth, spent a night with him over pancakes and Athole brose; and I never expected to hear his match in my lifetime. But stop—the curtain rises."

The screen was indeed withdrawn, and displayed Hermia, Helena, and their lovers, in attitudes corresponding to the scene of confusion occasioned by the error of Puck.

Messrs Chatterley and the Painter played their parts neither better nor worse than amateur actors in general; and the best that could be said of them was, that they seemed more than half ashamed of their exotic dresses, and of the public gaze.

But against this untimely weakness Lady Penelope was supported, by the strong crutch of self-conceit. She minced, ambled, and, notwithstanding the slight appearance of her person, and the depredations which time had made on a countenance which had never been very much distinguished for beauty, seemed desirous to top the part of the beautiful daughter of Egeus. The sullenness which was proper to the character of Hermia, was much augmented by the discovery that Miss Mowbray was so much better dressed than herself,—a discovery which she had but recently made, as that young lady had not attended upon the regular rehearsals at the Well, save once, and then without her stage habit. Her ladyship, however, did not permit this painful sense of inferiority, where she had expected triumph, so far to prevail over her desire of shining, as to interrupt materially the manner in which she had settled to represent her portion of the scene. The nature of the exhibition precluded much action, but Lady Penelope made amends by such a succession of grimaces, as might rival, in variety at least, the singular display which Garrick used to call "going his rounds." She twisted her poor features into looks of most desperate love towards Lysander; into those of wonder and offended pride, when she turned them upon Demetrius; and finally settled them on Helena, with the happiest possible imitation of an incensed rival, who feels the impossibility of relieving her swollen heart by tears alone, and is just about to have recourse to her nails.

No contrast could be stronger in looks, demeanour, and figure, than that between Hermia and Helena. In the latter character, the beautiful form and foreign dress of Miss Mowbray attracted all eyes. She kept her place on the stage, as a sentinel does that which his charge assigns him; for she had previously told her brother, that though she consented, at his importunity, to make part of the exhibition, it was as a piece of the scene, not as an actor, and accordingly a painted figure could scarce be more immovable. The expression of her countenance seemed to be that of deep sorrow and perplexity, belonging to her part, over which wandered at times an air of irony or ridicule, as if she were secretly scorning the whole exhibition, and even herself, for condescending to become part of it. Above all, a sense of bashfulness had cast upon her cheek a colour, which, though sufficiently slight, was more than her countenance was used to display; and when the spectators beheld, in the splendour and grace of a rich oriental dress, her whom they had hitherto been only accustomed to see attired in the most careless manner, they felt the additional charms of surprise and contrast; so that the bursts of applause which were vollied towards the stage, might be said to be addressed to her alone, and to vie in sincerity with those which have been forced from an audience by the most accomplished performer.

"Oh, that puir Lady Penelope!" said honest Mrs Blower, who, when her scruples against the exhibition were once got over, began to look upon it with particular interest,—"I am really sorry for her puir face, for she gars it work like the sails of John Blower's vesshel in a stiff breeze.—Oh, Doctor Cacklehen, dinna ye think she would need, if it were possible, to rin ower her face wi' a gusing iron, just to take the wrunkles out o't?"

"Hush, hush! my good dear Mrs Blower," said the Doctor; "Lady Penelope is a woman of quality, and my patient, and such people always act charmingly—you must understand there is no hissing at a private theatre—Hem!"

"You may say what you like, Doctor, but there is nae fule like an auld fule—To be sure, if she was as young and beautiful as Miss Mowbray—hegh me, and I didna use to think her sae bonnie neither but dress—dress makes an unco difference—That shawl o' hers—I daur say the like o't was ne'er seen in braid Scotland—it will be real Indian, I'se warrant."

"Real Indian!" said Mr Touchwood, in an accent of disdain, which rather disturbed Mrs Blower's equanimity,—"why, what do you suppose it should be, madam?"

"I dinna ken, sir," said she, edging somewhat near the Doctor, not being altogether pleased, as she afterwards allowed, with the outlandish appearance and sharp tone of the traveller; then pulling her own drapery round her shoulders, she added, courageously, "there are braw shawls made at Paisley, that ye will scarce ken frae foreign."

"Not know Paisley shawls from Indian, madam," said Touchwood; "why, a blind man could tell by the slightest touch of his little finger. Yon shawl, now, is the handsomest I have seen in Britain—and at this distance I can tell it to be a real *Tozie*."

"Cozie may she weel be that wears it," said Mrs Blower. "I declare, now I look on't again, it's a perfect beauty."

"It is called Tozie, ma'am, not cozie," continued the traveller; "the Shroffs at Surat told me in 1801, that it is made out of the inner coat of a goat."

"Of a sheep, sir, I am thinking ye mean, for goats hae nae woo'."

"Not much of it, indeed, madam; but you are to understand they use only the inmost coat; and then their dyes—that Tozie now will keep its colour while there is a rag of it left—men bequeath them in legacies to their grand-children."

"And a very bonnie colour it is," said the dame; "something like a mouse's back, only a thought redder—I wonder what they ca' that colour."

"The colour is much admired, madam," said Touchwood, who was now on a favourite topic; "the Mussulmans say the colour is betwixt that of an elephant and the breast of the *faughta*."

"In troth, I am as wise as I was," said Mrs Blower.

"The *faughta*, madam, so called by the Moors, for the Hindhus call it *hollah*, is a sort of pigeon, held sacred among the Moslem of India, because they think it dyed its breast in the blood of Ali.—But I see they are closing the scene.—Mr Cargill, are you composing your sermon, my good friend, or what can you be thinking of?"

Mr Cargill had, during the whole scene, remained with his eyes fixed, in intent and anxious, although almost unconscious gaze, upon Clara Mowbray; and when the voice of his companion startled him out of his reverie, he exclaimed, "Most lovely—most unhappy—yes —I must and will see her."

"See her?" replied Touchwood, too much accustomed to his friend's singularities to look for much reason or connection in anything he said or did; "Why, you shall see her and talk to her too, if that will give you pleasure.—They say now," he continued, lowering his voice to a whisper, "that this Mowbray is ruined.—I see nothing like it, since he can dress out his sister like a Begum. Did you ever see such a splendid shawl?"

"Dearly purchased splendour," said Mr Cargill, with a deep sigh; "I wish that the price be yet fully paid."

"Very likely not," said the traveller; "very likely it's gone to the book; and for the price, I have known a thousand rupees given for such a shawl in the country.—But hush, hush, we are to have another tune from Nathaniel—faith, and they are withdrawing the screen—Well, they have some mercy—they do not let us wait long between the acts of their follies at least—I love a quick and rattling fire in these vanities—Folly walking a funereal pace, and clinking her bells to the time of a passing knell, makes sad work indeed."

A strain of music, beginning slowly, and terminating in a light and wild allegro, introduced on the stage those delightful creatures of the richest imagination that ever teemed with wonders, the Oberon and Titania of Shakespeare. The pigmy majesty of the captain of the fairy band had no unapt representative in Miss Digges, whose modesty was not so great an intruder as to prevent her desire to present him in all his dignity, and she moved, conscious of the graceful turn of a pretty ankle, which, encircled with a string of pearls, and clothed in flesh-coloured silk, of the most cobweb texture, rose above the crimson sandal. Her jewelled tiara, too, gave dignity to the frown with which the offended King of Shadows greeted his consort, as each entered upon the scene at the head of their several attendants.

The restlessness of the children had been duly considered; and, therefore, their part of the exhibition had been contrived to represent dumb show, rather than a stationary picture. The little Queen of Elves was not inferior in action to her moody lord, and repaid, with a look of female impatience and scorn, the haughty air which seemed to express his sullen greeting,

> Ill met by moonlight, proud Titania.

The other children were, as usual, some clever and forward, some loutish and awkward enough; but the gambols of childhood are sure to receive applause, paid, perhaps, with a mixture of pity and envy, by those in advanced life; and besides, there were in the company several fond papas and mammas, whose clamorous approbation, though given apparently to the whole performers, was especially dedicated in their hearts to their own little Jackies and Marias,—for *Mary*, though the prettiest and most classical of Scottish names, is now unknown in the land. The elves, therefore, played their frolics, danced a measure, and vanished with good approbation.

The anti-mask, as it may be called, of Bottom, and his company of actors, next appeared on the stage, and a thunder of applause received the young Earl, who had, with infinite taste and dexterity, transformed himself into the similitude of an Athenian clown; observing the Grecian costume, yet so judiciously discriminated from the dress of the higher characters, as at once to fix the character of a thick-skinned mechanic on the wearer. Touchwood, in particular, was loud in his approbation, from which the correctness of the costume must be inferred; for that honest gentleman, like many other critics, was indeed not very much distinguished for good taste, but had a capital memory for petty matters of fact; and while the most impressive look or gesture of an actor might have failed to interest him, would have censured most severely the fashion of a sleeve, or the colour of a shoe-tie.

But the Earl of Etherington's merits were not confined to his external appearance; for, had his better fortunes failed him, his deserts, like those of Hamlet, might have got him a fellowship in a cry of players. He presented, though in dumb show, the pragmatic conceit of Bottom, to the infinite amusement of all present, especially of those who were well acquainted with the original; and when he was "translated" by Puck, he bore the ass's head, his newly acquired dignity, with an appearance of conscious greatness, which made the metamorphosis, though in itself sufficiently farcical, irresistibly comic. He afterwards displayed the same humour in his frolics with the fairies, and the intercourse which he held with Messrs Cobweb, Mustard-seed, Pease-blossom, and the rest of Titania's cavaliers, who lost all command of their countenances, at the gravity with which he invited them to afford him the luxury of scratching his hairy snout.

The entertainment closed with a grand parade of all the characters which had appeared, during which Mowbray concluded that the young lord himself, unremarked, might have time enough to examine the outward form, at least, of his sister Clara, whom, in the pride of his heart, he could not help considering superior in beauty, dressed as she now was, with every advantage of art, even to the brilliant Amazon, Lady Binks. It is true, Mowbray was not a man to give preference to the intellectual expression of poor Clara's features over the sultana-like beauty of the haughty dame, which promised to an admirer all the vicissitudes which can be expressed by a countenance lovely in every change, and changing as often as an ardent and impetuous disposition, unused to constraint, and despising admonition, should please to dictate. Yet, to do him justice, though his preference was perhaps dictated more by fraternal partiality than by purity of taste, he certainly, on the present occasion, felt the full extent of Clara's superiority; and there was a proud smile on his lip, as, at the conclusion of the divertisement, he asked the Earl how he had been pleased. The rest of the performers had separated, and the young lord remained on the stage, employed in disembarrassing himself of his awkward vizor, when Mowbray put this question, to which, though general in terms, he naturally gave a particular meaning.

"I could wear my ass's head for ever," he said, "on condition my eyes were to be so delightfully employed as they have been during the last scene.—Mowbray, your sister is an angel!"

"Have a care that that head-piece of yours has not perverted your taste, my lord," said Mowbray. "But why did you wear that disguise on your last appearance? you should, I think, have been uncovered."

"I am ashamed to answer you," said the Earl; "but truth is, first impressions are of consequence, and I thought I might do as wisely not to appear before your sister, for the first time, in the character of Bully Bottom."

"Then you change your dress, my lord, for dinner, if we call our luncheon by that name?" said Mowbray.

"I am going to my room this instant for that very purpose," replied the Earl.

"And I," said Mowbray, "must step in front, and dismiss the audience; for I see they are sitting gaping there waiting for another scene."

They parted upon this; and Mowbray, as Duke Theseus, stepped before the screen, and announcing the conclusion of the dramatic pictures which they had had the honour to present before the worshipful company, thanked the spectators for the very favourable reception which they had afforded; and intimated to them, that if they could amuse themselves by strolling for an hour among the gardens, a bell would summon to the house at the expiry of that time, when some refreshments would wait their acceptance. This annunciation was received with the applause due to the *Amphitryon où l'on dîne;* and the guests, arising from before the temporary theatre, dispersed through the gardens, which were of some extent, to seek for or create amusement to themselves. The music greatly aided them in this last purpose, and it was not long ere a dozen of couples and upwards, were "tripping it on the light fantastic toe," (I love a phrase that is not hackneyed) to the tune of Monymusk.

Others strolled through the gardens, meeting some fantastic disguise at the end of every verdant alley, and communicating to others the surprise and amusement which they themselves were receiving. The scene, from the variety of dresses, the freedom which it gave to the display of humour amongst such as possessed any, and the general disposition to give and receive pleasure, rendered the little masquerade more entertaining than scenes of the kind for which more ample and magnificent preparations have been made. There was also a singular and pleasing contrast between the fantastic figures who wandered through the gardens, and the quiet scene itself, to which the old clipt hedges, the formal distribution of the ground, and the antiquated appearance of one or two fountains and artificial cascades, in which the naiads had been for the nonce compelled to resume their ancient frolics, gave an appearance of unusual simplicity and seclusion, and seemed rather to belong to the last than to the present generation.

Chapter Eight

PERPLEXITIES

For revels, dances, masques, and merry hours,
Fore-run fair Love, strewing his way with flowers.
Love's Labour's Lost

Worthies away—the scene begins to cloud.
Ibidem

MR TOUCHWOOD and his inseparable friend, Mr Cargill, wandered on amidst the gay groups we have described, the former censuring with great scorn the frequent attempts which he observed towards an imitation of the costume of the East, and appealing with self-complacence to his own superior representation, as he greeted, in Moors and in Persic, the several turban'd figures who passed his way; while the clergyman, whose mind seemed to labour with some weighty and important project, looked in every direction for the fair representative of Helena, but in vain. At length he caught a glimpse of the memorable shawl, which had drawn forth so learned a discussion from his companion; and, starting from Touchwood's side with a degree of anxious alertness totally foreign to his usual habits, he endeavoured to join the person by whom it was worn.

"By the Lord," said his companion, "the Doctor is beside himself! —the parson is mad!—the divine is out of his senses, that is clear; and how the devil can he, who scarce can find his road from the Cleikum to his own manse, venture himself unprotected into such a scene of confusion?—he might as well pretend to cross the Atlantic without a pilot—I must push off in chase of him, lest worse come of it."

But the traveller was prevented from executing his friendly purpose by a sort of crowd which came rushing down the alley, the centre of which was occupied by Captain MacTurk, in the very act of bullying two pseudo Highlanders, for having presumed to lay aside their breeches before they had acquired the Gaelic language. The sounds of contempt and insult with which the genuine Celt was overwhelming the unfortunate impostors, were not, indeed, intelligible otherwise than from the tone and manner of the speaker; but these intimated so much displeasure, that the plaided forms whose unadvised choice of a disguise had provoked it—two raw lads from a certain great manufac-

Even after a fever of the brain, we retain our recollection of the causes of our illness.—Come, you must and do understand me, when I say that I will not consent to your committing a great crime to attain temporal wealth and rank, no, not to make you an empress.—My path is a clear one; and should I hear a whisper breathed of your alliance with this Earl, or whatever he may be, rely upon it, that I will withdraw the veil, and make your brother, your bridegroom, and the whole world acquainted with the situation in which you stand, and the impossibility of your forming the alliance which you propose to yourself, I am compelled to say, against the laws of God and man."

"But, sir—sir," answered the lady, rather eagerly than anxiously, "you have not yet told me what business you have with my marriage, or what arguments you can bring against it."

"Madam," replied Mr Cargill, "in your present state of mind, and in such a scene as this, I cannot enter upon a topic for which the season is unfit, and you, I am sorry to say, are totally unprepared. It is enough that you know the grounds on which you stand. At a fitter opportunity, I will, as it is my duty, lay before you the enormity of what you are said to have meditated, with the freedom which becomes one, who, however humble, is appointed to explain to his fellow-creatures the laws of his Maker.—In the meantime, I am not afraid that you will take any hasty step after such a warning as this."

So saying, he turned from the lady with that dignity which a conscious discharge of duty confers, yet, at the same time, with a sense of deep pain, inflicted by the careless levity of her whom he addressed. She did not any longer attempt to detain him, but made her escape from the arbour by one alley, as she heard voices which seemed to approach it from another. The clergyman, who took the opposite direction, met in full encounter a whispering and tittering pair, who seemed, at his sudden appearance, to check their tone of familiarity, and assume an appearance of greater distance towards each other. The lady was no other than the fair Queen of the Amazons, who seemed to have adopted the recent partiality of Titania towards Bully Bottom, being in conference such and so close as we have described with the late representative of the Athenian weaver, whose recent visit to his chamber had metamorphosed him into the more gallant disguise of an ancient Spanish cavalier. He now appeared with cloak and drooping plume, sword, poniard, and guitar, richly dressed at all points, as for a serenade beneath his mistress's window; a silk masque at the breast of his embroidered doublet hung ready to be assumed in case of intrusion, as an appropriate part of the national dress.

It sometimes happened to Mr Cargill, as we believe it may to other men much subject to absence of mind, that, contrary to their wont, and much after the manner of a sunbeam suddenly piercing a deep mist, and illuminating one particular object in the landscape, some sudden recollection rushes upon them, and seems to compel them to act under it, as under the influence of complete certainty and conviction. Mr Cargill had no sooner set eyes on the Spanish cavalier, in whom he neither knew the Earl of Etherington, nor recognized Bully Bottom, than with hasty emotion he seized on his reluctant hand, and exclaimed, with a mixture of eagerness and solemnity, "I rejoice to see you!—Heaven has sent you here in its own good time."

"I thank you, sir," replied Lord Etherington, very coldly, "I believe you have the joy of the meeting entirely on your side, as I cannot remember having seen you before."

"Is not your name Bulmer?" said the clergyman. "I—I know—I am sometimes apt to make mistakes.—But I am sure your name is Bulmer."

"Not that ever I or my godfathers heard of—my name was Bottom half an hour ago—perhaps that makes the confusion," answered the Earl, with very cold and distant politeness;—"Permit me to pass, sir, and attend the lady."

"Quite unnecessary," answered Lady Binks; "I leave you to adjust your mutual recollections with your new old friend, my lord—he seems to have something to say." So saying, the lady walked on, not perhaps sorry of an opportunity to shew apparent indifference for his Lordship's society in the presence of one who had surprised them in what might seem a moment of exuberant intimacy.

"You detain me, sir," said the Earl of Etherington to Mr Cargill, who, bewildered and uncertain, still kept himself placed so directly before the young nobleman as to make it impossible for him to pass, without absolutely pushing him to one side. "I must really attend the lady," he added, making another effort to walk on.

"Young man," said Mr Cargill, "you cannot disguise yourself from me. I am sure—my mind assures me, that you are that very Bulmer whom Heaven hath sent here to prevent crime."

"And you," said Lord Etherington, "whom my mind assures me I never saw in my life, are sent hither by the devil, I think, to create confusion."

"I beg pardon, sir," said the clergyman, staggered by the calm and pertinacious denial of the Earl—"I beg pardon if I am in a mistake—that is, if I am *really* in a mistake—-but I am not—I am sure I am not!—That look—that smile—I am NOT mistaken. You *are* Valentine Bulmer—the very Valentine Bulmer whom I—but I will not make your private affairs any part of this exposition—enough, you *are* Valentine Bulmer."

"Valentine?—Valentine?—I am neither Valentine nor Orson—I wish you good morning, sir."

"Stay, sir, stay, I charge you," said the clergyman; "if you are unwilling to be known yourself, it may be because you have forgotten who I am—Let me name myself as the Rev. Josiah Cargill, Minister of Saint Ronan's."

"If you bear a character so venerable, sir,—in which, however, I am not in the least interested,—I think when you make your morning draught a little too potent, it might be as well for you to stay at home and sleep it off, before coming into company."

"In the name of Heaven, young gentleman, lay aside this untimely and unseemly jesting! and tell me if you be not, as I cannot but still believe you, that same youth, who, seven years since, left in my deposit a solemn secret, which, if I should unfold to the wrong person, woe would be my own heart, and evil the consequences which might ensue."

"You are very pressing with me, sir," said the Earl; "and, in exchange, I will be equally frank with you.—I am not the man whom you mistake me for, and you may go seek him where you will—It will be still more lucky for you if you chance to find your own wits in the course of your researches; for I must tell you plainly, I think they are gone somewhat astray." So saying, with a gesture expressive of a determined purpose to pass on, Mr Cargill had no alternative but to make way, and suffer him to proceed.

The worthy clergyman stood as if rooted to the ground, and, with his usual habit of thinking aloud, exclaimed to himself, "My fancy has played me many a bewildering trick, but this is the most extraordinary of them all!—What can this young man think of me? It must have been my conversation with that unhappy young lady, that has made such impression upon me as to deceive my very eye-sight, and causes me to connect with her history the face of the next person that I met—What must the stranger think of me?"

"Why, what every one thinks of thee that knows thee, prophet," said the friendly voice of Touchwood, accompanying his speech with an awakening slap on the clergyman's shoulder; "and that is, that thou art an unfortunate philosopher of Laputa, who has lost his flapper in the throng.—Come along—having me once more by your side you need fear nothing.—Why, now I look at you closer, you look as if you had seen a basilisk—not that there is any such thing, otherwise I must have seen it myself, in the course of my travels—but you seem pale and frightened—What the devil is the matter?"

"Nothing," answered the clergyman, "except that I have even this very moment made an egregious fool of myself."

"Pooh, pooh, that is nothing to sigh over, prophet.—Every man does so at least twice in the four-and-twenty hours," said Touchwood.

"But I had nearly betrayed to a stranger a secret deeply concerning the honour of a noble family."

"That was wrong, Doctor," said Touchwood; "take care of that in future; and, indeed, I would advise you not to speak even to your beadle, Willie Watson, until you have assured yourself, by at least three pertinent questions and answers, that you have the said Willie corporally and substantially in presence before you, and that your fancy has not invested some stranger with honest Willie's singed periwig and threadbare brown joseph.—Come along—come along."

So saying, he hurried forward the perplexed clergyman, who in vain made all excuses he could think of in order to effect his escape from the scene of gaiety, in which he was so unexpectedly involved. He pleaded head-ache; and his friend assured him that a mouthful of food, and a glass of wine, would mend it. He stated he had business; and Touchwood replied that he could have none but composing his next sermon, and reminded him that it was two days till Sunday. At length, Mr Cargill confessed that he had some reluctance again to see the stranger, on whom he had endeavoured with such pertinacity to fix an acquaintance, which he was now well assured existed only in his own imagination. The traveller treated his scruples with scorn, and said that guests meeting in this general manner, had no more to do with each other than if they were assembled in a caravansary.

"So that you need not say a word to him in the way of apology or otherwise—or, what will be still better, I, who have seen so much of the world, will make the pretty speech for you." As they spoke, he dragged the divine towards the house, where they were now summoned by the appointed signal, and where the company were assembling in the old saloon already noticed, previous to passing into the dining-room, where the refreshments were prepared. "Now, Doctor," continued the busy friend of Mr Cargill, "let us see which of all these people has been the subject of your blunder. Is it yon animal of a Highlandman?—or the impertinent brute that wants to be thought a boatswain?—or which of them all is it?—Ay, here they come, two and two, Newgate fashion—the young Lord of the Manor with old Lady Penelope—does he set up for Ulysses, I wonder?—the Earl of Etherington with Lady Bingo—methinks it should have been with Miss Mowbray."

"The Earl of what did you say?" quoth the clergyman, anxiously. "How is it you titled that young man in the Spanish dress?"

"Oho!" said the traveller; "what, I have discovered the goblin that has scared you?—Come along—come along—I will make you acquainted with him." So saying, he dragged him towards Lord Etherington; and before the divine could make his negative intelligible, the ceremony of introduction had taken place. "My Lord Etherington, allow me to present Mr Cargill, minister of this parish—a learned gentleman, whose head is often in the Holy Land, when his person seems present among his friends. He suffers extremely, my lord, under the sense of mistaking your lordship for the Lord knows who; but when you are acquainted with him, you will find that he can make a hundred stranger mistakes than that, so we hope that your lordship will take no prejudice or offence."

"There can be no offence taken where no offence is intended," said Lord Etherington, with much urbanity. "It is I who ought to beg the reverend gentleman's pardon, for hurrying from him without allowing him to make a complete eclaircissement. I beg his pardon for an abruptness which the place and the time—for I was immediately engaged in a lady's service—rendered unavoidable."

Mr Cargill gazed on the young nobleman as he pronounced these words with the easy indifference of one who apologizes to an inferior in order to maintain his own character for politeness, but with perfect indifference whether his excuses are or are not held satisfactory. And as the clergyman gazed, the belief which had so strongly clung to him that the Earl of Etherington and young Valentine Bulmer were the same individual person, melted away like frost-work before the morning sun, and that so completely, that he marvelled at himself for having ever entertained it. Some strong resemblance of features there must have been to have led him into such a delusion; but the person, the tone, the manner of expression, were absolutely different; and his attention being now especially directed towards these particulars, Mr Cargill was inclined to think the two personages almost totally dissimilar.

The clergyman had now only to make his apology, and fall back from the head of the table to some lower seat, which his modesty would have preferred, when he was suddenly seized upon by the Lady Penelope Penfeather, who, detaining him in the most elegant and persuasive manner possible, insisted that they should be introduced to each other by Mr Mowbray, and that Mr Cargill should sit beside her at table.—She had heard so much of his learning—so much of his excellent character—desired so much to make his acquaintance, that she could not think of losing an opportunity, which Mr Cargill's learned seclusion rendered so very rare—in a word, catching the Black Lion was the order of the day; and her ladyship, having trapped her prey, soon sat triumphant with him by her side, like Britannia with her ferine attendant on the reverse of a halfpenny.

A second separation was thus effected betwixt Touchwood and his friend; for the former, not being included in the invitation, or, indeed, at all noticed by Lady Penelope, was obliged to find room at a lower part of the table, where he excited much surprise by the dexterity with which he dispatched boiled rice with chop-sticks.

Mr Cargill being thus exposed, without a consort, to the fire of Lady Penelope, speedily found it so brisk and incessant, as to drive his complaisance, little tried as it had been for many years by small talk, almost to extremity. She began by begging him to draw his chair closer, for an instinctive terror of fine ladies had made him keep his distance. At the same time, she hoped "he was not afraid of her as an Episcopalian: her father had belonged to that communion for," she added, with what was intended for an arch smile, "we were somewhat naughty in the forty-five, as you may have heard;—but all that was over, and she was sure Mr Cargill was too liberal to entertain any dislike or shyness on that score.—Indeed, she was far from disliking the Presbyterian form—indeed she had often wished to hear it, where she was sure to be both delighted and edified (here a gracious smile) in the church of Saint Ronan's—and hoped to do so whenever Mr Mowbray had got a stove, which he had ordered from Edinburgh, on purpose to air his pew for her accommodation."

All this, which was spoken with wreathed smiles and nods, and so much civility as to remind the clergyman of a cup of tea over-sweetened to conceal its want of strength and flavour, required and received no farther answer than an accommodating look and an acquiescent bow.

"Ah, Mr Cargill," continued the inexhaustible Lady Penelope, "your profession has so many demands on the heart as well as the understanding—is so much connected with the kindnesses and charities of our nature—with our best and purest feelings, Mr Cargill. You know what Goldsmith says,

> ——to his duty prompt at every call,
> He watch'd, and wept, and felt, and pray'd for all.

And then Dryden has such a picture of a parish priest, so inimitable, one would think, did we not hear now and then of some living mortal presuming to emulate its features, (here another insinuating nod and expressive smile.)

> Refined himself to soul to curb the sense,
> And almost made a sin of abstinence,
> Yet had his aspect nothing of severe,
> But such a face as promised him sincere;
> Nothing reserved or sullen was to see,
> But sweet regard and pleasing sanctity."

While her ladyship declaimed, the clergyman's wandering eye confessed his absent mind; his thoughts travelling perhaps to accomplish a truce betwixt Saladin and Conrade of Mountserrat, unless they chanced to be occupied with some occurrences of that very day, so that the lady was obliged to recal her indocile auditor with the leading question, "You are well acquainted with Dryden, of course, Mr Cargill?"

"I have not the honour, madam," said Mr Cargill, starting from his reverie, and but half understanding the question he replied to.

"Sir!" said the lady, in surprise.

"Madam!—my lady!" answered Mr Cargill, in embarrassment.

"I asked you if you admired Dryden;—but you learned men are so absent—perhaps you thought I said Leyden."

"A lamp too early quenched, madam," said Mr Cargill; "I knew him well."

"And so did I," eagerly replied the lady of the cerulean buskin; "he spoke ten languages—how mortifying to poor me, Mr Cargill, who could only boast of five?—but I have studied a little since that time—I must have you to help me in my studies, Mr Cargill—it will be charitable—but perhaps you are afraid of a female pupil?"

A thrill, arising from former recollections, passed through poor Cargill's mind, with as much acuteness as the pass of a rapier might have done through his body; and we cannot help remarking, that a forward prater in society, like a busy bustler in a crowd, besides all other general points of annoyance, is eternally rubbing upon some tender point, and galling men's feelings, without knowing or regarding it.

"You must assist me, besides, in my little charities, Mr Cargill, now that you and I are become so well acquainted.—There is that Anne Heggie—I sent her a trifle yesterday, but I am told—I should not mention it, but only one would not have the little they have to bestow lavished on an improper object—I am told she is not quite proper—an unwedded mother, in short, Mr Cargill—and it would be especially unbecoming in me to encourage profligacy."

"I believe, madam," said the clergyman, gravely, "the poor woman's distress may justify your ladyship's bounty, even if her conduct has been faulty."

"O, I am no prude neither, I assure you, Mr Cargill," answered the Lady Penelope. "I never withdraw my countenance from any one but on the most irrefragable grounds. I could tell you of an intimate friend of my own, whom I have supported against the whole clamour of the people at the Well, because I believe, from the bottom of my soul, she is only thoughtless—nothing in the world but thoughtless—O, Mr

Cargill, how can you look across the table so intelligently?—Who would have thought it of you?—Oh fie, to make such personal applications!"

"Upon my word, madam, I am quite at a loss to comprehend——"

"Oh fie, fie, Mr Cargill," throwing in as much censure and surprise as a confidential whisper can convey—"you looked at my Lady Binks—I know what you think, but you are quite wrong, I assure you; you are entirely wrong.—I wish she would not flirt quite so much with that young man though, Mr Cargill—her situation is particular.—Indeed, I believe she wears out his patience; for see—he is leaving the room before we sit down—how singular!—And then, do you not think it very odd, too, that Miss Mowbray has not come down to us?"

"Miss Mowbray!—what of Miss Mowbray—is she not here?" said Mr Cargill, starting, and with an expression of interest which he had not yet bestowed on any of her ladyship's liberal communications.

"Ay, poor Miss Mowbray," said Lady Penelope, lowering her voice, and shaking her head; "she has not appeared—her brother went up stairs a few minutes since, I believe, to bring her down, and so we are all left here to look at each other.—How very awkward!—but you know Clara Mowbray."

"I, madam?" said Mr Cargill, who was now sufficiently attentive; "I really—I know Miss Mowbray—that is, I knew her some years since—but your ladyship knows she has been long in bad health—uncertain health at least, and I have seen nothing of the young lady for a very long time."

"I know it, my dear Mr Cargill—I know it," continued the Lady Penelope, in the same tone of deep sympathy; "I know, and most unhappy surely have been the circumstances that have separated her from your advice and friendly counsel.—All this I am aware of—and to say truth, it has been chiefly on poor Clara's account that I have been giving you the trouble of fixing an acquaintance upon you.—You and I together, Mr Cargill, might do wonders to cure her unhappy state of mind—I am sure we might—that is, if you could bring your mind to repose absolute confidence in me."

"Has Miss Mowbray desired your ladyship to converse with me upon any subject which interests her?" said the clergyman, with more cautious shrewdness than Lady Penelope had suspected him of possessing. "I will in that case be happy to hear the nature of her communication; and whatever my poor services can perform, your ladyship may command them."

"I—I—I cannot just assert," said her ladyship with hesitation, "that I have Miss Mowbray's direct instructions to speak to you, Mr Cargill, upon the present subject. But my affection for the dear girl is so very great—and then, you know, the inconveniences which may arise from this match."

"From which match, Lady Penelope?" said Mr Cargill.

"Nay, now, Mr Cargill, you really carry the privilege of Scotland too far—I have not put a single question to you, but you have answered it by another—let us converse intelligibly for five minutes, if you can but condescend so far."

"For any length of time which your ladyship may please to command," said Mr Cargill; "providing the subject regard your ladyship's own affairs or mine, could I suppose these last for a moment likely to interest you."

"Out upon you," said the lady, laughing affectedly; "you should really have been a Catholic priest instead of a Presbyterian. What an invaluable father confessor have the fair sex lost in you, Mr Cargill, and how dexterously you would have evaded any cross-examinations which might have committed your penitents!"

"Your ladyship's raillery is far too severe for me to withstand or reply to," said Mr Cargill, bowing with more ease than her ladyship expected; and, retiring gently backwards, he extricated himself from a conversation which he began to find somewhat embarrassing.

At that moment a murmur of surprise took place in the apartment, which was just entered by Miss Mowbray, leaning on her brother's arm. The cause of this murmur will be best understood, by narrating what had passed betwixt the brother and sister.

Chapter Nine

EXPOSTULATION

> Seek not the feast in these irreverent robes;
> Go to my chamber—put on clothes of mine.
>
> *The Taming of the Shrew*

IT WAS with a mixture of anxiety, vexation, and resentment, that Mowbray, just when he had handed Lady Penelope into the apartment where the tables were covered, observed that his sister was absent, and that Lady Binks was hanging on the arm of Lord Etherington, to whose rank it would properly have fallen to escort the lady of the house. An anxious and hasty glance cast through the room, ascertained that she was absent, nor could the ladies present give any account of her after she had quitted the gardens, excepting that Lady Penelope had spoken a few words with her in her own apartment, immediately after the scenic entertainment was concluded.

Thither Mowbray hurried, complaining aloud of his sister's laziness in dressing, but internally hoping that the delay was occasioned by nothing of a more important character.

He hastened up stairs, entered her little sitting-room without ceremony, and knocking at the door of her dressing-room, begged her to make haste.

"Here is the whole company impatient," he said, assuming a tone of pleasantry; "and Sir Bingo Binks exclaiming for your presence, that he may be let loose on the cold meat."

"Paddock calls," said Clara from within; "anon—anon!"

"Nay, it is no jest, Clara," continued her brother; "for Lady Penelope is miauling like a starved cat!"

"I come—I come, grimalkin," answered Clara, in the same vein as before, and entered the parlour as she spoke, her finery entirely thrown aside, and dressed in the riding habit which was her usual and favourite attire.

Her brother was both surprised and offended. "On my soul," he said, "Clara, this is behaving very ill. I indulge you in every freak upon ordinary occasions, but you might surely on this day, of all others, have condescended to appear something like my sister, and a gentlewoman receiving company in her own house."

"Why, dearest John," said Clara, "so that the guests have enough to eat and drink, I cannot conceive why I should concern myself about their finery, or they trouble themselves about my plain clothes."

"Come, come, Clara, this will not do," answered Mowbray; "you must positively go back into your dressing-room, and huddle your things on as fast as you can. You cannot go down to the company dressed as you are."

"I certainly can, and I certainly will, John—I have made a fool of myself once this morning to oblige you, and for the rest of the day I am determined to appear in my own dress; that is, in one which shews I neither belong to the world, nor wish to have anything to do with its fashions."

"By my soul, Clara, I will make you repent this!" said Mowbray, with more violence than he usually exhibited where his sister was concerned.

"You cannot, dear John," she coolly replied, "unless by beating me; and that I think you would repent of yourself."

"I do not know but what it were the best way of managing you," said Mowbray, muttering between his teeth; but commanding his violence, he only said aloud, "I am sure, from long experience, Clara, that your obstinacy will at the long run beat my anger. Do let us compound the point for once—keep your old habit, since you are so fond of making such a sight of yourself, and only throw the shawl round your shoulders—it has been exceedingly admired, and every woman in the house longs to see it closer—they can hardly believe it genuine."

"Do be a man, Mowbray," answered his sister; "meddle with your horse-sheets, and leave shawls alone."

"Do you be a woman, Clara, and think a little on them, when custom and decency render it necessary.—Nay, is it possible!—Will you not stir—not oblige me in such a trifle as this?"

"I would indeed if I could," said Clara; "but, since you must know the truth—do not be angry—I have not the shawl. I have given it away—given it up, perhaps I should say, to the rightful owner.—She has promised me something or other in exchange for it, however. I have given it to Lady Penelope."

"Yes," answered Mowbray, "some of the work of her own fair hands, I suppose, or a couple of her drawings, made up into fire-screens.—On my word—on my soul, this is too bad!—It is using me too ill, Clara—far too ill. If the thing had been of no value, my giving it to you should have fixed some upon it.—Good even to you; we will do as well as we can without you."

"Nay, but, my dear John—stay but a moment," said Clara, taking his arm as he sullenly turned towards the door; "there are but two of us on the earth—do not let us quarrel about a trumpery shawl."

"Trumpery!" said Mowbray; "It cost fifty guineas, by G—, which I can but ill spare—trumpery!"

"O, never think of the cost," said Clara; "it was your gift, and that should, I own, have been enough to have made me keep to my death's day the poorest rag of it. But really Lady Penelope looked so very miserable, and twisted her poor face into so many odd expressions of anger and chagrin, that I resigned it to her, and agreed to say she had lent it to me for the performance. I believe she was afraid that I would change my mind, or that you would resume it as a seignorial waif; for, after she had walked a few turns with it wrapped around her, merely by way of taking possession, she dispatched it by a special messenger to her own apartment at the Wells."

"She may go to the devil," said Mowbray, "for a greedy unconscionable jade, who has varnished over a selfish, spiteful heart, that is as hard as a flint, with a fine glosing of taste and sensibility!"

"Nay, but, John," replied his sister, "she really had something to complain of in the present case. The shawl had been bespoke on her account, or very nearly so—she shewed me the tradesman's letter—only some agent of yours had come in between with the ready money, which no tradesman can resist.—Ah, John! I suspect half of your anger is owing to the failure of a plan to mortify poor Lady Pen, and that she has more to complain of than you have.—Come, come, you have had the advantage of her in the first display of this fatal piece of finery, if wearing it on my poor shoulders can be called a display—e'en make her welcome to the rest for peace's sake, and let us go down to these good folks, and you shall see how pretty and civil I shall behave."

Mowbray, a spoiled child, and with all the petted habits of indulgence, was exceedingly fretted at the issue of the scheme which he had formed for mortifying Lady Penelope; but he saw at once the necessity of saying nothing more to his sister on the subject. Vengeance he privately muttered against Lady Pen, whom he termed an absolute harpy in blue stockings; unjustly forgetting, that, in the very important affair in question, he himself had been the first to interfere with and defeat her ladyship's designs on the garment in question.

"But I will blow her," he said, "I will blow her ladyship's conduct in the business! She shall not outwit a poor whimsical girl like Clara, without hearing of it on more sides than one."

With this Christian and gentleman-like feeling towards Lady Penelope, he escorted his sister into the eating-room, and led her to her proper place at the head of the table. It was the negligence displayed in her dress, which occasioned the murmur of surprise that greeted Clara on her entrance. Mowbray, as he placed his sister in her chair, made her general apology for her late appearance, and her riding-habit. "Some fairies," he supposed, "Puck, or such like tricky goblin, had been in her wardrobe, and carried off whatever was fit for wearing."

There were answers from every quarter—that it would have been too much to expect Miss Mowbray to dress for their amusement a second time—that nothing she chose to wear could misbecome Miss Mowbray—that she had set like the sun, in her splendid scenic dress, and now rose like the full moon in her ordinary attire, (this flight was by the Reverend Mr Chatterley)—and that "Miss Mowbray being at hame, had an unco guid right to please hersell;" which last piece of politeness, being at least as much to the purpose as any that had preceded it, was the contribution of honest Mrs Blower; and was replied to by Miss Mowbray with a particular and most gracious bow.

Mrs Blower ought to have rested her colloquial fame, as Dr Johnson would have said, upon a compliment so evidently acceptable, but no one knows where to stop. She thrust her broad, good-natured, delighted countenance forwards, and sending her voice from the bottom to the top of the table, like her umquhile husband when calling to his mate during a breeze, wondered "why Miss Clara Moubrie didna wear that grand shawl she had on at the play-making, and her just sitting upon the wind of a door. Nae doubt it was for fear of the soup, and the butter-boats, and the like;—but *she* had three shawls, which she really fand was twa ower mony—if Miss Mobrie wad like to wear ane o' them—it was but imitashon to be sure—but it wad keep her shouthers as warm as if it were real Indian, and if it were dirtied it was the less matter."

"Much obliged, Mrs Blower," said Mowbray, unable to resist the temptation which this speech offered; "but my sister is not yet of quality sufficient, to entitle her to rob her friends of their shawls."

Lady Penelope coloured to the eyes, and bitter was the retort that arose to her tongue; but she suppressed it, and nodding to Miss Mowbray in the most friendly way in the world, yet with a very particular expression, she only said, "So, you have told your brother of the little transaction which we have had this morning?—*Tu me lo pagherai* —I give you fair warning, take care none of your secrets come into my keeping—that is all."

Upon what mere trifles do the important events of human life sometimes depend! If Lady Penelope had given way to her first movement of resentment, the probable issue would have been some such half-comic, half-serious skirmish, as her ladyship and Mr Mowbray had often entertained the company withal. But revenge, which is suppressed and deferred, is always most to be dreaded; and to the effects of the deliberate resentment which Lady Penelope entertained upon this trifling occasion, must be traced the events which our history has to record. Secretly did she determine to return the shawl, which she had entertained hopes of making her own upon very reasonable terms; and as secretly did she determine to be revenged both upon brother and sister, conceiving herself already possessed, to a certain degree, of a clew to some part of their family history, which might serve for a foundation on which to raise her projected battery. The ancient offences and emulation of importance of the Laird of Saint Ronan's, and the superiority which had been given to Clara in the exhibition of the day, combined with the immediate cause of resentment; and it only remained to consider how her revenge could be most signally accomplished.

Whilst such thoughts were passing through Lady Penelope's mind, Mowbray was searching with his eyes for the Earl of Etherington, judging that it might be proper, in the course of the entertainment, or before the guests had separated, to make him formally acquainted with his sister, as a preface to the more intimate connection which must, in prosecution of the plan agreed upon, take place betwixt them. Greatly to his surprise, the young Earl was nowhere visible, and the place which he had occupied by the side of Lady Binks had been seized upon by Mr Winterblossom, as the best and softest chair in the room, and nearest to the head of the table, where the choicest of the entertainment is usually arranged. This honest gentleman, after a few insipid compliments to her ladyship upon her performance as Queen of the Amazons, had betaken himself to the much more interesting occupation of ogling the dishes, through the glass which hung suspended at his neck, by a gold chain of Maltese workmanship. After looking and wondering for a few seconds, Mowbray addressed himself to the old beau-garçon, and asked him what had become of Etherington.

"Retreated," said Winterblossom, "and left but his compliments to you behind him—a complaint, I think, in his wounded arm.—Upon my word, that soup has a most appetizing flavour!—Lady Penelope, shall I have the honour?—no!—nor you, Lady Binks?—you are too cruel!—I must comfort myself, like a heathen priest of old, by eating the sacrifice which the deities have scorned to accept of."

Here he helped himself to the plate of soup which he had in vain offered to the ladies, and transferred the further duty of dispensing it to Mr Chatterley; "It is your profession, sir, to propitiate the divinities—ahem!"

"I did not think Lord Etherington would have left us so soon," said Mowbray; "but we must do the best we can without his countenance."

So saying, he assumed his place at the bottom of the table, and did his best to support the character of a hospitable and joyous landlord, while on her part, with much natural grace, and delicacy of attention calculated to set everybody at their ease, his sister presided at the upper end of the board. But the vanishing of Lord Etherington in a manner so sudden and unaccountable—the obvious ill-humour of Lady Penelope—and the steady, though passive, sullenness of Lady Binks, spread among the company a gloom like that produced by an autumnal mist upon a pleasing landscape.—The women were low-spirited, dull, nay, peevish, they did not well know why; and the men could not be joyous, though the ready resource of old hock and champagne made some of them talkative.—Lady Penelope broke up the party by well-feigned apprehension of the difficulties, nay, dangers, of returning by so rough a road.—Lady Binks begged a seat with her ladyship, as Sir Bingo, she said, judging from his devotion to the green flask, was likely to need their carriage home. From the moment of their departure, it became bad ton to remain behind; and all, as in a retreating army, were eager to be foremost, excepting MacTurk and a few staunch topers, who, unused to meet with such good cheer every day of their lives, prudently determined to make the most of it.

We will not dwell on the difficulties attending the transportation of a large company by few carriages, though the delay and disputes thereby occasioned were of course more intolerable than in the morning, for the contending parties had no longer the hopes of a happy day before them, as a bribe to submit to temporary inconveniences. The impatience of many was so great, that, though the evening was raw, they chose to go on foot rather than await the dull routine of the returning carriages; and as they retired, they agreed, with one consent, to throw the blame of whatever inconvenience they might sustain on their host and hostess, who had invited so large a party before getting a shorter and better road made between the Well and Shaws-Castle.

"It would have been so easy to repair the path by the Buckstane!"

And this was all the thanks which Mr Mowbray received for an entertainment which had cost him so much trouble and expense, and had been looked forward to by the good society at the Well with such impatient expectation.

"It was an unc' pleasant show," said the good-natured Mrs Blower, "only it was a pity it was sae tediousome; and there was surely an awfu' waste of gauze and muslin."

But so well had Dr Quackleben improved his numerous opportunities, that the good lady was much reconciled to affairs in general, by the prospect of coughs, rheumatisms, and other maladies acquired upon the occasion, which were likely to afford that learned gentleman, in whose prosperity she much interested herself, a very profitable harvest.

Mowbray, somewhat addicted to the service of Bacchus, did not find himself freed by the secession of so large a proportion of the company from the service of the jolly god, although, upon the present occasion, he could well have dispensed with his orgies. Neither the song, nor the pun, nor the jest, had power to kindle his heavy spirit, mortified as he was by the event of his party being so different from the brilliant consummation which he had anticipated. The guests, staunch boon companions, suffered not, however, their party to flag for want of the landlord's participation, but continued to drink bottle after bottle, with as little regard for Mr Mowbray's grave looks, as if they had been carousing at the Mowbray Arms, instead of the Mowbray mansion-house. Midnight at length released him, when, with an unsteady step, he sought his own apartment; cursing himself and his companions, consigning his own person with all dispatch to his bed, and bequeathing those of the company to as many mosses and quagmires, as could be found betwixt Shaws-Castle and Saint Ronan's Well.

Chapter Ten

THE PROPOSAL

Oh! you would be a vestal maid, I warrant,
The bride of Heaven—Come—we may shake your purpose;
For here I bring in hand a jolly suitor
Hath ta'en degrees in the seven sciences
That ladies love best—He is young and noble,
Handsome and valiant, gay, and rich, and liberal.
The Nun

THE MORNING after a debauch is usually one of reflection, even to the most customary boon companion; and, in the retrospect of the preceding day, the young Laird of Saint Ronan's saw nothing very consolatory, unless that the excess was not, in the present case, of his own seeking, but had arisen out of the necessary duties of a landlord, or what were considered as such by his companions.

But it was not so much his dizzy recollections of the late carouse which haunted him on awakening, as the inexplicability which seemed to shroud the purpose and conduct of his new ally, the Earl of Etherington.

That young nobleman had seen Miss Mowbray, had declared his high satisfaction, had warmly and voluntarily renewed the proposal which he had made ere she was yet known to him—and yet, far from seeking an opportunity to be introduced to her, he had even left the party abruptly, in order to avoid the necessary intercourse which must there have taken place between them. His lordship's flirtation with Lady Binks had not escaped the attention of the sagacious Mowbray—her ladyship also had been in a hurry to leave Shaws-Castle; and Mowbray promised to himself to discover the nature of this connection through Mrs Gingham, her ladyship's attendant, or otherwise; vowing deeply at the same time, that no peer in the realm should make an affectation of addressing Miss Mowbray a cloak for another and more secret intrigue. But his doubts on this subject were in great measure removed by the arrival of one of Lord Etherington's grooms with the following letter.

"MY DEAR MOWBRAY,

"You would naturally be surprised at my escape from the table yesterday before you returned to it, or your lovely sister had graced it with her presence. I must confess my folly; and I may do so the more boldly, for, as the footing on which I first opened this treaty was not a very romantic one, you will scarce suspect me of wishing to render it such. But I did in reality feel, during the whole of yesterday, a reluctance which I cannot express, to be presented to the lady on whose favour the happiness of my future life is to depend, upon such a public occasion, and in the presence of so promiscuous a company. I had my mask, indeed, to wear while in the promenade, but, of course, that was to be laid aside at table, and, consequently, I must have gone through the ceremony of introduction; a most interesting moment, which I was desirous to defer till a fitter season. I hope you will permit me to call upon you at Shaws-Castle this morning, in the hope—the anxious hope—of being allowed to pay my duty to Miss Mowbray, and apologize for not waiting upon her yesterday. I expect your answer with the utmost impatience, being always yours, &c. &c. &c.

"ETHERINGTON."

"This," said Saint Ronan's to himself, as he folded up the letter deliberately, after having twice read it over, "seems all fair and above board, I could not wish anything more explicit; and, moreover, it puts into black and white, as old Mick would say, what only rested before on our private conversation. An especial cure for the headach, such a billet as this in a morning."

So saying, he sat him down and wrote an answer, expressing the pleasure he would have in seeing his lordship so soon as he thought proper. He watched even the departure of the groom, and beheld him gallop off, as one who knows that his speedy return was expected by an impatient master.

Mowbray remained for a few minutes by himself, and reflected with delight upon the probable consequences of this match;—the advancement of his sister—and, above all, the various advantages which must necessarily accrue to himself by so close an alliance with one whom he had good reason to think deep *in the secret*, and capable of rendering him the most material assistance in his speculations on the turf, and in the sporting world. He then sent a servant to let Miss Mowbray know that he intended to breakfast with her.

"I suppose, John," said Clara, as her brother entered the apartment, "you are glad of a weaker cup this morning than those you were drinking last night—you were carousing till after the first cock."

"Yes," said Mowbray, "that sand-bed, old MacTurk, upon whom whole hogsheads make no impression, did make a bad boy of me—but the day is over, and they will scarce catch me in such another scrape.—What did you think of the masques?"

"Supported as well," said Clara, "as such folks support the disguise of gentlemen and ladies during life; and that is, with a great deal of bustle and very little propriety."

"I saw only one good masque there, and that was a Spaniard," said her brother.

"O, I saw him too," answered Clara; "but he wore his vizor on. An old Indian merchant, or some such thing, seemed to me a better character—the Spaniard did nothing but stalk about and twangle his guitar, for the amusement of my Lady Binks, as I think."

"He is a very clever fellow, though, that same Spaniard," rejoined Mowbray—"Can you guess who he is?"

"No, indeed; nor shall I take the trouble of trying. To set to guessing were as bad as seeing the whole mummery again."

"Well," replied her brother, "you will allow one thing at least—Bottom was well acted—you cannot deny that."

"Yes," replied Clara, "that worthy really deserved to wear his ass's head to the end of the chapter—but what of him?"

"Only conceive that he should be the very same person with that handsome Spaniard," replied Mowbray.

"Then there is one fool fewer than I thought there was," replied Clara, with the greatest indifference.

Her brother bit his lip.

"Clara," he said, "I believe you are an excellent good girl, and clever to boot, but pray do not set up for wit and oddity; there is nothing in life so intolerable as pretending to think differently from other people. —That gentleman was the Earl of Etherington."

This annunciation, though made in what was meant to be an imposing tone, had no impression on Clara.

"I hope he plays the peer better than the Fidalgo," she replied, carelessly.

"Yes," answered Mowbray, "he is one of the handsomest men of the time, and decidedly fashionable—you will like him much when you see him in private."

"It is of little consequence whether I do or no," answered Clara.

"You mistake the matter," said Mowbray, gravely; "it may be of considerable consequence."

"Indeed?" said Clara, with a smile; "I must suppose myself, then, too important a person not to make my approbation necessary to one of your first-rates. He cannot pretend to pass muster at Saint Ronan's without it.—Well, I will depute my authority to Lady Binks, and she shall pass your new recruits instead of me."

"This is all nonsense, Clara," said Mowbray. "Lord Etherington calls here this very morning, and wishes to be made known to you. I expect you will receive him as a particular friend of mine."

"With all my heart—so you will engage, after this visit, to keep him down with your other particular friends at the Well—you know it is a bargain that you bring neither buck nor pointer into my parlour—the one worries my cat, and the other my temper."

"You mistake me entirely, Clara—this is a very different visitor from any I have ever introduced to you—I expect to see him often here, and I hope you and he will be better friends than you think of. I have more reasons for wishing this, than I have now time to tell you."

Clara remained silent for an instant, then looked at her brother with an anxious and scrutinizing glance, as if she wished to penetrate into his inmost purpose.

"If I thought—" she said, after a minute's consideration, and with an altered and disturbed tone; "but no—I will not think that Heaven intends me such a blow—least of all, that it should come from your hands." She walked hastily to the window, and threw it open—then shut it again, and returned to her seat, saying, with a constrained smile, "May Heaven forgive you, brother, but you frightened me heartily."

"I did not mean to do so, Clara," said Mowbray, who saw the necessity of soothing her; "I only alluded in joke to those chances that are never out of other girls' heads, though you never seem to calculate on them."

"I wish you, my dear John," said Clara, struggling to regain entire composure, "I wish *you* would profit by my example, and give up the science of chance also—it will not avail you."

"How d'ye know that?—I'll shew you the contrary, you silly wench," answered Mowbray—"Here is a banker's bill, payable to your own order, for the cash you lent me, and something over—don't let old Mick have the fingering, but let Bindloose manage it for you—he is the honester man between two d—d knaves."

"Will not you, brother, send it to the man Bindloose yourself?"

"No—no," replied Mowbray—"he might confuse it with some of my transactions, and so you forfeit your stake."

"Well, I am glad you are able to pay me, for I want to buy Campbell's new work."

"I wish you joy of your purchase—but don't scratch me for not caring about it—I know as little of books as you of the long odds.—And come now, be serious, and tell me if you will be a good girl—lay aside your whims, and receive this English young nobleman like a lady as you are."

"That were easy," said Clara—"but—but—Pray, ask no more of me than just to see him.—Say to him at once, I am a poor creature in body, in mind, in spirits, in temper, in understanding—above all, say that I can receive him only once."

"I shall say no such thing," said Mowbray, bluntly; "it is good to be plain with you at once—I thought of putting off this discussion—but since it must come, the sooner it is over the better.—You are to understand, Clara Mowbray, that Lord Etherington has a particular view in this visit, and that his view has my full sanction and approbation."

"I thought so," said Clara, in the same altered tone of voice in which she had before spoken; "my mind foreboded this last of misfortunes! —but, Mowbray, you have no child before you—I neither will nor can see this nobleman."

"How!" exclaimed Mowbray, fiercely; "do you dare return me so peremptory an answer?—Think better of it, for, if we differ, you will have the worst of the game."

"Rely upon it," she continued, with more vehemence, "I will see him nor no man upon the footing you mention—my resolution is taken, and threats and entreaties will prove equally unavailing."

"Upon my word, madam," said Mowbray, "you have, for a modest and retired young lady, plucked up a goodly spirit of your own!—But you shall find mine equals it. If you do not agree to see my friend Lord Etherington, ay, and to receive him with the politeness due to the consideration I entertain for him, by Heaven! Clara, I will no longer regard you as my father's daughter. Think what you are giving up—the affection and protection of a brother—and for what?—merely for an idle point of etiquette.—You cannot, I suppose, even in the workings of your romantic brain, imagine that the days of Clarissa Harlowe and Harriet Byron are come back again, when women were married by main force; and it is monstrous vanity in you to suppose that Lord Etherington, since he has honoured you with any thoughts at all, will not be satisfied with a proper and civil refusal—You are no such prize, methinks, that the days of romance are to come back for you."

"I care not what days they are," said Clara—"I tell you I will not see Lord Etherington, or any one else, upon such preliminaries as you have stated—I cannot—I will not—and I ought not.—Had you meant me to receive him, which can be a matter of no consequence whatever, you should have left him on the footing of an ordinary visitor—as it is, I will not see him."

"You *shall* see and hear him both," said Mowbray; "you shall find me as obstinate as you are—as willing to forget I am a brother, as you to forget that you have one."

"It is time then," replied Clara, "that this house, once our father's, should no longer hold us both. I can provide for myself, and may God bless you!"

"You take it coolly, madam," said her brother, stepping through the apartment with much anxiety both of look and gesture.

"I do," she answered; "for it is what I have often foreseen—Yes, brother, I have often foreseen that you would make your sister the subject of your plots and schemes, so soon as other stakes failed you. That hour is come, and I am, as you say, prepared to meet it."

"And where may you propose to retire to?" said Mowbray. "I think that I, your only relation and natural guardian, have a right to know that—my honour and that of my family is concerned."

"Your honour?" she retorted, with a keen glance at him; "your interest I suppose you mean, is somehow connected with the place of my abode.—But keep yourself patient—the den of the rock, the linn of the brook, should be my choice, rather than a palace without my freedom."

"You are mistaken, however," said Mowbray, sternly, "if you hope to enjoy more freedom than I think you capable of making a good use of. The law authorizes, and reason, and even affection, require that you should be put under restraint for your own safety, and that of your character. You roamed the woods a little too much in my father's time, if all stories be true."

"I did—I did indeed, Mowbray," said Clara, weeping; "God pity me, and forgive you for upbraiding me with my state of mind—I know I cannot sometimes trust my own judgment; but is it for you to remind me of this?"

Mowbray was at once softened and embarrassed.

"What folly is this?" he said; "you say the most cutting things to me —are ready to fly from my house—and when I am provoked to make an angry answer, you burst into tears."

"Say you did not mean what you said, my dearest brother!" exclaimed Clara; "O say you did not mean it!—Do not take my liberty from me—it is all I have left, and, God knows, it is a poor comfort in the sorrows I undergo. I will put a fair face on everything—will go down to the Well—will wear what you please, and say what you please —but O! leave me the liberty of my solitude here—let me weep alone in the house of my father—and do not force a broken-hearted sister to lay her death at your door—My span must be a brief one, but do not you shake the sand-glass!—Disturb me not—let me pass quietly—I do not ask this so much for my sake as for your own. I would have you think of me sometimes, Mowbray, after I am gone, and without the bitter reflections which the recollection of harsh usage will assuredly bring with it. Pity me, were it but for your own sake—I have deserved nothing but compassion at your hand—There are but two of us on earth, why should we make each other miserable?"

She accompanied these entreaties with a flood of tears, and the most heart-bursting sobs. Mowbray knew not what to determine. On the one hand, he was bound by promise to the Earl; on the other, his sister was in no condition to receive such a visitor; nay, it was most probable, that if he adopted the strong measure of compelling her to receive him, her behaviour would probably be such as totally to break off the projected match, on the success of which he had founded so many castles in the air. In this dilemma, he had again recourse to argument.

"Clara," he said, "I am, as I have repeatedly said, your only relation and guardian—if there be any real reason why you ought not to receive, and, at least, make a civil reply to such a negotiation as the Earl of Etherington has thought fit to open, surely I ought to be intrusted with it. You enjoyed far too much of that liberty which you seem to prize so highly during my father's lifetime—in the last years of it at least—have you formed any foolish attachment during that time, which now prevents you from receiving such a visit as Lord Etherington has threatened?"

"Threatened!—the expression is well chosen," said Miss Mowbray; "and nothing can be more dreadful than such a threat, excepting its accomplishment."

"I am glad your spirits are reviving," replied her brother; "but that is no answer to my question."

"Is it necessary," said Clara, "that one must have actually some engagement or entanglement, to make them unwilling to be given in marriage, or even to be pestered upon such a subject?—Many young men declare they intend to die bachelors, why may I not be permitted to commence old maid at three-and-twenty?—Let me do so, like a kind brother, and there were never nephews and nieces so petted and so scolded, so nursed and so cuffed by a maiden aunt, as your children, when you have them, shall be by aunt Clara."

"And why not say all this to Lord Etherington?" said Mowbray; "wait until he proposes such a terrible bugbear as matrimony, before you refuse to receive him. Who knows, the whim that he hinted at may have passed away—he was, as you say, flirting with Lady Binks, and her ladyship has a good deal of address as well as beauty."

"Heaven improve both, (in an honest way,) if she will but keep his lordship to herself!" said Clara.

"Well, then," continued her brother, "things standing thus, I do not think you will have much trouble with his lordship—no more, perhaps, than just to give him a civil denial. After having spoken on such a subject to a man of my condition, he cannot well break off without you give him an apology."

"If that is all," said Clara, "he shall, as soon as he gives me an opportunity, receive such an answer as will leave him at liberty to woo any one whatsoever of Eve's daughters, excepting Clara Mowbray. Methinks I am so eager to set the captive free, that I wish as much for his lordship's appearance as I feared it a little while since."

"Nay, nay, but let us go fair and softly," said her brother. "You are not to refuse him before he asks the question."

"Certainly," said Clara; "but I well know how to manage that—he shall never ask the question at all. I will restore Lady Binks's admirer, without accepting so much as a civility in ransom."

"Worse and worse, Clara," answered Mowbray; "you are to remember he is my friend and guest, and he must not be affronted in my house. Leave things to themselves.—Besides, consider an instant, Clara—were you not better take a little time for reflection in this case? The offer is a splendid one—title—fortune—and, what is more, a fortune which you will be well entitled to share largely in."

"This is beyond our implied treaty," said Clara. "I have yielded more than ever I thought I should have done, when I agreed that this Earl should be introduced to me on the footing of a common visitor—And now you talk favourably of his pretensions—this is encroachment, Mowbray, and now I shall relapse into my obstinacy, and refuse to see him at all."

"Do as you will," replied Mowbray, sensible that it was only by working on her affections that he had any chance of carrying a point against her inclination,—"Do as you will, my dear Clara; but, for heaven's sake, wipe your eyes."

"And behave myself," said she, trying to smile as she obeyed him,—"behave myself, you would say, like folks of this world; but the quotation is lost on you, who never read either Prior or Shakespeare."

"I thank heaven for that," said Mowbray. "I have enough to burthen my brain, without carrying such a lumber of rhymes in it as you and Lady Pen do.—Come, that is right; go to the mirror, and make yourself decent."

A woman must be much borne down indeed by pain and suffering, when she totally loses all respect for her external appearance. The mad-woman in Bedlam wears her garland of straw, with a certain air of pretension; and we have seen a widow whom we knew to be most sincerely affected by a recent deprivation, whose weeds, nevertheless, were arranged with a dolorous degree of grace, which amounted almost to coquetry. Clara Mowbray had also, negligent as she seemed to be of appearances, her own arts of the toilette, although of the most rapid and most simple character. She took off her little riding-hat, and, unbinding a lace of Indian gold which retained her locks, shook them in dark and glossy profusion over her very handsome form, which they overshadowed down to her slender waist; and while her brother stood looking on her with a mixture of pride, affection, and compassion, she arranged them with a large comb, and, without the assistance of any *femme d'atours*, wove them, in the course of a few minutes, into such a natural head-dress as we see on the statues of the Grecian nymphs.

"Now let me but find my best muff," she said; "come prince and peer, I will be ready to receive them."

"Pshaw! your muff—who has heard of such a thing this twenty years? Muffs were out of fashion before you were born."

"No matter, John," replied his sister; "when a woman wears a muff, especially a determined old maid like myself, it is a sign she has no intentions to scratch; and therefore the muff serves all the purposes of a white flag, and prevents the necessity of drawing on a glove, so prudentially recommended by the motto of our cousins, the McIntoshes."

"Be it as you will then," said Mowbray; "for other than you do will it, you will not suffer it to be.—But how is this!—another billet?—We are in request this morning."

"Now, Heaven send his lordship may have judiciously considered all the risks which he is sure to encounter on this charmed ground, and resolved to leave his adventure unattempted," said Miss Mowbray.

Her brother glanced a look of displeasure at her, as he broke the seal of the letter, which was addressed to him with the words, "Haste and secrecy," written on the envelope. The contents, which greatly surprised him, we remit to the commencement of the next chapter.

Chapter Eleven

PRIVATE INFORMATION

> ——Ope this letter,
> I can produce a champion that will prove
> What is avouched there.——
>
> *King Lear*

THE BILLET which Mowbray received, and read in his sister's presence, contained these words:—

"SIR,

"Clara Mowbray has few friends—none, perhaps, excepting yourself, in right of blood, and the writer of this letter, by right of the fondest, truest, and most disinterested attachment that ever man bore to woman. I am thus explicit with you, because, though it is unlikely that I should ever again see or speak with your sister, I am desirous that you should be clearly acquainted with the cause of that interest, which I must always, even to my dying breath, take in her affairs.

"The person calling himself Lord Etherington is, I am aware, in the neighbourhood of Shaws-Castle, with the intention of paying his addresses to Miss Mowbray; and it is easy for me to foresee, arguing according to the ordinary views of mankind, that he may place his proposals in such a light as may make them seem highly desirable. But ere you give this person the encouragement which his offers may seem to deserve, please to inquire whether his fortune is certain, or his rank indisputable; and be not satisfied with light evidence on either point. A man may be in possession of an estate and title, to which he has no better right than his own rapacity and forwardness of assumption; and supposing Mr Mowbray jealous, as he must be, of the honour of his family, the alliance of such a one cannot but bring disgrace. This comes from one who will make good what he has written."

On the first perusal of a billet so extraordinary, Mowbray was inclined to set it down to the malice of some of the people at the Well, anonymous letters being no uncommon resource of the small wits who frequent such places of general resort, as a species of deception safely and easily executed, and well calculated to produce much mischief and confusion. But upon closer consideration, he was shaken in this opinion, and, starting suddenly from the reverie into which he had fallen, asked for the messenger who had brought the letter. "He was in the hall," the servant thought, and Mowbray ran to the hall. No—the messenger was not there, but Mowbray might see his back as he walked up the avenue.—He hollo'd—no answer was returned—he ran after the fellow, whose appearance was that of a countryman. The man quickened his pace as he saw himself pursued, and when he got out of the avenue, threw himself into one of the numerous by-paths which wanderers, who strayed in quest of nuts, or for the sake of exercise, had made in various directions through the extensive copse which surrounded the Castle, and was doubtless the reason of its acquiring the name of Shaws, which signifies, in the Scottish dialect, a wood of this description.

Irritated by the fellow's obvious desire to avoid him, and naturally obstinate in all his resolutions, Mowbray pursued for a considerable way, until he fairly lost breath; and the man having been long out of sight, he recollected at length that his engagement with the Earl of Etherington required his attendance at the Castle.

The young lord, indeed, had arrived at Shaws-Castle, so few

minutes after Mowbray's departure, that it was wonderful they had not met in the avenue. The servant to whom he applied, conceiving that his master must return instantly, as he had gone out without his hat, ushered the Earl, without farther ceremony, into the breakfast-room, where Clara was seated upon one of the window-seats, so busily employed with a book, or perhaps with her own thoughts while she held a book in her hands, that she scarce raised her head, until Lord Etherington advancing, pronounced the words, "Miss Mowbray." A start, and a low scream, announced her deadly alarm, and these were repeated as he made one pace nearer, and in a firmer accent said, "*Clara.*"

"No nearer—no nearer," she exclaimed, "if you would have me look upon you and live!" Lord Etherington remained standing, as if uncertain whether to advance or retreat, while with incredible rapidity she poured out her hurried entreaties that he would begone, sometimes addressing him as a real person, sometimes, and more frequently, as a delusive phantom, the offspring of her own excited imagination. "I knew it," she muttered, "I knew what would happen, if my thoughts were forced into that fearful channel.—Speak to me, brother! speak to me while I have reason left, and tell me that what stands before me is but an empty shadow! But it is no shadow—it remains before me in all the lineaments of mortal substance!"

"Clara," said the Earl, with a firm, yet softened voice, "collect and compose yourself. I am, indeed, no shadow—I am a much injured man, come to demand rights which have been unjustly withheld from me. I am now armed with power as well as justice, and my claims shall be heard."

"Never—never!" replied Clara Mowbray; "since extremity is my portion, let extremity give me courage.—You have no rights—none —I know you not, and I defy you."

"Defy me not, Clara Mowbray," answered the Earl, in a tone, and with a manner—how different from those which delighted society! for now he was solemn, tragic, and almost stern, like the judge when he passes sentence upon a criminal. "Defy me not," he repeated. "I am your Fate, and it rests with you to make me a kind or severe one."

"Dare you speak thus?" said Clara, her eyes flashing with anger, while her lips grew white, and quivered for fear—"Dare you speak thus, and remember that the same heaven is above our heads, to which you so solemnly vowed you would never see me more without my own consent?"

"That vow was conditional—Francis Tyrrel, as he calls himself, swore the same—hath *he* not seen you?" He fixed a piercing look on her; "He has—you dare not disown it!—And shall an oath, which to him is but a cobweb, be to me a shackle of iron?"

"Alas! it was but for a moment," said Miss Mowbray, sinking in courage, and drooping her head as she spoke.

"Were it but the twentieth part of an instant—the least conceivable space of subdivided time—still, you *did* meet—he saw you—you spoke to him. And me also you must see—me also you must hear! Or I will first claim you for my own in the face of the world; and, having vindicated my rights, I will seek out and extinguish the wretched rival who has dared to interfere with them."

"Can you speak this?" said Clara—"Can you so burst through the ties of nature?—Have you a heart?"

"I have; and it shall be moulded like wax to your slightest wishes, if you agree to do me justice; but not granite, nor aught else that nature has of hardest, will be more inflexible if you continue an useless opposition!—Clara Mowbray, I am your Fate."

"Not so, proud man," said Clara, rising. "God gave not one potsherd the right to break another, save by His divine permission—my fate is in the will of Him, without whose will even a sparrow falls not to the ground.—Begone—I am strong in faith of heavenly protection."

"Do you speak thus in sincerity?" said the Earl of Etherington; "consider first what is the prospect before you. I stand here in no doubtful or ambiguous character—I offer not the mere name of a husband—propose to you not a humble lot of obscurity and hardship, with fears for the past and doubts for the future; yet to a suit like this you could once listen.—I stand high among the nobles of the country, and offer you, as my bride, your share in my honours, and in the wealth which becomes them.—Your brother is my friend, and favours my suit. I will raise from the ground, and once more render illustrious, your ancient house—your motions shall be regulated by your wishes, even by your caprices—I will even carry my self-denial so far, that you shall, should you insist on so severe a measure, have your own residence, your own establishment, and without intrusion on my part, until the most devoted love, the most unceasing attentions, shall make way on your inflexible disposition.—All this I will consent to for the future —all that is passed shall be concealed from the public.—But mine, Clara Mowbray, you must be."

"Never—never!" said she, with increasing vehemence. "I can but repeat a negative, but it shall have all the force of an oath.—Your rank is nothing to me—your fortune I scorn—my brother has no right, by the law of Scotland, or of nature, to compel my inclinations.—I detest your treachery, and I scorn the advantage you propose to attain by it.—Should the law give you my hand, it would but award you that of a corpse."

"Alas! Clara," said the Earl, "you do but flutter in the net; but I will urge you no farther now—there is another encounter before me."

He was turning away, when Clara, springing forward, caught him by the arm, and repeated, in a low and impressive voice, the commandment, "Thou shalt do no murther!"

"Fear not any violence," he said, softening his voice, and attempting to take her hand, "but what may flow from your own severity.—Francis is safe from me, unless you are altogether unreasonable.—Allow me but what you cannot deny to any friend of your brother, the power of seeing you at times—suspend at least the impetuosity of your dislike to me, and I will, on my part, modify the current of my just and otherwise uncontrollable resentment."

Clara, extricating herself, and retreating from him, only replied, "There is a heaven above us, and THERE shall be judged our actions towards each other! You abuse a power most treacherously obtained—you break a heart that never did you wrong—you seek an alliance with a wretch who only wishes to be wedded to her grave.—If my brother brings you hither, I cannot help it—and if your coming prevents bloody and unnatural violence, it is so far well.—But by my consent you come *not;* and were the choice mine, I would rather be struck with life-long blindness, than that my eyes should again open on your person—rather that my ears were stuffed with the earth of the grave, than that they should again hear your voice!"

The Earl of Etherington smiled proudly, and replied, "Even this, madam, I can bear without resentment. Anxious and careful as you are to deprive your compliance of every grace and of every kindness, I receive the permission to wait on you, as I interpret your words."

"Do not so interpret them," she replied; "I do but submit to your presence as an unavoidable evil. Heaven be my witness, that, were it not to prevent greater and more desperate evil, I would not even so far acquiesce."

"Let acquiescence, then, be the word," he said; "and so thankful will I be, even for your acquiescence, Miss Mowbray, that all shall remain private, which I conceive you do not wish to be disclosed; and, unless absolutely compelled to it in self-defence, you may rely, no violence will be resorted to by me in any quarter.—I relieve you from my presence."

So saying, he withdrew from the apartment.

Chapter Twelve

EXPLANATORY

——By your leave, gentle wax.
SHAKESPEARE

IN THE HALL of Shaws-Castle the Earl of Etherington met Mowbray, returned from his fruitless chase after the bearer of the anonymous epistle before recited; and who had but just learned, on his return, that the Earl of Etherington was with his sister. There was a degree of mutual confusion when they met; for Mowbray had the contents of the letter fresh in his mind, and Lord Etherington, notwithstanding all the coolness which he had endeavoured to maintain, had not gone through the scene with Clara without discomposure. Mowbray asked the Earl whether he had seen his sister, and invited him, at the same time, to return to the parlour; and his lordship replied, in a tone as indifferent as he could assume, that he had enjoyed the honour of the lady's company for several minutes, and would not now intrude farther upon Miss Mowbray's patience.

"You have had such a reception as was agreeable, my lord, I trust?" said Mowbray. "I hope Clara did the honours of the house with propriety during my absence?"

"Miss Mowbray seemed a little fluttered with my sudden appearance," said the Earl, "for the servant shewed me in rather abruptly; and, circumstanced as we are, there is always awkwardness in a first meeting, where there is no third party to act as master of ceremonies.—I suspect, from the lady's looks, you have not quite kept my secret, my good friend. I myself, too, felt a little consciousness in approaching Miss Mowbray—but it is over now; and the ice being fairly broken, I hope to have other and more convenient opportunities to improve the advantage I have just gained in acquiring your lovely sister's personal acquaintance."

"So be it," said Mowbray; "but, as you declare for leaving the Castle just now, I must first speak a single word with your lordship, for which this place is not altogether convenient."

"I can have no objection, my dear Jack," said Etherington, following him with a thrill of conscious feeling, somewhat perhaps like that of the spider when he perceives his deceitful web is threatened with injury, and sits balanced in the centre, watching every point, and uncertain which he may be called upon first to defend. Such is one part, and not the slightest, of the penance which never fails to wait on those, who, abandoning the "fair play of the world," endeavour to work out their purposes by a process of deception and intrigue.

"My lord," said Mowbray, when they had entered a little apartment, in which the latter kept his guns, fishing-tackle, and other implements of sport, "you have played on the square with me; nay, more—I am bound to allow you have given me great odds. I am therefore not entitled to hear any reports to the prejudice of your lordship's character, without instantly communicating them. There is an anonymous letter which I have just received. Perhaps your lordship may know the hand, and thus be enabled to detect the writer."

"I do know the hand," said the Earl, as he received the note from Mowbray; "and, allow me to say, it is the only one which could have dared to frame any calumny to my prejudice. I hope, Mr Mowbray, it is impossible for you to consider this infamous charge as anything but a falsehood?"

"My placing it in your lordship's hands, without further inquiry, is a sufficient proof that I hold it such, my lord; at the same time, that I cannot doubt for a moment that your lordship has it in your power to overthrow so frail a calumny by the most satisfactory evidence."

"Unquestionably I can, Mr Mowbray," said the Earl; "for, besides my being in full possession of the estate and title of my father, the late Earl of Etherington, I have my father's contract of marriage, my own certificate of baptism, and the evidence of the whole country, to establish my right. All these shall be produced with the least delay possible. You will not think it surprising that one does not travel with this sort of documents in one's post-chaise."

"Certainly not, my lord," said Mowbray; "it is sufficient they are forthcoming when called for.—But, may I inquire, my lord, who the writer of this letter is, and whether he has any particular spleen to gratify by this very impudent assertion, which is so easily capable of being disproved?"

"He is," said Etherington, "or, at least, has the reputation of being, I am sorry to say—a near—a very near relation of my own—in fact, a brother by the father's side, but illegitimate.—My father was fond of him—I loved him also, for he has uncommonly fine parts, and is accounted highly accomplished. But there is a strain of something irregular in his mind—a vein, in short, of madness, which breaks out in the usual manner, rendering the poor young man a dupe to vain imaginations of his own dignity and grandeur, which is perhaps the most ordinary effect of insanity, and inspiring the deepest aversion against his nearest relatives, and against myself in particular. He is a man extremely plausible, both in speech and manners; so much so, that many of my friends think there is more vice than insanity in the irregularities which he commits; but I may, I hope, be forgiven, if I have formed a milder judgment of one supposed to be my father's son. Indeed, I cannot help being sorry for poor Frank, who might have made a very distinguished figure in the world."

"May I ask the gentleman's name, my lord?" said Mowbray.

"My father's indulgence gave him our family name of Tyrrel, with his own Christian name Francis; but his proper name, to which alone he has a right, is Martigny."

"Francis Tyrrel?" exclaimed Mowbray; "why, that is the name of the very person who made some disturbance at the Well just before your lordship arrived.—You may have seen an advertisement—a sort of placard."

"I have, Mr Mowbray," said the Earl. "Spare me on that subject, if you please—it has formed a strong reason why I did not mention my connection with this unhappy man before; but it is no unusual thing for persons, whose imaginations are excited, to rush into causeless quarrels, and then to make discreditable retreats from them."

"Or," said Mr Mowbray, "he may have, after all, been prevented from reaching the place of rendezvous—it was that very day on which your lordship, I think, received your wound; and, if I mistake not, you hit the man from whom you got the hurt."

"Mowbray," said Lord Etherington, lowering his voice, and taking him by the arm, "it is true that I did so—and, truly glad I am to observe, that, whatever might have been the consequences of such an accident, they cannot have been serious.—It struck me afterwards, that the man by whom I was so strangely assaulted, had some resemblance to the unfortunate Tyrrel—but I had not seen him for years.—At any rate, he cannot have been much hurt, since he is now able to resume his intrigues to the prejudice of my character."

"Your lordship views the thing with a firm eye," said Mowbray; "firmer than I think most people would be able to command, who had so narrow a chance of a scrape so uncomfortable."

"Why, I am, in the first place, by no means sure that the risk existed," said the Earl of Etherington; "for, as I have often told you, I had but a very transient glimpse of the ruffian; and, in the second place, I *am* sure that no permanent bad consequences have ensued. I am too old a fox-hunter to be afraid of a leap after it is cleared, as they tell of the fellow who fainted in the morning at the sight of the precipice he had leaped over when he was drunk on the night before. The man who wrote that letter," touching it with his finger, "is alive, and able to threaten me; and if he did come to any hurt from my hand, it was in the act of attempting my life, of which I shall carry the mark to my grave."

"Nay, I am far from blaming your lordship," said Mowbray, "for what you did in self-defence, but the circumstance might have turned out very unpleasant.—May I ask what you intend to do with this unfortunate gentleman, who is in all probability in the neighbourhood?"

"I must first discover the place of his retreat," said Lord Etherington, "and then consider what is to be done both for his safety, poor fellow, and my own. It is probable, too, that he may find sharpers to prey upon what fortune he still possesses, which, I assure you, is sufficient to attract a set of folks, who may ruin while they humour.—May I beg that you, too, will be on the out-look, and let me know if you hear or see more of him?"

"I shall, most certainly, my lord," answered Mowbray; "but the only one of his haunts which I know, is the old Cleikum Inn, where he chose to take up his residence. He has now left it, but perhaps the old crab-fish of a landlady may know something of him."

"I will not fail to inquire," said Lord Etherington; and, with these words, took a kind farewell of Mowbray, mounted his horse, and rode up the avenue.

"A cool fellow," said Mowbray, as he looked after him, "d—d cool fellow, this brother-in-law of mine, that is to be—takes a shot at his father's son with as little remorse as at a black cock—what would he do with me, were we to quarrel?—Well, I can snuff a candle and strike out the ace of hearts; and so, should things go wrong, he has no Jack Raw to deal with, but Jack Mowbray."

Meanwhile, the Earl of Etherington hastened home to his own apartments at the Hotel; and, not entirely pleased with the events of the day, commenced a letter to his correspondent, agent, and confidant, Captain Jekyl, with which we have fortunately the means of presenting our readers.—

"FRIEND HARRY,

"THEY say a falling house is best known by the rats leaving it—a falling state, by the desertion of confederates and allies—and a falling man, by the desertion of his friends. If this be true augury, your last letter may be considered as ominous of my breaking down. Methinks, you have gone far enough, and shared deep enough with me, to have some confidence in my *savoir faire*—some little faith both in my means and management.—What cross-grained fiend has at once inspired you with what I suppose you wish me to call politic doubts and scruples of conscience, but which I can only regard as symptoms of fear and disaffection? You can have no idea of 'duels betwixt relations so nearly connected'—and 'the affair seems very delicate and intricate'—and again, 'the matter has never been fully explained to you'—and, moreover, 'if you are expected to take an active part in the business, it must be when you are honoured with my full and unreserved confidence, otherwise how could you be of the use to me which I might require?' Such are your expressions.

"Now, as to scruples of conscience about near relations, and so forth, all that has blown by without much mischief, and certainly is not likely to occur again—besides, did you never hear of friends quarrelling before? And are they not to exercise the usual privileges of gentlemen when they do? Moreover, how am I to know that this plaguy fellow *is* actually related to me?—They say it is a wise child knows its own father; and I cannot be expected wise enough to know to a certainty my father's son.—So much for relationship.—Then, as to full and unreserved confidence—why, Harry, this is just as if I were to ask you to look at a watch, and tell what it was o'clock, and you were to reply, that truly you could not inform me, because you had not examined the springs, the counter-balances, the wheels, and the whole internal machinery of the little time-piece.—But the upshot of the whole is this. Harry Jekyl, who is as sharp a fellow as any other, thinks he has his friend Lord Etherington at a dead-lock, and that he knows already so much of the said noble lord's history as to oblige his lordship to tell him the whole. And perhaps he not unreasonably concludes, that the custody of a whole secret is more creditable, and probably more lucrative, than that of a half one; and, in short,—he is resolved to make the most of the cards in his hand. Another, mine honest Harry, would take the trouble to recall to your mind past times and circumstances, and conclude with expressing a humble opinion, that if Harry Jekyl was asked *now* to do any service for the noble lord aforesaid, Harry had got his reward in his pocket aforehand. But I do not argue thus, because I would rather be leagued with a friend who assists me with a view to future profit, than from respect to benefits already received. The first lies like the fox's scent when on his last legs, increasing every moment; the other is a back-scent, growing colder the longer you follow it, until at last it becomes impossible to puzzle it out. I will, therefore, submit to circumstances, and tell you the whole story, though somewhat tedious, in hopes that I can conclude with such a trail as you will open upon breast high.

"Thus then it was.—Francis, fifth Earl of Etherington, and my much-honoured father, was what is called a very eccentric man—that is, he was neither a wise man nor a fool—had too much sense to walk into a well, and yet in some of the furious fits which he was visited with, I have seen him quite mad enough to throw any one else into it.

—Men said there was a lurking insanity—but it is an ill bird, &c., and I will say no more about it. This shatter-brained peer was, in other respects, a handsome accomplished man, with an expression somewhat haughty, yet singularly pleasing when he chose it—a man, in short, who might push his fortune with the fair sex.

"Lord Etherington, such as I have described him, being upon his travels in France, formed an attachment of the heart—ay, and some have pretended, of the hand also, with a certain beautiful orphan, Marie de Martigny. Of this union is said to have sprung, (for I am determined not to be certain on that point,) that most incommodious person, Francis Tyrrel, as he calls himself, but as I would rather call him, Francis Martigny; the latter suiting my views, as perhaps the former name agrees better with his pretensions. Now, I am too good a son to subscribe to the alleged regularity of the marriage between this lady and my right honourable and very good lord father, because my said right honourable and very good lord did, on his return to England, become wedded, in the face of the church, to my very affectionate and well-endowed mother, Anne Bulmer of Bulmer-hall, from which happy union sprung I, Francis Valentine Bulmer Tyrrel, the lawful inheritor of my father and mother's joint estates, as I was the proud possessor of their ancient names. But the noble and wealthy pair, though blessed with such a pledge of love as myself, lived mighty ill together, and the rather, when my right honourable father, sending for this other Sosia, this unlucky Francis Tyrrel, senior, from France, insisted, in the face of propriety, that he should reside in his house, and share, in all respects, in the opportunities of education by which the real Sosia, Francis Valentine Bulmer Tyrrel, then commonly called Lord Oakendale, hath profited in such an uncommon degree.

"Various were the matrimonial quarrels which arose between the honoured lord and lady, in consequence of this unseemly conjunction of the legitimate and illegitimate; and to these, we, the subjects of the dispute, were sometimes very properly, as well as decorously, made the witnesses. On one occasion, my right honourable mother, who was a free-spoken lady, found the language of her own rank quite inadequate to express the strength of her generous feelings, and borrowing from the vulgar two emphatic words, applied them to Marie de Martigny, and her son Francis Tyrrel. Never did Earl that ever wore coronet, fly a pitch of more uncontrollable rage, than did my right honourable father; and, in the ardour of his reply, he adopted my mother's phraseology, to inform her that if there *was* a whore and bastard connected with his house, it was herself and her brat.

"I was even then a sharp little fellow, and was incredibly struck with the communication, which, in an hour of uncontrollable irritation, had escaped my right honourable father. It is true, he instantly gathered himself up again; and he perhaps recollecting such a word as *bigamy*, and my mother, on her side, considering the consequences of such a thing as a descent from the Countess of Etherington into Mrs Bulmer, neither wife, maid, nor widow, there was an apparent reconciliation between them, which lasted for some time. But the speech remained deeply imprinted on my remembrance; the more so, that once, when I was exerting over my friend Francis Tyrrel, the authority of a legitimate brother, and Lord Oakendale, old Cecil, my father's confidential valet, was so much scandalized as to intimate a possibility that we might one day change conditions. These two accidental communications seemed to me a key to certain long lectures, with which my father used to regale us boys, but me in particular, upon the extreme mutability of human affairs,—the disappointment of the best-grounded hopes and expectations,—and the necessity of being so accomplished in all useful branches of knowledge, as might, in case of accidents, supply any defalcation in our rank and fortune;—as if any art or science could make amends for the loss of an Earldom, and twelve thousand a-year! All this prosing seemed to my anxious mind designed to prepare me for some unfortunate change; and when I was old enough to make such private inquiries as lay in my power, I became still more persuaded that my right honourable father nourished some thoughts of making an honest woman of Marie de Martigny, and a legitimate elder brother of Francis, after his death at least, if not during his life. I was the more convinced of this, when a little affair, which I chanced to have with the daughter of my Tu——, drew down my father's wrath upon me in great abundance, and occasioned my being banished to Scotland, along with my brother, under a very poor allowance, without introductions, except to one steady old professor, and with the charge that I should not assume the title of Lord Oakendale, but content myself with my maternal grandfather's name of Valentine Bulmer, that of Francis Tyrrel being pre-occupied.

"Upon this occasion, notwithstanding the fear which I entertained of my father's passionate temper, I did venture to say, that since I was to resign my title, I thought I had a right to keep my family name, and that my brother might take his mother's. I wish you had seen the look of rage with which my father regarded me when I gave him this spirited hint. 'Thou art,' he said, and paused, as if to find out the bitterest epithet to supply the blank —'thou art thy mother's child, and her perfect picture'—(this seemed the severest reproach that occurred to him.)—'Bear her name then, and bear it with patience and in secrecy; or I here give you my word, you shall never bear another the whole days of your life.' This sealed my mouth with a witness; and then, in allusion to my flirtation with the daughter of my Tu—— aforesaid, he enlarged on the folly and iniquity of private marriages, warned me that in the country I was going to, the matrimonial noose often lies hid under flowers, and that folks find it twitched round their neck when they least expect such a cravat; assured me, that he had very particular views for settling Francis and me in life, and that he would forgive neither of us who should, by any such rash entanglement, render them unavailing.

"This last minatory admonition was the more tolerable, that my rival had his share of it; and so we were bundled off to Scotland, coupled up like two pointers in a dog-cart, and—I can speak for one at least—with much the same uncordial feelings towards each other. I often, indeed, detected Francis looking at me with a singular expression, as of pity and anxiety, and once or twice he seemed disposed to enter on something respecting the situation in which we stood towards each other; but I felt no desire to encourage his confidence. Meantime, as we were called, by our father's directions, not brothers, but cousins, so we came to bear towards each other the habits of companionship, though scarcely of friendship. What Francis thought, I know not; for my part, I must confess, that I lay by on the watch for some opportunity when I might mend my own situation with my father, though at the prejudice of my rival. And Fortune, while she seemed to prevent such an opportunity, involved us both in one of the strangest and most complicated mazes that her capricious divinity-ship ever wove, and out of which I am even now struggling, by sleight or force, to extricate myself. I can hardly help wondering, even yet, at the odd conjunction, which has produced such an intricacy of complicated incidents.

"My father was a great sportsman, and Francis and I had both inherited his taste for field-sports, but I in a keener and more ecstatic degree. Edinburgh, which is a tolerable residence in winter and spring, becomes disagreeable in summer, and in autumn is the most melancholy sejour that ever poor mortals were condemned to. No public places are open, no inhabitant of any consideration remains in the town; those who cannot get away, hide themselves in obscure corners, as if ashamed to be seen in the streets—the gentry go to their country-houses—the citizens to their sea-bathing quarters—the lawyers to their circuits—the writers to visit their country clients—and all the world to the moors to shoot grouse. We, who felt the indignity of remaining in town during this deserted season, obtained, with some difficulty, permission from the Earl to betake ourselves to any obscure corner, and shoot grouse, if we could get leave to do so on our general character of English students at the University of

Edinburgh, without quoting anything more.

"The first year of our banishment we went to the neighbourhood of the Highlands; but finding our sport interrupted by game-keepers and their gillies, on the second occasion we established ourselves at this little village of Saint Ronan's, where there was then no Spaw, no fine people, no card tables, no quizzes, excepting the old quiz of a landlady, with whom we lodged. We found the place much to our mind; the old landlady had interest with some old fellow, agent of a non-residing nobleman, who gave us permission to sport over his moors, of which I availed myself keenly, and Francis with more moderation. He was, indeed, of a grave musing sort of habit, and often preferred solitary walks, in the wild and beautiful scenery with which the village is surrounded, to the use of the gun. He was attached to fishing moreover, that dullest of human amusements, and this also tended to keep us considerably apart. This gave me rather pleasure than concern;—not that I hated Francis at that time; nay, not that I greatly disliked his society; but merely because it was unpleasant to be always with one whose fortunes I apprehended to stand in direct opposition to my own. I also rather despised the indifference about sport, which indeed seemed to grow upon him; but my gentleman had better taste than I was aware of. If he sought no grouse on the hill, he had flushed a pheasant in the wood.

"Clara Mowbray, daughter of the Lord of the more picturesque than wealthy domain of Saint Ronan's, was at that time scarce sixteen years old, and as wild and beautiful a woodland nymph as the imagination can fancy—simple as a child in all that concerned the world and its ways, acute as a needle in every point of knowledge which she had found an opportunity of becoming acquainted with; fearing harm from no one, and with a lively and natural strain of wit, which brought amusement and gaiety wherever she came. Her motions were under no restraint, save that of her own inclination; for her father, though a cross, peevish, old man, was confined to his chair with the gout, and her only companion, a girl of somewhat inferior caste, bred up in the utmost deference to Miss Mowbray's fancies, served for company indeed in her strolls through this wild country on foot and on horseback, but never thought of controlling her will and pleasure.

"The extreme loneliness of the country, (at that time,) and the simplicity of its inhabitants, seemed to render their excursions perfectly safe. Francis, happy dog, became the companion of the damsels on such occasions through the following accident. Miss Mowbray had dressed herself and her companion like country wenches, with a view to surprise the family of one of their better sort of farmers. They had accomplished their purpose greatly to their satisfaction, and were hying home after sunset, when they were encountered by a country fellow—a sort of Harry Jekyl in his way, who, being equipped with a glass or two of whisky, saw not the nobility of blood through her disguise, and accosted the daughter of a hundred sires, as he would have done a ewe-milker. Miss Mowbray remonstrated—her companion screamed—up came cousin Francis with a fowling-piece on his shoulder, and soon put the sylvan to flight.

"This was the beginning of an acquaintance, which had gone great lengths before I found it out.—The fair Clara, it seems, found it safer to roam in the woods with an escort than alone, and my studious and sentimental relative was almost her constant companion. At their age, it was likely that some time might pass ere they came to understand each other; but full confidence and intimacy was established between them ere I heard of their amour.

"And here, Harry, I must pause till next morning, and send you the conclusion under a separate cover. The rap which I had over the elbow the other day, is still tingling at the end of my fingers, and you must not be critical upon my manuscript."

Chapter Thirteen

LETTER CONTINUED

——Must I then ravel out
My weaved-up follies?——
SHAKESPEARE

"I RESUME my pen, Harry, to mention, without attempting to describe my surprise, when, compelled by circumstances, Francis made me the confidant of his love-intrigue. My grave cousin in love, and very much in the mind of approaching the perilous verge of clandestine marriage—he who used every now and then, not much to the improvement of our cordial regard, to lecture me upon filial duty, just upon the point of slipping the bridle himself! I could not for my life tell whether surprise, or a feeling of mischievous satisfaction, was predominant. I tried to talk to him as he used to talk to me; but I had not the gift of persuasion, or he the power of understanding my words of wisdom. He insisted our situation was different—that his unhappy birth, as he termed it, freed him at least from dependence on his father's absolute will—that he had, by bequest from some relative of his mother, a moderate competence, which Miss Mowbray had consented to share with him; in fine, that he desired not my counsel but my assistance. A moment's consideration convinced me, I should be unkind, not to him only but to myself, unless I gave him all the backing I could in this his most dutiful scheme. I recollected our right honourable father's denunciations against Scotch marriages, and secret marriages of all sorts,—denunciations perhaps not the less vehement, that he might feel some secret prick of conscience on the subject himself. I remembered that my grave brother had always been a favourite, and I forgot not—how was it possible I could forget—those ominous expressions which intimated a possibility of the hereditary estate and honours being transferred to the elder, instead of the younger son. Now, it required no conjuror to foresee, that should Francis commit this inexpiable crime of secretly allying himself with a Scotch beauty, our sire would lose all wish to accomplish such a transference in his favour; and while my brother's merits were altogether obscured by such an unpardonable act of disobedience, my own, no longer overshadowed by prejudice or partiality, would shine forth in all their natural brilliancy. These considerations, which flashed on me with the rapidity of lightning, induced me to consent to hold Frank's backhand, during the perilous game he proposed to play. I had only to take care that my own share in the matter should not be so prominent as to attract my father's attention; and this I was little afraid of, for his wrath was usually of that vehement and forcible character, which, like lightning, is attracted to one single point, there bursting with violence as undivided as it was uncontrollable.

"I soon found the lovers needed my assistance more than I could have supposed; for they were absolute novices in a sort of intrigue, which to me seemed as easy and natural as lying. Francis had been detected by some tattling spy in his walks with Clara, and the news had been carried to old Mowbray, who was greatly incensed at his daughter, though little knowing that her crime was greater than admitting an unknown English student to form a personal acquaintance with her. He prohibited farther intercourse—resolved, in justice of peace phrase, to rid the country of us; and, prudently sinking all mention of his daughter's delinquency, commenced an action against Francis, under pretext of punishing him as an encroacher upon his game, but in reality to scare him from the neighbourhood. His person was particularly described to all the keepers and satellites about Shaws-Castle, and any personal intercourse betwixt him and Clara became impossible, except under the most desperate risks. Nay, such was their alarm, that Master Francis thought it prudent, for Miss Mowbray's sake, to withdraw as far as a town called Marchthorn, and there to conceal himself, maintaining his intercourse with Clara only by letter.

"It was then I became the sheet-anchor of the hope of the lovers; it was then my early dexterity and powers of contrivance were first put to the test; and it would be too long to tell you in how many shapes, and by how many contrivances, I acted as agent, letter-carrier, and go-between, to maintain the intercourse of these separated turtles.—I have had a good deal of trouble in that way on my own account, but never half so much as I took on account of this brace of lovers. I scaled walls and swam rivers, set blood-hounds, quarter-staves, and blunderbusses at defiance; and, excepting the distant prospect of self-interest which I have hinted at, I was neither to have honour nor reward for my pains. I will own to you, that Clara Mowbray was so very beautiful—so absolutely confiding in her lover's friend—and thrown into such close intercourse with me, that there were times when I thought that, in conscience, she ought not to have scrupled to have contributed a mite to reward the faithful labourer. But then, she looked like purity itself; and I was such a novice at that time of day, that I did not know how it might have been possible for me to retreat, if I had made too bold an advance—and, in short, I thought it best to content myself with assisting true love to run smooth, in hopes it would assure me, in the long-run, an Earl's title and an Earl's fortune.

"Nothing was therefore ventured on my part which could raise suspicion, and, as the confidential friend of the lovers, I prepared everything for their secret marriage. The pastor of the parish agreed to perform the ceremony, prevailed upon by an argument which I used to him, and which Clara, had she guessed it, would have little thanked me for. I led the honest man to believe, that, in declining to do his office, he might prevent a too successful lover from doing justice to a betrayed maiden; and the parson, who, I found, had a spice of romance in his disposition, resolved, under such pressing circumstances, to do them the kind office of binding them together, although the consequence might be a charge of irregularity against himself. Old Mowbray was much confined to his room, his daughter less watched since Frank had removed from the neighbourhood—the brother, (which, by the by, I should have said before) not then in the country—and it was settled that the lovers should meet at the Old Kirk when the twilight became deep, and go off in a chaise for England so soon as the ceremony was performed.

"When all this was arranged save the actual appointment of the day, you cannot conceive the happiness and the gratitude of my sage brother. He looked upon himself as approaching to the seventh heaven, instead of losing his chance of a good fortune, and encumbering himself at eighteen with a wife, and all the probabilities of narrow circumstances, and an increasing family. Though so much younger myself, I could not help wondering at his extreme want of knowledge of the world, and feeling ashamed that I had ever allowed him to take the airs of a tutor with me; and this conscious superiority supported me against the thrill of jealousy which always seized me when I thought of his carrying off the beautiful prize, which, without my address, he could never have made his own.—But at this important crisis, I had a letter from my father, which, by some accident, had long lain at our lodgings in Edinburgh; had then visited our former quarters in the Highlands; again returned to Edinburgh, and at length reached me at Marchthorn in a most critical time.

"It was in reply to a letter of mine, in which, among other matter, such as good boys send to their papas, descriptions of the country, account of studies, exercise, and so forth, I had, to fill up the sheet to a dutiful length, thrown in something about the family of Saint Ronan's, in the neighbourhood of whom I was writing. I had no idea what an effect the name must have produced on the mind of my right honourable father, but his letter sufficiently expressed it. He charged me to cultivate the acquaintance of Mr Mowbray as fast and as intimately as possible; and, if need were, to inform him candidly of our real character and situation in life. Wisely considering, at the same time, that his paternal admonition might be neglected if not backed by some sufficient motive, his lordship frankly let me into the secret of my granduncle by the mother's side, Mr S. Mowbray of Nettlewood's last will and testament, by which I saw, to my astonishment and alarm, that a large and fair estate was bequeathed to the eldest son and heir of the Earl of Etherington, on condition of his forming a matrimonial alliance with a lady of the house of Mowbray, of Saint Ronan's.—Mercy of heaven! how I stared! Here had I been making every preparation for wedding Francis to the very girl, whose hand would insure to myself wealth and independence!—And even the first loss, though great, was not like to be the last. My father spoke of the marriage like a land-surveyor, but of the estate of Nettlewood like an impassioned lover. He seemed to doat on every acre of it, and dwelt on its contiguity to his own domains, as a circumstance which rendered the union of the estates not desirable merely, but constituted an arrangement pointed out by the hand of nature. And although he observed, that, on account of the youth of the parties, a treaty of marriage could not be immediately undertaken, it was yet clear he would approve at heart of any bold stroke which would abolish the interval of time that might otherwise intervene ere Oakendale and Nettlewood became one property.

"Here, then, were shipwrecked my fair hopes. It was clear as sunshine, that a private marriage, unpardonable in the abstract, would become venial, nay, highly laudable, in my father's eyes, if it united his heir with Clara Mowbray; and if he really had, as my fears suggested, the means of establishing legitimacy on my brother's part, nothing was so like to tempt him to use them, as the certainty that, by his doing so, Nettlewood and Oakendale would be united into one. The very catastrophe which I had prepared, as sure to exclude my rival from his father's favour, was thus likely, unless it could be prevented, to become a strong motive and argument for my father's placing his rights above mine.

"I shut myself up in my bed-room; locked the door; read, and again read my father's letter; and, instead of giving way to idle passion, (beware of that, Harry, even in the most desperate circumstances,) I considered, with keen investigation, whether some remedy could not yet be found.—To break off the match for the time, would have been easy—a little private information to Mr Mowbray would have done that with a vengeance—But then the treaty might be renewed under my father's auspices;—at all events, the share which I had taken in the intrigue between Clara and my brother, rendered it almost impossible for me to become a suitor in my own person.—Amid these perplexities, it suddenly occurred to my adventurous heart and contriving brain—What if I should personate the bridegroom?—This strange thought, you will recollect, occurred to a very youthful brain—it was banished—it returned—returned again and again—was viewed under every different shape—became familiar—was adopted.—It was easy to fix the appointment with Clara and the clergyman, for I managed the whole correspondence—the resemblance between Francis and me in stature and in proportion—the disguise which we were to assume—the darkness of the church—the hurry of the moment—might, I trusted, prevent Clara from recognizing me. To the minister I had only to say, that, though I had hitherto talked of a friend, I myself was the happy man. My first name was Francis as well as his; and I had found Clara so gentle, so confiding, so flatteringly cordial in her intercourse with me, that, once within my power, and prevented from receding by shame, and a thousand contradictory feelings, I had, with the vanity of an *amoureux de seize ans*, the confidence to believe I could reconcile the fair lady to the exchange.

"There certainly never came such a thought into a madcap's brain; and, what is more extraordinary—but that you already know—it was so far successful, that the marriage ceremony was performed between us in the presence of a servant of mine, her accommodating companion, and the priest.—We got into the carriage, and were a mile from the church, when my unlucky or lucky brother stopped the chaise by force—through what means he had obtained knowledge of my little trick, I never have been able to learn. Solmes has been faithful to me in too many instances, that I should suspect him in this important crisis. I jumped out of the carriage, pitched fraternity to the devil, and, betwixt desperation and something very like shame, began to cut away with a couteau de chasse, which I had provided in case of necessity.—All was in vain—I was hustled down under the wheel of the carriage, and, the horses taking fright, it went over my body.

"Here ends my narrative; for I neither heard nor saw more until I found myself stretched on a sick-bed many miles from the scene of action, and Solmes engaged in attending on me. In answer to my passionate inquiries, he briefly informed me, that Master Francis had sent back the young lady to her own dwelling, and that she appeared to be extremely ill in consequence of the alarm she had sustained. My own health, he assured me, was considered as very precarious, and added, that Tyrrel, who was in the same house, was in the utmost perturbation on my account. The very mention of his name brought on a crisis in which I brought up much blood; and it is singular that the physician who attended me—a grave gentleman, with a wig—considered that this was of service to me. I know it frightened me heartily, and prepared me for a visit from Master Frank, which I endured with a tameness he would not have experienced, had the usual current of blood flowed in my veins. But sickness and the lancet make one very tolerant of sermonizing.—At last, in consideration of being relieved from his accursed presence, and the sound of his infernally calm voice, I slowly and reluctantly acquiesced in an arrangement, by which he proposed that we should for ever bid adieu to each other, and to Clara Mowbray. I would have hesitated at this last stipulation. 'She was,' I said, 'my wife, and I was entitled to claim her as such.'

"This drew down a shower of most moral reproaches, and an assurance that Clara disowned and detested my alliance, and that where there had been an essential error in the person, the mere ceremony could never be accounted binding by the law of any Christian country. I wonder this had not occurred to me; but my ideas of marriage were much founded on plays and novels, where such devices as I had practised are often resorted to for winding up the plot, without any hint of their illegality; besides, I had confided, as I mentioned before, a little too rashly perhaps, in my own powers of persuading so young a bride as Clara to be contented with one handsome fellow instead of another.

"Solmes took up the argument, when Francis released me by leaving the room. He spoke of my father's resentment, should this enterprize reach his ears—of the revenge of Mowbray of Saint Ronan's, whose nature was both haughty and rugged—of risk from the laws of the country, and God knows what bugbears beside, which, at a more advanced age, I would have laughed at. In a word, I sealed the capitulation, vowed perpetual absence, and banished myself, as they say in this country, forth of Scotland.

"And here, Henry, observe and respect my genius. Every circumstance was against me in this negotiation. I had been the aggressor in the war; I was wounded, and, it might be said, a prisoner in my antagonist's hands; yet I could so far avail myself of Monsieur Martigny's greater eagerness for peace, that I clogged the treaty with a condition highly advantageous to myself, and equally unfavourable to him.—Said Mr Francis Martigny was to take upon himself the burthen of my right honourable father's displeasure; and our separation, which was certain to give immense offence, was to be represented as his work, not as mine. I insisted, tender-hearted, dutiful soul, as I was, that I would consent to no measure which was to bring down papa's displeasure. This was a *sine qua non* in our negotiation.

Voilà ce que c'est d'avoir des talens!

Monsieur Francis would, I suppose, have taken the world on his shoulders, to have placed an eternal separation betwixt his turtle-dove and the falcon who had made so bold a pounce at her.—What he wrote to my father, I know not; as for myself, in all duty, I represented the bad state of my health from an accident, and that my brother and companion having been suddenly called from me by some cause which he had not explained, I had thought it necessary to get to London for the best advice, and only waited his lordship's permission to return to the paternal mansion. This I soon received, and found, as I expected, that he was in towering wrath against my brother for his disobedience; and, after some time, I even had reason to think, (as, how could it be otherwise, Harry?) that, on becoming better acquainted with the merits and amiable manners of his apparent heir, he lost any desire which he might formerly have entertained, of accomplishing any change in my circumstances in relation to the world. Perhaps the old peer turned a little ashamed of his own conduct, and dared not aver to the congregation of the righteous, (for he became saintly in his latter days,) the very pretty frolics which he seems to have been guilty of in his youth. Perhaps, also, the death of my right honourable mother operated in my favour, since, while she lived, my chance was the worse—there is no saying what a man will do to spite his wife.—Enough, he died—slept with his right honourable fathers, and I became, without opposition, Right Honourable in his stead.

"How I have borne my new honours, thou, Harry, and our merry set, know full well. Newmarket and Tattersal's may tell the rest.—I think I have been as lucky as most men where luck is most prized, and so I shall say no more on that subject.

"And now, Harry, I will suppose thee in a moralizing mood; that is, I will fancy the dice have run wrong—or your double-barrel has hung fire—or a certain lady has looked cross—or any such weighty cause of gravity has occurred, and you give me the benefit of your seriousness. —'My dear Etherington,' say you pithily, 'you are a precious fool!—Here you are, stirring up a business rather scandalous in itself, and fraught with mischief to all concerned—a business which might sleep for ever, if you let it alone, but which is sure, like a sea-coal fire, to burst into a flame if you go on poking it. I would like to ask your lordship only two questions,'—say you, with your usual graceful attitude of adjusting your perpendicular shirt-collar, and passing your hand over the knot of your cravat, which deserves a peculiar place in the *Tietania*—'only two questions—that is, Whether you do not repent the past? and, Whether you do not fear the future?' Very comprehensive queries, these of yours, Harry; for they respect both the time past and the time to come—one's whole life, in short. However, I shall endeavour to answer them as well as I may.

"Repent the past, said you?—Yes, Harry, I think I do repent the past—that is, not quite in the parson's style of repentance, which resembles yours when you have a head-ache, but as I would repent a hand at cards which I had played on false principles. I should have begun with the young lady—availed myself in a very different manner of Monsieur Martigny's absence, and my own intimacy with her, and thus superseded him, if possible, in the damsel's affections. The scheme I adopted, though there was, I think, both boldness and dexterity in it, was that of a novice of premature genius, who could not calculate chances. So much for repentance.—Do I not fear the future?—Harry, I will not cut your throat for supposing you to have put the question, but calmly assure you, that I never feared anything in my life. I was born without the sensation, I believe; at least, it is perfectly unknown to me. When I felt that cursed wheel pass across my breast, when I felt the pistol-ball benumb my arm, I felt no more agitation than at the bounce of a champagne-cork. But I would not have you think that I am fool enough to risk plague, trouble, and danger, (all of which, besides considerable expence, I am now prepared to encounter,) without some adequate motive,—and here it is.

"From various quarters, hints, murmurs, and surmises have reached me, that an attack will be made on my rank and status in society, which can only be in behalf of this fellow Martigny, for I will not call him by his stolen name of Tyrrel. Now, this I hold to be a breach of the paction betwixt us, by which—that is, by its true meaning and purport—he was to leave my right honourable father and me to settle our own matters without his interference, which amounted to a virtual resignation of his rights, if the scoundrel ever had any. Can he expect I am to resign my wife, and, what is a better thing, old Scrogie Mowbray's estate of Nettlewood, to gratify the humour of a fellow who sets up claims to my title and whole property? No, by ——. If he assails me in a point so important, I will retaliate upon him in one where he will feel as keenly; and that he may depend upon.—And now, methinks, you come upon me with a second edition of your grave remonstrances, about family feuds, unnatural rencontres, offence to all the feelings of all the world, et cætera, et cætera, which you might usher in most delectably with the old stave about brethren dwelling together in unity. I will not stop to inquire, whether all these delicate apprehensions are on account of the Earl of Etherington, his safety, and his reputation; or whether my friend Harry Jekyl be not considering how far his own interference with such a naughty business will be well taken at Head-quarters; and so, without pausing on that question, I will barely and briefly say, that you cannot be more sensible than I am of the madness of bringing matters to such an extremity—I have no such intention, I assure you, and it is with no such purpose that I invite you here.—Were I to challenge Martigny, he would refuse me the meeting; and all less ceremonious ways of arranging such an affair are quite old-fashioned.

"It is true, at our first meeting, I was betrayed into the scrape I told you of—just as you may have shot (or shot *at*, for I think you are no downright hitter,) a hen pheasant, when flushed within distance, by a sort of instinctive movement, without reflecting on the enormity you were about to commit. The truth is, there is an ignis fatuus influence, which seems to govern our house—it poured its wild fire through my father's veins—it has descended to me in full vigour, and every now and then its impulse is irresistible. There was my enemy, and here were my pistols, was all I had time to think about the matter. But I will be on my guard in future, the more surely, as I cannot receive any provocation from him; on the contrary, if I must confess the truth, though I was willing to gloss it a little in my first account of the matter, (like the Gazette, when recording a defeat,) I am certain he would never voluntarily have fired at me, and that his pistol went off as he fell. You know me well enough to be assured, that I will never be again in the scrape of attacking an unresisting antagonist, were he ten times our brother.

"Then, as to this long tirade about hating my brother—Harry, I do not hate him more than the first-born of Egypt are in general hated by those whom they exclude from entailed estates, and so forth—not one landed man in twenty of us that is not hated by his younger brothers, to the extent of wishing him quiet in his grave, as an abominable stumbling-block in their path of life; and so far only do I hate Monsieur Martigny. But for the rest, I rather like him as otherwise; and would he but die, would give my frank consent to his being canonized; and while he lives, I am not desirous that he should be exposed to any temptation from rank and riches, those main obstacles to the self-denying course of life, by which the Odour of Sanctity is attained.

"Here again you break in with your impertinent queries—If I have no purpose of quarrelling personally with Martigny, why do I come into collision with him at all?—why not abide by the treaty of Marchthorn, and remain in England, without again approaching Saint Ronan's, or claiming my maiden bride?

"Have I not told you, I want him to cease all threatened attempts upon my fortune and dignity? Have I not told you, that I want my wife, Clara Mowbray, and my estate of Nettlewood, fairly won by marrying her?—And to let you into the whole secret, though Clara is a very pretty woman, yet she goes for so little in the transaction with me, her unimpassioned bridegroom, that I hope to make some relaxation of my rights over her the means of obtaining the concessions which I think most important.

"I will not deny, that an aversion to awakening bustle, and encountering reproach, has made me so slow in looking after my interest, that the period will shortly expire, within which I ought, by old Scrog Mowbray's will, to qualify myself for becoming his heir, by being the accepted husband of Miss Mowbray of Saint Ronan's. Time was—time is—and, if I catch it not by the forelock as it passes, time will be no more—Nettlewood will be forfeited—and if I have in addition a law-suit for my title, and for Oakendale, I run a risk of being altogether capotted. I must, therefore, act at all risks, and act with vigour—and this is the general plan of my campaign, subject always to be altered according to circumstances. I have obtained—I may say, purchased—Mowbray's consent to address his sister. I have this advantage, that if she agrees to take me, she will for ever put a stop to all disagreeable reports and recollections, founded on her former conduct. In that case I secure the Nettlewood property, and am ready to wage war for my paternal estate. Indeed, I firmly believe, that should this happy consummation take place, Monsieur Martigny will be too much heart-broken to make further fight, but will e'en throw helve after hatchet, and run to hide himself, after the fashion of a true lover, in some desert beyond seas.

"But, supposing the lady has the bad taste to be obstinate, and will none of me, I still think that her happiness, or her peace of mind, will be as dear to Martigny, as Gibraltar is to the Spaniards, and that he will sacrifice a great deal to induce me to give up my pretensions. Now, I shall want some one to act as my agent in communicating with this fellow; for I will not deny that my old appetite for cutting his throat may awaken suddenly, were I to hold personal intercourse with him. Come thou, therefore, without delay, and hold my back-hand—Come, for you know me, and that I never left a kindness unrewarded. To be specific, you shall have means to pay off a certain inconvenient mortgage, without troubling the tribe of Issachar, if you will but be true to me in this matter—Come, therefore, without further apologies or further delay. There shall, I give you my word, neither be risk nor offence in the part of the drama which I intend to commit to your charge.

"Talking of the drama, we had a miserable attempt at a sort of bastard theatricals, at Mowbray's rat-gnawed mansion. There were two things worth noticing—One, that I lost all the courage on which I pique myself, and fairly fled from the pit, rather than present myself before Miss Clara Mowbray, when it came to the push. And upon this I pray you to remark, that I am a person of singular delicacy and modesty, instead of being the Drawcansir and Daredevil that you would make of me. The other memorable is of a more delicate nature, respecting the conduct of a certain fair lady, who seemed determined to fling herself at my head. There is a wonderful degree of free-masonry among us folks of spirit; and it is astonishing how soon we can place ourselves on a footing with neglected wives and discontented daughters. If you come not soon, one of the rewards held out to you in my former letter, will certainly not be forthcoming. No school-boy keeps gingerbread for his comrade, without feeling a desire to nibble at it; so, if you come not to look after your own interest, say you had fair warning. For my own part, I am rather embarrassed than gratified by the prospect of such an affair, when I have on the tapis another of a different nature. This enigma I will explain at meeting.

"Thus finishes my long communication. If my motives of action do not appear explicit, think in what a maze fortune has involved me, and how much must necessarily depend on the chapter of accidents.

"Yesterday I may be said to have opened my siege, for I presented myself before Clara. I had no very flattering reception—that was of little consequence, for I did not expect one. By alarming her fears, I made an impression thus far, that she acquiesces in my appearing before her as her brother's guest, and this is no small point gained. She will become accustomed to look on me, and will remember with less bitterness the trick which I played her formerly; while I, on the other hand, by a similar force of habit, will get over certain awkward feelings with which I have been compunctiously visited whenever I look upon her.—Adieu! Health and brotherhood. "Thine,

"ETHERINGTON."

END OF VOLUME SECOND

SAINT RONAN'S WELL

VOLUME III

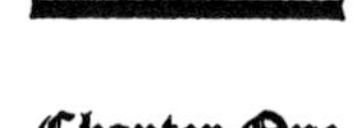

Chapter One

THE REPLY

> Thou bearest a precious burthen, gentle post,
> Nitre and sulphur—See that it explode not.
>
> *Old Play*

"I HAVE received your two long letters, my dear Etherington, with equal surprise and interest; for what I knew of your Scotch adventures before, was by no means sufficient to prepare me for a statement so perversely complicated. The Ignis Fatuus which, you say, governed your father, seems to have ruled the fortunes of your whole house, there is so much eccentricity in all that you have told me. But n'importe, Etherington, you have been my friend—you held me up when I was completely broken down; and, whatever you may think, my services are at your command, much more from reflections on the past, than hopes for the future. I am no speech-maker, but this you may rely on while I continue to be Harry Jekyl. You have deserved some love at my hands, Etherington, and you have it.

"Perhaps I love you the better since your perplexities have become known to me; for, my dear Etherington, you were before too much an object of envy to be entirely an object of affection. What a happy fellow! was the song of all who named you. Rank, and a fortune to maintain it—luck sufficient to repair all the waste that you could make in your income, and skill to back that luck, or supply it, should it for a moment fail you.—The cards turning up as if to your wish—the dice rolling, it almost seemed, at your wink—it was rather your look than the touch of your cue that sent the ball into the pocket.—You seemed to have fortune in chains, and a man of less honour would have been almost suspected of helping his luck by a little art.—You won every bet; and the instant that you were interested, one might have named the winning horse—it was always that which you were to gain most by. —You never held out your piece but the game went down—and then the women!—with face, manners, person, and, above all, your tongue —what wild work have you made among them!—Good heaven! and have you had the old sword hanging over your head by a horse-hair all this while?—Has your rank been doubtful?—your fortune unsettled? —and your luck, so constant in everything else—has that, as well as your predominant influence with the women, failed you, when you wished to form a connection for life, and when the care of your fortune required you to do so?—Etherington, I am astonished!—The Mowbray scrape I always thought an inconvenient one, as well as the quarrel with this same Tyrrel, or Martigny; but I was far from guessing the complicated nature of your perplexities.

"But I must not run on in a manner which, though it relieves my own marvelling mind, cannot be very pleasant to you. Enough, I look on my obligations to you as lighter, now I have some chance of repaying them to a certain extent; but, even were the full debt paid, I would remain as much attached to you as ever. It is your friend who speaks, Etherington; and, if he offers his advice in somewhat plain language, do not, I entreat you, suppose that your confidence has encouraged an offensive familiarity, but consider me as one who, in a weighty matter, writes plainly to avoid the least chance of misconstruction.

"Etherington, your conduct hitherto has resembled anything rather than the coolness and judgment which are so peculiarly your own when you choose to display them. I pass over the masquerade of your marriage—it was a boy's trick, which could hardly have availed you much, even if successful; for what sort of a wife would you have acquired, had this same Clara Mowbray proved willing to have accepted the change which you had put upon her, and transferred herself, without repugnance, from one bridegroom to another?—Poor as I am, I know that neither Nettlewood nor Oakendale should have bribed me to marry such a——I cannot decorously fill up the blank.

"Neither, my dear Etherington, can I forgive you the trick you put on the clergyman, in whose eyes you destroyed the poor girl's character to induce him to consent to perform the ceremony, and have thereby perhaps fixed an indelible stain on her for life—this was not a fair *ruse de guerre*.—As it is, you have taken little by your stratagem—unless, indeed, it should be difficult for the young lady to prove the imposition put upon her—for that being admitted, the marriage certainly goes for nothing. At least, the only use you can make of it, would be to drive her into a more formal union, for fear of having this whole unpleasant discussion brought into a court of law; and in this, with all the advantages you possess, joined to your own arts of persuasion, and her brother's influence, I should think you very likely to succeed. All women are necessarily the slaves of their reputation. I have known some who have given up their virtue to preserve their character, which is, after all, only the shadow of it. I therefore would not conceive it difficult for Clara Mowbray to persuade herself to become a countess, rather than be the topic of conversation for all Britain, while a law-suit betwixt you is in dependence; and that may be for the greater part of both your lives.

"But, in Miss Mowbray's state of mind, it may require time to bring her to such a conclusion; and I fear you will be thwarted in your operations by your rival—I will not offend you by calling him your brother. Now, it is here that I think with pleasure I may be of some use to you,—under this special condition, that there shall be no thoughts of farther violence taking place between you. However you may have smoothed over your rencontre to yourself, there is no doubt that the public would have regarded any accident which might have befallen on that occasion, as a crime of the deepest dye, and that the law would have followed it with the most severe punishment. And for all that I have said of my serviceable disposition, I would fain stop short on this side of the gallows—my neck is too long already. Without a jest, Etherington, you must be ruled by counsel in this matter. I detect your hatred to this man in every line of your letters, even when you write with the greatest coolness; even where there is an affectation of gaiety, I read your sentiments on this subject, and they are such as—I will not preach to you—I will not say a good man—but such as every wise man—every man who wishes to live on fair terms with the world, and to escape general malediction, and perhaps a violent death, where all men will clap their hands and rejoice at the punishment of the fratricide,—would, with all possible speed, eradicate from his breast. My services therefore, if they are worth your acceptance, are offered, on the condition that this unholy hatred be subdued with the utmost force of your powerful mind, and that you avoid everything which can possibly lead to such a catastrophe as you have twice narrowly escaped. I do not ask you to like this man, for I know well the deep root which your prejudices hold in your mind; I merely ask you to avoid him, and to think of him as one, who, if you do meet him, can never be the object of personal resentment.

"On these conditions, I will instantly join you at your Spaw, and wait but your answer to throw myself into the post-chaise. I will seek out this Martigny for you, and I have the vanity to think I shall be able to persuade him to take the course which his own true interest, as well as yours, so plainly points out—and that is, to depart and make us free of him. You must not grudge a round sum of money, should that prove necessary—we must make wings for him to fly with, and I must be empowered by you to that purpose. I cannot think you have anything serious to fear from a law-suit. Your father threw out this sinister hint at a moment when he was enraged at his wife, and irritated by his son; and I have little doubt that his expressions were merely flashes of anger at the moment, though I see they have made a deep impression on you. At all events, he spoke of a preference to his illegitimate son, as something which it was in his own power to give or to withhold; and he has died without bestowing it. The family seem addicted to irregular matrimony, and some left-handed marriage there may have been used to propitiate the modesty, and save the conscience, of the French lady; but, that anything of the nature of a serious and legal ceremony took place, nothing but the strongest proof can make me believe.

"I repeat, then, that I have little doubt that the claims of Martigny, whatever they are, may be easily compounded, and England made clear of him. This will be more easily done, if he really entertains such a romantic passion, as you describe, for Miss Clara Mowbray. It would be easy to shew him, that whether she is disposed to accept your lordship's hand or not, her quiet and peace of mind must depend on his leaving the country. Rely on it, I shall find out the way to smooth him down, and whether distance or the grave divide Martigny and you, is very little to the purpose; unless in so far as the one point can be attained with honour and safety, and the other, if attempted, would only make all concerned the subject of general execration and deserved punishment.—Speak the word, and I attend you, as your truly grateful and devoted

"HENRY JEKYL."

To this admonitory epistle, the writer received, in the course of post, the following answer:—

"My truly grateful and devoted Henry Jekyl has adopted a tone, which seems to be exalted without any occasion. Why, thou suspicious monitor, have I not repeated a hundred times that I repent sincerely of the foolish rencontre, and am determined to curb my temper, and be on my guard in future—And what need you come upon me, with your long lesson about execration, and punishment, and fratricide, and so forth?—You deal with an argument as a boy does with the first hare he shoots, which he never thinks dead till he has fired the second barrel into her. What a fellow you would have been for a lawyer! how long you would have held forth upon the plainest cause, until the poor bothered judge was almost willing to decide against justice, that he might be revenged on you. If I must repeat what I have said twenty times, I tell you I have no thoughts of proceeding with this fellow as I would with another. If my father's blood be in his veins, it shall save the skin his mother gave him. And so come, without more parade, either of stipulation or of argument. Thou art, indeed, a curious animal! One would think, to read your communication, that you had yourself discovered the propriety of acting as a negotiator, and the reasons which might, in the course of such a treaty, be urged with advantage to induce this fellow to leave the country. Why, this is the very course chalked out in my last letter! You are bolder than the boldest gipsy, for you not only steal my ideas, and disfigure them that they may pass for yours, but you have the assurance to come a-begging with them to the door of the original parent! No man like you for stealing other men's inventions, and cooking them up in your own way. However, Harry, baiting a little self-conceit and assumption, thou art as honest a fellow as ever man put faith in—clever, too, in your own style, though not quite the genius you would fain pass for.—Come on thine own terms, and come as speedily as thou canst. I do not reckon the promise I made the less binding, that you very generously make no allusion to it. Thine,

"ETHERINGTON.

"P.S. One single caution I must add—do not mention my name to any one at Harrogate, or your prospect of meeting me, or the route which you are about to take. On the purpose of your journey, it is unnecessary to recommend silence. I know not whether such doubts are natural to all who have secret measures to pursue, or whether nature has given me an unusual share of anxious suspicion; but I cannot divest myself of the idea, that I am closely watched by some one whom I cannot discover. Although I concealed my purpose of coming hither from all mankind but you, whom I do not for an instant suspect of blabbing, yet it was known to this Martigny, and he is down here before me. Again, I said not a word—gave not a hint to any one of my views towards Clara, yet the tattling people here had spread a report of a marriage depending between us, even before I could make the motion to her brother. To be sure, in such society there is nothing talked of but marrying and giving in marriage; and this, which alarms me, as connected with my own private purposes, may be a bare rumour, arising out of the gossip of the place. Yet I feel like the poor woman in the old story, who felt herself watched by an eye that glared upon her from behind the tapestry.

"I should have told you in my last, that I had been recognized at a public entertainment by the old clergyman, who pronounced the matrimonial blessing on Clara and me, nearly eight years ago. He insisted upon addressing me by the name of Valentine Bulmer, under which I was then best known. It did not suit me at present to put him into my confidence, so I cut him, Harry, as I would an old pencil. The task was the less difficult, that I had to do with one of the most absent men who ever dreamed with his eyes open. I verily believe he might be persuaded that the whole transaction was a vision, and that he had never in reality seen me before. Your pious rebuke, therefore, about what I told him formerly concerning the lovers, is quite thrown away. After all, if what I said was not accurately true, as I certainly believe it was an exaggeration, it was all Saint Francis of Martigny's fault, I suppose. I am sure he had love and opportunity on his side.

"Here you have a postscript, Harry, longer than the letter, but it must conclude with the same burthen—Come, and come quickly."

Chapter Two

THE FRIGHT

As shakes the bough of trembling leaf,
When sudden whirlwinds rise;
As stands aghast the warrior chief,
When his base army flies.
MICKLE

IT HAD BEEN settled by all who took the matter into consideration, that the fidgetty, fiery, old Nabob would soon quarrel with his landlady, Mrs Dods, and become impatient of his residence at Saint Ronan's. A man so kind to himself, and so inquisitive about the affairs of others, could have, it was supposed, a limited sphere for gratification either of his tastes or of his curiosity, in the Aulton of Saint Ronan's; and many a time the precise day and hour of his departure were fixed by the idlers at the Spaw. But still old Touchwood appeared amongst them when the weather permitted, with his nut-brown visage, his throat carefully wrapped up in an immense Indian kerchief, and his gold-headed cane, which he never failed to carry over his shoulder; his short, but stout limbs, and his active step, shewing plainly that he bore it rather as a badge of dignity than a means of support. There he stood, answering shortly and gruffly to all questions proposed to him, and making his remarks aloud upon the company, with great indifference as to the offence which might be taken; and as soon as the ancient priestess had handed him his glass of the salutiferous water, turned on his heel with a brief good morning, and either marched back to hide himself in the Manse, with his crony Mr Cargill, or to engage in some hobby-horsical pursuit connected with his neighbours in the Aulton.

The truth was, that the honest gentleman having, so far as Mrs Dods would permit, put matters to right within her residence, wisely abstained from pushing his innovations any farther, aware that it is not every stone which is capable of receiving the last degree of polish. He next set himself about putting Mr Cargill's house into order; and without leave asked or given by that reverend gentleman, he actually accomplished as wonderful a reformation in the Manse, as could have been effected by a benevolent Brownie. The floors were sometimes swept—the carpets were sometimes dusted—the plates and dishes were cleaner—there was tea and sugar in the tea-chest, and a joint of meat at proper times was to be found in the larder. The elder maid-servant wore a good stuff gown—the younger snooded up her hair, and now went about the house a damsel so trig and neat, that some said she was too handsome for the service of a bachelor divine; and others, that they saw no business so old a fool as the Nabob had to be meddling with a lassy's busking. But for such evil bruits Mr Touchwood cared not, even if he happened to hear of them, which was very doubtful. Add to all these changes, that the garden was weeded, and the glebe was regularly laboured.

The talisman by which all this desirable alteration was wrought, consisted partly in small presents, partly in constant attention. The liberality of the singular old gentleman gave him a perfect right of scolding when he saw things wrong; the domestics, who had fallen into total sloth and indifference, began to exert themselves under Mr Touchwood's new system of rewards and surveillance; and the minister, half unconscious of the cause, reaped the advantage of the exertions of his busy friend. Sometimes he lifted his head, when he heard workmen thumping and bouncing in the neighbourhood of his study, and demanded the meaning of the clatter which annoyed him; but on receiving for answer that it was by order of Mr Touchwood, he resumed his labours, under the persuasion that all was well.

But even the Augean task of putting the Manse in order, did not satisfy the gigantic activity of Mr Touchwood. He aspired to universal dominion in the Aulton of Saint Ronan's; and, like most men of an ardent temper, he contrived, in a great measure, to possess himself of the authority which he longed after. Then was there war waged by him with all the petty, but perpetual nuisances which infest a Scottish town of the old stamp. Then was the hereditary dunghill, which had reeked before the window of the cottage for fourscore years, transported behind the house—then was the broken wheelbarrow, or unserviceable cart, removed out of the foot-path—the old hat or blue petticoat, taken from the window into which it had been stuffed, to "expel the winter's flaw," was consigned to the gutter, and its place supplied with good perspicuous glass. The means by which such reformation was effected, were the same as resorted to in the Manse—money and admonition. The latter given alone would have met little attention—perhaps would have provoked opposition—but, softened and sweetened by a little present to assist the reform recommended, it sunk into the hearts of the hearers, and in general overcame their objections. Besides, an opinion of the Nabob's wealth was high among the villagers; and an idea prevailed amongst them, that, notwithstanding his keeping no servants or equipage, he was able to purchase, if he pleased, half the land in the country. It was not grand carriages and fine liveries that made heavy purses, they rather helped to lighten them; and they said, who pretended to know what they were talking about, that old Turnpenny and Mr Bindloose to boot, would tell down more money on Mr Touchwood's mere word, than upon the joint bond of half the fine folks at the Wells. Such an opinion smoothed everything before the path of one, who shewed himself neither averse to give nor to lend; and it by no means diminished the reputation of his wealth, that in transactions of business he was not carelessly negligent of his interest, but plainly shewed he understood the value of what he was parting with. Few, therefore, cared to withstand the humours of a whimsical old gentleman, who had both the will and the means of obliging those disposed to comply with his fancies; and thus the singular stranger contrived, in the course of a brief space of days or weeks, to place the villagers more absolutely at his devotion, than they had been to the pleasure of any individual since their ancient lords had left the Aulton. The power of the Baron-baillie himself, though the office was vested in the person of old Micklewhame, was a subordinate jurisdiction, compared to the voluntary allegiance which the inhabitants paid to Mr Touchwood.

There were, however, recusants, who declined the authority thus set up amongst them, and, with the characteristical obstinacy of their countrymen, refused to hearken to the words of the stranger, whether they were for good or for evil. These men's dunghills were not removed, nor the stumbling-blocks taken from the foot-path, where it passed the front of their houses. And it befel, that while Mr Touchwood was most eager in abating the nuisances of the village, he had very nearly experienced a frequent fate of great reformers—lost his life by means of one of those enormities which as yet had subsisted in spite of all his efforts.

The Nabob finding his time after dinner hang somewhat heavy on his hand, and the moon being tolerably bright, had, one harvest evening, sought his usual remedy for dispelling ennui by a walk to the Manse, where he was sure, that, if he could not succeed in engaging the minister himself in some disputation, he would at least find something in the establishment to animadvert upon and to restore to order.

Accordingly, he had taken the opportunity to lecture the younger of the minister's lasses upon the duty of wearing shoes and stockings; and, as his advice came fortified by a present of six pair of white cotton hose, and two pair of stout leathern shoes, it was received, not with respect only, but with gratitude, and the chuck under the chin that rounded up the oration, while she opened the outer door for his honour, was acknowledged with a blush and a giggle.—Nay, so far did Girzy carry her sense of Mr Touchwood's kindness, that, observing the moon was behind a cloud, she very carefully offered to escort him to the Cleikum Inn with a lantern, in case he should come to some harm by the gate. This the traveller's independent spirit scorned to listen to; and, having briefly assured her that he had walked the streets of Paris and of Madrid whole nights without such an accommodation, he stoutly strode off on his return to his lodgings.

An accident, however, befel him, which, unless the police of Madrid and Paris be belied, might have happened in either of those two splendid capitals, as well as in the miserable Aulton of Saint Ronan's.—Before the door of Saunders Jaup, a feuar of some importance, "who held his land free, and caredna a bodle for any one," yawned that odoriferous filthy gulph, ycleped, in Scottish phrase, the jaw-hole, in other words, an uncovered common sewer. The local situation of this receptacle of filth was well known to Mr Touchwood; for Saunders Jaup was at the very head of those who held out for the practices of their fathers, and still maintained those ancient and unsavoury customs which our traveller had in so many instances succeeded in abating. Guided, therefore, by his nose, he made a considerable circuit to avoid the displeasure and danger of passing this filthy puddle at the nearest, and by that means fell upon Scylla as he sought to avoid Charybdis. In plain language, he approached so near the bank of a little rivulet, which in that place passed betwixt the foot-path and the horse-road, that he lost his footing, and fell into the channel of the streamlet from a height of three or four feet. It was thought that the noise of his fall, or, at least, his call for assistance, should have been heard in the house of Saunders Jaup; but that honest person was, according to his own account, at that time engaged in the exercise of the evening; an excuse which passed current, although Saunders was privately heard to allege, that the town would have been the quieter "if the auld, meddling busy-body had bidden still in the burn for gude and a'."

But Fortune had provided better for poor Touchwood, whose foibles, as they arose out of the most excellent motives, would have ill deserved so severe a fate. A passenger, who heard him shout for help, ventured cautiously to the side of the bank, down which he had fallen; and, after ascertaining the nature of the ground as carefully as the darkness permitted, was at length, and not without some effort, enabled to assist him out of the channel of the rivulet.

"Are you hurt materially?" said this good Samaritan to the object of his care.

"No—no—d—n it—no," said Touchwood, extremely angry at his disaster, and the cause of it. "Do you think I, who have been at the summit of Mount Athos, where the precipice sinks a thousand feet on the sea, care a farthing about such a fall as this is?"

But, as he spoke, he reeled, and his kind assistant caught him by the arm to prevent his falling.

"I fear you are more hurt than you suppose, sir," said the stranger; "permit me to go home along with you."

"With all my heart," said Touchwood; "for, though it is impossible I can need help in such a foolish matter, yet I am equally obliged to you, friend; and if the Cleikum Inn be not out of your road, I will take your arm so far, and thank you to boot."

"It is much at your service, sir," said the stranger; "indeed, I was thinking to lodge there for the night."

"I am glad to hear it," resumed Touchwood; "you shall be my guest, and I will make them look after you in proper fashion—You seem to be a very civil sort of fellow, and I do not find your arm inconvenient—it is the rheumatism makes me walk so ill—the pest of all that have been in hot climates when they settle among these d—d fogs."

"Lean as hard and walk as slow as you will, sir," said again the benevolent assistant—"this is a rough street."

"Yes, sir—and why is it rough?" answered Touchwood. "Why, because the old pig-headed fool, Saunders Jaup, will not allow it to be made smooth. There he sits, sir, and obstructs all rational improvement; and, if a man would not fall into his infernal putrid gutter, and so become an abomination to himself and odious to others, for his whole life to come, he runs the risk of breaking his neck, as I have done to-night."

"I am afraid, sir," said his companion, "you have fallen on the most dangerous side.—You remember Swift's proverb, 'The more dirt, the less hurt.'"

"But why should there be either dirt or hurt in a well-regulated place?" answered Touchwood—"Why should not men be able to go about their affairs at night, in such a quiet place as this, without either endangering necks or noses?—Our Scottish magistrates are worth nothing, sir—nothing at all.—Oh, for a Turkish Cadi now to trounce the scoundrel—or the Mayor of Calcutta to bring him into his court—or were it but an English justice of the peace that is newly included in the commission, they would abate the villain's nuisance with a vengeance on him.—But here we are—this is the Cleikum Inn.—Hallo—hilloa—house!—Jane Anderson!—Susie Chambermaid!—boy Boots!—Mrs Dods!—are you all of you asleep and dead?—Here have I been half murthered, and you let me stand yawling here—Mrs Dods—"

Jane Anderson came with a light, and so did Susie Chambermaid with another—but no sooner did they look upon the pair who stood in the porch under the huge sign that swung to and fro with heavy creaking, than Susie screamed, flung away her candle, although a four in the pound, and in a newly japanned candlestick, and fled one way, while Jane Anderson, echoing the yell, brandished her light round her head like a Bacchante flourishing her torch, and ran off in another direction.

"Ay—I must be a bloody spectacle," said Mr Touchwood, letting himself fall heavily upon his assistant's shoulder, and wiping his face, which trickled with wet—"I did not think I had been so seriously hurt; but I find my weakness now—I must have lost much blood."

"I hope you are still mistaken," said the stranger; "but here lies the way to the kitchen—we shall find light there, since no one chooses to bring it to us."

He assisted the old gentleman into the kitchen, where a lamp, as well as a bright fire, was burning, by the light of which he could easily discern that the supposed blood was only water of the rivulet, and, indeed, none of the cleanest, although much more so than the sufferer would have found it a little lower, where the stream is joined by the superfluities of Saunders Jaup's palladium. Relieved by his new friend's repeated assurances that such was the case, the Senior began to bustle up a little, and his companion, desirous to render him every assistance, went to the door of the kitchen to call for a basin and water. Just as he was about to open the door, the voice of Mrs Dods was heard as she descended the stairs, in a tone of indignation by no means unusual to her, yet mingled at the same time with a few notes that sounded like unto the quaverings of consternation.

"Idle limmers—silly sluts—I'll warrant nane o' ye will ever see onything waur than yoursell, ye silly tawpies—Ghaist, indeed!—I'll warrant it's some idle dub-skelper frae the Waal, coming after some o' yoursells on nae honest errand—Ghaist, indeed!—Haud up the candle, John Ostler—I'se warrant it a twa-handed ghaist, and the door left on the sneck—There's somebody in the kitchen—gang forward wi' the lantern, John Ostler."

At this critical moment the stranger opened the door of the kitchen, and beheld the Dame advancing at the head of her household troops. The ostler and hump-backed postilion, one bearing a stable-lantern and a hay-fork, the other a rushlight and a broom, constituted the advanced guard; Mrs Dods herself formed the centre, talking loud, and brandishing a pair of tongs; while the two maids, like troops not to be much trusted after their recent defeat, followed, cowering in the rear. But notwithstanding this admirable disposition, no sooner had the stranger shewn his face, and pronounced the words "Mrs Dods," than a panic seized the whole array. The advanced guard recoiled in confusion, the ostler upsetting Mrs Dods in the confusion of his retreat; while she, grappling with him in her terror, secured him by the ears and hair, and they joined their cries together in hideous chorus. The two maidens resumed their former flight, and took refuge in the darksome den, entitled their bed-room, while the hump-backed postilion fled like the wind into the stable, and, with professional instinct, began, in the extremity of his terror, to saddle a horse.

Meanwhile, the gentleman who had caused this combustion, plucked the roaring ostler from above Mrs Dods, and pushing him away with a hearty slap on the shoulder, proceeded to raise and encourage the fallen landlady, inquiring, at the same time, "What, in the devil's name, was the cause of all this senseless confusion?"

"And what is the reason, in Heaven's name," answered the matron, keeping her eyes firmly shut, and still shrewish in her expostulation, though in the very extremity of terror, "what is the reason that you should come and frighten a decent house, where you met naething but the height o' civility?"

"And why should I frighten you, Mrs Dods? or, in one word, what is the meaning of all this nonsensical terror?"

"Are not you," said Mrs Dods, opening her eyes a little as she spoke, "the ghaist of Francis Tirl?"

"I am Francis Tyrrel, unquestionably, my old friend."

"I ken'd it! I ken'd it!" answered the honest woman, relapsing into her agony; "and I think ye might be ashamed of yoursell, that are a ghaist, and have nae better to do than to frighten a puir auld ale-wife."

"On my word, I am no ghost, but a living man," answered Tyrrel.

"Were ye no murdered than?" said Mrs Dods, still in an uncertain voice, and only partially opening her eyes—"Are ye very sure ye werena murdered?"

"Why, not that ever I heard of, certainly, dame," replied Tyrrel.

"But I shall be murdered presently," said old Touchwood from the kitchen, where he had hitherto remained a mute auditor of this extraordinary scene—"I shall be murdered, unless you fetch me some water presently."

"Coming, sir, coming," answered Dame Dods, her professional reply being as familiar to her as that of poor Francis's 'Anon, anon, sir.' "As I live by honest reckonings," said she, fully collecting herself, and giving a glance of more composed temper at Tyrrel, "I believe it is yoursell, Maister Frank, in blood and body after a'—-And see if I dinna gie a proper sorting to yon twa silly jauds, that gar'd me mak a bogle of you, and a fule of mysell—Ghaists! my certie, I sall ghaist them—If they had their heads as muckle on their wark as on their daffing, they wad play nae sic pliskies—it's the wanton steed that scaurs at the windle-strae—Ghaists! wha e'er heard of ghaists in an honest house? Naebody need fear bogles that hae a conscience void of offence.—But I am blythe that MacTurk hasna murdered ye when a' is dune, Maister Frauncie."

"Come this way, Mother Dods, if you would not have me do you a mischief!" exclaimed Touchwood, grasping a plate which stood on the dresser, as if he were about to heave it at the landlady, by way of recalling her attention.

"For the love of heaven, dinna break it!" exclaimed the alarmed landlady, knowing that Touchwood's effervescence of impatience sometimes expended itself at the expense of her crockery, though it was afterwards liberally atoned for. "Lord, sir, are ye out of your wits!—it breaks a set, ye ken—Godsake, put doun the cheeny plate, and try your hand on the delf-ware!—it will just make as good a jingle—But, Lord haud a grip o' us! now I look at ye, what can hae come ower ye, and what sort of a plight are ye in!—Wait till I fetch water and a towel."

In fact, the miserable guise of her new lodger now overcame the dame's curiosity to inquire after the fate of her earlier acquaintance, and she gave her instant and exclusive attention to Mr Touchwood, with many exclamations, while aiding him to perform the task of ablution and abstersion. Her two fugitive handmaidens had by this time returned to the kitchen, and endeavoured to suppress a smuggled laugh at the recollection of their mistress's panic, by acting very officiously in Mr Touchwood's service. By dint of washing and drying, the token of the sable stains was at length removed, and the veteran became, with some difficulty, satisfied that he had been more dirtied and frightened than hurt.

Tyrrel, in the meantime, stood looking on with wonder, imagining that he beheld in the features which emerged from a masque of mud, the countenance of an old friend. After the operation was ended, he could not help addressing himself to Mr Touchwood, to demand whether he had not the pleasure to see a friend to whom he had been obliged when at Smyrna, for some kindness respecting his money matters?

"Not worth speaking of—not worth speaking of," said Touchwood, hastily. "Glad to see you, though—glad to see you.—Yes, here I am, you will find me the same good-natured old fool that I was at Smyrna —never look how I am to get in money again—always laying it out. Never mind—it was written in my forehead, as the Turk says.—I will go up now and change my dress—you will sup with me when I come back—Mrs Dods will toss us up something—a brandered fowl will be best, Mrs Dods, with some mushrooms, and get us a jug of mulled wine—plottie, as you call it—-to put the recollection of the old Presbyterian's common sewer out of my head."

So saying, up stairs marched the traveller to his own apartment, while Tyrrel, seizing upon a candle, was about to do the same.

"Mr Touchwood is in the blue room, Mrs Dods; I suppose I may take possession of the yellow one?"

"Suppose naething about the matter, Maister Frauncie Tirl, till ye tell me downright where ye have been a' this time, and whether ye hae been murdered or no?"

"I think you may be pretty well satisfied of that, Mrs Dods?"

"Troth! and so I am in a sense; and yet it gars me grew to look upon ye, sae mony days and weeks it has been since I thought ye were rotting in the moulds. And now to see ye standing before me hale and feir, and crying for a bed-room like other folk!"

"One would almost suppose, my good friend," said Tyrrel, "that you were sorry at my having come alive again."

"It's no for that," replied Mrs Dods, who was peculiarly ingenious in the mode of framing and stating what she conceived to be her grievances; "but is it no a queer thing for a decent man like yoursel, Maister Tirl, to be leaving your lodgings without a word spoken, and me put to a' these charges in seeking for your dead body, and very near taking my business out of honest Maister Bindloose's hands, because he ken'd the cantrips of the like of you better than I did.—And than they hae put up an adverteezement down at the Waal yonder, wi' a' their names at it, setting ye forth, Maister Frauncie, as ane of the greatest blackguards unhanged; and wha, div ye think, is to keep ye in a creditable house, if that's the character ye get?"

"You may leave that to me, Mrs Dods—I assure you that matter shall be put to rights to your satisfaction; and I think, so long as we have known each other, you may take my word that I am not undeserving the shelter of your roof for a single night, (I shall ask it no longer,) until my character is sufficiently cleared. It was for that purpose I chiefly came back again."

"Came back again!" said Mrs Dods.—"I profess ye made me start, Maister Tirl, and you looking sae pale too.—But I think," she added, straining after a joke, "if ye were a ghaist, being we are such auld acquaintance, ye wadna wish to spoil my custom, but would just walk decently up and down the auld castle wa's, or maybe down at the kirk yonder—there have been awfu' things dune in that kirk and kirk-yard—I whiles dinna like to look that way, Maister Frauncie."

"I am much of your mind, mistress," said Tyrrel, with a sigh; "and indeed I do in one sense resemble the apparitions you talk of; for, like them, and to as little purpose, I stalk about scenes where my happiness departed.—But I speak riddles to you, Mrs Dods—the plain truth is, that I met with an accident on the day I last left your house, the effects of which detained me at some distance from Saint Ronan's till this very day."

"Hegh, sirs, and ye were sparing of your trouble, that wadna write a bit line, or send a bit message!—Ye might hae thought folks wad hae been vexed aneugh about ye, forbye undertaking journeys, and hiring folk to seek for your deid body."

"I shall willingly pay all reasonable charges which my disappearance may have occasioned," answered her guest; "and I assure you once for all, that my remaining for some time quiet at Marchthorn arose partly from illness, and partly from business of a very pressing and particular nature."

"At Marchthorn!" exclaimed Dame Dods, "heard ever man the like o' that!—And where did ye put up in Marchthorn? an ane may mak bauld to speer."

"At the Black Bull," replied Tyrrel.

"Ay, that's auld Tam Lowrie's—a very decent man, Thamas—and a douce, creditable house—nane of your flisk-ma-hoys—I am glad ye made choice of sic gude quarters, neighbour; for I am beginning to think ye are but a queer ane—ye look as if butter wadna melt in your mouth, but I sall warrant cheese no choak ye.—But I'll thank ye to gang your ways into the parlour, for I am no like to get mickle mair out of ye it's like; and ye are standing here just in the gate, when we hae the supper to dish."

Tyrrel, glad to be released from the examination to which his landlady's curiosity had, without ceremony, subjected him, walked into the parlour, where he was presently joined by Mr Touchwood, newly attired and high in spirits.

"Here comes our supper!" he exclaimed.—"Sit ye down, and let us see what Mrs Dods has done for us.—I profess, mistress, your plottie is excellent, ever since I taught you to mix the spices in the right proportion."

"I am glad the plottie pleases ye, sir—but I think I ken'd gay weel how to make it before I saw your honour—Mr Tirl can tell that, for mony a browst of it I hae brewed lang syne for him and the callant Valentine Bulmer."

This ill-timed observation extorted a groan from Tyrrel; but the traveller, running on with his own recollections, did not appear to notice his emotion.

"You are a conceited old woman," said Mr Touchwood; "how the devil should any one know to mix spices so well as one that has been where they grow?—I have seen the sun ripening nutmegs and cloves, and here, it can hardly fill a peascod, by Jupiter!—Ah, Tyrrel, the merry nights we had at Smyrna!—Gad, I think the gammon and the good wine taste all the better in a land where folks hold them to be sinful indulgences—Gad, I believe many a good Moslem is of the same opinion—that same prohibition of their prophets gives a flavour to the ham, and a relish to the Cyprus.—Do you remember old Cogia Hussein, with his green turban?—I once played him a trick, and put a pint of brandy into his sherbet. Egad, the old fellow took care never to discover the cheat until he had got to the bottom of the flagon, and then he strokes his long white beard, and says, 'Ullah Kerim,'—that is, 'Heaven is merciful,' Mrs Dods, Mr Tyrrel knows the meaning of it.—Ullah Kerim, says he, after he had drunk about a gallon of brandy-punch!—Ullah Kerim, says the hypocritical old rogue, as if he had done the finest thing in the world!"

"And what for no? What for shouldna the honest man say a blessing after his drap punch?" demanded Mrs Dods; "it was better, I ween, than blasting, and blawing, and swearing, as if folks shouldna be thankful for the creature-comforts."

"Well said, old Dame Dods," replied the traveller; "that is a right hostess's maxim, and worthy of Mrs Quickly herself. Here is to thee, and I pray ye to pledge me before ye leave the room."

"Troth, I'll pledge naebody the night, Mr Touchwood; for, what wi' the upcast and tirrivie that I got a wee while syne, and what wi' the bit taste that I behoved to take of the plottie while I was making it, my head is sair aneugh stressed the night already.—Maister Tirl, the yellow room is ready for ye when ye like; and, gentlemen, as the morn is the Sabbath, I canna be keeping the servant queans out of their beds to wait on ye ony langer, for they will mak it an excuse for lying till aught o'clock on the Lord's day. So, when your plottie is done, I'll be mickle obliged to ye to light the bed-room candles, and put out the double moulds, and een shew yoursells to your beds; for douce folks, sic as the like of you, should set an example by ordinary.—And so, gude night to ye baith."

"By my faith," said Touchwood, as she withdrew, "our dame turns as obstinate as a Pacha with three tails!—We have her gracious permission to finish our mug, however; so, here is to your health once more, Mr Tyrrel, wishing you a hearty welcome to your own country."

"I thank you, Mr Touchwood," answered Tyrrel; "and I return you the same good wishes, with, as I sincerely hope, a much greater chance of their being realized.—You relieved me, sir, at a time when the villainy of an agent, prompted, as I have reason to think, by an active and powerful enemy, occasioned my being for a time pressed for funds.—I made remittances to the *Ragion* you dealt with, to acquit myself at least of the pecuniary part of my obligation; but the bills were returned, because, it was stated, you had left Smyrna."

"Very true—very true—left Smyrna, and here I am in Scotland—as for the bills, we will speak of them another time—something due for picking me up out of the gutter."

"I shall make no deduction on that account," said Tyrrel, smiling, though in no jocose mood; "and I beg you not to mistake me. The circumstances of embarrassment, under which you found me at Smyrna, were merely temporary—I am most able and willing to pay my debt; and, let me add, I am most desirous to do so."

"Another time—another time," said Mr Touchwood—"time enough before us, Mr Tyrrel—besides, at Smyrna, you talked of a law-suit—Law is a lick-penny, Mr Tyrrel—no counsellor like the pound in purse."

"For my law-suit," said Tyrrel, "I am fully provided."

"But, have you good advice?—Have you good advice?" said Touchwood; "answer me that."

"I have advised with my lawyers," answered Tyrrel, internally vexed to find that his friend was much disposed to make his generosity upon the former occasion a pretext for prying farther into his affairs than he thought polite or convenient.

"With your counsel learned in the law—eh, my dear boy? But the advice you should take is that of some travelled friend, well acquainted with mankind and the world—some one that has lived double your years, and is maybe looking out for some bare young fellow that he may do a little good to—one that might be willing to help you farther than I can pretend to guess—for, as to your lawyer, you get just your guinea's worth from him—not even so much as the baker's bargain, thirteen to the dozen."

"I think I should not trouble myself to go far in search of a friend such as you describe," said Tyrrel, who could not affect to misunderstand the senior's drift, "when I was near Mr Peregrine Touchwood; but the truth is that my affairs are at present so much implicated with those of others, whose secrets I have no right to communicate, that I cannot have the advantage of consulting you, or any other friend. It is possible I may be soon obliged to lay aside this reserve, and vindicate myself before the whole public. I will not fail, when that time shall arrive, to take an early opportunity of confidential communication with you."

"That is right—confidential is the word—No person ever made a confidant of me who repented it—Think what the Pacha might have made of it, had he taken my advice, and cut through the isthmus of Suez.—Turk and Christian, men of all tongues and countries, used to consult old Touchwood, from the building of a mosque down to the settling of an *agio*.—But come—Good night—good night."

So saying, he took up his bed-room light, and, extinguishing one of those which stood on the table, nodded to Tyrrel to discharge his share of the duty imposed by Mrs Dods with the same punctuality, and they withdrew to their several apartments, entertaining very different sentiments of each other.

"A troublesome, inquisitive, old gentleman," said Tyrrel to himself; "I remember him narrowly escaping the bastinado at Smyrna, for thrusting his advice on the Turkish cadi—and then I lie under a considerable obligation to him, giving him a sort of right to annoy me—Well, I must parry his impertinence as I can."

"A shy cock this Frank Tyrrel," thought the traveller; "a very complete dodger!—But no matter—I shall wind him, were he to double like a fox—I am resolved to make his matters my own, and if *I* cannot carry him through, I know not who can."

Having formed this philanthropic resolution, Mr Touchwood threw himself into bed, which luckily declined exactly at the right angle, and, full of self-complacence, consigned himself to slumber.

Chapter Three

MEDIATION

——So, begone!
We will not now be troubled with reply;
We offer fair, take it advisedly.
King Henry IV. Part I

IT HAD BEEN the purpose of Tyrrel, by rising and breakfasting early, to avoid again meeting Mr Touchwood, having upon his hands a matter in which that officious gentleman's interference was likely to prove troublesome. His character, he was aware, had been assailed at the Spaw in the most public manner, and in the most public manner he was resolved to demand redress, conscious that whatever other important concerns had brought him to Scotland, must necessarily be postponed to the vindication of his honour. He was determined, for this purpose, to go down to the rooms when the company was assembled at the breakfast hour, and had just taken his hat to set out, when he was interrupted by Mrs Dods, who, announcing "a gentleman that was speering for him," ushered into the chamber a very fashionable young man in a military surtout, covered with silk lace and fur, and wearing a foraging-cap; a dress now too familiar to be distinguished, but which at that time was used only by geniuses of a superior order. The stranger was neither handsome nor plain, but had in his appearance a good deal of pretension, and the cool easy superiority which belongs to high breeding. On his part, he surveyed Tyrrel; and, as his appearance differed, perhaps, from that for which the exterior of the Cleikum Inn had prepared him, he abated something of the air with which he had entered the room, and politely announced himself as Captain Jekyl, of the —— Guards, (presenting, at the same time, his ticket.)

"He presumed he spoke to Mr Martigny."

"To Mr Francis Tyrrel, sir," replied Tyrrel, drawing himself up—"Martigny was my mother's name—I have never borne it."

"I am not here for the purpose of disputing that point, Mr Tyrrel, though I am not entitled to admit what my principal's information leads him to doubt."

"Your principal, I presume, is Sir Bingo Binks," said Tyrrel. "I have not forgotten that there is an unfinished affair between us."

"I have not the honour to know Sir Bingo Binks," said Captain Jekyl. "I come on the part of the Earl of Etherington."

Tyrrel stood silent for a moment, and then said, "I am at a loss to know what the gentleman who calls himself Earl of Etherington can have to say to me, through the medium of such a messenger as yourself, Captain Jekyl. I should have supposed that, considering our unhappy relationship, and the terms on which we stand towards each other, the lawyers were the fitter negotiators between us."

"Sir," said Captain Jekyl, "you are misunderstanding my errand. I am come on no message of hostile import from Lord Etherington. I am aware of the connection betwixt you, which would render such an office altogether contradictory to common sense and the laws of nature; and I assure you, I would lay down my life rather than be concerned in an affair so unnatural. I would act, if possible, as a mediator betwixt you."

They had hitherto remained standing. Mr Tyrrel now offered his guest a seat; and, having assumed one himself, he broke the awkward pause which ensued by observing, "I should be happy, after experiencing such a long course of injustice and persecution from your friend, to learn, even at this late period, Captain Jekyl, anything which can make me think better either of him or of his purpose towards me and towards another."

"Mr Tyrrel," said Captain Jekyl, "you must allow me to speak with candour. There is too great a stake betwixt your brother and you to permit you to be friends; but I do not see it is necessary that you should therefore be mortal enemies."

"I am not my brother's enemy, Captain Jekyl," said Tyrrel—"I have never been so—His friend I cannot be, and he knows but too well the insurmountable barrier which his own conduct has placed between us."

"I am aware," said Captain Jekyl, slowly and expressively, "generally, at least, of the particulars of your unfortunate disagreement."

"If so," said Tyrrel, colouring, "you must be also aware with what extreme pain I feel myself compelled to enter on such a subject with a total stranger—a stranger, too, the friend and confidant of one who ——But I will not hurt your feelings, Captain Jekyl, but rather endeavour to suppress my own. In one word, I beg to be favoured with the import of your communication, as I am obliged to go down to the Spaw this morning, in order to put to rights some matters there which concern me nearly."

"If you mean the cause of your absence from a meeting with Sir Bingo Binks," said Captain Jekyl, "the matter has been already completely explained. I pulled down the offensive placard with my own hand, and rendered myself responsible for your honour to any who should presume to hold it in farther doubt."

"Sir," said Tyrrel, very much surprised, "I am obliged to you for your intention, the more so as I am ignorant how I have merited such interference. It is not, however, quite satisfactory to me, because I am accustomed to be the guardian of my own honour."

"An easy task, I presume, in all cases, Mr Tyrrel," answered Jekyl, "but peculiarly so in the present, when you will find no one so hardy as to assail it.—My interference, indeed, would have been unjustifiably officious, had I not been at the moment undertaking a commission implying confidential intercourse with you. For the sake of my own character, it became necessary to establish yours. I know the truth of the whole affair from my friend, the Earl of Etherington, who ought to thank Heaven so long as he lives, that saved him on that occasion from the commission of a very great crime."

"Your friend, sir, has had, in the course of his life, much to thank Heaven for, but more for which to ask God's forgiveness."

"I am no divine, sir," replied Captain Jekyl, with spirit; "but I have been told that the same may be said of most men alive."

"I, at least, cannot dispute it," said Tyrrel; "but, to proceed.—Have you found yourself at liberty, Captain Jekyl, to deliver to the public the whole particulars of a rencontre so singular as that which took place between your friend and me?"

"I have not, sir," said Jekyl—"I judged it a matter of great delicacy, and which each of you had the like interest to preserve secret."

"May I beg to know, then," said Tyrrel, "how it was possible for you to vindicate my absence from Sir Bingo's rendezvous otherwise?"

"It was only necessary, sir, to pledge my word as a gentleman and man of honour, characters in which I am pretty well known to the world, that, to my certain personal knowledge, you were hurt in an affair with a friend of mine, the further particulars of which prudence required should be sunk into oblivion. I think no one will venture to dispute my word, or to require more than my assurance—if there should be any one very hard of faith on the occasion, I shall find a way to satisfy him. In the meanwhile, your outlawry has been rescinded in the most honourable manner; and Sir Bingo, in consideration of his share in giving rise to reports so injurious to you, is desirous to drop all further proceedings in his original quarrel, and hopes the whole matter will be forgot and forgiven on all sides."

"Upon my word, Captain Jekyl," answered Tyrrel, "you lay me under the necessity of acknowledging obligation to you. You have cut a knot which I should have found it very difficult to unloose; for I frankly confess, that, while I was determined not to remain under the stigma put upon me, I should have had great difficulty in clearing myself, without mentioning circumstances, which, were it only for the sake of our father's memory, should be buried in eternal oblivion. I hope your friend feels no continued inconvenience from his hurt?"

"His lordship is nearly quite recovered," said Jekyl.

"And I trust he did me the justice to own, that, so far as my will was concerned, I am totally guiltless of the purpose of hurting him?"

"He does you full justice in that and everything else," replied Jekyl; "regrets the impetuosity of his own temper, and is determined to be on his guard against it in future."

"That," said Tyrrel, "is so far well; and now, may I ask once more, what communication you have to make to me on the part of your friend?—Were it from any one but him, whom I have found so uniformly false and treacherous, your own fairness and candour would induce me to hope that this unnatural quarrel might be in some sort ended by your mediation."

"I then proceed, sir, under more favourable auspices than I expected," said Captain Jekyl, "to enter on my commission.—You are about to commence a law-suit, Mr Tyrrel, if Fame does not wrong you, for the purpose of depriving your brother of his estate and his title?"

"The case is not fairly stated, Captain Jekyl," replied Tyrrel; "I commence a lawsuit, when I do commence it, for the sake of ascertaining my own just rights."

"It comes to the same thing eventually," said the mediator; "I am not called upon to decide upon the justice of your claims, but they are, you will allow, newly started. The late Countess of Etherington died in possession—open and undoubted possession—of her rank in society."

"If she had no real claim to it, sir," replied Tyrrel, "she had more than justice who enjoyed it so long; and the injured lady whose claims were postponed, had just so much less.—But this is no point for you and me to discuss between us—it must be tried elsewhere."

"Proofs, sir, of the strongest kind, will be necessary to overthrow a right so well established in public opinion, as that of the present possessor of the title of Etherington."

Tyrrel took a paper from his pocket-book, and handing it to Captain Jekyl, only answered, "I have no thoughts of asking you to give up the cause of your friend; but methinks the documents of which I give you a list, may shake your opinion of it."

Captain Jekyl read, muttering to himself, "'*Certificate of marriage, by the Revd. Zadock Kemp, chaplain to the British Embassy at Paris, between Marie de Bellroche, Comptesse de Martigny, and the Right Honble. John Lord Oakendale—Letters between John Earl of Etherington and his lady, under the title of Madame de Martigny—Certificate of baptism—*

Declaration of the Earl of Etherington on his death-bed.'—All this is very well—but may I ask you, Mr Tyrrel, if it is really your purpose to go to extremity with your brother?"

"He has forgot that he is one—he has lifted his hand against my life."

"You have shed his blood—twice shed it," said Jekyl; "the world will not ask which brother gave the offence, but which received, which inflicted, the severest wound."

"Your friend has inflicted one on me, sir," said Tyrrel, "that will bleed while I have the power of memory."

"I understand you, sir," said Captain Jekyl; "you mean the affair of Miss Mowbray?"

"Spare me on that subject, sir!" said Tyrrel. "Hitherto I have disputed my most important rights—rights which involved my rank in society, my fortune, the honour of my mother, with something like composure, but do not say more on the topic you have touched upon, unless you would have before you a madman!—Is it possible for you, sir, to have heard even the outline of this story, and to imagine that I can ever reflect on the cold-blooded and most inhuman stratagem, which this friend of yours prepared for two unfortunates, without ——" He started up, and walked impetuously to and fro. "Since the Fiend himself interrupted the happiness of perfect innocence, there was never such an act of treachery—never such schemes of happiness destroyed—never such inevitable misery prepared for two wretches who had the ideocy to repose perfect confidence in him!—Had there been passion in his conduct, it had been the act of a man—a wicked man, indeed, but still a human creature, acting under the influence of human passions—but his was the deed of a calm, cold, calculating demon, actuated by the basest and most sordid motives of self-interest, joined, as I firmly believe, to an early and inveterate hatred of one whose claims he considered as at variance with his own."

"I am sorry to see you in such a temper," said Captain Jekyl, calmly; "Lord Etherington, I trust, acted on very different motives than those you impute to him; and if you will but listen to me, perhaps something may be struck out which may accommodate these unhappy disputes."

"Sir," said Tyrrel, sitting down again, "I will listen to you with calmness, as I would remain calm under the probe of a surgeon tenting a festered wound. But when you touch me to the quick, when you prick the very nerve, you cannot expect me to endure it without wincing."

"I will endeavour, then, to be as brief in the operation as I can," replied Captain Jekyl, who possessed the advantage of the most admirable composure during the whole conference. "I conclude, Mr

Tyrrel, that the peace, happiness, and honour of Miss Mowbray are dear to you."

"Who dare impeach her honour!" said Tyrrel, fiercely; then checking himself, added, in a more moderate tone, but one of deep feeling, "They are dear to me, sir, as my eye-sight."

"My friend holds them in equal regard," said the Captain; "and has come to the resolution of doing her the most ample justice."

"He can do her justice no otherwise, than by ceasing to haunt this neighbourhood, to think, to speak, even to dream of her."

"Lord Etherington thinks otherwise," said Captain Jekyl; "he believes that if Miss Mowbray has sustained any wrong at his hands, which, of course, I am not called upon to admit, it will be best repaired by the offer to share with her his title, his rank, and his fortune."

"His title, rank, and fortune, sir, are as much a falsehood as he is himself," said Tyrrel, with violence—"Marry Clara Mowbray? never!"

"My friend's fortune, you will observe," replied Jekyl, "does not rest entirely upon the event of the law-suit with which you, Mr Tyrrel, now threaten him.—Deprive him, if you can, of the Oakendale estate, he has still a large patrimony by his mother; and besides, as to his marriage with Clara Mowbray, he conceives, that unless it should be the lady's wish to have the ceremony repeated, to which he is most desirous to defer his own opinion, they have only to declare that it has already passed between them."

"A trick, sir!" said Tyrrel, "a vile, infamous trick! of which the lowest wretch in Newgate would be ashamed—the imposition of one person for another."

"Of that, Mr Tyrrel, I have seen no evidence whatsoever. The clergyman's certificate is clear—Francis Tyrrel is united to Clara Mowbray in the holy bands of wedlock—such is the tenor—there is a copy—nay, stop one instant, if you please, sir. You say there was an imposition in the case—I have no doubt but you speak what you believe, and what Miss Mowbray told you. She was surprised—forced in some measure from the husband she had just married—ashamed to meet her former lover, to whom, doubtless, she had made many a vow of love, and ne'er a true one—what wonder that, unsupported by her bridegroom, she should have changed her tune, and thrown all the blame of her own inconstancy on the absent swain?—A woman, at a pinch so critical, will make the most improbable excuse, rather than be found guilty on her own confession."

"There must be no jesting in this case," said Tyrrel, his cheek becoming pale, and his voice altered with passion.

"I am quite serious, sir," replied Jekyl; "and there is no law court in

Britain that would take the lady's word—all she has to offer, and that in her own cause—against a whole body of evidence, direct and circumstantial, shewing that she was by her own free consent married to the gentleman who now claims her hand.—Forgive me, sir—I see you are much agitated—I do not mean to dispute your right of believing what you think is most credible—I only use the freedom of pointing out to you the impression which the evidence is likely to make on the minds of indifferent persons."

"Your friend," answered Tyrrel, affecting a composure, which, however, he was far from possessing, "may think by such arguments to screen his villainy; but it cannot avail him—the truth is known to Heaven—it is known to me—and there is, besides, one indifferent witness upon earth, who can testify that the most abominable imposition was practised on Miss Mowbray."

"You mean her cousin,—Hannah Irwin, I think, is her name," answered Jekyl; "you see I am fully acquainted with all circumstances of the case. But where is Hannah Irwin to be found?"

"She will appear, doubtless, in Heaven's good time, and to the confusion of him who now imagines the only witness of his treachery—the only one who could tell the truth of this complicated mystery—either no longer lives, or, at least, cannot be brought forward against him, to the ruin of his schemes. Yes, sir, that slight observation of yours has more than explained to me why your friend, or, to call him by his true name, Mr Valentine Bulmer, has not commenced his machinations sooner, and also why he has commenced them now. He thinks himself certain that Hannah Irwin is not now in Britain, or to be produced in a court of justice—he may find himself mistaken."

"My friend seems perfectly confident of the issue of his cause," answered Jekyl; "but for the lady's sake, he is most unwilling to prosecute a suit which must be attended with so many circumstances of painful exposure."

"Exposure, indeed!" answered Tyrrel; "thanks to the traitor who laid a mine so fearful, and who now affects to be reluctant to fire it.—Oh! how I am bound to curse the affinity that restrains my hands! I would be content to be the meanest and vilest of society, for one hour of vengeance on this unexampled hypocrite!—One thing is certain, sir—your friend will have no live victim. His persecution will kill Clara Mowbray, and fill up the cup of his crime, with the murder of one of the sweetest——I shall grow a woman, if I say more on the subject."

"My friend," said Jekyl, "since you like best to have him so defined, is as desirous as you can be to spare the lady's feelings; and with that view, not reverting to former passages, he has laid before her brother a proposal of alliance, with which Mr Mowbray is highly pleased."

"Ha!" said Tyrrel, starting—"And the lady?"

"And the lady has so far proved favourable, as to consent that Lord Etherington shall visit Shaws-Castle."

"Her consent must have been extorted!" exclaimed Tyrrel.

"It was given voluntarily," said Jekyl, "as I am led to understand; unless, perhaps, in so far as the desire to veil these very unpleasing transactions may have operated, I think naturally enough, to induce her to sink them in eternal secrecy, by accepting Lord Etherington's hand.—I see, sir, I give you pain, and I am sorry for it.—I have no title to call upon you for any exertion of generosity; but, should such be Miss Mowbray's sentiments, is it too much to expect of you, that you will not compromise the lady's honour by insisting upon former claims, and opening up disreputable transactions so long past?"

"Captain Jekyl," said Tyrrel, solemnly, "I have no claims. Whatever I might have had, were cancelled by the act of treachery through which your friend endeavoured too successfully to supplant me. Were Clara Mowbray as free from her pretended marriage as law could pronounce her, still with me—*me*, at least, of all men in the world—the obstacle must ever remain, that the nuptial benediction has been pronounced over her, and the man whom I must for once call *brother.*—" He stopped at that word, as if it had cost him agony to pronounce it, and then resumed:—"No, sir, I have no views of personal advantage in this matter—they have been long annihilated—But I will not permit Clara Mowbray to become the wife of a villain—I will watch over her with thoughts as spotless as those of her guardian angel. I have been the cause of all the evil she has sustained—I first persuaded her to quit the path of duty—I, of all men who live, am bound to protect her from the misery—from the guilt which must attach to her as this man's wife. I will never believe that she wishes it—I will never believe, that in calm mind and sober reason, she can be brought to listen to such a guilty proposal.—But her mind—alas!—is not of the firm texture it once could boast; and your friend knows well how to press on the springs of every passion that can agitate and alarm her. Threats of exposure may extort her consent to this most unfitting match, if they do not indeed drive her to suicide, which, I think, the more likely termination. I will therefore be strong where she is weak.—Your friend, sir, must at least strip his proposals of their fine gilding. I will satisfy Mr Mowbray of Saint Ronan's of his false pretences, both to rank and fortune; and I rather think he will protect his sister against the claim of a needy profligate, though he might be dazzled with the alliance of a wealthy peer."

"Your cause, sir, is not yet won," answered Jekyl; "and when it is, your brother will retain property enough to entitle him to marry a greater match than Miss Mowbray, besides the large estate of Nettlewood, to which that alliance must give him right. But I would wish to make some accommodation between you if it were possible. You profess, Mr Tyrrel, to lay aside all selfish wishes and views in this matter, and to look entirely to Miss Mowbray's safety and happiness?"

"Such, upon my honour, is the exclusive purpose of my interference—I would give all I am worth to procure her an hour of quiet—for happiness she will never know again."

"Your anticipations of Miss Mowbray's distress," said Jekyl, "are, I understand, founded upon the character of my friend. You think him a man of light principle, and because he over-reached you in a juvenile intrigue, you conclude that now, in his more steady and advanced years, the happiness of the lady in whom you are so much interested ought not to be trusted to him."

"There may be other grounds," said Tyrrel, hastily; "but you may argue upon those you have named, as sufficient to warrant my interference."

"How, then, if I should propose some accommodation of this nature? Lord Etherington does not pretend to the ardour of a passionate lover. He lives much in the world, and has no desire to quit it. Miss Mowbray's health is delicate—her spirits variable—and retirement would most probably be her choice.—Suppose—I am barely putting a supposition—suppose that a marriage between two persons so circumstanced was rendered necessary or advantageous to both—suppose that such a marriage was to secure to one party a large estate—was to insure the other against all the consequences of an unpleasant exposure—still, both ends might be obtained by the mere ceremony of marriage passing between them. There might be a previous contract of separation, with suitable provisions for the lady, and stipulations, by which the husband should renounce all claim to her society. Such things happen every season, if not on the very marriage day, yet before the honey-moon is over.—Wealth and freedom would be the lady's, and as much rank as you, sir, supposing your claims just, may think proper to leave them."

There was a long pause, during which Tyrrel underwent many changes of countenance, which Jekyl watched carefully, without pressing him for an answer. At length he replied, "There is so much in your proposal, Captain Jekyl, which I might be tempted to accede to, as one manner of unloosing this Gordian knot, and a compromise by which Miss Mowbray's future tranquillity would be in some degree provided for. But I would rather trust a fanged adder than your friend, unless I saw him fettered by the strongest ties of interest. Besides, I am certain the unhappy lady could never survive the being connected with him in this manner, though but for the single moment when they should appear together at the altar. There are other objections——"

He checked himself, paused, and then proceeded in a calm and self-possessed tone. "You think, perhaps, even yet, that I have some selfish and interested views in this business; and perhaps you may feel yourself entitled to entertain the same suspicion towards me, which I avowedly harbour respecting every proposition which originates with your friend.—I cannot help it—I can but meet these disadvantageous impressions with plain-dealing and honesty; and it is in the spirit of both that *I* make a proposition to *you*.—Your friend is attached to rank, fortune, and worldly advantages, in the usual proportion at least in which they are pursued by men of the world—this you must admit, and I will not offend you by supposing more."

"I know few people who do not desire such advantages," answered Captain Jekyl; "and I frankly own, that he affects no particular degree of philosophic indifference respecting them."

"Be it so," answered Tyrrel. "Indeed, the proposal you have just made indicates that his pretended claim on this young lady's hand is entirely, or almost entirely, dictated by motives of interest, since you are of opinion that he would be contented to separate from her society on the very marriage-day, provided that, in doing so, he was assured of the Nettlewood property."

"My proposition was unauthorized by my principal," answered Jekyl; "but it is needless to deny, that its very tenor implies an idea, on my part, that Lord Etherington is no passionate lover."

"Well then," answered Tyrrel. "Consider, sir, and let him consider well, that the estate and rank he now assumes depend upon my will and pleasure—that, if I prosecute the claims of which that scroll makes you aware, he must descend from the rank of an earl into that of a commoner, stripped of by much the better half of his fortune—a diminution which would be far from compensated by the estate of Nettlewood, even if he could obtain it, which could only be by means of a law-suit, precarious in the issue, and most dishonourable in its very essence."

"Well, sir," replied Jekyl, "I perceive your argument—What is your proposal?"

"That I will abstain from prosecuting my claim on those honours and that property—that I will leave Valentine Bulmer in possession of his usurped title and ill-deserved wealth—that I will bind myself under the strongest penalties never to disturb his possession of the Earldom of Etherington, and estates belonging to it—on condition that he allows the woman, whose peace of mind he has ruined for ever, to walk through the world in her wretchedness, undisturbed either by his marriage-suit, or by any claim founded upon his own most treacherous conduct—in short, that he forbear to molest Clara Mowbray, either by his presence, word, letter, or through the intervention of a third party, and be to her in future as if he did not exist."

"This is a singular offer," said the Captain; "may I ask if you are serious in making it?"

"I am neither surprised nor offended at the question," said Tyrrel. "I am a man, sir, like others, and affect no superiority to that which all men desire the possession of—a certain consideration and station in society. I am no romantic fool, to undervalue the sacrifice I am about to make. I renounce a rank, which is and ought to be the more valuable to me, because it involves (he blushed as he spoke) the fame of an honoured mother—because, in failing to claim it, I disobey the commands of a dying father, who wished that by doing so I should declare to the world the penitence which hurried him perhaps to the grave, and the making which public he considered might be some atonement for his errors. From an honoured place in the land, I descend voluntarily to become a nameless exile; for, once certain that Clara Mowbray's peace is assured, Britain no longer holds me.—All this I do, sir, not in an idle strain of overheated feeling, but seeing, and knowing, and dearly valuing, every advantage which I renounce—yet I do it, and do it willingly, rather than be the cause of further evil to one, on whom I have already brought too—too much."

His voice, in spite of his exertions, faultered as he concluded the sentence, and a big drop which rose to his eye, required him for the moment to turn towards the window.

"I am ashamed of this childishness," said he, turning again to Captain Jekyl; "if it excites your ridicule, sir, let it be at least a proof of my sincerity."

"I am far from entertaining such sentiments," said Jekyl, respectfully—for, in a long train of fashionable follies, his heart had not been utterly hardened—"very far indeed. To a proposal so singular as yours, I cannot be expected to answer—except thus far—the character of the peerage is, I believe, indelible, and cannot be resigned or assumed at pleasure. If you are really Earl of Etherington, I cannot see how your resigning the right may avail my friend."

"You, sir, it might not avail," said Tyrrel, gravely, "because you, perhaps, might scorn to exercise a right, or hold a title, that was not legally yours. But your friend will have no such compunctious visitings. If he can act the Earl to the eye of the world, he has already shewn that his honour and conscience will be easily satisfied."

"May I take a copy of the memorandum, containing this list of documents," said Captain Jekyl, "for the information of my constituent?"

"The paper is at your pleasure, sir," replied Tyrrel; "it is itself but a copy.—But, Captain Jekyl," he added, with a sarcastic expression, "is, it would seem, but imperfectly let into his friend's confidence—he may be assured his principal is completely acquainted with the contents of this paper, and has accurate copies of the deeds to which it refers."

"I think it scarce possible," said Jekyl, angrily.

"Possible and certain!" answered Tyrrel. "My father, shortly preceding his death, sent me—with a most affecting confession of his errors—this list of papers, and acquainted me that he had made a similar communication to your friend. That he did so I have no doubt, however Mr Bulmer may have thought proper to disguise the circumstance in communication with you. One circumstance, among others, stamps at once his character, and confirms me of the danger he apprehended by my return to Britain. He found means, through a scoundrelly agent, who had made me the usual remittances from my father while alive, to withhold those which were necessary for my return from the Levant, and I was obliged to borrow from a friend."

"Indeed?" replied Jekyl. "It is the first time I have heard of these papers—May I inquire where the originals are, and in whose custody?"

"I was in the East," answered Tyrrel, "during my father's last illness, and these papers were by him deposited with a respectable commercial house, with which he was connected. They were enclosed in a cover directed to me, and that again in an envelope, addressed to the principal person in their firm."

"You must be sensible," said Captain Jekyl, "that I can scarcely decide on the extraordinary offer which you have been pleased to make, of resigning the claim founded on these documents, unless I had a previous opportunity of examining them."

"You shall have that opportunity—I will write to have them sent down by the post—they lie but in small compass."

"This, then," said the Captain, "sums up all that can be said at present.—Supposing these proofs to be of unexceptionable authenticity, I certainly would advise my friend Etherington to put to sleep a claim so important as yours, even at the expense of resigning his matrimonial speculation—I presume you design to abide by your offer?"

"I am not in the habit of altering my mind—still less of retracting my word," said Tyrrel, somewhat haughtily.

"We part friends, I hope," said Jekyl, rising, and taking his leave.

"Not enemies certainly, Captain Jekyl. I will own to you I owe you my thanks, for extricating me from that foolish affair at the Well—nothing could have put me to more inconvenience than the necessity of following to extremity a frivolous quarrel at the present moment."

"You will come down among us then?" said Jekyl.

"I certainly shall not wish to seem to hide myself," answered Tyrrel; "it is a circumstance might be turned against me—I have a party who will avail himself of every advantage. I have but one path, Captain Jekyl—that of truth and honour."

Captain Jekyl bowed, and took his leave. So soon as he was gone, Tyrrel locked the door of the apartment, and drawing from his bosom a portrait, gazed on it with a mixture of sorrow and tenderness, until the tears dropped from his eye.

It was the picture of Clara Mowbray, such as he had known her in the days of their youthful love, and taken by himself, whose early turn for painting had already developed itself. The features of the blooming girl might be yet traced in the fine countenance of the more matured original. But what was now become of the glow which had shaded her cheek?—what of the arch, yet subdued pleasantry, which lurked in the eye?—what of the joyous content, which composed every feature to the expression of an Euphrosyne?—Alas! these were long fled!—Sorrow had laid his hand upon her—the purple light of youth was quenched—the glance of innocent gaiety was exchanged for looks now moody with ill concealed care, now animated by a spirit of reckless and satirical observation.

"What a wreck! what a wreck!" exclaimed Tyrrel; "and all of one wretch's making.—Can I put the last hand to the work, and be her murtherer outright? I cannot—I cannot!—I will be strong in the resolve I have formed—I will sacrifice all—rank—station—fortune—and fame. Revenge!—revenge itself, the last good left me—revenge itself I will sacrifice to obtain her such tranquillity as she may be yet capable to enjoy."

In this resolution he sat down, and wrote a letter to the commercial house with whom the documents of his birth, and other relative papers, were deposited, requesting that the packet containing them should be forwarded to him through the post-office.

Tyrrel was neither unambitious, nor without those sentiments respecting personal consideration, which are usually united with deep feeling and an ardent mind. It was with a trembling hand, and a watery eye, but with a heart firmly resolved, that he sealed and dispatched the letter; a step towards the resignation, in favour of his mortal enemy, of that rank and condition in life, which was his own by right of inheritance, but had so long hung in doubt betwixt them.

Chapter Four

INTRUSION

By my troth, I will go with thee to the lane's-end!—I
am a kind of burr—I shall stick.

Measure for Measure

IT WAS now far advanced in autumn. The dew lay thick on the long grass, where it was touched by the sun; but where the sward lay in shadow, it was covered with hoar frost, and crisped under Jekyl's foot, as he returned through the woods of Saint Ronan's. The leaves of the ash trees detached themselves from the branches, and without an air of wind fell spontaneously on the path. The mists still lay lazily upon the heights, and the huge old tower of Saint Ronan's was entirely shrouded with vapour, excepting where a sun-beam, struggling with the mist, penetrated into its wreaths so far as to shew a projecting turret upon one of the angles of the old fortress, which, long a favourite haunt of the raven, was popularly called the Corbie's Tower. Beneath, the scene was open and lightsome, and the robin red-breast was chirping his best, to atone for the absence of all other choristers. The fine foliage of autumn was seen in many a glade, running up the sides of each little ravine, russet-hued and golden-specked, and tinged frequently with the red hues of the mountain-ash; while here and there a huge old fir, the native growth of the soil, flung his broad shadow over the rest of the trees, and seemed to exult in the permanence of his dusky livery over the more showy, but transitory brilliance by which he was surrounded.

Such is the scene, which, so often described in prose and in poetry, yet seldom loses its effect upon the ear or upon the eye, and through which we wander with a strain of mind congenial to the decline of the year. There are few who do not feel the impression; and even Jekyl, though bred to far different pursuits than those most favourable to such contemplation, relaxed his pace to admire the uncommon beauty of the landscape.

Perhaps, also, he was in no hurry to rejoin the Earl of Etherington, towards whose service he felt himself more disinclined since his interview with Tyrrel. It was clear that nobleman had not fully reposed in his friend the confidence promised; he had not made him aware of the existence of those important documents of proof, on which the whole fate of his negotiation appeared now to hinge, and in so far had deceived him. Yet, when he pulled from his pocket, and re-read Lord

Etherington's explanatory letter, he could not help being more sensible than he had been on the first perusal, how much the present possessor of that title felt alarmed at his brother's claims; and he had some compassion for the natural feeling that must have rendered him shy of communicating at once the very worst view of his case, even to his most confidential friend. Upon the whole, he remembered that Lord Etherington had been his benefactor to an unusual extent; that he had promised him his active and devoted assistance, in extricating him from the difficulties with which he seemed at present surrounded; that, in quality of his confidant, he had become acquainted with the most secret transactions of his life; and that it could only be some very strong cause indeed, which could justify breaking off from him at this moment. Yet he could not help wishing either that his own obligations had been less, his friend's cause better, or, at least, the friend himself more worthy of assistance.

"A beautiful morning, sir, for such a foggy, d—d climate as this?" said a voice close by Jekyl's ear, which made him at once start out of his contemplation. He turned half round, and beside him stood our honest friend Touchwood, his throat muffled in his large Indian handkerchief, huge gouty shoes thrust upon his feet, his bob-wig well powdered, and his gold-headed cane in his hand, carried upright as a serjeant's halbert. One glance of contemptuous survey entitled Jekyl, according to his modish ideas, to rank the old gentleman as a regular-built Quiz, and to treat him as gentlemen of his Majesty's Guards think themselves entitled to use every unfashionable variety of the human species. A slight inclination of a bow, and a very cold "You have the advantage of me, sir," dropped as it were unconsciously from his tongue, were meant to repress the old gentleman's advances, and moderate his ambition to be hail fellow well met with his betters. But Mr Touchwood was callous to the intended rebuke; he had lived too much at large upon the world, and was far too confident of his own merits to take a repulse easily, or to permit his modesty to interfere with any purpose which he had formed.

"Advantage of you, sir?" he replied; "I have lived too long in the world not to keep all the advantages I have, and get all I can—and I reckon it one that I have overtaken you, and shall have the pleasure of your company to the Well."

"I should but interrupt your worthier meditations, sir," said the other; "besides, I am a modest young man, and think myself fit for no better company than my own—moreover, I walk slow—very slow.—Good morning to you, Mr A—A—I believe my treacherous memory has let slip your name, sir."

"My name!—Why, your memory must have been like Pat Murtough's greyhound, that let the hare go before he caught it. You never heard my name in your life. Touchwood is my name. What d'ye think of it, now you know it?"

"I am really no connoisseur in surnames," answered Jekyl; "and it is quite the same to me whether you call yourself Touchwood or Touchstone. Don't let me keep you from walking on, sir. You will find breakfast far advanced at the Well, sir, and your walk has probably given you an appetite."

"Which will serve me to luncheon-time, I promise you," said Touchwood; "I always drink my coffee so soon as my feet are in my pabouches—it's the way all over the East. Never trust my breakfast to their scalding milk and water at the Well, I assure you; and for walking slow, I have had a touch of the gout."

"Have you?" said Jekyl; "I am sorry for that; because, if you have no mind to breakfast, I have—and so, Mr Touchstone, good morrow to you."

But, although the young soldier went off at double quick time, his pertinacious attendant kept close by his side, displaying an activity which seemed inconsistent with his make and his years, and talking away the whole time, so as to shew that his lungs were not in the least degree incommoded by the unusual rapidity of motion.

"Nay, young gentleman, if you are for a good smart walk, I am for you, and the gout may be d—d. You are a lucky fellow, to have youth on your side; but yet, so far as between the Aulton and the Well, I think I could walk you for your sum, barring running—all heel and toe—equal weight, and I would match Barclay himself for a mile."

"Upon my word, you are a gay old gentleman!" said Jekyl, relaxing his pace; "and if we must be fellow-travellers, though I can see no great occasion for it, I must even shorten sail for you."

So saying, and as if another means of deliverance had occurred to him, he slackened his pace, took out an ivory case for segars, and, lighting one with his *briquet*, said, while he walked on, and bestowed as much of its fragrance as he could upon the face of his intrusive companion, "Vergeben sie mein herr—ich bin erzogen in kaiserlicher dienst—muss rauchen ein kleine wenig."

"Rauchen sie immer fort," said Touchwood, producing a huge meerschaum, which, suspended by a chain from his neck, lurked in the bosom of his coat, "habe auch mein pfeifchen—Sehen sie den lieben topf;" and he began to return the smoke, if not the fire, of his companion, in full volumes, and with interest.

"The devil take the twaddle," said Jekyl to himself, "he is too old and too fat to be treated after the manner of Professor Jackson; and, on my life, I cannot tell what to make of him.—He is a residenter too —I must tip him the cold shoulder, or he will be pestering me eternally."

Accordingly, he walked on, sucking his segar, and apparently in as abstracted a mood as Mr Cargill himself, without paying the least attention to Touchwood, who, nevertheless, continued talking, as if he had been addressing the most attentive listener in Scotland, whether it were the favourite nephew of a cross, old, rich bachelor, or the aid-de-camp of some old, rusty, fire-lock of a general, who tells stories of the American war.

"And so, sir, I can put up with any companion at a pinch, for I have travelled in all sort of ways, from a caravan down to a carrier's cart; but the best society is the best everywhere; and I am happy I have fallen in with a gentleman who suits me so well as you—that grave, steady attention reminds me of Elfi Bey—you might talk to him in English, or anything he understood least of—you might have read Aristotle to Elfi, and not a muscle would he stir—give him his pipe, and he would sit on his cushion as if he took in every word of what you said."

Captain Jekyl threw away the remnant of his segar, with a little movement of pettishness, and began to whistle an opera air.

"There again, now!—That is just so like the Marquis, another dear friend of mine, that whistles all the time you talk to him—He says he learned it in the reign of terror, when a man was glad to whistle to shew his throat was whole.—And, talking of great folks, what do you think of this affair between Lord Etherington and his brother, or cousin, as some folks call him?"

Jekyl absolutely started at the question; a degree of emotion, which, had it been witnessed by any of his fashionable friends, would for ever have ruined his pretensions to rank in their first order.

"What affair?" he asked, so soon as he could command a certain degree of composure.

"Why, you know the news surely? Francis Tyrrel, whom all the company voted a coward the other day, turns out as brave a fellow as any of us; for, instead of having run away to avoid having his own throat cut by Sir Bingo Binks, he was at the very moment engaged in a gallant attempt to murder his elder brother, or his more lawful brother, or his cousin, or some such near relation."

"I believe you are misinformed, sir," said Jekyl dryly, and then resumed, as deftly as he could, his proper character of a pococurante.

"I am told," continued Touchwood, "one Jekyl acted as a second to them both on the occasion—a proper fellow, sir—one of those fine gentlemen that we pay for polishing the pavement in Bond Street, and looking at a thick shoe and a pair of worsted stockings, as if the wearer were none of their paymasters. However, I believe the Commander-in-Chief is like to discard him when he hears what has happened."

"Sir!" said Jekyl, fiercely—then, recollecting the folly of being angry with an original of his companion's description, he proceeded more coolly, "You are misinformed—Captain Jekyl knew nothing of any such matter as you refer to—you talk of a person you know nothing of—Captain Jekyl is——" (Here he stopped, a little scandalized, perhaps, at the very idea of vindicating himself to such a personage from such a charge.)

"Ay, ay," said the traveller, filling up the chasm in his own way, "he is not worth our talking of, certainly—but I believe he knew as much of the matter as either you or I do, for all that."

"Sir, this is either a very great mistake, or wilful impertinence. However absurd or intrusive you may be, I cannot allow you, either in ignorance or incivility, to use the name of Captain Jekyl with disrespect.—I am Captain Jekyl, sir."

"Very like, very like," said Touchwood, with the most provoking indifference; "I guessed as much before."

"Then, sir, you may guess what is likely to follow, when a gentleman hears himself unwarrantably and unjustly slandered," replied Captain Jekyl, surprised and provoked that his annunciation of name and rank seemed to be treated so lightly. "I advise you, sir, not to proceed too far upon the immunity of your age and insignificance."

"I never presume farther than I have good reason to think necessary, Captain Jekyl," answered Touchwood, with great composure. "I am too old, as you say, for any such idiotical a business as a duel, which no nation I know of practises but our silly fools of Europe—and then, as for your switch, which you are grasping with so much dignity, that is totally out of the question. Look you, young gentleman; four-fifths of my life have been spent among men who do not set a man's life at the value of a button on his collar—every man learns, in such cases, to protect himself as he can; and whoever strikes me must stand to the consequences. I have always a brace of bull-dogs about me, which put age and youth on a level."

So saying, he exhibited a very handsome, highly-finished, and richly mounted pair of pistols.

"Catch me without my tools," said he, significantly buttoning his coat over the arms, which were concealed in a side-pocket, ingeniously contrived for that purpose. "I see you do not know what to make of me," he continued, in a familiar and confidential tone; "but, to tell you the truth, everybody that has meddled in this Saint Ronan's business is a little off the hooks—something of a *tête exaltée*, in plain words, a little crazy, or so; and I do not affect to be much wiser than other people."

"Sir," said Jekyl, "your manners and discourse are so unprecedented, that I must ask your meaning plainly and decidedly—Do you mean to insult me, or no?"

"No insult at all, young gentleman—all fair meaning, and above board—I only wished to let you know what the world may say, that is all."

"Sir," said Jekyl, hastily, "the world may tell what lies it pleases; but I was not present at the rencontre between Etherington and Mr Tyrrel —I was some hundred miles off."

"There now," said Touchwood, "there *was* a rencontre between them—the very thing I wanted to know."

"Sir," said Jekyl, aware too late that, in his haste to vindicate himself, he had committed his friend, "I desire you will found nothing on an expression hastily used to vindicate myself from a false aspersion —I only meant to say, if there was an affair such as you talk of, I knew nothing of it."

"Never mind—never mind—I shall make no bad use of what I have learned," said Touchwood; "were you to eat your words with the best fish-sauce, (and that is Burgess's,) I have got all the information from them I wanted."

"You are strangely pertinacious, sir," replied Jekyl.

"O, a rock, a piece of flint for that—What I have learned, I have learned, but I will make no bad use of it.—Hark ye, Captain, I have no malice against your friend—perhaps the contrary—but he is in a bad course, sir—has kept a false reckoning, for as deep as he thinks himself; and I tell you so, because I hold you (your finery out of the question) to be, as Hamlet says, indifferent honest; but, if you were not, why, necessity is necessity; and a man will take a Bedouin for his guide in the desert, whom he would not trust with an asper in the cultivated field; so I think of reposing some confidence in you—have not made up my mind yet, though."

"On my word, sir, I am greatly flattered, sir, both by your intentions and your hesitation," said Captain Jekyl. "You were pleased to say just now, that every one concerned with these strange matters was something particular."

"Ay, ay—something crazy—a little mad, or so. That was what I said, and I can prove it."

"I should be glad to hear the proof," said Jekyl—"I hope you do not except yourself?"

"Oh! by no means," answered Touchwood; "I am one of the maddest old boys ever slept out of straw, or went loose. But you can put fishing questions in your turn, Captain, I see that—you would fain know how much, or how little, I am in all these secrets. Well, that is as thereafter may be. In the meantime, here are my proofs.—Old Scrogie Mowbray was mad, to like the sound of Mowbray better than that of Scrogie. Young Scrogie was mad, not to like it as well. The old Earl of Etherington was not sane when he married a French wife in secret, and devilish mad indeed when he married an English one in public. Then for the good folks here, Mowbray of Saint Ronan's is cracked, when he wishes to give his sister to he knows not precisely whom: She is a fool not to take him, because she *does* know who he is, and what has been between them; and your friend is maddest of all, that seeks her under such a heavy penalty;—and you and I, Captain, go mad gratis, for company's sake, when we mix ourselves with such a mess of folly and frenzy."

"Really, sir, all that you have said is an absolute riddle to me."

"Riddles may be read," said Touchwood, nodding; "if you have any desire to read mine, pray, take notice, that this being our first interview, I have exerted myself *faire les frais de conversation*, as Jack Frenchman says; if you want another, you may come to Mrs Dods's, at the Cleikum Inn, any day before Saturday, at three precisely, when you will find none of your half-starved, long-limbed bundle of bones, which you call poultry at the table d'hote, but a right Chitty-gong fowl—I got Mrs Dods the breed from old Ben Vandewash, the Dutch broker—stewed to a minute, with rice and mushrooms.—If you can eat without a silver fork, and your appetite serves you, you shall be welcome—that's all.—So, good morning to you, good master lieutenant, for a captain in the Guards is but a lieutenant after all."

So saying, and ere Jekyl could make any answer, the old gentleman turned short off into a path which led to the healing fountain, branching away from that which conducted to the Hotel.

Uncertain with whom he had been holding a conversation so strange, Jekyl remained looking after him, until his attention was roused by a little boy, who crept out from an adjoining thicket, with a switch in his hand, which he had been just cutting,—probably against regulations to the contrary effect made and provided, for he held himself ready to take cover in the copse again, in case any one were in sight who might be interested in chastising his delinquency. Captain Jekyl easily recognized in him one of that hopeful class of imps, who pick up a precarious livelihood about such places of public resort, by going errands, brushing shoes, doing the groom's and coachman's work in the stables, driving donkies, opening gates, and so forth, for about one-tenth part of their time, spending the rest in gambling, sleeping in the sun, and otherwise qualifying themselves to exercise the profession of thieves and pickpockets, either separately, or in conjunction with those of waiters, grooms, and postilions. The little outcast had an indifferent pair of pantaloons, and about half a jacket, for, like Pentapolin with the naked arm, he went on action with his right shoulder bare; a third part of what had once been a hat covered his hair, bleached white by the sun, and his face, as brown as a berry, was illumined by a pair of eyes, which, for spying out either peril or profit, might have rivalled those of the hawk.

"Come hither, ye unhanged whelp," said Jekyl, "and tell me if you know the old gentleman passed down the walk just now—yonder he is, still in sight."

"It is the Naboab," said the boy; "I could swear to his back amang all the backs at the Waal, your honour."

"What do you call a Naboab, you varlet?"

"A Naboab—a Naboab?" answered the scout; "odd, I believe it is ane comes frae foreign parties, with mair siller than his pouches can haud, and spills it aw through the country—they are as yellow as orangers, and maun hae a' thing their ain gate."

"And what is this Naboab's name, as you call him?" demanded Jekyl.

"His name is Tuchwud," said his informer; "ye may see him at the Waal every morning."

"I have not seen him at the ordinary."

"Na, na," answered the boy; "he is a queer auld cull, he disna frequent wi' other folk, but lives up by at the Cleikum.—He gave me half a crown yince, and bade me no to play it awa' at pitch and toss."

"And you disobeyed him, of course?"

"Na, I didna dis-obeyed him—I plaid it awa' at neevie-neevie-nick-nack."

"Well, there is sixpence for thee; lose it to the devil if thou think'st proper."

So saying, he gave the little galopin his donative, and a slight rap on the pate at the same time, which sent him scouring from his presence. He himself hastened to Lord Etherington's apartments, and, as luck would have it, found the Earl alone.

Chapter Five

DISCUSSION

I will converse with iron-witted clowns
And unrespective fools—none are for me
That look into me with suspicious eyes.
Richard III

"How now, Jekyl!" said Lord Etherington, eagerly; "what news from the enemy?—Have you seen him?"

"I have," replied Jekyl.

"And in what humour did you find him?—in none that was very favourable, I dare say, for you have a baffled and perplexed look, that confesses a losing game. I have often warned you how your hang-dog look betrays you at brag—And then, when you would fain brush up your courage, and put a good face on a bad game, your bold looks always remind me of a standard hoisted only half-mast high, and betraying melancholy and dejection, instead of triumph and defiance."

"I am only holding the cards for your lordship at present," answered Jekyl; "and I wish to Heaven there may be no one looking over the hand."

"How do you mean by that?"

"Why, I was beset, on returning through the wood, by an old bore, a Nabob, as they call him, and Touchwood by name."

"I have seen such a quiz about," said Lord Etherington—"What of him?"

"Nothing," answered Jekyl; "excepting that he seemed to know much more of your affairs than you would wish or are aware of. He smoked the truth of the rencontre betwixt Tyrrel and you, and what is worse—I must needs confess the truth—he contrived to wring out of me a sort of confirmation of his suspicions."

"'Slife! wert thou mad?" said Lord Etherington, turning pale; "His is the very tongue to send the story through the whole country—Hal, you have undone me."

"I hope not," said Jekyl; "I trust in Heaven I have not!—His knowledge is quite general—only that there was some scuffle between you—Do not look so dismayed about it, or I will e'en go back and cut his throat, to secure his secrecy."

"Cursed indiscretion!" answered the Earl—"how could you let him fix on you at all?"

"I cannot tell," said Jekyl—"he has powers of boring beyond ten of the dullest of all possible doctors—stuck like a limpet to a rock—a perfect double of the Old Man of the Sea, who I take to have been the greatest bore on record."

"Could you not have turned him on his back like a turtle, and left him there?" said Lord Etherington.

"And had an ounce of lead in my body for my pains? No—no—we have already had foot-pad work enough—I promise you the old buck was armed, as if he meant to bing folks on the low toby."

"Well—well—But Martigny, or Tyrrel, as you call him—what says he?"

"Why Tyrrel, or Martigny as your lordship calls him," answered Jekyl, "will by no means listen to your lordship's proposition. He will not consent that Miss Mowbray's happiness shall be placed in your lordship's keeping; nay, it did not meet his approbation a bit the more, when I hinted at the acknowledgment of the marriage, or the repetition of the ceremony, attended by an immediate separation, which I thought I might venture to propose."

"And on what grounds does he refuse so reasonable an accommodation?" said Lord Etherington—"Does he still seek to marry the girl himself?"

"I believe he thinks the circumstances of the case render that impossible," replied his confidant.

"What? then he would play the dog in the manger—neither eat nor let eat?—He shall find himself mistaken. She has used me like a dog, Jekyl, since I saw you; and, by Jove! I will have her, that I may break her pride, and cut him to the liver with the agony of seeing it."

"Nay, but hold—hold!" said Jekyl; "perhaps I have something to say on his part, that may be a better compromise than all you could have by teazing him. He is willing to purchase what he calls Miss Mowbray's tranquillity, at the expense of his resignation of his claims to your father's honours and estate; and he surprised me very much, my lord, by shewing me this list of documents, which, I am afraid, makes his success more than probable, if there really are such proofs in existence." Lord Etherington took the paper, and seemed to read with much attention, while Jekyl proceeded,—"He has written to procure these evidences from the person with whom they are deposited."

"We shall see what like they are when they arrive," said Lord Etherington; "they come by post, I suppose?"

"Yes; and may be immediately expected," said Jekyl.

"Well—he is my brother on one side of the house, at least," said Lord Etherington; "and I should not much like to have him lagged for forgery, which I suppose will be the end of his bolstering up an unsubstantial plea by fabricated documents—I should like to see these papers he talks of."

"But, my lord," replied Jekyl, "Tyrrel's allegation is, that you *have* seen them; and that copies, at least, were made out for you, and are in your possession—such is his averment."

"He lies," answered Lord Etherington, "so far as he pretends I know of such papers. I consider the whole story as froth—foam—fudge, or whatever is most unsubstantial. It will prove such when the papers appear, if indeed they ever shall appear. The whole is a bully from beginning to end; and I wonder at thee, Jekyl, for being so thirsty after syllabub, that you can swallow such whip'd cream as that stuff amounts to.—No, no—I know my advantage, and shall use it so as to make all their hearts bleed. As for these papers, I recollect now that my agent talked of copies of some manuscripts having been sent him, but the originals were not forthcoming; and I'll bet the long odds that they never are—mere fabrications—If I thought otherwise, would I not tell you?"

"Certainly, I hope you would, my lord," said Jekyl; "for I see no chance of my being useful to you, unless I have the honour to enjoy your confidence."

"You do—you do, my friend," said Etherington, shaking him by the hand; "and since I must consider your present negotiation as failed, I must devise some other mode of settling with this mad and troublesome fellow."

"No violence, my lord," said Jekyl, once more, and with much emphasis.

"None—none—none, by heaven!—Why, thou suspicious wretch, must I swear, to quell your scruples?—On the contrary, it shall not be my fault, if we are not on decent terms."

"It would be infinitely to the advantage of both your characters if you could bring that to pass," answered Jekyl; "and if you are serious in wishing it, I will endeavour to prepare Tyrrel. He comes to the Well or to the ordinary to-day, and it would be highly ridiculous to make a scene."

"True, true; find him out, my dear Jekyl, and persuade him how foolish it will be to bring our family quarrels out before strangers, and for their amusement. They shall see the two bears can meet without biting.—Go—go—I will follow you instantly—go, and remember you have my full and exclusive confidence.—Go, half-bred, startling fool!" he continued, the instant Jekyl had left the room, "with just spirit enough to ensure your own ruin, by hurrying you into what you are not up to. But he has character in the world—is brave—and one of those whose countenance gives a fair face to a doubtful business. He is my creature, too—I have bought and paid for him, and it would be idle extravagance not to make use of him—But as to confidence—no confidence, honest Hal, beyond that which cannot be avoided. If I wanted a confidant, here comes a better than thou by half—Solmes has no scruples—he will always give me money's worth of zeal and secrecy *for* money."

His lordship's valet at this moment entered the apartment, a grave, civil-looking man, past the middle age, with a sallow complexion, a dark, thoughtful eye, slow, and sparing of speech, and sedulously attentive to all the duties of his situation.

"Solmes," said Lord Etherington, and then stopped short.

"My lord—" There was a pause; and when Lord Etherington had again said, "Solmes!" and his valet had answered, "Your lordship," there was a second pause; until the Earl, as if recollecting himself, "Oh! I remember what I wished to say—it was about the course of post here. It is not very regular, I believe?"

"Regular enough, my lord, so far as concerns this place—the people in the Aulton do not get their letters in course."

"And why not, Solmes?" said his lordship.

"The old woman who keeps the little inn there, my lord, is on bad terms with the post-mistress—the one will not send for the letters, and the other will not dispatch them to the village; so, betwixt them, they are sometimes lost, or mislaid, or returned to the general post-office."

"I wish that may not be the case of a packet which I expect in a few days—it should have been here already, or, perhaps, it may arrive in the beginning of the week—it is from that formal ass, Freeman the quaker, who addresses me by my Christian and family name, Francis Tyrrel. He is like enough to mistake the inn, too, and I should be sorry it fell into Monsieur Martigny's hands—I suppose you know he is in that neighbourhood. Look after its safety, Solmes—quietly, you understand; because people might put odd constructions, as if I were wanting a letter which was not my own."

"I understand perfectly, my lord," said Solmes, without exhibiting the slightest change in his sallow countenance, though perfectly comprehending the nature of the service required.

"And here is a note will pay for postage," said the Earl, putting into his valet's hand a bank-bill of considerable value; "and you may keep the balance for occasional expenses."

This was also fully understood; and Solmes, too politic and cautious even to look intelligence, or acknowledge gratitude, made only a bow of acquiescence, put the note into his pocket-book, and assured his lordship that his commands should be punctually attended to.

"There goes the agent for my money, and for my purpose," said Lord Etherington, exultingly; "no extorting of confidence, no demanding of explanations, no tearing off the veil with which a delicate manœuvre is *gazé*—all excuses are received as *argent comptant*, providing only, that the best excuse of all, the *argent comptant* itself, come to recommend them.—Yet I will trust no one—I will out, like a skilful general, and reconnoitre in person."

With this resolution, Lord Etherington put on his surtout and cap, and sallying from his apartments, took the way to the bookseller's shop, which also served as post-office and circulating library; and being in the very centre of the parade, (for so is termed the broad terrace walk which leads from the inn to the Well,) it formed a convenient lounging-place for newsmongers and idlers of every description.

The Earl's appearance created, as usual, a sensation upon the public promenade; but, whether it was the suggestion of his own alarmed conscience, or that there was some real cause for the remark, he could not help thinking his reception was of a more doubtful character than usual. His fine figure and easy manners produced their usual effect, and all whom he spoke to received his attention as an honour; but none offered, as usual, to unite themselves to him, or to induce him to join their party. He seemed to be looked on rather as an object of observation and attention, than as making one of the company; and to escape from a distant gaze, which became rather embarrassing, he turned into the little emporium of news and literature.

He entered unobserved, just as Lady Penelope had finished reading some verses, and was commenting upon them with all the alacrity of a *femme sçavante*, in possession of something which no one is to hear repeated oftener than once.

"Copy—no, indeed!" these were the snatches which reached Lord Etherington's ear, from the group of which her ladyship formed the centre—"honour bright—I must not betray poor Chatterley—besides, his lordship is my friend, and a person of rank, you know—so one would not—You have not got the book, Mr Pot?—you have not got Statius?—you never have anything one longs to see."

"Very sorry, my lady—quite out of copies at present—I expect some in my next monthly parcel."

"Good lack, Mr Pot, that is your never-failing answer," said Lady Penelope; "I believe if I were to ask you for the last new edition of the Alcoran, you would tell me it was coming down in your next monthly parcel."

"Can't say, my lady, really," answered Mr Pot; "have not seen the work advertised yet; but I have no doubt, if it is likely to take, there will be copies in my next monthly parcel."

"Mr Pot's supplies are always in the *paullo post futurum* tense," said Mr Chatterley, who was just entering the shop.

"Ah! Mr Chatterley, are you there?" said Lady Penelope; "I lay my death at your door—I cannot find this Thebaid, where Polynices and his brother——"

"Hush, my lady!—hush, for Heaven's sake!" said the poetical divine, and looked towards Lord Etherington. Lady Penelope took the hint, and was silent; but she had said enough to call up the traveller Touchwood, who raised his head from the newspaper which he was studying, and, without addressing his discourse to any one in particular, ejaculated, as if in scorn of Lady Penelope's geography—

"Polynices?—Polly Peachum.—There is no such place in the Thebais—the Thebais is in Egypt—the mummies come from the Thebais—I have been in the catacombs—caves very curious indeed—we were lapidated by the natives—pebbled to some purpose, I give you my word. My janizary threshed a whole village by way of retaliation."

While he was thus proceeding, Lord Etherington, as if in a listless mood, was looking at the letters which stood ranged on the chimney-piece, and carrying on a languid dialogue with Mrs Pot, whose person and manners were not ill adapted to her situation, for she was good-looking, and vastly fine and affected.

"Number of letters here which don't seem to find owners, Mrs Pot?"

"Great number, indeed, my lord—it is a great vexation, for we are obliged to return them to the post-office, and the postage is charged against us if they are lost; and how can one keep sight of them all?"

"Any love-letters among them, Mrs Pot?" said his lordship, lowering his tone.

"Oh, fie! my lord, how should I know?" answered Mrs Pot, dropping her voice to the same cadence.

"Oh! every one can tell a love-letter—that has ever received one, that is—one knows them without opening—they are always folded hurriedly and sealed carefully—and the direction manifests a kind of tremulous agitation, that marks the state of the writer's nerves—that now,"—pointing with his switch to a letter upon the chimney-piece, "that *must* be a love-letter."

"He, he, he!" giggled Mrs Pot. "I beg pardon for laughing, my lord—but—he, he, he!—that is a letter from one Bindloose, the banker body, to the old woman Luckie Dods, as they call her, at the change-house in the Aulton."

"Depend upon it then, Mrs Pot, that your neighbour, Mrs Dods, has got a lover in Mr Bindloose—unless the banker has been shaking hands with the palsy. Why do you not forward her letter?—you are very cruel to keep it in durance here."

"Me forward!" answered Mrs Pot; "the cappernoity, old, girning ale-wife may wait long enough or I forward it—She'll not loose the letters that come to her by the King's post, and she must go on troking wi' the old carrier, as if there was no post-house in the neighbourhood. But the solicitor will be about with her one of these days."

"Oh! you are too cruel—you really should send the love-letter; consider, the older she is, the poor soul has the less time to lose."

But this was a topic on which Mrs Pot understood no jesting. She was well aware of our matron's inveteracy against her and her establishment, and she resented it as a place-man resents the efforts of a radical. She answered something sulkily, "That they that loosed letters should have letters; and neither Luckie Dods, nor any of her lodgers, should ever see the scrape of a pen from the Saint Ronan's office, that they did not call for and pay for."

It is probable that this declaration contained the essence of the information which Lord Etherington had designed to extract by his momentary flirtation with Mrs Pot, for when, retreating as it were from this sore subject, she asked him, in a pretty mincing tone, to try his skill in pointing out another love-letter, he only answered carelessly, "that in order to do that he must write her one;" and leaving his confidential station by her little throne, he lounged through the narrow shop, bowed slightly to Lady Penelope as he passed, and issued forth upon the parade, where he saw a spectacle which might well have appalled a man of less self-possession than himself.

Just as he left the shop, little Miss Digges entered almost breathless, with the emotion of impatience and of curiosity. "Oh la! my lady, what do you stay here for?—Mr Tyrrel has just entered the other end of the parade this moment, and Lord Etherington is walking that way—they must meet each other.—O Lord! come, come away, and see them meet!—I wonder if they'll speak—I hope they won't fight—Oh la! do come, my lady!"

"I must go with you, I find," said Lady Penelope; "it is the strangest thing, my love, that curiosity of yours about other folks' matters—I wonder what your mamma will say to it."

"Oh! never mind mamma—nobody minds her—papa, nor nobody—Do come, dearest Lady Pen, or I will run away by myself.—Mr Chatterley, do make her come!"

"I must come, it seems," said Lady Penelope, "or I shall have a pretty account of you."

But, notwithstanding this rebuke, and forgetting, at the same time, that people of quality ought never to seem in a hurry, Lady Penelope, with such of her satellites as she could hastily collect around her, tripped along the parade with unusual haste, in sympathy, doubtless, with Miss Digges's curiosity, as her ladyship declared she had none of her own.

Our friend, the traveller, had also caught up Miss Digges's information; and, breaking off abruptly an account of the Great Pyramid which had been naturally introduced by the mention of the Thebais, and echoing the fair alarmist's words, "hope they won't fight," he rushed upon the parade, and bustled along as hard as his sturdy supporters could carry him. If the gravity of the traveller, and the delicacy of Lady Penelope, were surprised into unwonted haste from their eagerness to witness the meeting of Tyrrel and Lord Etherington, it may be well supposed that the decorum of the rest of the company was a slender restraint on their curiosity, and that they hurried to witness the expected scene, with the alacrity of gentlemen of the fancy hastening to a set-to.

In truth, though the meeting afforded little sport to those who expected dire conclusions, it was, nevertheless, sufficiently interesting to those spectators who are accustomed to read the language of suppressed passion, betraying itself at the moment when the parties are most desirous to conceal it.

Tyrrel had been followed by several loiterers so soon as he entered the public walk; and their numbers were now so much reinforced, that he saw himself with pain and displeasure the centre of a sort of crowd who watched his motions. Sir Bingo and Captain MacTurk were the first to bustle through it, and to address him with as much politeness as they could command.

"Servant, sir," mumbled Sir Bingo, extending the right hand of fellowship and reconciliation, ungloved. "Servant—sorry that anything should have happened between us—very sorry, on my word."

"No more need be said, sir," replied Tyrrel; "the whole is forgotten."

"Very handsome, indeed—quite the civil thing—hope to meet you often, sir."—And here the knight was silent.

Meanwhile, the more verbose Captain proceeded, "Och, py Cot, and it was an awfu' mistake, and I could draw the penknife across my finger for having written the word.—By my sowl, and I scratched it till I scratched a hole in the paper.—Och! that I should live to do an uncivil thing by a gentleman that had got himself hit in an honourable affair! But you should have written, my dear; for how the devil could we guess that you were so well provided in quarrels, that you had to settle two in one day?"

"I was hurt in an unexpected—an accidental manner, Captain MacTurk. I did not write, because there was something in my circumstances at the moment which required secrecy; but I was resolved, the instant I recovered, to put myself to rights in your good opinion."

"Och! and you have done that," said the Captain, nodding sagaciously; "for Captain Jekyl, who is a fine child, has put us all up to your honourable conduct. They are pretty boys, these guardsmen, though they may play a little fine sometimes, and think more of themselves than peradventure they need for to do, in comparison with us of the line.—But he let us know all about it—and, though he said not a word of a certain fine lord, with his foot-pad, and his hurt, and what not, yet we all knew how to lay that and that together.—-And if the law would not right you, and there were bad words between you, why should not two gentlemen right themselves? And as to your being kinsmen, why should not kinsmen behave to each other like men of honour? Only, some say you are father's sons, and that *is* something too near.—I had once thoughts of calling out my uncle Dougal myself, for there is no saying where the line should be drawn; but I thought, on the whole, there should be no fighting, as there is no marriage, within the forbidden degrees. As for first cousins—wheugh!—that's all fair—fire away, Flanigan.—But here is my lord, just upon us like a stag of the first head, and the whole herd behind him."

Tyrrel stepped forward a little before his officious companion, his complexion rapidly changing into various shades, like that of one who forces himself to approach and touch some animal or reptile for which he entertains that deep disgust and abhorrence which was anciently ascribed to constitutional antipathy. This appearance of constraint put upon himself, with the changes which it produced on his countenance, was calculated to prejudice him somewhat in the opinion of the spectators, when compared with the steady, stately, yet, at the same time, easy demeanour of the Earl of Etherington, who was equal to any man in England in the difficult art of putting a good countenance on a bad cause. He met Tyrrel with an air as unembarrassed, as it was cold; and, while he paid the courtesy of a formal and distant salutation, he said aloud, "I presume, Mr Tyrrel de Martigny, that, since you have not thought fit to avoid this awkward meeting, you are disposed to remember our family connection so far as to avoid making sport for the good company."

"You have nothing to apprehend from my passion, Mr Bulmer," replied Tyrrel, "if you can assure yourself against the consequences of your own."

"I am glad of that," said the Earl, with the same composure, but sinking his voice so as only to be heard by Tyrrel; "and as we may not again in a hurry hold any communication together, I take the freedom to remind you, that I sent you a proposal of accommodation by my friend, Mr Jekyl."

"It was inadmissible," said Tyrrel—"altogether inadmissible—both from reasons which you may guess, and others which it is needless to detail.—I sent you a proposition, think of it well."

"I will," replied Lord Etherington, "when I shall see it supported by those alleged proofs, which I do not believe ever had existence."

"Your conscience holds another language from your tongue," said Tyrrel; "but I disclaim reproaches, and decline altercation. I will let Captain Jekyl know when I have received the papers, which, you say, are essential to your forming an opinion on my proposal.—In the meanwhile, do not think to deceive me—I am here for the very purpose of watching and defeating your machinations; and, while I live, be assured they shall never succeed.—And now, sir—or my lord—for the titles are in your choice—fare you well."

"Hold a little," said Lord Etherington. "Since we are condemned to shock each other's eyes, it is fit the good company should know what they are to think of us.—You are a philosopher, and do not value the opinion of the public—a poor worldling like me is desirous to stand fair with it.—Gentlemen," he continued, raising his voice, "Mr Winterblossom, Captain MacTurk, Mr—what is his name, Jekyl?—ay, Micklehen—You have, I believe, all some notion, that this gentleman, my near relation, and I, have some undecided claims on each other, which prevent our living upon good terms.—We do not mean, however, to disturb you with our family quarrels; and, for my own part, while this gentleman, Mr Tyrrel, or whatever he may please to call himself, remains a member of this company, my behaviour to him will be the same as to any stranger who may have that advantage.—Good morrow to you, sir—Good morning, gentlemen—we all meet at dinner, as usual.—Come, Jekyl."

So saying, he took Jekyl by the arm, and, gently extricating himself from the sort of crowd, walked off, leaving most of the company prepossessed in his favour, by the ease and apparent reasonableness of his demeanour. Sounds of depreciation, forming themselves indistinctly into something like the words, "my eye, and Betty Martin," did indeed issue from the neckcloth of Sir Bingo, but they were not much attended to; for it had not escaped the observation of quick-sighted gentry at the Well, that the Baronet's feelings towards the noble Earl were in the inverse ratio of those displayed by Lady Binks, and that, though ashamed to testify, or perhaps incapable of feeling, any anxious degree of jealousy, his temper had been for some time considerably upon the fret; a circumstance concerning which his fair moiety did not think it necessary to give herself any concern.

Meanwhile the Earl of Etherington walked onward with his confidant, in the full triumph of successful genius.

"You see," he said, "Jekyl, that I can turn a corner with any man in England. It was a proper blunder of yours, that you must extricate the fellow from the mist which accident had flung round him—you might as well have published the story of our rencontre at once, for every one can guess it, by laying time, place, and circumstance together; but never trouble your brains for a justification. You marked how I assumed my natural superiority over him—towered up in the full pride of legitimacy—silenced him, even where the good company most do congregate. This will go to Mowbray through his agent, and will put him still madder on my alliance. I know he looks jealously on my flirtation with a certain lady—the dasher yonder—nothing makes a man sensible of the value of an opportunity, but the chance of losing it."

"I wish to Heaven you would give up thoughts of Miss Mowbray!" said Jekyl; "and take Tyrrel's offer, if he has the means of making it good."

"Ay, if—if. But I am quite sure he has no such right as he pretends to, and that his papers are all a deception.—Why do you fix your eyes on me as steady as if you were pointing some most wonderful secret?"

"I wish I knew what to think of your real *bona fide* belief respecting these documents," said Jekyl, not a little puzzled by the steady and unembarrassed air of his friend.

"Why, thou most suspicious of coxcombs," said Etherington; "what the devil would you have me say to you?—Can I, as the lawyers say, prove a negative? or, is it not very possible, that such things may exist, though I have never seen or heard of them? All I can say is, that of all men I am the most interested to deny the existence of such documents; and, therefore, certainly will not admit of it, unless I am compelled to do so by their being produced; nor then either, unless I am at the same time well assured of their authenticity."

"I cannot blame you for your being hard of faith, my lord," said Jekyl; "but still I think if you can cut out with your earldom, and your noble hereditary estate, I would in your case pitch Nettlewood to the devil."

"Yes, as you pitched your own patrimony, Jekyl; but you took care to have the spending of it first.—What would *you* give for such an opportunity of piecing your fortunes by marriage?—Confess the truth."

"I might be tempted, perhaps," said Jekyl, "in my present circumstances; but if they were what they have been, I should despise an estate that was to be held by petticoat tenure, especially when the lady of the manor was a sickly fantastic girl, that hated me, as this Miss Mowbray has the bad taste to hate you."

"Umph—sickly?—no, no, she is not sickly—she is as healthy as any one in constitution—And, on my word, I think her paleness only renders her more interesting. The last time I saw her, I thought she might have rivalled one of Canova's finest statues."

"Yes; but she is indifferent to you—you do not love her," said Jekyl.

"She is anything but indifferent to me," said the Earl; "she becomes daily more interesting—for her dislike piques me; and besides, she has the insolence openly to defy and contemn me before her brother, and in the eyes of all the world. I have a kind of loving hatred—a sort of hating love for her; in short, thinking upon her is like trying to read a riddle, and makes one make quite as many blunders, and talk just as much nonsense. If ever I have the opportunity, I will make her pay for all her airs."

"What airs?" said Jekyl.

"Nay, the devil may describe them, for I cannot; but, for example—Since her brother has insisted on her receiving me, or I should rather say on her appearing when I visit Shaws-Castle, one would think her invention has toiled in discovering different ways of shewing want of respect to me, and dislike to my presence. Instead of dressing herself as a lady should, especially on such occasions, she chooses some fantastic, or old-fashioned, or negligent bedizening, which makes her at least look odd, if it cannot make her ridiculous—such triple tiaras of various-coloured gauze on her head—such pieces of old tapestry, I think, instead of shawls and pelisses—such thick-soled shoes—such tan-leather gloves—mercy upon us, Hal, the very sight of her equipment would drive mad a whole conclave of milliners! Then her postures are so strange—she does so stoop and lollop, as the women call it, so cross her legs and square her arms—were the goddess of grace to look down on her, it would put her to flight for ever!"

"And you are willing to make this awkward, ill-dressed, unmannered dowdy, your Countess, Etherington; you, for whose critical eye half the town dress themselves," said Jekyl.

"It is all a trick, Hal—all an assumed character to get rid of me, to disgust me, to baffle me; but I am not to be had so easily. The brother is driven to despair—he bites his nails, winks, coughs, makes signs, which she always takes up at cross-purposes.—I hope he beats her after I go away; there would be a touch of consolation, were one but certain of that."

"A very charitable hope, truly, and might lead the lady to judge what she may expect after wedlock. But," added Jekyl, "cannot you, so skilful in fathoming every mood of the female mind, devise some mode of engaging her in conversation?"

"Conversation!" replied the Earl; "why, ever since the shock of my first appearance was surmounted, she has contrived to vote me a nonentity; and that she may annihilate me the more completely, she has chosen, of all occupations, that of working a stocking! From what cursed old antediluvian, who lived before the invention of spinning-jennies, she learned this craft, Heaven only knows; but there she sits, with her work pinned to her knee—not the pretty taper silken fabric, with which Jeannette of Amiens coquetted, while Tristram Shandy was observing her progress; but a huge worsted bag, designed for some flat-footed old pauper, with heels like an elephant—But there she sits, counting all the stitches as she works, and refusing to speak, or listen, or look up, under pretence that it disturbs her calculation!"

"An elegant occupation, truly, and I wonder it does not work a cure upon her noble admirer," said Jekyl.

"Confound her—no—she shall not trick me. And then amid this affectation of vulgar stolidity, there break out such sparkles of exultation, when she thinks she has succeeded in baffling her brother, and in plaguing me, that, by my faith, Hal, I could not tell, were it at my option, whether to kiss or to cuff her."

"You are determined to go on with this strange affair, then," said Jekyl.

"On—on—on, my boy!—Clara and Nettlewood for ever," answered the Earl. "Besides, this brother of hers provokes me too—he does not do for me half what he might—what he ought to do. He stands on points of honour, forsooth, this broken-down horse-jockey, who swallowed my two thousand pounds as a pointer would a pat of butter.—I can see he wishes to play fast and loose—has some suspicions, like you, Hal, upon the strength of my right to my father's titles and estate, as if with the tythe of the Nettlewood property alone, I would not be too good a match for one of his beggarly family. He must scheme, forsooth, this half-baked Scotch cake—He must hold off and on, and be cautious, and wait the result, and try conclusions with me, this lump of oatmeal dough.—I am much tempted to make an example of him in the course of my proceedings."

"Why, this is vengeance horrible and dire," said Jekyl; "yet I give up the brother to you; he is a conceited coxcomb, and deserves a lesson. But I would fain intercede for the sister."

"We shall see," replied the Earl; and then suddenly, "I tell you what it is, Hal; her caprices are so diverting, that I sometimes think out of mere contradiction, I almost love her; at least, if she would but clear old scores, and forget one unlucky prank of mine, it should be her own fault if I made her not a happy woman."

Chapter Six

A DEATH-BED

> It comes—it wrings me in my parting hour,
> The long-hid crime—the well-disguised guilt.
> Bring me some holy priest to lay the spectre.
> *Old Play*

THE GENERAL expectation of the company had been much disappointed by the pacific termination of the meeting betwixt the Earl of Etherington and Tyrrel, the anticipation of which had created so deep a sensation. It had been expected that some appalling scene would have taken place; instead of which, each party seemed to acquiesce in a sullen neutrality, and leave the war to be carried on by their lawyers. It was generally understood that the cause was removed out of the courts of Bellona into that of Themis; and although the litigants continued to inhabit the same neighbourhood, and once or twice met at the public walks or public table, they took no notice of each other, farther than by exchanging on such occasions a grave and distant bow.

In the course of two or three days, people ceased to take interest in a feud so coldly conducted; and if they thought of it at all, it was but to wonder that both the parties should persevere in residing near the Spaw, and in chilling, with their unsocial behaviour, a party met together for the purpose of health and amusement.

But the brothers, as the reader is aware, however painful their occasional meetings might be, had the strongest reasons to remain in each other's neighbourhood—Lord Etherington to conduct his design upon Miss Mowbray, Tyrrel to disconcert his plan, if possible, and both to await the answer which should be returned by the house in London, who were depositaries of the papers left by the late Earl.

Jekyl, anxious to assist his friend as much as possible, made in the meantime a visit to old Touchwood at the Aulton, expecting to find him as communicative as he had formerly been on the subject of the quarrel betwixt the brothers, and trusting to discover, by dint of address, whence he had derived his information concerning the affairs of the noble house of Etherington. But the confidence which he had been induced to expect on the part of the old traveller was not reposed. Ferdinand Mendez Pinto, as the Earl called him, had changed his mind, or was not in the vein of communication. The only proof of his confidence worth mentioning, was his imparting to the young officer a valuable receipt for concocting curry-powder.

Jekyl was therefore reduced to believe that Touchwood, who appeared all his life to have been a great intermeddler in other people's affairs, had puzzled out the information which he appeared to possess of Lord Etherington's affairs, through some of those obscure sources whence very important secrets do frequently, to the astonishment and confusion of those whom they concern, escape to the public. He thought this the most likely, as Touchwood was by no means critically nice in his society, but was observed to converse as readily with a gentleman's gentleman, as with the gentleman to whom he belonged, and with a lady's attendant, as with the lady herself. He that will stoop to this sort of society, who is fond of tattle, being at the same time disposed to pay some consideration for gratification of his curiosity, and not over scrupulous respecting its accuracy, may always command a great quantity of private anecdote. Captain Jekyl naturally enough concluded, that this busy old man became in some degree master of other people's affairs by such correspondences as these; and he could himself bear witness to his success in cross-examination, as he had been surprised into avowal of the rencontre between the brothers, by an insidious observation of the said Touchwood. He reported, therefore, to the Earl, after this interview, that, on the whole, he thought he had no reason to fear much on the subject of the traveller, who, though he had become acquainted, by one means or other, with some leading facts of his remarkable history, only possessed them in a broken, confused, and desultory manner, insomuch, that he seemed to doubt whether the parties in the expected law-suit were brothers or cousins, and appeared totally ignorant of the facts on which it was to be founded.

It was the next day after this eclaircissement on the subject of Touchwood, that Lord Etherington dropped as usual into the bookseller's shop, got his papers, and skimming his eye over the shelf on which lay, till called for, the postponed letters destined for the Aulton, saw with a beating heart the smart post-mistress toss amongst them, with an air of sovereign contempt, a pretty large packet, addressed to Francis Tyrrel, Esq., &c. He withdrew his eye, as if conscious that even to have looked on this important parcel might engender some suspicion of his purpose, or intimate the deep interest which he took in the contents of the missive which was so slightly treated by his friend Mrs Pot. At this moment the door of the shop opened, and Lady Penelope Penfeather entered, with her eternal *pendante*, the little Miss Digges.

"Have you seen Mr Mowbray?—Has Mr Mowbray of Saint

Ronan's been down this morning?—Do you know anything of Mr Mowbray, Mrs Pot?" were questions which the lettered lady eagerly huddled on the back of each other, scarcely giving time to the lady of letters to return a decided negative to all and each of them.

"Mr Mowbray was not about—was not coming there this morning—his servant had just called for letters and papers, and announced as much."

"Good Heaven! how unfortunate," said Lady Penelope, with a deep sigh, and sinking down on one of the little sofas in an attitude of studied desolation, which called the instant attention of Mr Pot and his good woman, the first uncorking a small vial of salts, for he was a pharmacopolist as well as vender of literature and transmitter of letters, and the other hastening for a glass of water. A strong temptation thrilled from Lord Etherington's eyes to his finger-ends.—Two steps might have brought him within arm's length of the unwatched packet, on the contents of which, in all probability, rested the hope and claims of his rival in honour and fortune; and in the general confusion, was it impossible to possess himself of it unobserved? But no—no—no—the attempt was too dreadfully dangerous to be risked; and, passing from one extreme to another, he felt as if he was incurring suspicion by suffering Lady Penelope to play off her airs of affected distress and anxiety, without seeming to take that interest in them which her rank at least might be supposed to demand. Stung with this apprehension, he hastened to express himself so anxiously on the subject, and to demonstrate so busily his wish to assist her ladyship, that he presently stood committed a great deal farther than he had intended.—Lady Penelope was infinitely obliged to his lordship—indeed, it was her character in general not to permit herself to be overcome by circumstances; but something had happened, so strange, so embarrassing, so melancholy, that she owned it had quite overcome her—notwithstanding, she had at all times piqued herself on supporting her own distresses, better than she was able to suppress her emotions in viewing those of others.

"Could he be of any use?" Lord Etherington asked. "She had inquired after Mr Mowbray of Saint Ronan's—his servants were at her ladyship's command, if she chose to send to command his attendance."

"Oh! no, no!" said Lady Penelope; "I dare say, my dear lord, you will answer the purpose a great deal better than Mr Mowbray—that is, providing you are a Justice of Peace."

"A Justice of Peace!" said Lord Etherington, much surprised; "I am in the commission unquestionably, but not for any Scotch county."

"O, that does not signify," said Lady Penelope; "and if you will trust yourself with me a little way, I will explain to you how you can do one of the most charitable, and kind, and generous things in the world."

Lord Etherington's delight in the exercise of charity, kindness, and generosity, was not so exuberant as to prevent his devising some means for evading Lady Penelope's request, when, looking through the sash-door, he had a distant glance of his servant Solmes approaching the post-office.

I have heard of a sheep-stealer who had rendered his dog so skilful an accomplice in his nefarious traffic, that he used to send him out to commit acts of felony by himself, and had even contrived to impress on the poor cur the caution that he should not, on such occasions, even seem to recognize his master, if they met accidentally. Apparently, Lord Etherington conducted himself upon a similar principle; for he had no sooner a glimpse of his agent, than he seemed to feel the necessity of leaving the stage free for his machinations.

"My servant," he said, with as much indifference as he could assume, "will call for my letters—I must attend Lady Penelope;" and, instantly proffering his services as Justice of the Peace, or in whatever other quality she chose to employ them, he hastily presented his arm, and scarce gave her ladyship time to recover from her state of languor to the necessary degree of activity, ere he hurried her from the shop; and, with her thin hatchet-face chattering close to his ear, her yellow and scarlet feathers crossing his nose, her lean right honourable arm hooking his elbow, he braved the suppressed titters and sneers of all the younger women whom he met as they traversed the parade.—One glance of intelligence, though shot at a distance, passed betwixt his lordship and Solmes; and the former left the public walk under the guidance of Lady Penelope, his limbs indeed obeying her pleasure, and ears dinned with her attempts to explain the business in question, but his mind totally indifferent where he was going, or ignorant upon what purpose, and exclusively occupied with the packet in Mrs Pot's heap of postponed letters, and its probable fate.

At length, an effort of recollection made Lord Etherington sensible that his abstraction must seem strange, and, as his conscience told him, even suspicious, in the eyes of his companion; putting therefore the necessary degree of constraint upon himself, he expressed, for the first time, curiosity to know where their walk was to terminate. It chanced, as it happened, that this was precisely the question which he needed not have asked, if he had paid the slightest attention to the voluble communications of her ladyship, which had all turned upon this subject.

"Now, my dear lord," she said, "I must believe you lords of the creation think us poor simple women the vainest fools alive. I have told you how much pain it costs me to speak about my little charities, and yet you come to make me tell you the whole story over again. But I hope, after all, your lordship is not surprised at what I have thought it my duty to do in this sad affair—perhaps I have listened too much to the dictates of my own heart, which are apt to be so deceitful."

On the watch to get at something explanatory, yet afraid, by demanding it directly, to shew that the previous tide of narrative and pathos had been lost on an inattentive ear, Lord Etherington could only say, that Lady Penelope could not err in acting according to the dictates of her own judgment.

Still the compliment had not spice enough for the lady's sated palate; so, like a true glutton of praise, she began to help herself with the soup-ladle.

"Ah! judgment?—how is it you men know us so little, that you think we can pause to weigh sentiment in the balance of judgment?—that is expecting rather too much from us poor victims of our feelings. So that you must really hold me excused if I forgot the errors of this guilty and unhappy creature, when I looked upon her wretchedness—Not that I would have my little friend, Miss Digges, or your lordship, suppose that I am capable of palliating the fault, while I pity the poor, miserable sinner. Oh, no—Walpole's verses express beautifully what one ought to feel on such occasions—

For never was the gentle breast
  Insensible to human woes;
Feeling, though firm, it melts distress'd
  For weaknesses it never knows."

"Most accursed of all *précieuses*," thought his lordship, "when wilt thou, amidst all thy chatter, utter one word sounding like sense or information!"

But Lady Penelope went on—"If you knew, my lord, how I lament my limited means on these occasions! but I have gathered something among the good people at the Well. I asked that selfish wretch Winterblossom to walk down with me to view her distress, and the heartless beast told me he was afraid of infection!—infection from a puer—puerperal fever! I should not perhaps pronounce the word, but science is of no sex—however, I have always used thieves' vinegar since, and never have gone farther than the threshold."

Whatever were Etherington's faults, he did not want charity, so far as it consists in giving alms.

"I am sorry," he said, taking out his purse; "your ladyship should have applied to me."

"Pardon me, my lord, we only beg from our friends; and your

lordship is so constantly engaged with Lady Binks, that we have rarely the pleasure of seeing you in what I call *my* little circle."

Lord Etherington, without farther answer, again tendered a couple of guineas, and observed, that the poor woman should have medical attendance.

"Why so I say," answered Lady Penelope; "and I asked the brute Quackleben, who, I am sure, owes me some gratitude, to go and see her; but the sordid monster answered, 'Who was to pay him?'—He grows every day more intolerable, now that he seems sure of marrying that fat blowsy widow. He could not, I am sure, expect that I—out of my pittance—And besides, my lord, is there not a law that the parish, or the county, or the something or other, shall pay for physicking the poor?"

"We will find means to secure the Doctor's attendance," said Lord Etherington; "and I believe my best way will be to walk back to the Well, and send him to wait on the patient. I am afraid I can be of little use to a poor woman in a child-bed fever."

"Puerperal, my lord, puerperal," said Lady Penelope, in a tone of correction.

"In a puerperal fever, then," said Lord Etherington; "why, what can I do to help her?"

"Oh! my lord, you have forgotten that this Anne Heggie, that I told you of, came here with one child in her arms—and another—in short, about to become a mother again—and settled herself in this miserable hut I told you of—And some people think the minister should have sent her to her own parish, but he is a strange, soft-headed, sleepy sort of man, not over active in his parochial duties. However, there she settled, and there was something about her quite beyond the style of a common pauper, my lord—not at all the disgusting sort of person that you give a sixpence to while you look another way—but some one that seemed to have seen better days—one that, as Shakespeare says, could a tale unfold—though, indeed, I have never thoroughly learned her history—only, that to-day, as I called to know how she was, and sent my maid into her hut with some trifle, not worth mentioning, I find there is something hangs about her mind concerning the Mowbray family here of Saint Ronan's—and my woman says the poor creature is dying, and is raving either for Mr Mowbray or for some magistrate to receive a declaration; and so I have given you the trouble to come with me, that we may get out of the poor creature, if possible, whatever she has got to say.—I hope it is not murder—I hope it is not —though young Saint Ronan's has been a strange, wild, daring, thoughtless creature—*sgherro insigne*, as the Italian says.—But here is the hut, my lord—pray, walk in."

The mention of the Saint Ronan's family, and of a secret relating to them, banished the thoughts which Lord Etherington began to entertain of leaving Lady Penelope to execute her works of devoted charity without his assistance. It was now with an interest equal to her own, that he stood before a most miserable hut, where the unfortunate woman, her distresses not greatly relieved by Lady Penelope's ostentatious bounty, had resided both previous to her confinement, and since that event had taken place, with an old woman, one of the parish poor, whose miserable dole the minister had augmented, that she might have some means of assisting the stranger.

Lady Penelope lifted the latch and entered, after a momentary hesitation, which proceeded from a struggle betwixt her fear of infection, and her eager curiosity to know something, she could not guess what, that might affect the Mowbrays in their honour or fortunes. The latter soon prevailed, and she entered, followed by Lord Etherington. The lady, like other comforters of the cabins of the poor, proceeded to rebuke the grumbling old woman, for want of order and cleanliness—censured the food which was provided for the patient, and inquired particularly after the wine which she had left to make caudle with. The crone was not so dazzled with Lady Penelope's dignity or bounty as to endure her reprimand with patience. "They that had their bread to won wi' ae arm," she said, for the other hung powerless by her side, "had mair to do than to swoop houses; if her leddyship wad let her ain idle quean of a maid take the besom, she might make the house as clean as she liked; and madam wad be a' the better of the exercise, and wad hae done, at least, ae turn of wark at the week's end."

"Do you hear the old hag, my lord?" said Lady Penelope. "Well, the poor are horrid ungrateful wretches.—And the wine, dame—the wine?"

"The wine!—there was hardly half a mutchkin, and puir, thin, fusionless skink it was—the wine was drank out, ye may swear—we didna fling it ower our shouther—if ever we were to get good o't, it was by taking it naked, and no wi' your sugar and your slaisters—I wish, for ane, I had ne'er kend the sour smack o't—if the bedral hadna gien me a drap of usquebaugh, I might e'en hae died of your leddyship's liquor, for——"

Lord Etherington here interrupted the grumbling crone, thrusting some silver into her hand, and at the same time begging her to be silent. The hag weighed the crown-piece in her hand, and crawled to her chimney-corner, muttering as she went,—"This is something like—this is something like—no like rinning into the house and out of the house, and geeing orders, like mistress and mair, and than a puir shilling again Saturday at e'en."

So saying, she sat down to her wheel, and seized, at the same time, her jetty-black cutty pipe, from which she soon sent such clouds of vile mundungus vapour as must have cleared the premises of Lady Penelope, had she not been strong in purpose to share the expected confession of the invalid. As for Miss Digges, she coughed, sneezed, retched, and finally ran out of the cottage, declaring she could not live in such a smoke, if it were to hear twenty sick women's last speeches; and that, besides, she was sure to know all about it from Lady Penelope, if it was ever so little worth telling over again.

Lord Etherington was now standing beside the miserable flock-bed, in which lay the poor patient, distracted in what seemed to be her dying moments, with the peevish clamour of the elder infant, to which she could only reply by low moans, turning her looks as well as she could from its ceaseless whine, to the other side of her wretched couch, where lay the unlucky creature to which she had last given birth; its shivering limbs imperfectly covered with a blanket, its little features already swollen and bloated, and its eyes scarce open, apparently insensible to the evils of a state from which it seemed about to be speedily released.

"You are very ill, poor woman," said Lord Etherington; "I am told you desire a magistrate."

"It was Mr Mowbray of Saint Ronan's whom I desired to see—John Mowbray of Saint Ronan's—the lady promised to bring him here."

"I am not Mowbray of Saint Ronan's," said Lord Etherington; "but I am a justice of peace, and a member of the legislature—I am, moreover, Mr Mowbray's particular friend, if I can be of use to you in any of these capacities."

The poor woman remained long silent, and when she spoke it was doubtfully.

"Is my Lady Penelope Penfeather there?" she said, straining her darkened eyes.

"Her ladyship is present, and within hearing," said Lord Etherington.

"My case is the worse," answered the dying woman, for so she seemed, "if I must communicate such a secret as mine to a man of whom I know nothing, and a woman of whom I only know that she wants discretion."

"I—I want discretion!" said Lady Penelope; but at a signal from Lord Etherington she seemed to restrain herself; nor did the sick woman, whose powers of observation were greatly impaired, seem to be aware of the interruption. She spoke, notwithstanding her situation, with an intelligible and even emphatic voice; her manner in a great measure betraying the influence of the fever, and her tone and language seeming much superior to her most miserable condition.

"I am not the abject creature which I seem," she said; "at least, I was not born to be so. I wish I *were* that utter abject! I wish I were a wretched pauper of the lowest class—a starving vagabond—a husbandless mother—ignorance and insensibility would make me bear my lot like the outcast animal that dies patiently on the side of the common, where it has been half-starved during its life. But I—but I—born and bred to better things, have not lost the memory of them, and they make my present condition—my shame—my poverty—my infamy—the sight of my dying babes—the sense that my own death is coming fast on—they make these things a foretaste of hell!"

Lady Penelope's self-conceit and affectation were broken down by this fearful exordium. She sobbed, shuddered, and, for once perhaps in her life, felt the real, not the assumed necessity of putting her handkerchief to her eyes. Lord Etherington also was moved.

"Good woman," he said, "as far as relieving your personal wants can mitigate your distress, I will see that is fully performed, and that your poor children are attended to."

"May God bless you!" said the poor woman, with a glance at the wretched forms beside her; "and may you," she added, after a momentary pause, "deserve the blessing of God, for it is bestowed in vain on those who are unworthy of it."

Lord Etherington felt, perhaps, a twinge of conscience, for he said, something hastily, "Pray go on, good woman, if you really have anything to communicate to me as a magistrate—it is time your condition was somewhat mended, and I will cause you to be cared for directly."

"Stop yet a moment," she said; "let me unload my conscience before I go hence, for no earthly relief will long avail to prolong my time here. I was well-born, the more my present shame!—well educated, the greater my present guilt!—I was always, indeed, poor, but I felt not of the ills of poverty. I only thought of it when my vanity demanded idle and expensive gratification, for real wants I knew none. I was companion of a young lady of higher rank than my own, my relative however, and one of such exquisite kindness of disposition, that she treated me as a sister, and would have shared with me all that she had on earth——I scarce think I can go farther with my story!—something rises to my throat when I recollect how I rewarded her sisterly love!—I was elder than Clara—I should have directed her reading, and confirmed her understanding; but my own bent led me to peruse only works, which, though they burlesque nature, are seductive to the imagination. We read these follies together, until we had fashioned out for ourselves a little world of romance, and prepared ourselves for a maze of adventures. Clara's imaginations were as pure as those of angels; mine were—but it is unnecessary to tell them. The fiend, always watchful, presented a tempter at the moment when it was most dangerous."

She paused here, as if she found difficulty in expressing herself; and Lord Etherington, turning, with great appearance of interest, to Lady Penelope, began to inquire "Whether it were quite agreeable to her ladyship to remain any longer an ear-witness of this unfortunate's confession?—it seems to be verging on some things—things that it might be unpleasant for your ladyship to hear."

"I was just forming the same opinion, my lord; and, to say truth, was about to propose to your lordship to withdraw, and leave me alone with the poor woman. My sex will make her necessary communications more frank in your lordship's absence."

"True, madam; but then I am called here in my capacity of a magistrate."

"Hush!" said Lady Penelope; "she speaks."

"They say every woman that yields, makes herself a slave to her seducer; but I sold my liberty not to a man, but a demon! He made me serve him in his vile schemes against my friend and patroness—and oh! he found in me an agent too willing, from mere envy, to destroy the virtue which I had lost myself. Do not listen to me any more—Go, and leave me to my fate; I am the most detestable wretch that ever lived—detestable to myself worst of all, because even in my penitence there is a secret whisper that tells me, that were I as I have been, I would again act over all the wickedness I have done, and much worse. Oh! for Heaven's assistance, to crush the wicked thought!"

She closed her eyes, folded her emaciated hands, and held them upwards in the attitude of one who prays internally; presently the hands separated, and fell gently down on her miserable couch; but her eyes did not open, nor was there the slightest sign of motion on the features. Lady Penelope shrieked faintly, hid her eyes, and hurried back from the bed, while Lord Etherington, his looks darkening with a complication of feelings, remained gazing on the poor woman, as if eager to discern whether the spark of life was totally extinct. Her grim old assistant hurried to the bedside, with some spirits in a broken glass.

"Have ye no had pennyworths for your charity?" she said, in spiteful scorn. "Ye buy the very life o' us wi' your shillings and sixpences, your groats and your bodles—ye hae gar'd the puir wretch speak till she swarfs, and now ye stand as if ye never saw a woman in a dwam before. Let me till her wi' the dram—mony words mickle drought, ye ken—Stand out o' my gate, my leddy, if sae be that ye are a leddy;

there is little use of the like of you when there is death in the pot."

Lady Penelope, half affronted, but still more frightened by the manners of the old hag, now gladly embraced Lord Etherington's renewed offer to escort her from the hut. He left it not, however, without bestowing an additional gratuity on the old woman, who received it with a whining benediction.

"The Almighty guide your course through the troubles of this wicked warld—and the muckle deevil blaw wind in your sails," she added, in her natural tone, as the guests vanished from her miserable threshold—"A wheen cork-headed, barmy-brained gowks! that winna let puir folk sae muckle as die in quiet, wi' their sossings and their swoopings."

"This poor creature's declaration," said Lord Etherington to Lady Penelope, "seems to refer to matters which the law has nothing to do with, and which, perhaps, as they seem to implicate the peace of a family of respectability, and the character of a young lady, we ought to inquire no further after."

"I differ from your lordship," said Lady Penelope; "I differ extremely—I suppose you guess whom her discourse touched upon?"

"Indeed, your ladyship does my acuteness too much honour."

"Did she not mention a Christian name?" said Lady Penelope; "your lordship is strangely dull this morning?"

"A Christian name?—No, none that I heard—yes, she said something about a Catherine, I think it was."

"Catherine! No, my lord, it was Clara—rather a rare name in this country, and belonging, I think, to a young lady of whom your lordship should know something, unless your evening flirtations with Lady Binks have blotted entirely out of your memory your morning visits to Shaws-Castle. You are a bold man, my lord. I would advise you to include Mrs Blower amongst the objects of your attention, and then you will have maid, wife, and widow upon your list."

"Upon my honour, your ladyship is too severe," said Lord Etherington; "you surround yourself every evening with all that is clever and accomplished among the people here, and then you ridicule a poor secluded monster, who dare not approach your charmed circle, because he seeks for some amusement elsewhere. This is to tyrannize and not to reign—it is Turkish despotism!"

"Ah! my lord, I know you well, my lord—Sorry would your lordship be, had you not power to render yourself welcome to any circle which you may please to approach."

"That is to say, you will pardon me if I intrude on your ladyship's coterie this evening?"

"There is no society which Lord Etherington can think of frequenting, where he will not be a welcome guest."

"I will plead then at once my pardon and privilege this evening—And now (speaking as if he had succeeded in establishing some confidence with her ladyship,) what do you really think of this blind story?"

"O, I must believe it concerns Miss Mowbray. She was always an odd girl—something about her I could never endure—a sort of effrontery—that is, perhaps, a harsh word, but a kind of confidence—so that though I kept on a footing with her, because she was an orphan girl of good family, and because I really knew nothing positively bad of her, yet she sometimes absolutely shocked me."

"Your ladyship, perhaps, would not think it right to give publicity to the story; at least, till you know exactly what it is," said the Earl, in a tone of suggestion.

"Depend upon it, that it is quite the worst, the very worst—You heard the woman say that she had exposed Clara to ruin—and you know she must have meant Clara Mowbray, because she was so anxious to tell the story to her brother, Saint Ronan's."

"Very true—I did not think of that," answered Lord Etherington; "still it would be hard on the poor girl if it should get abroad."

"Oh, it will never get abroad for me," said Lady Penelope; "I would not tell the very wind of it. But then I cannot meet Miss Mowbray as formerly—I have a station in life to maintain, my lord—and I am under the necessity of being select in my society—it is a duty I owe the public, if it were even not my own inclination."

"Certainly, my Lady Penelope," said Lord Etherington; "but then consider, that, in a place where all eyes are necessarily observant of your ladyship's behaviour, the least coldness on your part to Miss Mowbray—and, after all, we have nothing like assurance of anything being wrong there—would ruin her with the company here, and with the world at large."

"Oh! my lord," answered Lady Penelope, "as for the truth of the story, I have some private reasons of my own for 'holding the strange tale devoutly true;' for I had a mysterious hint from a very worthy, but a very singular man, (your lordship knows how I adore originality,) the clergyman of the parish, who made me aware there was something about Miss Clara—something that—your lordship will excuse my speaking more plainly—Oh, no!—I fear—I fear it is all too true—You know Mr Cargill, I suppose, my lord?"

"Yes—no—I—I think I have seen him," said Lord Etherington. "But how came the lady to make the parson her father-confessor?—they have no auricular confession in the Kirk—it must have been with the purpose of marriage, I presume—let us hope that it took place—perhaps it really was so—did he, Cargill—the minister, I mean—say anything of such a matter?"

"Not a word—not a word—I see where you are, my lord, you would put a good face on't.—

> They call'd it marriage, by that specious name
> To veil the crime, and sanctify the shame.

Queen Dido for that. How the clergyman came into the secret, I cannot tell—he is a very close man.—But I know he will not hear of Miss Mowbray being married with any one, unquestionably because he knows that, in doing so, she would introduce disgrace into some honest family—and, truly, I am much of his mind, my lord."

"Perhaps Mr Cargill may know the lady is privately married already," said the Earl; "I think that is the more natural inference, begging your ladyship's pardon for presuming to differ."

Lady Penelope seemed determined not to take this view of the case.

"No, no—no, I tell you," she replied; "she cannot be married, for if she were married, how could the poor wretch say that she was ruined?—You know there is a difference betwixt ruin and marriage."

"Some people are said to have found them synonymous, Lady Penelope," answered the Earl.

"You are smart on me, my lord; but still, in common parlance, when we say a woman is ruined, we mean quite the contrary of her being married—it is impossible for me to be more explicit upon such a topic, my lord."

"I defer to your ladyship's better judgment," said Lord Etherington. "I only entreat you to observe a little caution on this business—I will make the strictest inquiries at this woman, and acquaint you with the result; and I hope, out of regard to the respectable family of Saint Ronan's, your ladyship will be in no hurry to intimate anything to Miss Mowbray's prejudice."

"I certainly am no person to spread scandal, my lord," answered the lady, drawing herself up; "at the same time, I must say, the Mowbrays have little claim on me for forbearance. I am sure I was the first person to bring this Spaw into fashion, which has been a matter of such consequence to their estate; and yet Mr Mowbray set himself against me, my lord, in every possible sort of way, and encouraged the under-bred people about him to behave very strangely.—There was the business of building the Belvidere, which he would not permit to be done out of the stock-purse of the company, because I had given the workmen the plan and the orders—and then, about the tea-room—and the hour for beginning dancing—and about the subscription for

Mr Rymour's new Tale of Chivalry—in short, I owe no consideration to Mr Mowbray of Saint Ronan's."

"But the poor young lady," said Lord Etherington.

"Oh! the poor young lady?—the poor young lady can be as saucy as a rich young lady, I promise you.—There was a business in which she used me scandalously, Lord Etherington—it was about a very trifling matter—a shawl. Nobody minds dress less than I do, my lord; I thank Heaven my thoughts turn upon very different topics—but it is in trifles that disrespect and unkindness is shewn; and I have had a full share of both from Miss Clara, besides a good deal of impertinence from her brother upon the same subject."

"There is but one way remains," thought the Earl, as they approached the Spaw, "and that is, to work on the fears of this d—d vindictive blue-stocking'd wild-cat.—Your ladyship," he said aloud, "is aware what severe damages have been awarded in late cases where something approaching to scandal has been traced to ladies of consideration—the privileges of the tea-table have been found insufficient to protect some fair critics against the consequences of too liberal animadversion upon the characters of their friends. So, pray remember, that yet we know very little on this subject."

Lady Penelope loved money, and feared the law; and this hint, fortified by her acquaintance with Mowbray's love of his sister, and his irritable and revengeful disposition, brought her in a moment much nigher the temper in which Lord Etherington wished to leave her. She protested, that no one could be more tender than she of the fame of the unfortunate, even supposing their guilt was fully proved—promised caution on the subject of the pauper's declaration, and hoped Lord Etherington would join her tea party early in the evening, as she wished to make him acquainted with one or two of her *protégés*, whom, she was sure, his lordship would find deserving of his advice and countenance. Being by this time at the door of her own apartment, her ladyship took leave of the Earl with a most gracious smile.

Chapter Seven

DISAPPOINTMENT

On the lee-beam lies the land, boys,
  See all clear to reef each course;
Let the fore-sheet go, don't mind, boys,
  Though the weather should be worse.
The Storm

What prodigy is this? what subtle devil
Hath razed out the inscription?
A New Way to Pay Old Debts

"IT DARKENS round me like a tempest," thought Lord Etherington, as, with slow step, folded arms, and his white hat slouched over his brows, he traversed the short interval of space betwixt his own apartments and those of the Lady Penelope. In a buck of the old school, one of Congreve's men of wit and pleasure about town, this would have been a departure from character; but the present fine man does not derogate from his quality, even by exhibiting all the moody and gentlemanlike solemnity of Master Stephen. So, Lord Etherington was at liberty to carry on his reflections, without attracting observation.—"I have put a stopper into the mouth of that old vinegar cruet of quality, but the acidity of her temper will soon dissolve the charm. And what to do?"

As he looked round him, he saw his trusty valet Solmes, who, touching his hat with due respect, said, as he passed him, "Your lordship's letters are in your private dispatch-box."

Simple as these words were, and indifferent the tone in which they were spoken, their import made Lord Etherington's heart bound as if his fate had depended on the accents. He intimated no farther interest in the communication, however, than to desire Solmes to be below, in case he should ring; and with these words entered his apartment, and barred and bolted the door, even before he looked on the table where his dispatch-box was placed.

Lord Etherington had, as is usual, one key to the box which held his letters, his confidential servant being entrusted with the other; so that, under the protection of a patent lock, his dispatches escaped all risk of being tampered with,—a precaution not altogether unnecessary on the part of those who frequent hotels and lodging-houses.

"By your leave, Mr Bramah," said the Earl, as he applied the key, jesting, as it were, with his own agitation, as he would have done with that of a third party. The lid was raised, and displayed the packet, the appearance and superscription of which had attracted his observation but a short while since in the post-office. *Then* he would have given much to be possessed of the opportunity which was now in his power; but many pause on the brink of a crime, who have contemplated it at a distance without scruple.—Lord Etherington's first impulse had led him to poke the fire; and he held in his hand the letter which he was more than half tempted to commit, without even breaking the seal, to the fiery element. But, though sufficiently familiarized with guilt, he was not as yet acquainted with it in its basest shapes—he had not yet acted with meanness, or at least with what the world terms such. He had been a duellist, the manners of the age authorized it—a libertine, the world excused it to his youth and condition—a bold and successful gambler, for that quality he was admired and envied; and a thousand other inaccuracies, to which these practices and habits lead, were easily slurred over in a man of quality, with fortune and spirit to support his rank. But his present meditated act was of a different kind. Tell it not in Bond Street, whisper it not on Saint James's pavement! —it amounted to an act of petty larceny, for which the code of honour would admit of no composition.

Lord Etherington, under the influence of these recollections, stood for a few moments suspended—But the devil always finds logic to convince his followers. He recollected the wrong done to his mother, and to himself, her offspring, to whom his father had, in the face of the whole world, imparted the hereditary rights, of which he was now, by a posthumous deed, endeavouring to deprive the memory of the one, and the expectations of the other. Surely, the right being his, he had a full title, by the most effectual means, whatever such means might be, to repel all attacks on that right, and even destroy, if necessary, the documents by which his enemies were prosecuting their unjust plans against his honour and interest.

This reasoning prevailed, and Lord Etherington again held the devoted packet above the flames; when it occurred to him, that, his resolution being taken, he ought to carry it into execution as effectually as possible; and to do so, it was necessary to know, that the packet actually contained the papers which he was desirous to destroy.

Never did a doubt arise in juster time; for no sooner had the seal burst, and the envelope rustled under his fingers, than he perceived, to his utter consternation, that he held in his hand only the copies of the deeds for which Francis Tyrrel had written, the originals of which he had too sanguinely concluded would be forwarded according to his requisition. A letter from a partner of the house in which they were deposited, stated, that they had not felt themselves at liberty, in the absence of the head of their firm, to whom these papers had been committed, to part with them even to Mr Tyrrel; though they had proceeded so far as to open the parcel, and now transmitted to him formal copies of the papers contained in it, which, they presumed, would serve Mr Tyrrel's purpose for consulting counsel, or the like. They themselves, in a case of so much delicacy, and in the absence of their principal partner, were determined to retain the originals, unless called to produce them in a court of justice.

With a solemn imprecation on the formality and absurdity of the writer, Lord Etherington let the letter of advice drop from his hand into the fire, and throwing himself into a chair, passed his hand across his eyes, as if their very power of sight had been blighted by what he had read. His title, and his paternal fortune, which he thought but an instant before might be rendered unchallengeable by a single movement of his hand, seemed now on the verge of being lost for ever. His rapid recollection failed not to remind him of what was less known to the world, that his early and profuse expenditure had greatly dilapidated his maternal fortune; and that the estate of Nettlewood, which five minutes ago he only coveted as a wealthy man desires increase of his store, must now be acquired, if he would avoid being a very poor and embarrassed spendthrift. To impede his possessing himself of this property, fate had restored to the scene the penitent of the morning, who, as he had too much reason to believe, was returned to this neighbourhood, to do justice to Clara Mowbray, and who was not unlikely to put the whole story of the marriage on its right footing. She, however, might be got rid of; and it might still be possible to hurry Miss Mowbray, by working on her fears, or through the agency of her brother, into an union with him, while he still preserved the title of Lord Etherington. This, therefore, he resolved to secure, if effort or if intrigue could carry the point; nor was it the least consideration, that should he succeed, he would obtain over Tyrrel, his successful rival, such a triumph, as would be sufficient to embitter the tranquillity of his whole life.

In a few minutes, his rapid and contriving invention had formed a plan for securing the sole advantage which seemed to remain open for him; and conscious that he had no time to lose, he entered immediately upon the execution.

The bell summoned Solmes to his lord's apartment, when the Earl, as coolly as if he had hoped to dupe his experienced valet by such an assertion, said, "You have brought me a packet designed for some man at the Aulton—let it be sent to him—Stay, I will re-seal it first."

He accordingly re-sealed the packet, containing all the writings, excepting the letter of advice, (which he had burned,) and gave it to the valet, with the caution, "I wish you would not make such blunders in future."

"I beg your lordship's pardon—I will take better care again—thought it was addressed to your lordship."

So answered Solmes, too knowing to give the least look of intelligence, far less to remind the Earl that his own directions had occasioned the mistake of which he complained.

"Solmes," continued the Earl, "you need not mention your blunder at the post-office; it would only occasion tattle in this idle place—but be sure that the gentleman has his letter.—And, Solmes, I see Mr Mowbray walk across—ask him to dine with me to-day at five. I have a head-ache, and cannot face the clamour of the savages who feed at the public table.—And—let me see—make my compliments to Lady Penelope Penfeather—I will certainly have the honour of waiting on her ladyship this evening to tea, agreeable to her very boring invitation received—write her a proper card, and word it your own way. Bespeak dinner for two, and see you have some of that batch of Burgundy." The servant was retiring, when his master added, "Stay a moment—I have a more important business than I have yet mentioned.—Solmes, you have managed devilishly ill about the woman Irwin!"

"I, my lord?" answered Solmes.

"You, you, sir—did you not tell me she had gone to the West Indies with a friend of yours, and did not I give them a couple of hundred pounds for passage-money?"

"Yes, my lord," replied the valet.

"Ay, but now it proves *no*, my lord," said Lord Etherington; "for she has found her way back to this country in miserable plight—half-starved, and, no doubt, willing to do or say anything for a livelihood—How has this happened?"

"Biddulph must have taken her cash, and turned her loose, my lord," answered Solmes, as if he had been speaking of the most common-place transaction in the world; "but I know the woman's nature so well, and am so much master of her history, that I can carry her off the country in twenty-four hours, and place her where she will never think of returning, provided your lordship can spare me so long."

"About it directly—but I can tell you, that you will find the woman in a very penitential humour, and very ill to boot."

"I am sure of my game," answered Solmes; "with submission to your lordship, I think if death and her good angel had hold of one of that woman's arms, the devil and I could make a shift to lead her away by the other."

"Away and about it, then," said Etherington. "But, hark ye, Solmes, be kind to her, and see all her wants relieved.—I have done her mischief enough—though nature and the devil had done half the work to my hand."

Solmes at length was permitted to withdraw to execute his various commissions, with an assurance that his services would not be wanted for the next twenty-four hours.

"Soh!" said the Earl, as his agent withdrew, "there is a spring put in motion, which, well oiled, will move the whole machine—And here, in lucky time, comes Harry Jekyl—I hear his whistle on the stairs.—There is a silly lightness of heart about that fellow, which I envy, while I despise it; but he is welcome now, for I want him."

Jekyl entered accordingly, and broke out with, "I am glad to see one of your fellows laying a cloth for two in your parlour, Etherington—I was afraid you were going down among these confounded bores again to-day."

"*You* are not to be one of the two, Hal," answered Lord Etherington.

"No?—then I may be a third, I hope, if not second."

"Neither first, second, nor third, Captain.—The truth is, I want a tête-à-tête with Mr Mowbray of Saint Ronan's," replied the Earl; "and, besides, I have to beg the very particular favour of you to go again to that fellow Martigny. It is time that he should produce his papers, if he has any—of which, for one, I do not believe a word. He has had ample time to hear from London; and I think I have delayed long enough in an important matter upon his bare assertion."

"I cannot blame your impatience," said Jekyl, "and I will go on your errand instantly. As you waited by my advice, I am bound to find an end to your suspense.—At the same time, if the man is not possessed of such papers as he spoke of, I must own he is happy in a command of consummate assurance, which might set up the whole roll of attorneys."

"You will be soon able to judge of that," said Lord Etherington; "and now, off with you.—Why do you look at me so anxiously?"

"I cannot tell—I have strange forebodings about this tête-à-tête with Mowbray. You should spare him, Etherington—he is not your match—wants both judgment and temper."

"Tell him so, Jekyl," answered the Earl, "and his proud Scotch stomach will up in an instant, and he will pay you with a shot for your pains.—Why, he thinks himself Cock of the walk this moment, notwithstanding the lesson I gave him before—And what do you think?—he has the impudence to talk about my attentions to Lady Binks as inconsistent with the prosecution of my suit to his sister! Yes, Hal—

this awkward Scotch laird, that has scarce tact enough to make love to a ewe-milker, or, at best, to some daggle-tailed soubrette, has the assurance to start himself as my rival!"

"Then, good night to Saint Ronan's!—this will be a fatal dinner to him.—Etherington, I know by that laugh you are bent on mischief—I have a great mind to give him a hint."

"I wish you would," answered the Earl; "it would all turn to my accompt."

"Do you defy me?—Well, if I meet him, I will put him on his guard."

The friends parted; and it was not long ere Jekyl encountered Mowbray on one of the public walks.

"You dine with Etherington to-day?" said the Captain—"Forgive me, Mr Mowbray, if I say one single word—Beware."

"Of what should I beware, Captain Jekyl," answered Mowbray, "when I dine with a friend of your own, and a man of honour?"

"Certainly Lord Etherington is both, Mr Mowbray; but he loves play, and is too hard for most people."

"I thank you for your hint, Captain Jekyl—I am a raw Scotchman, it is true; but yet, I know a thing or two. Fair play is always presumed amongst gentlemen; and that taken for granted, I have the vanity to think I need no one's caution on the subject, not even Captain Jekyl's, though his experience must needs be so superior to mine."

"In that case, sir," said Jekyl, bowing coldly, "I have no more to say, and I hope there is no harm done.—Conceited coxcomb!" he added, mentally, as they parted, "how truly did Etherington judge of him, and what an ass was I to intermeddle!—I hope Etherington will strip him of every feather."

He pursued his walk in quest of Tyrrel, and Mowbray proceeded to the apartments of the Earl, in a temper of mind well suited to the purposes of the latter, who judged of his disposition accurately when he permitted Jekyl to give his well-meant warning. To be supposed by a man of acknowledged fashion, so decidedly inferior to his antagonist—to be considered as an object of compassion, and made the subject of a good-boy warning, was gall and bitterness to his proud spirit, which, the more that he felt a conscious inferiority in the arts which they all cultivated, struggled the more to preserve the footing of apparent equality.

Since the first memorable party at piquet, Mowbray had never hazarded his luck with Lord Etherington, except for trifling stakes; but his conceit led him to suppose, that he now fully understood his play, and, agreeably to the practice of those who have habituated themselves to gambling, he had, every now and then, felt a yearning to try for his revenge. He wished also to be out of Lord Etherington's debt, feeling galled under a sense of pecuniary obligation, which hindered his speaking his mind to him fully upon the subject of his flirtation with Lady Binks, which he justly considered as an insult to his family, considering the footing on which the Earl seemed desirous to stand with Clara Mowbray. From these obligations a favourable evening might free him, and Mowbray was, in fact, indulging in a waking dream to this purpose, when Jekyl interrupted him. His untimely warning only excited a spirit of contradiction, and a determination to shew the adviser how little he was qualified to judge of his talents; and in this humour, his ruin, which was the consequence of that afternoon, was far from even seeming to be the premeditated, or even the voluntary work of the Earl of Etherington.

On the contrary, the victim himself was the first to propose play—deep play—double stakes—while Lord Etherington, on the contrary, often proposed to diminish their game, or to break off entirely; but it was always with an affectation of superiority, which only stimulated Mowbray to farther and more desperate risks; and, at last, when Mowbray became his debtor to an overwhelming amount, (his circumstances considered,) the Earl threw down the cards, and declared he should be too late for Lady Penelope's tea-party, to which he was positively engaged.

"Will you not give me my revenge?" said Mowbray, taking up the cards, and shuffling them with fierce anxiety.

"Not now, Mowbray; we have played too long already—you have lost too much—more than perhaps is convenient for you to pay."

Mowbray gnashed his teeth, in spite of his resolution to maintain an exterior, at least, of firmness.

"You can take your time, you know," said the Earl; "a note of hand will suit me as well as the money."

"No, by G——," answered Mowbray, "I will not be so taken in a second time—I had better have sold myself to the devil than to your lordship.—I have never been my own man since."

"These are not very kind expressions, Mowbray," said the Earl; "you *would* play, and they that will play must expect sometimes to lose—"

"And they who win will expect to be paid," said Mowbray, breaking in. "I know that as well as you, my lord, and you shall be paid—I will pay you—I will pay you, by G——! Do you make any doubt that I will pay you, my lord?"

"You look as if you thought of paying me in sharp coin," said Lord Etherington; "and I think that would scarce be consistent with the terms we stand upon towards each other."

"By my soul, my lord," said Mowbray, "I cannot tell what these terms are; and to be at my wit's end at once, I should be glad to know. You set out upon paying addresses to my sister, and with your visits and opportunities at Shaws-Castle, I cannot find the matter makes the least progress—it keeps moving without advancing, like a child's rocking-horse. Perhaps you think that you have curbed me so tightly, that I dare not stir in the matter; but you will find it otherwise.—Your lordship may keep a haram if you will, but my sister shall not enter it."

"You are angry, and therefore you are unjust," said Etherington; "you know well enough it is your sister's fault that there is any delay. I am most willing—most desirous to call her Lady Etherington —nothing but her unlucky prejudices against me have retarded a union which I have so many reasons for desiring."

"Well," replied Mowbray, "that shall be my business. I know no reason she can pretend to decline a marriage so honourable to her house, and which is approved of by me, that house's head. That matter shall be arranged in twenty-four hours."

"It will do me the most sensible pleasure," said Lord Etherington; "you shall soon see how sincerely I desire your alliance; and as for the trifle you have lost——"

"It is no trifle to me, my lord—it is my ruin—but it shall be paid—And let me tell your lordship, you may thank your good luck for it more than your good play."

"We will say no more of it at present, if you please," said Lord Etherington, "to-morrow is a new day; and if you will take my advice, you will not be too harsh with your sister. A little firmness is seldom amiss with young women, but severity——"

"I will pray your lordship to spare me your advice on this subject. However valuable it may be in other respects, I can, I take it, speak to my own sister in my own way."

"Since you are so caustically disposed, Mowbray," answered the Earl, "I presume you will not honour her ladyship's tea-table to-night, though I believe it will be the last of the season?"

"And why should you think so, my lord?" answered Mowbray, whose losses had rendered him testy and contradictory upon every subject that was started. "Why should not I pay my respects to Lady Penelope, or any other tabby of quality? I have no title, indeed, but I suppose that my family——"

"Entitles you to become a canon of Strasburgh, doubtless—But you do not seem in a very Christian mood for taking orders. All I meant to say was, that you and Lady Pen were not used to be on such a good footing."

"Well, she sent me a card for her blow-out," said Mowbray; "and so I am resolved to go. When I have been there half an hour, I will ride up to Shaws-Castle, and you shall hear of my speed in wooing for you to-morrow morning."

Chapter Eight

A TEA-PARTY

> Let fall the curtains, wheel the sofa round;
> And while the bubbling and loud hissing urn
> Throws up a steamy column, and the cups
> That cheer, but not inebriate, wait on each,
> Thus let us welcome peaceful evening in.
>
> COWPER'S *Task*

THE APPROACH of the cold and rainy season had now so far thinned the company at the Well, that, in order to secure the necessary degree of crowd upon her tea-nights, Lady Penelope was obliged to employ some coaxing towards those whom she had considered as much under par in society. Even the Doctor and Mrs Blower were graciously smiled upon—for their marriage was now an arranged affair; and the event was of a nature likely to spread the reputation of the Spaw among wealthy widows, and medical gentlemen of more skill than practice. So in they came, the Doctor smirking, gallanting, and performing all the bustling parade of settled and arranged courtship, with much of that grace wherewith a turkey-cock goes through the same ceremony. Old Touchwood had also attended her ladyship's summons, chiefly, it may be supposed, from his restless fidgetty disposition, which seldom suffered him to remain absent even from those places of resort, of which he usually professed his detestation. There was, besides, Mr Winterblossom, who, in his usual spirit of quiet epicurism and self-indulgence, was, under the fire of a volley of compliments to Lady Penelope, scheming to secure for himself an early cup of tea. There was Lady Binks also, with the wonted degree of sullenness on her beautiful face, angry at her husband as usual, and not disposed to be pleased with Lord Etherington for being absent, when she desired to excite Sir Bingo's jealousy. This she had discovered to be the most effectual way of tormenting the Baronet, and she rejoiced in it with the savage glee of a hackney coachman, who has found a *raw*, where he can make his poor jade feel the whip. The rest of the company were also in attendance as usual. MacTurk himself was present, notwithstanding that he thought it an egregious waste of hot water, to bestow it upon compounding any mixture, saving punch. He had of late associated himself a good deal with the traveller; not that they by any means resembled each other in temper or opinions, but rather because there was that degree of difference betwixt them which furnished perpetual subject for dispute and discussion. They were not long, on the present occasion, ere they lighted on a fertile source of controversy.

"Never tell me of your points of honour," said Touchwood, raising his voice altogether above the general tone of polite conversation—"all humbug, Captain MacTurk—mere hair-traps to springe woodcocks—men of sense break through them."

"Upon my word, sir," said the Captain, "and myself is surprised to hear you—for, look you, sir, every man's honour is the breath of his nostrils—Cot tamn!"

"Then, let men breathe through their mouths and be d—d," returned the controversialist. "I tell you, sir, that, besides its being forbidden both by law and gospel, it's an idiotical and totally absurd practice, that of duelling. An honest savage has more sense than to practise it—he takes his bow or his gun, as the thing may be, and shoots his enemy from behind a bush. And a very good way; for you see there can, in that case, be only one man's death between them."

"Saul of my body, sir," said the Captain, "gin ye promulgate sic doctrines among the good company, it's my belief you will bring somebody to the gallows."

"Thank ye, Captain, with all my heart; but I stir up no quarrels—I leave war to them that live by it. I only say, that, except our old, stupid ancestors in the north-west here, I know no country so silly as to harbour this custom of duelling. It is unknown in Africa, among the negroes—in America."

"Don't tell me that," said the Captain; "a Yankee will fight with muskets and buck-shot rather than sit still with an affront. I should know Jonathan, I think."

"Altogether unknown among the thousand tribes of India."

"I'll be tamned, then!" said Captain MacTurk. "Was I not in Tippoo's prison at Bangalore? and, when the joyful day of our liberation came, did we not solemnize it with fourteen little affairs, whereof we had been laying the foundation in our house of captivity, as holy writ has it, and never went farther to settle them than the glacis of the fort? By my soul, you would have thought there was a smart skirmish, the firing was so close; and did not I, Captain MacTurk, fight three of them myself, without moving my foot from the place I set it on?"

"And pray, sir, what might be the result of this Christian mode of giving thanks for your deliverance?" demanded Mr Touchwood.

"A small list of casualties, after all," said the Captain; "one killed on the spot, one died of his wounds—two severely wounded—three ditto, slightly, and little Duncan Macphail reported missing. We were out of practice, after such long confinement. So you see how we manage matters in India, my dear friend."

"You are to understand," replied Touchwood, "that I spoke only of the heathen natives, who, heathen as they are, live in the light of their own moral reason, and among whom ye shall therefore see better examples of practical morality than among such as yourselves; who, though calling yourselves Christians, have no more knowledge of the true acceptation and meaning of your religion, than if you had left your religion at the Cape of Good Hope, as they say of you, and forgot to take it up when you came back again."

"Py Cot, and I can tell you, sir," said the Captain, elevating at once his voice and his nostrils, and snuffing the air with a truculent and indignant visage, "that I will not permit you or any man to throw any such scandal on my character.—I thank Cot, I can bring good witness that I am as good a Christian as another, for a poor sinner, as the best of us are; and I am ready to justify my religion with my sword—Cot tamn!—Compare my own self with a parcel of black heathen bodies and natives, that were never in the inner side of a kirk whilst they lived, but go about worshipping stocks and stones, and swinging themselves upon bamboos, like peasts, as they are!"

An indignant growling in his throat, which sounded like the acquiescence of his inward man in the indignant proposition which his external organs thus expressed, concluded this haughty speech, which, however, made not the least impression on Touchwood, who cared as little for angry tones and looks as he did for fair speeches. So that it is likely a quarrel between the Christian preceptor and the peace-maker might have occurred for the amusement of the company, had not the attention of both, but particularly that of Touchwood, been diverted from the topic of debate by the entrance of Lord Etherington and Mowbray.

The former was, as usual, all grace, smiles, and gentleness. Yet, contrary to his wonted custom, which usually was, after a few general compliments, to attach himself particularly to Lady Binks, the Earl, on the present occasion, avoided the side of the room on which that beautiful but sullen idol held her station, and attached himself exclusively to Lady Penelope Penfeather, enduring, without flinching, the strange variety of conceited *bavardage*, which that lady's natural parts and acquired information enabled her to pour forth with unparalleled profusion.

An honest heathen, one of Plutarch's heroes, if I mistake not, dreamed once upon a night, that the figure of Proserpina, whom he had long worshipped, visited his slumbers with an angry and vindictive countenance, and menaced him with vengeance, in resentment of his having neglected her altars, with the usual fickleness of a Polytheist, for those of some more fashionable divinity. Not that goddess of the infernal regions herself could assume a more haughty or more displeased countenance than that with which Lady Binks looked from time to time upon Lord Etherington, as if to warn him of the consequence of this departure from the allegiance which the young Earl had hitherto manifested towards her, and which seemed now, she knew not why, unless it were for the purpose of public insult, to be transferred to her rival. Perilous as her eye-glances were, and much as they menaced, Lord Etherington felt at this moment the importance of soothing Lady Penelope to silence on the subject of the invalid's confession of that morning to be more pressing than that of appeasing the indignation of Lady Binks. The former was a case of the most pressing necessity—the latter, if he was at all anxious on the subject, might, he perhaps thought, be trusted to time. Had the ladies continued on a tolerable footing together, he might have endeavoured to conciliate both. But the bitterness of their long suppressed feud had greatly increased, now that it was probable the end of the season was to separate them, probably for ever; so that Lady Penelope had no longer any motive for countenancing Lady Binks, or the lady of Sir Bingo for desiring Lady Penelope's countenance. The wealth and lavish expense of the one was no longer to render more illustrious the suite of her right honourable friend, nor was the society of Lady Penelope likely to be soon again useful or necessary to Lady Binks. So that neither were any longer desirous to suppress symptoms of the mutual contempt and dislike which they had long nourished for each other; and whosoever should, in this decisive hour, take part with one, had little henceforward to expect from the other. What farther and more private reasons Lady Binks might have to resent the defection of Lord Etherington, have never come with certainty to our knowledge; but it was said there had been high words between them on the floating report that Lord Etherington's visits to Shaws-Castle were dictated by the wish to find a bride there.

Women's wits are said to be quick in spying the surest means of avenging a real or supposed slight. After biting her pretty lips, and revolving in her mind the readiest means of vengeance, fate threw in her way young Mowbray of Saint Ronan's. She looked at him, and endeavoured to fix his attention with a nod and a gracious smile, such as in an ordinary mood would have instantly drawn him to her side. On receiving in answer only a vacant glance and a bow, she was led to observe him more attentively, and was induced to believe, from his wavering look, varying complexion, and unsteady step, that he had been drinking unusually deep. Still his eye was less that of an intoxicated than of a disturbed and desperate man, one whose faculties were engrossed by deep and turbid reflection, which withdrew him from the passing scene.

"Do you observe how ill Mr Mowbray looks?" said she, in a loud whisper; "I hope he has not heard what Lady Penelope was just now saying of his family."

"Unless he hears it from you, my lady," answered Mr Touchwood, who, upon Mowbray's entrance, had broken off his discourse with MacTurk, "I think there is little chance of his learning it from any other person."

"What is the matter?" said Mowbray, sharply, addressing Chatterley and Winterblossom; but the one shrunk from the question, protesting, he indeed had not been precisely attending to what had been passing among the ladies, and Winterblossom bowed out of the scrape with quiet and cautious politeness—he really had not given particular attention to what was passing—"I was negotiating with Mrs Jones for an additional lump of sugar to my coffee.—Egad, it was so difficult a piece of diplomacy," he added, sinking his voice, "that I have an idea her ladyship calculates the West India produce by grains and pennyweights."

The innuendo, if designed to make Mowbray smile, was far from succeeding. He stepped forwards with more than usual stiffness in his air, which was never entirely free from self-consequence, and said to Lady Binks, "May I request to know of your ladyship what particular respecting my family had the honour to engage the attention of the company?"

"I was only a listener, Mr Mowbray," returned Lady Binks, with evident enjoyment of the rising indignation which she read in his countenance; "not being queen of the night, I am not at all disposed to be answerable for the turn of the conversation."

Mowbray, in no humour to bear jesting, yet afraid to expose himself by further inquiry in a company so public, darted a fierce look at Lady Penelope, then in close conversation with Lord Etherington, —advanced a step or two towards them,—then, as if checking himself, turned on his heel, and left the room. A few minutes afterwards, and when certain satirical nods and winks were circulating among the assembly, a waiter slid a piece of paper into Mrs Jones's hand, who, on looking at the contents, seemed about to leave the room.

"Jones—Jones!" exclaimed Lady Penelope, in surprise and displeasure.

"Only the key of the tea-caddie, your ladyship," answered Jones, "I will be back in an instant."

"Jones—Jones!" again exclaimed her mistress, "here is enough—" of tea, she would have said, but Lord Etherington was so near her, that she was ashamed to complete the sentence, and had only hope in Jones's quickness of apprehension, and the prospect that she would be unable to find the key which she went in search of.

Jones, meanwhile, tripped off to a sort of housekeeper's apartment, of which she was *locum tenens* for the evening, for the more ready supply of whatever might be wanted on Lady Penelope's night, as it was called. Here she found Mr Mowbray of Saint Ronan's, whom she instantly began to assail with "La! now, Mr Mowbray, you are such another gentleman!—I am sure you will make me lose my place—I'll swear you will—what can you have to say, that you could not as well put off for an hour?"

"I want to know, Jones," answered Mowbray, in a different tone, perhaps, from what the damsel expected, "what your lady was just now saying about my family."

"Pshaw!—was that all?" answered Mrs Jones. "What should she be saying?—nonsense—Who minds what she says?—I am sure I never do, for one."

"Nay, but, my dear Jones," said Mowbray, "I insist upon knowing —I must know, and I *will* know."

"La! Mr Mowbray, why should I make mischief?—as I live, I hear some one coming! and if you were found speaking with me here—indeed, indeed, some one is coming!"

"The devil may come, if he will!" said Mowbray, "but we do not part, pretty mistress, till you tell me what I wish to know."

"Lord, sir, you frighten me!" answered Jones; "but all the room heard it as well as I—it was about Miss Mowbray—and that my lady would be shy of her company hereafter—for that she was—she was—"

"For that my sister was *what?*" said Mowbray, fiercely, seizing her arm.

"Lord, sir, you terrify me," said Jones, beginning to cry; "at any rate, it was not I that said it—it was Lady Penelope."

"And what was it the old, adder-tongued madwoman dared to say of Clara Mowbray?—Speak out plainly, and directly, or, by Heaven, I'll make you!"

"Hold, sir—hold, for God's sake!—you will break my arm," answered the terrified hand-maiden. "I am sure I know no harm of Miss Mowbray; only, my lady spoke as if she was no better than she ought to be.—Lord, sir, there is some one listening at the door!"—and making a spring out of his grasp, she hastened back to the room in which the company were assembled.

Mowbray stood petrified at the news he had heard, ignorant alike what could be the motive for a calumny so atrocious, and uncertain what he were best to do to put a stop to the scandal. To his farther confusion, he was presently convinced of the truth of Mrs Jones's belief that they had been watched, for, as he went to the door of the apartment, he was met by Mr Touchwood.

"What has brought you here, sir?" said Mowbray, sternly.

"Hoitie toitie," answered the traveller, "why, how came *you* here, if you go to that, squire?—Egad, Lady Penelope is trembling for her souchong, so I just took a step here to save her ladyship the trouble of looking after Mrs Jones in person, which, I think, might have been a worse interruption than mine, Mr Mowbray."

"Pshaw, sir, you talk nonsense," said Mowbray; "the tea-room is so infernally hot, that I had sat down here a moment to draw breath, when the young woman came in."

"And you are going to run away, now the old gentleman is come in," said Touchwood—"Come, sir, I am more your friend than you may think."

"Sir, you are intrusive—I want nothing that you can give me," said Mowbray.

"That is a mistake," answered the Senior; "for I can supply you with what most young men want—money and wisdom."

"You will do well to keep both till they are wanted," said Mowbray.

"Why, so I would, squire, only that I have taken something of a fancy for your family; and they are supposed to have wanted cash and good counsel for two generations, if not for three."

"Sir," said Mowbray, angrily, "you are too old either to play the buffoon, or to get buffoon's payment."

"Which is like monkey's allowance, I suppose," said the traveller, "more kicks than halfpence—Well—at least I am not young enough to quarrel with boys for bullying. I'll convince you, however, Mr Mowbray, that I know some more of your affairs than what you give me credit for."

"It may be," answered Mowbray; "but you will oblige me more by minding your own."

"Very like; meantime, your losses to-night to my Lord Etherington are no trifle, and no secret neither."

"Mr Touchwood, I desire to know where you had your information?" said Mowbray.

"A matter of very little consequence compared to its truth or falsehood, Mr Mowbray," answered the old gentleman.

"But of the last importance to me, sir," said Mowbray. "In a word, had you such information by or through means of Lord Etherington?

—Answer me this single question, and then I shall know better what to think on the subject."

"Upon my honour," said Touchwood, "I neither had my information from Lord Etherington directly or indirectly. I say thus much to give you satisfaction, and I now expect you will hear me with patience."

"Forgive me, sir," interrupted Mowbray, "one farther question. I understand something was said in disparagement of my sister just as I entered the tea-room?"

"Hem—hem—hem," said Touchwood, hesitating. "I am sorry your ears have served you so well—something there *was* said lightly, something that can be easily explained, I dare say.—And now, Mr Mowbray, let me speak a few serious words with you."

"And now, Mr Touchwood, we have no more to say to each other—good evening to you."

He brushed past the old man, who in vain endeavoured to stop him, and, hurrying to the stable, demanded his horse. It was ready saddled, and waited his orders; but even the short time that was necessary to bring it to the door of the stable was exasperating to Mowbray's impatience. Not less exasperating was the constant interceding voice of Touchwood, who, in tones alternately plaintive and snappish, kept on a string of expostulations.

"Mr Mowbray, only five words with you—Mr Mowbray, you will repent this—Is this a night to ride in, Mr Mowbray?—My stars, sir, if you would but have five minutes patience!"

Curses not loud but deep, muttered in the throat of the impatient laird, were the only reply until his horse was brought out, when, staying no farther question, he sprung into the saddle. The poor horse paid for the delay, which could not be laid to his charge. Mowbray struck him hard with his spurs so soon as he was in his seat—the noble animal reared, bolted, and sprung forward like a deer, over stock and stone, the nearest road—and we are aware it was a rough one—to Shaws-Castle. There is a sort of instinct by which horses perceive the humour of their riders, and are furious and impetuous, or dull and sluggish, as if to correspond with it; and Mowbray's gallant steed seemed on this occasion to feel all the stings of his master's internal ferment, although not again urged with the spur. The ostler stood listening to the clash of the hoofs succeeding each other in thick and close gallop, until they died away in the distant woodland.

"If Saint Ronan's reach home this night, with his neck unbroken," muttered the fellow, "the devil must have it in keeping."

"Mercy on us!" said the traveller, "he rides like a Bedouin Arab! but in the desert there are neither trees to cross the road, nor cleughs, nor linns, nor floods, nor fords. Well, I must set to work myself, or this gear will get worse than even I can mend.—Here you, ostler, let me have your best pair of horses instantly to Shaws-Castle."

"To Shaws-Castle, sir?" said the man, with some surprise.

"Yes—do you not know such a place?"

"In troth, sir, sae few company go there, except on the great ball day, that we have had time to forget the road to it—but Saint Ronan's was here even now, sir."

"Ay, what of that?—he has ridden on to get supper ready—so, turn out without loss of time."

"At your pleasure, sir," said the fellow, and called to the postilion accordingly.

Chapter Nine

DEBATE

Sedet post equitem atra cura.——

Still though the headlong cavalier,
O'er rough and smooth, in wild career,
Seems racing with the wind;
His sad companion,—ghastly pale,
And darksome as a widow's veil—
CARE keeps her seat behind.
HORACE

WELL WAS IT that night for Mowbray, that he had always piqued himself on his horses, and that the animal on which he was then mounted was as sure-footed and sagacious as he was mettled and fiery. For those who observed next day the print of the hoofs on the broken and rugged track through which the creature had been driven at full speed by his furious master, might easily see, that in more than a dozen of places the horse and rider had been within a few inches of destruction. One bough of a gnarled and stunted oak tree, which stretched across the road, seemed in particular to have opposed an almost fatal barrier to the horseman's career. In striking his head against this impediment, the force of the blow had been broken in some measure by a high-crowned hat, yet the violence of the shock was sufficient to shiver the branch to pieces. Fortunately, it was already decayed; but, even in that state, it was subject of astonishment to every one that no fatal damage had been sustained in so formidable an encounter. Mowbray himself was unconscious of the accident.

Scarce aware that he had been riding at an unusual rate, scarce sensible that he had ridden faster perhaps than ever he followed the hounds, Mowbray alighted at his stable door, and flung the bridle to his groom, who held up his hands in astonishment when he beheld the condition of the favourite horse; but, concluding that his master must be intoxicated, he prudently forbore to make any observations.

No sooner did the unfortunate traveller suspend that rapid motion by which he seemed to wish to annihilate, as far as possible, time and space, in order to reach the place he had now attained, than it seemed to him as if he would have given the world that seas and deserts had lain between him and the house of his fathers, as well as that only sister with whom he was now about to have a decisive interview.

"But the place and the hour are arrived," he said, biting his lip with anguish; "this explanation must be decisive; and whatever evils may attend it, suspense must be ended now, at once and for ever."

He entered the Castle, and took the light from the old domestic, who, hearing the clatter of his horse's feet, had opened the door to receive him.

"Is my sister in her parlour?" he asked, but in so hollow a voice, that the old man only answered the question by another, "Was his honour well?"

"Quite well, Patrick—never better in my life," said Mowbray; and, turning his back on the old man, as if to prevent his observing whether his countenance and his words corresponded, he pursued his way to his sister's apartment. The sound of his step upon the passage roused Clara from a reverie, perhaps a sad one; and she had trimmed her lamp, and stirred her fire, so slow did he walk, before he at length entered her apartment.

"You are a good boy, brother," she said, "to come thus early home; and I have some good news for your reward. The groom has fetched back Trimmer—He was lying by the dead hare, and he had chased him as far as Drumlyford—the shepherd had carried him to the shieling, till some one should claim him."

"I would he had hanged him, with all my heart," said Mowbray.

"How?—hanged Trimmer?—your favourite Trimmer, that has beat the whole county?—and it was only this morning you were half-crying because he was amissing, and like to murder man and mother's son."

"The better I like any living thing," answered Mowbray, "the more reason I have for wishing it dead and at rest; for neither I, nor anything that I love, will ever be happy more."

"You cannot frighten me, John, with these flights," answered Clara, trembling, although she endeavoured to look unconcerned—"You have used me to them too often."

"It is well for you, then; you will be ruined without the shock of surprise."

"So much the better—We have been," said Clara,

> "So constantly in poortith's sight,
> The thoughts on't gie us little fright.

So say I with honest Robert Burns."

"D—n Burns and his trash!" said Mowbray, with the impatience of a man determined to be angry with everything but himself, who was the real source of the evil.

"And why damn poor Burns?" said Clara, composedly; "it is not his fault if you have not risen a winner, for that, I suppose, is the cause of all this uproar."

"Would it not make any one lose patience," said Mowbray, "to hear a woman quoting the rhapsodies of a hobnail'd peasant, when a man is speaking of the downfall of an ancient house! Your ploughman, I suppose, becoming one degree poorer than he was born to be, would only go without his dinner, or without his usual potation of ale. His comrades would cry 'poor fellow!' and let him eat out of their kit, and drink out of their bicker without scruple, till his own is full again. But the poor gentleman—the downfallen man of rank—the degraded man of birth—the disabled and disarmed man of power!—it is he that is to be pitied, who loses not merely drink and dinner, but honour, situation, credit, character, and name itself!"

"You are declaiming in this manner in order to terrify me," said Clara; "but, friend John, I know you and your ways, and I have made up my mind upon all contingencies that can take place. I will tell you more—I have stood on this tottering pinnacle of rank and fashion, if our situation can be termed such, till my head is dizzy with the instability of my eminence; and I feel that strange desire of tossing myself down, which the devil is said to put into folks' heads when they stand on the top of steeples—at least, I had rather the plunge were over."

"Be satisfied then, if that will satisfy you—the plunge *is* over, and we are—what they used to call it in Scotland—gentle beggars—creatures to whom our second, and third, and fourth, and fifth cousins may, if they please, give a place at the side-table, and a seat in the carriage with the lady's maid, if driving backwards will not make us sick."

"They may give it to those who will take it," said Clara; "but I am determined to eat bread of my own buying—I can do twenty things, and I am sure some one or other of them will bring me all the little money I will need. I have been trying, John, for several months, how little I can live upon, and you would laugh if you heard how low I have brought the account."

"There is a difference, Clara, between fanciful experiments and real poverty—the one is a masquerade, which we can end when we please, the other is wretchedness for life."

"Methinks, brother," replied Miss Mowbray, "it would be better for you to set me an example how to carry my good resolutions into effect, than to ridicule them."

"Why, what would you have me do?" said he, fiercely—"turn postilion, or rough-rider, or whipper-in?—I don't know anything else that my education, as I have used it, has fitted me for—and then some of my old acquaintances would, I dare say, give me a crown to drink now and then for old acquaintance sake."

"This is not the way, John, that men of sense think or speak of serious misfortunes," answered his sister; "and I do not believe that this is so serious as it is your pleasure to make it."

"Believe the very worst you can think," replied he, "and you will not believe bad enough!—You have neither a guinea, nor a house, nor a friend;—pass but a day, and it is a chance that you will not have a brother."

"My dear John, you have drunk hard—rode hard."

"Yes—such tidings deserved to be carried express, especially to a young lady who receives them so well," answered Mowbray, bitterly. "I suppose, now, it will make no impression, if I were to tell you that you have it in your power to stop all this ruin?"

"By consummating my own, I suppose—Brother, I said you could not make me tremble, but you have found a way to do it."

"What, you expect I am again to urge you with Lord Etherington's courtship?—that *might* have saved all, indeed—But that day of grace is over."

"I am glad of it, with all my spirit," said Clara; "may it take with it all that we can quarrel about!—But till this instant, I thought it was for this very point that this long voyage was bound, and that you were endeavouring to persuade me of the reality of the danger of the storm, in order to reconcile me to the harbour."

"You are mad, I think, in earnest," said Mowbray; "can you really be so absurd as to rejoice you have no way left to relieve yourself and me from ruin, want, and shame?"

"From shame, brother?" said Clara. "No shame in honest poverty, I hope."

"That is according as folks have used their prosperity, Clara.—I must speak to the point.—There are strange reports going below—By Heaven! they are enough to disturb the ashes of the dead! Were I to mention them, I should expect my poor mother to enter the room.—Clara Mowbray, can you guess what I mean?"

It was with the utmost exertion, yet in a faultering voice, that she was able, after an ineffectual effort, to utter the monosyllable, "*No!*"

"By Heaven! I am ashamed—I am even afraid to express my own meaning!—Clara, what is there which makes you so obstinately reject every proposal of marriage?—Is it that you feel yourself unworthy to be the wife of an honest man?—Speak out!—Evil Fame has been busy with your reputation—Speak out!—Give me the right to cram these lies down the throats of the inventors, and when I go among them to-morrow, I shall know how to treat those who cast reflections on you! The fortunes of our house are ruined, but no tongue shall slander its honour.—Speak—speak, wretched girl! Why are you silent?"

"Stay at home, brother," said Clara; "stay at home, if you regard our house's honour—murther cannot mend misery—Stay at home, and let them talk of me as they will,—they cannot say worse than I deserve!"

The passions of Mowbray, at all times ungovernably strong, were at present inflamed by wine, by his rapid journey, and the disturbed state of his mind. He set his teeth, clenched his hands, looked on the ground, as one that forms some horrid resolution, and muttered almost unintelligibly, "It were charity to kill her."

"Oh! no—no—no!" exclaimed the terrified girl, throwing herself at his feet; "Do not kill me, brother. I have wished for death—thought of death—prayed for death—but, oh! it is frightful to think that he is near—Oh! not a bloody death, brother, nor by your hand!"

She held him close by the knees as she spoke, and expressed, in her looks and accents, the utmost terror. It was not, indeed, without reason; for the extreme solitude of the place, the lateness of the hour, the violent and inflamed passions of her brother, and the desperate circumstances to which he had reduced himself, seemed all to concur to render some horrid act of violence not an improbable termination of this strange interview.

Mowbray folded his arms, without unclenching his hands, or raising his head, while his sister continued on the floor, clasping him round the knees with all her strength, and begging piteously for her life and for mercy.

"Fool!" he said, at last, "let me go!—Who cares for thy worthless life?—who cares if thou live or die? Live, if thou canst—and be the hate and scorn of every one else, as much as thou art mine!"

He grasped her by the shoulder with one hand, pushed her from him, and, as she arose from the floor and again pressed to throw her arms around his neck, he repulsed her with his arm and hand, with a push—a blow—it might be termed either one or the other,—violent enough, in her weak state, to have again extended her on the ground, had not a chair received her as she fell. He looked at her with ferocity, grappled a moment in his pocket; then ran to the window, and throwing the sash violently up, thrust himself as far as he could without falling, into the open air. Terrified, and yet her feelings of his unkindness predominating even above her fears, Clara continued to exclaim, "Oh, brother, say you did not mean this!—Oh, say you did not mean to strike me!—Oh, whatever I have deserved, be not you the executioner!—It is not manly—it is not natural—there are but two of us in the world!"

He returned no answer; and, observing that he continued to stretch himself from the window, which was in the second story of the building, and overlooked the paved court, a new cause of apprehension mingled, in some measure, with her personal fears. Timidly, and with streaming eyes and uplifted hands, she approached her angry brother, and fearfully, yet firmly, seized the skirt of his coat, as if anxious to preserve him from the effects of that despair, which so lately seemed turned against her, and now against himself.

He felt the pressure of her hold, and drawing himself angrily back, asked her sternly what she wanted.

"Nothing," she said, quitting her hold of his coat; "but what—what did he look after so anxiously?"

"After the devil!" he answered, fiercely; then drawing in his head, and taking her hand, "By my soul, Clara—it is true, if ever there was truth in such a tale!—He stood by me just now, and urged me to murther thee!—What else could have put my hunting-knife into my thought?—Ay, by God, and into my very hand—at such a moment?—Yonder I could almost fancy I see him fly, the wood, and the rock, and the water, gleaming back the dark-red furnace-light, that is shed on them by his dragon wings! By my soul, I can hardly suppose it fancy!—I can hardly think but that I was under the influence of an evil spirit—under an act of fiendish possession! But gone as he is, gone let him be—and thou, too ready implement of evil, be thou gone after him!" He drew from his pocket his right hand, which had all this time held his hunting-knife, and threw the implement into the court-yard as he spoke; then, with a mournful quietness and solemnity of manner, shut the window, and led his sister by the hand to her usual seat, which her tottering steps scarce enabled her to reach. "Clara," he said, after a pause of mournful silence, "we must think what is to be done, without passion or violence—there may be something for us in the dice yet, if we do not throw away our game. A blot is never a blot till it is hit—dishonour concealed, is not dishonour in some respects.—Dost thou attend to me, wretched girl?" he said, suddenly and sternly raising his voice.

"Yes, brother—yes indeed, brother," she hastily replied, terrified even by delay again to awaken his ferocious and ungovernable temper.

"Thus it must be, then," he said. "You must marry this Etherington—there is no help for it, Clara—you cannot complain of what your own vice and folly have rendered inevitable."

"But, brother—" said the trembling girl.

"Be silent. I know all that you would say. You love him not, you would say. I love him not, no more than you. Nay, what is more, he loves you not—if he did, I might scruple to give you to him, you being such as you have owned yourself. But you shall wed him out of hate, Clara—or for the interest of your family—or for what reason you will—But wed him you shall and must."

"Brother—dearest brother—one single word!"

"Not of refusal or expostulation—that time is gone by," said her brother. "When I believed thee what I thought thee this morning, I might advise you, but I could not compel. But, since the honour of our family has been disgraced by your means, it is but just, that, if possible, its disgrace should be hidden; and it shall,—ay, if selling you for a slave would tend to conceal it!"

"You do worse—you do worse by me! A slave in an open market may be bought by a kind master—you do not give me that chance—you wed me to one who——"

"Fear him not, nor the worst that he can do, Clara," said her brother. "I know on what terms he marries; and, being once more your brother, as your obedience in this matter will make me, he had better tear his flesh from his bones with his own teeth, than do thee any displeasure! By Heaven, I hate him so much—for he has outreached me every way—that methinks it is some consolation that he will not receive in thee the excellent creature I thought thee!—Fallen as thou art, thou art still too good for him."

Encouraged by the more gentle and almost affectionate tone in which her brother spoke, Clara could not help saying, although almost in a whisper, "I trust it will not be so—I trust he will consider his own condition, honour, and happiness, better than to share them with me."

"Let him utter such a scruple if he dares," said Mowbray—"But he dares not hesitate—he knows that the instant he recedes from addressing you, he signs his own death-warrant or mine, or perhaps that of both; and his views, too, are of a kind that will not be relinquished on a point of scrupulous delicacy merely. Therefore, Clara, nourish no such thought in your heart as that there is the least possibility of your escaping such a marriage! The match is booked—Swear you will not hesitate."

"I will not," she said, almost breathlessly, terrified lest he was about to start once more into the fit of unbridled fury which had before seized on him.

"Do not even whisper or hint an objection, but submit to your fate, for it is inevitable."

"I will—submit—" answered Clara, in the same trembling accent.

"And I," he said, "will spare you—at least at present—and it may be for ever—all inquiry into the guilt which you have confessed. Rumours there were of misconduct, which reached my ears even in England; but who could have believed them that looked on you daily, and witnessed your late course of life?—On this subject I will be at present silent—perhaps may not again touch on it—that is, if you do nothing to thwart my pleasure, or to avoid the fate which circumstances render unavoidable.—And now it is late—retire, Clara, to your bed—think on what I have said as what necessity has determined, and not my selfish pleasure."

He held out his hand, and she placed, but not without reluctant terror, her trembling palm in his. In this manner, and with a sort of mournful solemnity, as if they had been in attendance upon a funeral, he handed his sister through a gallery hung with old family pictures, at the end of which was Clara's bed-chamber. The moon, which at this moment looked out through a huge volume of mustering clouds that had long been boding storm, fell on the two last descendants of that ancient family, as they glided hand in hand, more like the ghosts of the deceased than like living persons, through the hall and amongst the portraits of their forefathers. The same thoughts were in the breasts of both, but neither attempted to say, while they cast a flitting glance on the pallid and decayed representations, "How little did these anticipate this catastrophe of their house!" At the door of the bed-room Mowbray quitted his sister's hand, and said, "Clara, you should to-night thank God, that saved you from a great danger, and me from a deadly sin."

"I will," she answered—"I will." And, as if her terror had been anew excited by this allusion to what had passed, she bid her brother hastily good night, and was no sooner within her apartment, than he heard her turn the key in the lock, and draw two bolts besides.

"I understand you, Clara," muttered Mowbray between his teeth, as he heard one bar drawn after another. "But, if you could earth yourself under Ben Nevis, you could not escape what fate has destined for you.—Yes!" he said to himself, as he walked with slow and moody pace through the moonlight gallery, uncertain whether to return to the parlour, or to retire to his solitary chamber, when his attention was roused by a noise in the court-yard.

The night was not indeed far advanced, but it had been so long since Shaws-Castle received a guest, that, had Mowbray not heard the rolling of wheels in the court-yard, he might have thought rather of housebreakers than of visitors. But, as the sound of a carriage and horses was distinctly heard, it instantly occurred to him, that the guest must be Lord Etherington, come, even at this late hour, to speak with him on the reports which were current to his sister's prejudice, and perhaps to declare his addresses to her were at an end. Eager to know the worst, and to bring matters to a decision, he re-entered the apartment he had just left, where the lights were still burning, and, calling loudly to Patrick, whom he heard in communion with the postilion, commanded him to shew the visitor to Miss Mowbray's parlour. It was not the light step of the young nobleman which came tramping, or rather stumping, through the long passage, and up the two or three steps at the end of it. Neither was it Lord Etherington's graceful figure which was seen when the door opened, but the stout square substance of Mr Peregrine Touchwood.

Chapter Ten

A RELATIVE

Claim'd kindred there, and had his claims allow'd.
Deserted Village

STARTING at the unexpected and undesired apparition which presented itself, in manner described at the end of the last chapter, Mowbray yet felt, at the same time, a kind of relief, that his meeting with Lord Etherington, painfully decisive as that meeting must be, was for a time suspended. So it was with a mixture of peevishness and internal satisfaction, that he demanded what had procured him the honour of a visit from Mr Touchwood at this late hour.

"Necessity, that makes the old wife trot," replied Touchwood; "no choice of mine, I assure you—Gad, Mr Mowbray, I would rather have crossed Saint Gothard, than run the risk I have done to-night, rumbling through your break-neck roads in that damned old wheel-barrow.—On my word, I believe I must be troublesome to your butler for a draught of something—I am as thirsty as a coal-heaver that is working by the piece. You have porter, I suppose, or good old Scotch two-penny?"

With a secret execration on his visitor's effrontery, Mr Mowbray ordered the servant to put down wine and water, of which Touchwood mixed a goblet full, and drank it off.

"We are a small family," said his entertainer; "and I am seldom at home—still more seldom receive guests, when I chance to be here—I am sorry I have no malt liquor, if you prefer it."

"Prefer it?" said Touchwood, compounding, however, another glass of sherry and water, and adding a large piece of sugar, to correct the hoarseness which, he observed, his night journey might bring on, —"to be sure I prefer it, and so does everybody, excepting Frenchmen and dandies.—No offence, Mr Mowbray, but you should order a hogshead from Meux—the brown-stout, wired down for exportation to the colonies, keeps for any length of time, and in every climate—I have drank it where it must have cost a guinea a quart, if interest had been counted."

"When I *expect* the honour of a visit from you, Mr Touchwood, I will endeavour to be better provided," answered Mowbray; "at present your arrival has been unexpected, and I would be glad to know if it has any particular object."

"That is what I call coming to the point," said Mr Touchwood, thrusting out his stout legs, accoutred as they were with the ancient defences, called boot-hose, so as to rest his heels upon the fender. "Upon my life, the fire turns the best flower in the garden at this season of the year—I'll take the freedom to throw on a log.—Is it not a strange thing, by the by, that one never sees a faggot in Scotland? You have much small wood, Mr Mowbray, I wonder you do not get down some fellow from the midland counties, to teach your people how to make a faggot."

"Did you come all the way to Shaws-Castle," asked Mowbray, rather testily, "to instruct me in the mystery of faggot-making?"

"Not exactly—not exactly," answered the undaunted Touchwood; "but there is a right and a wrong way in everything—a word by the way, on any useful subject, can never fall amiss.—As for my immediate and more pressing business, I can assure you, that it is of a nature sufficiently urgent, since it brings me to a house in which I am much surprised to find myself."

"The surprise is mutual, sir," said Mowbray, gravely, observing that his guest made a pause; "it is full time you should explain it."

"Well, then," replied Touchwood; "I must first ask you whether you have never heard of a certain old gentleman, called Scrogie, who took it into what he called his head, poor man, to be ashamed of the name he bore, though owned by many honest and respectable men, and chose to join to it your surname of Mowbray, as having a more chivalrous Norman-sounding, and, in a word, a gentleman-like twang with it?"

"I have heard of such a person, though only lately," said Mowbray. "Reginald Scrogie Mowbray was his name. I have reason to consider his alliance with my family as undoubted, though you seem to mention it with a sneer, sir. I believe Mr S. Mowbray regulated his family settlements very much upon the idea that his heir was to intermarry with our house."

"True, true, Mr Mowbray," answered Touchwood; "and certainly it is not your business to lay the axe to the root of the genealogical tree, that is like to bear golden apples for you—ha!"

"Well, well, sir—proceed—proceed," answered Mowbray.

"You may also have heard that this old gentleman had a son, who would willingly have cut up the said family-tree into faggots; who thought Scrogie sounded as well as Mowbray, and had no fancy for an imaginary gentility, which was to be attained by the change of one's natural name, and the disowning, as it were, of one's actual relations."

"I think I have heard from Lord Etherington," answered Mowbray, "to whose communications I owe most of my knowledge about these Scrogie people, that old Mr Scrogie Mowbray was unfortunate in a son, who thwarted his father on every occasion,—would embrace no opportunity which fortunate chances held out, of raising and distinguishing the family,—had imbibed low tastes, wandering habits, and singular objects of pursuit,—on account of which his father disinherited him."

"It is very true, Mr Mowbray," proceeded Touchwood, "that this person did happen to fall under his father's displeasure, because he scorned forms and flummery,—loved better to make money as an honest merchant, than to throw it away as an idle gentleman,—never called a coach when walking on foot would serve the turn,—and liked the Royal Exchange better than Saint James's Park. In short, his father disinherited him, because he had the qualities for doubling the estate, rather than those for squandering it."

"All this may be very true, Mr Touchwood," replied Mowbray; "but pray, what has this Mr Scrogie, junior, to do with you or me?"

"Do with you or me?" said Touchwood, as if surprised at the question; "he has a great deal to do with me at least, since I am the very man myself."

"The devil you are!" said Mowbray, opening wide his eyes in turn; "Why, Mr A—a—your name is Touchwood—P. Touchwood—Paul, I suppose, or Peter—I read it so in the subscription book at the Well."

"Peregrine, sir, Peregrine—my mother would have me so christened, because Peregrine Pickle came out during her confinement; and my poor foolish father acquiesced, because he thought it genteel. I don't like it, and I always write P. short, and you might have remarked an S. also before the surname—I use at present P. S. Touchwood. I had an old acquaintance in the city, who loved his jest

—He always called me Postscript Touchwood."

"Then, sir," said Mowbray, "if you are really Mr Scrogie, *tout court*, I must suppose the name of Touchwood is assumed?"

"What the devil!" replied Mr P. S. Touchwood, "do you suppose there is no name in the English nation will couple up legitimately with my paternal name of Scrogie, except your own, Mr Mowbray?—I assure you I got the name of Touchwood, and a pretty spell of money along with it, from an old godfather, who admired my spirit in sticking by commerce."

"Well, sir, every one has his taste—Many would have thought it better to enjoy a hereditary estate, by keeping your father's name of Mowbray, than to have gained another by assuming a stranger's name of Touchwood."

"Who told you Mr Touchwood was a stranger to me?" said the traveller; "for aught I know, he had a better title to the duties of a son from me, than the poor old man who made such a fool of himself, by trying to turn gentleman in his old age. He was my grandfather's partner in the great firm of Touchwood, Scrogie, and Co.—Let me tell you, there is as good inheritance in house as in field—a man's partners are his fathers and brothers, and a head clerk may be likened to a kind of first cousin."

"I meant no offence whatever, Mr Touchwood Scrogie."

"Scrogie Touchwood, if you please," said the Senior; "the scrog branch first, for it must become rotten ere it become touchwood—ha, ha, ha!—you take me."

"A singular old fellow this," said Mowbray to himself, "and speaks in all the dignity of dollars; best be civil to him, till I can see what he is driving at.—You are facetious, Mr Touchwood," he proceeded aloud. "I was only going to say, that although you set no value upon your connection with my family, yet I cannot forget that such a circumstance exists; and therefore I bid you heartily welcome to Shaws-Castle."

"Thank ye, thank ye, Mr Mowbray—I knew you would see the thing right. To tell you the truth, I should not have much cared to come a-begging for your acquaintance and cousinship, and so forth; but that I thought you would be more tractable in your adversity, than was your father in his prosperity."

"Did you know my father, sir?" said Mowbray.

"Ay, ay—I came once down here, and was introduced to him—saw your sister and you when you were children—had thoughts of making my will then, and should have clapped you both in before I set out to double Cape Horn. But, gad, I wish my poor father had seen the reception I got! I did not let the old gentleman, Mr Mowbray of Saint

Ronan's that was then, smoke my money-bags—that might have made him more tractable—not but that we went on indifferent well for a day or two, till I got a hint that my room was wanted, for the Duke of Devil-knows-what was expected, and my bed was to serve his valet-de-chambre.—'Oh, damn all gentle cousins!' said I, and off I set on the pad round the world again, and thought no more of the Mowbrays till a year or so ago."

"And, pray, what recalled us to your recollection?"

"Why," said Touchwood, "I was settled for some time at Smyrna, (for I turn the penny go where I will—I have done a little business even since I came here.)—But being at Smyrna, as I said, I became acquainted with Francis Tyrrel."

"The natural brother of Lord Etherington," said Mowbray.

"Ay, so called," answered Touchwood; "but by and by he is more like to prove the Earl of Etherington himself, and t'other fine fellow the bastard."

"The devil he is!—You surprise me, Mr Touchwood."

"I thought I should—I thought I should—Faith, I am sometimes surprised myself at the turn things take in this world. But the thing is not the less certain—the proofs are lying in the strong chest of our house at London, deposited there by the old Earl, who repented of his roguery to Miss Martigny long before he died, but had not courage enough to do his legitimate son justice till the sexton had housed him."

"Good Heaven, sir!" said Mowbray; "and did you know all this while, that I was about to bestow the only sister of my house upon an impostor?"

"What was my business with that, Mr Mowbray?" replied Touchwood; "you would have been very angry had any one suspected you of not being sharp enough to look out for yourself and your sister both. Besides, Lord Etherington, bad enough as he may be in other respects, was, till very lately, no impostor, or an innocent one, for he only occupied the situation in which his father had placed him. And, indeed, when I understood, upon coming to England, that he was gone down here, and, as I conjectured, to pay his addresses to your sister, to say truth, I did not see he could do better. Here was a poor fellow that was about to cease to be a lord and a wealthy man; was it not very reasonable that he should make the most of his dignity while he had it? and if, by marrying a pretty girl while in possession of his title, he could get possession of the good estate of Nettlewood, why, I could see nothing in it but a very pretty way of breaking his fall."

"Very pretty for him, indeed, and very convenient too," said Mowbray; "but pray, sir, what was to become of the honour of my family?"

"Why, what was the honour of your family to me?" said Touchwood; "unless it was to recommend your family to my care, that I was divorced on account of it. And if this Etherington or Bulmer had been a good fellow, I would have seen all Mowbrays that ever wore broad cloth at Jericho, before I interfered."

"I am really much indebted to your kindness," said Mowbray, angrily.

"More than you are aware of," answered Touchwood; "for though I thought this Bulmer, even when declared illegitimate, might be a reasonable good match for your sister, considering the estate which was to accompany the union of their hands; yet now I have discovered him to be a scoundrel—every way a scoundrel—why, I would not wish any decent girl to marry him, were they to get all Yorkshire, instead of Nettlewood. So I have come to put you right."

The strangeness of the news which Touchwood so bluntly communicated, made Mowbray's head turn round like that of a man who grows dizzy at finding himself on the verge of a precipice. Touchwood observed his consternation, which he willingly construed into an acknowledgment of his own brilliant genius.

"Take a glass of wine, Mr Mowbray," he said, complacently; "take a glass of old sherry—nothing like it for clearing the ideas—and do not be afraid of me, though I come thus suddenly upon you with such surprising tidings—you will find me a plain, simple, ordinary man, that have my faults and my blunders, like other people. I acknowledge that much travel and experience have made me sometimes play the busy body, because I find I can do things better than other people, and I love to see folks stare—it's a way I have got. But, after all, I am *un bon diable*, as the Frenchman says; and here I have come four or five hundred miles to lie quiet among you all, and put all your little matters to rights, just when you think they are most desperate."

"I thank you for your good intentions," said Mowbray; "but I must needs say, that they would have been more effectual had you been less cunning in my behalf, and frankly told me what you knew of Lord Etherington; as it is, the matter has gone fearfully far. I have promised him my sister—I have come under personal obligations to him—And there are other reasons why I fear I must keep my word to this man, earl or no earl."

"What!" exclaimed Touchwood; "would you give up your sister to a worthless rascal, who is capable of robbing the post-office, and of murdering his brother, because you have lost a trifle of money to him? Are you to let him go off triumphantly, because he is a gamester as well as a cheat?—You are a pretty fellow, Mr Mowbray of Saint Ronan's—you are one of the happy sheep that go out for wool, and come home shorn. Egad, you think yourself a mill-stone, and turn out a sack of grain—You flew abroad a hawk, and came home a pigeon—You snarled at the Philistines, and they have drawn your eye-teeth with a vengeance!"

"This is all very witty, Mr Touchwood," replied Mowbray; "but wit will not pay this man Etherington, or whatever he is, so many hundreds as I have lost to him."

"Why, then, wisdom must do what wit cannot," said old Touchwood; "I must advance for you, that is all. Look ye, sir, I do not go afoot for nothing—if I have laboured, I have reaped—and, like the fellow in the old play, 'I have enough, and can maintain my humour'—it is not a few hundreds or thousands either can stand betwixt old P. S. Touchwood and his purpose; and my present purpose is to make you, Mr Mowbray of Saint Ronan's, a free man of the forest.—You still look grave on it, young man?—Why, I trust you are not such an ass as to think your dignity offended, because the plebeian Scrogie comes to the assistance of the terribly great and old house of Mowbray?"

"I am indeed not such a fool," answered Mowbray, with his eyes still bent on the ground, "to reject assistance that comes to me like a rope to a drowning man—but there is a circumstance——" he stopped short, and drank a glass of wine—"a circumstance to which it is most painful to me to allude—but you seem my friend—and I cannot intimate to you more strongly my belief in your professions of regard than by saying, that the language held by Lady Penelope Penfeather on my sister's account, renders it highly proper that she were settled in life; and I cannot but fear, that the breaking off this affair with the man might be of great prejudice to her at this moment. They will have Nettlewood, and they may live separate—he has offered to make settlements to that effect, even on the very day of marriage. Her condition as a married woman will put her above scandal, and above necessity, from which I am sorry to say I cannot hope long to preserve her."

"For shame!—for shame!—for shame!" said Touchwood, accumulating his words thicker than usual on each other; "would you sell your own flesh and blood to a man like this Bulmer, whose character is now laid before you, merely because a disappointed old maid speaks scandal of her? A fine veneration you pay to the honoured name of Mowbray! If my poor, old, simple father had known what the owners of these two grand syllables could have stooped to do for merely insuring subsistence, he would have thought as little of the noble Mowbrays as of the humble Scrogies. And, I dare say, the young lady is just such another—eager to get married—no matter to whom."

"Excuse me, Mr Touchwood," answered Mowbray; "my sister

entertains sentiments so very different from what you ascribe to her, that she and I parted on the most unpleasant terms, in consequence of my pressing this man's suit upon her. God knows, that I only did so, because I saw no other outlet from this most unpleasant dilemma. But, since you are willing to interfere, sir, and aid me to disentangle these complicated matters, which have, I own, been made worse by my own rashness, I am ready to throw the matter completely into your hands, just as if you were my father arisen from the dead. Nevertheless, I must needs express my surprise at the extent of your intelligence in these affairs."

"You speak very sensibly, young man," said the traveller; "and as for my intelligence, I have for some time known the finesses of this Master Bulmer as perfectly as if I had been at his elbow when he was playing all his dog's tricks with this family. You would hardly suspect now," he continued, in a confidential tone, "that what you were so desirous a while ago should take place, has in some sense actually happened, and that the marriage ceremony has really passed betwixt your sister and this pretended Lord Etherington."

"Have a care, sir!" said Mowbray, fiercely; "do not abuse my candour—this is no place, time, or subject for impertinent jesting."

"As I live by bread, I am serious," said Touchwood; "Mr Cargill performed the ceremony; and there are two living witnesses who heard them say the words, 'I, Clara, take you, Francis,' or whatever the Scottish church puts in place of that mystical formula."

"It is impossible," said Mowbray; "Cargill dared not have done such a thing—a clandestine proceeding, such as you speak of, would have cost him his living. I'll bet my soul against a horse-shoe, it is all an imposition; and you come to disturb me, sir, amid my family distress, with legends that have no more truth in them than the Alkoran."

"There are some true things in the Alkoran, (or rather, the Koran, for the Al is merely the article prefixed,) but let that pass—I will raise your wonder higher before I am done. It is very true, that your sister was indeed joined in marriage with this same Bulmer, that calls himself by the title of Etherington; but it is just as true, that the marriage is not worth a maravedi, for she believed him at the time to be another person—to be, in a word, Francis Tyrrel, who is actually what the other pretends to be, a nobleman of fortune."

"I cannot understand one word of all this," said Mowbray. "I must to my sister instantly, and demand of her if there be any real foundation for these wonderful averments."

"Do not go," said Touchwood, detaining him, "you shall have a full explanation from me; and, to comfort you under your perplexity, I can assure you that Cargill's consent to celebrate the nuptials, was only obtained by an aspersion thrown on your sister's character, which induced him to believe, that speedy marriage would be the sole means of saving her reputation; and I am convinced in my own mind it is only the revival of this report which has furnished the foundation of Lady Penelope's chattering."

"If I could think so"—said Mowbray, "if I could but think this is truth—and it seems to explain, in some degree, my sister's mysterious conduct—if I could but think it true, I should fall down and worship you as an angel from heaven!"

"A proper sort of angel," said Touchwood, looking modestly down on his short, sturdy supporters—"Did you ever hear of an angel in boot-hose? Or, do you suppose angels are sent to wait on broken-down horse-jockeys?"

"Call me what you will, Mr Touchwood; only, make out your story true, and my sister innocent!"

"Very well spoken, sir," answered the Senior, "very well spoken! But then I understand you are to be guided by my prudence and experience? None of your G— damme doings, sir—your duels or your drubbings. Let *me* manage the affair for you, and I will bring you through with a flowing sail."

"Sir, I must feel as a gentleman," said Mowbray.

"Feel as a fool," said Touchwood, "for that is the true case. Nothing would please this Bulmer better than to fight through his rogueries—he knows very well, that he who can slit a pistol-ball on the edge of a penknife, will always preserve some sort of reputation amidst his scoundrelism—but I shall take care to stop that hole. Sit down—be a man of sense, and listen to the whole of this strange story."

Mowbray sat down accordingly; and Touchwood, in his own way, and with many characteristic interjectional remarks, gave him an account of the early loves of Clara and Tyrrel—of the reasons which induced Bulmer at first to encourage their correspondence, in hopes that his brother would, by a clandestine marriage, altogether ruin himself with his father—of the change which took place in his views when he perceived the importance annexed by the old Earl to the union of Miss Mowbray with his apparent heir—of the desperate stratagem which he endeavoured to play off, by substituting himself in the room of his brother—and all the consequences, which it is unnecessary to resume here, as they are detailed at length by the perpetrator himself, in his correspondence with Captain Jekyl.

When the whole communication was ended, Mowbray, almost stupified by the wonders he had heard, remained for some time in a sort of reverie, from which he only started to ask what evidence could be produced of a story so strange.

"The evidence," answered Touchwood, "of one who was a deep agent in all these matters, from first to last—as complete a rogue, I believe, as the devil himself, with this difference, that our mortal fiend does not, I believe, do evil for the sake of evil, but for the sake of the profit which attends it. How far this plea will avail him in a court of conscience, I cannot tell; but his disposition was so far akin to humanity, that I have always found my old acquaintance as ready to do good as harm, providing he had the same *agio* upon the transaction."

"On my soul," said Mowbray, "you must mean Solmes! whom I have long suspected to be a deep villain—and now he proves traitor, to boot. How the devil could you get into his intimacy, Mr Touchwood?"

"The case was particular," said Touchwood. "Mr Solmes, too active a member of the community, to be satisfied with managing the affairs which his master entrusted to him, adventured in a little business on his own accompt; and thinking, I suppose, that the late Earl of Etherington had forgotten fully to acknowledge his services, as valet to his son, he supplied that defect by a small cheque on our house for L.100, in name, and bearing the apparent signature, of the deceased. This small mistake being detected at our house, Mr Solmes, *porteur* of the little billet, would have been consigned to the custody of a Bow-street officer, but that I found means to relieve him, on condition of his making known to me the points of private history which I have just been communicating to you. What I had known of Tyrrel at Smyrna, had given me much interest in him, and you may guess it was not lessened by the distresses which he had sustained through his brother's treachery. By this fellow's means, I have counterplotted all his master's fine schemes. For example, so soon as I learned that Bulmer was coming down here, I contrived to give Tyrrel an anonymous hint, well knowing he would set off like the devil to thwart him, and so I should have the whole dramatis personæ together, and play them all off against each other, after my own pleasure."

"In that case," said Mr Mowbray, "your expedient brought about the rencontre between the two brothers, when both might have fallen."

"Can't deny it—can't deny it—a mere accident—no one can guard every point.—Egad, but I had like to have been baffled again, for Bulmer sent the lad Jekyl, who is not such a black sheep neither but what there are some white hairs about him, upon a treaty with Tyrrel, that my secret agent was not admitted to. Gad, but I discovered the whole—you will scarce guess how."

"Probably not, indeed, sir," answered Mowbray; "for your sources of intelligence are not the most obvious, any more than your mode of acting is simple, or easily comprehended."

"I would not have it so," said Touchwood; "simple men perish in their simplicity—I carry my eye-teeth about me.—And for my source of information—why, I played the eaves-dropper, sir—listened—knew my landlady's cupboard with the double door—got into it as she has done many a time.—Such a fine gentleman as you would rather cut a man's throat, I suppose, than listen at a cupboard door, though the object were to prevent murther."

"I cannot say I should have thought of the expedient, certainly, sir," said Mowbray.

"I did though, and learned enough of what was going on, to give Jekyl a hint that sickened him of his commission, I believe—so the game is all in my own hands. Bulmer has no one to trust to but Solmes, and Solmes tells me all."

Here Mowbray could not suppress a movement of impatience.

"I wish to God, sir, that since you were so kind as to interest yourself in affairs so intimately concerning my family, you had been pleased to act with a little more openness towards me. Here have I been for weeks the intimate of a damned scoundrel, whose throat I ought to have cut for his scandalous conduct to my sister. Here have I been rendering her and myself miserable, and getting myself cheated every night by a swindler, whom you, if it had been your pleasure, could have unmasked by a single word. I do all justice to your intentions, sir; but, upon my soul, I cannot help wishing you had conducted yourself with more frankness and less mystery; and I am truly afraid your love of mystery has been too much for your ingenuity, and that you have suffered matters to run into such a skean of confusion, as you yourself will find difficulty in unravelling."

Touchwood smiled, and shook his head in all the conscious pride of superior understanding. "Young man," he said, "when you have seen a little of the world, and especially beyond the bounds of this narrow island, you will find much more art and dexterity necessary in conducting these businesses to an issue, than occurs to a blunt John Bull, or a raw Scotchman. You will be then no stranger to the policy of life, which deals in mining and countermining,—now in making feints, now in making forthright passes. I look upon you, Mr Mowbray, as a young man spoiled by staying at home, and keeping bad company; and will make it my business, if you submit yourself to my guidance, to inform your understanding, so as to retrieve your estate.—Don't—don't answer me, sir! because I know too well, by experience, how young men answer on these subjects—they are conceited, sir, as conceited as if they had been in all the four quarters of the world. I hate to be answered, sir, I hate it. And, to tell you the truth, it is because Tyrrel has a fancy of answering me, that I rather make you my confidant on this occasion, than him. I would have had him throw himself into my arms, and under my directions; but he hesitated—he hesitated, Mr Mowbray—and I despise hesitation. If he thinks he has art enough to manage his own matters, let him try it—let him try it. Not that I will not do all that I can for him, in fitting time and place; but I will let him dwell in his perplexities and uncertainties for a little while longer. And so, Mr Mowbray, you see what sort of an odd old fellow I am, and you can satisfy me at once whether you mean to come into my measures—Only speak out at once, sir, for I abhor hesitation."

While Touchwood thus spoke, Mowbray was forming his resolution internally. He was not so inexperienced as the Senior supposed; at least, he could plainly see that he had to do with an obstinate, capricious, old man, who, with the best intentions in the world, chose to have every thing in his own way; and, like most petty politicians, was disposed to throw intrigue and mystery over matters which had much better be prosecuted boldly and openly. But he perceived, at the same time, that Touchwood, as a sort of relation, wealthy, childless, and disposed to become his friend, was a person to be conciliated, the rather that the traveller had himself frankly owned that it was Francis Tyrrel's want of deference toward him, which had forfeited, or at least abated, his favour. Mowbray recollected, also, that the circumstances under which he himself stood, did not permit him to trifle with returning gleams of good fortune. Subduing, therefore, the haughtiness of temper, proper to him as an only son and heir, he answered respectfully, that, in his condition, the advice and assistance of Mr Scrogie Touchwood was too important, not to be purchased at the price of submitting his own judgment to that of an experienced and sagacious friend.

"Well said, Mr Mowbray," replied the Senior, "well said. Let me once have the management of your affairs, and we will brush them up for you without loss of time.—I must be obliged to you for a bed for the night, however—it is as dark as a wolf's-mouth; and if you will give orders to keep the poor devil of a postilion, and his horses too, why, I will be the more obliged to you."

Mowbray applied himself to the bell. Patrick answered the call, and was much surprised, when the old gentleman, taking the word out of his entertainer's mouth, desired a bed to be got ready, with a little fire in the grate; "for I take it, friend," he went on, "you have not guests here very often.—And see that my sheets be not damp, and bid the house-maid take care not to make the bed upon an exact level, but let it slope from the pillow to the foot-posts, at a declivity of about eighteen inches.—And hark ye—get me a jug of barley-water, to place by my bed-side, with the squeeze of a lemon—or stay, you will make it as sour as Beelzebub—bring the lemon on a saucer, and I will mix it myself."

Patrick listened like one of sense forlorn, his head turning like a mandarin, alternately from the speaker to his master, as if to ask the latter whether this was all reality. The instant that Touchwood stopped, Mowbray added his fiat.

"Let everything be done to make Mr Touchwood comfortable, in the way he wishes."

"Aweel, sir," said Patrick, "I sall tell Mally, to be sure, and we maun do our best, and—but it's unco late, and——"

"And, therefore," said Touchwood, "the sooner we get to bed the better, my old friend. I, for one, must be stirring early—I have business of life and death—it concerns you too, Mr Mowbray—but no more of that till to-morrow.—And let the lad put up his horses, and get him a bed somewhere."

Patrick here thought he had gotten upon firm ground for resistance, for which, displeased with the dictatorial manner of the stranger, he felt considerably inclined.

"Ye may catch us at that, if ye can," said Patrick; "there's nae post-cattle come into our stables—What do we ken, but that they may be glandered, as the groom says?"

"We must take the risk to-night, Patrick," said Mowbray, reluctantly enough—"unless Mr Touchwood will permit the horses to come back early next morning?"

"Not I, indeed," said Touchwood; "safe bind safe find—it may be once away and aye away, and we shall have enough to do to-morrow morning. Moreover, the poor carrion are tired, and the merciful man is merciful to his beast—and, in a word, if the horses go back to Saint Ronan's Well to-night, I go there for company."

It often happens, owing, I suppose, to the perversion of human nature, that subserviency in trifles is more difficult to a proud mind, than compliance in matters of more importance. Mowbray, like other young gentlemen of his class, was finically rigid in his stable discipline, and even Lord Etherington's horses had not been admitted into that *sanctum sanctorum*, into which he now saw himself obliged to induct two wretched post-hacks. But he submitted with the best grace he could; and Patrick, while he left their presence, with lifted up hands and eyes, to execute the orders he had received, could scarcely help thinking that the old man must be the devil in disguise, since he could thus suddenly control his fiery master, even in the points which he had hitherto seemed to consider as of most vital importance.

"The Lord in his mercy haud a grip of this puir family! for I, that was born in it, am like to see the end of it." Thus ejaculated Patrick.

Chapter Eleven

THE WANDERER

'Tis a naughty night to swim in.
King Lear

THERE WAS a wild uncertainty about Mowbray's ideas after he started from a feverish sleep on the morning succeeding this memorable interview, that his sister, whom he really loved as much as he was capable of loving anything, had dishonoured him and her name; and the horrid recollection of their last interview was the first idea which his waking imagination was thrilled with. Then came Touchwood's tale of exculpation—and he persuaded himself, or strove to do so, that Clara must have understood the charge he had brought against her as referring to her attachment to Tyrrel, and its fatal consequences. Again, still he doubted how that could be—still feared that there must be more behind than her reluctance to confess the fraud which had been practised on her by Bulmer; and then, again, he strengthened himself in the first and more pleasing opinion, by recollecting that, averse as Clara was to espouse the person he proposed to her, it must have appeared to her the completion of ruin, if he, Mowbray, should obtain knowledge of the clandestine marriage.

"Yes—O yes," he said to himself, "she would think that this story would render me more eager in the rascal's interest, as the best way of hushing up such a discreditable affair—faith, and she would have judged right too; for, had he actually been Lord Etherington, I do not see what else she could have done. But, not being Lord Etherington, and an anointed scoundrel into the bargain, I will content myself with cudgelling him to death so soon as I can get out of the guardianship of this old, meddling, obstinate, self-willed busy-body.—Then, what is to be done for Clara?—This mock marriage was a mere bubble, and both parties must draw stakes. She likes this grave Don, who proves to be the stick of the right tree, after all—so do not I, though there be something lordlike about him. I was sure a strolling painter could not have carried it off so. She may marry him, I suppose, if the law is not against it—then she has the earldom, and the Oaklands, and Nettlewood, all at once.—Gad, we should come in winners, after all—and, I dare say, this old boy Touchwood is as rich as a Jew—worth a hundred thousand at least—He is too peremptory to be cut up for sixpence under a hundred thousand.—And he talks of putting me to rights—I must not wince—must stand still to be curried a little—Only, I wish the law may permit Clara's being married to this other earl.—A woman cannot marry two brothers, that is certain;—but then, if she is not married to the one of them in good and lawful form, there can be no bar to her marrying the other, I should think—I hope the lawyers will talk no nonsense about it—I hope Clara will have no foolish scruples.—But, by my word, the first thing I have to hope is, that the thing is true, for it comes through but a suspicious channel. I'll away to Clara instantly—get the truth out of her—and consider what is to be done."

Thus partly thought and partly spoke the young Laird of Saint Ronan's, hastily dressing himself, in order to inquire into the strange chaos of events which perplexed his imagination.

When he came down to the parlour where they had supped last night, and where breakfast was prepared this morning, he sent for a girl who acted as his sister's immediate attendant, and asked, "if Miss Mowbray was yet stirring?"

The girl answered, "she had not rung her bell."

"It is past her usual hour," said Mowbray, "but she was disturbed last night. Go, Martha, tell her to get up instantly—say I have excellent good news for her—or, if her head aches, I will come and tell them to her before she rises—go like lightning."

Martha went, and returned in a minute or two. "I cannot make my mistress hear, sir, knock as hard as I will. I wish," she added, with that love of evil presage which is common in the lower ranks, "that Miss Clara may be well, for I never knew her sleep so sound."

Mowbray jumped from the chair into which he had thrown himself, ran through the gallery, and knocked smartly at his sister's door; there was no answer. "Clara, dear Clara!—Answer me but one word—say but you are well. I frightened you last night—I had been drinking wine—I was violent—forgive me!—Come, do not be sulky—speak but a single word—say but you are well."

He made the pauses longer betwixt every branch of his address, knocked sharper and louder, listened more anxiously for an answer; at length he attempted to open the door, but found it locked, or otherwise secured. "Does Miss Mowbray always lock her door?" he asked the girl.

"Never knew her do it before, sir; she leaves it open that I may call her, and open the window-shuts."

She had too good reason for precaution last night, thought her brother, and then remembered having heard her bar the door.

"Come, Clara," he continued, greatly agitated, "do not be silly; if you will not open the door, I must force it, that's all; for how can I tell but that you are sick, and unable to answer?—if you are only sullen, say so.—She returns no answer," he said, turning to the domestic, who was now joined by Touchwood.

Mowbray's anxiety was so great, that it prevented his taking any notice of his guest, and he proceeded to say, without regarding his presence, "What is to be done?—she may be sick—she may be asleep—she may have swooned; if I force the door, it may terrify her to death in the present weak state of her nerves.—Clara, dear Clara! do but speak a single word, and you shall remain in your own room as long as you please."

There was no answer. Miss Mowbray's maid, hitherto too much fluttered and alarmed to have much presence of mind, now recollected a back-stair which communicated with her mistress's room from the garden, and suggested she might have gone out that way.

"Gone out," said Mowbray, in great anxiety, and looking at the heavy fog, or rather small rain, which blotted the November morning,—"Gone out, and in weather like this!—But we may get into her room from the back-stair."

So saying, and leaving his guest to follow or remain as he thought proper, he flew rather than walked to the garden, and found the private door which led into it, from the bottom of the back-stair abovementioned, was wide open. Full of vague, yet fearful apprehensions, he rushed up to the door of his sister's apartment, which opened from her dressing-room to the landing-place of the stair; it was ajar, and that which communicated betwixt the bed-room and dressing-room was half open. "Clara, Clara!" exclaimed Mowbray, invoking her name rather in an agony of apprehension, than as any longer hoping for a reply. And his apprehension was but too prophetic.

Miss Mowbray was not in that apartment; and, from the order in which it was found, it was plain she had neither undressed on the preceding night, nor occupied the bed. Mowbray struck his forehead in an agony of remorse and fear. "I have terrified her to death," he said; "she has fled into the woods, and perished there!"

Under the influence of this apprehension, Mowbray, after another hasty glance around the apartment, as if to assure himself that Clara was not there, rushed again into the dressing-room, almost overturning the traveller, who, in civility, had not ventured to enter the inner apartment. "You are as mad as a *Hamako*,"* said the traveller; "let us consult together, and I am sure I can contrive——"

* A fool is so termed in Turkey.

"Oh, d—n your contrivance!" said Mowbray, forgetting all proposed respect in his natural impatience, aggravated by his alarm; "if you had behaved straight forward, and like a man of common sense, this would not have happened!"

"God forgive you, young man, if your reflections are unjust," said the traveller, quitting the hold he had laid upon Mowbray's coat; "and God forgive me too, if I have done wrong while endeavouring to do for the best. But may not Miss Mowbray have gone down to the Well? I will order my horses, and set off instantly."

"Do, do," said Mowbray, recklessly; "I thank you, I thank you;" and hastily traversing the garden, as if desirous to get rid at once of his visitor and his own thoughts, he took the shortest road to a little postern-gate, which led into the extensive copsewood, through some part of which Clara had caused a walk to be cut to a little summer-house built of rough shingle, covered with creeping shrubs.

As Mowbray hastened through the garden, he met the old man by whom it was laboured, a native of the south country, and an old dependant on the family. "Have you seen my sister?" said Mowbray, hurrying words on each other with the eagerness of terror.

"What's your wull, Saint Ronan's?" answered the old man, at once dull of hearing, and slow of apprehension.

"Have you seen Miss Clara?" shouted Mowbray, and muttered an oath or two at the gardener's stupidity.

"In troth have I," replied the gardener, deliberately; "what suld ail me to see Miss Clara, Saint Ronan's?"

"When, and where?" eagerly demanded the querist.

"Ou, just yestreen, after tey-time—afore ye came hame yoursell galloping sae fast," said old Joseph.

"I am as stupid as he, to put off my time in speaking to such an old cabbage-stock," said Mowbray, and hastened on to the postern-gate already mentioned, leading from the garden into what was usually called Miss Clara's walk. Two or three domestics, whispering to each other, and with countenances that shewed grief, fear, and suspicion, followed their master, desirous to be employed, yet afraid to force their services on the fiery young man.

At the little postern he found some trace of her he sought. The pass-key of Clara was left in the lock. It was then a plain evidence that she must have passed that way; but at what hour, or for what purpose, Mowbray dared not conjecture. The path, after running a quarter of a mile or more through an open grove of oaks and sycamores, attained the verge of the large brook, and became there steep and rocky, difficult to the infirm, and alarming to the nervous; often approaching the brink of a precipitous ledge of rock, which in this place overhung the stream, in some places brawling and foaming in hasty currents, and in others seeming to slumber in deep and circular eddies. The temptations which this dangerous scene must have offered an excited and desperate spirit, came on Mowbray like the blight of the Simoom, and he stood a moment to gather breath and overcome these horrible anticipations, ere he was able to proceed. His attendants felt the same apprehension. "Puir thing—puir thing!—O, God send she may not have been left to hersell!—God send she may have been upholden!" were whispered by Patrick to the maidens, and by them to each other.

At this moment the old gardener was heard behind them, shouting, "Master—Saint Ronan's—Master—I have fund—I have fund—"

"Have you found my sister?" exclaimed the brother, with breathless anxiety.

The old man did not answer till he came up, and then, with his usual slowness of delivery, he replied to his master's repeated inquiries, "Na, I haena fund Miss Clara, but I hae fund something ye wad be wae to lose—your braw hunting knife."

He put the implement into the hand of its owner, who, recollecting the circumstances under which he had flung it from him last night, and the now too probable consequences of that interview, bestowed on it a deep imprecation, and again hurled it from him into the brook. The domestics looked at each other, and recollecting each at the same time that the knife was a favourite tool of their master, who was rather curious in such articles, had little doubt that his head was affected, in a temporary way at least, by his anxiety on his sister's account. He saw their confused and inquisitive looks, and assuming as much composure and presence of mind as he could command, directed Martha, and her female companions, to return and search the walks on the other side of Shaws-Castle; and, finally, ordered Patrick back to ring the bell, "which," he said, assuming a confidence that he was far from entertaining, "might call Miss Mowbray home from some of her long walks." He farther desired his groom and horses might meet him at the Clattering Brig, so called from a noisy cascade which was formed by the brook, above which was stretched a small foot-bridge of planks. Having thus shaken off his attendants, he proceeded himself, with all the speed he was capable of exerting, to follow out the path in which he was at present engaged, which, being a favourite walk with his sister, she might perhaps have adopted from mere habit, when in a disturbance of mind, which, he had too much reason to fear, must have put choice out of the question.

He soon reached the summer-house, which was merely a seat covered overhead and on the sides, open in front, and neatly paved with pebbles. This little bower was perched, like a hawk's nest, almost upon the edge of a projecting crag, the highest point of the line of rock which we have noticed; and had been selected by poor Clara, on account of the prospect which it commanded down the valley. One of her gloves lay on the small rustic table in the summer-house. Mowbray caught it eagerly up. It was wet—the preceding day had been dry; so that, had she forgot it there in the morning, or in the course of the day, it could not have been in that state. She had assuredly been there during the night, when it rained heavily.

Mowbray, thus assured that Clara had been in this place, while her passions and fears were so much afloat as they must have been at her flight from her father's house, cast a hurried and terrified glance from the brow of the precipice into the deep stream that eddied below. It seemed to him that, in the sullen roar of the water, he heard the last groan of his sister—the foam-flakes caught his eye, as if they were a part of her garments. But a closer examination shewed that there was no trace of such a catastrophe. Descending the path on the other side of the bower, he observed a foot-print in a place where the clay was moist and tenacious, which, from the small size, and the shape of the shoe, appeared to him must be a trace of her whom he sought. He hurried forward, therefore, with as much speed, as yet permitted him to look out keenly for similar impressions, of which it seemed to him he remarked several; although less perfect than the former, being much obliterated by the quantity of rain that had since fallen,—a circumstance seeming to prove that several hours had elapsed since the person had passed.

At length, through the various turnings and windings of a long and romantic path, Mowbray found himself, without having received any satisfactory intelligence, by the side of the brook, called Saint Ronan's Burn, at the place where it was crossed by foot-passengers, by the Clattering Brig, and by horsemen through a ford a little lower. At this point the fugitive might have either continued her wanderings through her paternal woods, by a path, which, after winding about a mile, returned to Shaws-Castle, or she might have crossed the bridge, and entered a broken horse-way, common to the public, leading to the Aulton of Saint Ronan's.

Mowbray, after a moment's consideration, concluded that the last was her most probable option. He mounted his horse, which the groom had brought down according to order, and commanding the man to return by the foot-path, which he himself could not examine, he proceeded to ride towards the ford. The brook was swollen during the night, and the groom could not forbear intimating to his master, that there was considerable danger in attempting to cross it. But Mowbray's mind and feelings were too high-strung to permit him to listen to cautious counsel. He spurred the snorting and reluctant horse into the torrent, though the water, rising high on the upper side, broke both over the pummel and the croupe of his saddle. It was by exertion of great strength and sagacity, that the good horse kept the ford-way. Had the stream forced him down among the rocks, which lie below the crossing-place, the consequences must have been fatal. Mowbray, however, reached the opposite side in safety, to the joy and admiration of the servant, who stood staring at him during the adventure. He then rode hastily towards the Aulton, determined, if he could not hear tidings of his sister in that village, that he would spread the alarm, and institute a general search after her, since her elopement from Shaws-Castle could, in that case, no longer be concealed. We must leave him, however, in his present state of uncertainty, in order to acquaint our reader with the reality of those evils, which his foreboding mind and disturbed conscience could only anticipate.

Chapter Twelve

THE CATASTROPHE

What sheeted ghost is wandering through the storm?
For never did a maid of middle-earth
Choose such a time or spot to vent her sorrows.
Old Play

GRIEF, Shame, Confusion, and Terror, had contributed to overwhelm the unfortunate Clara Mowbray, at the moment when she parted with her brother, after the stormy and dangerous interview which it was our task to record in a former chapter. For years, her life, her whole tenor of thought, had been haunted by the terrible apprehension of a discovery, and now the thing which she feared had come upon her. The extreme violence of her brother, which went so far as to menace her personal safety, had joined to the previous conflict of passions, to produce a rapture of fear, which probably left her no other free agency, than that which she derived from the blind instinct which urges flight, as the readiest resource in danger.

We have no means of exactly tracing the course of this unhappy young woman. It is probable she fled from Shaws-Castle, on hearing the arrival of Mr Touchwood's carriage, which she might mistake for that of Lord Etherington; and thus, while Mowbray was looking forward to the happier prospects which the traveller's narrative seemed to open, his sister was contending with rain and darkness, amidst the difficulties and dangers of the mountain path which we have described. These were so great, that a young woman more delicately brought up, must either have lain down exhausted, or have been compelled to turn her steps back to the residence she had abandoned. But the solitary wanderings of Clara had inured her to fatigue and to night-walks; and the deeper causes of terror which urged her to flight, rendered her insensible to the perils of her way. She had passed the bower, as was evident from her glove remaining there, and had crossed the foot-bridge; though it was almost wonderful, that, in so dark a night, she should have followed with such accuracy a track, where missing a single turn by a cubit's length might have precipitated her into eternity.

It is probable, that Clara's spirits and strength began in some degree to fail her, after she had proceeded a little way on the road to the Aulton; for she had stopped at the solitary cottage inhabited by the old female pauper, who had been for a time the hostess of the penitent and dying Hannah Irwin. Here, as the inmate of the cottage acknowledged, she had made some knocking, and she owned she had heard her moan bitterly, as she entreated for admission. The old hag was one of those whose hearts adversity turns to very stone, and obstinately kept her door shut, impelled more probably by general hatred to the human race, than by the superstitious fears which seized her; although she perversely argued that she was startled at the supernatural melody and sweetness of tone, with which the benighted wanderer made her supplication. She admitted, that when she heard the poor petitioner turn from the door, her heart was softened, and she did open with the intention of offering her, at least, a shelter; but that "before she could hirple to the door, and get the bar taken down," the unfortunate supplicant was not to be seen; which strengthened the old woman's opinion, that the whole was a delusion of Satan.

It is conjectured, that the repulsed wanderer made no other attempt to awaken pity or obtain shelter, until she came to Mr Cargill's Manse, in the upper room of which a light was still burning, owing to a cause which requires some explanation.

The reader is aware of the reasons which induced Bulmer, or the titular Lord Etherington, to withdraw from the country the sole witness, as he conceived, who could, or at least who might choose, to bear witness to the fraud which he had practised on the unfortunate Clara Mowbray. Of three persons present at the marriage, besides the parties, the clergyman was completely deceived. Solmes he conceived to be at his own exclusive devotion; and therefore, if by his means this Hannah Irwin could be removed from the scene, he argued plausibly that all evidence to the treachery which he had practised would be effectually stifled. Hence his agent, Solmes, had received a commission, as the reader may remember, to effect her removal without loss of time, and had reported to his master that his efforts had been effectual.

But Solmes, since he had fallen under the influence of Touchwood, was constantly employed in counteracting the schemes which he seemed most active in forwarding, while the traveller enjoyed (to him an exquisite gratification) the amusement of countermining, as fast as Bulmer could mine, and had in prospect the pleasing anticipation of blowing up the pioneer with his own petard. For this purpose, so soon as Touchwood learned that his house was to be applied to for the original deeds left in charge by the deceased Earl of Etherington, he expedited a letter, directing that only the copies should be sent, and thus rendered nugatory Bulmer's desperate design of destroying that evidence. For the same reason, when Solmes announced to him his master's anxious wish to have Hannah Irwin conveyed out of the country, he appointed him to cause the sick woman to be carefully transported to the Manse, where Mr Cargill was easily induced to give her temporary refuge.

To this good man, who might be termed an Israelite without guile, the distress of the unhappy woman would have proved a sufficient recommendation; nor was he likely to have inquired whether her malady might not be infectious, or to have made any of those other previous investigations which are sometimes clogs upon the bounty or hospitality of more prudent philanthropists. But, to stimulate him yet farther, Mr Touchwood informed him by letter, that the patient (not otherwise unknown to him) was possessed of certain most material information affecting a family of honour and consequence, and that he himself, with Mr Mowbray of Saint Ronan's in the quality of a magistrate, intended to be at the Manse that evening, to take her declaration upon this important subject. Such, indeed, was the traveller's purpose, which might have been carried into effect but for his own self-important love of manœuvring on the one part, and the fiery impatience of Mowbray on the other, which, as the reader knows, sent the one at full gallop to Shaws-Castle, and obliged the other to follow him post haste. This necessity he intimated to the clergyman by a note, which he dispatched express as he himself was in the act of stepping into the chaise. He requested, that the most particular attention should be paid to the invalid—promised to be at the Manse with Mr Mowbray early on the morrow—and, with the lingering and inveterate self-conceit which always induced him to conduct everything with his own hand, directed his friend, Mr Cargill, not to proceed to take the sick woman's declaration or confession until he arrived, unless in case of extremity.

It had been an easy matter for Solmes to transfer the invalid from the wretched cottage to the clergyman's Manse. The first appearance of the associate of much of her guilt had indeed terrified her; but he scrupled not to assure her, that his penitence was equal to her own, and that he was conveying her where their joint deposition would be formally received, in order that they might, so far as possible, atone for the evil of which they had been jointly guilty. He also promised her kind usage for herself, and support for her children; and she willingly accompanied him to the clergyman's residence, he himself resolving to abide in concealment the issue of the mystery, without again facing his master, whose star, as he well discerned, was about to shoot speedily from its exalted sphere.

The clergyman visited the unfortunate patient, as he had done frequently during her residence in his vicinity, and desired that she might be carefully attended. During the whole day, she seemed better; but, whether the means of supporting her exhausted frame had been too liberally administered, or whether the thoughts which gnawed her conscience had returned with double severity when she was released from the pressure of immediate want, it is certain that, about midnight, the fever began to gain ground, and the person placed in attendance on her came to inform the clergyman, then deeply engaged with the siege of Ptolemais, that she doubted if the woman would live till morning, and that she had something lay heavy at her heart, which she wished, as the emissary expressed it, "to make a clean breast of" before she died, or lost possession of her senses.

Awakened by such a crisis, Mr Cargill at once became a man of this world, clear in his apprehension, and cool in his resolution, as he always was when the path of duty lay before him. Comprehending, from the various hints of his friend Touchwood, that the matter was of the last consequence, his own humanity, as well as inexperience, dictated his sending for skilful assistance. His man-servant was accordingly dispatched on horseback to the Well for Dr Quackleben; while, upon the suggestion of one of his maids, "that Mrs Dods was an uncommon skeely body about a sick-bed," the wench was dismissed to supplicate the assistance of the gudewife of the Cleikum, which she was not, indeed, wont to refuse wherever it could be useful. The male emissary proved, in Scottish phrase, a "corbie messenger;" for either he found not the doctor, or he found him better engaged than to attend the sick-bed of a pauper, at a request which promised such slight remuneration as that of a parish minister. But the female ambassador was more successful; for, though she found our friend Luckie Dods preparing for bed at an hour unusually late, in consequence of some anxiety on account of Mr Touchwood's unexpected absence, the good old dame only growled a little about the minister's fancies in taking puir bodies into his own house; and then, instantly donning cloak, hood, and pattens, marched down the gate with all the speed of the good Samaritan, one maid bearing the lantern before her, while the other remained to keep the house, and to attend to the wants of Mr Tyrrel, who engaged willingly to sit up to receive Mr Touchwood.

But, ere Dame Dods had arrived at the Manse, the patient had summoned Mr Cargill to her presence, and required him to write her confession while she had life and breath to make it.

"For I believe," she added, raising herself in the bed, and rolling her eyes wildly around, "that, were I to confess my guilt to one of a less sacred character, the Evil Spirit, whose servant I have been, would carry away his prey, both body and soul, before they had severed from each other, however short the space that they must remain in partnership!"

Mr Cargill would have spoken some ghostly consolation, but she answered with pettish impatience, "Waste not words—waste not words!—Let me speak that which I must tell, and sign it with my hand; and do you, as the more immediate servant of God, and therefore bound to bear witness to the truth, take heed you write that which I tell you, and nothing else. I desired to have told this to Saint Ronan's —I have even made some progress in telling it to others—but I am glad I broke short off—for I know you, Josiah Cargill, though you have long forgotten me."

"It may be so," said Cargill. "I have indeed no recollection of you."

"You once knew Hannah Irwin, though," said the sick woman; "who was companion and relation to Miss Clara Mowbray, and who was present with her on that sinful night, when she was wedded in the kirk of Saint Ronan's."

"Do you mean to say that you are that person?" said Cargill, holding the candle so as to throw some light on the face of the sick woman. "I cannot believe it."

"No?" replied the penitent; "there is indeed a difference between wickedness in the act of carrying through its successful machinations, and wickedness surrounded by all the horrors of a death-bed!"

"Do not yet despair," said Cargill. "Grace is omnipotent—to doubt this is in itself a great crime."

"Be it so!—I cannot help it—my heart is hardened, Mr Cargill; and there is something here," she pressed her bosom, "which tells me that, with prolonged life and renewed health, even my present agonies would be forgotten, and I should become the same I have been before. I have rejected the offer of grace, Mr Cargill, and not through ignorance, for I have sinned with my eyes open. Care not for me, then, who am a mere outcast." He again endeavoured to interrupt her, but she continued, "Or if you really wish my welfare, let me relieve my bosom of that which presses it, and it may be that I shall then be better able to listen to you. You say you remember me not—but if I tell you how often you refused to perform in secret the office which was required of you—how much you urged that it was against your canonical rules—if I name the argument to which you yielded—and remind you of your purpose, to acknowledge your transgression to your brethren in the church courts, to plead your excuse, and submit to their censure, which you said could not be a light one—you will be then aware, that, in the voice of the miserable pauper, you hear the words of the once artful, gay, and specious Hannah Irwin."

"I allow it—I allow it!" said Mr Cargill; "I admit the tokens, and believe you to be indeed her whose name you assume."

"Then one painful step is over," said she; "for I would ere now have lightened my conscience by confession, saving for the cursed pride of spirit, which was ashamed of poverty, though not of guilt.—Well—In these arguments, which were urged to you by a youth best known to you by the name of Francis Tyrrel, though more properly entitled to that of Valentine Bulmer, we practised on you a base and gross deception.—Did you not hear some one sigh?—I trust there is no one in the room—I trust I shall die when my confession is signed and sealed, without my name being dragged through the public—I hope ye bring not in your menials to gaze on my abject misery—I cannot brook that."

She paused and listened; for the ear, usually deafened by pain, is sometimes, on the contrary, rendered morbidly acute. Mr Cargill assured her, there was no one present but himself. "O most unhappy woman," he said, "what does your introduction prepare me to expect?"

"Your expectation, be it ever so ominous, shall be fully satisfied. That Bulmer, when he told you that a secret marriage was necessary to Miss Mowbray's honour, thought that he was imposing on you—But he told you a fatal truth, so far as concerned Clara. She had indeed fallen, but Bulmer was not her seducer—knew nothing of the truth of what he so strongly asseverated."

"*He* was not her lover, then?—And how came he, then, to press to marry her?—Or, how came you—"

"Hear me—but question not.—Bulmer had gained the advantage over me which he pretended to have had over Clara. From that moment my companion's virtue became at once the object of my envy and hatred; yet, so innocent were the lovers, that, despite of the various arts which I used to entrap them, they remained guiltless until the fatal evening when Tyrrel met Clara for the last time ere he removed from the neighbourhood—and then the devil and Hannah Irwin triumphed. Much there was of remorse—much of resolutions of separation, until the church should unite them—but these only forwarded my machinations—for I was determined she should wed Bulmer, not Tyrrel."

"Wretch!" exclaimed the clergyman; "and had you not then done enough? Why did you expose the paramour of one brother to become the wife of another?"

She paused, and answered sullenly, "I had my reasons—Bulmer had treated me with scorn—He told me plainly, that he used me but as a stepping-stone to his own purposes; and that these finally centred in wedding Clara.—I was resolved he should wed her, and take with her misery and infamy to his bed."

"This was too horrible," said Cargill, endeavouring, with a trembling hand, to make minutes of her confession.

"Ay," said the sick woman, "but I contended with a master of the game, who played me stratagem for stratagem. If I destined for him a dishonoured wife, he contrived, by his agent Solmes, to match me with a husband imposed on me by his devices as a man of fortune,—a wretch who maltreated me—plundered me—sold me.—Oh! if fiends laugh, as I have heard they can, what a jubilee of scorn will there be, when Bulmer and I enter their place of torture!—Hark!—I am sure of it—some one draws breath, as if shuddering!"

"You will distract yourself if you give way to these fancies. Be calm—speak on—but, oh! at last, and for once, speak the truth!"

"I will, for it will best gratify my hatred against him, who, having first robbed me of my virtue, made me a sport and a plunder to the basest of the species. For that I wandered here to unmask him. I had heard he again stirred his suit to Clara, and I came here to tell young Mowbray the whole.—But do you wonder that I shrunk from doing so till this last decisive moment?—I thought of my conduct to Clara, and how could I face her brother?—And yet I hated her not after she had lost the advantage over me—and I was sorry that she was not to fall to the lot of a better man than Bulmer;—and I pitied her after she was rescued by Tyrrel, and prevailed on you to conceal her marriage—"

"I remember," answered Cargill, "alleging danger from her family. I did conceal it, until reports that she was again to be married reached my ears."

"Well, then," said the sick woman, "Clara Mowbray ought to forgive me—since what ill I have done her was inevitable.—I must see her, Mr Cargill—I must see her before I die—I shall never pray till I see her—I will never profit by word of godliness till I see her! If I cannot obtain the pardon of a worm like myself, how can I hope for that of——"

She started at these words with a faint scream; for slowly, and with a feeble hand, the curtains of the bed opposite to the side at which Cargill sat, were opened, and the figure of Clara Mowbray, her clothes and long hair drenched and dripping with rain, stood by the bedside. The dying woman sat upright, her eyes starting from their sockets, her lips quivering, her face pale, her emaciated hands grasping the bed-clothes, as if to support herself, and looking as much aghast as if her confession had called up an apparition of her betrayed friend.

"Hannah Irwin," said Clara, with her usual sweetness of tone, "my early friend—my unprovoked enemy!—Betake thee to Him who hath pardon for us all, and betake thee with confidence—for I pardon thee as freely as if you had never wronged me—as freely as I desire my own pardon.—Farewell—Farewell!"

She retired from the room ere the clergyman could convince himself that it was more than a phantom which he beheld. He ran down stairs—he summoned assistants, but no one would attend his call; for the deep ruckling groans of the patient satisfied every one that she was breathing her last; and Mrs Dods, with the maid-servant, ran into the bed-room, to witness the death of Hannah Irwin, which shortly after took place.

That event had scarce occurred, when the maid-servant who had been left in the inn, came down in great terror to acquaint her mistress, that a lady had entered the house like a ghost, and was dying in Mr Tyrrel's room. The truth of the story we must tell our own way.

In the irregular state of Miss Mowbray's mind, a less violent impulse than that which she had received from her brother's arbitrary violence, added to the fatigues, dangers, and terrors of her night walk, might have exhausted the powers of her body, and alienated those of her mind. We have before said, that the lights in the clergyman's house had probably attracted her attention, and in the temporary confusion of a family, never remarkable for its regularity, she easily mounted the stairs, and entered the sick chamber undiscovered, and thus overheard Hannah Irwin's confession, a tale sufficient to have greatly aggravated her mental malady.

We have no means of knowing whether she actually sought Tyrrel, or whether it was, as in the former case, the circumstance of a light still burning where all around was dark, that attracted her; but her next apparition was close by the side of her unfortunate lover, then deeply engaged in writing, when something suddenly gleamed on a large, old-fashioned mirror, which hung on the wall opposite. He looked up, and saw the figure of Clara, holding a light (which she had taken from the passage) in her extended hand. He stood for an instant with his eyes fixed on this fearful shadow, ere he dared turn round on the substance which was thus reflected. When he did so, the fixed and pallid countenance almost impressed him with the belief that he saw a vision, and he shuddered when, stooping beside him, she took his hand. "Come away!" she said, in a hurried voice—"come away—my brother follows to kill us both. Come, Tyrrel, let us fly—we shall easily escape him.—Hannah Irwin is on before—but, if we are overtaken, I will have no more fighting—you shall promise me that—we have had but too much of that—but you will be wise in future."

"Clara Mowbray!" exclaimed Tyrrel. "Alas! is it thus?—Stay—do not go," for she turned to make her escape—"stay—stay—sit down."

"I must go," she replied, "I must go—I am called—Hannah Irwin is gone before to tell all, and I must follow. Will you not let me go?—Nay, if you will hold me by force, you know I must sit down—but you will not be able to keep me for all that."

A convulsive fit followed, and seemed, by its violence, to explain that she was indeed bound for the last and darksome journey. The maid, who at length answered Tyrrel's earnest and repeated summons, fled terrified at the scene she witnessed, and carried to the Manse the alarm which we before mentioned.

The old landlady was compelled to exchange one scene of sorrow for another, wondering within herself what fatality could have marked this single night with so much misery. When she arrived at home, what was her astonishment to find there the daughter of the house, which, even in their alienation, she had never ceased to love, in a state little short of distraction, and tended by Tyrrel, whose state of mind seemed scarce more composed than that of the unhappy patient. The oddities of Mrs Dods were merely the rust which had indeed accumulated upon her character, but without impairing its native strength and energy; and her sympathies were not of a kind acute enough to disable her from thinking and acting as decisively as circumstances required.

"Mr Tyrrel," she said, "this is nae sight for men folk—ye maun rise and gang to another room."

"I will not stir from her," said Tyrrel—"I will not remove from her either now, or as long as she or I may live."

"That will be nae lang space, Master Tyrrel, if ye winna be ruled by common sense."

Tyrrel started up, as if half comprehending what she said, but remained motionless.

"Come, come," said the compassionate landlady; "do not stand looking on a sight sair enough to break a harder heart than yours, hinny—your ain sense tells ye, ye canna stay here—Miss Clara shall be well cared for, and I'll bring word to your room-door frae half-hour to half-hour how she is."

The necessity of the case was undeniable, and Tyrrel suffered himself to be led to another apartment, leaving Miss Mowbray to the care of the hostess and her female assistants. He counted the hours in an agony, less by the watch than by the visits which Mrs Dods, faithful to her promise, made from interval to interval, to tell him that Clara was no better—that she was worse—and, at last, that she did not think that she could live over morning. It required all the deprecatory influence of the good landlady to restrain Tyrrel, who, calm and cold on common occasions, was proportionally fierce and impetuous when his passions were afloat, from bursting into the room, and ascertaining, with his own eyes, the state of the beloved patient. At length there was a long interval—an interval of hours—so long, indeed, that Tyrrel caught from it the agreeable hope that Clara slept, and that sleep might bring refreshment both to mind and body. Mrs Dods, he concluded, was prevented from moving, for fear of disturbing her patient's slumber; and, as if actuated by the same feeling which he imputed to her, he ceased to traverse his apartment, as his agitation had hitherto dictated, and throwing himself into a chair, forbore to move even a finger, and withheld his respiration as much as possible, just as if he had been seated by the pillow of the patient. Morning was far advanced, when his landlady appeared in his room with a grave and anxious countenance.

"Mr Tyrrel," she said, "ye are a Christian man."

"Hush, hush, for Heaven's sake!" he replied; "you will disturb Miss Mowbray."

"Naething will disturb her, puir thing," answered Mrs Dods; "they have mickle to answer for that brought her to this."

"They have—they have indeed," said Tyrrel, striking his forehead; "and I will see her avenged on every one of them!—Can I see her?"

"Better not—better not," said the good woman; but he burst from her, and rushed into the apartment.

"Is life gone?—Is every spark extinct?" he exclaimed eagerly to a country surgeon, a sensible man, who had been summoned from Marchthorn in the course of the night. The medical man shook his head—He rushed to the bedside, and was convinced by his own eyes that the being whose sorrows he had both caused and shared, was now insensible to all earthly calamity. He raised almost a shriek of despair, as he threw himself on the pale hand of the corpse, wet it with tears, devoured it with kisses, and played for a short time the part of a distracted person. At length, on the repeated expostulation of all present, he suffered himself to be again conducted to another apartment, the surgeon following, anxious to give such sad consolation as the case admitted of.

"As you are so deeply concerned for the untimely fate of this young lady," he said, "it may be some satisfaction to you, though a melancholy one, to know, that it has been occasioned by a pressure on the brain, probably accompanied by a suffusion; and I feel authorized in stating, from the symptoms, that if life had been spared, reason would, in all probability, never have returned. In such a case, sir, the most affectionate relation must own, that death, in comparison to life, is a mercy."

"Mercy?" answered Tyrrel; "but why, then, is it denied to me?—I know—I know!—My life is spared till I revenge her."

He started from his seat, and rushed eagerly down stairs. But, as he was about to rush from the door of the inn, he was stopped by Touchwood, who had just alighted from his carriage, with an air of stern anxiety imprinted on his features, very different from their usual expression.

"Whither would ye? Whither would ye?" he said, laying hold of Tyrrel, and stopping him by force.

"For revenge—for revenge!" said Tyrrel; "Give way, I charge you, on your peril!"

"Vengeance belongs to God," replied the old man, "and his bolt has fallen.—This way—this way," he continued, dragging Tyrrel into the house. "Know," he said, so soon as he had led or forced him into a chamber, "that Mowbray of Saint Ronan's has met Bulmer within this half hour, and has killed him on the spot."

"Killed whom?" answered the bewildered Tyrrel.

"Valentine Bulmer, the titular Earl of Etherington."

"You bring tidings of death to the house of death," answered Tyrrel; "and there is nothing in this world left that I should live for."

Chapter Thirteen

CONCLUSION

Here come we to our close—for that which follows
Is but the tale of dull, unvaried misery.
Steep crags and headlong linns may court the pencil,
Like sudden haps, dark plots, and strange adventures;
But who would paint the dull and fog-wrapt moor,
In its long track of sterile desolation?

Old Play

WHEN MOWBRAY crossed the brook, as we have already detailed, his mind was in that wayward and uncertain state, which seeks something whereon to vent the self-engendered rage with which it labours like a volcano before eruption. On a sudden, a shot or two, followed by loud voices and laughing, reminded him he had promised, at that hour, and in that sequestered place, to decide a bet respecting pistol-shooting, to which the titular Lord Etherington, Jekyl, and Captain MacTurk, to whom such a pastime was peculiarly congenial, were parties as well as himself. The prospect this recollection afforded him, of vengeance on the man whom he regarded as the author of his sister's wrongs, was, in the present state of his mind, too tempting to be relinquished; and, setting spurs to his horse, he rushed through the copse to the little glade, where he found the other parties, who, despairing of his arrival, had already begun their amusement. A jubilee shout was set up as he approached.

"Here comes Mowbray, dripping, py Cott, like a watering-pan," said Captain MacTurk.

"I fear him not," said Etherington, (we may as well still call him so;) "he has ridden too fast to have steady nerves."

"We will soon see that, my Lord Etherington, or rather Mr Valentine Bulmer," said Mowbray, springing from his horse, and throwing the bridle over the bough of a tree.

"What does this mean, Mr Mowbray?" said Etherington, drawing himself up, while Jekyl and Captain MacTurk looked at each other in surprise.

"It means, sir, that you are a rascal and impostor," replied Mowbray, "who have assumed a name to which you have no right."

"That, Mr Mowbray, is an insult I cannot carry farther than this spot," said Etherington.

"If you had been willing to do so, you should have carried with it something still harder to be borne," answered Mowbray.

"Enough, enough, my good sir; no use in spurring a willing horse.

—Jekyl, you will have the kindness to stand by me in this matter."

"Certainly, my lord," said Jekyl.

"And, as there seems to be no chance of taking up the matter amicably," said the pacific Captain MacTurk, "I will be most happy, so help me, to assist my worthy friend, Mr Mowpray of Saint Ronan's, with my countenance and advice.—Very goot chance that we were here with the necessary weapons, since it would have been an unpleasant thing to have such an affair long upon the stomach, any more than to settle it without witnesses."

"I would fain know first," said Jekyl, "what all this sudden heat has arisen about."

"About nothing," said Etherington, "except a mare's nest of Mr Mowbray's discovering. He always knew his sister played the mad-woman, and he has now heard a report, I suppose, that she has likewise in her time played the —— fool."

"O, crimini!" cried Captain MacTurk, "my goot Captain, let us pe loading and measuring out—for, by my soul, if these sweetmeats be passing between them, it is only the twa ends of a handkercher that can serve the turn—Cot tamn!"

With such friendly intentions, the ground was hastily meted out. Each was well known as an excellent shot; and the Captain offered a bet to Jekyl of a mutchkin of Glenlivat, that both would fall by the first fire. The event shewed that he was nearly right; for the ball of Lord Etherington grazed Mowbray's temple, at the very second of time when Mowbray's pierced his heart. He sprung a yard from the ground, and fell down a dead man. Mowbray stood fixed like a pillar of stone, his arm dropped to his side, his hand still clenched on the weapon of death, reeking at the touch-hole and muzzle.—Jekyl ran to raise and support his friend, and Captain MacTurk, having adjusted his spectacles, stooped on one knee to look him in the face. "We should have had Quackleben here," he said, wiping his glasses, and returning them to the shagreen case, "though it would have been only for form's sake—for he is as dead as a toor-nail, poor boy.—But come, Mowbray, my bairn," he said, taking him by the arm, "we must pe ganging our ain gait, you and me, before waur comes of it. I have a bit powney here, and you have your horse till we get to Marchthorn.—Captain Jekyl, I wish you a good morning. Will you have my umbrella back to the inn, for I surmeese it is going to rain?"

Mowbray had not ridden a hundred yards with his guide and companion, when he drew his bridle, and refused to proceed a step further, till he had learned what was become of Clara. The Captain began to find he had a very untractable pupil to manage, when, while they were arguing together, Touchwood drove past in his hack chaise.

As soon as he recognized Mowbray, he stopped the carriage to inform him that his sister was at the Aulton, which he had learned from finding there had been a messenger sent from thence to the Well for medical assistance, which could not be afforded, the Esculapius of the place, Dr Quackleben, having been privately married to Mrs Blower on that morning, by Mr Chatterley, and having set out on the usual nuptial tour.

In return for this intelligence, Captain MacTurk communicated the fate of Lord Etherington. The old man earnestly pressed instant flight, for which he supplied at the same time ample means, engaging to furnish every kind of assistance and support to the unfortunate young lady; and representing to Mowbray, that if he staid in the vicinity, a prison would soon separate them. Mowbray and his companion then departed southwards upon the spur, reached London in safety, and from thence went together to the Peninsula, where the war was then at the hottest.

There remains little more to be told. Mr Touchwood is still alive, forming plans which have no object, and accumulating a fortune, for which he has apparently no heir. The old man had endeavoured to fix this character, as well as his general patronage, upon Tyrrel, but the attempt only determined the latter to leave the country; nor has he been since heard of, although the title and estates of Etherington lie vacant for his acceptance. It is the opinion of many, that he has entered into a Moravian mission, for the use of which he had previously drawn considerable sums.

Since Tyrrel's departure, no one pretends to guess what old Touchwood will do with his money. He often talks of his disappointments, but can never be made to understand, or at least to admit, that they were in some measure precipitated by his own talent for intrigue and manœuvring. Most people think that Mowbray of Saint Ronan's will be at last his heir. This gentleman has of late shewn one quality which usually recommends men to the favour of rich relations, namely, a close and cautious care of what is already his own. Captain MacTurk's military ardour having revived when they came within smell of gunpowder, the old soldier contrived not only to get himself on full pay, but to induce his companion to serve for some time as a volunteer. He afterwards obtained a commission, and nothing could be more strikingly different than was the conduct of the young Laird of Saint Ronan's and of Lieutenant Mowbray. The former, as we know, was gay, venturous, and prodigal; the latter lived on his pay, and even within it—denied himself comforts, and often decencies, when doing so could save a guinea; and turned pale with apprehension, if on any extraordinary occasion he ventured sixpence a corner at whist.

This meanness, or closeness of disposition, prevents his holding the high character to which his bravery and attention to his regimental duties might otherwise entitle him. The same close and accurate calculation of pounds, shillings, and pence, marked his communications with his agent Micklewhame, who might otherwise have had better pickings out of the estate of Saint Ronan's, which is now at nurse, and thriving full fast; especially since some debts, of rather an usurious character, have been paid up by Mr Touchwood, who contented himself with more moderate usage.

On the subject of this property, Mr Mowbray, generally speaking, gave such minute directions for acquiring and saving, that his old acquaintance, Mr Winterblossom, tapping his mosaic snuff-box with the sly look which intimated the coming of a good thing, was wont to say, that he had reversed the usual order of transformation, and was turned into a grub after having been a butterfly. After all, this narrowness, though a more ordinary modification of the spirit of avarice, may be founded on the same desire of acquisition, which in his earlier days sent him to the gaming-table.

But there was one remarkable instance in which Mr Mowbray departed from the rules of economy, by which he was guided in all others. Having acquired, for a large sum of money, the ground which he had formerly feued out for erection of the Hotel, lodging-houses, shops, &c. at Saint Ronan's Well, he sent positive orders for the demolition of the whole, nor would he permit the existence of any house of entertainment on his estate, except that in the Aulton, where Mrs Dods reigns with undisputed sway, her temper by no means improved either by time, or by the total absence of competition.

Why Mr Mowbray, with his acquired habits of frugality, thus destroyed a property which might have produced a considerable income, no one could pretend to affirm. Some said that he remembered his own early follies; and others, that he connected the buildings with the misfortunes of his sister. The vulgar reported, that Lord Etherington's ghost had been seen in the ball-room, and the learned talked of the association of ideas. But it all ended in this, that Mr Mowbray was independent enough to please himself, and that such was Mr Mowbray's pleasure.

The little watering-place has returned to its primitive obscurity; and lions and lionesses, with their several jackalls, blue surtouts, and bluer stockings, fiddlers and dancers, painters and amateurs, authors and critics, dispersed like pigeons by the demolition of a dove-cot, have sought other scenes of amusement and rehearsal, and have deserted SAINT RONAN'S WELL.

THE END

IN THE PRESS,

And speedily will be published,

BY ARCHIBALD CONSTABLE AND CO. EDINBURGH,

AN ACCOUNT OF

THE SIEGE OF PTOLEMAIS,

BEING A SPECIMEN OF THE AUTHOR'S GENERAL HISTORY OF THE CRUSADES;

BY

THE REV. JOSIAH CARGILL,

Minister of the Gospel at St Ronan's.

ESSAY ON THE TEXT

1. THE GENESIS OF *SAINT RONAN'S WELL* 2. THE COMPOSITION OF *SAINT RONAN'S WELL*: the Manuscript; from Manuscript to First Edition 3. THE LATER EDITIONS: octavo *Tales and Romances*; duodecimo *Tales and Romances*; eighteenmo *Tales and Romances*; the Interleaved Set and the Magnum 4. THE PRESENT TEXT: Capitalisation, Punctuation and Orthography; Verbal Emendations from the Manuscript; Later-edition Emendations; Editorial Emendations.

The following conventions are used in transcriptions from Scott's manuscript: deletions are enclosed ⟨thus⟩ and insertions ↑thus↓; superscript letters are lowered without comment; the letters 'NL' (new line) are Scott's own, and indicate that he wished a new paragraph to be opened in spite of running on the text, whereas the words '[new paragraph]' are editorial and indicate that Scott opened a new paragraph on a new line. The same conventions are used as appropriate for indicating variants between the printed editions.

1. THE GENESIS OF *SAINT RONAN'S WELL*

Sir Walter Scott was committed to *Saint Ronan's Well* before he knew either its name or its nature. Before *The Fortunes of Nigel* issued from the press on 27 May 1822, Scott had already arranged with his publisher, Archibald Constable, to produce four additional 'works of fiction'.[1] The following note among Constable's miscellaneous papers indicates the payment schedule for the four novels:

> New Works of the Author of Waverley (contracted for and not published:)
>
> | | |
> |---|---|
> | No 5 March 11th 1822 | £3000 |
> | No 6 May 3rd 1822 | £3000 |
> | No 7 Oct 8th „ | £2,500 |
> | No 8 March 10th 1823 | £2,500 |
> | | £11000.[2] |

In a letter to Constable on 5 February 1823, his partner Robert Cadell confirmed that 'we have large advances to him for *work to be done*'.[3] Scott delivered. In little more than two years from the original agreement, he wrote *Peveril of the Peak*, *Quentin Durward*, *Saint Ronan's Well*, and *Redgauntlet*.

According to Lockhart, the idea of *Saint Ronan's Well* began thus:

> As he, Laidlaw, and myself were lounging on our ponies, one fine calm afternoon, along the brow of the Eildon hill where it overhangs Melrose, he mentioned to us gaily the *row*, as he called it, that

> was going on in Paris about Quentin Durward, and said, "I can't but think that I could make better play still with something German." Laidlaw grumbled at this, and said, like a true Scotchman, "Na, na, sir—take my word for it, you are always best, like Helen MacGregor, when your foot is on your native heath; and I have often thought that if you were to write a novel, and lay the scene *here* in the very year you were writing it, you would exceed yourself."—"Hame's hame," quoth Scott, smiling, "be it ever sae hamely. There's something in what you say, Willie. What suppose I were to take Captain Clutterbuck for a hero, and never let the story step a yard beyond the village below us yonder?"—"The very thing I want," says Laidlaw; "stick to Melrose in July 1823."—"Well, upon my word," he answered, "the field would be quite wide enough—and *what for no?*"—(This pet phrase of Meg Dods was a *Laidlawism.*)—Some fun followed about the different real persons in the village that might be introduced with comical effect; but as Laidlaw and I talked and laughed over our worthy neighbours, his air became graver and graver; and he at length said, "Ay, ay, if one could look into the heart of that little cluster of cottages, no fear but you would find materials enow for tragedy as well as comedy. I undertake to say there is some real romance at this moment going on down there, that, if it could have justice done to it, would be well worth all the fiction that was ever spun out of human brains." He then told us a tale of dark domestic guilt which had recently come under his notice as Sheriff, and of which the scene was not Melrose, but a smaller hamlet on the other side of the Tweed, full in our view; but the details were not of a kind to be dwelt upon;—any thing more dreadful was never conceived by Crabbe, and he told it so as to produce on us who listened all the effect of another *Hall of Justice*.[4] It could never have entered into his head to elaborate such a tale; but both Laidlaw and I used to think that this talk suggested St Ronan's Well—though my good friend was by no means disposed to accept that as payment in full of his demand, and from time to time afterwards would give the Sheriff a little poking about "Melrose in July."[5]

Whatever Lockhart and Laidlaw may have thought, it is unlikely that this talk inspired *Saint Ronan's Well* for by July more than half of the first volume had been written. On 13 May 1823, Cadell wrote to Constable, 'Sir Walter has just been here in great glee—has begun the New—it is a Scotch story'.[6] On 19 May, Cadell continued, 'about this day week Ballantyne had a letter from Sir Walter (in consequence of one of Jas B saying after Quentin Durward was done he would have to pay off 20 men) saying "do not pay off any of your men—I shall give you new copy on my arrival in town"'.[7] Shortly afterwards, Cadell confirmed, 'the Printer has got 14 pages or about 1/5 of Volume first of the new—and great progress promised—no name—and titles to the Chapters as formerly'.[8] Scott's 'great progress' accelerated. On 24 May Cadell testified that 'the new work . . . goes on fast fast—30 pages of Copy in the hands of the Printer, and it is like to Continue'.[9] On the same date, Scott confirmed to Constable that 'Vol. I is pushing on at a handsome rate'.[10] And on 28 May, little more than two weeks after Scott had begun, Cadell wrote to Constable, 'half Volume first of the new book is in the hands of the Printer . . . the Author expects to make great progress before he leaves town—he writes a portion of it every day'.[11]

Scott returned corrected proofs of the early chapters with the following letter to James Ballantyne, his printer:

> I will be delighted to see you to-morrow with scrip and scrippage[12] at breakfast-time. The resemblance between Lovel[13] and Tyrrel is only that of situation. I have thoughts of making the tale tragic, having 'a humour to be cruel'.[14] It may go off, however. If not, it will be a pitiful tragedy, filled with the most lamentable mirth.[15] I find I must have a peep at the revise of sheet *c*; or, stay, insert the following addition and corrections:—
>
> *Del.* the alteration, line 2, p. 65, and *stet* as before, *I wadna*, etc.
>
> P. 66, line 2, add—And Nanny, ye may tell them he has an illustrated poem—illustrated—mind the word, Nanny, that is to be stuck as fou o' the likes o' that as ever turkey was larded wi' slabs o' bacon.[16]

Grierson dates this letter '*c. July* 1823'. But since Cadell's letter of 28 May revealed that half of the first volume was already in the hands of the printer, it seems more likely that Scott had corrected the proofs of page 66 in June.[17] Already on 13 June Cadell was making financial arrangements for *Saint Ronan's Well* and was planning to announce a 'New Work by Author of Waverley in July'.[18]

At this point, the rapid writing of *Saint Ronan's Well* was deliberately slowed. Scott had produced eight novels in the past three and a half years. *Quentin Durward*, which had followed *Peveril of the Peak* within five months, was not selling as quickly as they had hoped; on 13 June, Hurst, Robinson, Constable's co-publisher in London, still had 'upwards 1500 Copies' left, and no new orders.[19] Constable was worried about excessive supply, and Cadell agreed: '*We may gorge the public*'.[20] On 17 June Cadell wrote to his partner:

> I shall state to him with candour, that he must not stop with that now in hand—he must not allow himself to be beaten or appear to be beaten—he calculated on it being ready in August—I shall council to go on and finish it by Octr (V.I is almost done). . . . I shall further say to him 'go on Sir Walter with a Novel so soon as that now in hand is done, but perhaps it may be as well to calculate on its employing you say for 6 moth'.[21]

The following day, Cadell reported to Constable that he had used Ballantyne to convey his counsel:

> James B. repeated his and my conversation yesterday and on saying 'Mr Cadell is quite decided' he observed Sir Walter Knit his brows

> and look as if displeased supposing perhaps that something disagreeable was coming—B went on 'Mr C is quite decided as to your not stopping with the book now in progress but in place of finishing it in August finish it in October' the Baronets face brightened up instantly and he said 'that is exactly my own conclusion I shall write three sheets a week which is mere amusement to me—but between and October I shall think of something else' he said afterwards 'I will not stop the Novels I may take them more leisurely, but we must have something else to make up the blank' . . . he left me with the expression 'Sir Walter is quite pleased'.[22]

On 21 June Constable replied:

> I am glad the New Novel is not to be published till [November?] being fully satisfied—that Summer & Autumn are not by any means the Season for publishing books—the best things may be over done. I need not say to you how long and how anxiously it has been my wish—that the Great Unknown Should not come before the public quite so rapidly—there is however little harm done yet[23]

Scott, who began on a three-month pace, ended up taking nearly eight months to complete *Saint Ronan's Well.*

Among the letters for 1823, Grierson publishes two brief messages to James Ballantyne, noting that the manuscripts are 'stuck together as one'.[24] In the first, dated 'Friday', Scott says: 'I inclose the end of Vol. I. and have no doubt to redeem my pledge. I had a letter from Messrs. Constable & Co of a very satisfactory nature and trust we shall have no more rubs in that quarter'. In the second, endorsed 'Recd on 30 April 1823', he writes: 'I inclose the *finale* with a book and letter to ballast it which pray send safe'. Grierson believed that both notes refer to *Quentin Durward*, but while 'the *finale*' surely refers to *Quentin Durward*, which was completed at the end of April 1823, 'the end of Vol. I' refers to *Saint Ronan's Well.* The correct date of the *Saint Ronan's* note is almost certainly Friday, 12 September 1823. The reference in it to the satisfactory resolution of the 'rubs' with Constable and Co. is related to a letter of Tuesday, 9 September, from Constable to Cadell:

> I went to Abbotsford on Saturday after 12 & returned early yesterday. I found Sir Walter in the best health—& in no respect offended with me or at our later Correspondence and what passed on the Occasion was Calculated I hope to do no harm but to Cement & add to the Stability of our future dealings—St Ronans advances & the next after it is already chalked out.[25]

James C. Corson believes that the completion of Volume one of *Saint Ronan's Well* by early September means that 'Scott must have set it aside all summer and resumed it about September'.[26] But a complete suspension would be alien to Scott, who liked to keep his hand active. In mid-June, when the first volume was still incomplete, Scott planned to write three sheets a week, the equivalent of 13 pages of text, a paltry amount for him. On 19 August Constable testifies that *Saint Ronan's* is 'now in progress'.[27] It seems probable, then, that after a rapid start, Scott curtailed his work during the summer, finishing the first volume in late August or early September.

In a letter of 6 September 1823 to Constable, Cadell took up the question of the number of copies required, saying 'it is clear that we *overprint*'. He pointed out that of the 8180 copies of *Quentin Durward* that were sent to Hurst, Robinson, and Co., 1340 were still on hand. Robinson believed 'the anxiety of the public for these books is as high as ever', but so many readers now waited for the collected editions that 'the sale of the first editions are diminished'. Consequently, instead of the usual printing of 10,000, Cadell concludes:[28]

say H R Co	7000
our sale	2,400
	9,400
over book	400

Eventually, 7000 copies of *Saint Ronan's Well* were indeed shipped to Hurst, Robinson on 16 December.[29]

In September Scott's pace accelerated. In a letter that Grierson dates the 14th, Scott told Constable: 'I send you two proofs and a lot of copy. . . . The work is about half finishd or more'.[30] On the 19th, Constable wrote to Black, Young and Young, booksellers in London, 'With this we send you Volume 1st Complete of the New Work by the Author of Waverley we hope before 10 days pass to send the half of Volume 2d'.[31] On the 21st, Scott complained to Ballantyne: 'My difficulties are greatly increased by the proofs not being returnd in order of reading and I beg they may be so sent in future. I send you also a lot of copy.'.[32]

A lucky accident allows us to pinpoint Scott's further progress. Blurred markings from Scott's correspondence somehow got absorbed onto f. 150v of the manuscript. Among the few legible signifiers (when the sheet is held up to a mirror) are 'Abbotsford' and '15 Oct 1823', indicating that page 38 of Volume three (262 of the present text) had been completed by that date. On 29 October there is a sense of finality in his letter to Daniel Terry, the actor and director, when Scott says his 'last affair now in progress' is 'within, or may be easily compressed into, dramatic time; whether it is otherwise qualified for the stage, I cannot guess'.[33]

Scott was therefore on schedule for the planned publication in November.[34] Well into Volume three on 15 October, he normally would have completed the novel at the end of the month or in early November. But something happened. On 26 November, Constable wrote James Mitchell, bookseller in London, 'We fear that St Ronan's Well will hardly be ready at the time your leaving London',[35] and on 28 November, he told Keys and Co., London, 'all that we can say with certainty is this the work of the Author of Waverley now in progress is nearly done'.[36] What caused this unexpected delay? The biographies and letters reveal no untoward events in Scott's life at this time. I would suggest that the lengthy disagreement over the conclusion of *Saint Ronan's Well* and Scott's reluctant concession to alter the penultimate chapter in proof (see the discussion of this subject in 'The Present Text') pushed back the completion of the novel and, of course, its publication. In a letter that Grierson dates in November, but Corson places more convincingly in December,[37] Scott told Ballantyne there 'are but two or three pages more'.[38] Finally, after nearly eight months of work, *Saint Ronan's Well* was published in three volumes, post octavo, at one and a half guineas (£1.57), on 27 December 1823.[39]

2. THE COMPOSITION OF *SAINT RONAN'S WELL*

The Manuscript. Study of the manuscript provides a unique insight into the development of the text and the imagination of the artist. Scott's mind reveals itself in the handling of hundreds of minute particulars. The approximately 200,000 words of the extant manuscript of *Saint Ronan's Well* are written on 215 rectos and 156 versos of bifolia. Two leaves of manuscript (ff. 41 and 42), containing the end of Chapter 7 and the beginning of Chapter 8 (69.24–73.4), are missing. The main text is written on the rectos which are crammed full: Scott uses all practicable space, except for a slight break between chapters and at the end of volumes, and jams in additions and corrections above the line or along the left margin. Further additions and corrections appear on the versos, which may have anything from a single word to a full page of writing. In manuscript, the main text of the three volumes is written on the rectos of 70, 72, and 73 folios respectively, and 55, 53, and 48 of the versos contain additional matter. Each volume contains 13 chapters. There is a decrease in the number of changes as the manuscript progresses.[40]

If one counts everything, from a single letter that is crossed out to a paragraph-long addition, then there are approximately 3500 verbal changes in the manuscript. They are often dynamic and multi-layered but, for purposes of analysis, may be divided into several major categories.

1] *Narrative additions.* The most striking feature of Scott's manuscript is that he frequently adds new material and corrects old material; he rarely eliminates. He makes use of what he has, and increases it. Narrative additions range from a single word (Solmes is an '↑experienced↓' (317.39) valet) to paragraphs. On the most basic level, the narrator adds descriptive details: Meg has '↑grey eyes, thin lips↓' (8.13–14); Tyrrel's horse is put into a 'clean ↑and comfortable↓' stall (12.14); Tyrrel's avowal is '↑made without the least appearance of shame or retenue↓' (45.25–26); but Lady Binks disfigures her lovely face

'↑with sullenness↓' (52.17). Clara's countenance is described as antique: 'eyes something hollowed—care has dug caves for them'; Scott then adds, '↑caves of the most beautiful marble arched with jet↓' (54.40–41). Originally, the heraldic bearings of Scrogie Mowbray are described flippantly: '⟨the arms of your house being with a suitable difference born quarterly with God knows what⟩'; Scott revises in order to particularise: '↑a white lion for Mowbray to be born quarterly with three stunted or scrog bushes for Scrogie↓' (171.26–27).

On a more advanced level, the narrator adds description and interpretation together. Captain MacTurk went up and down '↑upon the points of his toes rising up on his instep with a jerk which at once expressed vexation and defiance↓' (105.4–6). In a defining moment, at the end of the chapter, 'Mediation', in which Tyrrel has displayed his generosity throughout, the narrator adds a final paragraph:

> ↑Tyrrel was neither unambitious nor without those feelings respecting personal consideration which are usually united with deep feeling and an ardent mind It was with trembling hand and with a watery eye but with a heart firmly resolved that he sealed and dispatchd the letter a step towards the resignation in favour of his mortal enemy of that rank and condition in life which was his own by right of inheritance but had so long hung in doubt betwixt them↓ (279.37–43)

A large proportion of the additional narrative material is humorous. For example, '⟨a hump backd⟩' postilion becomes an 'old fellow in a postilion's jacket, whose grey hairs escaped on each side of an old-fashioned velvet jockey-cap, and whose left shoulder was so considerably elevated above his head, that it seemed as if, with little effort, his ⟨head⟩ ↑neck↓ might have been tucked under his arm, like that of a roasted grouse-cock' (124.32–37). The humour is often conveyed by the introduction of an incongruous simile. For example, the various plays of a literary anthology were associated '⟨with as little regard to⟩ ↑like the passengers in a mail coach without the least attempt at selection or arrangement↓' (183.28–29). Likewise, in the final sentence of the manuscript, all the visitors to Saint Ronan's Well have '↑dispersed like pigeons by the demolition of a dove cot↓' (372.40). Humour also arises from those tumbling lists of things that seem to anticipate Dickens: 'for down came masons and murgeon-makers, and preachers and player-folk, and episcopals and methodists, ↑and fools and fiddlers and papists and pye bakers and doctors and drugsters↓' (21.1–3).

Narrative additions often reveal the thoughts and feelings of characters. Tyrrel is '↑somewhat surprised↓' (53.30–31). When threatened, Sir Bingo '↑thought it prudent somewhat to recoil↓' (75.5–6). Tyrrel answers Clara '↑in the bitterness of his heart↓' (85.2–3). And Scott adds three paragraphs to explain Mowbray's antipathy towards Tyrrel.

Scott's narrative additions often employ literary allusions, usually for purposes of humour and elucidation. The young men of the Helter Skelter and Wildfire Clubs cared little '↑for the exuberant frolics of Megs temper which were to them only "pretty Fanny's way"—the *dulces Amaryllidis irae*↓' (10.23–25). Likewise, '↑Nor must we omit among Megs steady customers "faithful amongst the unfaithful found" the copper-nosed sheriff-clerk↓' (10.32–33). Scott adds a paragraph on Lady Penelope's impersonation of Hermia, which he compares with Garrick's '↑going his rounds↓' (190.36–37). Similarly, he compares Etherington's behaviour with that of '↑a buck of the old school one of Congreves men of wit and pleasure about town↓' (315.14–15).

The narrator will sometimes add material at the end of a description to bring it into final focus. Thus, after presenting many vivid details about Winterblossom, the narrator concludes:

> ↑In a word he was possessd of some taste in the fine arts though both in painting and music it was rather of the technical kind than of that which warms the heart and elevates the feelings. There was indeed about Mr Winterblossom nothing that was either warm or elevated. He was shrewd selfish and sensual↓ ... (29.34–35)

All of these kinds of narrative addition—descriptive detail, interpretation, humour, the revelation of thoughts and feelings, literary allusion, and summation—can be observed in Scott's presentation of Josiah Cargill. Cargill is a potentially unattractive figure who commits a disastrous act, but Scott adds details throughout the manuscript to make him increasingly sympathetic. The narrator stresses that Cargill was '↑almost always solitary↓' (146.41) when young. When the mature Cargill falls in love with his female pupil, the narrator adds, '↑Every feeling heart will excuse a weakness which we will presently find carried with it its own severe punishment↓' (148.21–22), and then favourably contrasts Cargill's conduct with that of Jonathan Swift under similar circumstances. To balance the portrait, the narrator adds a passage on Cargill's '↑desultory longing after knowledge↓'that '↑promised little utility to mankind at large↓' (151.18–21). Nevertheless, his 'many ludicrous habits ↑tinged though they did not altogether obscure the natural civility of an amiable disposition as well as the acquired habits of politeness which he had learned↓' (151.25–27). Although his parishioners were sometimes '↑more astonished than edified by his learning↓', all '↑the neighbourhood acknowleged Mr Cargill's serious↓ and devout discharge of his ministerial duties' (151.18–20). To the epicurean Mr Touchwood who, like Dr Johnson, held

> ↑his dinner the most important business of the day Cargill did not act up to this definition and was therefore in the eyes of his new acquaintance so far ignorant and uncivilized—What then he was still a sensible intelligent man however abstemious and bookish↓. (158.41–159.2)

Near the end of the novel, the narrator reveals that the clergyman visited the suffering Anne Heggie '↑frequently during her residence in his vicinity↓' (361.14). There is much more. Throughout the manuscript, Scott's imagination becomes more fully engaged with its own creation, and he strives to present a balanced and complex portrait of Josiah Cargill.

One final example reveals the power of Scott's narrative additions. At the dramatic climax, when Clara and Tyrrel meet for the last time, Scott originally wrote, 'something ⟨familiarly touchd him on the Shoulder⟩'. Reconsidering, Scott writes,

> something ↑suddenly gleamd on ⟨the⟩ a large ⟨Glass mirr⟩ old fashiond mirror which hung on the wall opposite↓ He lookd up and saw the figure of Clara holding a light which (she had taken from the passage) in her extended hand. He stood for an instant with his eyes fixd on this ⟨hor⟩ fearful shadow ere he dared turn round on the substance ⟨of⟩ which was thus reflected. When he did so the fixd and pallid countenance almost impressd him with the belief that he saw a vision and he shudderd ... (365.42–366.6)

Thus, the master craftsman turns a familiar touch on the shoulder into a visionary experience.

2] *Expansion of speeches.* Scott frequently expands the speeches of his characters. The added words are not merely consistent with the speakers' other utterances; they are characteristic, expressing the essence of the speakers, and sometimes verging on self-parody. Mowbray adds that Winterblossom '↑won't stand the ironing↓' (37.7–8), complains about '↑unqualified↓' (73.42) people shooting on his lands, and ridicules Sir Bingo about his wagers. Lady Penelope adds another one of her literary allusions: '↑As Orlando leaves his verses in the forest of Ardennes↓' (55.32). Her duet of '↑dear . . . dearest . . . *dear*↓' (58.5–9) with Lady Binks is an afterthought of Scott's. The hypochondriacal Mrs Blower adds, Doctor Quackleben's instructor '↑wad ken something of my case↓' (60.2–3). When Clara is with the Wellers, she adds to her frequent use of animal imagery: 'My brother I suppose will bring his own peculiar regiment of bears which with ↑the usual assortment of monkeys seen in all caravans will complete the menagerie↓' (67.32–35). But when she is with her brother, she pleads, '↑there are but two of us on earth why should we make each other miserable↓' (219.40–41), an appeal that is repeated later in the text. Always itching for a fight, MacTurk adds, '↑and if you think I have used you like a spoon as you say↓' (117.18–19) and so forth in the bellicose vein. When asked about the Mowbrays of Saint Ronan's, Mr Cargill begins a disquisition on the fourteenth-century Duke of Norfolk. Characteristically, Etherington denigrates the Scots, ridicules his own father, mocks Jekyl's failures at gambling, and adds, '↑I'll bet the long odds↓' (290.16).

In contrast, Tyrrel laments the '↑insurmountable barrier his [Etherington's] own conduct↓' (268.27) has placed between the two brothers and renounces 'a rank which ↑is and↓ ought to be the more valuable to me because it involves . . . the fame of an honourd mother' (277.12–14).

The two characters who are given the most additional speech are Meg Dods and Peregrine Touchwood. Meg is prominent from the beginning, but Touchwood grows on Scott as the novel proceeds. Many of Touchwood's most memorable remarks are afterthoughts of Scott. He complains about the mercenary Scotsmen of today and about the weak tea at the Spa. He fears '↑I must have lost much blood↓'(259.25) after tumbling into Saunders Jaup's jaw-hole. He asks Mowbray, '↑you have porter I suppose or good old Scotch two-penny↓' (339.34–35). He refers to '↑what he [Scrogie] calld↓' his head (340.37). He fulminates against fasting. He insists upon proper attentions from Mowbray's servant, '↑and hark ye—get me a jug of barley-water to place by my bedside with the squeeze of a lemon—or stay you will make it as sour as Beelzebub—bring lemon on a saucer and I will mix it myself↓' (351.2–5).

With Meg, Scott's strategy is to grant her, after an already lengthy speech, a conclusive punch line. This happens at least four times, once even in a letter to James Ballantyne that Scott asked to be added to the manuscript material. The effect is like that of one of Dickens's villains popping his head back inside the door and making one more outrageous remark. Scott also adds considerable material to Meg's memorable confrontation with MacTurk and is often crafting her language, 'its an ill world since such ↑prick-my-dainty doings came in fashion↓' (106.43).

These speech expansions often pay particular attention to the language of country and of profession. For example, Micklewhame says, '↑but I doubt mickle if ⟨Miss Clara⟩ she would care a bodle for thae braw things Ye ken yoursell↓' and so forth (167.15–16), in dialect. When speaking to Mowbray about gaining money from Etherington, Micklewhame reverts to legalese.

3] *Exactness of meaning.* Scott makes mistakes, but he is not careless. He pays attention to minute particulars, corrects errors when he sees them, and improves details that are already adequate. The narrator claims that the prosperity of Scotland has accelerated over the last '↑half↓' century (1.11–12). The cottages of the poor, originally described as '⟨habitable⟩', are '↑inhabited, though scarce habitable↓' (3.30). Meg's 'linen' becomes '↑table-linen, bed-linen, and so forth↓' (7.2–3). Instead of '⟨eighteen pence⟩', Meg charges '↑3 shillings↓' for dinner (7.15). Nelly Trotter must '↑re↓pass the Aulton' (39.13). A pistol-case is 'six ⟨or eight⟩' inches broad (51.13). Mrs Blower is advised to take a '⟨thimbleful⟩ ↑table-spoonful↓' of spirits

(60.30–31). Later, Dr Quackleben gives her 'three ⟨spoon⟩ tea-spoonfulls'. As Sir Bingo approaches the duelling ground, his whistling '⟨soften⟩ sunk into silence' (115.22).

Meg gave Mr Bindloose '⟨twa⟩ ↑a↓ note' (127.27) for his troubles in Tyrrel's behalf. Mr Cargill thinks back to Thomas Mowbray, Duke of Norfolk, in the '⟨twelfth⟩ ↑14th↓' century (160.31). When Bulmer tricked Clara into marriage, he was an '*amoureux de* ⟨quinze⟩ ↑*seize*↓ *ans*' (240.34). Jekyl gives his young informer '⟨another half crown⟩ ↑sixpence↓' (287.30). Captain MacTurk describes fourteen little affairs, in which one was killed on the spot, one died of his wounds, '⟨three⟩ ↑two↓ severely wounded' (324.43), three slightly wounded, and so on. Mr Touchwood had thought no more of the Mowbrays till 'a ⟨mont⟩ year' (343.7) or so ago. Mowbray struck his '⟨shoulder⟩ forehead' (354.34) in an agony of remorse and fear. Mowbray and MacTurk depart '⟨northwards⟩ southwards' to London and eventually go together to the '⟨Continent⟩ Peninsula' (371.14–15).

The popular image of Scott as a natural genius, warbling his native woodnotes wild, is inadequate. Genius he may be, but he is also a painstaking craftsman, straining to communicate as precisely as he can.

4] *More vivid and appropriate words and phrases.* This category, though related to the preceding, is more subjective. Still, it shows in even greater detail that Scott is the dedicated craftsman, rejecting first (and second) thoughts, searching for the best expression. On the most basic level, a more precise and vivid word is substituted for a more general word. A '⟨ride⟩' becomes a canter (9.30); Tyrrel's '⟨walk⟩' (24.32) becomes sauntering. Meg's desire to '⟨communicate⟩' with Nelly becomes a longing to '↑pour forth↓' (25.18). Sir Bingo 'croaked' (36.1) instead of '⟨said⟩'. Tyrrel's drawings are composed of 'scratches' (46.21), not '⟨things⟩'. Mrs Blower's husband was as deep as any '⟨man⟩ skipper' (62.30). Mrs Blower imagines Clara '⟨riding⟩ ↑scampering↓' (66.10) on Leith sands. First, the '⟨paper⟩ ↑envelope↓' rustled under Etherington's fingers (316.38); shortly afterwards, the ⟨paper⟩ '↑letter of advice↓' (317.10) dropped from his hand. Clara was overwhelmed by 'Grief, Shame, Remorse, and ⟨Fear⟩ Terror' (358.22).

Scott often replaces a pronoun with its referent. Sir Bingo curses Touchwood, 'D—n ⟨him⟩ the old quiz' (197.33–34). Etherington mocks '⟨his⟩ ↑my brother's↓ merits' (237.13), but soon afterwards, '⟨my brother⟩' becomes the more appropriate 'my rival' (240.5). Tyrrel retaliates in a similar vein: '⟨he⟩ ↑his honour and conscience↓ will be easily satisfied' (277.42).

Scott seeks a truer or more appropriate word for one that is not quite right. Thus, Lady Penelope is described as '⟨virtuous⟩ ↑adorable↓' (40.42). Speaking ironically, Etherington desires that Tyrrel not be exposed to the temptations of rank and '⟨birth⟩ riches' (245.7). The old pauper woman mutters after Lady Penelope, 'geeing orders like

⟨master⟩ ↑mistress↓ and mair' (307.42). And when Tyrrel is forced to depart from the dying Clara, he is described as '⟨abandoning⟩ leaving Miss Mowbray to the care of the hostess and her female assistants' (367.6–7).

Scott refines his phrases and sentences with the same conscientiousness that he bestows upon individual words. Speaking of Lady Penelope's attempt to establish a civilised enclave at Saint Ronan's Well, the narrator begins to use the epigrammatic '*Rus in urbe*' (49.35), but Scott writes only '⟨Rus⟩' before revising to the more appropriate '*Urbs in rure*'. Meg changes the rather formal, 'You will maybe find ⟨it difficult to bring that about⟩', to 'You will maybe find ↑that easier said than dune↓'. For Touchwood's feast, Cargill changes into his '⟨preaching clothes⟩ ↑Sundays suit↓' (158.28). To describe Lady Pen's literary predilections, the narrator alters the conventional '⟨Blue Stocking⟩' to 'lady of the cerulean buskin' (205.16). Saunders Jaup's jaw-hole changes from '⟨ill savourd⟩' to an '↑odoriferous↓ filthy gulph' (257.26). Hannah Irwin describes how Etherington 'first ⟨seduced me⟩ robbed me of my virtue' (364.28), perhaps an indication of Scott's squeamishness about discussing sexual matters in print.

With regard to sexual matters, several of Scott's most interesting changes involve the relationship between Tyrrel and Clara. Speaking of her 'peace, happiness, and honour', Tyrrel says, 'They are dear to me sir as the ⟨apple of⟩ my eye-sight' (272.5). Apparently, Scott was going to write 'the apple of my eye', then realising the weakness of that cliché, changed it—by a process of association—to 'my eye-sight'. Looking at a picture of the young Clara, Tyrrel regrets the loss of her 'glance of ⟨joyous pleasure⟩ innocent gaiety'. And in the penultimate paragraph, Mowbray associates Saint Ronan's Well with '⟨those follies of his sis⟩ the misfortunes of his sister' (372.31–32).

Sometimes Scott's changes seem idiosyncratic. For example, when Mowbray and Etherington become deeply involved in gambling, '⟨luck⟩ fortune altogether deserted him who stood most in need of her favour' (168.31–32). Likewise, when Etherington reflects on his and Tyrrel's lives, he writes, '⟨fate⟩ ↑Fortune↓ . . . involved us both in one of the strangest and most complicated mazes her capricious divinity-ship ever wove' (234.22–25). One wonders about that capital 'F' and Scott's curious preference for 'Fortune' over 'luck' or 'fate'.

Scott would sometimes be unhappy with his improvements, and so revise his revisions. The narrator writes of the actors gaining 'secret access from their ⟨tiring separate⟩ green-room' (189.20). Tyrrel speaks of Etherington's 'cold-blooded and most inhuman ⟨trickery⟩ ↑falsehood↓', which then becomes 'stratagem' (271.19) in the first edition. Touchwood complains about the '⟨cold hot⟩ ↑scalding↓ milk . . . at the Well', moving from 'cold' to 'hot' to 'scalding' (282.13). Mowbray fears 'the temptations which this ⟨spot⟩ region ['dangerous scene' in the first edition] must have offerd' Clara (356.2–3). In later editions of *Saint Ronan's Well*, Scott was still striving to improve his text. The search for the best word or expression ended only with his death.

5] *Scots*. Scott changes English into Scots a dozen times in the manuscript. Since this process intensifies dramatically in published editions, the manuscript suggests that Scott himself was less interested in this kind of change than some of the intermediaries who were involved in the publication of his novels. The changes are given to Mrs Blower, Micklewhame, MacTurk, and especially Meg, perhaps because she '⟨hates those p⟩ canna bide their yanking way of knapping English at every word' (14.15–16).

6] *Improved rhetorical movement*. Scott improves the rhythm of his prose, as might have been expected from a poet-novelist. The majority of the changes are given, perhaps necessarily, to the narrator. Originally, he wrote that Sir Bingo's friends 'would rather have seen his bones broken ⟨than saved by retreat⟩'; this is amended to 'would rather have seen his bones broken in conflict bold than his honour injured by a discreditable retreat' (75.7–8). Later, the narrator writes that the economical damsels '↑twisted handkerchiefs into turbans and converted petticoats into pantaloons↓ shaped and sewd cut and clipd and spoild many a decent gown and petticoat to produce some thing like a Grecian habit' (186.38–41). Among his characters, Scott is especially concerned with the speech rhythms of Clara Mowbray, whose language tends to be highly rhetorical, if not poetic. She asks Tyrrel, 'And wherefore should not sorrow be the end of sin and of folly—And when did happiness come of disobedience ↑And when did↓ sound sleep visit a bloody pillow?' (83.4–6). Speaking of their buried hopes, 'Ay—buried is the word—↑she replied crushd down and↓ buried when they budded fairest' (83.37–38).

7] *Elimination of repetitions*. Scott eliminates eighteen verbal repetitions in the manuscript. For example, 'A consciousness that many scrupled to hold intercourse with her in society renderd her disagreeably ⟨jealous⟩ ↑tenacious↓ of her rank and jealous of everything which appeared like neglect' (51.34–37). On one occasion, Scott eliminates a sound repetition: 'glowing with dark purple heath or with the golden ⟨bloom⟩ ↑lustre↓ of the broom and gorse' (2.13–14). These mechanical changes become interesting on the two occasions when they lead to a more precise or vivid word. Tyrrel worries that 'to shew himself at a distance might give the lady an opportunity of turning back and . . . might be attended with danger to the ⟨lady⟩ rider' (81.21–25). Sir Bingo's 'coarse spirit was now thoroughly ⟨heated⟩ ↑kindled↓ and like iron or any other baser metal which is slow in receiving heat' (117.38–39). This minor concern with repetitions in the manuscript becomes a major anxiety in the first edition.

8] *Explicit references to language*. Because of Scott's continuous engagement with his own language throughout the manuscript, it is hardly surprising that he adds explicit references to the subject. They all appear early. Meg says to Tyrrel, 'Maybe ye think we have the fashion of the table-dot ⟨down by yonder⟩ as they ca' their bit newfangled ordinary down by yonder' (17.36–37). A little later, she says to him, 'Was it not the ⟨other g day⟩ ↑last season as they ca't↓' (23.4). Another addition slides from a speech by Dinah into a comment by the narrator: '"at the ⟨Aul'ton yonder⟩ ↑Cleek'um of Aultoun yonder"—A name by the way which the Inn had acquired from the use which the ⟨Devil wr⟩ Saint upon the sign-post was making of his hook↓' (33.14–16). Later, the narrator adds, '↑the *Cleikum* (pronounced Anglice)↓' (37.17–18). Tyrrel professes that he 'read with reluctance all but the ↑productions of the↓ very first rate ⟨productions⟩ poets and some of these . . . he should have liked better in ⟨prose⟩ humble prose' (46.3–5). Finally when Meg announces that Saint Ronan 'was nane of your idolatrous Roman Saunts but a Chaldee', the narrator interposes, '↑(meaning probably a Culdee)↓' (141.31–32).

9] *Finding the right name.* Study of the manuscript reveals that Scott took trouble to find the right names for places and characters. Saint Ronan's was originally Saint Duttrocks, the Fox Hotel was the Bull, Air Castle was Featherhed-house, and Shaws-Castle was The Tower of Shaws. Chatterley was originally named Saint John, Bonnyrig was Raunlitree, Etherington was first Heatherinton and Heatherington and then Wetherington, and Winterblossom was called Silverblossom, a name that keeps popping up throughout the manuscript. Early on, Scott leaves a space after 'Capt.', which the first edition fills in with 'MacTurk'. Likewise, where the manuscript reads, 'the woman says in the farce', the first edition specifies (incorrectly) 'Mrs Highmore' (69.12–13). But Scott left a space after 'the prince' that was never filled in until this edition supplied 'Ahmed' (68.14).

10] *Correction of errors.* Scott corrects those errors that he sees, although he overlooks many more. These interludes are amusing but perhaps significant only to those interested in word association and in the conflict between Scott's rapid imagination and his desire for accuracy. Meg refers to Bulmer's '⟨cheeps⟩ cheeks like roses' (18.25), while Lady Penelope notes the absence of colour in Clara's '⟨cheep⟩ cheek' (55.1). Lady Pen asks to see what objects Tyrrel, the painter, has '⟨rested⟩ rescued from natural decay' (55.24). Clara says she spoke to 'Lady ⟨Bingo⟩ Binks' (68.30). Jekyl reassures Etherington that his father merely threw out a 'sinister ⟨hit⟩ hint' (252.5). Twice, Lady Pen calls Mrs Jones, her waiting-lady, '⟨John⟩' (327.40, 42). In one instance, Scott seems to have gone to some trouble to correct his mistakes. He originally quoted Walpole's verses from memory:

For never was the gentle ⟨heart⟩ breast
Insensible to human woes

⟨Soft⟩ Feeling though firm it melts distressd
For weaknesses it never knows (305.24–27)

The manuscript indicates that he immediately looked up the lines and corrected them.

11] *Missing chapter titles, mottoes, and notes.* The titles of 11 of the 39 chapters were added after the composition of the main text: Volume 1, Chapters 10, 11, 12, 13; Volume 2, Chapters 6, 7 (called 'The fete' in MS), 8; Volume 3, Chapters 5, 7, 9, 10.

The mottoes of 12 chapters were added after the composition of the main text: Volume 1, Chapters 1, 3, 5, 9; Volume 2, Chapters 7, 9, 10; Volume 3, Chapters 1, 3, 7 (the second motto of this chapter is added, strangely, between the third and fourth paragraphs), 10, 11 (the original motto for this chapter was used for the next chapter).

Four footnotes were added to the main text: Volume 1, Chapter 1 (added on verso), and Chapter 4 (added on verso); Volume 2, Chapter 7 (added on verso); Volume 3, Chapter 11 (added in left margin).

12] *Cuts.* Scott cuts infrequently. He would rather add to or correct material than eliminate it. But he cuts when the logic of the situation demands it. Touchwood says, 'Not know Paisley shawls from Indian madam . . . why a blind ⟨and deaf⟩ man could tell by the slightest touch of his little finger' (192.3–4). The narrator describes how 'The ⟨dry⟩ leaves of the ash tree detachd themselves from the tree and without an air of wind fell spontaneously on the path' (280.9–11). In a friendly exchange, Touchwood offers, '⟨But let me alone for finding you good quarters⟩', and Tyrrel responds, '⟨Are you the landlord of the Cleikum inn Sir⟩' (f. 150r). But this response is awkward and involves Tyrrel in uncharacteristic subterfuge, so Scott cut the exchange.

13] *Genius.* Study of the manuscript necessarily emphasises Scott the craftsman, the man of second thoughts who is adding to, correcting, and generally striving to improve his text. But here the argument must reverse itself and ask what evidence the manuscript supplies of Scott the creative artist. Which material, for example, required the least change? By far the cleanest chapter is 'The Meeting', the dramatic confrontation between Clara and Tyrrel. Even Lady Louisa Stuart, who disliked the novel, acknowledged the power of this scene.[41] According to the evidence of the manuscript, Scott's imagination is immediately kindled, and he writes surely and swiftly throughout. The few changes are all minor. Likewise, the three major scenes between John and Clara Mowbray that carry so much of the emotional force of the novel over three volumes, 'Fraternal Love', 'The Proposal', and 'Debate', are relatively clean in manuscript.[42] Scott rises to the occasion when his imagination is fully engaged. He himself criticised the plot of *Saint Ronan's Well* as 'contorted and unnatural', and by classical standards it is.[43] But as the evidence of the manuscript suggests, this plot generates dramatic confrontations of the kind that Scott handles so masterfully.

From Manuscript to First Edition. One major change, unique among the Waverley Novels, occurred in the plot of *Saint Ronan's Well* as it proceeded from manuscript to publication. Lockhart testifies:

> Sir Walter had shown a remarkable degree of good-nature in the completion of this novel. When the end came in view, James Ballantyne suddenly took vast alarm about a particular feature in the history of the heroine. In the original conception, and in the book as actually written and printed, Miss Mowbray's mock marriage had not halted at the profaned ceremony of the church; and the delicate printer shrunk from the idea of obtruding on the fastidious public the possibility of any personal contamination having been incurred by a high-born damsel of the nineteenth century. Scott was at first inclined to dismiss his friend's scruples as briefly as he had done those of Blackwood in the case of the Black Dwarf:—"You would never have quarrelled with it," he said, "had the thing happened to a girl in gingham. The silk petticoat can make little difference." James reclaimed with double energy, and called Constable to the rescue;—and after some pause, the author very reluctantly consented to cancel and rewrite about twenty-four pages, which was enough to obliterate, to a certain extent, the dreaded scandal—and in a similar degree, as he always persisted, to perplex and weaken the course of his narrative, and the dark effect of its catastrophe.[44]

Although Lockhart recognises the general problem, he gets the details wrong. Clara did not have sexual intercourse with Etherington; their speeding carriage was overtaken only a mile from the church. The true account lies in the manuscript where Hannah Irwin confesses to Josiah Cargill that Clara and Tyrrel had sexual intercourse seven years before the action of the novel begins. Likewise, the manuscript reveals that Scott did not 'cancel and rewrite about twenty-four pages' but about twenty-four lines, thus leaving all too many perplexing and unexplained traces of 'the dreaded scandal' throughout the text.

No proof sheets of *Saint Ronan's Well* are now known to exist. But in 1893, Alexander Ballantyne made the cancelled proof sheet of the original ending available to *The Athenaeum* with the following note: 'This sheet, the only copy in existence, contains 'The Catastrophe' as originally written by Sir Walter Scott. He altered it, much against his will, at the suggestion of friends'.[45] The copy of the proof contains several refinements of the manuscript version and supports Lockhart's claim that Scott's capitulation came late in the publishing process.

Of the 50,000 changes between manuscript and first edition, the overwhelming majority involve the supplying of punctuation and the standardising of spelling. The system of punctuation and spelling in the manuscript is inappropriate to the printed texts of the period. Except for the omnipresent and all-purpose dash, Scott punctuated sparingly, expecting that the printing house would punctuate in accordance with the conventions of the time. Thus, the Scott manuscript remains a potential work of art; the first edition is an actual work. Only a mistaken scholarly fidelity would rely on holograph mannerisms that were never meant by the author to be translated into type.[46]

More interesting are the approximately 2,750 verbal changes between manuscript and first edition. Most of these continue the processes begun by Scott in the manuscript itself—narrative additions, expansion of speeches, more vivid and appropriate words and phrases, correction of errors, occasional cuts, the stabilisation of proper names, the completion of chapter titles and mottoes, the changing of English into Scots (and, to a lesser extent, Scots into English), and the elimination of repetitions. The last two processes are intensified. But whereas the changes within the manuscript were all attributable to Scott and could almost always be justified aesthetically, the new changes in the first edition often remain problematic as to source and value. Some are clearly improvements, some seem neutral or mechanical, and others are based on misreadings or misunderstandings of the manuscript. It is tempting to attribute the improvements, especially when they appear in clusters, to Scott, and to foist off less happy changes upon intermediaries but, in the absence of proof sheets, the argument remains circular.

The least interesting verbal changes are the many additions of the 'he said' variety, often with accompanying characterisation or description. These are usually mechanical enough but, even in this category, the creative imagination of Scott can be seen. When, in a dramatic confrontation between brother and sister, the first edition reads, '"I wish you, my dear John," ↑said Clara, struggling to regain entire composure, "I wish you↓"', the scene is heightened and vivified (217.21–22). Often, pronouns are mechanically replaced by their referents, especially at the beginning of paragraphs. But sometimes they are replaced by unexpectedly vivid referents: 'she' becomes 'her giddy charge' (50.5); 'it' becomes 'thy long visage' (169.9); 'he' becomes 'our mortal fiend' (348.4–5). At the beginning of a paragraph, 'She' (Clara) becomes 'The poor young lady' (85.13). Later in the novel, Etherington's sarcastic reference to 'him' (Tyrrel) is changed to 'the poor young man' (228.38). Are these two remarkably similar changes in the first edition a mere coincidence or another artistic linking of the tragic young lovers? At the end of the novel, 'He' becomes 'The old man' (371.19); the formerly vigorous Touchwood, having failed in all of his schemes, has become impotent.

One significant addition is irrefutably Scott's. In a letter of July, 1823, to James Ballantyne, he instructs the printer to conclude Meg's speech (26.13–20) with the following: 'And Nanny, ye may tell them he has an illustrated poem—illustrated—mind the word, Nanny, that is to be stuck as fou o' the likes o' that as ever turkey was larded wi' slabs o' bacon'.[47] That has the authentic ring to it and may serve as a touchstone for other changes. Scott's are imaginative and creative, adding humour, revealing character, clarifying story, and dramatising action.

Certain characters keep growing on Scott as he continues working on the text. Meg gets many additional lines, often a parting shot at the end of a paragraph. MacTurk too is given a number of humorous additions, including this intrusive paragraph:

> "By Cot, madam," said Captain MacTurk, "I should be proud to obey your Leddyship's commands—but, by Cot, I never call first on any man that never called upon me at all, unless it were to carry him a friend's message, or such like." (36.42–37.2)

Touchwood's many additions convey humour and social criticism but, as the tragic climax approaches, take on a darker tone. Near the end, he tells Mowbray, '↑So I have come to put you right↓' (344.14). He conceives of himself as a *deus ex machina*, a theatre director, or a kind of Walter Scott. He has gathered the dramatis personae together and now will '↑play them all off against each other, after my own pleasure↓' (348.33–34). That is why '↑I, for one, must be stirring early—I have business of life and death—it concerns you too, Mr Mowbray—but no more of that till to-morrow↓' (351.15–17). But that very night the catastrophe occurs, and this pseudo-novelist proves unable to control people or events. The additions reveal that it was during the time between the writing of the manuscript and the publication of the first edition that Scott reconsidered his own role as a writer of fictions.

Actions are clarified. How did Clara see Tyrrel when she visited the tea-table and avoid him when she left? Arriving, she tells Lady Penelope, 'There was much growling and snarling in the lower den ↑when I passed it↓' (68.7–8). Leaving, she says, '↑However, on second thoughts, I will take the back way, and avoid them.—What says honest Bottom? / For if they should as lions come in strife / Into such place, 'twere pity of their life↓' (68.16–19). And indeed, 'she tripped out of the room ↑by a side passage↓' (69.7). Similarly, the groundwork for the dramatic entertainment in 'Theatricals' (changed in the first edition from 'The fete') is effectively laid for the first time by being announced in the Mowbray invitation (160.3–5), criticised by Touchwood (160.5–15), and explained by the narrator (182.28–183.12).

Drama is heightened. For example, Scott intensifies the final confrontation between John and Clara. Spurring home, Mowbray strikes his head against the bough of an oak tree, shivering the branch to pieces. The narrator now adds, 'Mowbray himself was unconscious of the accident' (331.38). Ridiculing Clara's preparations for a life of poverty, he declaims, 'There is a difference, Clara, between fanciful experiments and real poverty—the one is a masquerade, which we can end when we please, ↑the other is wretchedness for life↓' (333.42–334.1). When he seems to be releasing her from Etherington's courtship, Clara says, 'I am glad of it, with all my spirit . . . ↑may it take with it all that we can quarrel about!↓' (334.27–28). But at the climax, Mowbray now ends his rant, '↑The match is booked—Swear you will not hesitate↓' (337.41–42). Clara swears and does not hesitate, but in a sense that her brother never intended.

The first edition also introduces numerous errors, largely based on misreading or misunderstanding of the manuscript. For example, in the first edition, John asks Clara,

> do you remember, when there was a report of a bogle in the upper orchard, when we were both children?—Do you remember how you were perpetually telling me to take care of the bogle, and keep away from its haunts?—And do you remember my going on purpose to detect the bogle, finding the cow-boy, with a shirt about him, busied in pulling pears, and treating him to a handsome drubbing? (103.4–10)

The suspect word is 'shirt'. Why should the wearing of a 'shirt' make the boy appear ghost-like? A careful look at the manuscript reveals a clear 'sh' at the beginning of the word and a final 't'. In between come two upstrokes. Since Scott dots approximately 20% of his i's in this manuscript, there is a negative presumption that this undotted first upstroke is more likely an 'e'. The second stroke is the same, lacking the horizontal line of Scott's r. The word is 'sheet', which makes perfect sense. In confirmation, the poetic epigraph to the penultimate chapter refers to a 'sheeted ghost', and the relevant word is formed exactly as it is in John Mowbray's speech.

According to James Thorpe, the first principle governing textual work 'is the necessity for the editor to have a thorough knowledge of the work he is to edit, along with a thorough knowledge of other works by the same author and of other related works'.[48] In the first edition, after having been frightened by another sham ghost, Meg Dods refuses Mr Touchwood's offer of a drink,

> Troth, I'll pledge naebody the night, Mr Touchwood; for, what wi' the upcast and terror that I got a wee while syne, and what wi' the bit taste that I behoved to take of the plottie while I was making it, my head is sair aneugh stressed the night already. (264.38–41)

Unlike the previous example, this speech makes perfectly good sense, yet it differs in one material respect from the manuscript version. A careful reading of the manuscript reveals that 'terror' is incorrect. There is an initial 't', the familiar upstroke for a vowel, two 'r's, and then at least four letters, the penultimate having a dot over it. Perhaps only the student of Scott will recognise the final word of the climactic sixty-ninth Chapter of *Waverley*, 'tirrivie'.

The first edition introduces many plausible errors. In the manuscript, Winterblossom never permitted the attendants upon the 'public table' to wait upon others before himself; in the first edition, it becomes 'public taste' (29.42–43). The 'canny' chemist in the wilds of Glenlivat now becomes 'cunning' (119.3). The beautifully balanced 'pantaloond and buskind beaux' become 'buckskin'd' (120.37–38). The Town Council, which was 'nightly' busied in preparing the fourth part of a member of Parliament, is now 'mightily' busied (123.29). Etherington calls Jekyl a 'knaving' hand, not a 'knowing' hand (181.1). Touchwood refers to 'a blunt John Bull, or a raw Scotchman', not a 'blind' John Bull (349.35). Worried about infection from a puerperal fever, Lady Penelope has 'always used thieves' vinegar since', not 'thieves vinegar essence' (305.37–38). In addition, the first edition misses considerable material —from single words to sentences—in the manuscript. It is little wonder that the first edition, the base-text, requires nearly 1500 emendations.[49]

3. THE LATER EDITIONS

The Second Edition. The one copy of the second edition that was discovered and examined, that of University College, London, proved to be a first edition fronted by new title pages.

Editions of *Tales and Romances*. *Saint Ronan's Well* was included in three different editions of *Tales and Romances of the Author of Waverley* (*Saint Ronan's Well*, *Redgauntlet*, *Tales of the Crusaders*, and *Woodstock*). On 25 May 1826, the Trustees in charge of Scott's financial arrangements since his ruin authorised Cadell, who had become Scott's publisher, to publish octavo, duodecimo, and 18mo editions of *Tales and Romances*, each of 1,500 copies. On 1 June Cadell offered £1,500; on 13 June Scott advised acceptance of the offer,[50] but the Trustees decided first to consult Longman and Murray, the London publishers. On 12 July the Trustees intimated that they had decided to print the editions themselves, whereupon Cadell declared himself 'much pleased at not getting these books'.[51] Nevertheless, the whole impression—the three editions of *Tales and Romances*, each consisting of 1,000 copies—was sold in 1827 by the Trustees to Cadell and Longman for £4,000. Out of this sum, the Trustees paid out £2,500 for paper, printing, and engraving, the latter furnished by Lizars of Edinburgh for about £400.[52] *Saint Ronan's Well* formed Volume one and the first half of Volume two of the seven-volume octavo, which was available by 20 July 1827;[53] it formed the first two volumes of the nine-volume duodecimo, which was advertised in *The Edinburgh Evening Courant* of 28 July; and it formed Volume one and the first half of Volume two of the seven-volume 18mo, which has a publication date of '1728' on the only copy I have been able to examine.[54]

Serious consideration was later given to adding 1,000 copies to the octavo edition. On 8 January 1828 Scott wrote in his *Journal*:

> My post brings serious intelligence to-day and of a very pleasing description. Longman and Coy, with a reserve which marks all their proceedings, suddenly inform Mr. Gibson [the leader of the three Trustees] that they desire 1000 of the 8vo. edition of *Saint*

> *Ronan's Well* and the subsequent series of novels thereunto belonging for that they have only *seven* remaining, and wish it to be sent to three printers and pushd out in three months. . . . In the present case this may do because I will make neither alteration nor addition till our *grande opus* the Improved Edition goes to press. But ought we to go to press with this 1000 copies knowing that our project will supersede and render equivalent to waste paper such of them as may not reach the public before our plan is publickly known and begins to operate? I have I acknowlege doubt as to this. No doubt I feel perfectly justified in letting Longman and Coy look to their own interest since they have neither consulted me nor attended to mine, but the loss might extend to the retail booksellers and to hurt the men through whom my works are ultimately to find their way to the public would be both unjust and impolitic.[55]

On the same day he wrote to Cadell: 'The business of Saint Ronans Well etc presses and I should wish James and you to take a quiet beefsteak with me in Shandwick place on Tuesday at five o'clock and talk it over'.[56] But on 11 January he noted in the *Journal*, 'I observe by a letter from Mr Cadell that I had somewhat misunderstood his last. It is he not Longman that wish to publish the thousand copies of *Saint Ronan's* Series'.[57] Scott's ethical and politic reservations may have won out over the financial temptations, for I have seen no further evidence of an addition to the original octavo edition.

Although significantly different from each other in many details, the three versions of *Saint Ronan's Well* share 217 verbal variants from the first edition, suggesting the same ultimate source for all three, perhaps a corrected version of the first edition. For example, in the first edition, Etherington ridicules Tyrrel for 'encumbering himself at eighteen with a wife' (238.40–41). But in all three versions of *Tales and Romances*, the number is changed to 'nineteen'. Likewise, when Mowbray urges Clara to wear the Indian shawl, she admits, 'I have given it away—given it up, perhaps I should say, to the rightful owner.—She has promised me something or other in exchange for it, however'. Mowbray replies, 'Yes, some of the work of her own fair hands, I suppose' (209.10–15), and the conversation changes direction. But someone now realised that the 'she' has not been identified. It could be Lady Binks who is 'the rightful owner', since Scott had earlier identified her as the one who ordered this special shawl. At any rate, a final sentence is added to Clara's speech in all three versions: 'I have given it to Lady Penelope'.

A complication arises when the three versions all make a change in slightly different forms. When the dramatic pictures from *A Midsummer Night's Dream* are about to commence, Touchwood exclaims, 'But stop—the curtain rises' (190.11–12), and the narrator continues, 'It did indeed arise'. But someone remembered that this is an outdoor performance and corrected to 'The screen was indeed withdrawn' or, perhaps, as the 18mo prints it, 'The screen was withdrawn indeed'. More curiously, the first edition compares Micklewhame to a dog who looks at his master's face 'with a piteous gaze, to assure him that he partakes of his trouble, though he neither comprehends the cause or the extent of it' (91.13–15). The three versions all make an addition to the end of the original sentence:

> nor has the power to remove it. (8vo)
> nor has the power to alleviate or remove it. (12mo)
> nor has the power to diminish or remove it. (18mo)

It is impossible that these additions could have been made independently of each other; they must be derived from the same source. What, then, can account for the differences between them?

But the biggest question of all is, what role did Scott play in the revision of the text for the first collected edition? In his *Journal* entry for 28 July 1826, he wrote, 'Read through and corrected *Saint Ronan's Well*. I am no good judge but I think the language of this piece rather good. . . . I have corrected it for the press'.[58] Two days before, he had written to James Ballantyne, 'I send you a few leaves of Saint Ronans that you may be going on. The rest of volume with next parcel'.[59] In his *Journal* entry for 8 January 1828, when he was considering the addition of 1,000 copies to the octavo edition, he wrote, 'In the present case this may do because I will make neither alteration nor addition',[60] indicating that in the previous case he did make changes. The literal meaning of Scott's words in his *Journal*, the praise for the language of the novel (rare self-congratulation), and the existence of significant revisions in large clusters suggest to me that Scott himself actively revised his text for the collected edition. Specific revisions would account for the identical changes among the three versions; incomplete or unclear revisions or mere indicia that revisions are desired might explain the slightly different changes among the three versions.

One thing is clear. The main line of development in the printed texts of *Saint Ronan's Well* runs from the first edition through the octavo *Tales and Romances*, which was used as the basis for Scott's Interleaved Set, to the Magnum Opus. The duodecimo and 18mo *Tales and Romances* are textual dead ends. When the octavo alone corrects the first edition ('The next billet . . . ⟨run⟩ ↑ran↓ thus': 40.29–30), that correction makes its way into the Interleaved Set and, from there, into the Magnum. The reverse is also true. In the first edition, Meg tells Bindloose that Tyrrel agreed to duel with Sir Bingo 'the neist day' (129.35). The duodecimo corrects to 'that vara day', and the 18mo corrects to 'that vera day'. But the octavo misses the needed correction, which, therefore, does not appear in the printed text of the Interleaved Set. Thus, the stemma, or family tree of editions, is as listed opposite.

The Octavo *Tales and Romances*. The octavo has 1281 variants from

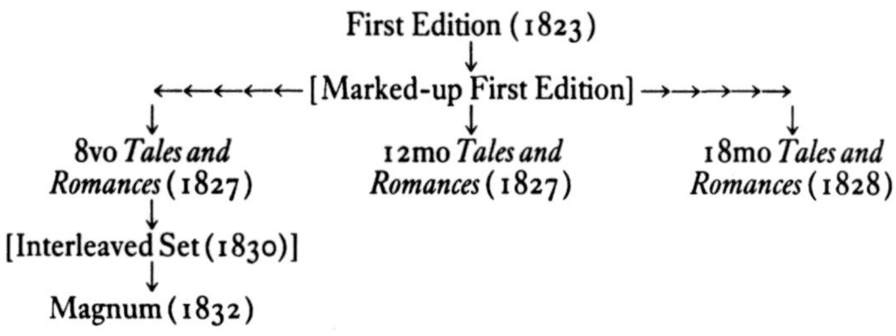

the first edition. Of these, 1002 are non-verbal variants. Most prominent are the following:

287 changes in spelling
174 commas added
108 commas deleted
31 commas into semicolons
14 semicolons into commas
17 semicolons added
54 hyphens added
21 hyphens deleted
42 lower-case letters raised
26 capitals lowered

The overall movement is toward a more standardised spelling and from an aural to a more grammatical system of punctuation.

There are 279 verbal variants—52 additions, 33 deletions, and 194 alterations. Of these verbal variants the octavo shares 17 with the duodecimo only, 22 with the 18mo only, and 217 with both the duodecimo and 18mo. The 23 verbal variants that are unique to the octavo are mostly dubious changes and downright mistakes. For example, in the first edition, Mowbray exclaims, 'necessity is as unrelenting a leader as any Vizier or Pacha, whom Scanderbeg ever fought with or Byron has sung' (165.24–25). The octavo incorrectly changes the key word to 'relenting'. Interestingly, the 18mo changes the same word to 'relentless', again suggesting that the different editions may have had a common source but that the source may, at times, have merely indicated the need for a change without spelling it out. In any case, the verbal variants of interest in the octavo are those it shares with the duodecimo and 18mo.

The Duodecimo *Tales and Romances*. The duodecimo has 2149 variants from the first edition. Of these, 1711 are non-verbal variants. Most prominent are the following:

380 changes in spelling
281 commas added
216 commas deleted
39 commas into semicolons
24 semicolons into commas

36 other comma changes
141 permutations involving dashes

The process begun in the octavo is intensified in the duodecimo.

There are 438 verbal variants—69 additions, 38 deletions, and 331 changes. Of these verbal variants, the duodecimo shares 17 with the octavo only, 125 with the 18mo only, and 217 with both the octavo and 18mo. The 79 verbal variants that are unique to the duodecimo are of no textual value. Scott was wrong when he wrote that the meeting between Dr Johnson and Wilkes was held at Strahan's; the duodecimo compounds the error by changing the name to Strachan. Several of the revisions shared by the duodecimo and 18mo are right. They both correct the speaker in the motto of Volume 1, Chapter 13, from Slender to Simple, and they both correctly eliminate Meg's reference to the morrow as the Sabbath (264.42–43). But the most significant verbal variants are those that the duodecimo shares with the other two versions.

The 18mo *Tales and Romances*. The 18mo pushes the process of revision to its outer limits. It has 2898 variants from the first edition, of which 2236 are non-verbal. Most prominent are the following:

509 changes in spelling
366 commas added
327 commas deleted
54 commas into semicolons
34 semicolons into commas
95 lower-case letters raised
72 capitals lowered
110 hyphens added
54 hyphens deleted

The aural system of punctuation in the manuscript has now become grammatical.

There are 662 verbal variants—107 additions, 92 deletions, and 463 changes. Of these verbal variants, the 18mo shares 22 with the octavo only, 125 with the duodecimo only, and 217 with both the octavo and duodecimo. The 298 verbal variants that are unique to the 18mo are the most significant of the three versions. Although they are scattered everywhere, many can be found concentrated in several heavy clusters. The busy text sometimes introduces trivia and errors. For example, 'Oberon, the King of Shadows, whose sovereign gravity . . . was somewhat indifferently represented by the silly ⟨gaiety⟩ ↑gait↓ of Miss in her Teens' (184.35–37). Etherington complains of Clara's 'affectation of vulgar ⟨stolidity⟩ ↑solidity↓' (300.19). Immediately afterwards, he complains of Mowbray's standing 'on points of honour, forsooth, this broken-down horse-jockey, who swallowed my two thousand pounds as a pointer would a ⟨pat⟩ ↑pot↓ of butter' (300.28–30).

In addition to errors, the 18mo introduces a new squeamishness into the text. The narrator describes Augusta Bidmore's progress, 'as different from that of her brother, as the fire of heaven differs from that grosser element which the peasant ⟨piles⟩ ↑nourishes↓ upon his smouldering hearth' (148.11–13). Soon afterwards, he assures the reader that Cargill would never 'involve his pupil in the toils of a mutual ⟨passion⟩ ↑affection↓' (148.36). Later, he changes a 'petticoat' into a generic 'under garment' (256.2).

Nevertheless, the 18mo contributes genuine improvements. The motto of Volume 2, Chapter 3, is rightly attributed to Goldsmith rather than to Dryden out of Chaucer. The incomprehensible 'marriage between my right honourable and very good lord father' is finally remedied: 'marriage between this lady and my right honourable and very good lord father' (232.14–15). Hannah Irwin's 'a wifeless mother' is deleted. Clara Mowbray's appeal is corrected: 'I trust he will consider his own condition, honour, and happiness, better than to share ⟨it⟩ ↑them↓ with me' (337.32–34). These are not the imaginative touches of the creative artist but, rather, the necessary corrections of an alert editor. Still, the 18mo was a textual dead end.

The Interleaved Set. The Interleaved Set of the Waverley Novels contains Scott's textual revisions, introductions, and notes for the Magnum Opus.[61] Scott used a copy of the octavo edition of *Tales and Romances* to work on *Saint Ronan's Well* during the latter part of 1830. Cadell's diary records that copy was in the publisher's hands by 19 January 1831.[62]

There were 53 non-verbal variants:

- 11 commas deleted
- 10 sets of quotation marks added
- 6 single quotation marks added
- 1 quotation mark location changed
- 6 periods added
- 7 periods deleted
- 1 italic added
- 8 dashes added
- 1 hyphen added
- 1 hyphen deleted
- 1 semicolon deleted

The changes are logical; the effect is negligible.

There were 179 verbal changes—111 additions, 2 deletions, and 66 alterations. The most frequent verbal addition—36 examples—was of the 'he said' variety. Most of these are mechanical enough, but a few are accompanied with important characterisation. For example, 'said her brother half repentant of his purpose' (Magnum, 33.203.11) exculpates Mowbray to some degree. Clara herself is characterised as 'the simple-hearted girl' (33.203.14). Meg is described as 'determined to be pleased with no supposition of ⟨Mr Bindloose⟩ her lawyer' (33.263.25), while Bindloose 'felt his own accompt in the modern improvements' (33.275.26).

Scott makes six lengthy additions. At one point, his imagination suddenly kindling, he literally creates a new character on the spot:

> Mowbray had also in his found a fitting representative for Puck in queer looking small eyed boy of the Aulton of Saint Ronans with large ears projecting from his head as turrets corbeld out from ⟨the⟩ a Gothic building. This exotick animal personified the merry and mocking spirit of Hobgoblin with considerabl power so that the ⟨whole⟩ groupe bore some resemblance to the well known and exquisite delineation of Puck by Sir Joshua in the select collection of the Bard of Memory.[63] It was the ruin of Saint Ronans ⟨?⟩ Robin Good fellow fell who did no good afterwards "gaed an ill gate" as Meg Dods said and "took on" with a party of strolling players (33.395.18)[64]

Another addition, later in the Interleaved Copy, confirms the continuing vitality of this appealing vagrant (34.81.10).

Mrs Blower, a character who grew on Scott, is given a couple of new observations. She says that Mowbray's 'sisters a very decent woman' (33.377.26), and she now deplores actors and actresses:

> And then the changing the name which was given them at baptism is I think an awful falling away from our vows and though ⟨B⟩ Thisby which I take to be Greek for Tibbie may be a very good yet Margaret was I christend and Margaret will I die. (33.377.5)

Touchwood, another character who grew on Scott, is given significant additions, including his description of Saint Ronan's Well—'no well in your swamps tenanted by such a conceited colony of clamorous frogs' (33.277.6)—and his warning to Jekyl, 'So suppose me horse⟨v⟩-whippd and pray at the same time suppose yourself shot through the body—The same exertion of imagination will serve for both purposes' (34.76.18).

Scott makes a dozen brief additions, from a word to a short phrase. A single touch can increase the humour of an already funny scene, as when Touchwood comments on Jekyl's whistling: 'That is just so like the Marquis ↑of Roccambole↓ (34.74.1), another dear friend of mine, that whistles all the time you talk to him—He says he learned it in the reign of terror, when a man was glad to whistle to show his throat was whole'. The narrator describes peace-officers who 'carry bludgeons to break folks heads' (33.62.7). Several of these brief additions are descriptive. On her first appearance Widow Blower is wearing 'a flowered ↑black↓ silk gown' (33.121.9). Clara addressed the Wellers 'with an affectation of interest and politeness ↑which thinly conceald scorn and contempt↓' (33.139.22).

Scott takes pains to correct errors, or what he deems to be such. Most commonly, he changes a word to avoid verbal repetition in a sentence.

He corrects verb tenses and changes 'whosoever' to 'whomsoever'. He finally corrects the spelling of '⟨lanmer⟩ ↑lamer↓ beads' (90.11). In an example that is relevant today, he corrects 'different genders' to 'different sexes' (70.8). He makes Tyrrel 'the ↑in↓direct' occasion of Mowbray's predicament (43.10). He changes 'a Mainot' to 'an Arnout' (184.25). He tries to be exact with numbers. The Town-Council of Marchthorn, 'at the end of every ⟨six or seven⟩ ↑five or six↓ years', weaved 'the fourth ↑or fifth↓ part of a member of Parliament' (124.1–3).[65] Touchwood wants his dinner ready 'at ⟨four⟩ ↑*three*↓ to an instant' (145.41). Mrs Blower 'had three shawls, which she really fand was ⟨twa⟩ ↑ane↓ ower mony' (211.1–2). 'Willie Watson', the beadle, becomes 'Johnie Tirlsneck' (202.8), which is the name the beadle was given earlier (187.40). The same striving after exactness that Scott exhibited in the manuscript continues on to the final edition.

Likewise, Scott is still seeking to replace an adequate word or phrase with a better. Winterblossom's handwriting, like his character, 'was most accurate and common-place, though betraying an affectation both of flourish and of ⟨precision⟩ ↑facility↓' (40.26–28). The ladies, like the hunters of Buenos-Ayres, 'prepare their ⟨cord and their loop⟩ ↑*lasso*↓' (49.18). Jekyl's 'ivory' case of cigars becomes 'morocco' (282.32). Because of Lady Penelope's sated palate, 'the compliment had not ⟨spice⟩ ↑sauce↓ enough' (305.12). Scott continues his search for the right name, even for the most minor of characters; thus Lady Penelope's maid, 'Jones', becomes 'Gingham' and then, finally, 'Jones' again (327.17, 40, 42; 328.1).

The Interleaved Set also adds an introduction and 32 notes to the novel.

The Magnum Opus. *Saint Ronan's Well* appeared as volumes 33 and 34 of the Magnum Opus in February and March of 1832. The volumes were physically attractive, in royal 18mo, and cost five shillings each.[66]

In addition to the 232 changes that Scott himself made in the text of the Interleaved Set, the Magnum contains almost 2,000 changes, nearly 300 of which are verbal. Many of these alterations follow a recurrent pattern. The punctuation at the end of interrupted dialogue is consistently changed from —' to '—. 'Micklewham' becomes 'Meiklewham', 'inquiry' becomes 'enquiry', adjectives like 'scarce' are changed into their adverbial form, 'kenn'd' becomes 'kend', 'recognize' becomes 'recognise', 'Scotch' becomes 'Scottish', 'folks' becomes 'folk' and 'whatsoever' becomes 'whatever'. Many of the other changes are errors, either of commission or omission. The most serious is the loss in transmission of an entire paragraph, which turns the two surrounding paragraphs into nonsense.[67] More pervasive than error, however, is the attempt to regularise, tone down, or 'correct' Scott's writing. In the terrifying last interview between John and Clara Mowbray on the climactic night of action, Clara exclaimed,

> "Stay at home, brother, . . . stay at home, if you regard our house's honour—murther cannot mend misery—Stay at home, and let them talk of me as they will,—they cannot say worse than I deserve!" (335.11–14)

The emotional climax is refined to 'they can scarcely say worse of me than I deserve!'. Mowbray, 'with a mournful quietness and solemnity of manner, shut the window, and led his sister by the hand to her usual seat, which her tottering steps scarce enabled her to reach' (336.34–36). But 'mournful' is changed to 'sad' because there is a 'mournful silence' in the next sentence. They soon have the following exchange:

> "Brother—dearest brother—one single word!"
> "Not of refusal or expostulation—that time is gone by," said her brother. (337.12–14)

The final 'brother' is changed to 'stern censurer'. The final paragraph of the chapter begins, 'The night was not indeed far advanced' (338.43); now, somebody writes, 'The night was not indeed very far advanced'. It is hard to believe that Scott had a hand in any of these changes.

Nine of the verbal alterations improve the text. Six of them are corrections. The epigraph of Volume 2, Chapter 3, is now attributed to Goldsmith's *Deserted Village* rather than Dryden's version of Chaucer. The quotation from *Richard III*, which forms the epigraph of Volume 3, Chapter 5, is corrected. In addition to these literary allusions, the Magnum corrects three internal errors. Mowbray is now advancing in the 'same' (rather than the 'opposite') direction as his sister when he rides from the Fox Hotel to Shaws-Castle (86.21). Meg now informs Bindloose that the duel between Tyrrel and Sir Bingo was scheduled for 'that same day' (129.31) rather than 'the neist day'. The statement that Touchwood 'stopped the carriage to inform him that his sister was at the Aulton, which he had learned from finding there had been a messenger sent there for medical assistance' is corrected for the first time to 'there had been a messenger sent from thence to the Well' (371.3).

One of the verbal changes promotes concision; a wordy sentence is helped by reducing 'betwixt him and that part of his property' to 'near':

> Here, while the party were assuming their hats, for the purpose of joining the ladies' society, (which old-fashioned folks used only to take up for that of going into the open air,) Tyrrel asked a smart footman who stood betwixt him and that part of his property, to hand him the hat which lay on the table beyond. (74.21–26)

Finally, two verbal additions provide appropriate material. During his first interview with Clara, Mowbray requests a cup of tea (99.12), which is forgotten until the Magnum adds that he '↑sipped a cup of tea which had for some time been placed before him↓'. Meg's belief in ghosts is given a characteristic twist when she asks Tyrrel, 'what is the reason that you should come and frighten a decent house, where you met naething, ↑when ye was in the body,↓ but the height of civility?' (260.31–33). It appears likely to me that Scott contributed these verbal additions, but the other changes seem well within the scope of a conscientious editor.

The introduction to *Saint Ronan's Well*, which first appeared in the Interleaved Set, was extensively corrected for the Magnum and includes two new paragraphs at the end on the reception of the novel in England and Scotland. This additional material was almost certainly written by Scott. The new notes from the Interleaved Set all appear in the Magnum.

4. THE PRESENT TEXT

This edition restores Scott's original conclusion. Lockhart's account of what happened (see 390 above) contains two material errors. First, the manuscript reveals that Scott cancelled and rewrote about twenty-four lines rather than twenty-four pages. Second, Clara never had sexual intercourse with Etherington. Since their speeding carriage was overtaken only a mile from the church, it would have had to have been a rather rapid coupling under terribly difficult circumstances. Rather, in the manuscript account, Hannah Irwin confesses to Cargill that Clara had sexual intercourse with Tyrrel seven years before the action of the novel begins. This information clicks shut the plot, explaining Tyrrel's feelings of remorse and Clara's burden of guilt. But in trying to conceal the real issue, Scott did not excise carefully enough, so vestiges of the original story remain sprinkled throughout the text. For example, in their first meeting after seven years of separation, Clara remarks, 'And wherefore should not sorrow be the end of sin and of folly? And when did happiness come of disobedience?—And when did sound sleep visit a bloody pillow?' (83.4–6). A little later in the meeting, she continues,

> Tyrrel, when was it otherwise with engagements formed in youth and in folly? You and I would, you know, become men and women, while we were yet scarcely more than children—We have run, while yet in our nonage, through the passions and adventures of youth, and therefore we are now old before our day, and the winter of our life has come on ere its summer was well begun. (85.4–9)

There is no objective correlative to such statements in the printed editions.

The question of self-censorship is one of general significance to nineteenth-century fiction, involving many of the major writers. In a theoretical discussion, Donald Pizer has formulated four 'tests for accepting the belief that self-censorship has occurred and that restoration of an earlier state of the text is required':

> 1 Evaluating evidence regarding the composition and publication history of a work,
> 2 Evaluating evidence bearing on the author's motives in making revisions,
> 3 Evaluating through critical analysis the relative merits of different versions,
> 4 Considering whether the published version is a well known historical artifact that should continue to occupy the role of general reading text.[68]

G. Thomas Tanselle points out that the last two tests are not relevant to accepting the belief that self-censorship has occurred, although they do 'represent two possible approaches to making textual decisions'.[69] In any case, all four of Pizer's criteria require the restoration of the manuscript conclusion to the printed text of *Saint Ronan's Well*. It is clear from Lockhart's account that Scott was pressured for a long time to cancel his original conception and that he finally consented 'very reluctantly'. In addition, Alexander Ballantyne made the cancelled proof sheet of the original ending available to *The Athenaeum*, in 1893, with the following note:

> This sheet, the only copy in existence, contains 'The Catastrophe' as originally written by Sir Walter Scott. He altered it, much against his will, at the suggestion of friends.[70]

The copy of the proof reveals several refinements of the manuscript version and supports Lockhart's contention that Scott's capitulation came late in the publishing process. Lockhart also testifies that Scott 'always persisted' that the changes weakened and distorted the course of his narrative. Scott was correct. A reading text incorporating the manuscript version of the catastrophe—or, better still, its later development in proof—is superior in quality to the version of the story in the first edition. Finally, with regard to Pizer's last test, *Saint Ronan's Well* is hardly such a well known historical artifact that changing it will offend people's sensibilities.

Aside from the catastrophe, the first edition provides the basis for the present text. The inadequate punctuation of the manuscript rules it out as a base-text. Scott expected his holograph mannerisms to be translated into a coherent system of punctuation appropriate to the printed texts of the period. The manuscript remains a potential work of art; the first edition is an actual work. Of the nearly 50,000 changes between manuscript and first edition, the overwhelming majority involve the supplying of punctuation. Approximately 2,750 verbal changes are made. But the complexity of the publishing process—the secrecy, the difficulty of Scott's handwriting, the use of a transcriber and other intermediaries—resulted in the introduction of many errors into the first edition, which the present text attempts to correct. Consequently, this edition makes a total of 1,471 emendations to the first edition, including 817 verbal emendations, 307 emendations designed to standardise the spelling of proper names, and 347 emendations involving punctuation and spelling. For a full-length novel by Scott, this is a low number of emendations, which may be attributable to the leisurely pace (eight months) at which Scott wrote and corrected the novel. The great majority of emendations come from the manuscript.

Capitalisation, Punctuation, and Orthography. Scott originally began the penultimate chapter, 'Grief, Shame, Remorse, and Fear had contributed to overwhelm the unfortunate Clara Mowbray'. In the manuscript, 'Fear' was changed to 'Terror'; in the first edition, 'Remorse' was changed to 'confusion' and all the capital letters were dropped except for the obligatory 'Grief'. The present text restores all of the capitals, which Scott used to convey a sense of the overwhelming pressures on his mad heroine (358.22). Similarly, the sheriff-clerk of the county advertised that his 'Prieves' or 'Comptis' were to proceed 'within the House of Margaret Dods, Vintner in Saint Ronan's' (10.36–38). Understanding the nature of puffs, Scott capitalised 'House' and 'Vintner', and such braggadocio is restored in the present text. Lady Penelope says, 'Mr Tyrrel, you do not know how I dote upon your "serenely silent art", second to Poetry—equal—superior perhaps—to Music' (55.25–27). Scott knew that Lady Penelope would not only quote Thomas Campbell but also speak in capitals when referring to Poetry and Music.

The present text works in reverse also. It restores the lower-case letters of the manuscript when they have been unjustifiably changed to capitals in the first edition. Thus, fakirs, dervises, and bonzes are reduced to the same level as monks and mendicants, all five groups appearing in the same sentence and all lacking capitals in the manuscript (145.18–19). But among the many examples of this kind of emendation, the most important are those in which the structure and rhythm of speech are changed. For example, in one of her tirades, Meg rambles on,

> It was not for the profit—there was little profit at it;—profit?—there was a dead loss;—but she wad not be dung by any of them—they maun hae a hottle, maun they?—and an honest public canna serve them—they may hoddle on that likes; but they shall see that Luckie Dods can hoddle on as lang as the best of them—Ay, though they . . .

and so on for another six lines (8.37–9.5). Inexplicably, someone broke up this characteristically breathless ramble into three distinct sentences by twice putting in full stops and capitalising the 't' of 'they'. Such alterations begin to shade into larger questions of punctuation.

The compositor and other intermediaries had the difficult task of putting Scott's manuscript into a form appropriate for publication.

Except for his all-purpose dashes, Scott generally eschewed formal punctuation. Of the nearly 45,000 changes in punctuation that the intermediaries made for the first edition, approximately 99% are unexceptionable. But every alteration must be considered on its own merits and, in 1% of the cases, a return to Scott's original manuscript punctuation is necessary. In the preceding example, the intermediaries incorrectly broke up an uninterrupted harangue. They also commit the opposite error of running-on a sentence where Scott requires a break. It often depends upon critical judgment, but in some cases the solution is clear. For example, Meg says,

> The deil's in him, for he winna bide being thrawn. And I think the deil's in me too for thrawing him, sic a canny lad, and sae gude a customer;—and I am judging he has something on his mind . . .

and so on for another 8 lines (87.34–88.2). A glance at the manuscript reveals that the last 'and' above has a capital letter; a more careful look reveals that the word is 'Odd'. So this involves a change not only in sentence structure and rhythm but also in diction. Likewise, the first edition reads, 'He grasped her by the shoulder, with one hand pushed her from him; and . . .'. But the manuscript reads, 'He grasped her by the shoulder with one hand ⟨and⟩ pushd her from him and . . .'. The cancelled 'and' reveals the true structure and rhythm of the sentence: 'He grasped her by the shoulder with one hand, pushed her from him, and . . .' (335.38–39).

Because Scott uses formal punctuation so scantly, his periods, colons, question marks, exclamation points, italics, and paragraph indentations acquire special force. The present text retains them, except in the face of compelling evidence to the contrary. For example, to justify the bullying of his sister, Mowbray refers to 'my honour and that of my family'. Clara responds, 'Your honour?' (219.7–8). The logic of the dialogue and the punctuation of the manuscript both require the question mark, but the first edition changes it—here, and in more than a dozen other instances —to an exclamation point. When Etherington approaches Clara for the first time since his marriage trick of seven years ago, he 'in a firmer accent said, "*Clara*"' (224.10–11). The first edition ignores Scott's underlining. But the opposite too is almost always true in these matters, and the first edition italicises words—naive, coterie, remora, pro and con, honoraria, magnum, ton—that Scott's manuscript and the *OED* indicate were already Anglicised.

Scott, as we have seen (388), experimented with proper names, and the names of some minor characters and places were never stabilised. The present text standardises all proper names, a process that involves the very title of the novel. In the manuscript, 'Saint Ronan's' appears 184 times; 'St Ronan's', the traditional spelling, never appears. The present text reverts to Scott's spelling. It restores Scott's correct spelling of actual persons and places, like 'Pontey', 'Niel Gow', and 'Oronoko'. It corrects first-edition misreadings of 'Hussein' and 'Freeman' and restores Meg's affectionate references to 'Frauncie' Tyrrel.

Verbal Emendations. Besides the familiar errors that occur in the development of any lengthy hand-written manuscript, such as the alteration of tenses and the transposition of words, Scott's handwriting engenders certain recurrent mistakes. In addition, the intermediaries omitted words, inserted words, and altered dialect forms inappropriately.

1] *Correction of common errors.* Scott's vowels are often indistinguishable, his 'r' and 'n' are similar, and it is sometimes hard to tell whether a word ends with an 's', an 'e', or a flourish. In *Saint Ronan's Well*, the following words have been misread because of a confusion over vowels (the MS reading is given first): mere / more; these / those; an / on; further / farther; in / on; on / in; Mack / Mick; tune / tone; and many more. The following words have been misread because of a confusion over 'r' and 'n': ever / even; there / then; where / when; wherever / whenever. The following words provide a sample of those that reveal a confusion over the final stroke: book / books; hands / hand; manners / manner; strange / stranger; twaddle / twaddler; drawing / drawings; spoke / spoken; degradations / degradation; knees / knee; regards / regard; road / roads; large / larger; soothe / sooth; reins / rein; folk / folks; philosopher / philosophers. The last example above can be read confidently only because the specific philosopher who is alluded to can be identified.

2] *Correction of Omissions.* Some manuscript material got lost during transmission, and some was cut by Scott; how much of each is difficult to determine and ultimately depends upon critical judgment. The evidence of the manuscript shows that Scott is reluctant to cut. Several omissions in the first edition clearly result from accident because they lead to untenable readings. For example, 'This recollection had not escaped Tyrrel, to whom the whole scenery was familiar, who now hastened to the spot' requires the 'and' before 'who' that is found in the manuscript (77.17–19). Several omissions occur because of difficulties in reading Scott's manuscript. For example, 'the others . . . were glad to make a matter of importance out of the most trivial occurrence' (35.10–12) loses its 'out' because the word is hard to find on the verso where it was added. But the majority of instances depend upon critical judgment. Was the old hump-backed postillion 'an assistant' (first edition) or 'an occasional assistant' (MS) to a still more aged hostler (9.15)? Sometimes, a consideration of the entire text tips the balance back to the manuscript reading. Lady Penelope, who orates about the battle of the sexes, probably said, 'That is always the way with us girls' (first edition loses 'girls'), especially since she refers to 'these conceited male wretches amongst us' in the next sentence (59.10–11). Likewise, she probably said 'good Queen Bess' (first edition: 'Queen Bess'), when she blessed the memory of her power and virginity (64.17). Even the narrator carries on this sub-text when he asks, 'how can mere masculine eyes' (first edition loses 'mere') judge room arrangements (89.36). The present text restores omissions when there is grammatical, thematic, or stylistic justification.

The examples above all involve a single word, but the present text also restores six phrases and a sentence from the manuscript. Miss Digges's costume is described as follows: 'Muslin trowsers, adorned with spangles, a voluminous turban of silver gauze, and wings of the same, together with an embroidered slipper, with a pretty ankle peeping out above it' (184.32–34). The omission of the final phrase intimates the prudishness of James Ballantyne. One of Meg Dods's conclusions—'And besides a' that I see them a' down the black gate before I change my auld ways or charge them a penny mair than I have done this twenty years' (9.3–5)—was probably omitted because the caret sign that points to the addition on the verso is obscure.

3] *Correction of Insertions.* Once again, the reverse process also occurs. The first edition is nearly as liable to add unnecessary material as it is to omit necessary. Many of these additions seem superfluous: 'his ear alertly awake to every sound which mingled with the passing breeze or ↑with↓ the ripple of the brook' (81.1–3), or 'the copper-nosed sheriff-clerk of the county, who, when summoned by official duty to that district ↑of the shire↓' (10.33–34). Sometimes, they strain to enhance the utterances of low characters. Thus, Sir Bingo's epistle is improved:

> Sur—Jack Moobray has betted with me that the samon you killed ↑on↓ Saturday last weyd ni to eiteen pounds,—I say nyer sixteen. —So you being a spurtsman, 'tis refer'd. (41.22–24)

Likewise, Meg's directness is blunted: 'They had ⟨leave⟩ ↑been↓ ower the neighbour's ground ↑they had leave on↓ up to the march' (24.22). In several instances, the incorrect insertion results from an ignorance of Scott's allusion or idiom. Thus, the first-edition quotation from Mat Lewis's 'A Gay, Gold Ring',

> 'This ring ↑my↓ Lord Brooke from his daughter took',

destroys both accuracy and rhythm (54.25). Similarly, 'Never did Earl . . . fly ↑into↓ a pitch of more uncontrollable rage' (232.37–38) alters a perfectly legitimate figure of speech.[71] The editor of Scott learns a new respect for his author's command of the language.

4] *Dialect.* Scott grants his lower-class characters distinctive speech patterns and vocabularies, carefully distinguishing between the language of Mrs Blower of the Bow-head and Captain MacTurk of the Highlands. The first edition inconsistently corrects anomalies and regularises dialect. The following are a few of the words spoken by Scottish characters in the manuscript that are regularised in the first edition: wi' / with; pit / put; frae / from; aff / off; whan / when; dauncing / dancing; ane / one; toun / town; o' / of; fo'k / folk; suner / sooner; a' / all; nae / no; doun / done; na / no; wad / would; ony / any; fand / found; powed / pulled.

Mrs Blower's 'Keckleben' and 'Cacklehen' are corrected to Quackleben, her 'Sir Bungo' is corrected to Bingo, and her 'vesshel', 'forshaken', and 'doun' are converted into 'proper' English. MacTurk's 'goot', 'peg' (for beg), 'Binco', 'gentlemans', 'py Cott', 'Mowpray', and much more are changed into King's English. The point of the scene between Captain Jekyl and the young vagabond at the end of Volume 3, Chapter 4, is blunted because of an itch to correct.

Again, the opposite process also occurs. In some instances the first edition has changed the English of the manuscript into Scots.

Verbal Emendations: Individual Words. In addition to the kinds of verbal emendation listed above, the present text corrects over sixty individual words of the first edition by returning to the reading of the manuscript. These corrections are necessitated by a variety of errors that were made in the creation of the first edition.

1] *Avoidance of Repetition.* The intermediaries had standing orders to avoid the repetition of words in close proximity. In some instances, however, their jugglings resulted in a loss of meaning or the substitution of an inferior word. For example, in the manuscript, Bindloose says, '"You do not seem much pleased with our improvements, sir"', and Touchwood replies, '"Pleased?"' (135.19–22). The mocking echo is lost when the first edition alters the first 'pleased' to 'delighted'.

Likewise, Meg originally complains, 'Vera bonnie wark this!—vera bonnie wark indeed!—a decent house to be disturbed at these hours—Keep a public—as weel keep a bedlam!' (87.1–3). The first edition weakens this complaint by changing the second 'bonnie' to the unlikely 'creditable'.

Mowbray originally complains to Touchwood, 'I cannot help wishing you had conducted yourself with more frankness and less mystery and I am truly afraid your love of mystery has been too much for your ingenuity' (349.26–28). In his anxiety to avoid repetition, an intermediary has replaced the second 'mystery' with the dubious 'dexterity'.

2] *Misunderstandings.* The first edition sometimes goes astray because of a misunderstanding of Scott's allusions or diction. Its 'there was a play filled' misses the 'fitted' of *A Midsummer Night's Dream* (185.7), and its 'were he ten times my brother' misses the 'our' of *Hamlet* (244.39–40). The first edition describes Cargill as being 'of a dark complexion', but the manuscript reading—'of an adust complexion' (154.7)—is more

original and appropriate. And of course 'tirrivie', discussed above (393), is also restored.

3] *Misreadings.* Anyone who has struggled with Scott's manuscripts can sympathise with the transcriber and other intermediaries. The secretive and complex process of printing the books, the indistinguishable vowel signs and consonantal confusions of Scott's handwriting, his neglecting to check proofs against manuscript, all contribute to the misreading of many words from the manuscript. As we have seen (393–94), the misreadings range from the curious to the ludicrous, and they have now been emended.

4] *Bad Alterations.* Some word changes in the first edition cannot be explained in terms of avoidance of repetition, misunderstanding, or misreading; they are just bad changes. It is assumed that Scott neither initiated nor sanctioned them, and so a return to the manuscript is made. For example, the change of Meg's exclamation, 'God guide us!' (161.32) to 'Gude guide us!' suggests the fastidiousness of James Ballantyne. Clara originally protests, 'God gave not one potsherd the right to break another' (225.16–17); the change of 'right' to 'power' subverts the meaning of the text.

5] *Cruxes.* Three words in the manuscript remain unreadable. An educated guess can be made at one of them. Near the climax of the action, Mowbray traces his sister along a favourite walk that 'she might perhaps have adopted from mere habit, when in a state of mind, which, he had too much reason to fear, must have put choice out of the question' (356.38–40). The word 'state' from the first edition resembles not the word in the manuscript. That word begins 'dis-' at the right edge of the manuscript, continues 'tur' at the left edge, and then breaks off. The rest of the word is then written in a different ink and on a slightly higher level. Perhaps, when Scott resumed writing, he glanced to the right and saw 'dis-' as 'li-', looked to the left and saw 'tur' as 'ter', and so added 'ature' to complete 'literature'. The present edition speculates that Scott originally intended to write about Clara's 'disturbance of mind'.

The other two cruxes are baffling. Mowbray claims, 'there are better dogs bred in the kennel than in the parlour' (167.36–37). But the word in the manuscript is not 'parlour'. It looks a little like 'barrel' but is something else again. Likewise, Clara says, 'Bring Lady Binks, if she has the condescension to honour us' (67.29). But the word in the manuscript is not 'condescension'. It looks a little like 'least' or 'lust' or 'bust'. So the present text has been forced to retain the substituted readings, 'parlour' and 'condescension', of the first edition.

Later-edition Emendations. The present text includes 50 necessary emendations, including 22 verbal emendations, drawn from later editions of *Saint Ronan's Well.* For example, in both the manuscript and first edition, Meg told Bindloose that the duel between Tyrrel and Sir

Bingo was to be held 'the neist day'. But the conversation between Tyrrel and MacTurk emphasised that the meeting was scheduled for one o'clock that same afternoon (110.28). The 12mo emended to 'that vara day', and the Magnum emended to 'that same day', but the present text uses the 18mo reading of 'that vera day' (129.35) because it is most consistent with Meg's speech patterns.

The change from 'It did indeed arise' to 'The screen was indeed withdrawn' is needed because, at this outdoor performance of *A Midsummer Night's Dream*, there was no curtain but only a screen (190.13). The additional sentence, 'I have given it to Lady Penelope' (209.12–13), is needed to make clear to Mowbray (and the reader) that the rival for Clara's shawl is not Lady Binks, but Lady Penelope.

Editorial Emendations. The present text includes 14 editorial emendations that are entirely original. Eleven of these emendations are indispensable. For example, Hannah Irwin referred to herself as a 'wifeless mother', an absurdity that was noted only by the 18mo, which deleted the expression. The present text chooses, rather, to correct it to a 'husbandless mother' (309.4–5), although tempted by the contemporary 'a single mother'.

The other 3 editorial emendations are more debatable. Forgetting the danger to British citizens, Scott has the cowardly Lady Penelope visit the Louvre in 1800. The present text changes the date to 1802 (54.39), the year of the Peace of Amiens. This is in accord with the policy of the Edinburgh Edition of the Waverley Novels to correct obvious errors of historical dating.

The other 2 emendations involve the Indian shawl, the chief stage property of the plot. Mowbray informs Micklewhame that he has got 'Lady Binks's maid to tell me what her mistress has set her mind on' (167.1–2) and that he wants the shawl for Clara: 'as Lady Binks writes by to-morrow's post, your order can go by to-night's mail' (167.8–9). These and other early references suggest that Scott originally intended to make Lady Binks the antagonist of Clara. But that role is quickly assumed by Lady Penelope. It was Lady Pen, according to Clara, who had ordered the shawl:

> she really had something to complain of in the present case. The shawl had been bespoke on her account, or very nearly so—she shewed me the tradesman's letter—only some agent of yours had come in between with the ready money, which no tradesman can resist.—Ah, John! I suspect half of your anger is owing to the failure of a plan to mortify poor Lady Pen, and that she has more to complain of than you have. (209.38–210.1)

As a result of this escalating rivalry, Lady Penelope precipitates the tragedy by exposing Clara's secret. Because Scott unwittingly changed agents in mid-stream, the present text emends Mowbray's two references above to read now, 'Lady Pen's maid' and 'Lady Penelope'.

NOTES

All manuscripts referred to are in the National Library of Scotland (NLS) unless otherwise stated.

1 J. G. Lockhart, *Memoirs of the Life of Sir Walter Scott, Bart.*, 7 vols (Edinburgh, 1837–38), 5.149.
2 MS 683, f. 36r.
3 Thomas Constable, *Archibald Constable and His Literary Correspondents: A Memorial*, 3 vols (Edinburgh, 1873), 3.240.
4 'The Hall of Justice' (1807) by George Crabbe (1754–1832) tells the story of a young woman driven towards madness by being forcibly married twice, to a father and son. For Scott's admiration of the poem, see *The Letters of Sir Walter Scott*, ed. H. J. C. Grierson and others, 12 vols (London, 1932–37), 6.254.
5 *Life*, 5.284–85.
6 MS 323, f. 398r.
7 MS 323, f. 400v.
8 MS 323, f. 401r.
9 MS 323, f. 403r.
10 *Letters*, 8.11
11 MS 323, ff. 410r.–11v.
12 *As You Like It*, 3.2.152.
13 The young hero of *The Antiquary* by Scott.
14 William Congreve, *The Way of the World*, 1.9.10–11.
15 See *A Lamentable Tragedy, Mixed Full of Mirth Conteyning the Life of Cambises, King of Percia*, by Thomas Preston.
16 *Letters*, 8.29.
17 See James C. Corson, *Notes and Index to Sir Herbert Grierson's Edition of 'The Letters of Sir Walter Scott'* (Oxford, 1979), 222.
18 MS 323, ff. 430–32.
19 MS 320, f. 138r.
20 Constable, 3.267.
21 MS 323, f. 439v.
22 MS 323, ff. 441r–42v.
23 MS 320, f. 149r.
24 *Letters*, 7.380–81.
25 MS 320, f.161r.
26 Corson, 216.
27 *Letters*, 8.71n.
28 MS 323, ff. 464v.–65v.
29 MS 792, pp. 176–77, 179, 181.
30 *Letters*, 8.88.
31 MS 792, p. 146.
32 *Letters*, 8.88–89.
33 *Letters*, 8.113.
34 An advertisement in *The Edinburgh Evening Courant* of 23 October

claimed that the novel was 'nearly ready'.

35 MS 792, p. 172.
36 MS 792, p. 173.
37 Corson, 227.
38 *Letters*, 8.123.
39 It was announced by *The Edinburgh Evening Courant* and reviewed by *The Literary Chronicle* and *Literary Gazette* on 27 December 1823.
40 The quarto-type leaves of the manuscript measure, with slight variations, 26.6 by 20.6 cm. Three watermarks are found throughout in the following general order: (1) A COWAN 1822, (2) a horn device (cf. Heawood 2774) and the date 1817, and (3) VALLEYFIELD 1817. The chain lines are approximately 2.5 cm. apart.
41 Lady Louisa Stuart, 'To Sir Walter Scott', 26 Mar. 1824, *Letters*, 8.241n.
42 For praise of the scenes between John and Clara Mowbray, especially the final one, see the above letter of Lady Louisa Stuart, and Sydney Smith, 'To Sir Walter Scott', 28 Dec. 1823, *The Letters of Sydney Smith*, ed. N. C. Smith (Oxford, 1953), 404–5; John Buchan, *Sir Walter Scott* (New York, 1932), 262; and Edgar Johnson, *Sir Walter Scott: The Great Unknown*, 2 vols (New York, 1970), 919–20.
43 *The Journal of Sir Walter Scott*, ed. W. E. K. Anderson (Oxford, 1972), 178.
44 *Life*, 5.315–6.
45 J. M. Collyer, '"The Catastrophe" in "St Ronan's Well"', *The Athenaeum*, No. 3406, 4 Feb. 1893: 154–55.
46 See John Updike, '"The Scandal of *Ulysses*": An Exchange', *The New York Review of Books*, 18 Aug. 1988, 63.
47 *Letters*, 8.29
48 James Thorpe, *Principles of Textual Criticism* (San Marino, 1972), 180.
49 The first edition of *Saint Ronan's Well* is textually stable. There were no textual variants in the ten copies of the first edition that were examined. There were six variations in press figures.
50 *Letters*, 10.56.
51 Corson, 268.
52 For these and additional details, see MS 113, pp. 199–200, and G. A. M. Wood, 'Scott's Continuing Revision: the Printed Texts of "Redgauntlet"', *The Bibliotheck* 6 (1973): 122–23.
53 MS 794, f. 178r.
54 My 'copy' was actually a composite. Volume one of this rare edition was made available to me by the University of Stirling Library, and a microfilm of volume two by the British Library.
55 *Journal*, 412.
56 *Letters*, 10.356.
57 *Journal*, 414.
58 *Journal*, 177–78.
59 *Letters*, 10.77.
60 *Journal*, 412.
61 For information, see *Scott's Interleaved Waverley Novels: An Introduction and Commentary*, ed. Iain Gordon Brown (Aberdeen, 1987).
62 MS 21021, f. 5v. See also *Journal*, 619, and Jane Millgate, *Scott's Last*

Edition: A Study in Publishing History (Edinburgh, 1987), 25.

63 *Puck*, the most successful of the Shakespearean pictures of Sir Joshua Reynolds (1723–92), was seen at the Academy in 1789 and was sold between 22 June 1789 and December 1790 for a hundred guineas. For complete information and a reproduction, see *Reynolds*, ed. Nicholas Penny (New York, 1986), 322–23.

64 Interleaved Set additions are given here in their original (MSS 23026–7) rather than their final Magnum form, but the references are to Volumes 33 and 34 of the Magnum Opus.

65 Scott is exact. Marchthorn is a Royal Burgh. After the Union of 1707, the Royal Burghs of Scotland (except for Edinburgh) were grouped together in a series of small groups of 4 or 5 to elect a member.

66 For information on the Magnum, see Millgate, *Scott's Last Edition*.

67 Sir Walter Scott, *St. Ronan's Well*, in *Waverley Novels*, 28 vols (1829–33), 33.114. The missing paragraph should appear between Mrs Blower's direct address to Mr Chatterley and the entrance of Mr Winterblossom.

68 Donald Pizer, 'Self-Censorship and Textual Editing', *Textual Criticism and Literary Interpretation*, ed. Jerome J. McGann (Chicago, 1985), 150–51.

69 G. Thomas Tanselle, *Textual Criticism since Greg: A Chronicle, 1950–1985* (Charlottesville, 1987), 132.

70 Collyer, 155.

71 *OED*, 'pitch', 18.

EMENDATION LIST

The base-text for this edition of *Saint Ronan's Well* is a specific copy of the first edition (1823), owned by the Edinburgh Edition of the Waverley Novels. All emendations to this base-text, whether verbal, orthographical, or punctuational, are listed below, with the exception of certain general categories of emendation described in the next paragraph, and of those errors which result from accidents of printing such as a letter dropping out, provided always that the evidence for the 'correct' reading has been found in at least one other copy of the first edition.

The following proper names have been standardised throughout on the authority of Scott's preferred usage as deduced from the manuscript: Saint Ronan's, Aulton, Buckstane, Shaws-Castle, Saint James's, Rachael Bonnyrig, Chatterley, Micklewhame (except where the spelling of this name reflects MacTurk's pronunciation), Quentin Quackleben, Pot, and Scrogie. The typographic presentation of mottoes, volume and chapter headings, letters, inset quotations, and the opening words of volumes and chapters has been standardised. Ambiguous end-of-line hyphens in the base-text have been interpreted in accordance with the following authorities (in descending order of priority): predominant first edition usage; octavo *Tales and Romances*; Magnum; MS.

Each entry in the list below is keyed to the text by page and line number; the reference is followed by the new EEWN reading, then in brackets the reason for the emendation and, after the slash, the base-text reading that has been replaced.

The great majority of emendations are derived from the manuscript. Most involve merely the replacement of one reading by another, and these are listed with the simple explanation '(MS)'. The spelling and punctuation of some emendations from the manuscript have been normalised in accordance with the prevailing conventions of the base-text, and where editorial intervention to normalise spelling or punctuation has been required, the exact manuscript reading is given in the form '(MS actual reading)'. Where the new reading has required editorial interpretation, in the provision of punctuation, for example, the explanation is given in the form '(MS derived: actual reading)'. Occasionally, some explanation of the editorial thinking behind an emendation is required, and this is provided in a brief note.

The following conventions are used in transcriptions from Scott's manuscript: deletions are enclosed ⟨thus⟩ and insertions ↑thus↓; an insertion within an insertion is indicated by double arrows ↑↑thus↓↓; superscript letters are lowered without comment; the letters 'NL' (new line) are Scott's own and indicate that he wished a new paragraph to be started, in spite of running on the text, whereas the words '[new paragraph]' are editorial and indicate that Scott opened a new paragraph on a new line. A question mark denotes an element of doubt about a reading.

Some errors and confusions in the manuscript persisted into the first edition. When straightening these the editor has studied the manuscript context so as to determine Scott's original intention, and where the original intention is discernible it is, of course, restored. But from time to time such confusions cannot be rectified in this way. In these circumstances Scott's own corrections in the Interleaved Set have more authority than the proposals of other editions, but if they have nothing to offer, the reading from the earliest edition to offer a satisfactory solution is adopted as the best means of rectifying a fault. Readings from the later editions and the Interleaved Set are indicated by '(8vo)', '(12mo)', '(18mo)', '(ISet)', and '(Magnum)'. Emendations that have not been anticipated by a contemporaneous edition are indicated by '(Editorial)'. In these cases it may be assumed that the manuscript reading is the same as that of the first edition unless otherwise indicated.

Title-page SAINT (Editorial) / ST
In the MS, 'Saint' appears (as part of 'Saint Ronan's') 184 times; St never appears.

Title-page "A jolly place," said he, "in times of old! / But something ails it now —the place is curst." (Editorial) / A merry place, 'tis said, in days of yore; / But something ails it now—the place is curst.
This edition restores Wordsworth's exact words in accordance with Scott's stated intention. Scott wrote to James Ballantyne, probably in December 1823, 'The title page may bear for motto the lines of Wordsworth / A merry place he said in days of yore / But something ails it now—the place is curst. / You may look up the exact words in the poem of Hartleap Well' (*Letters*, 8.123). Apparently Ballantyne failed to look up the 'exact words', which have been as now given since the second edition of *Lyrical Ballads* (1800).

1.18 History (MS) / history
3.22 to (MS) / with
3.23 mere (MS) / more
3.25 Scottish (MS) / Scotch
3.28 cottages (MS) / huts
4.2 repair—places essential, the (MS repair—places essential the) / repair; places essential—the
4.13 presbytery. And (MS presbytery And) / presbytery; and
4.21 assemblage (MS) / assembly
4.42 naive (MS) / *naïf*
5.5 these (MS) / those
5.9 his Castle (MS) / the Castle
5.18 these (MS) / those
5.34 Laurence (MS) / Lawrence
5.34 Crows (MS) / crows
5.40 episcopal (MS episcopopal) / Episcopal
6.3 "A jolly place," said he, "in times of old! / But something ails it now—the place is curst." (Editorial) / A merry place, 'tis said, in days of yore; / But something ails it now—the place is curst.
See the note above on the emendation to the Title-page.
6.25 desired (MS derived: desire) / desire

7.8 cleanliness (MS) / nicety
8.2 Woe to those (MS) / Those
8.3 Ronan's (8vo) / Ronans
8.3 Ronan's; well (MS Ronans, well) / Ronans, well
The semicolon is required after the restitution of the (MS) "Woe to those" at the beginning of the sentence.
8.4 pay them back (MS) / pay back
8.18 might be (MS) / is vouched to have been
8.39 them—they (MS) / them. They
8.40 them—they (MS) / them! They
8.41 hoddle (MS) / hottle
8.41 hoddle (MS) / hottle
8.42 Ay (MS) / ay
9.3 out. And besides ... this twenty years." (MS out. ↑And besides a' that" she concluded "I see them a down the black gate before I change my auld ways or charge them a penny mair than I have done this twenty years.↓) / out."
Scott's insertion on the verso was overlooked.
9.9 book (MS) / books
9.15 an occasional assistant (MS) / an assistant
9.35 wi' (MS) / with
9.42 heard (MS) / kenn'd
10.28 When (MS) / when
10.29 pit (MS) / put
10.30 And (MS) / and
10.34 district, (MS) / district of the shire,
10.38 House (MS) / house
10.38 Vintner (MS) / vintner
10.42 than their taste (MS) / than of their taste
11.32 possible some (MS) / possible that some
11.34 think that they (MS) / think they
13.10 and to apostrophize (MS) / and apostrophize
13.11 ever (MS) / even
13.32 frae (MS) / from
14.5 by (MS) / to
14.14 hands (MS) / hand
14.26 aff (MS) / off
14.28 on (MS) / upon
15.8 awakened. At (MS awakend. At) / awakened At
15.10 ye— (MS) / ye?—
15.11 parts. (MS) / parts?
15.30 Frauncie (MS) / Francie
15.34 further (MS) / farther
15.35 them—they (MS) / them. They
15.37 they (MS) / They
15.37 bye. They (MS) / bye—they
16.38 had it been called (MS had it been calld) / were it called
16.40 her he (MS) / her that he
16.43 in (MS) / on
17.4 make (MS) / awake
17.13 further (MS) / farther
17.40 wha's (MS) / which of the customers is
17.40 pothecaries' (MS pothecaries) / docter's
17.40 drugs (MS) / drogs
17.41 Scots (MS scots) / Scotch

17.41 them (MS) / their viols
18.7 When (MS) / when
18.13 wild-ducks (MS) / wild-duck
18.27 And (MS) / and
18.30 house—but (MS) / house.—And
19.1 whan (MS) / when
19.20 smore (MS) / smoor
19.22 yonder and (MS) / yonder. And
19.24 has no (MS) / hasna
19.25 think that if (MS) / think if
19.31 Scotswoman (MS) / Scotchwoman
19.31 dauncing (MS) / dancing
19.32 night o' (MS) / night in
19.35 days of (MS) / days in
19.37 wi' (MS) / with
19.43 papery (MS) / popery
20.1 ane (MS) / one
20.1 in't (MS) / in it
20.4 Frauncie (MS) / Francie
20.5 Frauncie (MS) / Francie
20.7 carvy (MS) / carvey
20.7 penny of (MS) / penny-worth of
20.8 twa three (MS) / twa or three
20.9 came (MS) / cam
20.14 receive (MS) / recover
20.19 as nae other body (MS) / some gate naebody
20.20 And (MS) / and
20.28 And (MS) / and
20.37 on bare (MS) / on the bare
21.2 episcopals (MS) / episcopalians
21.5 toun (MS) / town
21.14 landlady—ill (MS) / landlady. Ill
21.14 forbye (MS) / let be
21.15 An (MS) / an
21.16 Frauncie (MS) / Francie
21.19 verse for the property, (MS verse for the property) / verse,
21.19 whan (MS) / when
21.29 there is (MS) / there's
21.40 tother's slept (MS tothers slept) / t'other has slept
21.40 this (MS) / these
22.1 aneugh (MS) / eneugh
22.3 son—(MS) / son,
22.21 Frauncie (MS) / Francie
22.40 Francis (MS) / Francie
22.42 And (MS) / and
23.15 Mowbray,—keep (MS Mowbray—keep) / Mowbray, keep
23.22 Frauncie (MS) / Francie
24.18 brought baith him (MS) / brought him
24.20 howff (MS) / houff
24.22 leave (MS) / been
24.22 ground up (MS) / ground they had leave on up
24.30 directed (MS) / devoted
24.35 Frauncie (MS) / Francie
25.4 Frauncie (MS) / Francie
25.27 excellencies (MS) / xcellencies

25.29 o' (MS) / of
25.30 fo'k (MS) / folk
25.33 lown (MS) / loon
25.33 suner (MS) / sooner
25.37 a' (MS) / all
25.41 might (MS) / may
26.2 say't (MS) / say it
26.6 guineas (MS) / guines
26.7 o't (MS) / on't
26.22 slabs (*Letters*, 8.29) / dabs
In an undated letter to James Ballantyne Scott instructed that the sentence 'And Nanny... bacon' be added; the word 'slabs' must have been misread.
26.34 amongst (MS) / among
27.1 bitterness and wit (MS) / wit and bitterness
27.19 Scotsman (MS) / Scotchman
28.5 tea-room while the bottle continued to circulate; and on these occasions the Lady Penelope's suite was (MS tea-room while the bottle continued to circulate & on these occasions the Lady Penelope suite was) / tearoom; so that her society was
28.32 gifts. [new paragraph] *First* (MS gifts. NL *First*) / gifts. First
29.19 he spent (MS) / he had spent
29.31 on (MS) / in
29.43 table (MS) / taste
30.11 nose stood forth in the middle of (MS derived: nose stood forth in the of) / nose projected from the front of
Scott omitted a word as he moved from the end of one line to the beginning of the next. In those circumstances the correct emendation is the simplest.
30.29 took up (MS) / adopted
31.1 politeness, especially to (MS politeness especially to) / politeness to
31.5 to the great edification of all (MS) / to all
31.37 disordered nerves (MS disorderd nerves) / nervous disorders
32.28 Indian (MS) / India
32.29 And (MS) / and
32.29 go (MS) / Go
33.5 Indian (Editorial) / India
The adjectival form here makes it consistent with the MS reading 'Indian' at 32.28.
33.16 hook (MS) / crook
33.28 b—— I (Magnum) / b——I
34.11 Bingo," (MS) / Bingo,'
34.34 it (MS) / It
34.39 strange (MS) / stranger
34.42 Dorts's (MS derived: Dorts) / Dods's
35.4 curtesy (MS) / curtsey
35.12 importance out of (MS) / importance of
35.25 found an (MS) / found out an
35.27 Bing (MS) / Bingo
36.25 would," (MS would") / would,
36.26 think, "be (MS derived: think be) / think, be
The closing but not the opening inverted commas were provided in the MS.
36.36 in (MS) / on
37.9 But (MS) / but

37.14 their (MS) / that
37.27 their (MS) / the
38.12 their (MS) / the
38.21 remora (MS) / *remora*
38.27 Cleikum (8vo) / Cleekum
'Cleikum' appears 31 times in the base-text, 'Cleekum' this once only. The latter is based on a difficult MS reading because the second vowel is blotched.
38.31 Spaw (MS) / Spa
38.42 farther (MS) / further
39.4 in [purpose (MS) / [in purpose
39.13 repass (MS ↑re↓pass) / pass
39.18 twaddle (MS) / twaddler
39.19 coterie (MS) / *côterie*
40.5 further (MS) / farther
40.6 WELL (MS) / Well
40.30 ran (8vo) / run
41.22 killed Saturday (MS) / killed on Saturday
41.31 rivre (MS) / river
41.37 philosopher (MS) / philosophers
43.8 continue to (MS) / continue, to
43.31 and sensible (MS) / and was sensible
44.2 of (MS) / in
44.16 with a peculiar (MS) / with peculiar
44.22 nothing (MS) / Nothing
44.23 perhaps—or (MS) / perhaps.—Or
45.3 pro and con (MS) / *pro* and *con*
45.24 pleasing. [new paragraph] He (MS) / pleasing. He
An indentation on a new line indicates the opening of a new paragraph.
45.38 him (MS) / he
46.17 repair (MS) / have repaired
46.21 drawing (MS) / drawings
46.40 poney (MS) /*poney*
47.5 Micklewhame." [new paragraph] "See (12mo) / Micklewhame.—"See
A new paragraph is needed for a new speaker.
47.30 be now, (MS be now) / be,
48.7 Yes—with (MS) / Yes, with
49.29 bequest (MS) / inheritance
49.41 to. She (8vo) / to She
49.41 bottom well-principled, (MS) / bottom a well-principled woman,
49.43 in society (MS) / in her society
50.30 everything (MS) / every thing
50.39 and (MS) / or
51.11 stock. Out (MS) / stock; out
51.12 Andrea (MS) / Andrew
51.36 which (MS) / that
51.42 was the (MS) / was, the
52.27 on (MS) / to
53.17 the familiar dialogues (MS) / the 'Familiar Dialogues
53.18 occasions— (MS) / occasions'—
53.19 on (MS) / upon
53.20 has (MS) / hath
54.1 her—for (MS) / her.—For
54.15 come.—She (MS) / come—she

54.24 me! [new paragraph] "And (MS me [new paragraph] And) / me!" [new line] And
54.25 ring Lord Brooke (MS) / ring my Lord Brooke
Scott's original MS version is a correct quotation.
54.28 o'er [new paragraph] "You (MS oer [new paragraph] You) / o'er." [new line] You
Scott has a long indentation on a new line to indicate the opening of a new paragraph.
54.37 do not (MS) / don't
54.39 1802 (Editorial) / 1800
Until the Peace of Amiens in 1802, the War would have prevented Lady Penelope from going to Paris.
55.20 repose (MS) / bestow
55.26 Poetry (MS) / poetry
55.27 Music (MS) / music
56.1 having (MS) / my having
56.3 been only (MS) / only been
56.10 fairy (MS) / Fairy
56.25 his (MS) / the
56.30 these (MS) / the
58.5 dear (MS) / dearest
58.14 rink (MS) / ring
58.21 spoke (MS) / spoken
58.28 a (MS) / some
59.1 degradations (MS) / degradation
59.2 else no (MS) / else to be no
59.6 *âne* (12mo) / *ane*
59.7 *bien.*" [new paragraph] But (MS) / *bien!*" [new line] But
59.11 us girls, (MS) / us,
59.13 amongst (MS) / among
59.31 knees (MS) / knee
59.40 toddled (MS) / *toddled*
60.5 honoraria (MS) / *honoraria*
60.13 guid (MS) / gude
60.16 Keckleben (MS) / Quackleben
60.20 wine-glass (MS) / wine-glass-full
60.31 fo'k (MS) / folk
61.42 in: (MS) / in—
61.43 yours (MS) / your's
62.2 magnum (MS Magnum) / *magnum*
62.3 Bungo (MS) / Bingo
62.4 Cacklehen (MS) / Cocklehen
62.5 'in the wind's eye' (MS "in the winds eye") / in the wind's eye
62.6 Bungo (MS) / Bingo
62.14 na (MS) / nae
62.24 yours (MS) / your's
62.25 vesshel (MS) / vessel
62.31 forshaken (MS) / forsaken
62.32 the spirits—the spirits—the spirits (MS) / the spirits—the spirits
62.35 doun (MS) / done
63.18 and even (MS) / and that he had even
63.20 gallant, (MS) / gallant suitor,
63.23 regards (MS) / regard
63.34 do (18mo) / be
64.17 of good Queen (MS) / of Queen

64.31 come a funeral, (MS) / a funeral come of it,
65.3 the fondest tone of female (MS) / the tone of the fondest female
65.18 courtsying (MS) / curtseying
65.21 but she sate (MS) / but sat
65.22 courtsy (MS) / courtesy
65.27 halds (MS) / hauds
65.38 it is (MS) / it's
65.41 There is (MS) / There's
66.6 everything (MS) / every thing
66.23 here—what (MS) / here. What
67.1 Meantime (MS) / Meanwhile
67.4 new (MS) / favourite
67.38 a (MS) / *a*
67.38 *déjeuner* (ISet) / *dejeuner*
68.14 the prince Ahmed's quarters (MS derived: the prince [space] quarters) / the fairy prince's quarters
Scott left a large space in the MS after 'the prince', but the name has not been supplied until now.
68.21 only lions (MS) / lions only
73.5 and fain (MS) / and so I was fain
73.7 na (MS) / not
73.9 it's (8vo) / its
73.29 in (MS) / on
73.32 again (MS) / against
73.35 vagabonds— (MS) / vagabonds?—
73.35 can't (MS cant) / cannot
73.42 mention a fact (MS) / mention as a fact
74.15 there is something (MS) / there is a something
75.21 with (MS) / by
75.27 amongst (MS) / among
76.25 road (MS) / roads
76.29 copse-woods (MS) / copse-wood
76.40 Pontey (MS) / Ponty
The manuscript spelling of the name is correct.
77.19 familiar, and who (MS familiar and who) / familiar, who
77.20 behind (MS) / by
77.20 large (MS) / larger
77.23 whilst (MS) / while
77.43 goot (MS) / good
78.14 yours (MS) / your's
78.16 small-debt court (MS small debt court) / small debt-court
78.18 by (MS) / before
78.19 muckle (MS muikle) / meikle
78.20 peg (MS) / beg
78.35 amongst (MS) / among
78.40 *déjeuner* (ISet) / *dejeuner*
79.6 well (MS) / Well
80.25 *Souvenir* (MS) / *souvenir*
81.3 or the ripple (MS) / or with the ripple
81.17 forwards (MS) / forward
81.36 between (MS) / betwixt
81.38 stood (MS) / endured
81.38 presence—but (MS) / presence, but
82.3 real—enable (MS) / real, enable
82.3 endure (MS) / bear

82.4 you—are (MS) / you, are
82.26 soothe (MS) / sooth
82.32 And (MS) / and
82.40 obliges me to go into company sometimes (MS) / obliges me sometimes to go into company
83.8 mine—if (MS) / mine. If
83.10 is (MS) / Is
83.10 they (MS) / They
83.33 mine" (MS) / mine'
84.32 are now only (MS) / are only
85.2 Tyrell, unable in the bitterness of his heart any longer (MS) / Tyrell, in the bitterness of his heart, unable any longer
85.13 She (MS) / The poor young lady
85.23 were (MS) / was
85.34 please him? (Editorial) / please him—
It seems from the next emendation that an intermediary put the question mark in the wrong position.
85.35 pain— (MS) / pain?—
86.3 ever— (MS) / ever?—
86.15 reins (MS) / rein
86.21 same (Magnum) / opposite
87.1 bonnie (MS) / creditable
87.29 My bill? (MS) / My bill!
87.29 to-morrow? (MS tomorrw) / to-morrow!
This question mark is implied by the question mark immediately preceding.
87.36 customer.—Odd, I (MS customer—Odd I) / customer;—and I
87.40 wi' (MS) / with
87.41 there is (MS) / there's
87.41 o't (MS) / on't
87.43 nonsense splore the (MS) / nonsense the
88.13 assemble . . . Manor. (MS assemble the flower of the company now at Saint Ronans well in the halls of the Lord of the Manor.) / assemble in the halls of the Lord of the Manor the flower of the company now at St Ronan's Well.
88.20 he contrived (MS) / he generally contrived
88.21 his companions should be entertained where (MS his companions should be entertaind where) / to receive his companions where
88.28 that (MS) / which
88.30 trouble accordingly devolved (MS) / trouble devolved
88.38 after (MS) / in
89.2 to put things in some order to receive his guests (MS) / or opinion concerning the previous arrangements
89.5 ton (MS) / *ton*
89.7 The solid (MS) / The more solid
89.13 like (MS) / likely
89.19 stable (MS) / stables
89.36 can mere masculine (MS) / can masculine
90.11 lamer (MS) / lanmer
90.22 Oronoko (MS) / Oroonoko
91.18 order to the guidance of chance, (MS order to the guidance of chance) / order,
91.40 Senior (MS) / senior
92.9 say. Half (MS) / say—half
92.32 bog. Troth (MS bog Troth) / bog? Troth

93.5 na (MS) / no
93.10 there (MS) / then
93.15 this agent (MS) / his agent
93.29 folk (MS) / folks
94.6 if you were to lose (MS) / if you win them to lose
94.26 warks (MS) / wark
95.8 Mack (MS) / Mick
95.25 Mack (MS mack) / Mick
95.42 maist sib (MS) / nearest sib
96.18 wad (MS) / would
96.22 Ronan's (12mo) / Ronans
96.42 divert her. (8vo) / divert.
97.6 on (MS) / in
97.9 ye (MS) / you
97.15 me. So (MS) / me—so
97.39 Mack (MS) / Mick
98.6 Mack (MS) / Mick
99.25 male (MS) / thick
99.42 it will (MS) / that will
100.8 or a remonstrance (MS) / or remonstrance
100.19 please yourself (MS) / yourself please
101.3 and such mazareen-blue (MS) / and mazareen-blue
101.16 in (MS) / of
103.9 sheet (MS) / shirt
This misreading of the MS was not corrected by any other edition, despite making nonsense of the passage.
103.15 and a fanciful (MS) / and fanciful
103.18 from (MS) / out of
103.20 like (MS) / likely
103.21 Spaw (MS) / Spring
103.25 brother, John, and (MS brother John and) / brother, and
104.4 that (MS) / which
104.21 sort (MS) / sorts
104.28 he did (MS) / he "did
104.31 him. (MS) / him."
105.22 Spaw (MS) / Spa
106.11 Binco (MS) / Bingo
106.16 conditions (MS) / condition
106.21 and the door slam (MS) / and saw the door shut
106.43 an ill (MS) / a poor
107.7 ony (MS) / any
107.12 Mr (MS) / Maister
107.20 gentlemans (MS) / gentleman
107.29 aneugh (MS) / eneugh
108.14 sald (MS) / should
108.20 parlour he (MS) / parlour which he
108.32 cat-a-nine-tails (MS) / cat-o'-nine-tails
109.4 you were (Editorial) / you was
In the MS the original reading was 'I was'. Scott changed 'I' to 'you' but forgot to change 'was' to 'were'.
109.30 latest. You (MS latest You) / latest—you
110.7 inference? (MS) / inference.
110.28 *one* (MS) / one
110.40 intimates (MS) / intimate
110.40 th'ould (MS th ould) / the ould

110.41 him from (MS) / him unloosed from
110.41 petticoat-string (MS petticoat string) / petticoat
112.3 Binco (MS) / Bingo
112.5 it all (MS) / it at all
112.28 His (MS) / This
112.36 said, that (MS said that) / said, "that
112.43 him. (MS) / him."
113.7 of Mr Winterblossom (MS) / of Winterblossom
113.16 errand (MS) / occasion
113.34 from (MS) / for
113.39 like (MS) / likely
114.16 tooth-ache (MS) / tooth-ach
114.27 back-bone (MS) / back bone
114.41 it—no (MS) / it. No
116.7 looking at his (18mo) / looking his
116.10 wakened (MS wakend) / awakened
117.6 Bingo. (MS Bingo—) / Bingo?
117.27 Captain—out (MS) / Captain—Out
118.23 *procès* (ISet) / *proces*
118.29 on (MS) / in
119.3 canny (MS) / cunning
119.33 Tirrel (MS) / Tyrrel
The incorrect spelling of 'Tyrrel' throughout this statement seems to be deliberate.
119.36 Tirrel (MS) / Tyrrel
119.38 Tirrel (MS) / Tyrrel
120.1 Tirrel (MS) / Tyrrel
120.2 behalf. Which (MS) / behalf—which
120.4 Tirrel (MS) / Tyrrel
120.21 affiche (Magnum) / affiché
120.37 buskin'd (MS buskind) / buckskin'd
120.41 head (MS) / heads
121.3 wherever (MS) / whenever
121.5 be what (MS) / be he what
123.19 good (MS) / reasonable
123.24 take (MS) / make
123.29 nightly (MS) / mightily
124.21 whisky (MS) / whiskey
124.22 tim-whisky (MS) / tim-whiskey
124.30 no way (MS) / noway
124.41 whisky (MS) / whiskey
125.6 by (MS) / at
125.30 whisky (MS) / whiskey
125.34 draw (MS) / Draw
126.9 sit you down—sit you down—sit ye down (MS) / sit you down—sit you down—sit you down
126.12 ain (MS) / one
126.14 precious? (MS) / precious!
126.14 willywhaing (MS) / whullywhaing
126.35 compliment (MS) / compliments
126.37 matter? (12mo) / matter!
126.43 would have (MS) / would doubtless have
127.9 stand (MS) / become
127.20 cases, he quietly (MS) / cases, quietly
127.20 hers (MS) / her's

127.37 Mistress (MS) / Mrs
127.38 pro-fiscal (MS pro fiscal) / Procurator-fiscal
128.1 gledes (MS) / gleds
128.7 years (MS) / year
128.14 Francie (MS) / Francis
128.19 grey-hen (MS) / grey hen
128.26 doors (MS) / door
128.29 regular (MS) / regularly
129.8 Mistress (MS) / Mrs
129.9 hauld (MS) / haud
129.12 murther (MS) / murder
129.14 Murther (MS) / Murder
129.14 murther (MS) / murder
129.15 murther (MS) / murder
129.16 we (MS) / me
129.22 murthered (MS murtherd) / murdered
129.35 that vera day (18mo) / the neist day
The conversation between Tyrrel and MacTurk makes clear that the meeting was to be held at one that same afternoon. The 12mo emended the base-text to 'that vara day', and the Magnum emended to 'that same day'.
129.39 he (MS) / him
130.21 hand (MS) / hands
131.5 na (MS) / no
131.10 na (MS) / no
131.10 in (MS) / on
131.25 party (MS) / part
131.40 reasonable—consider (ISet) / reasonacble—onsider
131.40 isna (MS is na) / is no
132.2 sill— (MS) / siller
The MS reading is restored here on the assumption that Meg is being interrupted.
132.7 subject too (MS) / subject far too
132.8 subverted (MS) / converted
132.16 fand (MS derived: found) / fund
In the next chapter (135.39) Meg uses the form 'fand', which is more in accord with her speech pattern than 'found' or the base-text's 'fund'.
132.16 costs (MS) / cost
132.18 murthering (MS) / murdering
132.23 had but just (MS) / had just
133.4 their listening (MS) / them from listening
133.19 not (MS) / Not
133.19 cowrie (MS) / courie
133.24 about "the . . . trade." (MS about "the custom of the trade—") / about the custom of the trade.
133.25 Custom? (MS) / Custom!
133.39 my (MS) / me
134.8 courtsey (MS) / curtsey
134.17 burned (MS burnd) / burnt
134.20 by (MS) / with
134.32 braver (MS) / brawer
134.33 as if with (MS) / as with
135.15 powed (MS) / pulled
135.19 pleased (MS) / delighted
135.22 Pleased? (MS) / Pleased!

135.34 least (MS) / lest
135.36 weekdays (MS) / work days
135.37 doubted (MS) / doubtful
135.42 ballats (MS) / ballants
136.7 *gomerils* (MS) / gomerils
136.10 Scotsman (MS) / Scotchman
136.12 desert (MS) / desart
136.24 lords (MS) / lairds
136.38 and (MS) / And
136.38 it is (MS) / it's
137.28 amid (MS) / amidst
137.36 ye (MS) / you
137.41 old (MS) / Old
138.7 ye (MS) / you
138.10 been—this (MS) / been. This
138.13 so, sir," (MS so Sir") / so,"
138.19 forbearance: (MS) / forbearance;
139.5 wood (MS) / wud
139.7 Mr (MS) / Maister
140.1 rencontre (MS) / rencounter
140.16 Mistress (MS) / Mrs
140.17 has (MS) / had
140.19 there (MS) / There
140.27 whisky (MS) / whiskey
140.37 Bindloose, however, zealous (MS Bindloose ↑however↓ zealous) / Bindloose, zealous
141.27 ca'd (MS) / ca'ad
141.29 dared say (MS) / dared to say
141.40 ain (MS) / ane
141.42 Mr (MS) / Maister
142.1 doiled (MS doild) / doited
142.2 whisky (MS) / whiskey
142.5 ma'am, I (MS Maam I) / ma'am," answered the Oriental, "I
142.17 been fruitless (MS) / been found fruitless
143.22 incur himself (MS) / himself incur
143.37 attributes she (MS) / attributes which she
144.3 sometime (MS) / sometimes
144.19 Senior (MS) / senior
144.27 of man (MS) / of a man
144.27 be?" (12mo) / be?
144.28 men— (MS) / men?—
145.10 they that (MS) / them that
145.13 mickle (MS) / muckle
145.13 Mr (MS) / Maister
145.18 fakirs (MS) / Fakirs
145.18 dervises (MS) / Dervises
145.18 bonzes (MS) / Bonzes
145.22 doon (MS) / down
145.33 the true taste (MS) / the taste
145.41 three (ISet) / four
At 156.32 and 157.12 the dining hour is three.
145.42 out (MS) / me
145.42 Cockburn's (MS Cockburns) / Cockburn
145.42 particular Sherry (MS) / particular Indian Sherry
146.10 wad (8vo) / wald

146.18 reader. (MS) / reader
149.11 brother: (MS) / brother;
150.29 superintendent (MS) / superintendant
150.34 burned (MS burnd) / burnt
153.16 amongst (MS) / among
154.7 an adust (MS) / a dark
154.9 his (MS) / whose
155.29 Saint John (MS) / St John
156.13 which (MS) / that
158.2 wool-gathering: (MS) / wool-gathering;
158.9 us—why, you (MS us why you) /us—you
159.14 annal (MS) / annals
160.4 déjeuner (ISet) / dejeuner
160.5 a (Editorial) / A
The phrase 'A dramatic picture' is not in the MS and first appears in the base-text; when added it was not properly assimilated to the context.
160.19 Mr (MS) / Maister
160.32 till (MS) / until
160.42 about (MS) / of
161.16 Imaum (MS) / Imaun
161.27 whare's (MS) / where's
161.32 God (MS) / Gude
161.32 ye no weel (MS) / ye weel
161.43 least (MS) / lest
162.26 retreating (MS) / retracting
163.26 Barèges (MS Bareges) / Barege
163.30 *panpharmacon* (Magnum) / *panphamarcon*
165.8 ye (MS) / you
165.18 this (MS) / the
165.19 the Greeks?—the Greeks!—(MS the Greeks—the Greeks—) / the Greeks?—The Greeks!—
165.29 sound (MS) / whistle
It is necessary to return to the mansucript 'sound' because the base-text identifies a 'whistle' as a kind of groan.
166.7 frequent (MS) / frequeat
166.37 *paré* (8vo) / *parée*
166.40 tom-foolery (MS) / foolery
167.1 Lady Pen's maid (Editorial) / Lady Binks's maid
167.8 Lady Penelope (Editorial) / Lady Binks
This and the preceding emendation are made because it later becomes crucial to the plot that the shawl was sought by Lady Penelope.
167.14 na (MS) / not
168.35 favours (MS) / favour
169.33 And thus the poor devil," (MS And thus the poor devil") / And thus your friend, poor devil,"
169.38 loser. (MS loser—) / loser?
170.7 Mowbray. "You are but jesting—You (MS Mowbray "You are but jesting—You) / Mowbray; "you are but jesting—you
170.10 The Critic (MS the critic) / the Critic
170.17 nought (MS derived: not) / nothing
170.19 lord, undoubted heir (MS) / lord, an undoubted heir
172.7 is, as you (MS) / is, you
173.32 *lost* (MS) / lost
174.3 lordship is quite (MS) / lordshi p quite
174.12 and have (MS) / and I have

175.7 Mowbray? (MS) / Mowbray.
178.29 raw-head and bloody-bone (MS) / raw-head-and-bloody-bone
179.6 Sound (MS) / Well and sound
180.7 he could mingle with brother thanes and give (MS) / he could give
180.9 county (MS) / country
180.26 the disclosure (MS) / this partial disclosure
180.36 your coming (MS) / his coming
181.1 knaving (MS) / knowing
181.15 Yours (MS) / Your's
182.2 shelve, the difficulty namely (MS shelve the difficulty namely) / shelve, to wit, the difficulty
182.13 one in which, the (MS one in which the) / one, in which the
182.20 Commedia dell' arte (MS derived: Comedia del' arte) / Comedia del' Arte
182.26 presenters (MS) / personators
183.21 soothe (MS) / sooth
184.24 mountaineer, Egeus (MS) / mountaineer,—Egeus
184.34 slipper, with a pretty ankle peeping out above it, converted (MS slipper with a pretty ancle peeping out above it converted) / slipper, converted
185.7 fitted (8vo) / filled
This sentence is not in the MS. The first edition missed the quotation from *A Midsummer Night's Dream*.
185.9 present (MS) / represent
185.14 came (MS) / cam
185.16 eneugh (MS) / aneugh
185.19 a (MS) / a'
185.26 McDurk's (MS McDurks) / M'Durk's
185.37 in my line of practice (MS) / thus
185.38 easily (MS) /early
186.35 stone (MS) / stones
187.3 Christians. (MS) / Christians?
187.17 whisky (MS) / whiskey
187.25 curtains (MS) / curtain
187.29 Cleikum Inn, following (MS derived: Cleium inn following) / Cleikum, ever following
187.32 whisky (MS) / whiskey
187.34 actually discovered (MS) / actually at length discovered
188.5 Nabob (MS) / nabob
188.5 Minister (MS) / minister
188.26 the short avenue (MS) / the avenue
189.1 those who (MS) / others, who
189.32 humour (MS) / humours
190.2 rage. [new paragraph] And (MS rage [new line indented] And) / rage. [new line] And
190.9 Niel (MS) / Neil
190.13 The screen was indeed withdrawn (8vo) / It did indeed arise
Someone remembered that, at this outdoors theatre, there was no curtain to raise but a screen to be withdrawn.
190.20 supported (MS) / guarded
190.21 crutch (MS) / shield
191.34 neither but (MS) / neither—but
192.12 hae (MS) / has
194.15 newly acquired (MS) / newly-acquired
195.25 *où l'on dîne* (MS derived: *ou l'on dinent*) / *ou l'on dine*
195.32 gardens (MS) / grounds

196.2 and seemed (MS) / and which seemed
196.16 Moors (MS) / Moorish
197.13 Union (Magnum) / union
197.24 Dogs, and then were swamped at shooting the bridge, do (MS dogs and then were swampd at shooting the bridge do) / Dogs, do
198.31 have (MS) / Have
198.35 surface? Know (MS surface Know) / surface?—Know
199.1 our (MS) / a
199.42 may to (MS) / may chance to
201.32 must (MS) / *must*
202.38 the (MS) / The
203.19 words with (MS) / words, with
203.43 side, ... halfpenny. (MS side like Britannia with her ferine attendant on the reverse of a halfpenny.) / side.
204.11 closer (MS) / close
204.13 Episcopalian: (MS) / Episcopalian;
204.13 communion for (MS) / communion; for
204.17 score.—Indeed, she (MS score Indeed she) / score.—She
206.1 Who (MS) / who
209.1 such a sight (MS) / a sight
209.13 however. I have given it to Lady Penelope." (8vo) / however." The text must make clear to Mowbray (and the reader) that the rival for the shawl is Lady Penelope, not Lady Binks.
209.34 her own (MS) / her
209.39 bespoke (MS) / bespoken
210.16 of it (MS) / it
210.23 tricky (MS) / tricksy
210.32 guid (MS) / gude
210.39 forwards (MS) / forward
211.2 Mobrie (MS) / Moubrie
211.15 that is (MS) / that's
211.33 remained to (MS remaind to) / remained for her to
211.43 by Mr Winterblossom (MS) / by Winterblossom In the MS the sentence reads: 'the ↑place↓ ... had been seized upon as the best and softest chair in the room by Mr Winterblossom who after ...'. A verso addition, '↑and as placed near the head ... arranged↓', necessitated the rearrangement of the sentence, in the course of which 'Mr' was omitted.
212.13 honour?—no (MS honour—no) / honour to help you?—no
212.18 propitiate (MS) / propiate
212.41 it (MS) / the opportunity
213.2 the contending parties (MS the ↑contending↓ parties) / the parties
213.3 inconveniences (MS) / inconvenience
213.16 unc' (MS) / unca
213.29 had power (MS) / had any power
214.18 purpose (MS) / purposes
216.10 guessing were (MS) / guessing about it, were
216.10 mummery again (MS) / mummery over again
219.4 say (MS) / see
219.8 honour? (MS) / honour!
220.25 I not (MS) / not I
220.31 proposes (MS) / propose
221.17 visitor—And (MS) / visitor; and
221.18 pretensions—this (MS) / pretensions. This
221.18 is encroachment (MS) / is an encroachment

221.28 burthen (MS) / burden
222.8 this (MS) / these
222.15 McIntoshes (MS) / M'Intoshes
223.34 Castle (8vo) / castle
223.37 fellow's (MS fellows) / man's
223.39 man (MS) / flier
224.9 low (MS) / loud
224.11 *Clara* (MS) / Clara
224.16 person (MS) / personage
225.10 this (MS) / thus
225.17 right (MS) / power
225.24 future; yet to a suit like this you could once listen.—(MS future yet to a suit like this you could once listen—) / future; yet there *was* a time when to a suit like this you could listen favourably.—
227.9 the letter (MS) / the anonymous letter
227.22 Earl, "for the (MS Earl for the) / Earl; "the
227.25 looks, you (MS looks you) / looks, that you
227.34 objection (MS) / objections
228.16 further (MS) / farther
228.33 say—a (MS) / say, a
229.9 Tyrrel? (MS Tyrrel?—) / Tyrrel!
229.22 Lord Etherington (8vo) / his brother
Etherington is not 'his brother' (or brother-in-law), unless Etherington's 'marriage' to Clara is valid.
229.39 leaped (MS) / clambered
230.10 humour. (MS) / humour him.
230.14 old (MS) / Old
232.14 between this lady and my right honourable . . . father (18mo) / between my right honourable . . . father
The 18mo offers a neat solution to a problem that was recognised only by the 18mo and this edition.
232.18 Anne (MS) / Ann
232.19 Tyrrel, the lawful (MS) / Tyrrel, lawful
232.38 fly a pitch (MS) / fly into a pitch
233.29 professor (MS) / Professor
235.35 this (MS) / the
235.38 their (MS) / these
236.33 my words (MS) / the words
236.39 me, I (MS me I) / me, that I
239.10 matter (MS) / matters
239.20 paternal (Editorial) / filial
This error is now corrected for the first time.
240.3 like (MS) / likely
240.7 my father's (MS my fathers) / the Earl
240.20 What (MS) / what
241.27 was,' I said, 'my (MS was I said my) / was, I said, 'my
242.4 Henry (MS) / Harry
242.15 *qua* (8vo) / *quo*
242.16 Voilà (MS derived: Voila) / Voila
242.17 talens! [new paragraph] Monsieur (MS talens [new line indented] Monsieur) / talens! [new line] Monsieur
243.16 past? and, (MS past and) / past?—And,
243.22 yours (MS) / your's
243.39 murmurs (MS) / rumours
244.40 our brother. (MS) / my brothe .

The base-text missed the allusion to *Hamlet* and the last letter of 'brother'.

246.29 come (MS ↑come↓) / appear
250.7 your (MS) / Your
250.8 and (MS) / And
250.8 else—has (MS) / else, has
250.17 lighter (MS) / more light to be borne
251.24 letters (MS) / letter
252.1 yours (MS) / your's
252.3 for (8vo) / to
253.7 or of argument (MS) / or argument
253.10 country. Why (MS) / country—Why
253.13 yours (MS) / your's
253.40 place. Yet (MS) / place—Yet
254.22 MICKLE (MS) / [no attribution]
255.6 right (MS) / rights
255.42 stamp. Then (MS) / stamp—then
256.4 with (MS) / by
258.23 to boot (MS) / to the boot
259.3 quiet place (MS) / hamlet
259.4 Scottish (MS) / Scotch
259.12 stand yawling here—Mrs Dods—" (MS) / stand bawling at the door!"
260.24 gentleman (MS) / guest
260.43 ye (MS) / you
261.4 I (MS) / *I*
261.6 I (MS) / *I*
261.11 is (MS) / *is*
261.18 hae (MS) / has
261.21 do you a (MS) / do a
263.24 deid (MS) / dead
264.18 we had (MS) / we have had
264.23 Hussein (MS) / Hassein
264.39 tirrivie (MS) / terror
265.29 Law (MS) / law
265.39 is that of (MS) / is of
266.2 dozen." (MS) / dozen"
266.5 Senior's (Editorial) / senior's
The initial capital makes it consistent with all other uses of 'Senior' as a noun.
266.6 is that my (MS) / is, my
266.6 implicated (MS) / complicated
267.36 Binks," (MS Binks") / Binks?"
267.38 unfinished (MS unfinishd) / unfortunate
268.8 Etherington. I (MS) / Etherington—I
268.20 another (MS) / others
268.39 a meeting (MS) / an appointment
268.42 any who (MS) / any one who
268.43 farther (MS) / future
269.31 if (MS) / If
270.18 and his title?" (MS) / and title."
270.40 Revd. (MS revd.) / Rev.
270.41 Honble. (MS honble.) / Honourable
271.16 composure, but (MS composure but) / compo sure but
There is a space for the comma in the base-text.
271.39 endure it without (MS) / endure without

272.2 you." (MS you—") / you?"
272.37 tune (MS) / tone
273.16 all circumstances (MS) / all the circumstances
273.34 the (MS) / that
273.37 live (MS) / living
273.38 crime (MS) / crimes
273.40 subject. (MS) / subject!
274.2 lady?" (MS) / lady?"—
274.29 guilt which (MS) / guilt—which
274.34 springs (MS) / spring
At the end of f. 157 in the MS, the word is 'springs'; at the beginning of f. 158, it is 'spring'. The EEWN follows the reading of the catch-word.
274.37 more (MS) / most
275.15 him." (MS him—") / him?"
275.17 interference (MS) / interfeference
275.25 was (MS) / were
275.26 was (MS) / were
275.27 was (MS) / were
275.38 is so much (MS) / is much
276.6 perhaps (MS) / probably
277.21 an (MS) / any
277.28 said he (MS) / he said
279.28 murtherer (MS) / murderer
280.14 wreaths (MS) / wreath
282.32 for (MS) / of
282.39 pfeifchen (MS derived: pfeichen) / pfeichen
283.14 you—that (MS) / you. That
283.42 that (MS) / whom
284.8 stopped, a little scandalized (MS stopd a little scandalized) / stopped a little, scandalized
284.27 idiotical a business (MS) / idiotical business
285.31 asper (Editorial) / aspar
This correction first appeared in the Centenary (1870–71) and the Dryburgh (1892–94) editions of Scott.
285.36 these strange matters (MS) / these matters
286.3 thereafter (MS) / hereafter
286.5 Scrogie. Young (MS Scroggie—Young) / Scroggie; young
286.18 *conversation* (MS) / *conversations*
286.20 three (Editorial) / four
A second (and final) attempt to stabilise the precise hour of Touchwood's dinner.
286.21 bundle (MS) / bundles
286.27 in (MS) / of
286.39 about such places (MS) / about places
287.10 gentleman passed (MS) / gentleman that passed
287.12 amang (MS) / among
287.14 Naboab (MS) / Nabob
287.16 parties (MS) / parts
287.17 aw (MS) / a'
287.21 Tuchwud (MS) / Touchwood
287.26 bade me no to (MS) / forbade me to
287.29 nack." (MS nack—") / nack.'
288.12 game. I (MS) / game—I
288.27 would (MS) / should
288.39 him (MS) / h m

289.2 limpet (ISet) / lampit
'lampit' is a Scottish form, but Jekyl speaks English.
290.16 not forthcoming (MS) / not then forthcoming
290.42 spirit (MS) / spirits
291.28 Freeman (MS) / Trueman
292.29 *sçavante* (MS derived: *scavante*) / *scavante*
294.9 with (MS) / wi'
Mrs Pot's speech is markedly more Scottish in the MS, but was systematically anglicised between MS and Ed1. The base-text's substitution of 'wi" for 'with' is therefore a mistake.
294.34 won't (8vo) / wont
295.10 won't (8vo) / wont
295.25 numbers were (MS) / number was
296.21 wheugh (MS) / Wheugh
296.24 companion (MS) / companions
297.14 me—I (MS) / me. I
297.24 ay (MS) / Ay
298.21 right (MS) / rights
298.22 fix (MS) / put
298.22 eyes (MS) / eye
298.23 on (MS) / upon
298.23 steady (MS) / fixed
298.23 pointing (MS) / searching out
298.23 some most wonderful (MS) / some wonderful
298.28 me say (MS) / me to say
299.6 And (MS) / and
299.40 cross-purposes (MS cross purposes) / cross-purpose
300.2 devise (MS) / divine
300.6 annihilate me the more completely (MS derived: annihilate me the completely) / annihilate me completely
301.9 been much disappointed (MS) / been disappointed
301.24 purpose (MS) / purposes
302.5 people's affairs (MS peoples affairs) / peoples' affairs
302.9 most (MS) / more
302.30 eclaircissement (MS) / ecclaircissement
302.36 eye (MS) / eyes
303.10 studied (MS) / shocked
303.11 vial (MS) / phial
303.35 servants were (MS) / servant was
304.28 and (MS) / as
305.28 *précieuses* (ISet) / *precieuses*
305.32 these (MS) / those
305.37 thieves' vinegar since (MS Thieves vinegar since) / thieves vinegar essence
305.41 purse; your (MS purse your) / purse, your
305.41 should have (MS) / should not have
306.22 this (MS) / ths
306.25 And (MS) / and
307.23 swoop (MS) / soop
307.34 o't—if (MS) / o't. If
307.35 leddyship's (MS leddyships) / ladyship's
308.2 jetty-black (MS jetty black) / jet-black
309.4 vagabond—a husbandless mother (MS derived: vagabond—a wifeless mother) / vagabond—a wifeless mother
The absurdity of the MS phrase was noted only by the 18mo, which

deleted the expression. This edition chooses, rather, to correct it.
310.30 her (MS) / the
311.11 winna (MS) / wunna
311.12 swoopings (MS) / soopings
311.31 amongst (MS) / among
312.37 something about (MS) / something wrong about
313.16 differ." (MS) / differ in opinion."
314.29 *protégés* (MS derived: *proteges*) / *proteges*
315.8 What prodigy is this? what subtle devil
Hath razed out the inscription?
A New Way to Pay Old Debts
(MS derived: What prodigy is this what subtle devil
Hath razed out the inscription—
New way to pay Old Debts) / [motto omitted]
In the MS, between the third and fourth paragraphs of this chapter, there appears "Chapter. ⟨Hesitation⟩ Disappointment", followed by the quotation from Massinger. That this was intended to be at the chapter-head is clear, for this is the only indication of the chapter-title, 'Disappointment', which was adopted.
315.21 charm. And (MS) / charm—And
316.22 moments (MS) / minutes
316.27 his, (MS) / his own,
316.29 repel all (8vo) / repel himself of all
316.42 in (MS) / with
317.43 burned (MS burnd) / burnt
318.15 boring (MS boreing) / boreing
This error was not corrected until the Centenary edition (1870–71).
318.20 devilishly (MS) / devilish
318.39 ill to (MS) / ill in health to
319.19 second. (MS second—.) / second?
319.21 tête-à-tête (8vo) / tête-a-tête
319.28 by (MS) / on
319.35 tête-à-tête (8vo) / tête-a-tête
319.39 will up (MS) / will be up
319.40 walk this moment (MS) / walk, this strutting bantam
320.8 accompt (MS) / account
320.23 so superior (MS) / so much superior
320.38 of apparent (MS) / of at least apparent
321.15 double stakes—while (MS) / double stakes. While
322.6 me so (MS) / me up so
322.22 And (MS) / and
323.15 coaxing towards (MS) / coaxing, towards
323.31 on (MS) / in
325.26 fair (MS) / fine
326.39 and a gracious (MS) / and gracious
327.7 family. (MS family—) / family?
327.16 —he (MS) / —"he
327.17 —"I (MS derived: —I) / —I
327.22 innuendo (ISet) / inuendo
327.23 forwards (MS) / forward
327.33 further (MS) / farther
328.41 at (MS) / to
329.3 best to do (MS) / best do
329.21 Senior (MS) / senior
330.12 say.—And (MS derived: say And) / say;—and

331.20 veil— (MS veil) / veil,
331.21 CARE keeps (MS) / CARE—keeps
332.32 hanged (MS) / hang
332.33 county (MS) / country
333.12 a woman (MS) / her
334.25 that (MS) / That
334.40 my (MS) / our
335.1 afraid (MS) / *afraid*
335.6 these (MS) / their
335.9 Why (MS) / why
335.12 murther (MS) / murder
335.16 the disturbed (MS the disturbd) / the previously disturbed
335.38 shoulder with one hand, pushed her from him, and, as she arose from the floor and again (MS shoulder with one hand ⟨and⟩ pushd her from him and as she again) / shoulder, with one hand pushed her from him; and, as she arose from the floor, and again
The cancelled 'and' in the MS indicates that the comma should come after 'hand' and not after 'shoulder'.
335.41 a blow (MS) / or blow
336.11 paved court (MS) / court
337.3 you (MS) / You
337.33 them (18mo) / it
The plural referent is 'condition, honour, and happiness'.
339.10 communion with (MS derived: communing on) / communing with
339.13 stumping (MS) / stamping
340.14 unexpected (MS) / without notice
340.22 get down some (MS) / get some
340.39 to it (MS) / it to
340.40 Norman-sounding (MS) / Norman sounding
341.7 you—ha (MS) / you.—Ha
341.30 Touchwood," (8vo) / Touchwood,'
The MS supplied no punctuation here.
341.32 me? (MS) / me!
342.23 Senior (MS) / senior
342.27 best be civil (MS) / but I will be civil
342.34 much cared (MS) / cared much
343.3 Devil-knows-what (12mo) / Devil knows what
344.3 divorced (MS) / disinherited
344.4 all Mowbrays (MS) / all the Mowbrays
344.12 scoundrel—why, (MS scoundrel—why) / scoundrel,
344.35 I have come under (MS) / I have laid myself under
344.35 And (MS) / and
345.2 came home (MS) / have come home
345.40 would have thought (8vo) / would thought
346.18 Etherington. (MS Etherington—) / Etherington?
348.17 accompt (MS) / account
348.30 learned that Bulmer (MS) / learned Bulmer
349.1 not, (MS) / not easily,
349.3 easily comprehended (MS) / easily to be comprehended
349.10 murther (MS) / murder
349.28 mystery (MS) / dexterity
The base-text avoids the repetition of "mystery", but it provides a less appropriate word.
349.35 blunt (MS) / blind
350.7 art (MS) / wit

350.8 Not that I will not do (MS) / Not but I will do
350.20 of relation (MS) / of a relation
350.22 had himself (MS) / himself had
350.23 toward (MS) / towards
351.12 sall (MS) / shall
352.22 Clara (MS ↑Clara↓) / she
353.27 hard (MS) / loud
354.25 yet (MS) / but
355.15 shingle (MS) / shingles
355.19 hurrying words (MS) / hurrying his words
355.27 came (MS) / cam
355.37 then a plain evidence that (MS) / then plain that
356.1 currents (MS) / current
356.24 head (MS) / mind
356.38 disturbance (MS derived: disturature) / state
Scott wrote "dis-" at the right edge of the folio, continued with "tur" at the left edge, and then apparently stopped writing because the rest of the word is completed in a different ink and on a slightly higher level. It seems that when he resumed writing, he saw the 'dis-' as 'li-', and the 'tur' as 'ter' (errors which are not unlikely with Scott's handwriting), and so finished off the word 'literature'. The final letters are smudged, as though he realised his mistake and tried to erase it.
357.14 groan (MS) / groans
357.19 shoe, appeared (MS) / shoe, it appeared
358.14 reader (MS) / readers
358.22 Shame, Confusion, and Terror (MS Sham Remorse and ⟨Fear⟩ Terror) / shame, confusion, and terror
359.8 though (MS) / although
359.10 where missing (MS) / where the missing
359.10 length might (MS) / length, might
359.26 did open (MS) / did intend to open
359.27 "before she could hirple (MS) / before she could "hirple
359.42 plausibly that (MS) / plausibly, that
360.13 destroying (MS) / possessing himself of
360.24 stimulate (MS) / interest
361.36 wherever (MS) / whenever
361.38 found not (MS) / did not find
363.21 Valentine (8vo) / Leonard
363.28 "O most unhappy ... he contrived [364.19] (Proof and MS)/ "But, O, most unhappy woman!" he said, "what does your introduction prepare me to expect?"

"Your expectation, be it ever so ominous, shall be fully satisfied.—I was the guilty confidante of the false Francis Tyrrel.—Clara loved the true one.—When the fatal ceremony passed, the bride and the clergyman were deceived alike—and I was the wretch—the fiend—who, aiding another yet blacker, if blacker could be—mainly helped to accomplish this cureless misery!"

"Wretch!" exclaimed the clergyman, "and had you not then done enough?—Why did you expose the betrothed of one brother to become the wife of another?"

"I acted," said the sick woman, "only as Bulmer instructed me; but I had to do with a master of the game. He contrived

The present text is based on the proof of the passage as printed in *The Athenaeum*, 4 Feb. 1893, 155, except in two cases of word order—

'Tyrrel met Clara' and 'misery and infamy'—where it returns to the original MS.

364.33 after she had lost the advantage over me—and I was sorry (MS) / after I learned her utter wretchedness—her deep misery, verging even upon madness—I hated her not then. I was sorry

364.36 and prevailed on you to conceal her marriage—"
"I remember," answered Cargill, "alleging danger from her family. (MS and prevaild on you to conceal her marriage—" "I remember" answerd Cargill "alleging danger from her family) / and you may remember it was I who prevailed on you to conceal her marriage."
"I remember it," answered Cargill, "and that you alleged, as a reason for secrecy, danger from her family.

364.41 inevitable. (MS inevitable) / inevitable, while the good I did was voluntary.

365.6 stood by (MS) / stood in the opening by

365.14 pardon thee (MS) / pardon you

366.7 away—my (MS) / away, my

366.10 that— (MS) / that we shall not—

366.16 you know (MS) / I know

366.30 had indeed accumulated (MS had ↑indeed↓ accumulated) / had accumulated

367.10 no better (MS) / not better

367.31 this." (MS this—") / this

369.14 laughing (MS) / laughter

369.25 py Cott (MS) / by Cot

370.5 Mowpray (MS) / Mowbray

370.16 goot Captain (MS) / good Major

370.31 had Quackleben (MS) / had Dr Quackleben

370.37 Captain (MS) / Major

370.41 further (MS) / farther

371.3 from thence to the Well (Magnum) / there
The Magnum offers a neat solution to a problem that had gone unrecognised.

372.12 mosaic (MS) / morocco

END-OF-LINE HYPHENS

All end-of-line hyphens in the present text are soft unless included in the list below. The hyphens listed are hard and should be retained when quoting.

7.2	table-linen
7.36	two-penny
8.11	elf-locks
9.13	post-horses
12.27	sauce-pans
18.5	new-fangled
20.7	rye-meal
20.26	road-makers
21.16	sheriff-clerk's
23.24	hand-maidens
25.18	fish-woman
28.28	self-denying
30.8	loud-voiced
30.39	red-herring
37.25	shower-bath
40.13	folding-bed
48.25	dinner-bell
50.30	neck-or-nothing
51.1	help-mate
56.31	picture-books
57.31	common-place
60.9	table-spoonful
61.30	tea-spoonfulls
62.37	seal-skin
67.24	Shaws-Castle
71.21	hearth-rug
74.20	dining-parlour
78.39	Shaws-Castle
79.42	Shaws-Castle
82.20	Shaws-Castle
86.24	lurking-place
86.31	heart-strings
90.28	tea-leaves
90.32	silver-smith
91.19	aid-de-camp
93.34	Small-debt
108.31	cat-a-nine-tails
112.29	public-spirited
116.13	dial-plate
124.7	brass-hammered
124.18	two-wheeled
124.33	old-fashioned
130.5	cross-examination
130.26	Helter-skelter
130.36	four-nooked
132.24	she-publican
136.2	bed-ridden
137.4	Spaw-waal
137.27	powder-monkeys
139.15	land-louping
155.25	ink-standish
157.26	elbow-chair
158.8	night-gown
162.12	hat-bands
167.8	to-night's
172.43	grand-uncle's
176.35	grand-uncle's
181.37	Shaws-Castle
186.10	lime-and-stane
187.12	post-horses
193.15	flesh-coloured
194.7	shoe-tie
194.30	sultana-like
196.14	self-complacence
204.24	over-sweetened
209.15	fire-screens
212.30	low-spirited
213.9	Shaws-Castle
224.4	breakfast-room
231.33	back-scent
237.17	back-hand
237.36	Shaws-Castle
238.3	go-between
238.8	self-interest
239.21	grand-uncle
245.7	self-denying
246.23	free-masonry
246.27	school-boy
254.31	nut-brown
255.15	maid-servant
271.29	self-interest
287.28	neevie-neevie-nick-nack
291.24	post-office
293.21	chimney-piece
293.23	good-looking
293.42	change-house

300.8 spinning-jennies
308.10 flock-bed
313.38 under-bred
318.28 half-starved
319.35 tête-à-tête
324.8 wood-cocks
332.33 half-crying
338.29 to-night
339.31 wheel-barrow
342.31 Shaws-Castle
343.4 valet-de-chambre
347.12 broken-down
351.22 post-castle
354.28 dressing-room
355.14 summer-house
369.15 pistol-shooting

HISTORICAL NOTE

Saint Ronan's Well is not an historical novel, and contains no historical characters, yet the timing and dating of the action are essential aspects of the novel's meaning and effect.

The time line in *Saint Ronan's Well* is clear in general, although sometimes vague and inconsistent in detail. The story begins when Tyrrel arrives at the Cleikum Inn on 'a fine summer's day' (12.7) with the 'purpose of remaining for several days' (24.9–10). During that period, he attracts the notice of the Wellers, who invite him to join them. 'After a long delay' (43.26) because of Nelly Trotter's negligence with the messages, Tyrrel visits Saint Ronan's Well on a Monday (88.11). He insults Sir Bingo, who empowers Captain MacTurk to 'carry a message to that damned strolling artist, by whom he had been insulted three days since' (105.41–43); MacTurk arranges the duel for one o'clock 'this very day' (110.28). After Tyrrel fails to appear, Sir Bingo, MacTurk and Winterblossom issue a 'Statement' which specifies that the duel was scheduled for 'Wednesday — August' (119.40), and Touchwood later says that Lord Etherington was shot 'upon Wednesday last' (139.28), thus confirming the Wednesday specified in the 'Statement'. The Wednesday is compatible with 'three days since' because in the early nineteenth century the phrase could imply on the third day previously, not three whole days before.

The first volume covers a period of between two and three weeks, for at the beginning of the second volume, Meg recounts to Bindloose that Tyrrel 'came back again about a fortnight sin syne' (127.33) or, more plausibly, 'lived then at the Cleikum . . . for mair than a fortnight' (128.24–25).

Early in Volume 2, a month or so glides swiftly away. Chapters 3 and 4 present narrative summaries, in which Touchwood begins his new life in the Aulton, gets bored (at 144.5–6 'Ennui finds entrances into every scene, when the gloss of novelty is over'), and develops a 'companionship' with Cargill (159.16). The one specific date in the novel is now established. Touchwood receives an invitation to attend the theatricals at Shaws-Castle 'on the twentieth current' (160.3–4). This must be 20 October because, in the next chapter, 'Our history must now look a little backwards' (162.35) to present the card game between Mowbray and Etherington on 'a drizzly autumnal evening' (168.5). At the theatricals, Touchwood tells Cargill that he still has 'two days till Sunday' (202.19), establishing that 20 October is a Friday. 'The Morning after' (214.10), Etherington confronts Clara and begins his letter to Jekyl, which he completes the following day (246.36), Sunday, 22 October. The second volume ends.

At the beginning of Volume 3, a short but indefinite period of time passes. Replying to Etherington's letters, Jekyl writes, 'I will instantly join you at your Spaw' (251.40) and 'Speak the word, and I attend you' (252.27). Etherington urges him to 'Come, and come quickly' (254.15). Jekyl complies, for he is soon negotiating with Tyrrel. The narrator says of that day, 'It was now far advanced in Autumn' (280.6), and describes it so as to suggest early November. That same day, Tyrrel and Etherington meet but, 'in the course of two or three days' (301.20), the public loses interest in their rivalry. 'In the meantime' (301.31–32), Jekyl visits Touchwood but obtains no information. 'The next day' (302.30), Etherington drops into the bookseller's shop, visits a death-bed, ruins Mowbray at cards, and accompanies him to Lady Penelope's tea-party. There, Mowbray overhears rumours about Clara, rushes home, and assaults her. While he is discussing his troubles with Touchwood, Clara escapes into the storm, hears the death-bed confession of Hannah Irwin, meets Tyrrel for the last time and, early the next morning, dies. Remarkably all of the action from Chapter 6, i.e. from Etherington's visit to the bookshop, to the end takes place within 24 hours.

Thus the following is a plausible chronology of the major events in *Saint Ronan's Well* (days of the week are listed when they are specified in the text):

14 August	arrival of Tyrrel
Monday, 28 August	meeting between Tyrrel and Clara
Wednesday, 30 August	duel between Tyrrel and Etherington
4 September	meeting between Meg and Touchwood at Marchthorn
29 September	card game between Etherington and Mowbray
4 October	invitation to theatricals
Friday, 20 October	theatricals
21 October	meeting between Etherington and Clara
Saturday, 4 November	reappearance of Tyrrel
5 November	meeting between Tyrrel and Etherington
10 November	death of Clara.

Scott's handling of time in *Saint Ronan's Well* seems appropriate in at least two major ways. First, the compression of so many events into a period of about three months, with the action accelerating on that whirlwind last day, increases the tension and suggests the inevitability of the emerging tragedy. Second, the movement from the opening 'fine summer's day' (12.7) to the final 'cold and rainy season' (323.12) accords with the increasing grimness of the plot.

But can we place these events within a particular year? References in the text imply any time between 1803 and 1818. In the opening chapter, the narrator establishes that 'the nineteenth century had commenced' (7.18). More specifically, he implies a time 'about twenty years since' (1.24–25). But the wording is vague ('about' twenty years since), and in any case the year 1803 is not essential to *Saint Ronan's Well*, unlike 1745 to *Waverley*, which was subtitled ''Tis Sixty Years Since'. To avoid anachronisms completely, the year would have to be pushed up to at least 1818. Bindloose boasts about the modern improvements, including 'the auld reekie dungeons powed down' (135.14–15). This surely must include a reference to the old Edinburgh prison, demolished in 1817, and referred to by Scott in 'L'Envoy' to *The Heart of Mid-Lothian*, (1818). Furthermore, the narrator refers to Dr Redgill (29.1), a character in *Marriage: a Novel* by Susan Ferrier, published in 1818. And Etherington refers to *Tietania* (243.15), an obscure pamphlet entitled *Neckclothitania, or Tietania, being an Essay on Starchers, by One of the Cloth*, and also published in 1818. The difficulty is that this late date blatantly contradicts the narrator's claim on the first page that he is describing a time 'about twenty years since'.

But it is easily remembered dates that are most significant in assigning the action to a specific time, and so, when at the end of the novel Mowbray and MacTurk escape to the Peninsula 'where the war was then at the hottest' (371.15–16), most of the original readers would have placed the action in the period between 1808 when the first British forces landed in Portugal, and 1813 when British troops left Spain and entered southern France.

Other references propose 1809 or 1812 as the most probable dates. Clara tells her brother, 'I want to buy Campbell's new work' (217.32–33), pointing to either the *Poems* (1803) or *Gertrude of Wyoming* (1809); as the more celebrated work the latter is more likely. More important, between 1797 and 1815, the only year in which 20 October fell on a Friday was 1809. On the other hand, Miller's 'Modern and Ancient Drama' is consulted in the discussion of which play to present (183.26); *The Ancient British Drama* was published in 1810, and *The Modern British Drama* in 1811. Lady Penelope mentions John Leyden, and Cargill replies 'a lamp too early quenched' (205.13–14); Leyden died in August 1811. Touchwood is described as 'sixty years of age and upwards' (134.10) and later tells us that he was born in 1751 (341.39). Mowbray quotes the first canto of *Childe Harold's Pilgrimage*, published in 1812 (165.21–22), and a dispute on the appropriateness of MacTurk's costume at the déjeunée is resolved on the 'authority of Childe Harold' (184.21–22).

It seems clear that Scott does not have a precise year in mind but, rather, a particular period. As the notes to this edition indicate, the novel is saturated with references to historical and local events, to persons and characters, to works of art and ephemerae that cumulatively suggest the period between 1803 and 1818. But as the Peninsular War lasted from 1808–13, and as the two best known contemporary works to be cited, *Gertrude of Wyoming* and *Childe Harold's Pilgrimage* were published in 1809 and 1812 respectively, it seems that 1809–12 is the most likely time in which to place the action of *Saint Ronan's Well*. And that is appropriate; the company at the Well is turned in on itself, prevented from travelling except to exotic places, culturally incestuous. It is a microcosm of British 'society' towards the end of a very long war.

Sources. Lockhart implies that the source of *Saint Ronan's Well* lies in something Scott had recently found out about a Border family: 'He then told us a tale of dark domestic guilt which had recently come under his notice as Sheriff, and of which the scene was not Melrose, but a smaller hamlet on the other side of the Tweed, full in our view; but the details were not of a kind to be dwelt upon'.[1] The story may or may not have had some bearing on the novel; as Lockhart divulges no details it is impossible to say. But John W. Cairns has argued convincingly that Scott's awareness of the long legal case involving John William Henry Dalrymple and Johanna Gordon 'fed into aspects of the plot of *Saint Ronan's Well*'.[2] In essence, Dalrymple came to Edinburgh as a young officer in 1804, and formed a liaison with Johanna Gordon, involving promises of marriage. Dalrymple left Scotland, served abroad for some time, and on his return to England in 1808 went through a regular wedding with Laura Manners. Johanna Gordon took legal action to assert her rights as his wife, and in 1811 the courts found in her favour, arguing that Dalrymple and she were married in 1804 according to the law of Scotland, and that the marriage to Laura Manners was accordingly void and bigamous. It took until 1820 to unravel the mess.

Many of the legal issues in the case are echoed in *Saint Ronan's Well*: Dalrymple's actions are similar to those of the 5th Earl of Etherington, father of Francis Tyrrel and Valentine Bulmer; Lady Binks goes to law to nail Sir Bingo; Tyrrel and Clara have a prenuptial sexual relationship involving promises of marriage. Two facts relate the case to the novel. Firstly, the final stage of the legal proceedings was heard before Lord Meadowbank in the First Division of the Court of Session, where Scott was one of the clerks; and secondly, near both the beginning and the end of the manuscript of the novel, Scott calls his tragic heroine not 'Clara' but 'Laura'. The mistake may be explained if Scott did indeed have the predicament of Laura Manners in mind.

But the chief sources of *Saint Ronan's Well* are to be found in literature rather than history. Robert C. Gordon, for example, pointed out that Scott's story has its roots in British dramas, including Sheridan's *The Rivals* and Otway's *The Orphan*.[3] Sidney Smith objected to the names of the characters, finding 'Sir Bingo Binks' especially ludicrous.[4] But most of the names—Lady Penelope Penfeather, Mr Simon Chatterley, Dr Quackleben, Mr Winterblossom, Captain MacTurk, are emblematic and derived from a long line of literary satires. Chapter headings include 'Theatricals', 'A Death-Bed', and 'The Catastrophe'. Lines from Shakespearean tragedy are sprinkled liberally throughout the text. Clara Mowbray is compared to Ophelia (69.4), the Dark Ladye (53.27), the Ancient Mariner (53.39–40), Mat Lewis's Spectre Lady (54.17–18), Lady Clementina (69.3), Betty Foy (80.7), Emmeline (100.42), Ethelinda (100.42), Helena from *A Midsummer Night's Dream*, (184.10), Clarissa Harlowe (218.24), Harriet Byron (218.25), and Lady Macbeth (75.12). In short, there is ample warrant in the text for Clara's comparing herself to 'all distressed heroines' (100.40). It is hard to imagine a character in a novel being conceived in more theatrical terms.

The centrepiece of *Saint Ronan's Well* is literally a series of theatricals performed by the disguised characters, but this scene also serves as a metaphor for what is happening throughout the novel. Almost all of the characters are playing roles. As Clara says, 'I do carry on the farce of life . . . We are but actors, you know, and the world but a stage' (84.43–85.1). Tyrrel replies in key, 'And ours has been a sad and tragic scene' (85.2). But the most versatile of all the actors is the Earl of Etherington, who performs the roles of Bottom the weaver, the ass into which Bottom is transformed, the Spanish cavalier, and his one 'real-life' character, the Earl. Always striving to switch roles with his elder brother, he rearranges the cast at the fake marriage ceremony, the mainspring of the plot. In summary, whereas Scott regularly distances his material in time through the use of history, here—in his only novel dealing with 'events' of the nineteenth century—he achieves the effect of distancing by calling attention to the novel's overwrought theatricality and literary provenance.

NOTES

1 *Life*, 5.149.
2 John W. Cairns, 'A Note on *The Bride of Lammermoor*: Why Scott did not Mention the Dalrymple Legend until 1830', *Scottish Literary Journal*, 20:1 (May, 1993), 19–36.
3 Robert C. Gordon, *Under Which King?: A Study of the Scottish Waverley Novels* (New York, 1969), 140.
4 Sydney Smith, 'Sydney Smith on the novels 1819–23', in *Scott: the Critical Heritage*, ed. John O. Hayden (New York, 1970), 175.

EXPLANATORY NOTES

In these notes a comprehensive attempt is made to identify Scott's sources, and all quotations, references, historical events, and historical personages, to illuminate contemporary usages, to explain proverbs, and to translate difficult or obscure language. (Phrases are explained in the notes while single words are treated in the glossary.) The notes are designed to offer information rather than critical comment or exposition. When a quotation or allusion has not been recognised this is stated: any new information from readers will be welcomed. When quotations reproduce their sources accurately, the reference is given without comment; verbal differences in the source are indicated by a prefatory 'see'. References are to standard editions or to editions that Scott himself used. Proverbs are identified by reference to the six different volumes listed below. Books in the Abbotsford Library are identified by reference to the appropriate page of the *Catalogue of the Library at Abbotsford*. Biblical references are to the Authorised Version. Plays by Shakespeare are cited without authorial ascription, and references are to *William Shakespeare: The Complete Works*, edited by Peter Alexander (London and Glasgow, 1951, frequently reprinted).

The following items are distinguished by abbreviations, or are given without the names of their authors, in the notes and essays:

Apperson G. L. Apperson, *English Proverbs and Proverbial Phrases: A Historical Dictionary* (London, 1929; rpt. 1969).

Cairns John W. Cairns, 'A Note on *The Bride of Lammermoor*: Why Scott did not mention the Dalrymple Legend until 1830', *Scottish Literary Journal*, 20:1 (May, 1993), 19–36.

Child Francis James Child, *The English and Scottish Popular Ballads*, 5 vols (Boston and New York, 1882–98).

CLA J. G. Cochrane, *Catalogue of the Library at Abbotsford* (Edinburgh, 1838).

Corson James C. Corson, *Notes and Index to Sir Herbert Grierson's Edition of 'The Letters of Sir Walter Scott'* (Oxford, 1979).

Johnson Paul Johnson, *The Birth of the Modern: World Society 1815–1830* (New York, 1991).

Journal *The Journal of Sir Walter Scott*, ed. W. E. K. Anderson (Oxford, 1972).

Kelly James Kelly, *A Complete Collection of Scotish Proverbs Explained and made Intelligible to the English Reader* (London, 1721); *CLA*, 169.

Letters *The Letters of Sir Walter Scott*, ed. H. J. C. Grierson and others, 12 vols (London, 1932–37).

Life J. G. Lockhart, *Memoirs of the Life of Sir Walter Scott, Bart.*, 7 vols (Edinburgh, 1837–38).

Magnum Walter Scott, *Waverley Novels*, 48 vols (Edinburgh, 1829–33). Volumes 33 and 34 contain *St Ronan's Well*.

Minstrelsy Walter Scott, *Minstrelsy of the Scottish Border*, ed. T. F. Henderson, 4 vols (Edinburgh, 1902).

Prose Works *The Prose Works of Sir Walter Scott, Bart.*, 28 vols (Edinburgh, 1834–36).

ODEP *The Oxford Dictionary of English Proverbs*, 3rd edn, rev. F. P. Wilson (Oxford, 1970).

OED *The Oxford English Dictionary*, 12 vols (Oxford, 1933).

Ramsay *A Collection of Scots Proverbs*, in *The Works of Allan Ramsay*, 6 vols,

Scottish Text Society, vol. 5, ed. Alexander M. Kinghorn and Alexander Law (Edinburgh, 1972), 59–133.

Ray John Ray, *A Compleat Collection of English Proverbs*, 3rd edn (London, 1737); *CLA*, 169.

SMM *The Scots Musical Museum*, ed. James Johnson, 6 vols (Edinburgh, 1787–1803).

Tilley Morris Palmer Tilley, *A Dictionary of the Proverbs in England in the Sixteenth and Seventeenth Centuries* (Ann Arbor, Michigan, 1950).

Weber Henry Weber, *Tales of the East: Comprising the most popular Romances of Oriental Origin, and the best imitations by European Authors, etc.*, 3 vols (Edinburgh, 1812); *CLA*, 43.

All manuscripts referred to in the notes are in the National Library of Scotland. The following edition of *Saint Ronan's Well* has proved helpful: The Dryburgh Edition, 25 vols (London, 1892–94), vol. 17. For legal matters the detailed notes sent to me by Dr John W. Cairns of the University of Edinburgh have proved invaluable. Information derived from the notes of the late Dr J. C. Corson is indicated by '(Corson)'.

title-page Saint Ronan several saints of that name are mentioned in the Irish martyrologies, but practically no historical details about them survive. The connection, if any, of these Irish Ronans with the homonym venerated in Scotland under the name Mo-Rónóc has led to differentiations and identifications that have been 'more ingenious than enlightening' (*New Catholic Encyclopedia*, 12.662).

title-page Waverley (1814) Scott's 1st novel; *Quentin Durward* (1823) was his 15th. *Saint Ronan's Well*, his 16th and the only one set in the 19th century, was published on 27 December 1823.

epigraph Scott wrote to James Ballantyne, probably in Dec. 1823: 'The title page may bear for motto the lines of Wordsworth/ 'A merry place he said in days of yore/ But something ails it now—the place is cursed'./ You can look at the exact words in the poem of Hartleap Well' (*Letters*, 8.123). Apparently Ballantyne failed to look up the 'exact words', which, from the second edition of *Lyrical Ballads* (1800), have always been '"A jolly place," said he, "in times of old!/ But something ails it now: the spot is curst."' ('Hart-Leap Well', Part 2, lines 123–24). This edition restores Wordsworth's exact words in accordance with Scott's original intention.

1 **motto** see John Skelton (1460?–1529), 'The Tunning of Elynour Rummynge' (*c.* 1521), lines 101–03.

1.12 **Sultan Mahmoud's owls** Mahmoud (971?–1030), of Ghazni in Afghanistan, the first prince to assume the title of 'Sultan', wrought great desolation in India during several invasions. In one of the many stories about him, the vizier Khasayas had recourse to a fable. He told Sultan Mahmoud that he understood the language of birds, and revealed they were talking about His Majesty. One owl had a son, the other a daughter. The father of the male consented to a marriage, provided that the other would provide with his daughter a dowry of 50 ruined villages. The father of the female promised 500: 'God grant a prosperous long life to the sultan Mahmoud, and as long as he continues king of Persia we shall never want destroyed villages'. Sultan Mahmoud learned his lesson. He rebuilt the villages and afterwards thought of nothing but the good of his people. See 'The Fable of the Two Owls', in Weber, 3.193.

1.19 **Macpherson** David Macpherson (1746–1816), author of *Geographical Illustrations of Scottish History* (1796).

2.1 **river** usually identified as the River Tweed.

2.4 **enclosed** i.e. the common land in these parts has, by Act of Parliament, been allocated to proprietors, and is no longer rough pasture but under cultivation. The implication is that this is a modern agricultural community.

2.42 square tower the square fortified tower several stories high surrounded by a wall was the standard place of defence in medieval Scotland.

3.14–15 proud porter . . . rear'd himself see 'The Ballad of King Estmere', in *Reliques of Ancient English Poetry* (1765), ed. Thomas Percy, lines 171–74 (Child, 60).

3.20 Amphion's country-dances one of the twin sons born to Antiope and Zeus, Amphion made stones put themselves together under the magic of his lyre to form the wall of Thebes, in ancient Greece. However, no stories have been traced in which whole houses joined the dance. The same image is used in *The Antiquary*, 19.16.

3.24–25 humble plan . . . Scottish cottages single-storied, two-roomed buildings; the outer room would have an earth floor, unplastered walls and one window, with an open fire, while the inner room might be floored and the walls plastered.

4.6 landed proprietors the heritors who had the duty to pay certain public burdens in a parish, one of the most important of which was the upkeep and maintenance of the minister's manse.

4.13 brethren of the presbytery in the presbyterian system of church government the church is ruled by a series of courts, general assembly, synod, presbytery, and kirk session. The kirk session rules the parish; the presbytery consists of the minister and an elder from every kirk session in the presbytery's area.

4.24 Catholic times i.e. prior to the Scottish Reformation in 1560.

4.25 grace Scott puns; on the one hand he is talking of the proportions of the architecture, and on the other he refers to the operation of the Holy Spirit in human affairs. Protestants thought the Church of Rome had erred from the true faith.

4.27 crumbling hills of mortality i.e. the graveyard.

4.39–40 house of Douglas the dominant political family in Scotland in the late 14th and the 15th century.

4.42 our old naive historian Sir Robert Lindsay of Pitscottie (*c.* 1532–80). In a letter of 21 July 1823, Scott describes him as 'old Pitscottie whose events are told with so much naiveté and even humour and such individuality as it were that it places the actor and scenes before the reader' (*Letters*, 8.48). For the quotation see Lindsay's *The History of Scotland, From February 21, 1436 to March 1565*, 3rd edn (1778), 206; *CLA*, 259.

5.4 reign of James II 1437–60. At first allied with the Douglas clan, the King seized their lands in 1452 after discovering William Douglas, the 6th Earl, to be guilty of conspiracy.

5.8 unhappy battle of Dunbar on 3 September 1650 a Scottish army supporting the future King Charles II (reigned 1660–85) was defeated by Oliver Cromwell (Lord Protector 1653–58) at Dunbar, a port on the SE flank of the Firth of Forth.

5.14 Allan Ramsay's Sir William Worthy Ramsay (1684–1758), poet and bookseller, played an important role in the 18th-century revival of poetry in Scots. Sir William Worthy, a character in his principal work, *The Gentle Shepherd* (1725), returned from exile in 1660 to reclaim his estate.

5.15 after the Revolution i.e. in 1660, when the monarchy was restored after the Commonwealth.

5.35–36 owls and birds of the desart see Psalm 102.6.

5.38 Scottish Baron *Scots law* one who was a freeholder of the crown, but who had to have had his lands erected or confirmed by the king as being held *in liberam Baroniam*. This gave considerable jurisdiction in civil and criminal causes until such jurisdictions were abolished in 1747.

5.38 **auld lang syne** long ago, times past, as in the traditional song 'Auld lang syne', best known in Burns's version.
5.40 **devil's game-leg** i.e. the devil's lame leg. The devil is 'lame because of his fall from heaven; his knees are backward; . . . he has cloven hooves' (Jeffrey B. Russell, *The Prince of Darkness* (Ithaca, 1988), 114).
5.40 **episcopal crook** the pastoral staff of a bishop, abbot, or abbess, shaped like a shepherd's staff.
6.12–13 **portion off . . . younger son** i.e. marry off a daughter by providing a 'portion' or dowry, and purchase a position as an officer in the army for a younger son who would not inherit the estate.
6.14 **Meg Dods** 'On a fishing excursion to a loch near Howgate, among the Moorfoot Hills, Scott, Clerk, Irving, and Abercromby spent the night at a little public-house kept by one Mrs Margaret Dods. When St Ronan's Well was published, Clerk, meeting Scott in the street, observed, "That's an odd name; surely I have met with it somewhere before." Scott smiled, said, "Don't you remember Howgate?" and passed on. The name alone, however, was taken from the Howgate hostess.' (*Life*, 1.150)
6.21 **in single blessedness** *A Midsummer Night's Dream*, 1.1.78.
6.22 **Queen Bess** Queen Elizabeth of England (reigned 1558–1603), who lived and died unmarried.
6.23–24 **men servants . . . stranger within her gates** see Deuteronomy 5.14.
6.27 **Erasmus** (*c.* 1466–1536), of Rotterdam, the leading humanist scholar of the time.
6.28 **Quaere aliud hospitium** *Latin* look for some other inn. 'In a colloquy of Erasmus, called *Diversaria*, there is a very unsavoury description of a German inn of the period, where an objection of the guest is answered in the manner expressed in the text—a great sign of want of competition on the road.' (Magnum, 33.13)
6.29 **troop aff wi' ye** be off with you.
7.1 **minced collops** savoury dish made of veal, bacon, force-meat and other ingredients, all cut up very fine.
7.2 **Ferrybridge** coaching stop on the Great North Road, near Pontefract, Yorkshire. Mrs Hall has not been identified.
7.4 **a weary day** a sad or sorrowful day.
7.17–18 **even after the nineteenth century had commenced** in a Magnum note (33.14–15) Scott implies that Meg's prices were more appropriate to 1790; inflation was high during the years of the Revolutionary and Napoleonic Wars (1793–1815).
8.10 **Tony Lumpkin** character in Oliver Goldsmith's *She Stoops to Conquer* (1773). The phrase 'a concatenation accordingly' is actually spoken by one of the anonymous fellows at the ale-house, The Three Pigeons (Act 1).
8.16–17 **her bark was worse than her bite** proverbial: see Ramsay, 87; *ODEP*, 30.
8.21 **these light and giddy-paced times** see *Twelfth Night*, 2.4.6.
8.26–27 **speculative builder took land in feu** a builder acquired a feudal right to land (i.e. he purchased the feu or obtained a feudal grant from a feudal superior) to build houses etc. for sale. Here, Mowbray 'feued out' his land; i.e. by a feu-contract for a price, he created a relationship of superior and vassal with the builder as vassal. The builder would sell buildings to purchasers, who would come into his place in relationship with Mowbray, their feudal superior.
8.28 **tontine subscription** loan raised from individuals to build the hotel, each individual being granted an annuity for life in return. As each lender died, the annuities continued payable to the surviving lenders, so that the last survivor

took the whole. This was a relatively common mode of raising money for speculative ventures in this period.

8.32 well to pass well-off.

8.39 they maun hae a hottle 'This Gallic word (hôtel) was first introduced in Scotland during the author's childhood, and was so pronounced by the lower class.' (Magnum, 33.18)

8.43 breaths . . . in their nostrils see Isaiah 2.22.

9.4 down the black gate on the road to ruin, i.e. to hell.

9.5 this twenty years for this last twenty years.

9.12–13 shut up the windows . . . to baffle the tax-gatherer in 1789 a tax was imposed on glazed windows. As the tax was only applied to houses with more than 7, closing-up windows became a means of tax avoidance.

9.17–18 Dick Tinto Scott's own fictional sign-painter: see the introductory chapter to *The Bride of Lammermoor* (1819). The name is taken from the Italian 'tinto', which means 'tinted'.

9.24–25 Meg Dorts proverbial name for a bad-tempered, or sulky woman, the word *dorty* meaning 'bad-tempered' or 'sulky'. Compare Allan Ramsay, *The Gentle Shepherd* (1725), 1.1.125: 'Then fare ye well, *Meg Dorts*, and e'en's ye like'.

9.27 Killnakelty Hunt the name implies that the members of the hunt cannot even kill a salmon.

9.32 and what for no? and why not? Meg's familiar refrain was a 'Laidlaw-ism', a pet phrase of William Laidlaw, Scott's friend, neighbour, and amanuensis (*Life*, 5.285).

9.32–33 a Scots pint over-head each of them alike took his pint in full. The old Scots pint was about 3 imperial pints (1.696 litres).

9.35–36 puir quart . . . magnum two pints (1.14 litres) . . . four pints (2.27 litres).

9.41 pawky auld carles see 'The Gaberlunzie Man', line 1: a popular song attributed to James V (1512–42), in Allan Ramsay, *The Tea-table Miscellany*, first published in 1724. Scott owned the 13th edn (Edinburgh, 1762): *CLA*, 171.

9.41–42 kenn'd . . . buttered upon proverbial: see Ray, 179; Ramsay, 82; *ODEP*, 438.

10.9 metropolis Edinburgh.

10.24 pretty Fanny's way 'An Elegy, To an Old Beauty' (line 34) by Thomas Parnell (1679–1718). 'Pretty Fanny's way' has since become proverbial for some perverse or annoying habit that is regarded with toleration by the culprit's friends.

10.24–25 dulces Amaryllidis iræ *Latin* the sweet angers of Amaryllis. Amaryllis was a shepherdess in the pastorals of Theocritus (3rd century BC) and Virgil (70–19 BC) and has come to mean a rustic sweetheart. Compare Milton's 'Lycidas' (1637), line 68.

10.29 ye . . . auld head upon young shouthers proverbial: see *ODEP*, 589.

10.32–33 faithful amongst the unfaithful found see *Paradise Lost*, 5.896–97.

10.33 sheriff-clerk clerk to the Sheriff Court. In 1823 he was usually a local lawyer; since the Sheriff Court had a relatively wide jurisdiction, the office was of some importance.

10.36 "Prieves," or "Comptis," *Scots law* proofs and accounts. The clerk is gathering statements to determine the issues on which a criminal trial will take place, and is receiving or generating inventories, accounts etc. presumably for civil actions.

11.23 Dame Quickly Shakespeare's famous hostess of the Boar's Head

Tavern in Eastcheap: see *1 Henry IV*, *2 Henry IV* and *Henry V*.
11.35 the Giant Pope in the Pilgrim's Progress see John Bunyan, *The Pilgrim's Progress*, ed. James Blanton Wharey and Roger Sharrock (Oxford, 1960), 65.
12 motto (1) Quis ... Virgilium who is this young stranger? Dido, according to Virgil (Virgil, *The Aeneid*, 4.11).
12 motto (2) Cha'am ... Eneid not identified; probably by Scott.
12.19 rather high in bone i.e. rather thin.
12.38–39 Travellers ... Riders and Bagmen three names for commercial travellers.
13.4 Saint Ronan's Well Innerleithen, Gilsland, Moffat and other places have been suggested as prototypes.
13.12 deil's buckie thoroughly perverse person.
13.16 ghost ... speak first a ghost had to be spoken to before it could speak. See *Hamlet*, 1.1.42 and 45.
13.41 down by down there
13.42–43 bawbee rows halfpenny bread-rolls.
13.43 or I loose them before I give in to them.
14.1 Upsetting cutty assuming jade, one aping the manners of her superiors.
14.2 dreed penance suffered punishment; specifically, she had to sit on the stool of repentance in the parish kirk for fornication.
14.2 ante-nup shortened form of ante-nuptial, i.e. occurring in the time before marriage; specifically, antenuptial fornication.
14.16 knapping English speaking English in an affected or fancy way.
15.34–35 gang further, and be waur served proverbial: see *ODEP*, 306.
16.7–8 The merciful man ... beast see Proverbs 12.10.
16.9 by ordinar extraordinary, unusual.
16.35 the day today.
17.1 wine ... man's heart glad see Psalm 104.15.
17.34 what for why.
17.36 table-dot Meg's pronunciation of *table d'hôte*, a fixed menu for guests at a hotel or eating house, served at a stated hour and a fixed price.
17.40 wha's aught it who owns it.
18.4 maist feck the greatest part.
18.26–27 crap ... cheats the barber the fashion for conspicuously short hair began in the 1790s, and became general by the turn of the century; there was more work for barbers in tending long hair and wigs than in making hair short.
18.37 Bu'mer bay Boulmer Haven, north of Alnmouth, Northumberland. Spirits and tea were regularly smuggled into Scotland after the Union of Scotland and England in 1707 when English excise duties were extended to Scotland. For the smugglers' route from Northumberland into Scotland see *Rob Roy*, Vol. 2, Ch. 5.
19.12–13 but the deil flee awa' ... for Meg Dods let the devil fly away with the neighbours as far as Meg Dods is concerned.
19.21 link out i.e. pay down smartly.
19.22 fifty pounds the price per head for the tontine subscription.
19.22 ower head precipitately
19.24 four terms' rent in Scotland, there were four 'terms' yearly for the payment of rent or interest: Candlemas (2 Feburary), Whitsunday (15 May) Lammas (1 August), and Martinmas (11 November). Therefore, the landlord who leases the Fox hotel has paid no rent for a year.
19.29 Luckie Buchan Elspeth Simpson Buchan (*c.* 1738–91), known in Galloway as 'Luckie Buchan'. She gave herself out to be the third person in the

Godhead, and as the woman of Revelation 12, who was 'clothed with the sun', and pretended to have brought forth a man-child who was to rule all nations. Scott describes her as 'a species of Joanna Southcote, who long after death was expected to return and head her disciples on the road to Jerusalem' (Magnum, 33.38). Her adherents were known as Buchanites, and the sect appeared in the west of Scotland in 1783. See Joseph Train, *The Buchanites from First to Last* (Edinburgh, 1846).

19.36 Common Prayer-book the service book of the Anglican church.

19.41 pool of Bethesda see John 5.2–4.

20.3 Cuddie, or Culdee Meg confuses Culdees, solitary religious ascetics of the early Celtic church in Scotland, with cuddies, stupid fellows or donkeys.

20.18 it's like it seems.

20.21 has wit at wull *proverbial* is equal to the occasion, knows quite well what to do (see Tilley, 736; Apperson, 699; *ODEP*, 903).

20.22 Windywa's see the night-visiting song, 'Let me in this ae night': 'I am the laird of windy-wa's [i.e. my patrimony is the open air]/ I come na here without a cause,/ And I have gotten many fa's/ Upon a naked wame o!', in *Songs from David Herd's Manuscripts* (Edinburgh, 1904), 151; and *SMM*, no. 311.

20.24 clink verses i.e. produce verse with regular rhythms and pat rhymes.

20.24–25 Rob Burns the Scottish poet (1759–96).

20.26 chucky stanes pebbles.

20.28 ten-stringed instuments see Psalms 33.2, 92.3, 144.9.

20.41 or they wan hame before they reached home.

21.1 sin' syne since then, since that time.

21.15 Whitsunday and Martinmas the Scottish term days (see note to 19.24) on which people changed their employment.

21.18 charter and sasine *Scots law* the feu charter showing the title to heritable property, and the documentary instrument through which possession is established. The instrument is the only admissible evidence as to the delivery of possession, and is absolutely necessary by the law of Scotland for the transmission of landed property. The instrument had to be registered in the general register of sasines within 60 days.

21.18 special service the judicial proceedings 'serving' Meg as heir to the Inn, showing she has the right to be infeft in them (i.e. to have sasine). It is *special* service as distinct from *general* service, which is a general serving as heir.

21.18 to boot into the bargain.

21.28 Ashler a name derived from *ashlar* meaning 'smoothly cut stone' as distinct from rubble.

21.37–38 hunting moor-fowl . . . Mr Bindloose brought you neatly off there Tyrrel was charged with poaching, but Bindloose defended him successfully.

22.11 jinketting a nonce word which seems to combine 'jink', to move about quickly, and 'junket', to feast or make merry.

22.15 scauff and raff riff-raff.

22.15 writers' prentices those apprenticed to solicitors.

22.20–21 like draw to like proverbial: see Apperson, 367–68; Tilley, 381–82; *ODEP*, 465.

22.40 Never you fash your thumb don't worry, pay no heed.

22.41 Every Jack will find a Jill proverbial: see *A Midsummer Night's Dream*, 3.2.461; Apperson, 329; *ODEP*, 408.

23.5–7 Sir Bingo Binks . . . Miss Rachael Miss Bonnyrig has married Sir Bingo by one of the Scots forms of irregular (but perfectly valid) marriage: either by exchange of present consent to marriage, or promise of future marriage followed by sexual intercourse on the basis of that promise. See Cairns, 20–21.

23.7 Bonnyrig the name of a village near Edinburgh; the name also sug-

gests *bonny*, meaning 'beautiful', and *rig*, meaning 'hoax' or 'trick'.
23.7 **Loupengirth** the name means 'jumping out of a place of confinement', with a secondary implication of sexual union with a corpulent person.
23.10 **held him to his tackle** held him to his position.
23.10–11 **Commissary Court** the court that had jurisdiction over matters concerning marriage, legitimacy, etc. This suggests that Rachael Bonnyrig raised an action there of declarator of marriage to prove she and Sir Bingo were married.
23.35 **the faded hues of the glimmering landscape** see Thomas Gray (1716–71), 'Elegy Written in a Country Church-Yard' (1751), line 5.
23.37 **supper** dinner was taken at 3 or 4 p.m., supper about 9 or 10 p.m.
23.37 **a Welsh rabbit** cheese and butter melted together until smooth, when ale, pepper and salt are added; the whole is then poured over toast.
24 **motto** not identified; probably by Scott.
24.21 **start and an owerloup** said of a flock of sheep, when, being suddenly alarmed, they set off at full gallop and leap over the nearest fence; hence, an encroachment on a neighbour's property.
24.22 **leave ower the neighbour's ground . . . march** permission [to shoot] on the neighbour's property up to the boundary.
24.34 **the piper of Peebles** it is not known who the piper was, nor why he should be fishing. The reference in the novel may have been topical, but if so the note Scott added in the ISet ('The said piper was famous at the mystery') is misleading. There are records of medieval folk plays in Peebles (see Anna J. Mill, *Medieval Plays in Scotland* (1927)), but they do not identify a piper.
25.5 **munt up** set up, mount up.
25.10 **auld used** experienced.
25.10 **folk maun creep before they gang** *proverbial* folk must crawl before they walk: see *ODEP*, 120.
25.18 **Trotter** someone who trots, i.e. who moves about quickly; the name may also be derived from *trot*, meaning an 'old woman'.
25.42 **maunna fash our beards** mustn't bother ourselves.
26.14 **O the unbelieving generation** compare Psalm 78.8.
26.16 **sketchers** Meg confuses someone who sketches with the Scottish word for ice-skates.
26.33 **Nash** Richard 'Beau' Nash (1674–1762), a gambler who in 1705 established the Assembly Rooms at Bath and drew up a code of dress and etiquette, becoming the acknowledged and absolute master of ceremonies for the resort.
27.12 **et hoc genus omne** *Latin* and all this class (of people).
27.24 **Hymen** the Greek and Roman god of marriage.
27.34 **led forth . . . shady bower** see *Paradise Lost*, 5.367.
27.38 **To rave . . . land** see Alexander Pope (1688–1744), 'An Epistle from Mr. Pope, to Dr. Arbuthnot' (1735), line 6.
28.15 **the Loves of the Plants** Part II (1789) of *The Botanic Garden*, a poem by Erasmus Darwin (1731-1802).
28.31 **Fortunio** fairy-tale hero who, on the advice of her horse, hired 7 gifted servants, Strongback, Lightfoot, Marksman, Fine-ear, Boisterer, Trinquet, and Grugeon. See 'Belle-belle or Chevalier Fortuné' [also known as 'Fortunio or the Fortunate Knight'], in Countess d'Aulnoy, *Contes de Fées*, trans. J. R. Planché, 2nd edn (London, 1856).
29.1 **Dr Redgill** medical doctor with a particular interest in food in *Marriage* (1818), the novel by Scott's friend, Susan Ferrier (1782–1854).
29.2 **Dr Moncrieff of Tippermalloch** Dr John Moncrieff of Tippermalloch, author of *Tippermalluch's Receipts. Being a Collection of Many Useful and*

Easy Remedies for Most Distempers (Edinburgh, 1712), and *The Poor Man's Physician* (Edinburgh, 1716).

29.3 Dr Hunter of York Dr Alexander H. Hunter of York (1729–1809), author of *Culina Famulatrix Medicinae* (1804).

29.3 Dr Kitchiner of London Dr William K. Kitchiner (1775–1827) of London, a well-known epicure and author of *Apicius Redivivus; or, The Cook's Oracle* (1817).

29.6 ex officio *Latin* by virtue of office or position.

29.12 lantern jaws long thin jaws, giving a hollow appearance to the cheeks.

29.18 Bristol stones rock crystals resembling diamonds found in limestone near Clifton, Bristol.

29.18–19 seal-ring... Falstaff's see *1 Henry IV*, 3.3.80–81 and 103–04.

29.30 Garrick David Garrick (1717–79), English actor, dramatist, and manager of Drury Lane Theatre, London.

29.30 Foote Samuel Foote (1720–77), English actor, wit, playwright, and mimic.

29.30 Bonnel Thornton (1724–68), co-editor of *The Connoisseur* (a periodical which ran from 1754–56), and author of various books.

29.30 Lord Kellie Thomas Alexander Erskine (1732–81), 6th Earl of Kellie, musical composer, rake, *bon vivant*, and alcoholic. Boswell quotes Foote (see note to 29.30) to the effect that Kellie's face would ripen cucumbers. See *Boswell's London Journal, 1762–1763*, ed. Frederick A. Pottle (New York, 1950), 269 note.

29.43 to supply the wants of others see John Dryden (1631–1700), 'Ode to the Pious Memory of Mrs Anne Killegrew' (1685), line 72.

30.5 viis et modis by ways and means, a Scots law phrase (John Trayner, *Latin Maxims and Phrases*, (Edinburgh, 1861)).

30.9 Micklewhame i.e 'big belly'.

30.15 cutting up the Saint's-Well haugh Micklewhame, as Mowbray's lawyer, drafted the deeds dividing the area into separate feus.

30.16 building stances building plots.

30.22 per diem *Latin* per day, daily.

30.19–20 a Highland lieutenant on half-pay i.e. an officer of a Highland regiment on the half-salary paid to members of the forces who were not on active service.

30.24 Bow-street runners an early form of police-force, founded in 1749.

30.43 banks of Cam or Isis the rivers on which Cambridge and Oxford stand ('Isis' is the name given to the Thames at Oxford), sometimes used (as here) to signify the two universities.

31.9 zig-zags... parallels in a seige *parallels* were trenches (usually three) parallel to the place being attacked; *zig-zags* were trenches connecting the parallels and leading towards the beseiged place, but zigzagged to prevent defenders from shooting straight into them.

31.16 Jack Pudding buffoon, clown.

32 motto see Matthew Prior (1664–1721), 'Protogenes and Apelles' (1718), line 58.

32.10 curses, not loud, but deep *Macbeth*, 5.3.27.

32.12 Ganymedes personal waiters; *Ganymede* was a beautiful youth of Phrygia, who became the cup-bearer to the gods.

32.20 All his wants were well supplied see the translation by Joseph Addison (1672–1719) of Psalm 23, line 3, in the *Spectator*, No. 441, 26 July 1712; Isaac Watts, 'A Cradle Hymn', line 6, in *Divine Songs for the Use of Children* (1720).

32.35 **Belvidere** name for a summer-house placed on an eminence to see the view.
32.37 **Munt-grunzie** *munt* means 'mount'; *grunzie* is Scots for the 'snout of an animal'.
32.37–38 **stamped paper** paper used for deeds. The stamping of the paper showed that the tax on certain types of deed had been paid.
32.38 **ancient writs and evidents** the legal documents or deeds relating to the land.
33.2–3 **I have the honour . . . good health** see *Macbeth*, 3.4.89.
33.14 **Cleek'um** hook him.
33.20 **Trustees' school** private school as distinct from a burgh or parochial school.
33.23 **giff gaff** *proverbial* mutual help, give and take (see Tilley, 255; Apperson, 245; *ODEP*, 301).
33.41 **this Unknown** Scott is playing on his own designation, 'the great Unknown'.
34.34 **gipsy party** eating in the open air, having a picnic (*OED*).
35.8 **young Ascanius** the son of Aeneas in Virgil's *Aeneid*.
35.9 **tawny lion** person of note, a celebrity.
35.14 **Highland hills** an allusion to Scott himself.
35.15 **Lakes of Cumberland** the abode of the Lake poets, Wordsworth (1770–1850), Coleridge (1772–1834), and Southey (1774–1843).
35.15 **Sydenham Common** where the poet Thomas Campbell (1777–1844) made his home.
35.15–16 **Saint James's Place** where Samuel Rogers (1763–1855) had his house.
35.16 **the Banks of the Bosphorus** probably an allusion to Lord Byron (1788–1824).
35.23 **the reversion** legal term meaning a right to buy back property sold to another; here a comic reference to the practice of using the remains of a bottle when cooking the next day's food.
35.23–24 **furnish forth the feast of to-morrow** see *Hamlet*, 1.2.181.
35.34 **tide-ticks on his gills** i.e. sea-lice on the gills, an indication that this was a fish newly come up river from the sea.
35.40 **dozen of blue** i.e. a dozen blue-capped bottles of wine, identified later as claret.
35 footnote **in votis** *Latin* in the wishes, welcome to.
35 footnote **Optat . . . leonem** Virgil, *Aeneid*, 4.159: he wishes a wild boar or a tawny lion would descend from the hill.
36.33 **Vulcan** the Roman god of fire and craftsmanship; he was lame.
36.33 **Mars** the Roman god of war; here, Captain MacTurk.
36.34 **Mercury** the messenger of the gods, noted for his eloquence; here Mr Chatterley.
37.8 **Wogdens** pistols. Wogdens are 'the best quality English duellers of the late 1700s'. See Merrill Lindsay, *The Lure of Antique Arms* (New York, 1976), 118.
37.9 **hit the hay-stack** Mowbray is saying that Winterblossom is accurate enough with a pistol to do damage. Compare the note at 230.23.
37.19 **syrup of capillaire** syrup flavoured with orange-flower water.
38.7 **recruiting party** i.e. party of soldiers recruiting for the army.
39.2 **alterations in Pope's version of the Iliad** see Samuel Johnson (1709–84), 'Alexander Pope' (1781), in *The Lives of the Poets*.
39 **motto** see Matthew Prior (1664–1721), 'To a Person who wrote Ill, and spake Worse against Me' (1710), line 4.
40.12 **Lilliput-hall** Lilliput is the country of diminutive beings that

Lemuel Gulliver visits in Book I of Swift's *Gulliver's Travels* (1726).
40.34 Dryads and Naiads nymphs of trees and streams.
40.36 Apollo in Greek mythology, the god of the sun, prophecy, music, and poetry.
41.1 Nectar and Ambrosia the drink and food of the gods.
41.3 the Muses in Greek mythology, the nine daughters of Zeus and Mnemosyne, each of whom presided over a different art or science.
41.7 his narrow cot affords compare Thomas Gray (1716–71), 'Elegy Written in a Country Church-Yard' (1751), line 15.
41.8 Assuredly the thing is to be hired see *As You Like It*, 2.4.91.
41.10 Iris in Greek mythology the goddess who acted as the messenger of the gods, and whose sign was the rainbow.
41.29–30 Indian gout... black hakkels Indian gut for use as fishing line, and some flies.
41.37 the philosopher Scipio (236–183 BC) used to say that he was never less idle than when he had nothing to do and never less lonely than when he was alone: see Cicero, *De Officiis* (44 BC), 3.1.
42.8 Lycoris mistress of the Roman poet Gallus (*c.* 69–29 BC), immortalised in the tenth *Eclogue* of Virgil (70–19 BC), lines 2–3.
42.11 Gramachree Molly composed by George Ogle (1742–1814), and very popular at the end of the 18th century. The first line reads: 'As doun by Banna's banks I stray'd, one evening in May'. See *SMM*, no. 47. For further information, see *Love Songs of the Irish*, ed. James N. Healy (Dublin, 1977), 33–35.
42.16 the Misanthrope an allusion to *Le Misanthrope* (1666) by Molière (1622–73).
42.35 Timon another misanthrope. A citizen of Athens who lived about the time of the Peloponnesian War (431–404 BC), and the subject of the dialogue, 'Misanthropos', by Lucian (2nd century AD) and of *Timon of Athens* by Shakespeare.
42.37 Pirner the name suggests a 'pirn', the reel of a fishing-rod, or a small bobbin on which thread is wound.
45.1 all, or either, or one or other of them legal phraseology designed to cover every combination of two conditions or of two people acting either individually or together.
45.3 pro and con *Latin* pro and contra, for and against.
45.15 a morning dress dress intended for wear before dinner.
45.20 scales seemed to fall from the eyes see Acts 9.18.
45.34 Juno in Roman mythology, the wife of Jupiter.
46.12–13 real evidence technical term implying physical evidence to prove an allegation.
46.17 Mrs Weir not identified.
46.19 corpus delicti *Latin, literally* the body of the crime. A phrase from Scots criminal law which means that the substance of the offence must be made out, i.e. it must be shown that a crime took place, before a conviction can be made.
46.22 stand . . . confessed *Scots law* accept the proofs adduced against one.
47.19 leading strings reins used to control young children.
48.10 gentleman of elegant inquiry someone who asks questions in a graceful and polite way. The phrase is apparently a quotation (see *Letters*, 5.180), but has not been identified.
48 motto not identified; probably by Scott.
49.17 Amazonian chiefs chiefs of the legendary race of women warriors.
49.17–18 hunters of Buenos Ayres . . . cord and their loop the lasso

originated in that part of South America now called Argentina, and was used to capture wild horses.

49.31 **babble of green fields** see *Henry V*, 2.3.17.

49.35 **Urbs in rure** town life in the country. Compare *rus in urbe* ('the country in the midst of the town'): Martial, *Epigrammata*, 12.57.

50.4 **subscription tickets** *subscription* was a mode of selling books before publication, by getting individuals to *subscribe*, i.e. add their name to a list of those promising to purchase; the *ticket* is the promise to pay.

50.13–15 **new lights . . . Time was making** see Edmund Waller (1606–87), 'Of the Last Verses in the Book', lines 13-14; and compare Alexander Pope, *The Dunciad* (1742), 4.125–26.

50.29–30 **a girl must be bang up to everything** a girl must be quite up to the mark or up to the fashion in everything. The inverted commas probably indicate slang rather than a quotation.

50.37 **bone of his bone** see Genesis 2.23; the phrase is used in the context of the marriage service.

50.42 **pad on** tramp on.

51.1 **help-mate** see Genesis 2.20.

51.3 **Themis** Greek goddess of law and justice; hence Law or Justice personified.

51.5 **upon the tapis** *literally* on the tablecloth, i.e. under discussion or consideration.

51.6 **de par le monde** *French* the world over; i.e. as is the case everywhere.

51.8 **hack chaise** carriage kept for hire.

51.12 **Andrea Ferrara** sword named after the North Italian swordsmith of the late 16th century. His name became a mark of quality for Scotsmen in the 17th and 18th centuries, and many Scots swords bear his name, but it is doubted whether any of them are in fact his work.

51.12–13 **neat mahogany box** i.e. pistol case.

53.25 **seat unoccupied—the chair of Banquo** see *Macbeth*, 3.4.

53.27 **the Dark Ladye** see 'The Ballad of the Dark Ladié' (1798) by Coleridge (1772–1834).

53.39–40 **She glides . . . speech.** see Coleridge, 'The Rime of the Ancient Mariner' (1798), lines 586–87.

54.16–17 **Mat Lewis's Spectre Lady** see Matthew Gregory Lewis (1775–1818), 'The Gay Gold Ring', in *Tales of Wonder* (Kelso, 1800).

54.37–38 **the Louvre** palace of the French kings in Paris, which began its present role when the revolutionary government opened the Musée Central des Arts in the Grande Galerie in 1793; it soon became a major museum of fine art in the early 19th century as a result of Napoleon's conquests.

55.4 **Melpomene** the muse who presided over tragedy.

55.6 **Euphrosyne** one of the three Graces, Euphrosyne was associated with mirth and comedy.

55.11–12 **Il Penseroso** the poem (1632), associated with melancholy, by John Milton.

55.16–17 **we know . . . not what we may be** see *Hamlet*, 4.5.41–42.

55.18 **Elysium** in Greek mythology, the supposed state or abode of the blessed after death; figuratively, a place or state of ideal happiness.

55.26 **serenely silent art** Thomas Campbell (1777–1844), 'Stanzas to Painting' (1803), line 33.

55.32 **Orlando . . . Forest of Ardennes** see *As You Like It*, 3.2.1–10, 334–36.

56.6 **Arcadia** mountainous district in the central Peloponnese in Greece, taken as the ideal region of pastoral contentment.

56.10 **fairy favours** *A Midsummer Night's Dream*, 2.1.12.

56.28 de futuro *Latin* for the future.
56.28 tractus temporis in gremio *Latin* legal expression meaning a deed of temporary contract.
57 motto see William Cowper (1731–1800), *The Task* (1785), 4.39–40.
57.13 quantum sufficit *Latin* adequate supply.
57.13 tallow candles candles made from tallow, i.e. animal fat, which were more smelly and less refined than wax candles. Compare the note to 259.17–18.
57.15–16 on the light fantastic toe John Milton, 'L'Allegro' (1632), line 34.
57.21 the tea-table increasingly women were turning to tea and persuading men to do the same. Tea was brewed very strongly and, at 5*s.* (25p) a pound, was expensive. By 1820, the British were importing 30 million tons of tea annually, nearly all of it from China. Tea cost £40 a ton in Canton, and the duties on it when it reached Britain formed the biggest single item in the Exchequer's revenues. See Johnson, 756, 774.
57.22 souchong and congo teas imported from China.
57.23 ***fille de chambre*** *French* lady's maid.
58.3–4 their geese were all swans proverbial: see Tilley, 271; Apperson, 265; and *ODEP*, 298.
58.5 swan has proved but a goose see *Romeo and Juliet*, 1.2.87.
58.30–34 professional artist . . . gentleman see Scott's *Letters*, 3.54. The distinction between a 'man of letters' and 'gentleman' is more fully elaborated in Scott's 'Essay on Imitations of the Ancient Ballad' (1830), in *Minstrelsy*, 4.21–22.
59.4 Balaam . . . his ass see Numbers 22.21–35.
59.6 Mon . . . bien my ass talks and, what is more, talks well. The source of this quotation has not been identified, but in a letter of 11 May 1823, when Scott began writing *Saint Ronan's Well*, he quoted these same words: see *Letters*, 7.387.
59.9 pull caps *literally* snatch or pull off each other's caps, i.e. quarrel.
59.13 fern-seed before the mode of reproduction of ferns was understood, they were popularly supposed to produce an invisible seed, which was capable of communicating its invisibility to any person who possessed it.
59.13 fern-seed, and walk amongst us invisible see *I Henry IV*, 2.1.83–84. Scott uses the same quotation in a letter of 25 February 1823: see *Letters*, 7.342.
59.19–21 his eyes . . . Robert Burns see Maria Riddell's description in 'Memoir Concerning Burns', in the *Dumfries Journal*, 7 August 1796, many times reprinted in works on Burns by Currie, Chambers, Daiches, etc. However, the closest description to that in the text is Scott's own: 'the eye alone, I think, indicated the poetical character and temperament. It was large and of a dark cast, and glowed (I say literally *glowed*) when he spoke with feeling or interest. I never saw such another eye in a human head, though I have seen the most distinguished men in my time' (*Life*, 1.138).
60.1–2 passed on the other side see Luke 10.31–32 (the parable of the Good Samaritan).
60.19–21 My venerated instructor . . . old rum . . . after his dinner Dr William Cullen (1710–90), a medical professor of Edinburgh University (1775–90).
60.31 Macgregor Dr James Gregory (1776–1821), a leading physician in Edinburgh and medical professor in the University.
60.41–61.4 starving Doctor . . . generous diet physicians disagreed constantly on whether to use the lowering system (bleeding by means of leeches) or the raising (giving fortifying food and drink): see Johnson, 746.
61.25 Catch me without my tools see John Fletcher, *Monsieur Thomas*

(performed 1619; printed 1639), 3.1.244.
62.5 in the wind's eye nautical slang for intoxicated, the worse for liquor.
62.5–6 sang about a dog they ca'd Bungo folk-song with a spelling chorus: 'A farmer's dog jump'd over the stile, and I think his name was Bingo, B–I–N–G–O'. See the *Journal of the Folk-Song Society*, 1.242.
62.10–11 mad dog . . . no water hydrophobia is a classic symptom of rabies.
62.22 minister plenipotentiary minister invested with full powers, especially as the deputy or representative of a higher authority.
62.25–26 gie up . . . to be remembered in the prayers ask the congregation to pray for—an example of 18th-century presbyterian discourse.
62.30–31 Leith Roads sheltered water off Leith, the port of Edinburgh.
62.36 opening of my mind reveal my mind to spiritual view.
62.40 Leyden in Holland, the seat of a distinguished medical school, at which many eminent Scottish surgeons and physicians were trained.
63.3–4 comforts hae their cumbers compare the proverb 'Evils have their comforts' (*ODEP*, 233).
63.4 sair weird hard fate.
63.24 Fat, fair, and forty see John Dryden, *Secret Love, or The Maiden Queen* (1667), 3.1.353–54. Since Scott, the expression has become familiar, if not quite proverbial.
63.29 Stygian Creek i.e. the underworld; the river Styx was the principal river of Hades, where the dead went in classical mythology.
64.6–7 laughed till her eyes run over see *Troilus and Cressida*, 1.2.136–41.
64.13–14 let nineteen nay-says be a grant proverbial encouragement for those who have had denials from a Mistress to address her again (see Kelly, 268; Ramsay, 103; *ODEP*, 567).
64.26–27 12th of August first day of the grouse-shooting season.
64.27–28 skins the business up . . . break out elsewhere i.e. covers over the quarrel only for it to appear elsewhere: see *Hamlet*, 3.4.147–49.
64.29–30 bona fide *Latin* genuinely.
64.41 Angels and ministers of grace *Hamlet*, 1.4.39.
65.40 powder-monkey humorous term for a powder-boy, a boy chosen for his small size and employed on board ship to carry gunpowder.
66.11 fools of a feather i.e. fowls or birds of a feather. Proverbial: see Ray, 79; *ODEP*, 60.
66.34 secundum artem *Latin* in the light of science or knowledge.
66.43 inaudible in the gallery familiar expression in Parliamentary reports, meaning that what was said on the floor of the House of Commons was not audible in the gallery where the public sits.
67.17–18 like Ophelia's garlands, and wild snatches of melody see *Hamlet*, 4.7.167–84.
67.38 déjeuner à la fourchette *literally* a fork-lunch; i.e. a simple dinner.
67.41 old Nick familiar name for the devil.
68.3 Champagne and a chicken at last 'The Lover: a Ballad' (1747), line 26, by Lady Mary Wortley Montague (1689–1762).
68.7 Pidcock and Polito keepers of a wild-beast show.
68.14 the prince Ahmed's quarters of mutton see 'The Story of Prince Ahmed and the Fairy Pari Banou', in Weber, 1.432–54.
68.18–19 For if they should . . . pity of their life see *A Midsummer Night's Dream*, 5.1.222–23; but it is Snug the joiner who plays lion and speaks the speech.
68.25 Lord Chesterfield Philip Dormer Stanhope (1694–1773), 4th Earl of Chesterfield, author of *Letters to His Son* (1774), designed to teach him

how to become an accomplished man of the world.

68.33–34 Robert Rymar . . . Thomas Robert Rymar is fictitious. Thomas the Rhymer (Thomas of Erceldoune) was a 13th-century seer and poet, reputed author of a poem on the Tristram story which Scott had edited, and the subject of the famous ballad.

68.35 Keelavine the name is a word for a lead pencil.

69.3 Lady Clementina the long-suffering heroine of *Sir Charles Grandison* (1754) by Samuel Richardson (1689–1761). Like Clara's, her mind becomes deranged because of her unhappiness.

69.4–5 Ophelia . . . sweet ladies see *Hamlet*, 4.5.69–70.

69.6 my horse, my horse see *Richard III*, 5.4.13.

69.12–14 Mrs Highmore . . . impertinence see Henry Fielding (1707–54), *The Intriguing Chambermaid* (1733), 2.10.5–6. The character is actually called Mrs Highman, and she says, 'your madness is a poor excuse for this behaviour'.

69.20 Hate for arts which caused herself to rise see Alexander Pope, 'An Epistle from Mr. Pope, to Dr. Arbuthnot' (1735), line 200.

70 motto see Matthew Prior (1664–1721), 'Hans Carvel' (1700), lines 98–99.

71.32 licking trenchers, and scratching copper utensils used by the lower classes: 'trenchers' were wooden boards on which meat was cut and served, and by 'copper' Scott means a copper dish. The implied mode of eating is deliberately insulting.

71.33 sotto voce *Italian* in an undertone.

72.13–14 may I never die the black death may I never suffer the black death. The phrase 'black death' as the name of the great plague of the 14th century was in 1823 of recent origin.

72.16–17 the trouble of translating it 'We know from constant experience, that most highlanders after they have become compleat masters of English, continue to *think* in their own language and it is to me demonstrable that Macpherson *thought* almost every word of Ossian in Gaelic although he wrote it down in English.' (to Anna Seward, [probably September 1806], *Letters*, 1.323)

72.17 Ossian legendary Celtic hero and bard of the 3rd century AD. James Macpherson (1736–96) published *Fingal* (1762) and *Temora* (1763), epics purporting to be translations from the Gaelic of Ossian. A committee of the Highland Society chaired by Henry Mackenzie (1745–1831) decided in 1805 that Macpherson had translated Gaelic poems very freely and had added passages of his own.

72.20–22 setters . . . lying dogs . . . auld Scots statute there are a number of Scots Acts against setters or setting dogs, and against 'lying dogs', but the Acts of 1655 and 1661, while ratifying the authority given in 1617 to justices of the peace against lying dogs, change 'lying dogs' into 'setting dogs'. The identification of 'lying dogs' with 'setting dogs' is also to be found in Glendook, the standard edition of Scots statute law (Sir Thomas Murray of Glendook, *Acts and Laws of the Scottish Parliament made by King James the First, and His Royal Successors, Kings and Queen of Scotland*, 2 vols, 1682–83). Micklewhame's argument is thus based on the historical development of the statutes.

72.34 Saint Ronan's i.e. Mowbray, here given his territorial designation.

72.35–36 raised a summons against before the justices started an action against by seeking and gaining the legal document citing to appear before the justices of the peace for infringing the shooting rights of the old laird. The prosecution would have been under 13 George III c. 54 s. 8 (1773).

72.42–43 keep a calm sough *proverbial* keep quiet, say little or nothing (*ODEP*, 416).

72.43 intented the process instituted the action.

73.1 **Quarter Sessions** in Scotland, a court of review and appeal held quarterly by the justices of the peace on days appointed by statute.
73.1–2 **sheriff clerk stood the lad's friend** acted as a legal representative for him. Only 18, Tyrrel would then have been under age.
73.5 **let the process sleep** technical legal phrase meaning that a year and a day has elapsed without a judicial order or interlocutor being produced. An action of awakening used to be required to recommence the action.
73.9 **prescribed sax or seven years syne** technical legal term to the effect that the possibility of pursuing some legal right has lapsed due to the passage of time. The Statute 13 George III c. 54 (1773) (see note to 72.35–36) required prosecutions to be begun within six months of the commission of the offence.
73.14 **hap ye out of ae county and into anither** hop from one county into another; i.e. the poacher's defence would be that the offence happened over the boundary into the next county outwith the jurisdiction of the present court.
73.28–29 **the greatest improvement . . . since the year forty-five** the Whig lawyer is referring to the defeat of the Jacobites and the pacification of the Highlands in 1745–46.
74.6 **let sleeping dogs lie** proverbial (see *ODEP*, 456).
74.16–17 **regis ad exemplar** after the example of the king, or chief person.
74.41 **Fives-Court** prepared court where the game of fives (a game in which a ball is struck by the hand against the front wall of a three-sided court) is played, also used as a hall for boxing practice and matches.
74.42 **serve . . . out** administer corporal punishment.
75.12 **Are you a man?** *Macbeth*, 3.4.58.
75.13 **our inimitable Siddons** Sarah Siddons (1755–1831), queen of British tragic acting, whose performance of Lady Macbeth in 1785 was long famous.
75.43 **unfitness of the time** see *King John*, 3.3.26.
76.5 **he shews the white feather** *proverbial* he acts like a coward (see *ODEP*, 885).
76.34 **the fall of a stag** see 'Hart-Leap Well' (1800) by William Wordsworth, from which the lines of poetry on the title-page were taken.
76.40 **Pontey** William Pontey, author of *The Forest Pruner* (1808) and *The Profitable Planter* (1808). See Scott's description of 'this great forester' in his journal entry of 10 April 1831 (*Journal*, 647).
78.11–12 **scalding your lips in other folks' kale** proverbial: see Apperson, 552; Tilley, 384–85; and *ODEP*, 703.
78.16 **small-debt court** the Small Debt Act, 39 and 40 George III, c. 46 (1800), introduced a summary small-debt jurisdiction for justices of the peace. MacTurk is insulting Micklewhame.
79.6 **That qualification . . . be my speed** see *1 Henry IV*, 3.1.190.
79.22–23 **no lions . . . Cybele** Cybele was an Asiatic goddess who represented the fecundity of nature, and to whom the lion was sacred.
79.30 **lion rampant . . . lion passant** *heraldry* the lion rampant is rearing on the left hind leg with the forelegs elevated; the lion passant is walking toward the viewer's right with one front leg raised.
80.7 **Betty Foy's** see Wordsworth, 'The Idiot Boy' (1798), especially lines 112–16.
80.27 **age of the moon** the moon was associated with madness: 'lunacy' is derived from the Latin *luna*, the moon.
80 **motto** not identified; probably by Scott.
83.16 **poor in spirit** Matthew 5.3.
83.35 **after so many years of wandering** see Wordsworth, 'Tintern Abbey' (1798), line 156.
85.1 **We are but actors . . . a stage** see *As You Like It*, 2.7.139–40.

85.9 the winter of our life . . . summer see *Richard III*, 1.1.1–2.
86.5 while water can drown . . . steel pierce see *Othello*, 3.3.392–94.
86.35 Abigails waiting-women, probably derived from Abigail, the handmaid of David; see 1 Samuel 25.14–42.
86.35 waiter at Long's reference to either the busy ordinary in the Haymarket or Long's Hotel in Bond Street, where Scott stayed in 1815.
87.3 bedlam Bedlam, or St Mary of Bethlehem, was a hospital for the insane in London; from the 1660s, the term was used as a generic name for such institutions.
87.22–23 the fair-fashioned folk that can say My Jo, and think it no *proverbial* they can pretend friendship, where they have none: see Tilley, 487.
87.30 plack and bawbee to the last farthing, in full, every penny. A *plack* and a *bawbee* were Scots coins worth four pence Scots (0.14p) and six pence Scots (0.2p) respectively.
87.37 want of siller lack of money.
87.42 grund of the purse i.e. bottom of the purse.
87.43 the morn tomorrow.
88 motto not identified; probably by Scott.
90.10–11 pomander boxes cases in which perfume was carried, usually hollow balls of gold, silver, ivory, etc., often in the shape of an apple or orange.
90.13 unconsidered trifles *The Winter's Tale*, 4.3.27.
90.20–21 coral and bells infant's toys or teething equipment.
90.39–40 making the worse appear the better garnishment see *Paradise Lost*, 2.113–14.
91.3 comme il faut *French* as it should be, proper.
91.26 counsel learned in the law see *Henry IV*, 1.2.128–29.
91.37 het ha'-house *literally* hot hall-house, i.e. comfortable hall or mansion.
91.38 the Abbey Holyrood, in Edinburgh, the precincts of which were a sanctuary for debtors. Retiring to the sanctuary of the Abbey was an admission of bankruptcy, and the debtor was protected from being seized and put in prison.
92.9 a back-sliding generation see Hosea 4.16.
92.12 barking and fleeing on the verge of ruin.
92.14–15 grandfather's tailzie in Scotland a *tailzie* or entail secured the descent of a heritable estate to a designated series of heirs, preventing the current owner from selling or giving away or mortgaging either the whole or any part of it. By granting feus, not only has Mowbray reduced his rents ('mailing'), but has acted beyond what the entail permitted ('raxed ower the tether').
92.21 raxed ower the tether stretched out beyond the limits of one's rights or ability.
92.33–37 incurred an irritancy . . . sessions forfeited rights as heir of entail by acting contrary to the terms of the entail. Clara, as next heir of entail, or her husband as administrator of her heritable property, would have the right to raise an action of declarator of irritancy to deprive Mowbray of the entailed property, and might expect to succeed within 'twa or three sessions', i.e. 2 or 3 sessions of the Court of Session.
92.34 A. B. memorial request to an advocate for an opinion on a point of law, phrased in terms of A and B so that no parties are named.
92.41–42 bee in her bonnet 'loose screw'. Although proverbial (see Apperson, 33; and *ODEP*, 39) Scott does not use the saying in the usual way when it means a 'fantasy' or 'obsession'.
93.7–9 gie in . . . a petition to the Lords . . . Curator Bonis . . . affairs raise an action before the Lords of Session (the judges of the Court of Session, the supreme civil court in Scotland), to be appointed Clara's *curator bonis*, i.e. guardian to manage her property by reason of her mental incapacity.

93.23 **rerum dominos gentemque togatam** Virgil (70–19 BC), *Aeneid*, 1.282; in the quotation Jupiter tells Venus, '[I shall foster] the masters of the world, the race which wears the toga'. Scott plays on the use of *gens togata* to mean 'lawyers' as well as Virgil's meaning of 'Romans'.
93.27 **multiplepoinding** action about a sum of money brought by a person holding the sum but not knowing to whom it should be paid among several claimants; all potential claimants are called as parties to the action. Multiplepoindings were (and are) notoriously expensive.
93.33 **Outer-House** i.e. Parliament Hall in Parliament House in Edinburgh, where preliminary matters were dealt with by judges, but which was also the place where unemployed advocates lounged, waiting for a brief.
93.37–38 **ye might aye have gotten a Sheriffdom, or a Commissaryship** i.e. become a sheriff-depute of a county (as Scott did) or become one of the four judges (Commissaries) of the Commissary Court in Edinburgh, which had jurisdiction in matters relating to marriage, legitimacy, separation, divorce, defamation, and the execution of wills and testaments.
94.5 **fling the helve after the hatchet** *proverbial* add a new loss to that already incurred: see Tilley, 307; Apperson, 632; and *ODEP*, 368.
94.23–24 **the labourer is worthy of his hire** Luke 10.7.
94.30–31 **Land's-End to Johnnie Groat's** from the tip of Cornwall to the northern extremity of Scotland; from one end of Britain to the other.
94.37 **takes up his rents as he comes down** i.e. takes receipt on his way to the Well of the rents of his estates payable on Michaelmas (29 September).
95.8 **free of the company** i.e. freeman of, or admitted to the privileges of, the company of a company of traders (see *OED*, 'free', 29).
95.9 **trade on my own bottom** trade on my own behalf: compare *ODEP*, 845.
95.16 **three per cents** consols (consolidated annuities); i.e. government stocks on which interest at 3% was paid.
95.40 **service is nae inheritance** see *All's Well that Ends Well*, 1.3.24.
95.40–41 **friendship, it begins at hame** Micklewhame is mistaken. It is 'charity' that proverbially begins at home (Apperson, 91–92; Tilley, 93; and *ODEP*, 115).
96.1–2 **hasna sae mickle gentle blood ... hungry flea** see *Love's Labour's Lost*, 5.2.679–80.
96.7–8 **volunteer to the continent** i.e. volunteer to serve in the army in the Peninsular War.
96.28 **Bingo is got shy** 'gut shy' is a fishing term, usually applied to the fish, meaning it has been scared by the reflection of the sun on the gut.
97.7 **not me, for I advise nothing** Micklewhame wants to ensure that he is not accountable for counselling unethical, potentially fraudulent, conduct.
97.14 **care killed a cat** proverbial: see Ray, 84; *ODEP*, 103; and *Much Ado about Nothing*, 5.1.132.
97.18–19 **trustees for Miss Clara** Micklewhame and Turnpenny are Clara's trustees; the implication is that her aunt had wanted to make sure that Mowbray could not easily get possession of Clara's property.
97.24 **it's needless making twa bites of a cherry** proverbial: see Apperson, 653; and *ODEP*, 849.
97.30–31 **the wind will keep its way, preach ... like** see John 3.8. By Scott's time, it had become proverbial (see Kelly, 285).
97.32 **penny money** i.e. ready money.
97.33–34 **pitch and toss** game in which each player pitches a coin at a mark; the person whose coin comes nearest then tosses all the coins at the mark, and keeps those which turn up heads; the other player then does the same with the remaining ones, and so on, until all the coins are gone.

98.1–2 the best laid schemes will gang ajee see Robert Burns (1759–1796), 'To a Mouse' (1786), lines 39–40.
98.3 parish i.e. parish poor-relief; this was not notable for its generosity.
98 motto not identified; probably by Scott.
99.17 sufficient . . . evil thereof see Matthew 6.34.
99.23 Princess Caraboo Mary Wilcox (or Willcocks) who, early in the 19th century, posed at Bath as an Eastern princess. In 1817, she got to St Helena, and asked the governor, Sir Hudson Lowe, if he could get the Pope to dissolve Napoleon's marriage to Maria Louisa and let him marry Caraboo instead. For Scott's interest in her, see his letter of November 1823 to Maria Edgeworth (*Letters*, 8.121).
100.1–2 the goose which lays the golden egg proverbial: see *ODEP*, 422. The saying is derived from one of Aesop's fables: see *Aesop Without Morals*, trans. and ed. Lloyd W. Daly (New York, 1961), No. 87.
100.4 my natural guardian not legally. Clara is an adult and is legally competent.
100.29 [Fortune] favours the bold favourite expression of Latin writers: see Virgil, *Aeneid*, 10.398; Terence (*c.* 190–159 BC), *Phormio*, 1.203; the Younger Pliny (b. AD 61), Book 6, Letter 16.
100.42 Emmeline heroine of the romance by Charlotte Smith (1749–1806), *Emmeline, or the Orphan of the Castle* (1788).
100.42 Ethelinde heroine of the romance by Charlotte Smith, *Ethelinde, or the Recluse of the Lake* (1790).
101.14 go to the hammer go to auction.
101.43 playing on the square when play is fair and honest.
102.34 this morning portion of the day extending to dinner time at 3 or 4 p.m.
102.40 the Raw-head and Bloody-Bones the name of a nursery bugbear, or goblin, used to frighten children.
103.10 I am the same Jack Mowbray still see John Webster, *The Duchess of Malfi* (written 1612/13), 4.2.146.
103.30 Machiavel Niccolò Machiavelli (1469–1527), the Florentine statesman and political theorist. He became a symbol to the British of shrewd and labyrinthine diplomacy.
104 motto see Francis Beaumont (1584–1616) and John Fletcher (1579–1625), *A King and No King* (1619), 3.2.43–46.
105.11 peculiar cogniac i.e. cognac imported by the Baronet's himself.
105.33–34 on the road towards . . . Coventry *proverbial* to exclude a person from the society of which he is a member on account of objectionable conduct, to refuse to associate or have intercourse with him: see Apperson, 117; and *ODEP*, 149.
106.4–5 putting their spoon into other folks' dish proverbial: see *ODEP*, 767.
106.11 better late thrive than never do well proverbial: see Ramsay, 72; and *ODEP*, 54.
106.20 come up to the scratch come up to the line drawn across the boxing ring, to which boxers are brought for an encounter; the fight would end when one of the boxers could not come up to the scratch line at the beginning of a new round.
106.22 Jenny Sutton a reel. See Niel Gow (1727–1807), *A Second Collection of Strathspeys, Reels, etc.* (Edinburgh, 1788), 4.
107.7 Hector MacTurk . . . my name the name interprets the character. 'Hector' is the name of the Trojan hero in *The Iliad*, a name which gives rise to the English verb 'hector', meaning to 'bluster' or 'bully'. A 'Turk' suggests a savage, violent man.

107.11 Dumbarton drums the march of the Royal Scots Regiment. The name is said to come from George, Earl of Dumbarton, colonel of the regiment, 1645–88. It may be found in William Thomson, *Orpheus Caledonius* 2 vols (1733), 2.16; Niel Gow, *Complete Repository of Original Scots Slow Strathspeys and Dances*, Series 2 (Edinburgh, 1802), 11; and *SMM*, No. 161.
107.36–37 Saint George's guard one of the principal guards with the broadsword, St George's guard protects the head.
107.42 fasting from all but sin see Cervantes, *Don Quixote*, Part 2 (1615), Ch. 73, in Motteux's free translation (1700–03). The housekeeper says to Don Quixote, 'Troth, master, take my advice; I am neither drunk nor mad, but fresh and fasting from every thing but sin'. These words are retained in Lockhart's revised version of Motteux: *The History of the Ingenious Gentleman, Don Quixote of La Mancha*, 5 vols (1822), 5.316.
110.31 kettle of fish 'A kettle of fish is a *fête-champêtre* [open-air party in the country]. . . . A large cauldron is boiled by the side of a salmon river, containing a quantity of water, thickened with salt, to the consistence of brine. In this the fish is plunged when taken, and eaten by the company *fronde super viridi*.' (Magnum, 33.210). The Latin phrase means 'on a bed of green leaves', and comes from Virgil, *Eclogues*, 1.80.
111.24 the Ethic philosopher specifically, Aristotle (384–322 BC), but here probably any student of ethics.
111 motto see *The Merry Wives of Windsor*, 3.1.1–7. As the words of the first speech indicate, the second speaker should be Simple.
111.36 Belcher handkerchief neckerchief with blue ground, and large white spots having a dark blue spot or eye in the centre, and named after a celebrated pugilist, Jem Belcher (1781–1811).
112.22 bon vivant person who enjoys good food and drink and lives luxuriously.
113.35 entering for such a plate entering a horse race for a prize of a silver or gold cup, here specifically Lady Binks (if widowed).
114.17 carious molindinar decayed molar tooth.
114.28 secundum artem *Latin* according to rule.
115.5 nunquam non paratus *Latin* never unprepared.
115.17 straining like a greyhound in the slips see *Henry V*, 3.1.31–32.
116.28 time stands still with no man see *As You Like It*, 3.2.290–93.
117.30 short quarter-deck walk the 'quarter deck' was the short, upper deck in the stern of a sailing vessel on which the higher officers took exercise.
118.2–3 Bob Acres . . . good courage should be thrown away see Richard Brinsley Sheridan (1751–1816), *The Rivals* (1775), 4.1.81–82.
118.23 procès-verbal French legal term meaning the official minute or record of a legal process, recording findings of fact and giving reasons for decisions.
118.26 Machaon son of Asclepius, and one of the two surgeons of the Greek army in the Trojan war.
119.3 Glenlivat glen in Moray, famous for its whisky; but perhaps specific reference to the distillery of The Glenlivet is intended.
119.9–10 Dutch and French distilled waters i.e. schnapps (or gin), and brandy.
119.10 genuine Highland ware whisky.
119.11–12 if he can have the good fortune to come by it legally produced whisky was difficult to obtain because of the prohibition of small private stills in 1781, the drastic increases in duty from 1793 as one means of funding the war with France, and corn shortages which led to laws temporarily closing distilleries.

119.33 Tirrel the misspelling of 'Tyrrel' throughout this statement seems to be deliberate.
119.38 voluntarily engaged this legalistic language means bound by will or wish rather than by law.
120.13 M.D. . . . X.Z. while M.D., F.R.S. and B.L. are real honours and qualifications (Doctor of Medicine, Fellow of the Royal Society, and Bachelor of Laws), the other two are invented.
120.24 averment Scottish legal term meaning statement or allegation positively made and thus claimed to be true. The normal context is in written court proceedings, where averments are allegations of fact that will be proved at the actual proof.
120.26 a legislative enactment the Committee of Management is again acting as a legislative body as well as the executive body of the little republic of the Well.
121.5–6 to give the fellow his due . . .. like the devil proverbial: see Apperson, 143; Tilley, 153; and *ODEP*, 304.
123 motto see *Measure for Measure*, 2.1.127. In the play the speaker is Pompey.
123.28 more Scottico in the Scottish fashion.
123.30–124.3 Town-Council . . . member of Parliament Marchthorn is a Royal Burgh. After the Union of 1707 the Royal Burghs of Scotland (except for Edinburgh) were grouped together in fours or fives to select a member of Parliament. In a grouping of five Burghs, each Council would elect a representative internally, and a meeting of the five representatives would take place at which each would vote for a candidate. Parliamentary elections had to be held at least once in 7 years.
124.17 Piccadilly i.e. in the fashionable part of London.
125.37 in transitu *Latin* in transit or during conveyance (an instantly recognisable legal phrase).
125.39 in propria persona *Latin* in one's own person, rather than appearing or acting through an agent.
126.10 meat and mess food and a meal.
126.11 the spirit canna aye bear through the flesh *proverbial* the spirit is willing but the flesh is weak: see Matthew 26.41; Tilley, 626; *ODEP*, 765.
126.15 Deil ane not one.
126.23 it's an awful thing to die intestate the Romans' 'horror of intestacy' was proverbial among lawyers.
126.28 festina lente *Latin proverb* hasten slowly. This was a favourite saying of Augustus (63 BC–AD 14): see Suetonius (*c.* AD 70–*c.* 160), *The Twelve Caesars*, 25.
126.29 the true law language a reference to Scottish lawyers' love of Latin maxims, but there is also a mocking suggestion that 'hasten slowly' is the way that lawyers prefer to do business.
126.28 hoolly and fairly slowly and gently, but steadily.
126.41 banded debtors bonded debtors, i.e. debtors who had provided some kind of written undertaking to pay a debt. Such bonds could be personal or heritable (the latter usually involving the pledge of land).
127.6–7 Vita incerta, mors certissima *Latin* life is uncertain, death most sure.
127.28 no bring in a bill against i.e. not to bring in the document initiating the prosecution.
127.38 pro-fiscal procurator-fiscal, the official in Scottish sheriffdoms charged with overseeing the investigation and the prosecution of crime.
127.42 herd callant shepherd lad.
128.2 new lords new laws proverbial: see Apperson, 444; *ODEP*, 564.

128.19 marriage-contract ante-nuptial arrangement, normally entered into to avoid the full effects of the law on the property of married persons, and to provide for them and any children in the future.
128.38 Commissary Court business the Commissary Court had jurisdiction in matters of defamation of character: see note to 93.38, and Cairns.
129.20 scribes having authority see Matthew 7.29; Mark 1.22.
129.41 held sic a wark about made such an ado about, set such store by.
130.14 intra parietes *Latin* between walls, behind closed doors.
130.14 remotis testibus *Latin* with no witnesses being near, in the absence of witnesses.
131.10 making in forcing one's way into, interfering.
131.24 live and learn proverbial: see Tilley, 388; Apperson, 375; and *ODEP*, 473.
131.40 Corpus delicti *Latin* material evidence: see note to 46.19. The literal translation, the body of the crime, is also relevant here.
131.43 Habeas Corpus the English act of 1689 requiring prisoners to be brought speedily to trial and allowing them the right to be freed on bail, except in cases of treason and felony. The act never applied to Scotland, but the name was inaccurately used for a comparable Scottish act of 1701.
132.5 no proof that a crime has been committed 'For example, a man cannot be tried for murder merely in the case of the non-appearance of an individual; there must be proof that the party has been murdered.' (Magnum, 33.247)
132.31 Praiser of Past Times a translation of the Latin 'laudator temporis Acti': Horace, *Ars Poetica* (*c.* 19 BC), 173.
132 motto *King John*, 1.1.189–90.
133.19–22 Premium . . . call forty days par . . . remittances to London a Bank of England bill was one drawn on the Bank of England and payable at the Scottish bank for which Bindloose is agent (this would be the Royal Bank of Scotland as it alone of Scottish banks drew on the Bank of England). Touchwood argues that the bill should be exchanged at par, i.e. that the stated value of the bill should be paid; but Bindloose is apparently arguing that the Bank of England bill is at a premium, so that the person exchanging the bill will get less in cash than the sum stated. Touchwood says that he knows that when the Scottish bank sends money south it says it will pay in forty days at face value.
133.20 Bank of England founded in 1694 by William III (reigned 1689–1702) to finance his French wars, by 1810 the Bank had become the most powerful and august financial organ in the world.
133.28 Timbuctoo town in central Mali, in north Africa.
133.28 friends in the Strand probably Thomas Coutts and Co., bankers, then at 59 The Strand, London.
133.28–29 Bruce's from Gondar James Bruce (1730–94) travelled in Abyssinia (capital, Gondar) from 1769 to 1772. His narrative, *Travels to Discover the Source of the Nile* (he discovered that of the Blue Nile), was published in 1790.
133.36 Peregrine Touchwood *peregrine* means 'foreign', 'outlandish', or 'imported from abroad'; 'touchwood' is figuratively used of a person who easily 'takes fire', i.e. someone easily incensed.
133.36–37 Peregrine . . . the Willoughbies Peregrine Bertie (1555–1601), Baron Willoughby de Eresby, was named 'Peregrine' because he was born *in terra peregrina.* He succeeded to his mother's title as Lord Willoughby de Eresby in 1580. His valour in the war in the Netherlands, and especially at the siege of Bergen, made him one of the most admired soldiers of the time.
134.22–23 half boots boots reaching halfway to the knee.

134.24 cocked hat three-cornered hat with the brim permanently turned up.
134.29 well to pass well off, well to do.
135.6 heir of entail it was common practice to include in an entail a clause requiring those called to the succession as heirs of entail and the husbands of heirs-female to assume the surname and the arms of the maker of the entail.
135.6–7 deed of provision and tailzie Scott seems to be using 'provision' and 'tailzie' here as equivalent, but technically a provision would be related to a family settlement rather than a tailzie (or entail) as such.
135.14–15 the auld reekie dungeons powed down . . . good houses perhaps a reference to the old Edinburgh Tolbooth (prison), demolished in 1817; 'auld reekie' (old smoky) is a nickname for Edinburgh. In the late 18th and early 19th centuries many old buildings in the Old Town of Edinburgh were demolished, and at the same time the city expanded greatly with the building of the New Town to the north.
135.24–25 Unstable as water, ye shall not excel see Genesis 49.4.
135.38 Tom Paine and Voltaire Tom Paine (1737–1809), author of *Common Sense* (1776) and *The Rights of Man* (1791, 1792); François Marie Arouet, Voltaire (1694–1778), author of numerous rationalist, free-thinking works.
136.5 Regan or Goneril Lear's two evil daughters. But Meg confuses *Goneril* with 'gomeril', a fool or simpleton.
136.6 ye have skeel of our sect you have knowledge of our sex, you understand our sex.
136.15 Saint Giles sixth-century saint, famous for his humility, he refused presents offered to him by Childebert, King of France.
136.18 wealth makes wit waver proverbial: see Apperson, 671; Tilley, 713; and *ODEP*, 873.
136.26 Whitsunday and Martinmas see note to 19.24.
136.33 bill discounted bill of exchange payable some months in the future, but which had been sold by the payee to the banks at a discount on the face value, the discount representing the interest on what was, in effect, a loan. A bill of exchange was given as payment for goods or services to be delivered, but an accommodation bill, which worked like a bill of exchange, was given by the drawer not in respect of goods or services but to 'accommodate' the payee, and it was the payee who was liable to retire the bill on the due date; i.e. an accommodation bill was similar to a loan guaranteed by a 3rd party. Bindloose may be referring to either the bill of exchange or the accommodation bill, both of which 'accommodate' a client by providing credit.
136.37 one Air bank the collapse of the 'Ayr Bank' (properly Douglas, Heron and Company) in 1772 caused distress throughout Scotland and precipitated a financial crisis.
136.37–38 the whole country is an Air bank now i.e. all business is conducted on credit.
136.38 to pay the piper proverbial: see Tilley, 541; Apperson, 487; and *ODEP*, 615.
136.39 Babel see Genesis 11.1–9.
137.8 Vanity-fair see John Bunyan (1628–88), *The Pilgrim's Progress*, ed. James Blanton Wharey and Roger Sharrock (Oxford, 1960), 88–97.
137.20 Fong Qua not identified; probably fictional.
137.20 Celestial Empire translation of one of the native names for China.
137.21 Leadenhall-Street in the City of London, containing the head office of the East India Company.
137.30 Spectator periodical conducted by Joseph Addison (1672–1719) and Richard Steele (1672–1729) in 1711–12 and revived by Addison in 1714.
137.30 I might have laid my penny on the bar see *The Spectator*, No. 9,

Saturday, 10 March 1711. Among the rules of the Two-penny Club are 'If any member absent himself he shall forfeit a Penny for the Use of the Club'; paying such a forfeit for absences seems to have been a general practice in London convivial clubs, and was also an acceptable way of escaping from socialising.

137.43 Cheltenham water from the mineral springs discovered in 1716 at Cheltenham, in Gloucestershire.

138.22 two of his notes for L.100 each i.e accommodation bills for £100: see note to 136.33.

138.27 acceptances for their furnishings i.e. Mowbray pays for the supplies with bills of exchange: his agreement to pay is shown by writing 'accepted' with the date on which payment is to be made on the face of the bill.

138.29 Mowbray either on the back or front of it Mowbray may sign an accommodation bill on the face of the bill (see previous note), indicating willingness to repay the sum received on the due date, or on the back for someone else, thereby guaranteeing to pay the sum due should the acceptor fail to do so.

139.5 neither to haud nor to bind ungovernable, beyond control. Proverbial: see *ODEP*, 377, where this is the earliest citation.

139.5–6 ance wood and aye waur *proverbial* once mad and ever worse, i.e. once crazy, the malady gets worse instead of better: see Kelly, 271; *ODEP*, 595.

139.6 set them up and shute them forward expression of scornful contempt for another's pretensions or assumptions of superiority.

139.8–10 Lord of Session ... English lord ... Lord of Parliament a Lord of Session is a judge of the Court of Session, the supreme civil court in Scotland; he has the courtesy title of 'Lord', but is not a peer. After the Union of England and Scotland in 1707, all English peers (hence an 'English lord'), but only 16 Scottish peers (known as 'representative' peers because chosen by the Scottish peerage to represent them), were Lords of Parliament, i.e. members of the House of Lords.

139.10–11 flaw in the title i.e. his right to the peerage is not certain or undisputed.

139.24 the phœnix mythical bird, fabled to be the only one of its kind, and to live 500–600 years in the Arabian desert, after which it burns itself to ashes, only to emerge with renewed youth.

139.39–40 Tyrrel ... William Rufus Walter Tyrrell, or Tirel, was generally believed to have shot the arrow that killed William Rufus, King William II (reigned 1087–1100), but Tyrrell denied having done so.

140.8–9 Don Quixote ... Samson Carrasco see Miguel de Cervantes Saavedra (1547–1616), *Don Quixote*, Part 2 (1615), Chs 12–15.

140.18 taen the bent fled.

141.32 Chaldee, (meaning probably a Culdee,) a 'Chaldee' was a seer or astrologer of Chaldea; a 'Culdee' was a solitary religious ascetic of the early Celtic church in Scotland.

142.7 Queen Mab in a nut-shell see *Romeo and Juliet*, 1.4.53–69.

142 motto Oliver Goldsmith (1730?–74), *The Deserted Village* (1770), lines 141–42.

142.39–143.2 pastry-shop of Bedreddin Hassan ... without pepper see Weber, 1.91–109.

143.25 Burgess's sauces John Burgess and Son, established in 1760, became famous for its sauces, especially its fish sauce, which contained 'Original and Superior Essence of Anchovies', caught by the fleets of Gorgona fishing boats off Leghorn. Its admirers (besides Mr Touchwood) included Lord Nelson, Lord Byron (see *Beppo*), Lord Raglan, and Captain Scott, who took it on his expedition to the Antarctic in 1910. The fish sauce is even mentioned in *The Cook and Housewife's Manual: A Practical System of Modern Domestic Cookery and Family Management. By Mistress Margaret Dods, of the*

Cleikum Inn, St Ronan's, 5th edn (Edinburgh, 1833; first published 1826), 214–15.

143.34 the top of Tintock hill on the upper Tweed, celebrated in local rhyme: 'On Tintock tap there is a mist,/ And in the mist there is a kist,/ And in the kist there is a cap,/ And in the cap there is a drap,/ Tak' up the cap, drink out the drap,/ And set it down on Tintock tap'.

144.10 Sir John Sinclair (1754–1835), Scottish lawyer and author, editor of the first *Statistical Account of Scotland*, 29 vols (1791–98), first president of the board of agriculture and called by Abbé Gregoire, Bishop of Blois, 'the most indefatigable man in Britain'. This precise advice on beds has not been traced, but then the *Saint Ronan's* reference may be mocking; Sinclair discusses beds and bedclothes in *The Code of Health and Longevity*, 4 vols, 2nd edn (1807), 1.582–87.

144.34 gunpowder kind of fine green tea in which each leaf is rolled up so that it has a granular appearance.

145.13–14 he makes the Word gude 'the Word' here means 'God's word', specifically the requirement to look after the needy: see Mathew 25.34–40 and Luke 10.29–37.

145.23 potato bogle scarecrow.

145.26–27 black fasting . . . papestrie enduring a very severe fast, considered in those days in Scotland to be a Roman Catholic practice.

145.32 easier said than dune proverbial: see *ODEP*, 212.

145.37 nae Christian man . . . bowels compare *Boswell's Life of Johnson*, ed. R. W. Chapman (London, 1952), 331 (5 August 1763): 'for I look upon it, that he who does not mind his belly will hardly mind anything else'.

145.41 old hock wine called in German *hockheimer* and commercially extended to other white German wines.

145.42 Cockburn Robert Cockburn, a well-known wine-merchant of Edinburgh. See Alan Bell, 'Scott and His Wine-Merchant', *Blackwood's*, 310 (August 1971), 167–75.

145.42 particular sherry i.e. sherry imported by Cockburn's, and sold under their name.

146.26 Boanerges 'the sons of thunder': Mark 3.17. Later used to designate a loud, vociferous preacher or orator.

146.26 Donald Cargill (1619–81), covenanting minister ejected from his Glasgow parish in 1662 and put to death in 1681 in the covenanting troubles during the reign of Charles II (1660–1685) for the reasons enumerated in the text. Cargill was wounded, not killed, at Queensferry.

146.42 guilty of a sonnet see *Love's Labour's Lost*, 1.2.107–08.

147.9 swift feet of the stag in the fable see 'A Stag Drinking', in *Fables of Aesop, According to Sir Roger L'Estrange* (Paris, 1931), 1–2.

147.21 sine qua non *Latin, literally* without which not, i.e. an essential element or condition.

148.1 various readings the different readings of the manuscripts and editions of a text: see *OED*, 'various', III 8 (d).

148.22–30 Cadenus . . . the finest boy Jonathan Swift (1667–1745), 'Cadenus and Vanessa' (1712), lines 550–53.

149.41 patronage or advowson heritable right usually owned by a local landowner to present a minister to a church.

150.9 Episcopal see position of being a bishop in the Anglican Church or Episcopal Church in Scotland.

150.25 muckle wheel the great wheel of a spinning wheel; here probably the wheel of fortune.

150.32 Mago-Pico 'hero' (in a Cargillesque way) of a Scottish ecclesiastical satire on Alexander Pyott: Simon Haliburton and Thomas Hepburn, *The*

Memoirs of Magopico, 2nd edn (1761). See also Magnum, 33.287.
150.39 Beltenebros in the desert name assumed by Amadis of Gaul when, being in disgrace with Oriana, he retired to the wilderness to do penance: see *Amadis de Gaul*, trans. from the Spanish of Garci de Montalvo by Robert Southey, 4 vols (1803), Vol. 2, Chs 9–10. See also Cervantes, *Don Quixote*, Part 1 (1605), Ch. 25.
151.15 barren talent see Matthew 25.14–30.
152.13 concio ad clerum *Latin* address to the clergy.
152.21–26 heritors . . . repair of the old one heritors had the duty of building the manse and keeping it in repair.
152.23–24 suing an augmentation of stipend ministers could apply to the Teind Court for an augmentation of their stipend (salary). The teinds of a parish were one-fifth of the rentals of a parish, and if the minister could show that there was 'free teind', i.e. teinds not already allocated to his maintenance, he could obtain an increase in stipend. In an era of rapidly rising rentals (it is estimated that the rentals for Scotland were £1.5m. in 1795 and £5.5m. in 1815), increases were easily obtained, and had to be paid by the heritors.
153 motto not in Butler; not identified; probably by Scott.
153.17 here the hand of woman had been not identified, but close to proverbial: compare Kelly, 307; and Ramsay, 111 ('The foot at the cradle an' the hand at the reel,/ Is the sign of a woman that means to do weel').
153.22 that of the sluggard was only a type see Proverbs 20.4, 24.30–31. See also Isaac Watts (1674–1748), 'The Sluggard', lines 9–10, in *Divine Songs for the Use of Children* (London, 1720).
153.27–28 in flagrant delict *Latin* in flagrante delicto: in the very act, red-handed.
153.28 fled . . . like a guilty thing see *Hamlet*, 1.1.148–49.
153.35 no trespass could be committed i.e. the building was so ramshackle that walking through it was scarcely an illegal intrusion.
155.1 mite is insufficient see Mark 12.41–44.
155.29 Saint John d'Acre, to Jerusalem the distance is 80 miles, not 23.
155.36 Ingulphus Ingulf (d. 1109), Abbot of Croyland, secretary to William the Conqueror (reigned 1066–87), and erroneously believed to be the chronicler of *The Croyland History*, a forgery of the 15th century.
155.36–37 Jeffrey Winesauf Geoffrey de Vinsauf (fl. 1200), adherent of Richard I (reigned 1189–99), poet, historian of the Crusades, and author of a treatise on poetry, *Poëtria Nova*, a mixture of classical precept and medieval practice, which inspired Chaucer to call him 'my maister soverayne'.
156.5–7 Acre . . . Sir Sydney Admiral Sir Sidney Smith (1764–1840), a distinguished British commander in the French Revolutionary and Napoleonic Wars. He successfully defended Acre in 1799 and forced Napoleon to retreat.
156.7 Djezzar Pacha Turkish commandant of Acre at the time of Napoleon's repulse in March–May 1799.
156.25 one good turn deserves another proverbial: see Apperson, 470–71; *ODEP*, 325.
157.5 pin the dishclout to his tail said as a threat to men who interfere in the kitchen.
157.7–8 toiling in their fiery element see *Paradise Lost*, 1.52.
157.14–15 civil but sly see George Crabbe, *The Parish Register* (1807), Part 3, line 966 (Corson).
157.16 when a' was dune see Robert Burns (1759–96), 'It Was A' For Our Rightfu' King' (1796), stanza 2.
157.34–35 ex intervallo, as the lawyers express it *Latin* used in legal affairs with its meaning of 'after some passage of time', it has no special significance.

157.40–41 Pythagorean entertainment i.e. a vegetarian meal of fruit and vegetables.

158.1–2 your wits are fairly gone a wool-gathering *proverbial* you are absent-minded: see Apperson, 709; and *ODEP*, 905.

158.30–32 Boswell . . . Wilkes the famous dinner at Dilly's on 15 May 1776 in which Boswell brought together the 2 politically hostile celebrities, Johnson and Wilkes, also included Arthur Lee, John Miller, Dr Lettsom, and 'Mr Slater the druggist' (but not Strahan). James Boswell (1740–95) was Johnson's biographer. William Strahan (1715–85) was one of the foremost printers of his era: he printed Johnson's *Dictionary*. John Wilkes (1727–97) was a member of Parliament, and founded the periodical *The North Briton* in which he attacked the government of Lord Bute.

158.41–42 Johnson . . . dinner the most important business of the day see Hester Piozzi (1741–1821), *Anecdotes of the Late Samuel Johnson* (1786): 'a man seldom thinks with more earnestness of any thing than he does of his dinner' (149). See also note to 145.37.

159.13 William of Tyre (*c.* 1130–1185), Archbishop of Tyre from 1174. His *Historia* covers the period 1095 (the preaching of the First Crusade) to 1184, and is the primary authority from 1127. It was translated into French in the 12th or 13th century and in this form had a wide circulation.

159.13–14 Raymund of Saint Giles (*c.* 1043–1105), Count of Toulouse, a leader of the First Crusade. He went to the Holy Lands in October 1096, but was thwarted in his attempt to gain control of Antioch in 1098. He is regarded as the founder of the Latin stronghold of Tripoli.

159.14 Abulfaragi Gregorius Bar-Hebraeus (1226–86), a Christian of the Syrian church, consecrated Bishop of Aleppo in 1246 and Primate of the East in 1264. His *Universal History* professes to give a complete history of the world from creation, and his *Cream of Science* is an encyclopaedic work, Aristotelian in its approach to knowledge.

159.31 Still he welcomed, but with less of cost see Thomas Parnell (1679–1718), *The Hermit* (1722), line 213.

159.35 Saladin Sala-Ed-Din Yusuf Ibn Ayub (1137–93) became Sultan of Egypt about 1174, invaded Palestine, defeated the Christians, and captured Jerusalem. He was attacked by the Crusaders under Richard Coeur-de-Lion and Philip II of France, and forced to conclude a truce. See Scott's portrait of him in *The Talisman*.

159.35 Coeur de Lion Richard I of England (1157–99; reigned 1189–99), a leader of the Third Crusade. See Scott's portraits of him in *Ivanhoe*, *The Talisman*, and *The Betrothed*.

159.36 Hyder Ali (1722–82), Moslem of peasant stock, rose to command the army of the Hindu state of Mysore and by 1761 was virtual ruler of Mysore. He expanded the dominions of that kingdom at the expense of other Indian states and their British allies, until he was defeated in 1781 near Madras by Sir Eyre Coote.

159.36 Sir Eyre Coote (1726–83), British general distinguished for his service in India. His defeat of Hyder Ali in 1781 saved the Madras Presidency for the British.

160.6–7 choice phrases are ever commendable see *2 Henry IV*, 3.2.69–70.

160.13 Salam Alicum the Moslem greeting, meaning 'Peace be with you'.

160.16 the seventh heaven seven heavens were recognised by the Jews; the 7th, the highest, was the abode of God. Thus the phrase implies that Cargill is wholly abstracted from his current surroundings. See also note to 238.39–40.

160.27 Camden William Camden (1551–1623), antiquary and historian, author of *Britannia* (1586) and *Annales rerum Anglicarum et Hibernicarum reg-*

ante Elizabetha . . . ad annum 1589 (1615).
60.27–28 **Thomas Mowbray** (*c.* 1366–99), made Earl Marshal of Eng-
ınd for life in 1385, created 1st Duke of Norfolk in 1397. See Shakespeare's
ichard II for the end of his career.
60.33 **a startled hare** see *1 Henry IV*, 1.3.198.
60.40 **bal paré** full-dress ball. The phrase was used of a rather theatrical
ccasion, with suggestions of impropriety and rakishness.
61.34 **ottar of roses** attar of roses, a highly fragrant, volatile oil obtained
rom rose petals.
61.41 **pease bannock** scone made of pease-meal.
61.43 **nakedness of the land** see Genesis 42.9, 12.
62.8 **the tinkling cymbal** see 1 Corinthians 13.1.
62.10–11 **multure . . . mill** proverbial: don't pay for what you already
wn, i.e. look after your own interests. The 'multure' was a quantity of grain
iven as a payment to the proprietor or tenant of a mill for milling the grain; if
ou owned the mill you would not pay a multure to the miller.
62.16 **brown study** state of mental abstraction.
62.17 **boy of blackletter** i.e. slave to ancient materials. 'Blackletter' is
ısed of matter published before 1600 in 'gothic' type.
62.20 **Santon** European designation for a kind of Moslem monk or her-
nit; also, incorrectly, a yogi or Hindu ascetic.
62 **motto** see Colley Cibber (1671–1757), *The Provoked Husband* (1728),
.73–76.
63.8 **three black Graces** the *OED* quotes Mrs Catherine Gore 'The three
lack graces—law, physic, and divinity' (1846). Since Scott, writing in 1823, is
imself quoting an unidentified contemporary to the same effect, this designa-
ion of the 3 professions seems to have been familiar at the time. In classical
nythology, the Graces were the three sister goddesses in whom beauty was
leified.
63.12 **stood on tiptoe** see *Henry V*, 4.3.42.
63.25 **all the troubles which flesh is heir to** see *Hamlet*, 3.1.62–63.
63.26 **Barèges** village and spa in the Hautes Pyrénées, France, famous for
ts mineral water.
63.32 **the love of Alpheus for Arethusa** the river-god Alpheus fell in
ove with the nymph Arethusa when she bathed in his stream. Artemis trans-
ormed her into a fountain but, flowing under the sea, Alpheus was reunited
vith her.
64.43 **coming the old soldier over** deceiving, imposing upon.
65.1 **keeping up** keeping secret, undivulged.
65.14 **go through the mill** undergo a hard experience.
65.15 **money and money's worth** something that is worth money.
65.19 **Suliote** the Suliotes, a tribe of Greek-Albanian origin, renowned
or their resistance to Turkish rule. Of the 2,000 insurgents whom Byron
ollected, about 500 were Suliotes.
65.21–22 **I think not . . . the Vizier** see Lord Byron (1788–1824),
Childe Harold's Pilgrimage (1812), 2.72 (9.1–2).
65.24 **Pacha** Ali Pasha (1741–1822), the Lion of Janina, an Albanian
Moslem who gained power in Greece and whose barbarous court was observed
by Byron in 1809–10. See *Childe Harold's Pilgrimage* (1812), 2.72.
65.25 **Scanderbeg** George Castriot (1403–67), son of the hereditary
prince of a district in Albania. He was brought up as a hostage at the court of
Sultan Amurath (Murad II), became the successful champion of Albanian
ndependence, and for many years resisted the Ottoman Empire.
65.34 **When Greek . . . tug of war** see Nathaniel Lee (1653?–92), *The
Rival Queens, or The Death of Alexander the Great* (1677), 4.2.138.

165.38 Piquet card came played by 2 persons with a deck of 32 cards—7 (low) up to ace (high) in each suit. Each player receives 12 cards, and 8 cards are left on the table face down. The nondealer (the minor) discards 1 to 5 cards and picks up an equal number from the table. The dealer (the major or elder) is entitled to exchange the remaining number of cards. Trumps are not named. After the draw from the table, the hands are compared, and points are given for point (most cards in a suit), sequence (longest sequence) and highest set of three or four of a kind. Carte blanche, a hand without a face card, also scores points. Play of cards from the hands follows with points scored for tricks won. 100 points are needed to win.
166.8 friend of all hours i.e. Mowbray is spending all his time with Etherington. The phrase is a translation of the Latin 'amicus omnium horarum'.
167.2–3 Will Allan's eastern subjects Sir William Allan (1782–1850), Scottish historical painter and friend of Scott. He spent 9 years from 1805 in Russia, Georgia, the Caucasus, and Turkey.
167.3 But here's the rub see *Hamlet*, 3.1.65.
167.5 Gallery of Fashion Edinburgh shop. The following advertisement appeared in *The Edinburgh Advertiser* for Tuesday 23 March to Friday 26 March 1802 (vol. 77, no. 3990): 'INDIA SHAWLS Gilchrist and Co. have the pleasure to announce the Arrival of an Assortment of SHAWLS, the most beautifu texture and closest imitation of REAL INDIA ever yet discovered, being the invention of an eminent House in London, with whom G. & Co. have formed a connection for a regular supply; they are to have the exclusive privilege of selling them in Scotland. GALLERY OF FASHION March 25 1802.' Shortly afterwards, a similar advertisement added, 'Orders for the country punctually attended to' (*The Edinburgh Advertiser*, Friday 30 April to Tuesday 4 May 1802, vol. 77, no. 4001). The first mention of actual Indian shawls appeared in the issue of Tuesday 23 November to Friday 26 November 1802 (vol. 78, no. 4060): 'A few Real India shawls with a large assortment of the new Imitation Ditto, both White and Coloured Grounds, most beautiful patterns.'
167.24 a sair foot an emergency.
167.27 blaze them down dazzle them.
167.31 decerniture against him, with expenses court decree against him, with his paying the expenses of the action. The word 'decern' is the technical, operative word in a judgment, giving effect to the order that the court makes the person against whom the court has 'decerned' can be compelled to do something or to forbear from doing something.
167.31 that is the question *Hamlet*, 3.1.56.
167.34 great clubs e.g. White's, Boodle's and Brooks's, all in St James's St, London.
167.34–35 Superlatives and Inaccessibles not identified; probably fictional.
167.40 save my little Abigail's reputation i.e. be careful not to betray Lady Penelope's maid who gave Mowbray the information (167.1–2).
169.8 rueful countenance Don Quixote was known as 'the knight of the rueful countenance', a name given to him by Sancho Panza.
169.15–16 Revenge, they say, is sweet proverbial: see Tilley, 569; Apperson, 528; and *ODEP*, 673.
170.9–10 I may have seen . . . Puff says in The Critic see Richard Brinsley Sheridan (1751–1816), *The Critic* (1779), 2.1.28–31. But it is Tilburnia who is so susceptible, not Puff.
170.22–23 renown'd . . . barons bold not identified.
170.30 the vale of Bever the vale of Bever, or Belvoir, lies on the borders of Lincolnshire and Leicestershire.

171.1 sixteen quarters *heraldry* each quarter in a coat of arms divided into further 4 quarters is indicative of the nobility of all ascendants, and of an ancient pedigree.

171.3 city i.e. the City of London; Etherington says that one of his grandmothers came from a family of rich merchants.

171.3–172.23 grandfather . . . riddle is read

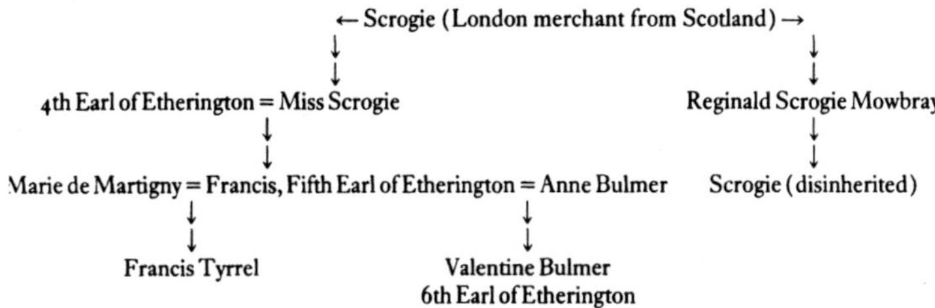

171.16 vulgar name of Scrogie the name means 'covered in undergrowth'.

171.18 Lyon, nor Marchmont, nor Islay, nor Snadoun the Court of the Lord Lyon, the authority on all matters heraldic in Scotland, is among the most ancient of Scottish institutions. Scotland has the one King of Arms, the Lord Lyon, who derives his name from the national escutcheon. From 1500 to 1866, there were six Heralds and six Pursuivants in Scotland, and among the Heralds were Islay, Marchmont, and Snowdon ('Snadoun').

171.25 argent and or heraldic names for silver and gold.

172.18–19 he settled it on me . . . on condition conditions in bequests restricting marriage are normally invalid if they amount to some form of total or near total prohibition. There are therefore the legal issues (hence the stress on taking legal advice) of whether this condition is valid (it probably is valid as not being too restrictive), but if invalid, whether the whole bequest would fall or whether this condition alone could be ignored.

172.27 a grain of a scruple of doubt a minute portion of a minute quantity: see *2 Henry IV*, 1.2.123–24.

172.30 Miss Mowbray's . . . sole guardian as Clara is over the age of 21, Mowbray's statement has no legal import.

173.10 keeping me in hand keeping me in expectation or suspense.

175.9–10 he must remain . . . bound a general principle of Scots law: if a man makes an offer, he is bound to hold it open for acceptance for any time he states, or, if no time is stated, for a reasonable time.

175.25 taking a little law redressing your own grievance.

177 motto see *Richard III*, 4.2.44–45.

177.10 Harrogate spa in Yorkshire.

177.16 Napoleon's new-made monarchs Napoleon installed his brothers Joseph, Louis and Jerome as kings of countries conquered by France. In addition Murat became King of Naples, and Bernadotte King of Sweden.

177.18 Saint James's coffee-house founded in 1705 at 87 St James's Street, London.

177.21 plucking of pigeons 'fleecing' of simpletons.

177.24 yeoman's service good, efficient, or useful service, such as is rendered by a faithful servant of good standing: *Hamlet*, 5.2.36.

178.18 et pour cause *French* and for a very good reason.

178.20 Kuchenritters variety of pistols, named after their maker.

178.29 raw-head and bloody-bone story see note to 102.40.

178.30 my gory locks see *Macbeth*, 3.4.51.
179.4–5 he could not have vanished . . . a bubble of the elements see *Macbeth*, 1.3.79–80.
179.20 Monsieur le Frere *French* the brother.
179.24 buck of the season see *The Merry Wives of Windsor*, 3.3.140.
179.27–28 the Isle of Saints Ireland.
179.32 mauvaise honte false shame, diffidence.
179.34 win the plate *horse racing* win the race and be given a gold or silver cup as the prize.
180.3 the clumsy gambols of the ass in the fable see 'An Asse and a Whelp', in *Fables of Aesop, According to Sir Roger L'Estrange* (Paris, 1931), 44.
180.5 to pass current to be generally accepted.
180.6 Northern Meeting i.e. northern horse-racing meeting.
180.11 this trout was not easily tickled see *Twelfth Night*, 2.5.20.
180.16–17 caught a Tartar tackled someone who unexpectedly proved too formidable.
181.3–4 by my life,/ . . . pretty wife see Charles Churchill, *The Rosciad* (1761), lines 319–20 (Corson).
181.6 Juno in beauty i.e. statuesque.
181 motto *Hamlet*, 2.2.600.
181.38 stage and scenery compare *A Midsummer Night's Dream*, 3.1.2–5.
182.6 top the part play the part to perfection, *or* overact the part.
182.15–16 Petruchio . . . mother wit see *The Taming of the Shrew*, 2.1.256.
183.23 circulating library library in which books are circulated among subscribers.
183.25–26 Bell's British Theatre John Bell (1745–1831), *Bell's British Theatre, consisting of the most esteemed English Plays*, 21 vols (London, 1776–81), and 37 vols (London, 1791–99). The latter edition includes 136 plays.
183.26 Miller's Modern and Ancient Drama William Miller (1769–1844), *The Ancient British Drama. A Collection of 57 Plays by various Authors, from 1547 to 1678*, 3 vols (London, 1810), and *The Modern British Drama. A Collection of Tragedies, Comedies, Operas, and Farces, from 1598 to 1783*, 5 vols (London, 1811). For Scott's contributions, see *Letters*, 10.118, and Bill Ruddick, 'Scott on the Drama: A Series of Ascriptions', *The Scott Newsletter*, No. 14 (Spring, 1989), 2–6.
183.40–41 such of his dramas as have not kept possession of the stage the only Shakespearean drama that was not acted in any of the major London theatres in the 18th century was *Love's Labour's Lost*. The following were not acted between 1751 and 1800: the 3 parts of *Henry VI*, *Pericles*, *Richard II*, *Titus Andronicus*, and *Troilus and Cressida*. *A Midsummer Night's Dream* stood 21st (out of 37) in popularity. The tragedies were more popular than the comedies and histories throughout the century, but only 4 plays were performed uninterruptedly: *Romeo and Juliet*, *Hamlet*, *Richard III*, and *Macbeth*. According to the historian of the subject, 'The most remarkable fact about the theatrical history of Shakespeare in the second half of the eighteenth century is the almost complete disappearance of those drastically rewritten versions of the original texts that are so frequently met with in the first half'. See Charles B. Hogan, *Shakespeare in the Theatre, 1701–1800* (Oxford, 1957), Appendix C, 716–19.
184.21–22 the authority of Childe Harold . . . costume 'The Arnaouts, or Albanese, struck me forcibly by their resemblance to the Highlanders of Scotland. . . . The kilt, though white; the spare, active form; their dialect, Celtic in its sound, and their hardy habits, all carried me back to Morvern.' (Byron's note to *Childe Harold's Pilgrimage*, Canto 2 (1812), stanza 38)
184.25 Mainot one of the Mainotes, a people of the Peloponnese in the

south of Greece. The district was mountainous and inaccessible, and the people famed for their ferocity and independent spirit.

184.26 walking gentlemen actors playing parts with little to say.

184.35 King of Shadows *A Midsummer Night's Dream*, 3.2.347.

184.37 Miss in her Teens play (1747) by David Garrick.

185.7 there was a play fitted see *A Midsummer Night's Dream*, 1.2.57.

185.12 Mrs Siddons see note to 75.13.

185.15–16 three frightsome carlines . . . sailor's wife see *Macbeth*, 1.3.3–25.

185.26 tobacconist's sign retailers formerly indicated the nature of their business by displaying signs; tobacconists were represented by the figure of a brightly attired Indian.

185.33–34 Mr Sowerbrowst the maltster's the name suggests a bitter brew.

186.2–3 vial of tincture i.e. bottle of liquid medicine.

186.5 losing cast losing social rank or status.

186.7 Popish disguises there was strong disapproval of drama among the presbyterian ministers and people of Scotland; Mrs Blower comically associates dressing-up with the wearing of surplices etc. in the Catholic Church, another practice condemned by presbyterians.

186.8 baith wife and lass both as woman and girl.

186.17 O'Keefe John O'Keefe (1747–83), Irish dramatist, who wrote some 50 comic and musical pieces.

186.35 Bristol stone see note to 29.18.

187.5 beau monde fashionable world.

187.8 taxed cart two-wheeled open cart drawn by one horse, and used mainly for agricultural or trade purposes, on which was charged only a reduced tax which was later removed altogether.

187.22 deil anither body's fit *emphatic* nobody else's foot.

187.23 Let every herring hing by its ain head proverbial: see Ray, 154; Kelly, 240; and *ODEP*, 370.

187.40 Tirlsneck the name means 'twist-neck'.

188.10 General Assembly the supreme court of the Church of Scotland.

188.20–21 James VI. of Scotland, and his unfortunate son King James VI of Scotland and I of England (reigned 1567–1625 in Scotland and from 1603 in England), and his son, King Charles I (reigned 1625–49), who was executed. The objection is to the eclectic nature of Jacobean architecture, and the way in which it used elements from different architectural traditions.

189.5–6 those principles . . . *Ars Topiaria* Scott added the following note to Ed2 of *The Antiquary* (1816): '*Ars Topiaria*, the art of clipping yew-trees and hedges into fantastic figures. A Latin poem, entitled *Ars Topiaria*, contains a curious account of the process' (19.42–43). The poem has not been identified or traced.

189.21 dramatis personae the characters in a story or play.

189.38–39 This green plot . . . in action *A Midsummer Night's Dream*, 3.1.3–5.

189.41 Gow's fiddle Nathaniel Gow (1766–1831), Scots violinist and composer, the youngest son of Niel Gow.

190.1 As through . . . Highland rage see Robert Burns, 'The Brigs of Ayr, a Poem' (1786), line 204.

190.3 the plaintive notes of Roslin Castle in Letter X of Scott's *Redgauntlet* (1824), Wandering Willie says, 'it's no a Scots tune, but it passes for ane —Oswald made it himsel' (81.1–2). Oswald is James Oswald (1715–69), musician and collector of Scottish traditional tunes. 'Roslin Castle' can be found in his compilation, *The Caledonian Pocket Companion* (1752), 4.3, and also in *SMM*, No. 8.

190.9 old Niel at Inver Niel Gow (1727–1807), Scots traditional violinist and composer, from Inver near Dunkeld in Perthshire.

190.10 Athole brose mixture of oatmeal, whisky, and honey.

190.14 scene of confusion see *A Midsummer Night's Dream*, 3.2.

190.36–37 Garrick . . . "going his rounds" David Garrick (1717–79), the greatest actor of the 18th century, was able to throw 'his features into the representations of Love, Hatred, Terror, Pity, Jealousy, Desire, Joy in so rapid and striking a manner as astounded the whole country' ('A Memoir of David Garrick Esq.', *The Universal Magazine* (October, 1776), 187).

191.26 gusing iron tailor's goose, i.e. tailor's iron for smoothing clothes.

191.32–33 nae fule like an auld fule proverbial: see Tilley, 231; *ODEP*, 276.

192.2 Paisley town just west of Glasgow, famous for its soft wool fabric with a woven, swirled and highly-coloured pattern of abstract curved shapes.

192.6–7 Tozie . . . Cozie garment of soft, carded wool . . . warm and comfortable. *Tozie* is 'soft like teased wool' (*OED*).

192.26 Ali 4th Caliph (*c.* 600–61), son-in-law of Mohammed, husband of Fatima, and especially reverenced by Shiite Moslems.

193.1–2 thousand rupees given for such a shawl about £100. In 1842 the usual price demanded for a pair of genuine *tozie* shawls was 3,000 rupees, but the rupee fell in value from about 2*s.* (10p) to 1*s.* 2*d.* (6p) in the course of the 19th century. See James Bischoff, *A Comprehensive History of the Woollen and Worsted Manufactures, and the Natural and Commercial History of Sheep, from the Earliest Records to the Present Period*, 2 vols (Leeds, 1842).

193.11–12 captain of the fairy band see *A Midsummer Night's Dream*, 3.2.110

193.26 Ill met by moonlight, proud Titania *A Midsummer Night's Dream*, 2.1.60.

193.42–194.1 thick-skinned mechanic see *A Midsummer Night's Dream*, 3.2.9 and 13.

194.11–12 a cry of players a company or pack of players: *Hamlet*, 3.2.272.

194.15 Bottom 'translated' by Puck *A Midsummer Night's Dream*, 3.1.92.

194.18–19 his frolics with the fairies *A Midsummer Night's Dream*, 3.1.148–81 and 4.1.5–36.

195.25 Amphitryon où l'on dîne in *Amphitryon* (1668) by Molière (1622–73), Sosia says, 'The true Amphitryon is the Amphitryon who provides the dinner' (3.5.1703–04). In Greek mythology, Zeus assumes the form of Amphitryon to seduce Alcmene, and their child is Heracles. The pun on 'l'on dîne' (l'Ondine) anticipates the reference to naiads in the next paragraph.

195.29–30 tripping it on the light fantastic toe see John Milton, 'L'Allegro' (1632), lines 33–34.

195.31 the tune of Monymusk see Niel Gow (1727–1807), *Complete Repository of Original Scots Slow Strathspeys and Dances*, Series 1 (1799), 10, and James Stewart-Robertson, *The Athole Collection of the Dance Music of Scotland* (Edinburgh, 1961), 158.

196 motto (1) see *Love's Labour's Lost*, 4.3.375–76.

196 motto (2) *Love's Labour's Lost*, 5.2.710.

197.5 Termagaunt name of an imaginary deity who, according to many Christians, was worshipped by Moslems. His violent character became familiar through medieval Morality plays, and the name came to represent a savage, violent, overbearing, or quarrelsome person.

197.13 Bethel Union a mission to sailors, often accommodated on an old ship in a port.

197.21 horse-marines imaginary corps of mounted marine soldiers, considered as a type of men out of their element; hence, men doing work for which they are not fitted.
197.24 Isle of Dogs not an island, but an area on the north bank in a loop of the Thames, opposite Greenwich, just three miles east of the City.
197.28 Abram-man one of a set of vagabonds who wandered about the country after the dissolution of the religious houses in 1536–40.
201.1 neither Valentine nor Orson twin brothers in an early French romance. Orson was reared as a wild man (i.e. in the wilderness, out of touch of society), Valentine as a knight. Valentine later conquers Orson and tames him. They share numerous adventures. Scott owned a chap-book version of the story (*CLA*, 104) and knew the ballad in Percy's *Reliques* (*CLA*, 172).
201.36 unfortunate philosopher of Laputa . . . his flapper flappers kept the theorising rulers of Laputa awake in Part III of *Gulliver's Travels* (1726). See *The Works of Jonathan Swift*, ed. Walter Scott, 19 vols (1814), 12.204.
202.36–37 two and two, Newgate fashion *1 Henry IV*, 3.3.89. Prisoners were conveyed to Newgate, the principal London prison until 1902, manacled together in pairs.
202.37–38 Lady Penelope . . . Ulysses Penelope was the patient, long-suffering wife of Ulysses in the *Odyssey*.
203.42 Black Lion Mr Cargill's complexion is 'adust' (154.7), and he is dressed in black.
203.43–204.1 Britannia with her ferine attendant Britannia, symbolising Britain, first appeared on the halfpenny in 1667; she was accompanied by a lion, which in heraldry symbolises sovereignty and power, and which in Spenser's *The Faerie Queene* symbolises truth.
204.15 naughty in the forty-five in the first half of the 18th century most Episcopalians were Jacobites, i.e. supporters of James VII and II (who lost his throne in the Revolution of 1688) and his descendants. Lady Penelope implies that her family took part in the Jacobite rebellion of 1745.
204.21–22 stove . . . to air his pew the laird would usually have his own boxed pew in a country church, and as churches were unheated he might take with him a 'stove' (which was like a footstool) containing burning charcoal.
204.23 wreathed smiles and nods see John Milton , 'L'Allegro' (1632), line 28.
204.33–34 to his duty prompt . . . pray'd for all see Oliver Goldsmith, *The Deserted Village* (1770), lines 165–66.
204.39–44 Refined himself to soul . . . pleasing sanctity see John Dryden, 'The Character of a Good Parson; Imitated from Chaucer, and Inlarg'd' (1699), lines 10–15.
205.3 Saladin see note to 159.35.
205.3 Conrade of Mountserrat (d. 1192), Marquis of Montserrat, King of Jerusalem (1192), a leading figure during the Third Crusade. See Scott's portraits of him in *Ivanhoe* and *The Talisman*.
205.13 Leyden Dr John Leyden (1775–1811), son of a farm manager from near Hawick in Roxburghshire, obtained a degree from Edinburgh University in 1796, mastered medicine, went to India in 1803 and made himself the first international authority on the languages of the Far East: at his death he is said to have known 34. He helped Scott in collecting material for *Minstrelsy of the Scottish Border* (1802–03).
207.4 privilege of Scotland to answer a question by asking another.
207 motto see *The Taming of the Shrew*, 3.2.108–09.
208.10 Paddock calls . . . anon see *Macbeth*, 1.1.9–10. 'Paddock' is a name for a toad; in *Macbeth*, it is the witch's familiar spirit.

208.13 I come—I come, grimalkin see *Macbeth*, 1.1.8. Grimalkin (a variant of Shakespeare's 'Graymalkin') is a name given to a cat, especially an old she-cat, which in *Macbeth* embodies a fiend.
209.4 Do be a man compare *Macbeth*, 3.4.58.
209.15 fire-screens movable screens to intercept the heat of the fire.
209.31 seignorial waif piece of property which is found ownerless and which if unclaimed within a fixed period falls to the lord of the manor.
209.36–37 a selfish, spiteful heart, that is as hard as a flint see Job 41.24.
210.36 colloquial fame . . . Johnson i.e. her reputation as a conversationalist: see Samuel Johnson, *The Rambler*, No. 201.
210.43 upon the wind of a door in a draught.
211.13 Tu me lo pagherai you will pay me for it.
212.14–15 heathen priest . . . eating the sacrifice among the Greeks and Romans the deity was a guest at a sacrifical feast, and many inscriptions enforce the necessity of eating the flesh within the holy precincts.
212.36–37 green flask i.e. a 'hunting-flask' (see 61.42), probably containing whisky.
213.25 Bacchus Greek god of wine; hence, wine itself.
214 motto not identified; probably by Scott.
214.10 The morning . . . one of reflection see Nicholas Rowe (1674–1718), *The Fair Penitent* (1703), 1.1.162.
215.35 you were carousing till after the first cock see *Macbeth*, 2.3.23–24. The crowing of the cock in the early morning has led to the expressions *first, second, third cock*, etc. to express points of time.
216.3 he wore his vizor on see *Hamlet*, 1.2.229.
217.32–33 Campbell's new work presumably *Gertrude of Wyoming* by Thomas Campbell (1777–1844), published in 1809. See the 'Historical Note'.
218.24 Clarissa Harlowe the oppressed heroine of *Clarissa Harlowe* (1747–48) by Samuel Richardson (1689–1761).
218.25 Harriet Byron the oppressed heroine of *Sir Charles Grandison* (1754) by Samuel Richardson. The connection with Clara Mowbray seems especially close in this case: Sir Hargrave Pollexfen attempts a secret marriage ceremony with Harriet, their coach is stopped, she is rescued by the hero, etc.
219.6 natural guardian this view has no legal import.
219.15–17 the law authorizes . . . your character a legal threat to have Clara declared insane or incapable and himself appointed her curator: see note to 93.7–9. Curators to the insane guarded the person as well as the property of the insane person.
220.6 castles in the air proverbial: see Tilley, 84–85; Apperson, 84–85; and *ODEP*, 107.
221.4 let us go fair and softly proverbial: see Apperson, 201; and *ODEP*, 238. In this phrase, 'fair' means gently, quietly, without haste or violence.
221.26 behave . . . like folks of this world not identified; the quotation appears in neither Shakespeare nor Prior. According to the *OED* ('behave', 1b) the expression *behave yourself before folk* is a 'modern Scottish maxim'.
221.27 Prior Matthew Prior (1664–1721), English diplomat and poet, frequently quoted by Scott.
222.3 femme d'atours *French* lady's maid (in charge of the wardrobe).
222.14–15 the McIntoshes 'The well-known crest of this ancient race, is a cat rampant, with a motto bearing the caution—"Touch not the cat, but [i.e. *be out*, or without] the glove".' (Magnum, 34.79)
222 motto *King Lear*, 5.1.40, 43–44.
225.16–17 potsherd see Isaiah 30.14, 45.9, and Psalms 2.9. A potsherd is a fragment of a broken earthenware pot, a broken piece of earthenware.

225.18–19 Him, without whose will even a sparrow falls not to the ground see Matthew 10.29.
225.42 Should the law give you my hand an allusion to the basic question: was the ceremony of marriage such that it would be upheld as valid in a court of law?
226.5 Thou shalt do no murther! see Exodus 20.13, and Deuteronomy 5.17.
226.14–15 There is a Heaven above us, and THERE shall be judged our actions towards each other Clara talks of Heaven's commands and judgments (and quotes Exodus, Deuteronomy, Psalms, Isaiah, and Matthew) in the scene—appealing to a superior Law.
227 motto see *Twelfth Night*, 2.5.85, and *King Lear*, 4.6.261.
227.27 the ice being fairly broken having disposed of the inhibitions preventing the discussion of the subject: proverbial (see *ODEP*, 83).
228.1 the fair play of the world proverbial: see Apperson, 199; and *ODEP*, 239–40.
228.5 played on the square dealt honestly, in a straightforward manner.
230.23–24 snuff a candle and strike out the ace of hearts Mowbray is boasting of his extreme accuracy with a pistol. Compare the note at 37.9.
230.32 falling house is best known by the rats leaving it proverbial: see *ODEP*, 664.
230.37 savoir faire ability to say or do the right thing in any situation.
231.11–12 They say it is a wise child knows its own father proverbial: see Ray, 86; and *ODEP*, 899.
231.20 at a dead-lock in a tight grip, so it is impossible to move.
231.37–38 trail as you will open upon breast high *breast-high* is used in hunting of a scent so strong that the hounds go at racing pace with their heads held high; thus Etherington continues the hunting metaphor to suggest that he has something which will really interest Jekyl.
232.1 it is an ill bird, &c *proverbial* it is an ill bird that pecks out the dam's eyes; i.e. it is not in one's interest to damage one's parent. See *ODEP*, 398.
232.6–28 Lord Etherington . . . Marie de Martigny . . . Anne Bulmer should the Earl's marriage in France be valid according to French law, the English courts would recognise it as a valid marriage, rendering the second (or English) marriage bigamous and void. For a contemporary case illustrating the legal complexities of such a situation see Cairns, 20–27.
232.24–27 this other Sosia . . . the real Sosia in John Dryden's *Amphitryon* (1690), a play adapted from the comedies of Plautus and Molière, the usual complications arise from the presence of two indistinguishable Sosias.
232.38 fly a pitch the height to which a falcon or other bird of prey soars before swooping down on its prey.
233.18–19 twelve thousand a-year equivalent now to between £1m and £1.2m per annum; this income would be largely derived from the rentals of his estates.
234.3–4 matrimonial noose referring to the Scots law on irregular marriages, either by declaration (*de praesenti*) or by a promise of marriage followed by sexual intercourse (*per verba de futuro subsequenta copula*). As 'lies hid under flowers' is a coy allusion to sexual intercourse, the latter possibility is intended here. Compare the similar situation of Sir Bingo and Rachael Bonnyrig (23.5–7 and note).
234.38 lawyers to their circuits the High Court, with its judges and officials, goes 'on circuit' to try serious criminal offences in districts outside Edinburgh. At the time *Saint Ronan's Well* was written, Circuit Courts were held in spring and autumn.

234.38 writers to visit their country clients i.e. solicitors visiting their country clients.
236 motto see *Richard II*, 4.1.228–29.
237.26 as easy and natural as lying see *Hamlet*, 3.2.348.
237.31–32 in justice of peace phrase, to rid the country of us justices of the peace had a general policing jurisdiction and had legal authority to banish someone from their jurisdictions.
238.14 a mite to reward the faithful labourer see Luke 10.7; 1 Timothy 5.18.
238.18 true love to run smooth see *A Midsummer Night's Dream*, 1.1.134.
238.22 their secret marriage the marriage, though clandestine, would be perfectly valid.
238.30 charge of irregularity ministers who married couples without proclaiming their 'banns of marriage' (their intention to marry) were subject to both civil and ecclesiastical penalties, unless there were urgent reasons preventing the proclamation. See note to 346.26–27.
238.39–40 seventh heaven stock phrase for 'perfect heaven', derived from the belief in seven as a perfect number, signifying wholeness. In both the Jewish and Moslem traditions, there are seven heavens, the highest of which (the 'heaven of heavens') is the abode of God. See also note to 160.16.
238.41 at eighteen Tyrrel was 18, Bulmer and Clara 16. None of them could at this time have married in England without parental consent, but could do so in Scotland.
239.22–23 S. Mowbray of Nettlewood's last will and testament see 172.7–23.
240.20 What if I should personate the bridegroom see the text at 271.11–273.8 for a discussion of error as to person, and the difficult issues it raises.
240.34 amoureux de seize ans *French* lover of sixteen years.
241.4 couteau de chasse *French* hunting-knife.
242.2–3 banished myself . . . forth of Scotland then a standard criminal penalty in Scotland.
242.15 sine qua non *Latin, literally* without which not, i.e. an essential condition.
242.16 Voilà . . . talens! *French* that's what it is to have talent. The quotation has not been identified.
242.42 Newmarket town, east of Cambridge, famous for its horse-races. In the 1820s, Newmarket had 7 meetings a year and was the national racing centre; 400 out of 1200 blood race-horses trained there.
242.42 Tattersal's an auction-room for horses, founded near Hyde Park Corner in 1766 by Richard Tattersal (1724–95), stud-groom to the second Duke of Kingston.
243.13–14 perpendicular shirt-collar . . . knot of your cravat fashionable men in the Regency period wore straight soft-collars and cravats. The cravats, which were more like fine scarves than modern ties, were wound twice round the neck and knotted at the front.
243.15 Tietania *Neckclothitania, or Tietania, being an Essay on Starchers, by One of the Cloth* (1818).
243.43 breach of the paction traditional Scottish legal terminology. Lord Stair famously wrote, 'every paction produceth action' in *Institutes of the Law of Scotland*, 2nd ed. (1693), 1.10.7.
244.13 brethren dwelling together in unity see Psalms 133.1.
244.28 ignis fatuus phosphorescent light seen flitting over marshy ground; the term is commonly used figuratively for any delusive hope, aim, etc.
244.36 Gazette *The London Gazette* (founded as *The Oxford Gazette* in 1665

as a newspaper). It had become by Scott's day the organ for making official announcements.

244.39–40 were he ten times our brother see *Hamlet*, 3.2.324.

244.42 the first-born of Egypt see Exodus 11.5–12.30.

245.8 Odour of Sanctity sweet smell supposedly given off by the bodies of eminent saints; the phrase came to imply any appearance of sanctity.

245.26–28 Time was—time is . . . time will be no more see Robert Greene (1560?–92), *Friar Bacon and Friar Bungay* (1594), 4.1.

245.27 if I catch it not by the forelock proverbial: see *ODEP*, 822. The complete version of the proverb is, 'catch time by the forelock for he is bald behind': time is traditionally represented as a bald-headed old man with a long forelock. To 'catch time by the forelock' is to seize the chance of controlling a future event.

245.39–40 throw helve after hatchet see note to 94.5.

246.1 Gibralter is to the Spaniards rock at the southern tip of Spain, captured by the British in 1704; its return has ever since been an object of Spanish policy.

246.9 the tribe of Issachar Issachar was one of the patriarchs of Israel, but the reference is to Jewish money lenders.

246.15 rat-gnawed mansion see the nursery rhyme 'This is the house that Jack built', in *The Oxford Dictionary of Nursery Rhymes*, ed. Iona and Peter Opie (Oxford, 1951), 229–32.

246.20 Drawcansir blustering bully in *The Rehearsal* (1672) by George Villiers (1628–87), 2nd Duke of Buckingham. Drawcansir helps to satirise the heroic tragedies of the day and specifically parodies Almanzor in Dryden's *The Conquest of Granada, or Almanzor and Almahide* (1670, 1671).

246.20 Daredevil the boastful title character of *The Atheist* (1684), a comedy by Thomas Otway (1652–85).

246.31 on the tapis see note to 51.5.

246.35 the chapter of accidents unforeseen course of events; see Philip Dormer Stanhope (1694–1773), 4th Earl of Chesterfield, *Letters*, 16 Feb 1753.

246.43–247.1 certain awkward feelings . . . compunctiously visited see *Macbeth*, 1.5.42.

249 motto not identified; probably by Scott.

249.14 n'importe *French* never mind, it doesn't matter.

249.19–20 You have deserved some love . . . and you have it see Molière, *Georges Dandin* (1668), 1.7.

250.6 old sword hanging over your head having extolled the good fortune of Dionysius, Damocles was invited to dine with the tyrant of Syracuse. In the midst of a royal banquet, he looked up and saw a sword hanging over his head, suspended by a single horse-hair.

250.39 ruse de guerre *French* stratagem of war.

250.43–251.1 to drive her . . . a court of law Jekyl suggests driving Clara into a more formal marriage to avoid litigation.

251.5 given up their virtue to preserve their character see Alexander Pope, *The Rape of the Lock* (1714), 4.105–06, and Henry Fielding, *Tom Jones* (1749), Bk 10, Ch. 7.

251.9 in dependence *law* pending, waiting to be settled.

252.3 wings to fly with proverbial: see *ODEP*, 271.

252.12 left-handed marriage morganatic marriage; a man of high rank marries a woman of lower station with the provisions that she remain in her former rank and that the issue have no claim to succeed. In the marriage ceremony, the bridegroom gave the bride his left hand.

253.25 Harrogate spa in Yorkshire.

253.39–40 the poor woman in the old story not identified.

254 motto see William Julius Mickle (1735–88), 'The Sorceress; or, Wolfwold and Ulla: An Heroic Ballad', lines 49–52. Previously, these lines have always been attributed to Scott.

255.12 Brownie benevolent spirit or goblin, of shaggy appearance, supposed to haunt old farmhouses in Scotland. See Scott's description of this 'useful domestic drudge, who served faithfully without fee and reward, food or raiment': *Letters on Demonology and Witchcraft* (1830), in *The Prose Works of Sir Walter Scott, Bart.*, 30 vols (Edinburgh, 1869–71), 29.338–39.

255.16 snooded up her hair tied up her hair with a ribbon round the forehead and tied at the back under the hair.

255.36 the Augean task the 6th task of Heracles. King Augeas's stable contained 3,000 oxen and had not been cleaned in 30 years. By turning the river Alpheus through it, Heracles purified it in a single day.

255.42 hereditary dunghill removing dunghills from sight was one of the symbols of improvement: compare John Galt, *The Annals of the Parish* (1821), Ch. 8.

256.3–4 expel the winter's flaw *Hamlet*, 5.1.210.

256.18–19 the joint bond written agreement to pay. For a money debt, each would be bound to pay only his share *pro rata* in general, though it would be possible to agree otherwise.

256.30 Baron-baillie Micklewhame is the judicial officer for the barony of Saint Ronan's. From 1747, such judicial functions were very restricted, but he would also have had other administrative duties.

256.36 refused to hearken to the words of the stranger see Psalms 58.5.

256.38 stumbling-blocks taken from the foot-path see Isaiah 57.14.

257.2 moon . . . harvest evening a harvest moon in November in Scotland is not implausible.

257.24 Saunders Jaup *jaup* means a spot of mud or dirty water, or (as verb) to bespatter with mud.

257.25–26 who held his land free . . . for any one this is almost certainly direct speech; if it is a quotation it has not been identified.

257.35 Scylla . . . Charybdis see Homer, *Odyssey*, Bk 12. Scylla was the rock upon the Italian side of the Straits of Messina, Charybdis the dangerous whirlpool on the coast of Sicily opposite. The two together came to mean the danger of running into one evil or peril while seeking to avoid another. Now proverbial: see Tilley, 588–89; *ODEP*, 707.

257.42 exercise of the evening evening worship.

258.10 good Samaritan see Luke 10.25–37.

258.14 Mount Athos peninsula which rises steeply from the sea to a height of 6400 ft (1950 m), stretching into the Aegean from the south coast of Turkey.

258.38 abomination common Biblical word.

258.43 the more dirt, the less hurt Scott also attributes the proverb to Jonathan Swift (1667–1745) in his 'Life of Swift', in *Prose Works*, 2.412, and in *Letters*, 9.331.

259.4–5 Our Scottish magistrates are worth nothing justices of the peace in Scotland were a less effective institution than those in England for a variety of social and legal reasons.

259.5 Turkish Cadi civil judge in a town or village in greater Turkey.

259.7–8 English justice of peace . . . newly included in the commission i.e. a 'new broom' acting with the wider powers conferred on English justices. The 'commission' is the document issued by the Crown, appointing certain named persons to be justices of the peace within a specific district, typically a county. 'Commission of the peace' is often a way of referring to the justices collectively.

259.8 abate . . . nuisance technical legal phrase, referring to the right of a person suffering from a nuisance to remedy it himself.
259.17–18 four in the pound a wax candle. All candles were taxed: tallow ones at 1*d*. a pound, and wax at 4*d*.
259.20 Bacchante female follower of Bacchus, or Dionysus, god of wine. Scott seems to have in mind women (who were often frenzied with wine) in one of the torchlight processions in Athens in honour of Dionysus.
259.22 bloody spectacle *2 Henry VI*, 4.1.144.
260.4 on the sneck only latched.
261.9–10 Anon, anon, sir *1 Henry IV*, 2.4.32–94.
261.16–17 it's the wanton steed that scaurs at the windle-strae it is the wild, unmanageable horse that takes fright at dried grass. Although this sounds proverbial it is not recorded as one.
261.18–19 void of offence without sin.
261.31 Lord haud a grip o' us Lord keep hold of us.
262.7 Smyrna chief port of Asia Minor, situated at the head of the gulf of the same name.
262.13 it was written in my forehead, as the Turk says Moslems believe that the decreed events of every man's life are impressed in divine characters on his forehead but are invisible to mortal eyes. The expression became proverbial in English (see Tilley, 236).
262.27 gars me grew gives me the creeps, terrifies me.
262.29 hale and feir safe and sound.
263.37–38 butter wadna melt in your mouth, but I sall warrant cheese no choak ye you look innocent enough but I am sure you are more experienced than you seem: see Jonathan Swift, *A Complete Collection of Polite and Ingenious Conversation* (1738), in *The Works of Jonathan Swift*, ed. Walter Scott, 19 vols (1814), 11.355.
263.40 it's like it's likely.
264.17–18 Ah, Tyrrel, the merry nights we had see *2 Henry IV*, 3.2.193.
264.26 Ullah Kerim God is merciful.
264.36 Mrs Quickly herself see note to 11.23.
264.39 a wee while syne a little time ago.
265.5 by ordinary out of the common run.
265.8 Pacha with three tails pasha of the highest rank, entitled to have three horse-tails on his war-standard.
265.29 Law is a lick-penny law makes the money go: proverbial (see *ODEP*, 446). But the only two examples of this proverb which use the word 'lick' come from Scott, here and from *The Heart of Mid-Lothian*, 4.39.15 (Ch. 39).
265.38 With your counsel learned in the law see *2 Henry IV*, 1.2.128–29.
266.15–16 cut through the isthmus of Suez a canal was proposed by Napoleon who in his 1798 invasion of Egypt took surveyors with him. In the late 18th century the route to India was of considerable importance to both Britain and France, and both powers vied to gain influence with the Turkish overlords in Egypt for rights of passage overland; Napoleon invaded Egypt to secure that end. The canal was eventually built in 1859–69.
267 motto *1 Henry IV*, 5.1.112–14.
267.20 foraging-cap 'the undress cap worn by infantry soldiers and known as the Glengarry' (*OED*).
271.21–22 Since the Fiend himself . . . perfect innocence see Genesis 3.1–21.
272.26 Newgate the principal London prison until 1902.
272.35–36 many a vow of love, and ne'er a true one see *The Merchant of Venice*, 5.1.19–20.

272.43–273.1 no law court in Britain . . . would take the lady's word Jekyl argues that Clara might find it difficult, because of the evidence on record, to establish that she was not married to Bulmer. Scott has been careful to construct one of the few plausible circumstances for finding a marriage void (that of error as to person) and in so doing has followed the suggestion of his teacher and colleague, Professor David Hume (see *Lectures*, 1.24). The argument points up the importance of the testimony of Hannah Irwin.

273.13–14 the most abominable imposition . . . on Miss Mowbray the trick would indeed make the marriage void. The argument arises from the nature of marriage as a contract based on consent. Clara consented to marry Tyrrel; she did not consent to marry Bulmer. Therefore, the marriage is void. The classic expression of this in Scots Law is in James Dalrymple, Viscount Stair, *Institutes of the Law of Scotland*, 2nd ed. (1693), 1.4.6 and 1.9.9. But why did Clara not instantly repudiate the marriage? As Jekyl suggests, a court would need convincing. This is why, for Clara to *prove* that her marriage to Bulmer was void, the evidence of Hannah Irwin is necessary. So, while in theory the marriage is undoubtedly void—i.e. of no legal effect or existence—proving this might be difficult.

273.39 I shall grow a woman i.e. I shall cry.

274.20–22 obstacle must ever remain . . . brother in Scott's day, it was technically incest for a man to have sex with his brother's wife, and a brother could not marry his deceased or divorced brother's wife. But if the marriage to the brother were declared void on the ground of error, it would be void from the start. Tyrrel is referring to a constraint that is other than legal.

275.40 unloosing this Gordian knot proverbial: see Tilley, 271; and *ODEP*, 328–29. Gordius, the King of Gordium in Phrygia, had a chariot whose pole was fastened to the yoke with an intricate knot that defied all efforts to untie it. An oracle stated that he who unloosed this Gordian knot would rule Asia; Alexander the Great cut the knot with his sword.

275.42 I would rather trust a fanged adder than your friend see *Hamlet*, 3.4.202–03.

277.34–35 the character of the peerage . . . cannot be resigned Jekyl is correct. A peer of the realm could not resign the dignity (he may, of course, need to establish it is his). So, if Tyrrel is the true Earl of Etherington, though not acknowledged as such, he cannot give it up.

277.40 no such compunctious visitings see *Macbeth*, 1.5.42.

278.34 they lie but in small compass they do not take up much space.

279.21 Euphrosyne see note to 55.6.

280 motto see *Measure for Measure*, 4.3.171–74.

281.29 hail fellow well met proverbial: see Tilley, 280; Apperson, 342; and *ODEP*, 277.

282.1–2 Pat Murtough's greyhound the allusion has not been identified, but both master and hound may be another of Touchwood's fictional creations.

282.6 Touchstone the court jester in *As You Like It*.

282.26 all heel and toe walking as opposed to running.

282.27 equal weight i.e. were my weight equal to Barclay's, or, were we carrying an equal weight (i.e. Barclay would carry weights, as in horse-racing, so that he had no advantage).

282.27 Barclay Robert Berkeley Allardice (1779–1854), commonly known as Captain Barclay, and famous for his pedestrian feats. In 1809 at Newmarket, walking in a lounging gait which raised his feet scarcely two inches above the ground, he covered 1,000 miles within a specified time to win a 2,000-guinea (£1,100) bet. See Johnson, 703–04.

282.35–36 Vergeben sie . . . wenig 'Forgive me, sir, I was bred in the

Imperial service, and must smoke a little' (Magnum, 34.188). Jekyl's German is slightly incorrect.

282.37–40 Rauchen sie . . . topf 'Smoke as much as you please; I have got my pipe, too.—See what a beautiful head!' (Magnum, 34.188). Touchwood's German is correct, but 'pfeifchen' is, more accurately, 'little pipe'.

282.43 Professor Jackson John Jackson (1769–1845), known as 'Gentleman John'. He was boxing champion of England (1795–1803), then kept a gym in Old Bond Street, earning more than a thousand pounds a year, teaching Byron and other wealthy patrons to box. Artists called him 'the finest formed man in Europe' (Johnson, 710).

283.10 American war the American War of Independence 1775–83.

283.15 Elfi Bey Mohammed Elfi Bey (d. 1807), Egyptian Mamluk leader, supported by the British during the struggle for power in Egypt in the early 19th century. See Stanford J. Shaw, *Between Old and New: The Ottoman Empire under Sultan Selim III, 1789–1807* (Cambridge, Mass., 1971), 275–90. In the spring of 1815 in London, Scott gave Byron 'a beautiful dagger mounted with gold, which had been the property of the redoubted Elfi Bey' (*Life*, 3.336).

283.16 Aristotle Greek philosopher 384–322 BC.

283.23 the reign of terror that period of the French Revolution from March 1793 to July 1794 when the ruling faction executed persons of both sexes and all ages and conditions whom they found obnoxious.

283.42 Bond Street in London, long famous for its fashionable shops.

284.34 brace of bull-dogs pair of pistols of large calibre.

284.43 tête exaltée a little queer.

285.21 fish-sauce . . . Burgess's see note to 143.25.

285.29 indifferent honest *Hamlet*, 3.1.122.

285.43 ever slept out of straw, or went loose Touchwood means that he is one of the maddest people not to be confined in Bedlam (where patients slept on straw and were locked up).

286.18 faire les frais de conversation *French* to sustain the burden of the conversation.

286.22 Chitty-gong a British port in India, near Calcutta.

286.26–27 So, good morning to you, good master lieutenant see Nicholas Rowe (1674–1718), *Lady Jane Grey* (1715), 5.1.

286.27 a captain in the Guards is but a lieutenant i.e. a lieutenant in the Guards (the collective name for the Grenadier, Coldstream, Scots, Irish, and Welsh Guards) is known by the courtesy title of 'captain'.

287.4 Pentapolin with the naked arm see Cervantes, *Don Quixote*, Part 1 (1605), Ch. 18.

287.26 pitch and toss see note to 97.33–34.

287.28–29 neevie-neevie-nick-nack guessing game in which something is held in one hand behind the back and the opponent has to guess which: 'Neevie-neevie-nick-nack,/ Which hand will ye tak,/ The right or the left?' See *The Oxford Dictionary of Nursery Rhymes*, ed. Iona and Peter Opie (Oxford, 1951), 197–98.

288 motto see *Richard III*, 4.2.28–30.

289.3 Old Man of the Sea see 'Story of Sinbad the Sailor', in *The Arabian Nights* (Weber, 1.80–82).

289.9 bing folks on the low toby slang for 'rob as a footpad', as translated by Scott (Magnum, 34.200).

289.24 dog in the manger see *Fables of Aesop: According to Sir Roger L'Estrange* (Paris, 1931), 79. The expression became proverbial (see Ray, 186; and *ODEP*, 195).

290.38–39 the two bears can meet without biting see *Much Ado about Nothing*, 3.2.69–70.

292.5 argent comptant *French* ready money.
292.29 femme sçavante learned woman; a blue-stocking.
292.36 Statius Publius Papinius Statius (1st century AD), Roman poet, author of the *Thebaid*, an epic in 12 books on the struggle between two brothers, Polynices and Eteocles of Thebes, who engaged in civil war when Eteocles refused to share the throne of Thebes with his brother. They killed each other.
292.41 Alcoran the Koran, the holy book of the Moslems.
293.3 paullo post futurum in the very near future, a phrase used to describe one of the tenses of Greek verbs.
293.6–7 Polynices and his brother see note to 292.36.
293.14 Polly Peachum heroine of *The Beggar's Opera* (1728) and its sequel, *Polly* (1729), by John Gay (1685–1732).
294.14–15 place-man ... radical person appointed to a position in the court or government to placate some interest regardless of that person's fitness for office; this was a prevalent practice which was attacked by radical politicians from both within and outside Parliament.
295.17–18 gentlemen of the fancy prize-fighters and their backers.
296.20–21 there is no marriage, within the forbidden degrees the marriage of relatives was forbidden within 3 degrees, (the number of steps up to a common ancestor and down from that ancestor inclusive of the parties concerned). Captain MacTurk's speech provides an important commentary on the situation between the two brothers and Clara.
296.21–22 fire away, Flanigan boastful Royalist commandant of a castle who, upon being challenged by Cromwell to 'fire away, Flanigan', fled without firing a shot.
297.37 my eye, and Betty Martin *proverbial* humbug, nonsense (see *ODEP*, 10).
298.12–13 even where the good company most do congregate see *The Merchant of Venice*, 1.3.44.
298.24 bona fide sincere, genuine.
298.29 prove a negative the difficulty of proving that something is not so or has not happened is proverbial among lawyers.
299.1–2 an estate that was to be held by petticoat tenure see Washington Irving (1783–1859), *Knickerbocker's History of New York* (1809), 4.4. The phrase should properly be used of the situation where a husband holds an estate in right of his wife, but this is *not* the case with Nettlewood, which is settled on the son of the 5th Earl of Etherington provided he marry a Mowbray.
299.8 one of Canova's finest statues Antonio Canova (1757–1822), Italian sculptor, whose statues were executed with extreme grace, polish, and purity of contour. His reputation was extremely high in the early 19th century, and his 'Three Graces' was the most admired and copied piece of sculpture in the century.
299.13–14 a kind of loving hatred—a sort of hating love see *Romeo and Juliet*, 1.1.173–74.
300.11 Jeannette of Amiens ... Tristram Shandy see Laurence Sterne (1713–68), *Tristram Shandy* (1760–67), Vol. 7, Ch. 9. When the narrator is at Montreuil, Janatone, the handsome inn-keeper's daughter, 'knits, and sews, and dances, and does the little coquetries very well'.
300.38 vengeance horrible and dire see John Milton, *Paradise Lost*, 2.128.
301 motto not identified; probably by Scott.
301.15–16 out of the courts of Bellona into that of Themis the Roman goddess of war, and of law and justice, respectively.
301.38 Ferdinand Mendez Pinto Fernqzao Mendes Pinto (1509?–83), a Portuguese traveller in Africa and Asia for 20 years, who left a colourful

narrative of his adventures, *Peregrinaçqzao* (1614), marked by a vivid imagination. Cervantes called him 'Prince of Liars', and Congreve called him 'Liar of the first Magnitude' (*Love for Love*, 2.5.76–77).

303.42 the commission see note to 259.7–8.

305.22 Walpole Horace Walpole (1717–97), 4th Earl of Orford, printer, poet, first Gothic novelist, and prolific letter-writer.

305.24–27 For never . . . weaknesses it never knows see Horace Walpole, 'Sonnet: To the Right Honourable Lady Mary Coke'. The poem was originally published with the 2nd edition of *The Castle of Otranto* (1765).

305.36 puerperal fever also called 'childbed fever', an infection of the endometrium and of the bloodstream following childbirth.

305.37 thieves' vinegar an infusion of rosemary tops, sage leaves, etc. in vinegar; formerly esteemed as an antidote against the plague.

306.11–13 is there not a law . . . for physicking the poor the infirm or diseased poor were entitled to poor relief but not to medical treatment; but individual kirk sessions had considerable discretion and could choose to pay for medical treatment.

306.25–26 the minister should have sent her to her own parish the parish was charged with supporting the poor of that parish. It was important to identify someone's own parish for this purpose, and there was a body of law (the law of settlement) that determined this. The heritors and kirk session administered the poor law, hence, Lady Pen's remark about the minister's negligence.

306.32 could a tale unfold *Hamlet*, 1.5.15.

306.37–38 some magistrate to receive a declaration she wants a justice of the peace to ensure that her depositions would be received as evidence in a court of law; otherwise, such statements would be rejected as hearsay.

306.42 sgherro insigne *Italian* notorious cut-throat

307.10 assisting the stranger see Matthew 25.35. As a 'stranger', Anne Heggie is not entitled to poor relief; hence, Cargill gives his own money to support Anne Heggie.

307.31 fusionless skink weak, ineffective drink.

308.2 her jetty-black cutty pipe snuff taking was an expensive and mainly a rich woman's habit; poorer women smoked pipes. But by the 1820s, pipe smoking among women was confined mostly to the elderly (Johnson, 760).

308.25 member of the legislature i.e. member of the House of Lords.

310.42 mony words mickle drought talking's dry work.

312.34–35 holding the strange tale devoutly true see William Collins (1721–59), 'Ode to Fear' (1746), line 57.

313.6–7 They call'd it marriage . . . sanctify the shame see Virgil, *The Aeneid*, trans. John Dryden (1697), 4.249–50.

313.8 Queen Dido in *The Aeneid* the Queen of Carthage who loved and lived 'in sin' with Aeneas.

314.1 Mr Rymour's new Tale of Chivalry Robert Rymour or Rymar, a fictitious writer mentioned as a visitor to the spa at 68.34.

314.15–16 damages . . . scandal allusion to the law of defamation. Actions of defamation before the Commissary Court in Edinburgh were described as 'actions of scandal'.

315 motto (1) not identified; probably by Scott.

315 motto (2) Philip Massinger (1583–1640), *A New Way to Pay Old Debts* (1633), 5.1.190–91.

315.15 Congreve's men of wit and pleasure about town William Congreve (1670–1729), author of comedies of manners, including *Love for Love* (1695) and *The Way of the World* (1700).

315.18 Master Stephen 'a country gull' in *Every Man in His Humour* (1598) by Ben Jonson (1572–1637). He says, 'I am somewhat melancholy'

(3.1.66), and asks, 'have you a stool there, to be melancholy upon?' (3.1.85).

315.38 By your leave *Twelfth Night*, 2.5.85.

315.38 Mr Bramah Joseph Bramah (1748–1814), English inventor of the safety lock, hydraulic press, beer pump, modern fire engine, fountain pen, and modern water closet.

316.18 Tell it not . . . whisper it not see 2 Samuel 1.20.

316.19 petty larceny *English law* minor theft.

319.40 Cock of the walk chief person in a circle of people.

320.35 good-boy warning warning intended to achieve some moral effect. 'Good-boy' is a Scott word: compare his letter of 16 January 1823 to Edgar Taylor: 'there is also a sort of wild fairy interest in them [fairy tales] which makes me think them fully better adapted to awaken the imagination and soften the heart of childhood than the good-boy stories which have been in later years composed for them' (*Letters*, 7.312).

320.35 gall and bitterness to his proud spirit see Acts 8.23.

321.8 waking dream day-dream.

321.29 note of hand note in the author's own handwriting promising to pay a specific sum to a specific person on a specific date.

321.41 sharp coin to pay anyone in his own *coin* is to treat him as he has treated others. Thus Etherington hints that Mowbray may retalitate with violence.

322.39 canon of Strasburgh sixteen quarterings (genealogical divisions of one's family tree) were necessary to be a canon of Strasbourg (the principal city of Alsace). In many German bishoprics, the canons or Domherren were obliged to be of noble blood, sometimes of the old nobility of the Empire. See Scott's *Letters*, 8.112 and 8.222, and *Life*, 5.312–13.

323 motto see William Cowper (1731–1800), *The Task* (1785), 4.37–41.

324.8 mere hair-traps to springe wood-cocks see *Hamlet*, 1.3.115. Now proverbial: see Tilley, 788; *ODEP*, 768.

324.11–12 every man's honour is the breath of his nostrils see Isaiah 2.22.

324.15–16 forbidden both by law and gospel . . . duelling an Act of 1600 made fighting a duel a capital offence in Scotland, even if no death resulted; an Act of 1696 made giving or accepting a challenge to a duel an offence punishable by banishment and confiscation of movable goods. These laws were reformed in 1819; now duels would result in charges of murder if death resulted, assault if either party were wounded, and breach of the peace where no injury resulted. Besides the Sixth Commandment ('Thou shalt not kill': Exodus 20.13), there was a long tradition of Christian homily against duelling.

324.30 Jonathan generic name for the people of the United States, a representative United States citizen.

324.32–33 Tippoo's prison at Bangalore Tippoo Sahib (1749–99), Indian ruler, Sultan of Mysore (1782–99), the son and successor of Hyder Ali (see note to 159.36). In 1792, he was defeated by a force under Cornwallis and forced to cede territory. In 1798, Wellesley invaded Mysore, and Tippoo was killed in 1799, defending his capital at Srirangapatna.

324.35 our house of captivity see Exodus 13.3.

325.12–13 elevating . . . his nostrils, and snuffing the air compare Job 39.19–25.

325.41–42 one of Plutarch's heroes . . . figure of Proserpina it was not one of the heroes of Plutarch (1st century AD) but the poet Pindar (*c.* 522–442 BC). In his old age, Pindar dreamt that Persephone, the Queen of the Underworld, came to him and said that of all the deities she alone had not received a poem from him in her honour, but that he should write a song for her also when he came to her. Pindar died in ten days. After his death, he appeared to an aged kinswoman and repeated to her a poem on Persephone, which she wrote down after she awoke. See Geoffrey S. Conway, *The Odes of Pindar* (London, 1972), xxv–xxvi.

326.35–36 **Women's wits . . . avenging** compare e.g. Molière, *Tartuffe* (1664): 'A woman always has her revenge ready' (2.2).

327.20 **West India produce** i.e. sugar.

328.7 **locum tenens** *Latin* (the one) holding the place.

328.40–41 **no better than she ought to be** said of a woman of doubtful moral character: proverbial (see *ODEP*, 568).

329.8 **Hoitie toitie** exclamation expressing surprise with some degree of contempt.

329.29–30 **monkey's allowance . . . more kicks than halfpence** see 'Monkey', in Francis Grose, *A Classical Dictionary of the Vulgar Tongue*, 3rd ed. (London, 1796). Now proverbial: see *ODEP*, 541.

330.25 **Curses not loud but deep** *Macbeth*, 5.3.27.

330.27 **staying no farther question** see *2 Henry IV*, 1.1.48.

331 **motto** Scott's free translation of Horace, *Odes*, 3.1.37–40.

333.2–3 **So constantly . . . little fright** see Robert Burns (1759–96), 'The Twa Dogs' (1786), lines 104–06.

334.6 **whipper-in** huntsman's assistant who keeps the hounds from straying by driving them back with the whip into the main body of the pack.

334.35 **No shame in honest poverty** see Robert Burns, 'Is There for Honest Poverty' (1795), line 1. The song is also known as 'Song: For a' that and a' that'.

336.39 **A blot is never a blot till it is hit** in backgammon a 'blot' is an exposed piece or 'man' liable to be taken or forfeited.

338.38 **Ben Nevis** 4,406 ft (1,343 m), the highest mountain in Britain, located on the west coast of Scotland near Fort William.

339 **motto** Oliver Goldsmith *The Deserted Village* (1770), line 154.

339.28 **Necessity, that makes the old wife trot** proverbial: see *ODEP*, 558.

339.30 **Saint Gothard** mountain pass in Switzerland (6,929 ft; 2,112 m).

339.34 **working by the piece** on piece-work, i.e. being paid for the work completed rather than for the time taken.

340.8 **hogshead from Meux** barrel of beer containing 52 1/2 gallons (239 litres) from Meux's Brewery in London.

340.8 **wired down** secured with wire (compare a champagne cork).

341.7 **golden apples** see Proverbs 25.11.

341.27 **Royal Exchange** the 'Burse' or Exchange, built in London by Sir Thomas Gresham (1519?–79) in 1566, and named the 'Royal Exchange' by Queen Elizabeth (reigned 1558–1603). It was the centre of business activity in London.

341.27 **Saint James's Park** place for fashionable loitering, because of its proximity to Saint James's Palace. It was developed by King Charles II (reigned 1660–85) after the Dutch gardens he had seen in exile, and remodelled on its present lines by John Nash (1752–1835) for King George IV (reigned 1820–30).

341.39 **Peregrine Pickle** the novel by Tobias Smollett (1721–71), published in 1751. This suggests that Touchwood is now about 60 years of age (see 'Historical Note'). For his earlier explanation of his name see 133.36–37 and note.

342.2 **tout court** *French* just that; that's all, and nothing more.

343.5–6 **on the pad** on the road, on the tramp.

344.5 **Jericho** ancient town in Palestine, in the Jordan valley, used (as here by Touchwood) in slang phrases for a place of retirement or concealment, or a place far distant and out of the way, perhaps in allusion to 2 Samuel 10.5. Proverbial: see Tilley, 346; Apperson, 332–33; and *ODEP*, 410.

344.27–28 **un bon diable** *French* a good devil.

344.43–345.1 **the happy sheep that go out for wool, and come home shorn** proverbial: see Tilley, 751; Apperson, 709; and *ODEP*, 913–14.

345.3 **the Philistines** alien warlike people who occupied the southern coast of Palestine, and in early times harassed the Israelites; applied figuratively (as here by Touchwood) to persons regarded as the enemy, into whose hands one may fall.

345.3 **they have drawn your eye-teeth** they have taken the conceit out of you.

345.10–11 **the fellow in the old play** not identified.

345.14 **free man of the forest** the son of a freeman of a burgh inherited his father's rights and privileges but not his debts; by analogy Touchwood is proposing to disencumber Mowbray of his problems.

346.26–27 **a clandestine proceeding . . . cost him his living** Cargill appears to have celebrated a marriage without the calling of banns. This was a criminal offence, but the punishment is unclear, as Cargill was a minister of the Church of Scotland: normally the celebrant of a clandestine marriage would have been a Roman Catholic priest who would have been banished for life. There was also an ecclesiastical offence (see 363.6–11). The presbytery, and ultimately the General Assembly, would have jurisdiction, and it may be that Cargill would be subject to deprivation of his pulpit. Scott leaves ambiguous what the punishment would be, probably because it was unclear.

348.23 **Bow-street officer** a constable. See note to 30.24.

349.5 **I carry my eye-teeth about me** I am wide awake.

349.35 **John Bull** a personification of England or the English; a typical Englishman. Proverbial: *ODEP*, 412–13.

350.35 **as dark as a wolf's mouth** proverbial: see Apperson, 135; *ODEP*, 167–68.

351.6 **like one of sense forlorn** see Samuel Taylor Coleridge, 'The Rime of the Ancient Mariner' (1798), line 623.

351.6–7 **like a mandarin** like a toy representing a grotesque seated figure in Chinese costume which nodded a long time after it was shaken.

351.28 **safe bind safe find** proverbial: see Apperson, 543.

351.30–31 **the merciful man is merciful to his beast** see Proverbs 12.10.

351.38 **sanctum sanctorum** *Latin* holy of holies.

352.3 **haud a grip of** look after, take into his care.

352 **motto** *King Lear*, 3.4.109–10.

352.37–38 **She may marry him . . . if the law is not against it** Mowbray's musings on a possible marriage between Clara and Tyrrel bring up again (and for the last time) the issue of whether or not Clara and Bulmer are validly married.

353.4 **must stand still to be curried a little** must suffer myself to be rubbed hard or groomed with a curry-comb.

355.20 **What's your wull?** what do you want?

356.4 **blight of the Simoom** hot dry suffocating sand wind which blows over the deserts of Africa and Asia in spring and summer. Compare Byron, *Manfred* (1817), 3.1.128–29: 'The red-hot breath of the most lone simoom,/ Which dwells but in the desert'.

358 **motto** not identified; probably by Scott.

358.27–28 **the thing which she feared had come upon her** see Job 3.25.

360.9 blowing up the pioneer with his own petard see *Hamlet*, 3.4.206–07.
360.19 an Israelite without guile see John 1.47.
361.22 the siege of Ptolemais Saint Jean d'Acre, on the coast of Syria, was the main point of entry to the Holy Land during the Crusades, and became the focal point of many sieges. Richard I, for example, regained the city for the Christians in 1191; its surrender to the Saracens in 1291 marked the end of the Crusades.
361.37 corbie messenger the raven sent out by Noah (see Genesis 8.7), hence a dilatory or unfaithful messenger.
362.4 good Samaritan see Luke 10.25–37.
363.7 it was against your canonical rules see note to 346.26–27.
363.31 Your expectation . . . shall be fully satisfied Hannah Irwin now gives the evidence necessary to demonstrate the invalidity of the marriage of Clara and Bulmer. This edition restores, for the first time, her entire confession.
365.18 phantom which he beheld Lockhart believed that this 'apparition' of Clara Mowbray was based on a ghost story that Scott liked to tell: see *Life*, 5.296–97, and *Letters on Demonology and Witchcraft* (1830), in *The Prose Works of Sir Walter Scott, Bart.*, 30 vols (Edinburgh, 1869–71), 29.368–71.
368.24 Vengeance belongs to God see Romans 12.19.
368.31 You bring tidings of death to the house of death see Ecclesiastes 7.2.
369 motto not identified; probably by Scott.
369.41 no use in spurring a willing horse proverbial: see Ray, 159; *ODEP*, 768.
370.12 mare's nest illusory discovery, especially one that displays foolish credulity.
370.18 twa ends of a handkercher in cases of mortal enmity, the duellists sometimes stood back to back, each holding the corner of a handkerchief; then, at a given signal, they turned and fired.
370.33 dead as a toor-nail proverbial: see Tilley, 171; Apperson, 137; and *ODEP*, 170.
370.34–35 we must pe ganging . . . before waur comes of it Mowbray and MacTurk must flee because they have contravened the laws against duelling (see note to 324.15–16). But even without those statutes, it was murder—Mowbray guilty as actor, MacTurk as art and part (i.e. accessory).
371.4 Esculapius Roman god of medicine; hence a physician.
371.15–16 the Peninsula, where the war was then at the hottest the War in the Iberian Peninsula (1808–13) between the English, Spanish, and Portuguese under Wellington (from 1809) and the French under Napoleon's generals. The text may be referring to the fierce battles of Talavera and Saragossa in 1809, or to the storming of Ciudad Roderigo and Badajoz at great cost in 1812, and the subsequent advance into Spain.
371.24 Moravian mission the Moravians, or Herrnhuters, a Protestant sect that originated in Bohemia (1457) and was revived in Saxony (1722), were active in missionary work.
371.37 volunteer . . . commission i.e. he volunteered for service in the army and subsequently became an officer.
371.43 corner at whist point in a rubber at whist.
372.6–7 at nurse said of an estate being administered by trustees.
372.14–15 reversed the usual order . . . butterfly see *Coriolanus*, 5.4.11–12.

GLOSSARY

This selective glossary defines single words; phrases are treated in the Explanatory Notes. It covers Scottish words, archaic and technical terms, and occurrences of familiar words in senses that are likely to be strange to the modern reader, which are unlikely to be in commonly-used one-volume dictionaries. For each word (or clearly distinguishable sense) glossed, up to four occurrences are normally noted; when a word occurs four or more times in the novel, only the first instance is normally given, followed by 'etc.'. Orthographical variants of single words are listed together, usually with the most common use first. Often the most economical and effective way of defining a word is to refer the reader to the appropriate explanatory note.

a' all 9.2 etc.
abigail waiting-woman, lady's maid 86.35, 90.32, 167.40
Abram-man vagabond, one who feigns sickness 197.28
absolvitor *Scots law* decision of a court in favour of the defender 73.16
abstersion act of wiping clean 261.38
accompt account 320.8, 348.17
adust in a dusty condition, affected by dust 157.4
advowson right of presentation to a parish or ecclesiastical office 149.41
ae one 18.35 etc.
aff off 6.29 etc.
affiche *French* poster, notice 120.21
afore before 355.27
aften often 22.11
afterhand afterwards, later 167.24
again towards, by 307.43
agio foreign-exchange transaction 266.18; percentage profit in a foreign-exchange transaction 348.9
ail *with infinitive* interfere with, prevent [from] 93.21, 355.24
ain own 9.3 etc.
ainsell, ainsells *literally* ownself; yourself 140.20, 185.29; themselves 25.6
airn iron 26.16
ajee awry 98.2
ale-posset drink of hot milk curdled with ale or other liquor, often with sugar and spices, used as a remedy for colds etc. 146.10
almaist almost 15.37
amang among 14.17 etc.
Amazon one of the legendary race of female warriors 49.17 etc.
ambrosia fabled food of the gods 41.1
an if 15.32
ance once 72.20 etc.
ane one 9.2 etc.
âne ass, donkey 159.6
anent in respect of, as regards 142.19
aneugh enough 22.1 etc.
angle fishing rod 9.37, 98.20
Anglice in the English form 37.18
anither another 18.20 etc.
ante-nup *i.e.* antenuptial fornication 14.2
Antigua rum, from the West Indian island so named 10.35
archon one of the 3, later 9, highest officers of the Athenian republic 24.5
arena aren't 17.24
argent *French* silver 171.25, 292.5, 292.6
asper Turkish silver coin of little worth 285.31
assoilzie *Scots law* acquit of a criminal charge 73.5
asteer astir 126.3
atween between 87.30
aught[1] possession 21.27; for 17.40 see note
aught[2] eight 265.2
auld old 5.38 etc.
averment *legal* allegation positively

made and thus claimed to be true 120.24, 290.6, 346.40
aw all 8.43
awa, awa' away 10.1 etc.
awe owe 62.35
aweel well 95.10 etc.
awfu' awful 62.17 etc.
awmry cupboard 17.38
ay, aye yes 8.42 etc.
aye always 16.8 etc.
bacchante female votary of Bacchus 259.20 (see note)
back-hand hidden cards, i.e. clandestine or devious purpose 177.9, 237.17, 246.6
bagman, bag-man commercial traveller 12.39, 14.11, 22.15
baillie see note to 256.30
bairn child 8.36 etc.
baith both 18.23 etc.
bal *French* ball
ballant, ballat ballad 56.31, 135.42
ballat ballad 135. 42
band bond 126.41, 272.30
bandeau head-band 52.20
bane bone 93.39
bangster winner, victor 96.33
bannock round flat cake, made from oat or pease-meal, and baked on a girdle 161.41
barking see note to 92.12
barmy-brained yeasty or frothy-brained, i.e. empty-headed 311.10
baron-baillie see note to 256.30
baronet man having a hereditary knighthood 27.21 etc.
basilisk fabulous reptile, whose breath and look were fatal 201.39
basket-beagles small dogs used to hunt a basket-hare (i.e. hare turned out of a basket to be coursed) 9.29
bastinado blow with a cudgel, esp. on the soles of the feet 266.25
bauld bold 263.32
bavardage *French* idle talk, prattle 325.8
bawbee copper coin worth 6 pence Scots (0.21p) 19.24
beadle parish officer or constable 4.33, 187.40, 202.8
beau-garçon fine fellow, handsome man 212.8
beaver-hat hat of beaver fur 65.28
bedral sexton or **beadle** 307.21
begum princess or lady of high rank in Hindustan 192.39
belang belong 62.6
Beltane 1 May 13.43
besom broom 111.4 etc.
bicker wooden drinking-bowl 333.17
bide stay 13.43 etc.; put up with 14.15, 87.35
bigg build 19.22, 21.27
bijouterie *French* collective appellation for jewellery and trinkets 90.19
bilked cheated 117.5, 117.6
bind capacity in drinking 9.32
bink wall-rack or shelf for dishes 12.31
birl spin 25.35
Bismillah *Turkish* in God's name 161.17
bit small 10.3 etc.
black-fisher one who catches salmon at night by torchlight 42.37
black-leg swindler on the turf and other forms of gambling 138.12
blackletter name for the form of type used by the early printers 162.17
blaw blow 311.8; boast 264.33
blawart flower of the bluebell or cornflower 185.27
blaw-in-my-lug flatterer 14.25
blithe happy, cheerful 18.21 etc.
blot exposed piece in backgammon 336.39
blude blood 127.32
blue-stocking woman having or affecting literary tastes and learning 137.32
blunt money 94.32
bob-wig wig having the bottom locks turned up into bobs (short curls) 281.20
boddle, bodle small copper coin worth 2 pence Scots (0.07p), something that is worthless 19.21 etc.
body person, man 9.41 etc.
boggle 'play fast or loose' (Johnson) 50.43
bogle ghost 103.5 etc.; scarecrow 145.23
bohea finest black Chinese tea 107.43
boltsprit bowsprit, a large spar running out from the stem of a vessel, to which the fore-mast stays are fastened 197.26
bombazine stuff of which the lawyer's gown was made 93.31
bonnet-laird one who farmed his

own ground but who in dress was not distinguishable from small tenant farmers 6.16, 7.35
bonnie, bonny pleasing to the sight, pleasant, beautiful 18.24 etc.
bonze term applied by Europeans to the Buddhist clergy 145.18
boot-hose coarse, worsted hose worn over hose of finer materials 340.18
bosky bushy 189.36
bourasque *French* outburst, upblazing 10.15
brag game of cards, essentially identical with modern poker 288.13
braid broad 191.36
Bramin member of the highest or priestly caste among Hindus 158.23
brander cook on the gridiron, grill 262.15
brank fine, showy 22.27
braw fine, splendid 167.16, 192.2, 356.17
briquet *French* lighter 282.33
brose for 190.10 see note
brownie benevolent spirit 255.12 (see note)
browst brew 264.9
bruick enjoy possession of 8.1
bruit rumour, report 255.20
buck dashing fellow, dandy 27.16; deer 76.23
buckie see note to 13.12
buckskins leather breeches 22.28
bully bluster 290.10
burn stream 2.34 etc.
buskin tragic actor's boot, here covering for the foot and leg up to the knee 184.6, 205.16
busking mode of dressing 255.20
butter-boat small vessel for holding melted butter 211.1
bye besides, in addition 21.3
bygane bygone 22.22
ca' call 9.43 etc.
cadi civil judge among the Turks, Arabs, Persians, etc., usually the judge of a town or village 259.5, 266.26
calash folding hood of a carriage 124.25
Caledonia Scotland 1.13
callant lad, fellow 9.34
caller fresh 10.4
cankered ill-tempered 72.32
canna can't 8.40
canny shrewd, prudent, sensible 87.36, 119.3
cantle crown of the head 129.31
cantrip trick, piece of mischief 262.39
canty lively, cheerful 18.22
capillaire syrup flavoured with orange-flower water 37.19
capot win very trick in piquet 166.33
cappernoity crabbed, irritable 249.5
cappie 'kind of beer between table-beer and ale, formerly drunk by the middling classes (Jamieson)' 129.1
caravanserail, caravansary large quadrangular building with a spacious court in the middle where caravans put up 141.19, 202.25
cardinal short cloak worn by ladies, originally of scarlet cloth with a hood 125.8
caredna didn't care 56.32, 257.25
carious decayed 114.11
carle fellow 9.41
carline witch, old woman 185.15
carrack large ship, galleon 63.26
carvy caraway seed 20.7, 20.8
cat-a-nine-tails whip with nine knotted lashes 108.32
catch-match match which is a catch or great advantage to one of the parties 50.32, 175.14
cattle horses 7.29, 140.31, 142.2; [human] beasts 73.31, 87.21
caudle warm drink of gruel and wine or ale, sweetened and spiced, and given to women in child-birth 146.9
cauld cold 10.3, 145.35
cerulean deep blue 205.16
chaff banter 46.43
Chaldee native of Chaldea, especially (as at Babylon) one skilled in occult learning 141.32 (see note)
change-house small inn or alehouse 73.34
charter for 21.18 see note
cheek-haffit locks at the side of the face or temple 16.10
cheeny china 261.28
chiffonier *French* junk, jumble 90.10
chucky see note to 20.26
chuse choose 38.7
cicatrized covered by a scar 163.23
cimelia *Latin* treasures, things laid up in store as valuable 90.3
clachan small village or settlement 8.3
claithes clothes 20.34

claver gossip, talk aimlessly 23.21
cleck hatch 128.36
cleek, cleik hook 23.6, 128.13
cleugh gorge or ravine 330.42
clew clue 211.28
clink see note to 20.24
closet inner room 21.17
clout patch 4.22
cock-a-leeky chicken and leek soup 6.43
cock-bree broth in which a chicken has been boiled 25.42
cockernonnie top-knot 129.6
cogue small wooden drinking vessel 10.4
collie sheep-dog 107.31
collops see note to 7.1
comptis financial accounts 10.36 (see note)
con[1] see note to 45.3
con[2] turn over in the mind, study 16.15
concatenation union by linking together 8.10 (see note)
condiddling pilfering, filching 37.4
congo black tea imported from China 37.22
Consul one of the 2 supreme officers of the Roman republic, elected annually 24.5
copt native Egyptian 156.22
corbie raven 280.16
corkit *of wine* tasting of cork, having an unsound cork that has let in air 18.8
corner point in a rubber at whist 298.5
corpus *Latin* body, corpse 46.19 etc.
coruscation quivering flash of light 54.31
Cot *Highland English* God 36.42 etc.
coterie set or circle of associates 39.9, 49.17, 311.43
couchant lying, recumbent 90.20
couldna couldn't 25.3, 73.3
cousin-german first cousin 173.25
cowrie shell used as money in Africa and southern Asia 133.19
cowt adolescent (human or animal) 10.30
crackit cracked 18.35
craig crag, rocky point 20.30 etc.
craniologist one who reads someone's character from the shape of his skull 111.23
crap crop, conspicuously short hair 18.26
craw crow 20.29
creel basket 10.3
crimini exclamation of astonishment 370.16
croupe hinder end of a saddle 358.3
croupier one who sits as assistant chairman at a dinner at the lower end of the table 10.18
crown coin worth five shillings (25p) 117.22, 307.39, 334.8
cruells scrofula 20.16
cruet small bottle for sauces etc. on the dining table 17.38, 315.20
cry pack, company [of actors] 194.11
cubit ancient unit of liner measure, usually from 18 to 22 ins (45 to 55 cms) 359.10
cuddie donkey, stupid fellow 20.3
cued *of hair* twisted behind like a tail 29.17
cuitle coax, flatter 14.26, 128.35
Culdee member of an ancient Scoto-Irish religious order, found from the 8th century 20.3 (see note), 141.32 (see note)
cull man, fellow 287.24
cumbers drawbacks troubles 63.4
curricle light, two-wheeled carriage, drawn by two horses abreast 187.8
curry rub down or dress (a horse) with a currycomb 353.4
cutty contemptuous name for a woman 14.1; short, stumpy 308.2
daffing fun, licentious behaviour 22.13
daft foolish, fun-loving, stupid 10.28 etc.
daggle-tailed *of a woman* untidy, slatternly 320.2
daub coarsely executed, inartistic painting 89.39
daunce dance 19.31
daur dare 23.12 etc.
decerniture *Scots law* decree of a court 167.31
declarator *Scots law* action in the Court of Session brought by an interested party to have some right or status declared, the legal consequences being left as a matter of course 92.36
deevil devil 136.1 etc.
defalcation diminution, reduction 233.17
deid dead 263.24

deil devil 13.12 etc.
déjeuner luncheon 67.38 etc.
delireet distracted 107.19
delf-ware glazed earthenware, originally made at Delf, the Netherlands; piece of pottery of this style 261.30
delicti *Latin* of the crime 46.19 etc.
demi-jour *French* softened light 89.36
dennet light open two-wheeled carriage akin to a gig 125.20
dervise Moslem friar who has taken vows of poverty and austere life 145.18
diablerie devil-lore, magic, sorcery 77.31
didna didn't 93.40 etc.
diet-loaf sponge-cake, cake without fruit 20.4, 65.40
dinna don't 16.3 etc.
dishclout dishcloth 157.5 (see note)
div do 262.42
divertisement diversion, amusement 185.23, 194.39
doiled stupid, crazed 142.1
doited stupid 132.19
donnart stupid 145.1
dookit ducked 141.28
doom *Scots law* judicial sentence or decree 175.27
doon down 145.22
dorts for 9.25 and 44.18 see note to 9.25
doubt fear, suspect 26.8, 44.17
douce quiet, sensible, respectable 9.35
dought was able, dared 60.13
doun down 128.35 etc.
dowcot dovecot, pigeon-house 21.17
down bye down yonder 15.34, 161.25
draggle-tailed having a skirt that trails on the ground, slovenly 20.33
drap drop 10.5
drappie drop of spirits 162.4
dree undergo, suffer 14.2
druse inhabitant of an area in eastern Lebanon and Syria 156.22
dub-skelper one who travels rapidly, regardless of the state of the roads 260.1
ducking-stool chair at the end of an oscillating plank, in which disorderly women were tied and plunged in water as a punishment 111.7
dune done 20.33
dung knocked, beaten 8.39, 145.1
dwam stupor 310.41
ebullition sudden outburst or boiling over 70.12
éclaircissement explanation 203.15
eclat lustre of reputation; renown 30.37
ee eye 94.19
e'en, een[1] even 13.28 etc.
e'en[2] evening 10.3, 307.43
een eyes 18.25 etc.
elf-locks tangled mass of hair 8.11
embrasure window recess 17.5
encoignure *French* corner table 90.15
eneugh enough 21.6 etc.
equerry officer in a royal court charged with the care of horses 124.37
exaltée *French* over-excited, heated 284.43
exordium introductory part of a discourse 309.13
fa' fall 19.20
fa'an fallen 20.18
facetious witty, amusing 242.28
fain *adjective and adverb* glad, happy; gladly, willingly 23.9 etc.
fair gently, quietly 221.4
fakir loosely applied to Hindu devotees and naked ascetics 145.18
fallow fellow 62.5 etc.
fand found 132.16, 135.9, 211.2
farthing coin worth ¼*d.* (0.1p)
fash trouble, annoy 22.40 etc.
fashery annoyance, trouble 22.42
fashious troublesome 18.34
faughta pigeon sacred among the Hindus 192.24
feck the greater part 18.4, 97.35
feckless ineffective, weak 130.38
feir for 262.29 see note
fern-seed for 59.13 see notes
feu for 8.27, 21.25, and 372.22, see note to 8.26–27
feuar one who holds lands in feu, i.e. has heritable possession of the land in payment of a feu duty to a superior 7.35, 257.24
fidalgo Portuguese noble 216.26
file dirty 13.43
fir-deal fir-wood cut into planks 4.22
fit foot 187.22
flapper for 201.36 see note
flaw squall, blast of wind 256.4

flee fly 20.7
fleech flatter, coax 19.41
flesher butcher 129.33
flichter flutter 22.12
flisk-ma-hoys something flashy or insubstantial 263.35
flock-bed bed stuffed with flock or other coarse material 308.10
flummery anything empty of meaning, humbug 341.24
flyte rail, scold, quarrel 18.28 etc.
foraging-cap for 267.20 see note
forbye besides, in addition to 20.31 etc.
forelock lock of hair growing from the fore part of the head 245.27 (see note)
fore-sheet fore-sail 315.5
fou, fow full 14.1 etc.
four-nooked four-cornered, square 130.35–37
frae from 13.32 etc.
frappant *French* striking, impressive 57.36
frontless unblushing, shameless 26.1
fudge contemptible nonsense 290.9
fule fool 19.41 etc.
funditus *Latin* thoroughly 165.7
fusionless weak, ineffective 307.31
gae go 13.13 etc.
gaed went 14.18 etc.
gaen, gane gone 13.13, 23.5
gaff for 33.23 see note
gallery long room in a large country house used to display ancestral portraits 147.30, 338.19, 338.40, 353.31
gaillard gallant, lively 22.24
gait way, road 138.42, 370.35
galopin errand-boy 287.32
gang go 9.43 etc.
gar make, cause [something to be done] *or* [someone to do something] 17.23 etc.
gate way, road 18.35 etc.
gaun going 87.21, 186.10
gay very, considerably 267.7
gazé *French* covered, veiled 292.5
gear business 330.1
geeing giving 307.22
geisen'd *of wooden containers* cracked, leaky 18.35
gentle well-born 22.30, 30.41, 96.1
gentles the well-born 22.31
ghaist ghost 259.43 etc.
gie give 13.39 etc.
giff for 33.23 see note
gill-flirt young woman of a wanton character 128.33
gillie lad 43.25; attendant on fisherman or game hunter in the Highlands 235.4
gill-stoup cup or tankard holding a gill (1/4 of a standard pint) 38.19
gin if 324.20
gin-twist mixed drink principally of gin 78.22
girn whine, grumble 126.15
glacis gently sloping bank in front of a fortification 324.36
glass eye-glass 63.42
glebe church land assigned to a parish minister to augment his stipend 255.23
glede bird of prey, kite128.1
gnostic knowing, sharp 48.4
gnostically knowingly, cleverly 35.28
gomeril fool, silly fellow 136.4, 136.7
goodman husband 22.25, 92.35; owner or tenant of a farm 170.28
gossip chum 26.28, 38.13, 43.21, 120.36
goupin double handful 25.32
gowd gold 25.32
gowk cuckoo, fool 161.25, 311.10
gree agree, come to terms 25.29
green-room room in a theatre provided for the accommodation of actors 188.41
grew to shiver 262.27
groat silver coin worth 4 pence Scots (0.14p) 310.40
grossart gooseberry 21.25
grouse small game bird 234.39, 234.42, 235.21
grund ground 20.37; for 87.42 see note
gude good 17.35
gudes possessions, property 63.3
gudewife landlady 361.35
gudgeon small fresh-water fish, credulous, gullible person 197.23
guide treat, manage, control 87.43, 126.17
gully large knife 129.33
guse goose 92.25
gusing for 191.26 see note
gymnosophist ancient Hindu philosopher of ascetic habits 158.24
ha' hall 13.13

habit dress appropriate to a particular occupation: riding-dress 65.28, 65.33, 208.15, 208.43; stage dress 190.30
hack chaise, hackney coach travelling carriage kept for hire 51.8 (see note), 370.43; 323.35
hadgi pious Moslem who has made the pilgrimage to Mecca 160.11, 161.17
hadna hadn't 307.34
hae have 8.39 etc.
haena haven't 356.16
hail, hale whole 14.18 etc.
halbert weapon combining spear and battle-axe 281.22
hald hold 65.27
hale see **hail**
half-pay for 30.20 etc. see note to 30.20
hamako fool, witless person 354.41
hame home 10.3 etc.
hap hop 73.14
hasna hasn't 96.1 etc.
haud hold 17.41 etc.
haugh flat alluvial land by the side of a river 30.15, 151.24
hauld hold 129.9
havena haven't 127.36
havrel foolish chatterer, gossip 141.27
heartsome cheerful, lively 21.6
heather-tap tuft or bunch of heather 18.26
hellicate giddy, wild, noisy 14.20
helve for 94.5 and 245.39 see note to 94.5
hempie roguish, romping 24.21; rogue 72.36
herd shepherd 127.42, 128.1
heritor proprietor of a heritable subject having a responsibility to pay, with the other heritors of a parish, the minister and school-master, and maintain the church, manse, school and school-house 152.21, 152.30
hersell herself 65.39 etc.
het hot 91.37
Hieland Highland 72.33
himsel, himsell himself 21.28 etc.
hinder-end bottom 18.19
hinny honey, dear 367.2
hirple limp, hobble 359.21
hobnail'd having boots with large nails in the soles 333.12
hock white Rhine wine 145.41 (see note)
hoddle hobble, waddle 8.41
hogshead large cask holding 52½ gallons 215.37, 340.8
Hollands grain spirit made in Holland, gin 18.37
holm level ground beside a stream 17.11, 21.25
hooly for 126.28 see note
horse-couper horse-dealer 6.16
horse-marine land-lubber on shipboard, someone out of their element 197.21
hostler man who attends to horses at an inn 9.16, 112.17
hotch jerk oneself along in a sitting posture to let someone else in 142.4
hottle hotel 8.39 etc.
hough thigh 185.27
house-tyke house dog 126.17
howff resort, public house 24.20, 25.36, 73.31
howk dig 21.27
humourist person subject to fancies or whims 4.19
hurley-hacket term of contempt applied to an ill-hung carriage 141.40
hussy *disparaging* servant-girl 10.13
ibidem *Latin* in the same place 196.10
ilk, ilka each, every 9.1 etc.
ill-redd-up disorderly, untidy 145.4
illustrate honour, shed lustre upon 171.14
imam, imaum officiating priest of a Moslem mosque 145.18, 161.16
indweller inhabitant 3.32
ink-standish stand containing ink, pens, and other writing materials, inkstand 155.25
instanter *Latin* instantly 97.21
intent *Scots law* raise, commence 72.43
intill't into it 187.23
irritancy nullification of a deed resulting from contravention of the agreement 92.33
I'se I shall 16.11 etc.
isna isn't 130.35, 131.40
itsel, itsell itself 19.32, 141.26
janizary Turkish soldier 293.18
japanned varnished with japan, a varnish of exceptional hardness, which

originally came from Japan 125.33, 259.18
jaud *disparaging* jade, woman 13.12, 261.13
jaug jag, leather bag, especially one used by a beggar 13.27
jaw-hole open entrance to a sewer 257.27
jee word of command to a horse 153.29
jeest jest 62.23
jer-faulcon large falcon 129.4
jink move quickly, dodge 73.13
jinketting for 22.11 and 91.36 see note to 22.11
jirbling emptying liquids from vessel to vessel 91.36
jo sweetheart, darling 87.23
Jonathan generic name for people of the United States 324.30
joseph long coat with a small cape and buttons down the front 202.12
kale cabbage soup, broth 78.12 (see note)
keepit kept 128.6, 131.28
ken know 9.41
khan unfurnished building for the accommodation of travellers, a caravanserai 141.19
kickshaw *contemptuous* insubstantial, fancy dish in cookery 91.30
kilt part of Highland dress, consisting of a skirt reaching from the waist to the knee 184.24
kirtle man's tunic or coat, originally a garment reaching to the knees or lower, sometimes forming the only body-garment 184.24
kitchen-fee dripping 20.5
kittle enliven, tease 21.8, 135.36
knap for 14.16 see note; knock, tap 20.25
kouscousou, African dish made of flour granulated, and cooked by steaming over the vapour of meat or broth 143.26
kuchenritter variety of pistol 178.20
ladye lady 53.27 etc.
lagged delivered up to justice and punished for crime 289.43
laird landowner who leased land to others to farm 5.22 etc.
lamer amber 90.11
landlouper charlatan, adventurer 128.32
lang long 5.38 etc.
lapidate pelt with stones 293.17
lass girl 26.4 etc.
lave remainder, what is left 93.38
lawing tavern reckoning 7.21
lea-rig ridge left in grass at the end of a ploughed field 128.26
least lest 161.43
leddy lady 22.25 etc.
leddyship ladyship 20.22 etc.
lee lie 162.4
leeving living 16.33
Levant countries of the eastern Mediterranean
limmer worthless creature, idle hussy 259.42
link link 8.43; pay quickly 19.21; link arms in a dance 22.13
linn deep narrow gorge 219.10; waterfall 330.43, 369.5
lippen trust, confide 26.19
list please, choose 21.19, 82.42
livery distinctive suit of clothes given to someone's retainers 137.28
lollop lounge or loll idly and awkwardly 299.31
loon rascal, scoundrel 131.27, 135.41
loot let, allowed 60.12
loosing-time time for stopping work 135.35
loup jump 23.10
lown loon, worthless person 25.33
luckie, lucky familiar name for an elderly woman, especially the mistress of an ale-house 8.41 etc.
lug ear 14.25 etc.
lugger small boat used for fishing, coasting, or smuggling 59.30
magnum bottle containing two quarts (4.54 litres) of wine or spirits 9.36, 62.2
mail-coach large coach of a construction intended to prevent overturning, like the stage coaches used to carry mail 23.6, 27.26, 183.28
mailing total rental of an estate 92.20 (see note)
mair more 9.5 etc.
maist most 19.19 etc.
maister master 15.30 etc.
mak make 17.35 etc.
maltster someone who makes malt for brewing 185.34
mandarin for 351.7 see note
manse house allocated to the minister

of a parish in Scotland 4.4 etc.
man-sworn perjured 129.37
maravedi old Spanish copper coin worth less than a farthing (0.1p)
march border, boundary [between estates] 24.22, 73.3
mask make or infuse [tea] 17.24
maun must 8.35 etc.
maunder mumble, talk aimlessly 12.31, 146.14
maunna mustn't 15.24, 25.42 etc.
mawkin hare 127.43
mazareen a deep rich blue 101.4
mechanic handicraftsman 194.1
meerschaum clay-pipe, the bowl of which is made of meerschaum 282.38
meith boundary-mark 24.23
mell meddle, interfere 94.41
memorable something worthy of being remembered 246.21
menstruum solvent; any liquid agent by which a solid substance may be dissolved 91.28
meridian mid-day dram 123.25
mess portion of food, meal 12.7, 126.10, 132.33
messuage *Scots Law* principal dwelling house, with its outbuildings and adjacent land, in a Barony 5.26
miaul cry as a cat 208.12
mickle much, great 93.40 etc.
minatory threatening, menacing 234.9
mind remember 14.1 etc.
mis-caa abuse, revile 131.25
missive letter, epistle 302.39
mista'en mistaken 13.26 etc.
modish according to the mode of prevailing fashion 281.23
moiety *literally* half; wife 298.2
molendinar molar tooth 114.17
mony many 14.20 etc.
Moors Urdu 196.16
morning portion of day extending to the fashionable dinner time, as late as 4 p.m. 42.20 etc.; morning dram 106.12
moulds[1] earth of the grave 262.29
moulds[2] candles made in a mould (as distinguished from dip-candles 265.4
muckle much, great 18.22 etc.
muff woman's accessory for keeping the hands warm 222.6, 222.8, 222.10, 222.12
muir moor 21.37 etc.
mulled of wine, made into a sweetened and spiced hot drink 10.19, 262.16
mullegatawny spiced Indian soup 144.8
multiplepoinding for 93.27 see note
multure for 162.10 se note
mundungus ill-smelling tobacco 308.3
murgeon-maker person who grimaces or engages in bodily antics 21.1
murther *Scots law* murder 129.12 etc.
mutch close-fitting cap worn by women 8.12
mutchkin liquid measure, about 3/4 of an imperial pint (0.4 litres)
mysel, mysell myself 15.40 etc.
mystery craft, profession, skill, art
na no 10.1 etc.
nabob one who has returned from India with a large fortune 15.31 etc.
nae no 16.35 etc.
naebody nobody 15.39 etc.
naething nothing 15.34 etc.
naiad river-nymph 40.34, 196.1
naig nag, horse 131.8
nane none 87.22 etc.
nectar the drink of the gods 41.1
needna needn't 130.23
neevie-neevie-nick-nack for 287.28 see note
negus mixture of wine and hot water, sweetened with sugar and flavoured with lemon and nutmeg 33.4
neist next 16.4
n'importe *French* never mind; it doesn't matter 294.14
no not 9.32 etc.
nonage immaturity, minority 85.7
nonce occasion 196.1
nook corner 135.25
o' of 9.34 etc.
odd-come-shortly some day in the near future 161.24
odoriferous of an unpleasant odour 257.26
œdomatous affected with oedema, dropsical 61.39
ohon exclamation expressing sorrow 18.36
ony any 9.41 etc.
o'on oven 20.9

or[1] before 13.24 etc.
or[2] *French* gold 171.25
ordinance regulation 28.29
ordinary for 16.9, 265.5 see note to 16.9; eating-house where meals were provided at a fixed price 17.37 etc.
originality quality of being independent or idiosyncratic 7.40, 312.36
Oronoko name of a variety of tobacco 90.22
o't of it 17.39 etc.
outrider mounted attendant who rides beside a carriage 105.13, 187.8
owerloup for 24.21 see note
ower over 16.32 etc.; for 19.22 see note
owerta'en overcome (with liquor) 9.35
pabouch heel-less Oriental slipper 282.12
pacha title borne in Turkey by officers of high rank, such as military commanders or governors of provinces 156.7 etc.
paction bargain, agreement 243.43
pad tramp 50.42; road 343.6
palaver conference, negotiation 51.14
palinode *Scots law* recantation by a defender in a trial 128.41
palanquin covered litter, usually for one person, used in Eastern countries 142.6
palladium anything on which the safety of an institution etc. is believed to depend 259.34
panpharmacon remedy against all diseases and poisons 163.30
papery popery 19.43
par for 133.21 see note to 133.19–22
paré *French* for 160.40 and 166.37 see note to 160.40
parritch porridge 10.1
Parsee member of a Zoroastrian religious sect in India 188.11
passant *heraldry* walking 79.30
pat *past tense* put 19.43
patronage heritable right to present a minister to a church 149.41
pawky shrewd, crafty, lively 9.41
peascod pea-pod 264.17
peccant causing disorder of the system, unhealthy 66.18
pelisse long mantle, worn by women, reaching to the ankles, and having arm-holes or sleeves 299.28
pendante *Italian* attendant, companion 302.41
Persic the Persian tongue 196.16
petard weapon of war, consisting of a cubical wooden box, charged with powder and fired by a fuse, used to blow in doors etc. 360.9
petted sulky 210.6; spoiled 220.27
pettifogger lawyer who is concerned only with trivia and paper 56.24
pharmacopeia collection or stock of drugs 61.26
phœnix mythical bird, the only one of its kind, that burns itself to ashes, only to emerge with renewed youth 139.24
pice Indian copper coin of little value 133.19
pickle small quantity 18.37
pigeon one who can be easily swindled, esp. in gaming 177.21, 345.2
pinfold fold for sheep, cattle etc. 1.22
piquant that stimulates keen interest or curiosity 54.3; pleasantly sharp in flavour 89.22
piqued having a peak; pointed 11.23
piquet card-game for two 165.38 (see note) etc.
pit put 10.29, 65.43
pitch[1] height to which a falcon or other bird of prey soars before swooping down on its prey 232.38 (see note)
pitch[2] for 287.26 see note
placebo medicine intended to pacify, rather than benefit medicinally 185.22
place-man for 294.14 see note to 294.14–15
plack small copper coin usually valued at 4 pennies Scots (0.14p) 87.30
platanus plane-tree 198.20
plea action at law, suit 290.2
plenipotentiary person invested with full powers 62.22
plethoric full of blood 114.30
pliskie trick 261.16
plottie hot drink, composed of wine or spirits, with hot water and spices 262.17 etc.
pluvious rainy 152.27
pock bag 21.15

pococurante careless or indifferent person 283.39
podagra gout 113.12
pomander mixture of aromatic substances; for 90.10 see note to 90.10–11
poney, pony the sum of £25 sterling 46.40, 46.41
poortith poverty 333.2
poutry poultry 15.36
port a fortified wine from Portugal 7.16, 91.28, 146.1
porter beer of dark brown colour 7.28, 339.34
porteur *French* bearer 348.22
portmantle portmanteau 129.40
post-chaise carriage hired from stage to stage, or drawn by horses so hired 141.35
postern-gate small gate at the back 355.13
post-horse horse kept for hire at a post-house or inn 7.26 etc.
postilion, postillion rider of one of a pair or 4 horses drawing a coach when there is no driver on the box 7.26 etc.
potation drink, draught 333.15
pothecary apothecary, chemist 17.40
pother fuss and bother 95.6
potsherd broken piece of earthenware, *hence* creature of clay 225.16 (see note)
pouches pockets 125.36, 287.1
pow[1] pull 135.15
pow[2] head, crown 108.10
powder-monkey boy employed on board ship to carry gunpowder, *hence* boy servant 65.40, 137.27
pownie, powney pony 22.26, 370.36
Praise God 21.13
précieuse *French* affected woman 305.28
prelatical *disparaging* Episcopal 19.34
presbytery in Presbyterian churches the court next above the kirk-session 4.13 (see note) etc.
prescribed *Scots law* being outside the temporal limit in which an action can be raised 73.9
prescription *Scots law* limitation or restriction of the time within which an action or claim can be raised 73.12, 73.16
prick-my-dainty excessively precise 106.43
prieve legal proof 10.36 (see note)
pro for 45.3 (see note)
procès-verbal French legal term for the official minute of a legal process, recording findings of fact and giving reasons for decisions 118.23
pro-fiscal *Scots law* procurator-fiscal, the official charged with overseeing the investigation and prosecution of crime 127.38
prononcé *French* pronounced, marked 49.23
protégé *French* follower, one under the guidance and supervision of another 314.29
public public house, inn offering food and drink to the public 6.29, 87.2
puerperal pertaining to child-birth 305.36 etc.
puir poor 9.35 etc.
pursuivant officer of the College of Arms, ranking below a herald 171.19
pyot a magpie
quackle quack, croak 69.1
quaigh shallow drinking-cup with two handles 18.36
quart-stoup drinking vessel holding a quart (3.4 litres) 18.35
quean girl, unmarried young woman 17.23, 150.33; impudent woman 307.24
quid piece of tobacco to be held in the mouth and chewed 115.33
quiz odd or eccentric person 36.7 etc.
raff worthless fellow, a nobody 22.15 (see note) etc.
ragion commercial or a trading company 265.16
rampant *heraldry* rearing up 79.30
ranting merry, boisterous 10.8
rattan cane or walking-stick made from rattan (climbing palm) 106.18, 133.34
raw sore or sensitive spot 323.36
rax stretch 92.21 (see note)
reckoning bill 285.27
recusant one who refuses to submit to authority 171.40, 256.34
redd tidy 22.35
reek smoke 255.42, 370.28
reekie smoky 135.14

reise-sac military travelling-bag 51.12
relative pertinent, relevant 279.34
relict widow 61.9
remora obstacle, hindrance 38.21
rencontre chance meeting 111.21; duel 140.1 etc.
residenter resident 283.1
residuum that which remains, residue 60.10
retenue *French* reserve 46.26
reticule small ladies' bag 80.28
reversion right to buy back property in the hands of another 35.23
ribband ribbon 135.43
rig trick, scheme 35.37
rin run 18.37 etc.
rink space within which a combat takes place 58.14
riven torn 185.13
rood measurement of land, 1 rood = 0.12 hectares 92.19
roof-tree ridge-pole of a roof, i.e. house, home 19.20
rough-rider horse-breaker 334.6
rouleau roll of coined money 47.3, 47.4
row bread-roll 13.43
ruckling rattling, making the death-rattle in the throat 365.20
rupee the monetary unit of India 193.1
sacerdotal priestly
sack white wine from Spain or the Canaries 146.8
sae so 14.26
saft *of the weather* damp but mild 134.35
sair sore, great, very 16.9 etc.
sald should 108.14
sall shall 16.10 etc.
salute kiss 10.20
salutiferous promoting or conducive to health 162.39, 184.40, 255.1
sanctum *Latin* sacred place or shrine 351.38 (see note)
sand-bed one who absorbs much liquor 215.37
sang song 9.32 etc.
Santon European designation for a kind of monk or hermit among Moslems 162.20
sasine instrument by which possession of feudal property in Scotland is proved 21.18 (see note)
saul soul 324.20
sax six 73.9
'Sbodikins God's bodikins, God's dear body 133.26
scauff *of persons* scum, refuse 22.15 (see note)
scallop shape into the form of a scallop-shell 101.5
scart scratch 107.1
scate large, flat fish 25.42
scate-rumple skate-tail 25.42
scauff see note to 22.15
scaur become frightened, to shy 261.17
sçavante *French* clever, well-informed 292.29 (see note)
sclate slate 130.37
scratch line drawn across the ring, to which boxers are brought for an encounter 106.20 (see note)
scratch-wig small, short wig 29.11
scrog stunted bush or scrub 171.27, 342.23
scrogie stunted, thorny 171.16 etc.
scruple very small quantity 172.27, 172.28
sea-coal coal, as distinct from charcoal 243.10
segar cigar 78.22, 282.32
seignorial pertaining to a feudal lord 209.31 (see note)
sejour place of abode 234.33
sell self 60.13 etc.
shagreen untanned leather with a rough granular surface 370.32
sharper cheat, swindler 230.8
shave slice 65.40
shaw thicket, copse 22.8 etc.
sheet-anchor that on which one places one's ultimate reliance 237.43
sheriff-clerk clerk to the sheriff-court 10.33 (see note), etc.
sheroot cigar made in southern India or Manila 142.9
shieling hut erected on or near a piece of pasture to accommodate a herd in the summer 332.30
shock-headed having the head covered with a thick crop of hair 157.35
shoe-tie shoe-lace 194.7
shool shovel 132.17
shouldna shouldn't 264.31, 264.33
shouther shoulder 10.29, 211.4
shroff banker or money-changer in

the East 187.27, 192.10
sib related by blood 95.42
sic such 18.17 etc.
siller money 87.37 etc.
simoom hot, dry, suffocating sand-wind 356.4 (see note)
sin', sin for 21.1 and 127.33 see note to 21.1
single-stick fighting with a stick provided with a guard and requiring only one hand 108.2
skean thread that is ravelled or tangled up 249.29
skeel skill 136.6
skeely skilful 361.34
skelper a tall, lanky youth
sketchers ice-skates 26.16
skink insipid drink, liquor 307.31
skylark trick 47.6
skylight *literally* daylight, i.e. opening to examination and disclosure 97.39
slaister wet or splashy mess 16.23, 307.33
'Slife God's life 288.31
sloan sharp retort, reproof 11.9
sluggard habitually inactive or lazy person 153.22
sma' small 22.7 etc.
smoke get an inkling of 288.28, 343.1
smore smother 19.20
snap scrap of food 13.42; ginger biscuit 19.19
sneck latch of a door or gate 260.4
sneck-drawing crafty, guileful 131.27
snood bind up with a headband 255.16
soft *of the weather* damp but mild 134.37, 134.39
sorning begging, taking meat and drink from others without paying for them 78.7, 145.16, 145.17
sort put to rights, manage, order 145.6, 261.13
soss eat in a messy way 311.11
souchong one of the finer varieties of black Chinese tea 57.22, 329.10
soubrette lady's maid, any flirtatious young woman 320.2
sough sigh 72.43 (see note)
souse drench, wet through 37.22, 70.20
Souvenir title of a kind of diary or illustrated annual publication 80.25
sowl soul 295.39
spake spoke 56.26
spaw spa 13.32 etc.
speer ask 13.20 etc.
spleuchan pouch for keeping tobacco 63.2
splore commotion, fuss 87.43
sponsible respectable 185.34
sprat small sea-fish 112.8
springe snare, trap 324.8 (see note)
stance building plot 30.16
stancheon upright iron bar 124.12
stane stone 20.26 etc.
startling fickle, irresolute 290.40
steer disturb, interfere with 131.30
stocks instrument of punishment, consisting of a heavy timber frame with holes for confining the ankles 108.30, 111.7; god made of wood 325.20; total share capital of a company or the public debt of a nation 120.38
stop stay 14.17
strap hang 132.19
strathspey Scottish dance, slower than a reel 190.1
streekit laid out 8.37
suffusion *either* inflammation *or* haemorrhage 368.8
suld should 20.2 etc.
sune soon 25.33, 129.6
surtout man's great-coat or overcoat 267.19, 372.38
sward stretch of grass 280.7
swarf swoon 310.41
swoop sweep 307.23, 311.12
syllabub sweet made of wine and cream 290.12
syndings slops, remains 17.39
syne since, ago 5.38 etc.; for 21.1 and 127.33 see note to 21.1
synod body of ministers and elders, constituting the ecclesiastical court next above the presbytery 144.40
table-dot *table d'hôte*, a common table for guests at an eating house 17.36
tackle see note to 23.10
ta'en taken 13.31 etc.
tailzie for 92.15, 92.16, and 135.7 see note to 92.14–15
talisman anything that acts as a charm, or by which extraordinary results are achieved 255.24
tamarind fruit used as a relish 33.6, 33.7
tandem two-wheeled vehicle drawn

by two horses, harnessed one before the other 124.20
tane one of two 22.30
tapis for 51.5 and 246.31 see note to 51.5
tappit-hen pewter vessel having a lid with a knob and taking a standard measure of liquor 9.33
tattler watch 47.12
tauld told 14.20, 20.40
taupie, tawpie awkward, careless girl 16.18 etc.
tea-cadie, tea-caddie small box for holding tea 125.33, 327.42
tent look after, watch 271.38
Termagaunt violent, boisterous, or quarrelsome person 197.5
tête head 284.43 (see note)
tête-à-tête private conversation between two persons 319.21 319.35
tether range of one's resources or abilities 92.21 (see note)
thae these, those 9.34 etc.
thane earl 180.7
thegither together 23.8
thereout in the open air 20.36
thirdsman third person called in as an intermediary or arbiter 115.13
thraw thwart, oppose 87.35, 87.36
threappit persisted, insisted upon 129.34
thumb-ring ring worn on the thumb, often engraved with a seal 90.20
tight smart 22.27
tilbury light open two-wheeled carriage 125.20
till until 8.36 etc.; to 13.32 etc.
till't to it 25.38
tim-whisky light carriage drawn by a single horse or by two driven tandem 124.22
tinkler tinker 20.37
tirrivie tantrum 264.39
tither the other 97.34
titular having only the title or name, so-styled 359.35
titupping lively, full of spirit 120.37
toast lady named as the person to whom the company is asked to drink, often the chief beauty of the season 49.27
toddy beverage of whisky with hot water, and sugar 30.21
tog'd dressed 35.28
toilette dressing-table 50.13, 158.25, 221.39; dressing and making-up 188.43
ton fashionable air or style 89.5, 212.38
tontine for 8.28, 39.35, and 40.23 see note to 8.28
toom empty 135.26
toper hard drinker 212.40
topping first-rate 6.15
tother, t'other the other or second of two 21.40, 22.31
touchhole small hole in the breech of a fire-arm 370.28
toun town 21.5
tourbillon whirlwind 27.40
tozie shawl made of the inner coat of a goat 192.6 etc.
trangum personal ornament, a trinket 167.6
trencher plate 12.27, 71.32 (see note)
troop see note to 6.29
troth *exclamation* truth 26.8
trow trust, believe 108.9 etc.
tryacle treacle 20.8
tryste arrange to meet at an agreed time and place 129.34; appointed meeting 129.36
turbinacious *of whisky* peaty 119.5
twa two 18.14 etc.
twal twelve 19.32
twangle twang a stringed instrument lightly 216.5
twig watch, look at 37.3
twopenny beer sold at twopence per Scots pint (3 imperial pints; 1.7 litres) 7.36, 339.35
ultroneous offered of one's own accord 56.41
umbrageous abounding in shade, 17.10
umquhile former, late 210.40
unco great 16.22, 20.41, 191.35; strange, extraordinary 62.3, 130.30, 146.5; very 210.32, 213.16, 351.13
underwood small trees or shrubs growing beneath higher trees 86.23
ungartered not wearing garters to hold up stockings 154.14
unriddler one who solves or explains 31.6
upcast upset, startling surprise 264.39
uphold affirm, warrant 78.23, 116.15; hold up, support 356.8
usage interest on money 372.9
usquebaugh *literally* water of life,

whisky 307.35
valet-de-chambre valet, man's personal servant 343.4
vamp refurbish, restore 46.16
vapouring acting in a pretentious or high-flown manner 21.7
varlet rascal 287.14
velitation wordy skirmish or encounter 70.23
venta inn 141.18
vera very 61.33 etc.
vertu love or knowledge of the fine arts 29.31
vestal chaste, pure 214.3
vex vexation 21.30
view-hollo shout given by a huntsman on seeing a fox break cover 197.11
vilipend slight, undervalue 8.28, 104.25
virago scold, bold, impudent woman 10.20, 38.21
vizier chief minister of an eastern sovereign 165.21, 165.23
voilà *French* there is 242.16
wa wall 263.11
waal well 73.27
wad would 7.33 etc.
wadna wouldn't 25.7 etc.
wae sad, woeful 129.20, 256.17
waif for 209.31 see note
walth wealth 16.31
wame-fou' bellyful 91.31
wan reached 20.41, 62.16
wark fuss, work, business 66.10, 94.26
warld world 16.4 etc.
warrant guarantee, be sure 25.9 etc.
warst worst 22.42
wasna wasn't 127.27 etc.
watering-pan watering-can 369.25
waur worse 9.34 etc.
weal well-being 4.2
weary wretched, dispiriting 7.4 etc.
wee small, little 20.4 etc.
weeds black clothing worn by a widow in mourning 64.32, 221.36
weel well 14.1 etc.
weel-doing good behaviour, hard work 125.36
ween think 264.32
weird destiny, lot
wha who 13.20 etc.
whan when 19.1 etc.
whare where 161.27
wheen [a] number [of], a few 20.29
whelp impertinent young fellow, puppy 287.9
whiles sometimes, occasionally 14.18 etc.
whilk which 8.43 etc.
whipper-in huntsman's assistant who whips stray hounds back into the pack 334.6
whipping-post post to which offenders were tied to be whipped 111.6
whisht quiet! sh! 72.42
whisky light carriage drawn by a single horse or by two driven tandem 124.41 etc.
whist game of cards 29.24
wi' with 6.29 etc.
willywhaing flattering, wheedling 126.14
wind turn or lead [a person] according to one's will, inveigle 266.30
windlestrae withered stalk of grass 261.17
winna won't 60.16 etc.
wis guess 25.8
Wogdens variety of pistols 37.8 (see note)
won win 307.22
wood mad 139.5
wot know 19.28
wrang wrong 98.1
writer lawyer, solicitor 22.15
wull will, wish 20.21, 157.37, 355.20
wuss wish 22.13
yawl shout, howl 259.12
yank jerk, twitch 14.15
ycleped called, named 257.26
yestreen last night 355.27
yince once 287.26
yont further along 142.4
yoursel, yourself yourself 13.28 etc.

LaVergne, TN USA
04 December 2009
166051LV00001B/1/A

9 780231 103985